MARRYING MOM

FASHIONABLY LATE

OLIVIA GOLDSMITH

MARRYING MOM

Encore

This omnibus edition published in 2000 by Diamond Books

An imprint of HarperCollins*Publishers*
77-85 Fulham Palace Road,
Hammersmith, London W6 8JB

Marrying Mom
Copyright © Olivia Goldsmith 1997
Fashionably Late
Copyright © Olivia Goldsmith 1994

The Author asserts the moral right to
be identified as the author of this work

A catalogue record for this book
is available from the British Library

ISBN 0 007 60396 7

Printed and bound in Great Britain by
Omnia Books Limited, Glasgow

To Nan, with abiding affection.
We'll always have Paris.

Thanks to:

Paul Smith for putting up with an insane schedule, and for giving me the house of my dreams.

Jim and Christopher Robinson for their understanding and sacrifice on behalf of this book.

Linda Grady, as fine a reader as she is a friend and writer.

Barbara Turner for her love, humor, and for giving me this plot in the first place. (Don't sue, sis.)

Paul Mahon because of all those trips to Montana, Ireland, Michigan, and the rest. Lucky I don't depend on you.

Jerry Young for never putting me on hold. What are you wearing, Jerry?

Sherry Lansing for sharing my vision, telling me jokes, and turning this book into a film.

Aida Mora for keeping me supplied with endless Diet Cokes and making things homey.

Allen Kirstein for encouragement when I needed it the most.

John Yunis for tempting me to look better than I ever have.

Flex (a.k.a. Angelo) for the streaks and blow job.

Gail Parent, whom I can't live without.

Chris Patusky, who tried to pick me up at a book signing. (Hope that trouble with the bar association clears up soon, Chris.)

Amy Bobrow for help with Wall Street lingo and with Matilda.

Harold Wise, the best, most caring internist in Manhattan. You were right about everything, Harold.

Diana Hellinger, the only girlfriend I have who will sing with me over the telephone.

Lorraine Kreahling for putting aside our project while this book consumed me; thanks for being my friend.

Acknowledgments

Amy Fine Collins for helping me with my ABCs. You know I'd always do it for you, girlfriend.

Mike Snyder for being one giant earlobe. You were so slow you hurt my whole family, but I love you.

John Botteri (a.k.a. Moe) for knowing exactly how many BTUs a girl writer needs.

Barry LaPoint for your artistic talent, integrity, and for knowing which of the hallway doors to change.

Laura Ziskin for kindly understanding and for giving this book up.

David Madden, even though you wouldn't marry me.

Robert Cort for giving me the really key advice about Mom's character. Wish this were an award, big guy.

Arlene Sorkin, girl screenwriter *extraordinaire*.

Andrew Fisher for his unmatchable expertise in dealing with the true professionals of the building trade.

Kelly Lange, because being Queen ain't easy.

Anthea Disney, a real woman, a real CEO, and a real pal.

Ruth Nathan, my inspiration in so many ways.

Lynn Goldberg, because I still worship you, Lynn. And by the way, when are you going to put me up on your wall?

Dwight Currie, superb book reader, bookseller, book writer, and bookkeeper (except for that last one).

Michael Kohlmann, still "the nice one" and still my friend.

Steve Rubin and Ed Town of Gallery North Star, Grafton, Vermont, for keeping me well fed and well hung.

Edgar Fabro at Copy Quest, because no one can duplicate his amazing talents.

Jody Post, because I miss you and I missed you.

Norman Currie at the Bettmann Archives for his inspirational help in filling the album.

"Old age is woman's hell."
—Ninon de Lenclos

one

*I*ra, I'm leaving you." It wasn't easy for Phyllis to give her husband of forty-seven years the news, but she was doing it. She had always told the truth. All her life people had called her "difficult" or "tough" or "insensitive," but actually she was just honest.

"I can't take it, Ira," she told him. "You know I never liked Florida. I came down here for you, because you wanted to." She paused. She didn't want to blame. It was a free country and Ira hadn't forced her. "Well, you'd always supported me," Phyllis admitted. "Let's face it: you earned the money, so I owed it to you. But it was your retirement, Ira, not mine. I wasn't ready to retire. But did you give me a choice?" Ira said nothing. Of course, she didn't expect him to. The fact was that in their forty-seven years of married life he'd rarely said much. Still, by some marital osmosis, she always knew what his position was on any given subject. Now she realized that the wave of disapproval that she expected to feel had not materialized. This meant that either Ira was sulking or that he wasn't there at all. She paused. Even for her, considered a loud mouth by everyone all her life, even for her it was hard to say this. But it had to be said. "You didn't pay enough attention to them, Ira. You needed me at the company, and I did what I had to do. But the children needed us. And I don't think they got enough of us,

Ira. Things have gone wrong for them. Sharon with Barney . . . Susan unmarried . . . and Bruce!" Phyllis paused and bit her lip. There were some things best left unsaid. "I don't want to criticize you, but I don't think you were there for them, Ira. You paid for the best schools, but they didn't learn how to live. They don't know what's important. And I think they need their mother. I'm going up to take care of the children, Ira. I wasn't a good enough mother to them then, but I can try and make up for it now."

Phyllis sighed deeply. The sun was merciless, and she thought of the skin cancer that Ira had developed on his bald head. She should wear a hat, but she couldn't stand hats or sunglasses or any of the extra *chazerai* that most people schlepped around in Florida: sunscreen, lip balm, eye shades, visors. Who had the time? Florida was the place that looked like paradise but wound up deadly. "Ira, Thanksgiving was unbearable. Eating a turkey in the Rascal House yesterday and having the kids calling only out of a sense of obligation? What kind of holiday was that? It wasn't good for them and it wasn't good for me. It was depressing, Ira." She lowered her voice. Phyllis wasn't vain, but she lied about her age. "My seventieth birthday is on the twelfth, Ira. It scares me. Then there's Hanukkah, Christmas, and New Year's coming, I won't survive if I try to do it down here. Do you understand?"

Nothing. No response. Phyllis told herself she shouldn't be surprised. Always she talked, he listened. But at least at one time he had listened. In Florida, in the last several years, he seemed to have collapsed in on himself. His world was only as large as his chest cavity and the illness that resided in it. Phyllis had made sure he took his pills, watched his diet, and that he'd exercised. But conversation? A luxury. Phyllis sighed again. What did she expect?

Phyllis turned her back on Ira and wiped moisture out of her eyes. She wasn't a crier. It was ridiculous to get all emotional. She knew that and fiercely told herself to stop it. She turned back. "You won't be alone here," she said. "Iris Blumberg is just over there by the willow tree, and Max Feiglebaum isn't far away." She paused. "I know you don't have patience for Sylvia, but she'll visit every week to tidy up."

There wasn't anything more to say. They had had a good marriage, she and Ira. There were those who saw her as pushy, as too outgoing, as egocentric. Not Ira. And he'd been wrong because she *was* all those things. You couldn't reach the age of sixty-nine, she mused, without knowing a little bit about yourself. Unless you were very pigheaded, or a man. Ira, a man, had never really understood her or learned a thing about himself. But then with men, how much was there to know?

With men, either they had a job or they didn't, they cheated or they didn't, they charmed you or they didn't. Ira had been an accountant before he retired, almost a decade ago. Ira was a good man. He worked and brought home his pay, didn't cheat, and didn't charm. But he had liked her. If he hadn't understood her, he had at least enjoyed her. And he'd given her three beautiful babies.

Phyllis thought of Susan, Bruce, and Sharon. Each had been so perfect, so gorgeous. Funny how babies grew up and became just as imperfect as any other adults.

She shook her head, dislodging the tangential thought. As she'd aged she hadn't, thank God, lost her memory. Instead, if anything, she remembered too much too often. "So anyway, Ira, I hope this doesn't come as a shock. You always knew I hated this place. Nobody down here but tourists, old Jews, and rednecks. I've *got* to leave you. It's for my mental health," she said, though she knew that Ira would hardly accept that as a legitimate excuse. "When did you become sane?" was one of the questions he'd frequently asked her. Despite his mild joke they both knew she was the voice of reason.

"I haven't told the children. I know they'll be upset. But I can't live only for them or you, Ira." Phyllis stooped down and picked up a stone from the ground beside the grave. She walked up to his headstone and laid the pebble beside the others that still remained from previous visits she or the children had made. Who would visit the grave now? Just her friend, Sylvia Katz? The *goyishe* groundskeeper she always gave five dollars to when she came in? Whoever it was, she knew Ira wouldn't like it. "Ira, I *have* to," she said as she picked up her purse and prepared to go. "It'll kill me if I stay here much longer."

∞

Virtually every morning for nine years and three months, Ira and Phyllis Geronomous had walked the strip of macadamized beachfront that was known throughout Dania, Florida, as "The Broadwalk." Now, since his death almost two years ago, Phyllis continued to walk it, more out of habit than desire. Today, Black Friday, the day after Thanksgiving, the beautiful weather did not match her mood, though she felt better after her talk with Ira. The sea, a Caribbean azure, winked at her as she made the turn from the shaded section of the path to the straightaway that led past the band shell, the cheap bathing suit and T-shirt boutiques, the snack shops, and greasy restaurants. In stark contrast, on the other side of the tarmac was a swath of flat pristine beach that met the aqua water. No one, not even the *meshuga* suntanners, was on the beach side yet. The Broadwalk was already peppered with pedestrians—dozens of people over sixty-five who found sleep impossible beyond 5 A.M. and did their morning constitutionals before the heat became too oppressive.

Phyllis didn't know why she was walking now. She had

walked with Ira because he had to: with congestive heart failure you had to keep the circulation moving, the weight down, and the fluids out of your lungs. Ira wouldn't walk without her, so every morning they'd both gotten up and she'd done the three miles down to the parking lot and the three miles back, past the Howard Johnson's, past the palm trees and cheap motels, all the way to the California Dream Inn before quitting for the day.

Now she passed the Pinehearst and, as usual, Sylvia Katz was sitting out in front on her webbed aluminum lawn chair, waiting, with her ubiquitous huge black patent leather purse perched on her lap. Sylvia Katz was in her mid-seventies, maybe more, though she wouldn't admit it. She was *zaftig*, short, and her hair had thinned. She wore it teased and colored red—the unnatural red of those poisonous maraschino cherries that they put on top of the Chinese food in the bad restaurants down here. She was from Queens—Kew Gardens—and had spent the last fifteen years of her married life living here. She was neither smart nor witty, but she was loyal and patient and the best that Phyllis could do in the friendship department right now. Here, friends had died or dispersed in the diaspora of the aging. "Can I walk with you?" Sylvia asked, as she always did.

"It's a free country," Phyllis answered with a shrug, completing the morning ritual in their usual way.

Sylvia Katz pushed herself up from the chair and stepped past the concrete balustrade that separated Pinehearst Gardens from The Broadwalk hoi polloi. They walked in near silence for a moment, the only sound being the noise of Sylvia's sandals shuffling, and the swishing of her purse rubbing against her shorts. Over and over again Phyllis had begged Sylvia both to leave the purse behind and to get a pair of Reeboks just like everybody else. But Sylvia wouldn't do it. You couldn't tell with Sylvia whether it was that she hated change or that she couldn't spend the money. Phyllis shrugged. What did it matter if Sylvia schlepped the purse or dragged her feet? So it made her walk more slowly. Big deal. They weren't going anywhere.

"I told Ira," Phyllis announced.

"Do you think he was upset?" Sylvia asked.

"How could I know?" Phyllis heard her own voice betraying the irritation that Sylvia so often made her feel. "Even when he was alive, you couldn't tell if Ira was feeling anything. In the hospital, with his lungs filled with fluid, he didn't complain."

They were past the band shell, empty except for the sign that announced the swing-band concert that night. Once a week The Broadwalk was thronged with couples joined together by the lindy. Sylvia, whose husband had deserted her a few years earlier after over twenty-one years of marriage, came regularly and sat watching, her patent leather purse firmly held on her lap. But no matter how often she invited Phyllis, Phyllis abstained. Sylvia never noticed and kept asking.

It wasn't that Phyllis didn't like the music, except maybe this Friday evening, when the sign said "The Mistletoes," the season's opening band, were playing a holiday medley. She needed chestnuts roasting like she needed a melanoma. Usually she loved music. Now, though, it made her too restless and sad. Somehow Sylvia could feel comfortable sitting on the sidelines, but for Phyllis, it was too painful knowing that she'd never dance again. People did dance on The Broadwalk, and then, in a blink of time, they were dead and gone. They might as well be under The Broadwalk, buried in the sand. Phyllis repressed a sigh. Ira had never been much of a dancer. Long ago, somehow, Phyllis had given it up. It was ridiculous at her age to care, but there was something about the music that got under her skin and didn't allow her to sit, blank and regret-less, along with Sylvia.

"You comin' tonight?" Sylvia asked, as predictable as Republican bank scandals.

"I can't," Phyllis told her. "I'm having dinner in Buckingham Palace."

"Don't kid me," Sylvia said, but there was enough doubt in her voice that Phyllis knew she could.

"Betty is very unhappy," Phyllis continued. "All of her children have disappointed her. I said 'Betty, that's what they're for.' We're talking it over tonight. You know, they say that Edward is like my Bruce. 'Gay, schmay,' I said to her. 'Just help him find a nice *faigela* and settle down.'"

"Prince Edward is like your Bruce?" Sylvia asked, her voice lowering.

"Wake up and smell the nitroglycerin," Phyllis told her friend, who also had a heart condition.

"What a tragedy," Sylvia tsked. "And in such a family."

"It's in *my* family, too," Phyllis snapped. "What are we, belly lox? Nothing wrong with it." Plenty was wrong with it, in Phyllis's opinion, and with Susan and Sharon, too, but it was no one's job but hers to point it out.

If Phyllis ever took Sylvia seriously she'd be offended. But, luckily, she knew how ridiculous it would be to be offended by anything Sylvia said. The woman had a strong constitution, a good heart, and a weak mind.

"I heard the Queen Mother had a colostomy," Sylvia said in a lowered voice. "Like my Sid." For the decade before Sid left her, Sylvia had coped with not only her own heart condition but also Sid's colon cancer. "Can you imagine? All those garden parties." Phyllis ignored the non sequitur. Who knew how Sylvia's mind worked?

They had reached the end of The Broadwalk and, as always, Sylvia had to touch the post implanted in the macadam to stop vehicular traffic.

"What would happen if, just once, we walked to the end and you didn't hit the barrier?" Phyllis asked.

"Everybody touches the post," Sylvia said. "You have to touch the post."

"No you don't. I don't."

"You. You're different."

"*Nu?* Tell me something I don't know."

Phyllis sighed. Different was fine. It was lonely that was the problem. She didn't know how long she'd been lonely. Certainly way before Ira died. After a while, it became a fact of life and you just didn't notice it any more. That was the danger. It was like smelling gas: if you didn't pay attention to it, it could kill you. In Florida, Phyllis hadn't had a really good friend, one who understood her and got her jokes. Even Ira, long before he died, had stopped responding much. But nobody talked to their husbands. What was there to say after forty-seven years? "Do you still like my brisket?" "Do you think that I ought to shorten this skirt?" "Should we pull our troops out of Bosnia?"

Phyllis still had a lot to say, but who wanted to listen? And who had anything interesting to say back? Which was why she was now walking down The Broadwalk with Sylvia Katz. Sylvia was no Madame Curie, didn't understand half of what Phyllis was talking about, but at least she wasn't offended by Phyllis's wisecracks.

Most of the women that Phyllis knew *were* offended by her. She had to face it, she had a big mouth. She always had. And if she offended most of the women she met down here, they in turn bored her. They'd talk about recipes, grandchildren, shopping, and more recipes. They bored her stiff. Sylvia was a relief. No kids, no recipes, no aggravation.

Phyllis's own children interested her, but not just to brag about. They interested her because they were interesting, not because they were hers. Susan was brilliant, Bruce was remarkably witty, and Sharon ... well, Sharon, she had to admit, favored her father's side of the family. Still, she loved them. Like Queen Betty must love her brood. It didn't mean she approved of their behavior, or that they approved of hers.

"This means you'll be with the kids for the holidays. Nice for you." She sounded wistful. "Nice for them." Sylvia paused. "Do they know you're going up?" she asked.

Phyllis was silent.

"You haven't told them, have you?" Sylvia asked accusingly.

"Not yet," Phyllis admitted.

"You have to. You have to," Sylvia said. Her own son had both refused a Thanksgiving invitation and not extended one to her. "If you don't tell them, I will."

"Don't you dare," Phyllis warned.

"When are you going to tell them?"

"Next Purim," Phyllis said, and opened the gate to Pinehearst for her friend.

two

*Y*ou're joking."

"You wish."

"Come on," Sig Geronomous said cavalierly. "It's just one of those empty threats. One of those nutty things she says that get us all jerked around for nothing. Like the time she corresponded with the Asian bride and wanted to import her for you."

"She means this," Sig's brother, Bruce, told her. "Todd, get over here and tell her that it's true." Bruce didn't live with Todd, but they had been spending a lot of time together. Whenever Sig asked if it was serious Bruce evaded the question.

"Bruce has the proof," Todd shouted into the receiver.

"How do you know?"

"Because she gave Mrs. Katz the rattan magazine rack," Bruce responded.

"The magazine rack? Oh my God!" Susan Geronomous—now known to her friends and business associates as Sigourney—accidentally dropped the telephone receiver. It crashed so hard against her granite countertop that her brother Bruce, at the other end of the phone, winced.

"What was that? Did you hurt yourself?"

"I wish." Sigourney had gotten control of the phone; now she just had to control herself. This couldn't really be happening . . .

nothing was ever as bad as it seemed . . . absence made the heart grow fonder . . . too many cooks—she stopped. She was going crazy. This couldn't be true. Christmas and her mother both coming? She might as well pull out the razor blades now. Sig looked down appraisingly at her elegant wrist. "She just casually mentioned that she gave away the rattan magazine rack?"

"I'm way ahead of you," Bruce sang. "Mom didn't tell me. It's not a setup. It was Mrs. Katz who called."

"When?"

"Twenty minutes ago."

"Mom could have put her up to it."

"I already called the building manager. Confirmation. *And* there's a garage sale this week."

"A garage sale? She doesn't even have a garage, for God's sake."

"Yard sale, lawn sale, tag sale. Sigourney, don't play your word games now. It's happening. So, what are we going to do?"

Sigourney tried to regain some control. "What did Mrs. Katz say when you talked to her? Exactly. Word for word."

"That Mom was leaving Florida for good. That she's packing up and moving to New York. She's getting a ticket today. She wants to arrive on Wednesday."

"Wednesday! That's only six days from now."

"Mmm. Good counting, Sig. That's why you earn the big bucks. Actually, it's five, since you don't officially count—".

"Don't be so anal, Bruce. And sarcasm is not necessary at this moment. We'll have more than we can handle starting Wednesday." Sigourney tapped the countertop. Her mother, living here in New York again. Calling her. Looking in her closets. Commenting. Criticizing. Oh God! Fear gripped Sig's chest like a Wonderbra. "This is the end of life as we know it, Bruce. How can we stop her?"

"Hmmm." He paused, ruminating. Bruce was smart. Maybe he'd have a solution. "How about plastic explosives in the cargo bay? We'd take down a lot of innocent lives, but we would know it was a small price to pay."

"Bruce!"

"Come on, Sig. It would be an act of kindness. People *love* tragedies at holiday time. It gives them something to watch on TV. Makes them feel better about the tragedy unfolding under their own Christmas trees."

"Amen, brother!" Todd yelled in the background. Todd had been raised a Southern Baptist in Tulsa, Oklahoma, before he ran off to New York City to become an agnostic photographer.

"Bruce!" Sigourney forced herself to exhale while simultaneously staring up at the immaculate blue ceiling of her seventy-thousand-dollar kitchen. Her home, her beautifully designed, luxurious, and comfortable home, was her haven, her safe place where perfection reigned. It comforted her as nothing else did. She breathed deeply. Then her eyes focused on a tiny line. Was that a crack right in the corner? Was the glaze going already, despite Duarto's assurances that the fourteen hand-lacquered layers would last ten lifetimes? She had picked up the pen and jotted a note to herself to call him before she realized what she was doing. This news, this shattering news had come, *and she was writing notes to her decorator*? Where were her values, her priorities? It could only be denial kicking in. She'd better focus. "Did you speak to Sharon yet?" she asked her brother.

"You *are* losing it. I don't bother to call her with *good* news—not that I've had any of *that* lately." Bruce, at his end of the phone, eyed his shabby brownstone apartment. The two rooms, though neat and cozy, were cluttered not only with all his worldly goods but also with what remained of his entire business stock—the gay greeting card line he'd created and marketed until his partner had absconded with most of the money last year. And the season wasn't going as well as he'd hoped. It had really only just begun but already stock had started being returned by Village shops Queer Santa wasn't selling as he'd expected. Bruce sighed. Sig was buzzing in his ear. He adored his older sister, but she was sometimes so controlling, especially when she was frightened. He interrupted her chatter. "Sig, if I called Sharon, which I wouldn't. she'd just tell me how it was going to be even worse for her than for us, that it was always worse for her." Bruce sighed again, this time explosively. "I know it's the middle-child syndrome, but you'd think at thirty-seven she'd get over it."

Sharon was their disappointed and disappointing sister— four years younger than Sig, and only a year older than Bruce. But she looked twice his age. She had let herself go—it wasn't just her weight, it was her frosted hair that looked ten years out of date, the Talbots clothes in size sixteen that even a skinny Connecticut WASP couldn't get away with, and more than anything else it was the way her eyes and her mouth and her shoulders drooped in parallel, descending bell curves.

"We have to call Sharon," Sigourney said, ignoring her brother. "This is too big to handle on our own."

"Well, she's bigger than both of us," Bruce laughed. "Not that she'll be any use."

Sigourney knew all about it. Bruce had almost no patience for Sharon, but Sigourney felt sorry for her fat, whiny, frustrated, younger sister. Maybe it was because Sharri made her feel guilty. Maybe it was because Sig herself was so successful. Whatever the reason, she had no time now to listen to Bruce's usual sniping. "*I'll* call her," Sigourney said. "Can you meet here Saturday? I'm giving a pre-Christmas brunch at eleven for my A-list clients. Sunday I'm doing the B-list with the leftovers. But three on Saturday would be good for me."

"Well, don't put yourself out," Bruce said nastily. "What does that make us? C-list?"

Sig knew he was probably hurt because she hadn't invited him and Todd to either brunch. Bruce didn't realize how badly her own business had fallen off and she was too proud to tell him. She was also embarrassed about her necessary small economies, like using the catering firm for one party and making it do for two. But this wasn't the eighties anymore. And she couldn't afford to have Todd and Bruce acting up and alienating prospects and clients.

"I'll come," Bruce finally agreed, "but there's nothing we can do." He began to recite aloud in a singsong: "Roses are red / Chickens are white / If you think you can stop her / You're not very bright."

"No wonder your greeting card business is in trouble," was all Sig answered. "I'm hanging up and calling Sharon."

"Well, don't let Barney come," Bruce begged, defeated. Barney was not just Sharon's loser husband; he was also a blowhard. He was big and barrel-chested and balding. But what Sig and Bruce found intolerable was that he managed to lose every job he'd ever had while making Sharon feel like a failure. Barney was the kind of person who explained to heart surgeons at cocktail parties some new technique he'd read about in *Reader's Digest*. In short, he was an asshole.

Now it was Sig's turn to sigh. "I'll try to make it just us, but lately Sharon hasn't been driving. She gets those panic attacks when she has to cross a bridge."

"Oh, come on. She's a victim of faux agoraphobia. She's just too lazy to drive into the city. She's probably just trying to get a handicapped parking permit. Totally faux."

"Bruce! That's not true."

"Oh, Sig, Sig, Sig, Sig! Sometimes life could do with a little embellishment."

"My God! You sounded *exactly* like Mother then."

"I did not."

"You *did*."

"It's started," Bruce sang out.

Sig paused, biting back the need to tell him it was his fault. "You're right," she admitted. "Okay. It's Saturday at three and now I'll call Sharon."

"See ya. Wouldn't wanna be ya!" Bruce yodeled. Sig merely shook her head and hung up the phone.

∞

Sig stood silently for a few moments in the center of her immaculate living room. She knew she shouldn't do it, but she was drawn irresistibly to the vanity in her bedroom. She looked around at the room and its beautiful decor. She'd have to sell the co-op, no doubt about it. She was behind in her maintenance payments and starting to get nasty looks from the co-op board president when she ran into him in the lobby.

Her client list had dropped, her commissions were down, and her own portfolio had taken a beating. Welcome to the nineties. Sig had done her best to downsize her expenses—she hadn't used her credit cards for months, had paid her phone bill and Con Ed on time, and had spent money only on the necessities. But it wasn't enough. Business had slowed to a trickle and even if she sold her stock now, she'd take a loss and have no possibility for the future. She'd just have to sell her apartment.

But this apartment was more than just equity: it was her haven. Maybe that was because she felt her mother had never made a home for her. As Phyllis had often said, "I'd be happy living out of a suitcase in a clean motel." The very thought made Sig shudder. Besides, the apartment was her visible sign of success, her security, and a place she could come after a long hard day of gambling with other people's money to lick her wounds. It was beautiful. It was perfect, and she'd have to face the fact that it was empty and she would have to sell it. The money would evaporate faster than good perfume out of an open flask and she would wind up destitute. Or worse: she'd wind up in an apartment in Fort Lee, New Jersey.

Sig looked into the mirror as she knew, irrevocably, what she would have to do. She didn't like what she saw. Was Bruce right? She wasn't just getting older, but also bitter? Were those new lines forming at the corner of her mouth? She stared more deeply into the mirror. And then her eyes flitted to the reflection in one pane of the three-sided glass. For a second something about the softness in the line of her jaw reminded her of . . . what? She was puckering, decaying, and withering. She was going the way of all flesh. Sig shuddered. But it wasn't just the age thing that gave her the shivers; she had looked like . . . her mother.

Sig moved her head but the trick of light, or the angle, was gone. Jesus, she would wind up alone. She wouldn't even have the comfort of three children to annoy and be annoyed by. Tears of self-pity and something else—a deeper sorrow—rose to her eyes. She *was* getting older, but she was also getting bitter. The thought of Phillip Norman made her sad. Sig had known he was no genius, but he was presentable, fairly successful—if a corporate lawyer could be considered that—and his warmth for her made up for some of her coolness. It was nice to be wanted, and Phillip seemed to want marriage and a child. She would have to at least compromise—she'd give up the idea of a soulmate for a friend, a partner, and a family. But she was starting to believe that Phillip was even less than a friend: he was an empty suit. He and all of the other empty suits and bad boys who had preceded him made her mouth tremble. She looked like shit and she felt worse.

It wasn't as if she hadn't been trying to find somebody, someone to settle down with, to marry. Even to have a family with, if it wasn't too late. Her mother acted as if it was Sig who was stopping it from happening. But the truth was there were no men who were interested. Despite her good haircut, her visible success, her careful makeup, her Armani suits—or maybe because of them—Sig couldn't remember the last time a new man had expressed any interest in her. The truth was, it wasn't like she had a choice except Phillip. Oh, she could have affairs with any of the more interesting but very married men she worked with, but she wasn't a Glenn Close/*Fatal Attraction* kind of girl. She didn't steal other women's husbands. And other than other women's husbands, who had looked at her lately? The Gristede's delivery boy? Her elevator operator? Women over thirty-five started to become invisible. She was losing it, and she was losing it fast.

She picked up a lipstick, about to paint a little color onto her lips when her hand froze in midair. Why bother, she thought. Why bother to paint it on. She was losing it—she had lost it. The bloom of youth, the promise of fecundity that attracted men, that even on some unconscious level promised them a breeder, was disappearing. Perhaps men her age wanted younger women not only for their looks but because of the hormonal message a young girl sent: that she could still carry their child. That she could demonstrate their virility to the world with her upright breasts and a bulging belly. Sig's periods were still regular. But how long would it last? She wasn't a breeder. The bloom of youth was gone, and she'd grow old alone.

She looked deeper into the mirror. Under her mother's brittle veneer, wasn't there a desperation? Wasn't there a gallantry that seemed to say to Sig that it was better to go down fighting, to be feisty and annoying, than to ever be perceived as pathetic and lonely?

Sig looked around once more at the bedroom and rose and wandered through all her perfect rooms. She wound up, as usual, in her kitchen. Her eyes immediately focused on the one flaw—the tiny crack in the lacquer finish. Had it grown? Perhaps she should have spent the money on smoothing her own wrinkles, in lacquering her own finish. Perhaps if she lost a few pounds more, did a little more time on the treadmill, and had her eyes done, she could attract someone more acceptable, more interesting, more human than Phillip Norman. Then again, maybe not. Sig reached for the door of her Subzero refrigerator, pulled open the freezer, and grabbed a pint container of Edy's low-fat double Dutch chocolate ice milk. She sat on the floor and, using a tablespoon, began to eat it all. She rarely gave herself over to this behavior, but the sweetness in her mouth was comforting. She understood how her sister had ballooned to over two hundred pounds. Thinking of Sharon, she realized she hadn't yet called her. Well, she'd call her later. After the Edy's was gone.

three

"hyllis Geronomous. A ticket to New York," she announced. "One way. For a December fourth arrival."

"Do you have reservations?"

"Plenty of them, but I'm going anyway." The agent didn't look up from her keyboard or even respond to Phyllis's little joke. Phyllis shrugged. She knew this type. Old women were usually invisible to them.

They were in a tiny, tacky office, desks lined up facing each other, and in the center was a small white Dynel Christmas tree with tiny pink Christmas bulbs hanging down. The travel agent had been recommended by her son-in-law—she was the young woman who owned the agency. Barney had said, "She'll get you a deal. She owes me." Phyllis didn't like to think of what this annoying Floridian with the big hair could possibly owe Barney for, but she had to get a ticket somewhere. The clerk looked at her for the first time, as if she now knew something was expected but wasn't sure what. "So . . . you're going to The Big Apple?" she asked.

"It looks that way." She smiled sweetly. The only advantage to being an old dame was that if she smiled she could get away with murder.

The agent consulted her screen, then made a baby mouth. "You should have planned ahead. Do you know that a one-way

ticket costs as much as a round trip?" She spoke in a condescending, louder voice, as if Phyllis were both stupid and hard
of hearing.

"We're in peak season for the holidays. You can't meet the
fourteen- or twenty-one-day advance ticket purchase deadline."

Tell me something I don't know, Phyllis thought, while the
agent continued. Where was the help or break in price Barney
had implied? Typical. Barney Big Mouth. Phyllis certainly wasn't
going to ask this woman for any favors. "Anyway," the agent continued, "don't you want a round trip, for when you're coming
back?"

"I'm never coming back!" Phyllis said vehemently. "I only
moved down in the first place because Ira wanted to. But he's
dead, so why stay?" Phyllis immediately realized she'd said too
much. God, next she'd be telling strangers on buses her entire
life story. The potential humiliation of loneliness was like a
direct kick to her pride. She took a breath. She'd fight back with
the only weapon she'd ever used—her tongue. "Who needs to
live in a place where everybody talks, but they're so deaf they
can't listen? No one was born here, they just die here. Feh!
Nothing has roots here, except the mangrove trees. I hate
Florida!"

"*I* was born in Gainesville," the younger woman said. "I *like*
Florida. Especially Miami."

Phyllis crossed her arms. "How can you like a city where the
local rock band is called Dead German Tourists?" she asked.

The condescending younger woman recoiled. "Well, the violence is bad for my business . . . " she began.

"Not too good for the German tourists, either," Phyllis added.
"But the survivors are enough to make you homicidal. And the
retirees!" Phyllis rolled her eyes. "I didn't like any of these people when they lived up in New York and were important and

pushy. Why the hell I should like them now, when they're just hanging around all day and still being pushy, is beyond me."

"Florida is a nice place for retirement. The weather's good and—"

"You call ninety-nine percent humidity *good* weather?" Phyllis asked. "Compared to what? Djakarta? You should see the fungus garden growing on my winter coat! And another thing: Who says that everyone the same age should hang out together? I don't want to be anywhere near these people. It's an age ghetto. This place isn't God's Waiting Room; it's Hell's Foyer. It's an elephant graveyard." Phyllis straightened herself up to her full height. "Well, I'm no elephant. I'm a New Yorker."

Coldly, the agent looked at her. "New York is a dangerous place, especially for an older lady alone." She was acting now as if Phyllis were incompetent, a doddering old wreck.

"You mean you think I'm incapacitated?"

"Uhh—no." The witch raised her brows. "Certainly not," she said, with the sincerity of a surgical nurse saying the procedure wouldn't hurt at all.

Why did every person under the age of fifty feel they could talk to an older woman as if she'd lost her marbles? Phyllis wondered. It made Phyllis feel more ornery than usual. "Look, just book me a seat. In first class. I'll get all the bad advice I need from my children."

Phyllis waited while the ticket printed out and took comfort in the idea that this girl would some day also be post-menopausal. In forty-five years she'd be plucking whiskers out of that recessive chin—if she could still see her chin, and had enough eye-hand coordination to hold a tweezers.

"Oh," the young woman cooed as she handed Phyllis the ticket. "Your *children* are up there. That's different. Well, I'm sure *they'll* be happy to see you."

"My eldest is a very successful stockbroker. She's got a gorgeous apartment on Central Park. And my youngest, my son, is an entrepreneur." Phyllis paused for a moment. She couldn't leave out Sharon. "My middle daughter has two adorable children."

"Which one will you be staying with?" the agent asked.

"Oh, I'm sure they'll all be fighting over *that*," Phyllis told the agent. "As soon as they know I'm coming."

"Don't they know?"

Phyllis shook her head. "Surprise is an essential part of the art of war." Mrs. Katz choked a little behind her. Phyllis turned her head. "Sylvia. Did you—"

"Do you want this?" the agent said, interrupting in a rude way.

Phyllis snatched the ticket from the agent and shook her head again. "Certainly. Just take the time from now on to show a little respect to your elders. Osteoporosis is in *your* future, too, you know." Phyllis got up from the chair, turned, and walked away.

four

Who's going to pick Mom up at the airport on Wednesday?" Sharon asked. The three siblings were together at their elder sister's, but Sharon was doing most of the talking. She was a big woman, though her hands and feet were dainty—almost abnormally tiny. Her eyes, buried in her pudgy cheeks, were the same dark brown as the unfrosted parts of her hair and darted nervously from side to side. She'd already obsessed about the airport for two and a half hours.

Sig sighed. Between now and Wednesday she had a lot to cram into four days. She had to prepare for the marketing meeting, complete a newsletter, start her Christmas shopping on a nonexistent budget, and prepare Christmas cards for her clients, as well as coping now with the arrival of her mother. She always had to do everything, she thought, including making all the arrangements, dealing with their mother's minimal finances, and regularly lending money to both her siblings. Sometimes you just had to draw the line. She waited. She knew that Sharon, like nature itself, abhorred a vacuum. She'd break the silence, and once she did. . .

"I'm not going to do it," Sharon responded, filling the gap. Her voice sounded firm, though her chin wobbled. "I'm *not*," she repeated. The sureness was already gone, a whine beginning. Sharon was an expert in fine whines. Sig continued to wait. When she closed a large order she used this technique. "Don't you have to go over the Triborough Bridge?" Sharon asked anxiously, waiting for a response. There was none, except a groan from Bruce as he exhaled cigarette smoke. "I don't think I could do a three-borough bridge," Sharon said in a little-girl voice. Sig began to feel sorry for her. "Let Bruce get her."

Bruce snorted. He was a greenish color, but it didn't stop him from smoking, Sig thought, annoyed. One sibling ate. One smoked. Oh well.

Before Bruce could react further, Sig intervened. "Bruce says he can't. He's meeting with some new potential partner." He always was, and nothing ever came of it, but. . . . "I'll just send a car," Sig said wearily.

"You can't do that! Mom will talk about it for the next ten years."

"Look, Sharon, I can't go, Sig can't go, and you can't go. What do you suggest?" Bruce asked nastily.

Sharon ignored her brother. "Sig, she'll never step into a limo. You know how she is about money. She'll try to get all of her luggage onto a Fugazy bus. And she'll have a stroke doing it. Then we'll all have to nurse her."

There was a long pause as all three siblings graphically imagined it.

"You're right. We'll all have to go," Sig said. She was feeling queasy. The brunch had not gone well and then Phillip had shocked her by—

"That's settled. Now what do we do with her once she's here?" Bruce asked, crushing out his cigarette in Sig's pristine Steuben crystal ashtray and lighting another.

"I have an idea." Sharon looked up from the sofa, which she was weighing down with her bulk. Despite her frightened eyes, she smiled hopefully at her two siblings. Bruce, sunk in his chair, was still recovering from a big Friday night. The upcoming holidays, the low reorders, and the news about his mother's imminent arrival had pushed him to overdo it.

Sig, overwhelmed by it all, stood up and began fussily picking up tiny specks off the rug, moving the holly-decorated candles and napkins around and wiping microscopic smears from the cleared-up remains of her client brunch. She had to keep things in order for her B-list brunch tomorrow. Neither Sig nor Bruce even looked over at Sharon, but Sig—in a voice that sounded less than interested—at last asked, "So?"

"Mommy, can I have some juice?" Jessie interrupted as she rubbed Sig's white cashmere throw compulsively against her cheek. Despite Sig's request to the contrary, Sharon had brought Barney and her daughter, though the former wasn't minding the latter as Sharon had promised.

"Here's my idea," Sharon said, ignoring her relentless daughter. "We put Mom in a home."

"Yeah. Right," Bruce said with disgust.

"Sharon, no home would take her. She's not physically incapacitated," Sigourney pointed out. "She isn't sick or crippled . . . "

" . . . Except emotionally," Bruce agreed. "Anyway, there's not a pen that could hold her. She'd start food riots. *The Big House*. Mom's Wallace Beery in drag. She'd tunnel her way out with her dentures."

There was a pause. "We could tell them she's mentally unstable," Sharon suggested.

"Hey. It just might work," Bruce said, opening his eyes to narrow slits. "We take her to some high-security retirement home and say she has senile dementia."

"She's *always* been demented, Bruce. It has nothing to do with her age," Sigourney reminded him. "Anyway, she knows what day of the week it is. And who the president is." Sigourney laughed bitterly. "When they ask her *that* one, they'll get a fifteen-minute tirade!"

"Mommy, can I have some juice?" Jessie asked again.

"Barney, would you give Jessie a drink?" Sharon nearly shrieked. Both Sig and Bruce recoiled and winced. Barney had planted his own bulk in the kitchen and was simultaneously scarfing down every bit of the leftovers and watching the Rams game. Bruce clutched at his head. Sharon didn't notice, nor did she move off the sofa. She certainly didn't lower the volume. "Jessie, be patient or you'll have to go sit in the thinking chair in the corner," she warned in a little-girl voice. Jessie hung her head, then went to hide behind Sig's eighty-dollar-a-yard Scalamandre silk curtains, taking the throw with her. "What if we say she's delusional?" Sharon continued desperately. "We could say she's not our mother—she only thinks she is."

For the first time Bruce sat up straight and fully opened his eyes. "Why Sharon, I'm proud of you. That's a truly devious idea. I like that in a person." He paused. "*Gaslight*. Mom as a small, Jewish Ingrid Bergman. We all play Charles Boyer. 'But Auntie Phyllis, you know you have no children!' Then we start hiding her hat in the closet."

"I hope you're having a good time with this nonsense," Sig said. "But Mom doesn't have a hat, you're out of the closet, and this nightmare begins in three days. Don't encourage Sharon, Bruce." Sig turned to her younger sister. "Sharri, no home would take Mom, and even if they did, she can't afford it. *I* can't afford it. Do you know what the DeWitt charges? Twenty thousand a month."

"Well, she doesn't have to be on East Seventy-ninth Street," Barney said, finally entering with the juice. His bare belly hung out under his Rams T-shirt. Despite his own girth he still criticized Sharon's weight. "She doesn't need anything that fancy. She's no friggin' duchess."

"Shut up, Barney," Sig and Bruce told him simultaneously.

"Just put her in a mental institution," Barney said as he was about to hand the brimming glass to Jessie. "A place for the criminally insane. That's where she belongs anyway. She's crazy."

"She's *not* crazy, Barney," Sig began in a voice calibrated to be understood even by four-year-olds. "She's not crazy: she's hostile. To you. There is a difference."

"Well, I say she's crazy."

Bruce raised his brows at his brother-in-law and looked over at Sharon. "Maybe it's time for Barney to go sit in the thinking chair in the corner?" he said in a little-girl voice. Without a word, Barney turned and walked toward the kitchen. "Ah, that's better," Bruce said, closing his eyes. "Now I can die in peace."

"Bruce, stop it. Have *you* got any ideas?" Sig asked, watching Jessie and the juice nervously. Was her niece wearing a hole in the cashmere? And why did she worry herself about material things when her whole life was coming apart?

"Well, I've been thinking. Mom is a kind of negative Auntie Mame." He paused. "Eureka! That's it: she's the Anti-Mame. Not to be confused with the Antichrist, although in the South I understand she has been." He paused. "What to do, what to do? Maybe we could spray her gold and sell her as a standing lamp at the Twenty-sixth Street flea market. She's very fifties."

"Would you get serious?" Sig snapped. Bruce wasn't stupid. It was just that he was always joking, right until he went bankrupt. She thought of a way to focus him. "Mrs. Katz called me, too. Apparently Mom told her she was planning to be at the Chelsea."

"Oh my God!" Bruce cried and nearly dropped his cigarette. "That's only three blocks from my apartment!"

"Isn't that where Sid Vicious and all those rock stars died of overdoses?" Sharon asked.

Bruce nodded, starting to feel well and truly panicked. "We should be so lucky. What would *she* die of? An overdose of Provera? The only way *that* stuff could kill you is if a carton of it fell on your head."

Sigourney ignored the two of them. She would have to handle her mother and the holidays and the end of her relationship with Phillip all at once. "Would both of you stop with the jokes and hysteria and try, for just a minute, to get a grip?"

Bruce looked up at his older sister through bloodshot eyes. "Only if *you'll* stop being so superior!" He clutched at his aching head. "You know, the minute Mom gets here she's going to start calling you 'Susan' again and you're going to lose it. She'll call you 'Susan' in front of all your brunch-eating, bond-dealing friends. And she'll follow you to the bathroom after you eat to make sure you don't vomit. You'll balloon back up to a hundred and seventy pounds in no time."

"Pthew. Phtew." Jessie said as she sprayed juice all over the carpet and drapes. "Pthew! This has stuff in it!"

"Yes, sweetie. It's called 'pulp.' It's part of the orange," Sharon explained serenely.

"It's fresh-squeezed," Sig said through clenched teeth, attempting to avoid a cerebral hemorrhage. "Barney, would you bring some paper towels and club soda in here?" she called, managing not to scream. "I'll wipe off your face and take away the juice," she said to her niece.

Jessie began to wail. Then, to Sig's astonishment, so did Jessie's mother. Sig and her brother looked at Sharon and then at one another in astonishment. Sig raised her brows in the international gesture for 'what gives?' Bruce shrugged in the answering symbol, 'who knows?' Even Jessie stopped crying and looked at her mother. Sig forgot about the stains and gingerly perched beside Sharon on the sofa. "What is it, Sharri?"

"I know you want Mom to come live with us. That's what this is about. I know it. But she can't. She just can't!" Sharon sobbed. "We don't have a place to put her. We don't have a car for her to drive. Barney is using the spare room as his office until he gets a new job and, anyway, it would just be too much for me."

Sharon continued sobbing, and picked up the corner of the cashmere throw to wipe her eyes. "I know you're going to try and make me, but I won't. I just can't. I can't let her live with Jessie and Travis," she whimpered. She fumbled in her voluminous purse for her inhaler. When she was upset she reached for her asthma medicine. "Last time she did we had to have six double sessions with the family therapist. Do you know what that costs?" Sharon wiped her nose on the throw, and Sig winced. "Travis was having nightmares every night. He thinks 'Nana' is a curse word. And Jessie went mute."

"Well, *that* would be a relief," Bruce muttered. "Worth every penny."

Barney reentered the living room. It was too late. Jessie had cleaned her mouth and tongue with the other end of the white cashmere throw. Sharon's sobs grew louder and uncontrollable. Sig now divided her concern equally between her sister and her afghan. She patted Sharon's bloated shoulder, and gently handed her a paper towel.

"Sharri, we don't expect that. We know it would ruin your life."

"Not that it isn't already ruined . . . " Bruce added. Sharon's wails increased.

Sig threw a now-look-what-you've-done look at Bruce. "We're not trying to trick you into taking Mom home with you. First of all, it wouldn't be fair. Secondly, Mom wouldn't go. She doesn't like Westchester." Sig figured it wasn't necessary to add that Phyllis also didn't like Barney. "Thirdly, it wouldn't really solve our problem. When she wasn't nagging and interfering in *your* life, she'd come into town and ruin ours." Sharri looked up. Slowly, her tears abated. "Listen," Sig continued, "we have to find a permanent solution. A way to really neutralize her and separate her from us once and for all. And I think I have the way to do it. It's got to be done right away. It's a fill or kill."

"Oh my God! You want us to murder her," Sharon gasped. She clapped her hands over Jessie's ears to protect her. "You're going to make us help you do it, aren't you? We'll all go to prison."

"Nope. Murder's out." Bruce said. "Not on moral grounds, mind you. It's just that the woman wrecked the first thirty years of my life. I'm not going to spend the second thirty in jail for her." He shuddered. "Can you imagine *me* in prison? God, every night would be prom night. I'll bet Todd wouldn't even visit." He looked seriously at Sigourney. "With all of those shady clients of yours, don't *you* know someone who will bump her off and keep us out of it?"

Sigourney rolled her eyes. Couldn't Bruce ever be serious and couldn't Sharon ever make sense? "We can't *kill* her," Sigourney explained through clenched and beautifully bonded teeth. Sometimes Sharon was a complete ditz. "First of all, she's our mother and, more importantly, I have no intention of taking up residence in the Menendez Brothers' Wing at the nearest correctional facility. Fill or kill is just market talk for completing an order right away or dropping it. You have to help me with this. This is an immediate fill." She looked at her younger siblings sternly, the way she used to do when they were kids and she forced them to play Monopoly until she landed on Boardwalk and Park Place *and* had hotels on both. "We need a plan, a strategy, and I've got one.

But we'll have to work together to get it to happen." Finally, for the first time, silence reigned and Sig had everyone's complete attention. That was just the way she liked it.

Her mind had been working at lightning speed, doing what she did best, when she was trading: pulling together a wide and diverse bunch of information and coming up with a cohesive, realistic program. She could deal with their weaknesses and play to their strengths. She knew she could motivate them, and maybe, for once, they could all work together. She saw, as the Iron Duke must have seen the Waterloo battle plan, the roles that each of them could play in not just winning this battle but ending the war. As it always happened when she was trading, she grew calm and it felt as if time stopped. She knew she could cover the short.

"Sharon, aside from more money coming in, you need something to do. You're bright, and you used to be a great librarian. We can use your skills." Sharon opened her small eyes as wide as she could. "Bruce, you need an investor for your rapidly failing business. And you also have a sense of style second to none. I need some new clients. And we *all* need Mom distracted so that she won't be driving us totally nuts." She paused again for the drama of it. "I have a way to accomplish it all."

Bruce cocked his head. "How?"

"We marry her off."

"We *what*?" Sharon, Bruce, and Barney asked simultaneously.

"We marry her off. Preferably to a wealthy guy with bad health and no heirs."

"Ahh," Bruce said, light dawning. "The old Anna Nicole Smith ploy."

"I prefer to call it 'Operation Geezer Quest,'" Sig announced with dignity. "If we work together, it could happen." She warmed to the sale, just the way she did when she was pushing

OTC equity or TFI bonds. "We set Mom up like a jewel in a velvet box. We dress her right. Bruce, that's your job. We put her in a good hotel—no, not just good, but the best. I'll take care of that. And then we present her to the prospects. Finding them is your job, Sharon. If we work it right it's a short sell—we get someone to go for it before Mom's price goes down."

"But what if it doesn't work?" Bruce asked.

"Then we got a street-side buy-in," Sig said, rolling her eyes. "I lose a lot of money covering the short."

"But what about Daddy?" Sharon asked. They all turned to look at her.

"Sharon, Dad's dead," Bruce reminded her.

"I know that! But that doesn't mean he would like it. And what does she want with an old guy? She never even took care of *us*. Why would she want to take care of some old geezer?" Sharon's eyes filled. "They're sick and they usually don't smell very good."

"Not for *her* to take care of *him*. For *him* to take care of *her*," Sig explained. "We want 'em sick. We have to marry off Mom to somebody really old and really wealthy. Somebody who likes us—likes us a *lot*. He can introduce me to some rich, powerful clients. He can give Barney a job, and pay for Jessie's and Travis's private school. He could even bail out Bruce's semibankrupt business."

"He'd have to be deaf, dumb, and blind," Bruce said.

Sigourney nodded. "That would be good," she agreed. She began counting off on her fingers. "Deaf, dumb, blind, old, and rich."

"Oh, come off it, Sig," Sharon almost sneered. "*You're* only forty-one. You're thin, you're successful. You have a weird first name, you're beautiful, and *you* can't get a decent date. Phillip Norman is a jerk. He doesn't even appreciate you. Men want young, beautiful, fresh girls. How in the world are we supposed to find a rich man for Mom?"

Sig recoiled. Phillip Norman had come to her A-list brunch and afterwards, as she cleaned up the mess and waited for Bruce and Sharon, he had told Sig that though he truly liked her he thought it was important for her to know that he didn't believe there was a future in their relationship. Sig hadn't known whether to laugh or cry. Phillip was such a compromise for her, such a corporate drone. She'd been with him mainly because of his enthusiasm for her. To find that he wasn't avid was almost a joke, but one that had an unpleasant irony to it. How low would she sink? Could she find another man anywhere? Next she'd be sleeping with Eldin the painter.

"Right," Bruce agreed. "If *I* haven't found one, why should *she* get one? And even if we *could* get ahold of such a commodity, how could we possibly get Mom to date him? You know what she's like." He shrugged. "To know her is to be permanently irritated."

Sigourney pulled herself together. It was now or never. She tried to do her best Andy Hardy imitation. "Oh, come on, kids. I'm not saying it's easy, but we're not licked yet. You haven't lost *all* your librarian skills, Sharri. You can do the research, finding the geezers. And Brucie, you still have all those dresses in your closet." He grimaced at her. "Okay. We'll buy costumes! But we can use your makeup. I'll write the script and direct the rehearsals. And Barney . . . " She paused, momentarily losing her enthusiasm. "Well, we'll find *something* you can handle. So, come on, kids. Let's put on a show!"

She dropped the fake energy and her tone became cold and as frightening as she could manage. "Because if we don't, let's face it: our lives will become even worse than they are now."

five

*A*lthough it was seventy-eight degrees and sunny, the Miami airport was incongruously decked out in fake firs and Christmas tinsel. Sylvia Katz, forlornly schlepping her oversized purse, looked at Phyllis and shook her head. "First class? It's such a bad idea. *And* a waste of money," she said.

"What the hell." Phyllis shrugged. "I've never flown first class in my life. And that travel agent of my son-in-law's looked at me with respect."

"For wasting money, she respects you?"

"Oh, life can always use some embellishment. If I play my cards right, I'll never fly again. Might as well go out with a bang, right, Sylvia?"

"God forbid. Don't even joke." Sylvia paused. "You sure you won't change your mind? I'll give you back the magazine rack."

"Tempting, but no cigar."

"*Cigars?*" Sylvia said. "What do cigars have to do with this?"

Phyllis leaned forward and kissed Sylvia on the cheek. She'd never known anyone as literal as Sylvia. Nine-tenths of what Phyllis said went right over Sylvia's overpermed head. "You're in a world of your own, Sylvia," Phyllis told her friend. "That's probably why you can stand me. I don't get on your nerves because you don't have any."

"Nerves? Who cares about nerves? I won't have any *friends*

now." A tear began to run down Sylvia's very wrinkled cheek.

Phyllis fished into her jacket pocket and pulled out a key chain. "Keys to the Buick," she said. "Stay off I-95 and don't get carjacked, if you can help it."

"You're giving me your car? Your car?"

"I won't need it in New York. No one has cars in New York. It's a civilized place. We have taxis."

"Your *car*?"

"Sylvia, stop repeating yourself. You sound like a demented toucan." Phyllis reached out, took Mrs. Katz's plump and wrinkled hand and put the keys in them. "A little Christmas present. From me to you."

"But you already gave me so much. The magazine rack, the plants . . . " Sylvia took out a crumpled handkerchief and noisily blew her nose.

"Sylvia, who uses handkerchiefs anymore?" Phyllis asked and looked at the wet cloth distastefully. "What are you going to do with it now?"

"Put it in my purse."

"Feh! You'll get mucus all over your wallet. Get with the times and get yourself some Kleenex."

"Don't you think you should call the children?" Sylvia asked. "Tell them."

"You mean warn them. No. Why should I? So they'll argue with me?" She paused. "Sylvia, did you interfere?"

Sylvia cast down her eyes guiltily. Phyllis didn't need to ask any further and let her friend off the hook.

"You still giving me your car?" Sylvia asked.

"Yes. And I won't put any of them out, Sylvia. I'll stay at a hotel. I'll get my own place. It will make a nice surprise." Phyllis wasn't altogether sure that "nice" was the word any of her three children would use, but it was a free country.

"I'm going to miss you, Phyllis."

"I know."

"If it doesn't work out, you can come back down and stay with me any time."

"I know."

The fat woman fumbled in her purse. "I only got you a little something. A token." She handed Phyllis a small box.

"I know. A woman who hasn't picked up a check for more than seven years is not going to suddenly begin handing out Harry Winston." Phyllis took the little package and opened it. "Oh. Handkerchiefs. What have I done without them?"

"What will I do without *you*?" Sylvia sighed, the sarcasm lost on her.

"Play a lot of canasta. The girls will let you back into the game now that I'm not around to insult them."

"They never should have banned you," Mrs. Katz said with fresh indignation.

"Sylvia. It was four years ago. Forget about it. Play canasta. Meld. May you draw many red threes. Go to Loehmann's, schlep around the Saw Grass Mall. You'll be fine." Phyllis had never been good with emotions. What was the point? Most things she deflected with a wisecrack. The rest she ignored.

Mrs. Katz mopped at her eyes. "I'm going to miss you."

"You're repeating yourself, Sylvia. I have to go." The two women hugged one another briefly, and then Phyllis turned and walked with the crowd, moving toward the security checkpoint and the waiting flights.

Phyllis passed under a big sign that said: "Come Back to Miami Soon. We'll Miss You." "Fat chance," she answered out loud to herself, her voice caustic. "I'm getting out alive."

∞

Sig sat at her dining room table, a tumbler of Chianti beside her. She was secretively filling in the real estate broker's form to put her apartment up for sale. She didn't know if she could renegotiate her home equity loan or if she could get a hiatus on her mortgage. But while she was trying both of those strategies it was best to take this frightening step. She was not in a good mood. She'd actually considered calling Phillip last night before she'd regained her dignity and sanity.

"This isn't easy," Sharon said from her seat at the other end of the table. She had spread its lacquered surface with dozens of files as well as her laptop and printer. "I don't know why I always get the hardest job." Before Sig had a chance to launch into just how difficult it was for her to conceive of and finance Operation Geezer Quest, the doorbell chimed. Before Sig could even rise, Bruce had turned the lock with his key and had come in and collapsed onto the love seat under the dining room window.

"I'm busy doing the research." They both looked at Sig.

"Yeah, and I'm busy working to pay for this entire sting operation," she reminded them. Each of them looked resentfully at their siblings. There was a pause that could have gone either way: they could all disintegrate into endless childish bickering or move on. Bruce decided to make a heroic effort.

"So, how is the research coming?"

Sharon, with some difficulty because of her bulk, got up, found her huge canvas sack, and pulled out even more armfuls of files, magazines, and clippings. Sig thought she might go mad.

"Okay. Operation Geezer Quest. Cross-referenced in different categories." Sharon began to sort colored folders, laying them in various piles on the coffee table. "What I have here are all unmarried men in the tristate metropolitan area, seventy or older, with a net worth of more than fifty million." She looked up at Bruce and Sig with a worried expression. "I didn't know if I should make the cutoff fifty million or a hundred million. But there weren't many at a hundred, so I arbitrarily picked fifty. I did keep an initial reference list so I can go back if you want me to."

"I think you made the right decision, Sharon," Bruce told her.

Sharon merely nodded into her categorized stack. "I sorted them by geographical location, religious affiliation, previous marriages . . . " She looked up. "I separated the widowed from the divorced. I wasn't sure, but I thought it might make a difference down the road. Among the divorced I listed the settlements, if any. I also categorized them by whether or not they require a prenuptial. Lastly, I listed their philanthropic histories. I figured we wanted to find the generous ones."

Sig poured the last of the coffee into the bone china service. She might order takeout, but she ate off porcelain. Sharon pulled out a list and handed it to Bruce and Sig as a justification. "Okay, here's my initial analysis. Bernard Krinz's on the list. So is John Glendon Stanford and Robert Himmelfarb. I thought those three would make a good first cut. They're all here in New York." She paused. "Well, Himmelfarb is out in Sands Point, but he socializes in Manhattan."

Sig looked over Sharon's findings. "Good targets," she agreed.

"This is where having an anal compulsive as a sister finally pays off," Bruce said.

Sharon's face crumpled like an empty beer can against a jock's forehead. "I worked very hard on this. You don't have to be so critical."

"Sharri, he's *not* being critical," Sig assured her. "It's Bruce's way of saying he thinks this is good."

Sharri looked at her brother. "You do? You think it's good?"

"I think it's superb! Sharri, it's wonderful."

"Honestly?"

Bruce put up a hand in a crossing-guard stop sign. "Sharon, shut up. You always go too far. No more praise. It's good, so now let's get to work."

Sig called out for more coffee—she never made her own but ordered it instead from the Greek joint at the corner. Mostly in silence, together the Sibs poured through Sharon's findings. They devoured the dish, whistling or exclaiming every now and then at the numbers of homes, numbers of ex-wives, and numerous offshore accounts.

"Sharri, this is *really* outstanding," Sig finally said. "You've done an excellent job." Sharon glowed from the praise.

Bruce looked at her appraisingly. "You know, Sharon, I need market research like this for my company."

"Sharon, why don't *you* get a job? Forget Barney's downsized career," Sig said. "You certainly need the money."

"Oh, I couldn't do that. Libraries aren't hiring." Sharon shrugged. "Anyway, Barney is the one who needs to boost his self-esteem."

"Just call her Cleopatra, Queen of Denial." Bruce shrugged.

"You don't need a librarian's job, Sharri. You could do this." Sig waved a sheaf of paper. "This is great market research. Really thorough."

Sharon just shook her head. "Who'd hire me?"

"You know what I've got here?" Bruce asked. The two others shook their heads. "I've got Mr. Right."

"I don't remember that name," Sharon said.

"Du-uuh! I'm not using it literally, Sharon." Bruce opened the file. "This guy lives right here in New York, he's loaded, he's a widower, *and* he gives a lot of money to charity."

"Who is he?" Sig wanted to know.

"Bernard E. Krinz."

"The architect?" Sig asked.

"Yeah." Bruce rolled his eyes upward and got what Sharon called his "movie look." "Hey, it could be just like Patricia Neal and Gary Cooper in *The Fountainhead*. Except for the sex scene," Bruce shuddered. "Boy, look at this." Bruce held up a page from the file. "Well, maybe not exactly. The 'E' stands for Egbert. His mother really hated *him*."

"Phyllis Krinz. Eeuw!" Sig said.

"You won't say that when you look at his P&L." Bruce handed the folder to his sisters. Both of them raised their eyebrows, deeply impressed.

"Well, what's in a name?" Sharon shrugged.

"Plenty," Bruce said. "Rothschild is good. Rockefeller is good. Gates is *very* good."

"Names! Don't talk to me about names! 'Susan!' Does it get any less original than that?" Sig asked angrily. "Is there any name more dated, more boring, more stereotypically dull than Susan?"

"Well, actually, 'Bruce' does seem rather like a self-fulfilling prophecy. She made me a *faigela*, wouldn't you say?" he asked.

Sharon looked up. "Oh, what do you two have to complain about? I was named for a woman who stuck her hand up Lamb Chop's ass to make a living."

Chastened, Sharri's sister and brother looked at one another and nodded. "She's got a point," Sig admitted.

"Let me see," Bruce ruminated. He waved the file. "If we pick our mark, how do we get Mom to meet him?" Bruce asked.

"Let's figure out what events he's planning to be at. These people all have public lives. They attend openings, theater, they go to dinners. Especially the charitable ones," Sig said. "I know all the events my firm helps underwrite and I think I can get access to seating arrangements. We have our target and we get next to it. Then we get a ticket for Mom to go, and make sure she meets him and he likes her."

"Yeah. How do we manage that last part?" Bruce asked. "You can bring a horse to water, but—"

"Obviously, one of us has to take her to the event, be sure we've got her near the mark, and make it happen."

"Not me," Bruce said. "It will be bad enough getting humiliated in a department store, let alone some—"

"Oh, I'd *like* to go to a party," Sharon volunteered.

"Not *you*," Bruce added. "Sig, you go with Phillip Norman."

Sig nearly blushed. She didn't have the strength to admit she'd been dissed by Phillip. "I don't think so," she said as casually as she could. "Look, this is going to be an expensive proposition," Sig told them. "The clothes, the tickets, a limo. Bruce, I think you and I should both go and make sure that we at least get Mom in front of the target." Sig turned to Sharon. "Sharon, we need you as the secret weapon. This was great work so far. But now you have to research the next phase."

"What's the next phase? I can't do anything else."

"Yes you can. Just find out the next big charity events in New York. I'll see which one my firm helps to sponsor and if any of these three clowns is going to attend. Then you dig out everything extra you can on our first target."

She handed the three folders back to Sharon. "Needless to say, Mr. Phelps, if anything goes wrong with this mission we will disavow all knowledge of—"

Bruce interrupted her. "You're right. This is Mission Impossible."

Sig put down the folder she held. "Well, one thing I know for sure: you can't catch fish without bait. Sharon's done her job and I'm doing mine. We'll see what you can do with Mom when she gets here."

six

At La Guardia airport all three Sibs waited nervously. A group of people was coming out of the jetway entrance like nothing so much as cattle moving down the slaughter shoot. Then, behind them, strode Phyllis. "It's amazing," Bruce said sotto voce. "She's like Keyser Söze in *Usual Suspects*. She limps among them without revealing her lethal talents."

"Shut up," Sig warned. "Here she comes. She'll hear you."

"Try to look happy to see her," Sharon said, but neither Sig nor Bruce were listening. "Hi, Mom," Sharon sang out in a falsely cheerful voice.

Phyllis walked up to the three of them. "How did you know I was coming?"

"Mrs. Katz called."

"Figures. She can't keep anything to herself." Phyllis nodded. "So? No flowers?" she asked. Then she looked directly at Sharon and said, "You must have gained another twenty pounds, Sharri." She looked her daughter over while Sharon shrank from her gaze. "I always gained weight when I was sexually frustrated. Has Barney become completely impotent?" she asked. Then she kissed her fat daughter, who recoiled.

"Let the games begin!" Bruce declared.

Phyllis turned to her son. "So, how's the gay greeting card business? Have you gone *mahula* yet?" She pecked Bruce on the cheek. Then she waved her hand in the air. "My God! You're wearing more perfume than I am!"

"At least it's *good* perfume."

Lastly Phyllis turned appraisingly to Sig. "A lot of people think red and black go together, Susan." She shrugged. "Don't ask me why."

"Maybe because they're a classic." Sig smiled.

"Or maybe because they're a cliché?" Phyllis responded and shrugged again. "But hey, if you *want* to look like a drum majorette . . . burr-rump-a-bum-bum." Phyllis winked at Sig, then glanced around at the cosmopolitan bustle of the airport. Here the Christmas *chazerei* looked good: tinsel, wreaths, red ribbons, and white snow—well, gray snow—out the window. "Let's get over to baggage claim before some jerk walks away with my luggage."

Numbly, the three shell-shocked Sibs began to walk beside her. She smiled expansively. "It's great to be in New York again! Talking to Floridians was like chewing on avocado: everyone down there is soft. Up here people are like bagels: when you chew on them your jaw gets some exercise. I had a lovely conversation on the plane."

"Can you imagine being stuck next to Mom?"

"Oh my God," Sharon breathed. "I'm getting claustrophobic just thinking of it. Where's my inhaler?"

"He asked for my phone number," Phyllis added in a self-satisfied tone.

"What was he selling?" Bruce asked, puffing on his Marlboro despite the No Smoking signs.

"What difference does it make? She doesn't have any money," Sig reminded him.

"Be like that," Phyllis sniffed. "He was very nice."

Bruce sighed deeply. "It's started," he said in a singsong.

"Sharri is fat / Mom is no fun / Sig is unmarried / And I'm a bad son."

Phyllis turned and looked at him and his cigarette disapprovingly. She waved her liver-spotted hand in front of his face. "You know, you're killing both of us with that smoke."

"Not fast enough," Bruce muttered.

Phyllis pretended not to hear and speeded up, heading toward baggage claim, looking ready to chew out everyone. Her three stunned children followed.

"Unbelievable. No matter how often I'm with her, in between sightings I forget what it's like," said Bruce.

"That's what they say about UFOs," Sig reminded him. "Yet doubters still persist."

"No wonder I'm fat," Sharon mumbled resentfully.

"No wonder I'm unmarried," Sig added.

"No wonder I'm gay."

"*Bruce, you're gay?*" Sig asked, pretending shock. Bruce looked at her murderously.

"Forget Operation Geezer Quest. Let's just kill her," Sharon suggested, blood in her eye. "And I *didn't* gain twenty pounds. Fifteen, tops."

"Twenty," their mother called back from way ahead of them.

"God, she still has her faculties," Bruce commented.

"Not for long," Sig threatened. "Come on. Let's get her to your place and brief her."

ळ

"My place? Why my place?" Bruce almost squeaked. "We're closer to *your* neighborhood," he told Sig.

"Yeah, but there's no room for her to stay over at your apartment. Plus there's Todd. He'll move her right along."

Despite the crowds, Phyllis had spotted her bags right away

and dived for them. She was still fast, for an old woman. In minutes they were standing in the cold outside of baggage claim, waiting for Todd to pick them up in his van. Even in her winter coat, Phyllis shivered. Sig tapped her foot, irritated and impatient. They had to indoctrinate their mother ASAP, get her to cooperate, and get her into the Pierre Hotel suite Sig had already reserved. But it wouldn't be an easy sell.

"Can't we do something else?" Bruce asked.

"No."

"Why?"

"Why? Because I say so, that's why," Sig told Bruce.

Phyllis laughed. "You sound just like me," she said to her daughter.

"I do not," Sig retorted.

"Do too." Bruce and Sharon confirmed with a nod. Just then, thank God, Todd drove up with his van. It took them almost fifteen precious minutes to load all the assorted crap into the battered vehicle that Bruce used for card deliveries.

"Do we need anything else?" Todd asked cheerfully when they were all settled in at last.

"Just Valium and a baseball bat," Sig said through her teeth.

seven

Forget it. I'm not even considering it," Phyllis told her children. They were sitting in Bruce's apartment, crowded into the front room of his tiny brownstone flat. Boxes of greeting cards towered above them, threatening to collapse, just as Bruce's business was. Phyllis paid no attention to either the disorder or her children's arguments.

"Mom, you don't understand. It's not that we don't want you here or staying with us," Sig lied, "it's just that you don't understand the realities in New York anymore. It's not as safe as it used to be. And it's not as cheap."

"Since when is a hotel cheap?" Phyllis asked.

"Not cheap, but safe. New York has changed," Bruce said. He was desperate to have her out of his already crowded space.

"Don't worry about me," Phyllis said. "I can take care of myself. I always have. I don't plan to be a burden on any of you." She paused. It was hard for her to admit her mistakes to anyone, much less her children. "Listen," she said, "I haven't come for a visit. And I haven't come for myself. I've come for you. I know that your father and I were so busy with the business that I didn't give you all the attention that you needed. If I had . . . " She shrugged her shoulders. "Well, things might be different."

"Mom, you—"

Phyllis held up her hand. "I couldn't stand those women at the PTA. I wasn't a Brownie leader or a den mother. I didn't help you with your homework. And I'd like to make up for that now. I'm here for the duration," she said as bravely as she knew how.

"The duration of what?" Sig asked. Her mother had been in Manhattan for only two hours and it already felt like a month to Sig.

Sharon let out a whimper, while Sig thought she heard her brother groan. "You mean you're serious about living up here permanently?" Sig asked.

"Well, at least until you straighten out your lives. I'm your mother. I'm here to help. And I'm *not* staying at some expensive hotèl." She patted her purse. "You don't have to worry about anything. I have a little put away, and my Social Security check. And I still get some of Ira's pension money. I'll be fine."

Sig smacked her forehead. Despite how often she'd begged her mother, she'd never gotten into TFIs or any other bonds. "Your Social Security check is six hundred and sixty-three dollars monthly," Sig said. "Daddy's pension is . . . what? Three hundred? Four hundred more?"

"Three eighty, but it's all tax-free."

Bruce covered his eyes with his hands. Sharon looked away. It was only Sig, as always, who had to continue relentlessly. "Great. So you have less than a thousand a month to live on here in Manhattan, the most expensive city in the world."

"No, Sig, I think Hong Kong and Tokyo now rank as slightly more expensive," Sharon corrected.

"Yes, Sharon, but Mom isn't thinking of living in Hong Kong or Tokyo," Sig said through gritted teeth.

"In my dreams," Bruce said under his breath.

"I heard that, Bruce," his mother snapped. "Susan, a thousand dollars is still a lot of money. And I *do* have a little something put aside," she repeated.

Sig shook her head bitterly. If her mother had only let her put some money into Paine Webber's Select Ten Portfolio, her yield could be twice as high. But no. "Mom, you just don't get it. Do you know what the rental on a small studio apartment is here? A *very* small studio apartment?"

"I'm not so out of touch, Susan. I'm willing to pay four fifty or five hundred if I have to."

Bruce laughed out loud. "A *parking spot* for a car in midtown is four hundred dollars, Mom," he laughed.

"Don't be ridiculous," his mother snapped and put down her teacup. Todd had served them and then discreetly disappeared into the tiny bedroom. "I may be old, but I'm not an idiot." She shook her head. "Four hundred dollars for a parking space? You think I just got off the boat?"

"No, you came from the Planet of the Senior Citizens. You believe in early bird specials and movie discounts. But now you have to live here in a really strange place—among humans on planet Earth."

"Worse than that: among New Yorkers in Manhattan," Sig said, and handed a folded newspaper to her mother. "In Manhattan we don't have early bird specials at dinnertime or discounts for senior citizens. Except during the day at the movies, when you only have to pay four fifty."

"Four fifty?" Phyllis cried. "In Florida we pay three dollars. What do regular people have to pay?"

"Eight fifty."

"Next you'll be telling me that tokens are a buck," Phyllis laughed.

Bruce rolled his eyes. "A subway ride will cost you a buck and a half, Mom. And that's if you *don't* get robbed."

"Meanwhile, we don't have senior housing. Read it and weep," Sig directed, pointing to the newspaper. "I've circled a few of the cheaper apartment ads for you."

For a few moments silence reigned while Phyllis perused the paper. Then she looked up at her children. "So I'll live in Queens," she said. "Manhattan was only my first choice. Queens is nice, and it's just a subway ride away." She paused.

Sig, prepared, handed Phyllis another newspaper with another group of circled ads. "Queens," she said smugly.

Phyllis realized again that it had never been easy to love her daughter. She scanned the listings, one after another, then threw the paper down. "All right. So I'll get a little job. A part-time job."

Wordlessly, Sig handed Phyllis yet another newspaper section, this one the classifieds. But nothing was circled here. "Ivy League college graduates are making minimum wage at fast-food joints, Mom," Sig explained. "Kids with MBAs will work for Reeboks. What, exactly, did you have in mind?"

Shaken, though too valiant to admit it, Phyllis stood up, brushed off her skirt, and tried to look nonchalant. "Look, I'll work it out. Just help me get my things over to the Chelsea Hotel and then I'll see. A career will develop."

"Photos develop, Mom. Careers are built."

"Anyway, Mom, you can't stay at the Chelsea," Bruce said. "Number one, you can't afford it and *b*, it's not safe for an old lady."

"I'm *not* an old lady," Phyllis barked. "I may be an old dame, or an old babe, or an old woman, but I'm certainly not an old lady, and don't you friggin' forget it."

"Slip of the tongue," Bruce apologized, reaching for a cigarette.

Now it was Sharon's turn to take a deep breath and pick up a butter cookie. "Do you think the éclairs are any good?" she asked. No one else had eaten anything with their coffee, despite the array of cookies and pastries that Todd had brought out. Everyone ignored her. They always ignored her, she thought resentfully.

"You don't need anything extra on your hips anyway." Phyllis took a sip of her coffee and settled back into her chair. She shook her head. "You know, I believe in this ecological movement. I have a theory: couples should only reproduce themselves. If they have three children they get to kill one." She paused. "So what's all of this really about anyway? I smell a rat. Which one of you is getting ready to set me up?"

Sharon gasped, from surprise or asthma or both. "Mom, it's nothing like—"

"Oh, I get it. You're just trying to get me back on that airplane to Florida, aren't you?"

"No, Mother," Sig said as reassuringly as she possibly could. "Actually, we're trying to get you into the Pierre."

∞

The lobby of the Pierre was always attractive and elegant, but at Christmas it had a special, discreet holiday decor that added extra glisten to the gilded wood and sparkling ormolu. There were no white Dynel Christmas trees here, Phyllis noted. Still, it wasn't until Phyllis got upstairs to suite 1604 that she looked around and let out an ear-piercing whistle. "This is where you think I should stay?" Phyllis asked. "Marie Antoinette would be uncomfortable here. It's too big. Too fancy-schmancy."

"Sometimes life can use some embellishment," Sig said wickedly.

"Yeah. Well, if I'd brought my tiara, I'd feel right at home," Phyllis told her, looking at the grand living room with a fireplace, the damask drapes framing a view of Central Park, the ebony baby grand piano and the plush carpet. Some kind of vase—it look Chinese to Phyllis—had been placed on a side table and it was filled with lilies, more lilies than Phyllis had seen at the last three funerals she'd been too. She opened one of the doors and found a bedroom, complete with canopy bed. Another door led to a smaller room with the sofa and shelves of books.

"You think I need all this to get a date?" Phyllis asked. "How much does this all cost?"

"I got the corporate rate," Sig lied. "Anyway, I look at it as a loss leader. Like when they have a special at the supermarket and sell something below its normal cost, so they get you to buy other things."

"What are you talking about?" Phyllis asked. "Have you turned into the Mayflower Madam here?" So far all of the pickup and conversation couldn't have gone worse, Sig thought. If we were an Israeli SWAT team, all the hostages would be dead. Sig had begun to pitch the idea of remarriage to what could be charitably described as a total lack of enthusiasm on Phyllis's part.

"Screw that," Phyllis said. She was as enthusiastic as a cow at a barbecue. "I need a man like a fish needs a bicycle," she said.

"I never did understand what that meant," Bruce commented.

"You're not a woman," Sig muttered bitterly, and thought of Phillip Norman.

Phyllis hadn't quite agreed on the idea of dating yet, but she was trying to listen to her children. That had been one of the problems when they were growing up. She hadn't listened.

"I thought you already agreed to try this," Sig said, exasperated.

Phyllis sighed. "Look, a woman needs a man for sex or

money. . . . I've had the first and I still have the second: ergo I don't need a man," Phyllis said.

Sig ignored her. "So back to this marriage plan. You see why we think it would be nice for you? No matter how much money you have, it would make the financial burden easier. Not just on you, but on us, too."

"Have I asked for a penny? For one penny?" Phyllis demanded.

"That's not the point. You need some security. And you need companionship. You need attention, and time. The three of us are so busy. It would be nice for you to have someone in your life who—"

"Cut the crap. You want me to marry for money and get out of your hair. But I'm not that kind of a girl."

"You haven't been a *girl* in sixty years, Mom."

"Oh, you know what I mean! I never mixed money in with it. You know, I could have had a stage career if I was willing to play hanky-panky for profit."

"Hanky-panky?" Bruce yodeled. "*Hanky-panky?*" He leaned back to laugh.

Phyllis ignored him. "Anyway," she said with some dignity, "I've never been attracted to a wealthy man in my life. They're all so arrogant. They're so controlling."

"Unlike anyone *else* in this room," Bruce muttered.

"We're not saying you should marry someone you don't like," Sharon said, trying to be helpful. "You could like him *and* he could also be rich."

"I was already married. Been there, done that."

"Exactly. You were married to Daddy, and you liked it. So why not get married again?"

"When I married your father, we married for life. Everyone did. Only movie stars got divorced, and even when they did, there was a scandal. Not that I think there's anything wrong with divorce," Phyllis added and looked pointedly at Sharon. "*Some* people need one. I wouldn't want to discourage it." Sharon, choosing to ignore Phyllis, picked a luscious, chocolate-covered strawberry and put half of it into her mouth. "Nowadays things are different," Phyllis continued. "Nowadays every woman should either stay single or make four marriages."

"*Four?*" Sig asked. Four weddings? She hadn't even had one. Her mother was as unpredictable as an Oklahoma twister, and almost as disorienting. "Four weddings and a funeral," she said sarcastically.

"Four," Phyllis repeated with the maddening assurance she always had about everything. "Let's face it: the first is always a mistake." Phyllis smiled at Sharon again and lifted her shoulders in a shrug. "You marry a Barney," she said to Sharon. "Or, in my case, I marry an Ira. Who knows anything?"

"Mom! What was wrong with Daddy?" Sharon bleated, her mouth full of the other half of the strawberry.

"He was a man. Other than that, nothing. Not for a first marriage. A first marriage teaches you how disappointing a man is."

"Thanks, Mom. No wonder I've had such gender confusion," Bruce said.

"Oh, don't take it so personally," Phyllis told him.

"So what should women marry again for?" Sig couldn't stop herself from asking.

"The second is for love. Ha! At least that's what they think it is for at the time." Phyllis shook her head. "You gotta work that stuff out of your system, or else you're doomed. Everyone with brains finally gives up on it." She looked at Bruce. "Except for you. You just keep chasing rainbows." She gestured with her chin toward Todd, who was taking pictures from the balcony.

The criticism slid off Bruce's well-moisturized back. "What about number three?" Bruce asked. His mother occasionally fascinated him, like O.J.'s ride in the Bronco. You knew it would end in tragedy, but you couldn't tear your eyes away.

Phyllis sat back in her chair. "The third marriage should be for L.F.S.—lifetime financial security. Somebody who will take care of you and make sure you won't ever be living on Social Security."

Sig felt mesmerized, a snake before the snake charmer. "And what's the fourth one for?"

"Companionship." Phyllis smiled, almost wistfully. "After all, a Sylvia Katz only goes so far."

"Well, all this just proves our point: you do need to get another husband. You're three short"

"It's too late for me. I was talking about you. I don't want a husband! I want more grandchildren."

"You have two already," Sharon reminded her. "Isn't that enough?"

"Yes, Sharon. You've delivered," Phyllis said, then lowered her voice. "It's the smart ones who never breed," Phyllis said bitterly, under her breath.

Bruce and Sig exchanged looks. "Not this again," Sig muttered.

"I thought you finally gave up on me, Mom," Bruce told her. "I mean once I came out."

"Once you came out! You made such a drama out of it. Like I didn't already know! Who used to sneak my mascara? And what other fourteen-year-old boy knew the name of every shoe designer in France?"

"You knew?" Bruce asked, truly shocked. His mother nodded.

"That's why your greeting-card business is going nowhere. Gay men don't need funny 'I've come out of the closet' announcement cards. Or queer Santas for Christmas. And lesbians don't need *anything* funny."

Bruce sank into a chair. "I have to take this in. I'm so confused I can't think straight."

"You never could, Bruce."

"But you were always nagging me to get married."

Phyllis lowered her voice. "Yes. Because I want you to be settled down. Pick someone and make a commitment." She jerked her head toward Todd snapping pictures of Central Park. "He seems nice. Did I ever say it had to be a girl?" Phyllis stood up. "Gender, shmender. Look at your sisters. Definitely *not* a recommendation for my sex." She raised her hand in a placating way to both Sig and Sharon. "Don't blame yourselves. You did the best you could for brunettes," she told them.

Then she leaned toward Bruce and put her hand on his knee. "I screwed up with them," she admitted sotto voce. "What's his name again?"

"Todd."

"Todd? You sure he's Jewish?"

"Yes, he's Jewish, but he's also too young and probably too dumb. He's a visual kind of guy. He looks a lot like David Hemmings in *Blow-Up*," Bruce sniffed. "Not to be confused with the remake. Travolta's adorable, but DePalma can't compare with Antonioni."

"Nothing wrong with young and dumb. They make good wives. Better than I was. You serious about him?"

"Ma, would you leave me alone? I like him. He's nice. But he needs his own space."

Phyllis shook her head. "I ought to rent a loft in New York for all the men who need more space," Phyllis said. "You and your sister Susan have run into at least a dozen of them. But *you* know how to have fun. Now, though, it's time to settle down.

Find a nice decorator who cooks. Stop living out of takeout boxes. Adopt a nice Chinese baby. You know?"

"Well, if you're so hot for marriage, why won't you *get* married?" Sig asked, totally exasperated. "Why aren't you cooperating?"

"Darling, I *was* married. I drove your father crazy for forty-seven years. Then he died. I think that's enough. Now it's *your* turn to drive somebody crazy."

They had come to a stalemate. Sig, as always, tried to think fast to come up with an approach—any approach—that might work.

"I want you children to know: I'm here for you. I'm going to make up for all the times I didn't stay home with you when you were sick. I'm going to make up for all the PTA meetings and the Girl Scout meetings I missed. I'm going to make up for—"

"Mom," Bruce said. "I understand you have regrets. I think all parents do. But you can make it up to us by going back to Florida."

Phyllis tried hard not to react. After all, Bruce was deeply hurt. Ira hadn't paid enough attention to him. Or maybe she hadn't. Or maybe she'd paid too much. Whatever it was, hadn't she or Ira made him into what he was? She turned to Sig.

"Mom," Sig said, "this is very important to me."

"And to me," Bruce added. Sharon was silent, but she was watching Phyllis intently, as if her life depended on it.

Then, suddenly, Phyllis realized what this was all about. She'd been on the right track. The children *did* need a mother, but that wasn't all. They needed a father, too. This was their cry for help, and this time she had to recognize it. She wouldn't fail them again the way she had before, or the way her mother and father had failed her.

But what would Ira think? In her whole life, Phyllis had never had any man but Ira. Wouldn't Ira have been hurt? And would any man but Ira have her? She considered the idea and bit her lip.

Maybe, just maybe, if she could serve as whatever they called it—a rolling model or something—then Sig could find a decent man, Bruce would finally settle down, and Sharon would leave that *shlub* Barney. Phyllis wasn't sure she could make it happen, but at least she could try. "I'll consider it," Phyllis said.

"So you'll cooperate? You'll meet some of these men we've searched out. You'll be nice to them?"

"Nice?" Phyllis asked. "I don't think we said anything about being *nice.*"

"You're right. That would be too much to expect. But you won't immediately pull a Lorena Bobbitt? You'll encourage them, as best you can?"

Phyllis sighed. "Garage space here is really four hundred a month?" She paused, ruminating. "If I hadn't given Sylvia Katz my Buick, I could have lived in the car." She stared for a while out the window onto the park. "Maybe I'll call Sylvia."

"Are you going to do it?" Sig asked after the silence had lengthened.

"Please, Mom," Sharon begged.

"With sugar on top," Bruce added.

God, when was the last time her children had been united on *anything*? This was important, deeply important to all three of them. And if a man would make them happy, if a surrogate father would do the job, who was she—or Ira for that matter—to object? Phyllis at last nodded.

"Then you'll do it?" Sig asked.

"Does the Pope write bestsellers?" Phyllis asked.

eight

Bruce was regarding his mother critically, as he always did. But this time there was a purpose. Sig had given Bruce some cash, a budget, and authorization to use her department store charges. Today was the day the transformation was to begin.

Bruce and his mother had met at the Pierre and the two of them were walking down Fifth Avenue past Tiffany's, the Plaza, and the Sherry Netherland. All the doorways and windows were dressed up in elegant New York Christmas decor—silk ribbons, real balsam, and ever-so-subtle dustings of artificial snow. It was only the crowd that looked bad. Bruce observed them in parkas, sweatpants, and ugly, lumpy winter gear and shuddered. His mother was as bad as any of them. Heterosexuals—they didn't know a thing about style. "We start with the hair."

"My hair? What's wrong with my hair?"

"Only everything," Bruce told his mother calmly. "The color. The cut. The . . . " he shuddered, "the perm. Why do all old women think 'blond' and 'perm'? We need a genius for this." He lifted a strand. "This is worse than the Hindenburg disaster. And you call that a part? Moses couldn't fix this. We need to get to an emergency room."

"Mount Sinai?" Phyllis asked sarcastically, because of the Moses wisecrack, but Bruce ignored her little joke.

"Flex. The Einstein of hair color."

"Flex? His mother named him Flex?"

"His real name is Angelo. Flex is his professional name."

"A hairdresser with a *nom des cheveaux*? Forget about it."

"You're going. *If* we can get an appointment."

"Bruce, if I can get an appointment with a genius, I'm not going to talk about coiffures. I've been dying my hair myself for twenty years and I already know how."

"You're always the expert. You know more about hair color than Flex, the style coordinator for Dramatics for Hair."

"Well . . . "

Bruce, always quick to give up his anger, took his mother's arm in an affectionate way. "Come on, Mom, cooperate. You're as stiff as Charlton Heston in *Ben Hur*. I know it's against your religion, but just this once, break a commandment."

"Excuse me. Isn't there one about honoring thy father and thy mother?"

"Yes, but not my mother's hairstyle. Come on, girlfriend. I'm taking you to Columbus Avenue."

∽

Columbus Avenue had been a blur of those new kind of boutiques, ones that Phyllis never went into, that seemed to either be crammed full of an overwhelming selection of insane choices or stripped down to empty, displaying only three black T-shirts each costing four hundred bucks. There was construction on the street, and piles of dirty snow, and Christmas crowds of young people all making their way easily through the chaos and cold. Phyllis hated to admit it, even to herself, but the temperature and the people were all a lot cooler than she had remembered. When was the last time she'd been in New York in the winter? The bustling and pushing and the temperature sapped her strength. After moving through three blocks of it, she was grateful to have Bruce take her arm and lead her into a warm haven.

Well, a kind of haven. The beauty parlor wasn't anything like the ones Phyllis was used to. There were no rows of women sitting in their own bell-shaped dryers. Instead, the music was blaring so loudly that Phyllis could hear nothing else. The very strange thing was that she also couldn't hear the music. It was that loud, or it was the way the singers—if you could call them that—sang. Skinny kids were running up and down the long, narrow shop wearing black and white outfits, clients were constantly coming in, conversing in shouts, being seated, and getting washed and blow-dried. Each workstation was framed with colored Christmas garlands that swayed whenever the gunlike hair dryers were on. Lights, those little white Christmas tree ones, were blinking all over. And that was aside from the hot pink and blue neon that outlined the reception desk and waiting area. It wasn't just her. The place, she decided, would definitely throw an epileptic into a seizure.

But it wasn't the conversations or lights that were so disorienting: it was the damn blaring noise over the radio, or hi-fi, or whatever they called it. It made a buzz in her ears and a kind of confusion in her brain. Phyllis didn't like it. After all, she prided herself on being alert. She wasn't one of those dotty old ladies— a Sylvia Katz—who barely knew what was going on. Yet she'd been robed and shampooed and coated with chemicals and rinsed and conditioned and she still couldn't hear what the loud music was about. She stopped thinking and concentrated on the words.

"Did that singer just say 'Hot tramp, I love you so'?" she asked.

Bruce, who had been deep in a shouted conversation with

Flex, looked up. He cocked his head and listened effortlessly for a moment. "Yeah. It's Bowie. 'Rebel, Rebel.' "

"You like Bowie?" Flex asked Phyllis.

"Who is she? Is she new?"

The two guys laughed. "Mom, he's a really famous rock star. He's been around forever. You know, Ground Control to Major Tom." Phyllis hadn't a clue, but she nodded. She wondered if this was what it would feel like if the Alzheimer's kicked in. She was tired. She had to admit to herself that, despite her temperament and her intentions, she didn't have the stamina that she used to.

Well, she was almost seventy, she told herself. What did she expect? These kids—no one in the beauty parlor seemed older than thirty—these kids were listening to their Frank Sinatra and using their energy just the way she had used up hers. Nothing to regret. Nothing unusual.

The music changed to a rap tune that Phyllis tried to hear. She actually thought it was "Jingle Bells," but it was such a different beat that she wasn't even sure if that was what she was hearing. She sighed. "Just a little longer," Flex said kindly. "Are you happy with the color?" Phyllis shrugged. She couldn't see in the mirror, though it covered the wall in front of her from ceiling to counter, but she wasn't going to ask to put her glasses on again because Flex had taken them off when her hair was washed and Bruce wouldn't give them back. He'd made that very clear. She squinted at the wall.

"Very nice," she said, feeling a little defeated by it all. Flex squeezed her shoulder kindly. He was really a very nice boy: his name wasn't Flex. It was Angelo, and all the other kids there had weird names that weren't their real ones—Ice and Storm and Electric and Heater. Why, Phyllis wondered, did children change their names? Why did Susan insist on being called

Sigourney? It hurt her. It was an ugly name. Susan was so pretty. Why would someone want to be called Sig, or Flex, or Heater? You were given a name by your mother. After all, it wasn't easy to give birth, and naming seemed the least a mother could expect in return for a life she had created. Phyllis sighed again and felt all of her sixty-nine years.

Flex tapped her shoulder gently, as if in response to her sigh. "All done," he said. "What do you think?" She looked toward the mirror, but could see nothing.

"Unbelievable," Bruce said. "Flex, you're a genius." Then he handed her glasses back to Phyllis. A woman stared out at her from the mirror, but—for a moment, in her fatigue and disorientation—Phyllis didn't recognize herself.

"My God," she said. "Not bad for a woman in her sixties."

"Yeah. And great for one about to be seventy."

"Seventy? Really?" Flex asked.

"Sixty-nine," Phyllis snapped. Seventy frightened her. She avoided their eyes and instead focused on her image in the mirror.

Her hair had been completely re-created. Instead of the permed, blondish mound that she wore, hers was now a thick, straight, silvery crown. She shook her head, just to clear it. Her hair moved around her face, leaving little wisps against her cheeks, where the ends curled, just slightly, onto her face. She stared, and almost dropped her jaw. Light bangs covered the deep wrinkles on her forehead and somehow the color or the cut made her skin seem brighter.

Behind her glasses, her eyes were nearly popping out. You could still see her chicken neck and she still looked like an old lady, but not so old and more like . . . a lady. Phyllis blinked behind her lenses.

"You don't like it?" Flex/Angelo asked in a voice full of concern.

The boy really cared about his work, she realized, just as she once had. But she was still speechless. She stared again at her image in the mirror and tilted her head to one side. Her hair moved, each strand, in a kind of waterfall. She was trying to define what this change had done, exactly. It wasn't that she was younger looking, but she looked . . . She paused. Phyllis looked the way rich women looked when they got older. She had never been beautiful, and she wasn't beautiful now, but she was transformed nonetheless.

"Come on, Mom, what do you think?" Bruce questioned.

"Not bad," Phyllis told him.

 споз

"Bergdorf's, Bruce? Are you crazy? Isn't that fortune we spent on my hair enough?" Of all the department stores in New York, Bergdorf Goodman was the most elegant. And now, with only twenty shopping days before Christmas, the place was thronged with exquisitely dressed clientele. It was definitely *not* the Saw Grass Mall.

"You need something to wear, Mom."

"I *have* something to wear. I have lots of things to wear. Look through all my luggage."

"I did, Mom. Frightening. I didn't know they still made Naugahyde jackets. You have nothing. Not a single decent thing. This is not Collins Avenue."

"What am I missing?" Phyllis asked.

"For one thing, you have no sportswear."

"Sportswear? Why do I need sportswear? Do I look like Andre Agassi?"

Bruce stopped next to the Plaza fountain and looked at his mother coldly. "Don't you know it's not appropriate to wear your old cocktail dresses for early morning grocery shopping?"

"Why not? Recycling is the modern thing to do, isn't it? Anyway, if I *do* need something why can't we go to Loehmann's?"

"Because, Mother, right now Loehmann's only has the things that didn't look good on anybody at Bergdorf *last* season." He paused and glanced beyond the fountain toward the Plaza Hotel. "This is the very spot where Barbra Streisand ran into Bob Redford in *The Way We Were*," he said with a sigh. "So poignant."

"Poignant? He was a putz and she was an idiot not to notice it."

Bruce dragged Phyllis past the Salvation Army band playing carols and through the revolving door. The Christmas season was upon them. Bruce threw five dollars of Sig's money into the pot. As he hustled his mother up the escalator, he looked her over. "You know, Mom, now that we got rid of that atrocious haircut, aside from your horrible makeup and frightening clothes, you're really not bad looking."

"Thank you, darling," she said coldly. "I can't tell you how much your approval means to me."

Bruce took another step up the escalator to give him some distance and squinted his eyes. "I'm looking at Phyllis Geronomous," he hummed, "but I'm seeing Carolina Herrera."

They stepped off the escalator onto the designer floor. Phyllis surveyed one of the mannequins dressed in yards of tulle and silk jersey. "Nipples? The dummies have nipples now?"

"Big deal," Bruce shrugged and took her by her upper arm.

Phyllis pulled it away and stopped to regard the dummies distastefully. "Listen, if you're going to get anatomically correct, how about potbellies or saddlebags?" she asked bitterly as she pointed to the mannequins' legs. "How about varicose veins and hammertoes and bunions?"

"God! Spare me!" Bruce cried. All he needed was for Phyllis to pull what he always thought of as her "Bella Abzug" in the middle of Designer Formal Wear.

But Phyllis merely shook her head. "America hates the reality of what women truly are," she said sadly.

"No they don't. Look at movie stars. Look at models. Women are making more money, they're more visible . . . " He took her arm again and began to move her to the designer sections.

"Get a grip! Men control everything and don't you forget it. They own the magazines that women edit and write in and read. They own every channel on television. They pick a few genetically female mutants to shill for them and mortify the rest of us. They hate aging women. They hate sagging and drooping and menopause. Old bellies. Old thighs. Men, no matter how old, how bald, how fat, think they're great. Unlike women, they don't have a biological clock. So they don't know what the hell time it is. They deny death."

Bruce had taken her arm and—with difficulty—was able to move her away from the mannequin and lead her through a maze of garments. They approached a rack of clothes. "This could be nice," Bruce said, trying to lift the tone and lifting up a hanger holding a black satin suit. "Satin is big this year."

"Nah. Too dull. I like more drama."

"It's a Karen Kahn. It's not dull, Mom. It's classy."

A thin, young saleswoman approached them. "Maybe I could help?"

Bruce smiled at her. "I think we're looking for a dinner suit. Something in black satin, perhaps." He looked down at his mother's slightly bulging stomach. "With a peplum," he added.

"I have just the thing," the saleswoman chirped. She went to another rack and lifted up a beaded jet jacket and dress. "Escada."

"Black. Why black?" Phyllis asked. "Nobody died. At least not yet. What's wrong with color, here? Let's be festive."

"Oh great. You probably want something red and green. You

want to look like a psychopathic Christmas elf?" Bruce complained. He pushed the Escada suit in front of her. Phyllis looked at the price tag.

"Oh my God, Bruce. This is more than your father's entire annual pension check."

Bruce put his hands on his hips. "Why do you always go for the price tag first? Since I'm a kid, whatever I wanted, first it was 'how much'! You haven't even *looked* at the dress."

The saleslady turned from one to the other, seeing her quick sale evaporate. "I'll let the two of you work it out," she said. "Talk among yourselves."

"That's what's wrong with you!" Bruce went on. "It was never the quality, always the price. When I was eleven and I wanted those two perfect Izod shirts, you bought me a dozen from J.C. Penney."

"Bruce, I could buy an entire condo in Del Ray for this!"

"Yeah, but you'd feel like shit in a condo in Del Ray. In this, you'll feel like Greer Garson in *Mrs. Miniver*. You'll feel like a queen."

"Isn't one queen enough in any family?" Phyllis sighed.

Bruce pursed his lips and put his hand on his hips. "Mother, are you going to cooperate?"

"*No.*" Phyllis seemed impervious. Bruce paused and actually tapped his foot. "Bruce, I am not going to try on a dress that costs forty-seven hundred dollars. I'm not going to do it."

Bruce looked up to the ceiling as if the writing on the wall wasn't crystal clear. "Okay," he said. "I'll try again, Mom. I don't think you understand the concept yet. You see, to attract money you have to look like you already have it. Don't think of this as spending money, think of it as an investment in our future."

"My future isn't long enough to amortize a forty-seven-hundred-dollar dress."

"Yeah, but *my* future is, and I'm going into bankruptcy court if something doesn't change." He looked at her, his face serious for the first time. "Mom, this company means something to me. It really does. I got three kids working for me, all out of my apartment. I got so far with the company. I was doing so well. And then that son of a bitch—"

Phyllis looked at him with a scolding expression. "You took out bank loans? You're paying interest?"

"Well . . . loans. Not from a bank, exactly. Banks wouldn't lend after Bill absconded. I had to borrow from a guy named Lefty. He has a *lot* of interest in this."

"But no principles, I bet," Phyllis tsked and shook her head. "Bruce, Bruce, Bruce." Giving in, at last, she followed Bruce to the dressing room.

∞

The interior of the dressing room on Bergdorf's third floor was as disarrayed as the inside of a schizophrenic's mind. A three-thousand-dollar sequined jacket lay crumpled on the floor. An Italian silk evening stole and matching turquoise gown hung disconsolately from a single hanger clasp, its four-figure price tag dangling. And the floor and the hooks were littered with enough rejects to rival Bruce's own suitor list. A faux leopard strapless sheath with matching bolero was thrown over one of the two tiny upholstered chairs, while Bruce sat on the other one, calm and resplendent.

Phyllis, exhausted, was struggling into yet another dress, this one in red accented by gold trim and buttons. She looked in the mirror. "Dowdy, dowdy, dowdy. Holy Baby Jesus! Am I supposed to be doing a Nancy Reagan impersonation?"

Bruce looked her over from head to foot, ignoring her comments completely. He turned to the saleswoman. "You know," he said. "For once she's not all wrong. It's a little too St. John. Too many buttons. I want something sleeker. Don't think Adolfo—think Lacroix as done by Calvin Klein."

The saleslady stood stock-still for a long moment.

"What language are you talking in?" Phyllis inquired. Bruce just sat there and the saleswoman didn't respond either. They seemed to be communicating on some deeper level.

"I think I know *exactly* what you mean," the saleswoman told him.

"That'll be a first," Phyllis said, sitting down on the other tiny chair, waiting for the next phase of her transformation.

∞

"Mission accomplished! God! I'm exhausted," Bruce said to his sisters as he collapsed onto a fauteuil and dumped a collection of glossy shopping bags around him. He lit a cigarette.

"God! How much did you spend?" Sig asked nervously.

"Don't worry. You can afford it."

"Where's Mom?" Sharon asked.

"She said she wanted a drink. She's in the bar."

"Mom wanted a drink? She doesn't drink," Sharon reminded her brother.

"I told you not to leave her alone," Sig added.

"She's not a child," Bruce said defensively. "Anyway, she's just here in the hotel."

"Drinking alone? Do you think she's been drinking alone down in Florida?"

"Alcoholism? Are you worried Mom's a lush? Hah! That's the least of our problems. I wish she *would* drink. It might take her edge off. Nothing like a nice gin and tonic at four or five o'clock to give one that false sense of well-being. If you could describe what was wrong with Mom, we could join some kind of support group. You know, like Adult Children of Alcoholics."

"Yeah. That might be a comfort," Sig said bitterly. "But first we have to diagnose her. How about 'Adult Children of Extremely Annoying, Stubborn, and Sarcastic Mothers Who Come Back Home to Live?'"

"A little long, but we could use an acronym," Bruce laughed. "You have no idea what I went through at Bergdorf's."

"Never mind Bergdorf's, where's Mom now?" Sharon whined. "You've lost Mom."

"Look, if you don't like the way I'm doing my job, *you* do it."

"*I'm* busy doing the research."

They both looked at Sig, as if she'd been tack-free.

"Yeah, and I'm busy working to pay for this entire sting operation," she reminded them. Each of them looked resentfully at their siblings. It was all so familiar. Sig had a sense of déjà vu. There was a pause that could have gone either way: they could all disintegrate into endless childish bickering or move on. This time it was Sig who decided to make a heroic effort. "Let's go find Mom," she said, and they did.

nine

Sig had worked behind the scenes since the Sibs had found a candidate. She had wangled three tickets to the Winter Wonderland Ball, held at the Plaza Hotel. Her firm had a table, but Sig had managed—through more than a dozen phone calls to people who were not altogether happy to hear from her—to get the seats moved to table eleven, the table that Bernard Krinz would be sitting at. That is, if he attended. During the holidays, a high point of the social season in New York, lots of people bought tickets but preferred to spend the season in the Caribbean. Sig would like to herself, and in the glory days of the eighties she had. But that was then and this was definitely the nineties.

Now, the day before the Wonderland Ball, all they had to do was indoctrinate Phyllis and then introduce her to Bernard or another rich, eligible old coot. Drag the guy to the Pierre, set the wheels in motion and hope that Cupid's bow would not misfire. They had to cast a spell, project the illusion that Phyllis Geronomous was a wealthy, stylish, charming, and available woman. It was a long shot, but Sig had long been used to playing the odds. It wasn't a bull market for rich widowers, so they'd have to make the most of this opportunity.

Sig got to the Pierre before work on Friday morning. She was almost wet through from the sleet that had been falling. She only hoped it hadn't spoiled the dress she had schlepped along with all her other accoutrements. She found that Bruce wasn't yet there with Todd, but that her sister had just arrived by train from Westchester.

Sharon took out a bag almost as large as she was. It wasn't full of formal wear. Instead it held research data. She began riffling through file folders. She finally pulled out a large one and snapped it open. "His name is Bernard Krinz. The architect," she explained to her mother. "Well, he started out as an architect. Then he became a developer. He built the Thompson building on East Fifty-fifth. He was the one that built the new wing for the museum; you know, the one that everyone talked about? He's done headquarters buildings for close to a dozen of the Fortune 100. We have pictures of them right here. Anyway, before all this he already had family money. As if that's not enough, his wife died eight years ago and left him more. They had no children, and he's never remarried." Sharon moved her finger down her notes. "Net worth in excess of fifty million dollars." She pulled out a clipping and handed it to Sig. "Here's his picture."

Sig looked at the photo. As Bruce might say in his movie mode, definitely *not* Gary Cooper in *The Fountainhead*. But then Mom was no Patricia Neal. "Your architect, Mr. Right," she said and handed the picture on to her mother. Phyllis eyed the wizened face, the bald pate, the narrow eyes.

"Looks like Frank Lloyd Wrong to me. Feh! Forget about it."

"Mother! You promised you were going to try. You haven't even met him."

"I don't need to."

"The next possibility would be John Glendon Stanford. He's about eighty-eight years old. But I couldn't get a picture of him," Sharon told them.

"That's perfect. One foot in the grave and the other on a

banana peel. We can all imagine what *he* looks like," Bruce said from the doorway. He and Todd had arrived, schlepping makeup, hair dryers, brushes, and God knows what else. They were going to do a dry run.

Sharon ignored her brother. "And last but not least is Robert Himmelfarb. He's younger than Stanford, but his net worth is lower."

"Well, if I really have to . . . " Phyllis began.

"You want us settled?" Bruce interrupted. "I need a father's influence."

"And more grandchildren? Don't you want that?" Sig joined in, jumping on the guilt bandwagon. Sometimes Bruce was shrewd. "You weren't there for us when we were kids. You go to the dinner and get a date with this guy now," Sig said.

Phyllis sighed. "What do I have to do?"

"Pull out the portfolio," Sig commanded. The spell was working and the preparation had to begin.

&

"To review, what's a corbel?" Bruce asked.

Phyllis crossed her eyes. "A cross between a corner and a dumbbell."

"Come on, Mom. Concentrate." Sharon had been prepping Phyllis all morning on architectural terms. "A corbel is a piece of stone or wood projecting from a wall and supporting a cornice or arch."

"Okay. If you say so," Phyllis shrugged.

"What's a dentil?"

"A female dentist? Or maybe the cousin of a corbel?"

"Mom! How are you going to impress Mr. Krinz if you're architecturally illiterate?"

"With my expensive haircut," Phyllis said.

"What's Bauhaus?" Sharon continued relentlessly.

"Corbels and dentils and Bauhaus with noodles, these are a few of my favorite things," Phyllis sang, parodying Maria in *The Sound of Music*. Sharon didn't even crack a smile. It was an endless mystery to Phyllis how she could have raised a daughter so completely devoid of humor.

"Would you stop it! Would you stop it and just concentrate!" Sharon moaned, exasperated. "Here's a portfolio of his buildings. Would you just study those at least?"

"Buildings? They look like melting ice cream."

"Another thing. Krinz loves the opera. He's a fanatic."

"Forget about it, I'm not doing opera," Phyllis said sternly.

"Now you know what I've been going through." Bruce said as he and Todd emptied their bags. Phyllis made sure to smile in a positive way at the boy. He was sweet. What did it matter if he wasn't successful? He'd make a nice wife for Bruce, and photography could become his hobby. "Time for a dress rehearsal," Bruce called. "And Todd is going to help."

∞

It was Saturday evening, and almost zero hour. Sig paced nervously, waiting for her mother to appear. Sharon sat on the sofa, eating cashews by the handful. We shouldn't have done it, Sig thought. It's ridiculous. I'm wasting time and money. "Are you almost done?" she yelled into the bathroom for what seemed like the fiftieth time.

"Almost," Todd sang out. Sig smoothed down the skirt of her dress. With all this pacing her feet would ache and she'd be a wrinkled mess before they even got to the party.

"I don't know why I can't come," Sharon said resentfully as she popped another handful of cashews into her mouth.

They must be at least a thousand calories, Sig thought. Sharon was impossible. Sig looked at her watch. "We'll be late," she called.

"Fashionably late," Bruce said and stepped into the room, turning toward the dressing-room door. "Ta-da!" he announced.

"Oh my God."

Phyllis Geronomous emerged from the dressing room of the bedroom suite. Sig stared, her eyes popping, Susan Sarandon style. Sharon actually allowed her jaw to drop. "Are you my mother?" she asked.

Phyllis did a slow pirouette. "I'm ready for my close-up, Mr. DeMille," she told them as Todd snapped her picture. The sateen coat with the matching sheath dress under it was in an indeterminate color, somewhere between lavender and gray. As she spun, the costly fabric's subtle sheen flashed in a most unflashy way. Phyllis's once-blond, frizzy hair was now coifed in the simple elegant bob and virtually all silver. Her makeup, immaculately applied, seemed nonexistent. Instead, her skin looked nourished with a sheen that rivaled the one on her dress. And instead of her usual turquoise eye makeup and clashing blue-red lipstick, there was only a hint of purplish shadow above her eyes, a shadow so natural that it enhanced the deep-set hood of her eyelids and could almost have been mistaken for her natural color—if she had any.

Her lips glistened, though the color there again seemed no more than the blush of a healthy mouth. Around her neck a large—very large—double strand of gray pearls covered some of the still-visible ravages of time. The only glitter was reflected off the diamanté clasp of the necklace, worn chicly to the side, and the matching earrings, which twinkled at her cheekbones.

"Oh my God!" Sig repeated. She managed to tear her eyes off the vision and looked at Bruce, proudly preening behind Phyllis. "You're a genius," she told her brother. He blushed, but Sig was too fascinated with her mother to notice.

Phyllis's legs were encased in some silken but magical mesh that managed to pick up the gleam of the coat and dress while also covering her varicose veins. The shoes were the finishing touch. Feminine, strappy sandals, they were ladylike, clearly expensive, and sexy all at once.

"Are those Blahniks?" Sig breathed. Six hundred dollars a pair.

"They're cripplers," Phyllis admitted. "I feel like Lady Astor's pet horse."

Bruce got the movie look. "It's just like the Ascot scene in *My Fair Lady*," he breathed. "You know, when Audrey Hepburn looks beautiful, but she still speaks like a guttersnipe."

"Nice way to talk about your mother," Phyllis complained genially and walked across the room to the table on which her evening bag lay.

Even in her gait some Pygmalion-like transformation had taken place. Was it the shoes? Sig wondered. Or did Phyllis walk differently because she felt differently? Phyllis almost . . . glided. "Can you do that for me?" Sig asked Bruce. "I could meet a decent man if you'd do that for me."

Bruce nodded enthusiastically.

"What about me?" Sharon asked, coming out of her trance.

"Impossible," Bruce told her. "I'm an artist, not a magician."

"Bruce, be nice." Phyllis warned. She turned from the table, purse in hand. Phyllis looked her eldest daughter over.

"So severe, and your skirt should be shorter," Phyllis said, staring at Sig. "Never wear a white top and black bottoms to an affair," she told Sig. "You'll be mistaken for the help."

Sig looked down at her black and white Moschino Cheap & Chic. God, sometimes she felt like strangling her mother!

"Okay. Now what?" Phyllis asked.

"Now we take Cinderella to the ball and she meets the prince," Bruce said.

ten

"My maiden name was Steen. Can you imagine? Phyllis Steen."

The architect didn't crack a smile. "One of the Cincinnati Steens? I built a home for them. They were in shipping."

"No, the Bushwick Steens. They were just in trouble."

"Excuse me?" Bernard Krinz said. He looked puzzled. Phyllis rolled her eyes.

"It was a joke, Bernie."

"Bernard," he said.

Sig shifted in her chair. The Winter Wonderland Ball had transformed the already beautiful Grand Ballroom at the Plaza into a Viennese Christmas card. The chandeliers were hung with faux icicles, and the tables were set with tiny Blue Danubes, complete with weensy ice-skaters. The band was playing nothing but waltzes. But nothing else was going right. Sig was sitting on the other side of the architect, their mark, and she could already tell that dinner was not progressing as she'd hoped. They had arrived at the Plaza, taken their seats, and made sure to arrange it so that Phyllis sat beside Krinz, who had come unescorted. But the conversation so far had been a collection of missed jokes, gaffes, and general cross-purposes.

"So, Bernie, have you decided to take early retirement?" Phyllis asked as Sig winced.

"Bernard," Krinz corrected again. "I prefer to be called Bernard."

"Why?" Phyllis asked. "Let's face it, Bernie isn't great, but Bernard! It's hardly the name a woman would call out in the throes of passion."

Bernard Krinz deliberately turned to Sig, who tried to salvage what she could. "My mother admires your work so much," Sig said. Krinz didn't even blink. "She has a really large portfolio," she gabbled, desperate to say something. "My brother's best friend is doing a photography book about some of your buildings." She meant to talk about how Phyllis had collected photos of all of Krinz's buildings, but her Wall Street background got in the way. Krinz misunderstood and turned immediately back to Phyllis.

"Oh. Do you dabble in the market? I'm absolutely fascinated by it."

"Dabble? No. I buy what I need and I get the hell out."

"So you're a plunger!"

"Are we talking shopping or are we talking plumbing?" Phyllis asked, momentarily confused.

"I'm talking about your portfolio."

Phyllis shrugged. "Oh that. The kids filled it. For research. I don't even know what's in there."

"Really? I'm not sure that's a good idea. You obviously have a sense of taste in style. Is that dress by Lacroix? They don't come cheap." He paused. "You know, many people think that those of us in the practical arts can't be practical ourselves. But I take pride in the profitable little investments I've made. I don't claim to be a professional, but I'd be happy to take a look at your portfolio, if you'd like me to."

"Forget about it," Phyllis said, and then Bruce, at her other side, jabbed her sharply under the perfectly cut armhole of her sheath. He bent across her and turned to Krinz.

"You know, Mother would really love that. We've said to her, over and over again, that she should show more interest in the market."

"When did you say that? You're the one who always makes me throw out my coupons."

"Throw out your coupons?" Bernard said, really disturbed. "My dear, you *do* need some kind of assistance."

"That's what my kids say: 'You need help.'"

Across the table a handsome older man laughed. He was probably seventy if he was a day, but he had a glowing tan, a head of mostly thick white hair, blue eyes, a noble profile, and, Sig noted, a very blond young woman with him who looked as if she was in her teens. Phyllis narrowed her eyes and stared at him and his very youthful companion. "I hope she's your daughter," Phyllis said loudly.

"She's not," the man taunted.

"Do you know one another?" Bernard asked. Phyllis shook her head. "Permit me." Bernard did the introductions. "This is Paul Cushing. We go way back. I built a corporate headquarters building for him. They may do another." He cleared his throat. "Paul, this is Phyllis Steen."

Paul Cushing laughed. "Somehow I already guessed that."

"You see! What a name. No wonder I married the first person who asked me!" Phyllis said. "I *had* to get married. Not for that reason. For a different name. Not that 'Geronomous' is any bargain. Sounds like I'm about to parachute-jump. Who knew then that you could go down to City Hall and change your birth certificate for twenty-five dollars?" She looked across at Cushing with contempt. "Have you seen that young lady's birth certificate?" she asked.

Sig felt as if she were about to explode, but, luckily, Bernard Krinz tried to smooth the situation. "Mr. Cushing is the ex-president and chairman of Whetherall Industries." He lowered his voice discreetly. "He's also a widower."

"Well, I'm Phyllis Geronomous," she told Cushing. "Ex-president of the Turnbury Island Ladies Canasta Club. Widow of Ira Geronomous. And who's your little friend?"

The girl beside Paul Cushing looked up. She giggled. "I'm Wendy. Wendy . . . "

"Just Wendy," Paul Cushing said, cutting her off and obviously rising to Phyllis's bait.

"Oh. First names only, huh?" Phyllis asked acidly.

"Need-to-know basis," Paul Cushing told her serenely.

"What are you, the Man from UNCLE?" Phyllis looked the pretty young girl over. "I just hope she's over eighteen, or you're in trouble, mister."

"Mother," Sig said, as a wide but insincere smile spread across her face. "I think Mr. Krinz wanted to tell you something."

"What's *your* name?" Paul Cushing asked Sig.

"Sigourney Geronomous."

"She's too old for you," Phyllis spit out. "*She's* only half your age."

"I'm sorry, Mr. Cushing," Sig said, "my mother . . . "

"Your mother is charming," Paul Cushing interrupted smoothly. He was *very* handsome, Sig thought, despite his age, and the wrinkles around his blue eyes made him more attractive. Her own were already making her consider an eye job. Life was so unfair.

"Mother *is* outspoken."

"I admire that in a woman," Paul Cushing said. He looked at his young companion. "My granddaughter does, too." Wendy giggled again. "What is it you do, Miss Geronomous? Or is it Mrs.?" he said to Sig.

Sig saw Wendy glance at her left hand. She didn't wear a wedding band, obviously, but on her fortieth birthday in a fit of despair, she had splurged and bought herself a fabulous emerald. She had realized then that no one else was going to buy one for her. She looked at it as an investment rather than just an indulgence. But it was an investment she could relish. She loved the ring and lost herself for a moment in extreme depths. "Miss," she said. "And I'm a broker."

"Well, it's my lucky day. I'm in the process of looking for a new apartment."

"I'm not that kind of broker." The man turned her off. Residential real estate brokers were morons. Didn't he know that? Sig did her best to make general conversation. She spoke about the Bonnard show she'd recently seen and a bit about market trends. She drew Wendy, the young girl, out about her figure skating. She tried hard to hint, from time to time, that her mother loved to dance, that she spent the season in Palm Beach doing it, but there were no takers.

During all of this, Bernard Krinz and Bruce had been conversing. At last he was helping out, Sig thought with some relief as their coffee was served. Then, just as she was beginning to relax, the oddest thing happened. A stranger approached the table and, finally, it was he who asked Phyllis to dance. "I'd love to, Monty," she said. Bruce and Sig looked at each other in surprise. The old man was short and tubby. His dinner jacket looked like it was from some other era.

"Who is *he*?" Sig asked her mother as Phyllis stood up.

"Oh, he's Monty. Monty Dunleathe. The guy I told you about. The one I met on the plane."

Phyllis started to walk off with the codger. "The guy she met on the plane?" Bruce asked. "What guy?" Sig stood up and put her hand out in a gesture of unknowingness. A fat matron in an expensive beaded dress pushed past the table and put an empty glass in Sig's outstretched hand.

"See?" Phyllis said, her voice raised with satisfaction as she reached the dance floor. "She thought you were the hired help."

Before Sig could react, Paul Cushing addressed Sig. "I was about to ask your mother to dance, but it seems that someone beat me to it. Since my granddaughter doesn't waltz, could I interest you?"

He was asking something about dancing. Sig was flustered. She put down the glass. "Me?" she asked.

Bruce nudged her. "Get his number," Bruce whispered. "A backup for Mom. We're going to need it."

"I'd love to," Sig smiled at Mr. Cushing. But she felt a strange reluctance. Cushing was smiling back, making his way to her. "We don't want him for Mom," Sig hissed at Bruce. "We've already got Bernie."

"I don't think that's going to work out," Bruce told her as she walked away.

"Don't be so negative," Sig criticized.

"I'm *not* negative," Bruce answered. "It's just that I'm certain." Paul joined Sig and took her hand.

"How can you be certain?" Sig asked Bruce over her shoulder as Paul Cushing led her away.

Bruce smiled. "Because Bernard just asked me to dance."

eleven

"I told you it was stupid," Sharon said as she lifted a toasted bagel with too much cream cheese to her mouth. The Sibs were eating in a diner close to Grand Central Station, for Sharon's convenience, since she'd taken the train in from Westchester for a progress report after the ball the night before. The station was thronged with suburban Christmas shoppers; it was a nasty place to meet since it was also inconvenient for Bruce and Sig *and* the food was bad. "You can't handle Mom as if she was a normal person," Sharon went on. "She *isn't* normal. I can't believe the two of you didn't expose her to some other guys. Who else was there?"

"*You* try to manage a rodeo," Sig snapped. "We're ruined." What was the use. Why complain or explain? They'd always thought of her as a moneybags, an endless font of financial flow. "I think it's time for us to pack this project in. I must have been crazy. I've spent God knows what at the Pierre already." She looked at Bruce bitterly. "That's not counting designer dresses or Blahnik shoes, thank you very much." She'd have to try to explain to them, even though it hurt her pride, the kind of financial shape she was in. She took a deep breath. "You know, since Black Monday things have been . . . well, dark gray. It's not the eighties any more. I have fewer and fewer investors. I'm making money for everybody, thank God, but I have fewer people to make money for. That means fewer commissions."

"Yeah, yeah, we know all about it," Bruce said dismissively.

"Listen to me, you ignorant pooftah," Sig said, her teeth clenched. "It wasn't necessary to charge up eight thousand dollars to dress Mom up. It's not like she appreciated it. I can't bankroll this thing much longer. I'm going to have to pack her up out of that suite by Christmas. Where is she going to go then? *Your* house, Bruce?" Sig asked nastily. He recoiled. Sharon actually snickered at his discomfort.

"Your house?" Sig asked Sharon, who visibly shriveled and looked away. "We had a perfect target," Sig said. "Bernard Krinz. I spent three hundred bucks a plate just to get into that stupid party and sit beside him. I figured we *might* meet a fallback—Sharon, you might look up that Paul Cushing guy—but to find that *Mother* found a fallback, inappropriate as he was, well, that tears it. The guy was a loser, but at least he was heterosexual," Sig said. "He wasn't as damned inappropriate as Bernard was, Sharon."

Bruce sighed. "Sharon, didn't you know that Bernie was gay? Wasn't that on the Internet or in the *Who's Who* or something?"

"If he was married once before, he could be married once again," Sharon said defensively.

"But not to Mom. Not to our Mom," Sig said bitterly. "She didn't even try to cooperate for thirty seconds. We got her the haircut, the clothes. Even the shoes. And then she pissed Bernard off . . . "

"Bernie," Bruce corrected.

Sig shot her brother a murderous look. "She pissed *Bernard* off from the very beginning. Plus she antagonized Paul Cushing. And then, even if we could cast around for another candidate, she wasted the rest of our evening *and* my money by dancing with some jerkoff in a suit that predated the War of 1812." She paused and rubbed her head. "I'm pulling the plug on this," Sig said. "It's hopeless."

"Paul Cushing?" Sharon asked. "Wasn't he chairman of Whetherall?"

"It doesn't matter if he was the president of the Czechoslovakia," Bruce said. "She accused him of statutory rape. You know, her usual dinner banter. He *didn't* like Mom," Bruce sighed. "He could join the club. It's a large and distinguished group."

"Oh, I don't know, Bruce. I thought she piqued his interest," Sig said.

"Can't you get in touch with reality?" Bruce asked Sig.

"Can't you be helpful and productive and practical? All those things I have to be," Sig snapped back.

"Oh, do I hear the martyr marimbas being played?" Bruce asked and began to mime Carmen Miranda while he sang to the tune of "Mañana." "My name is Sig the eldest, and my life is very bad. My mother treats me difficult, and I am very sad. I have to pay out money; it's money all the time. Nobody really likes me because martyrdom's my crime."

Sig glared across the Formica table at Bruce, who put down the salt and pepper shakers he'd been using as castanets. To Bruce and Sharri's complete surprise, tears welled up in Sig's eyes and began to roll over her lids and down her carefully Renova-ed cheeks. Then she burst into loud, wet sobs. "What are we going to do?" she asked. "Mom can't stay on at the Pierre for long and she can't live in some hovel." Sig sniffed and tried to control herself. "It's not fair to the neighborhood. And I can't afford an apartment for her. None of us want her living with us. This isn't working," she sobbed.

In a moment, both Bruce and Sharon had moved to either side of Sig. Sharon offered her Kleenex. Bruce patted her hand. "I just can't do it anymore." Sig continued to sob. "I'm up to my neck in debt. My commissions have dropped off to almost nothing. I haven't dared to use my Platinum American Express because I can't pay a bill at the end of the month. I'm going to have to sell my apartment and auction off my emerald." She took Sharon's Kleenex, put it up to her nose, and hiccuped.

Sharon and Bruce looked at each other in one of their few moments of bonding. "Broke. Yeah, right!" Bruce whispered. They'd been hearing Sig complain about money all their lives.

"We know how hard you're trying," Sharon soothed. "We appreciate what you're trying to do. I'm sorry about Bernard."

"That was in the days when men didn't come out of the closet," Bruce said. "He's out now. He's *way* out in front."

"Mom could cooperate just a little bit, just a little bit," Sig said angrily, brushing away at her eyes and her ruined eye makeup. "She could have *tried* with Bernard, for chrissake. She didn't have to make herself Enemy of the People."

"She should have, she could have, but she won't. That's our Mom," said Bruce.

"On top of everything else, to spend most of the evening chatting to some minor director of a charity! Some loser in a dinner jacket that I saw Leslie Howard wear in 1939 . . . "

"What was his name?" Sharon asked. "Monty what?"

"God, I don't know. It sounded like a game show host or a hairdresser," Bruce added.

Sig wiped her eyes and seemed to regain possession of herself. "Montague Dunleathe," she said. "Mom's Prince Charming. They could have danced all night. Look, I can't bankroll Operation Geezer Quest based on these results. But check the Dunleathe guy out, Sharon. And check on Paul Cushing." Sig looked over at her younger sister and just shrugged. "Bruce, you salvaged Bernard as best you could. Call him on some pretext or other.

Anyway, Mom didn't do what we wanted, but we'll give it one more shot. After that, I swear to God, I'll wash my hands of her."

∽∾∽

Phyllis opened her eyes, didn't know where she was, and for a moment had to recollect herself. The few times before, when she'd woken up disoriented, it had frightened her. But this morning—it was the morning—she felt not the slightest anxiety.

Where was she? It felt like a puzzle to play with more than it felt like a diamond. The bed was enormous and the sheets were so smooth—she stretched her arms over her head as she tried to recall what she'd been dreaming and where she was. Something about dancing, and the song that still ran through her head was that old rock 'n' roll one that Bruce and his friends used to sing about: being under the broadwalk down by the sea. It was all so very pleasant.

Then she awoke fully. It wasn't a dream. She'd been dancing all night with Monty, the man she'd met on the plane. Unlike Ira, Monty was a *very* good dancer. Phyllis shut her eyes for a moment. Her legs hurt her—there was no doubt about it—but she didn't care. Her feet hurt, too. Maybe that was a blister on the left heel? But Phyllis smiled. So? She'd put on a Band-Aid and take a couple of Motrin. It was worth it. She wasn't under The Broadwalk yet.

Her eyes swept across the vast white expanse of the bed. Then she remembered: the suite at the Pierre, the charity ball . . . the whole *megillah*. She pulled up the sheets to cover her shoulder. What size was this bed, anyway? It was bigger than any she'd ever seen. Was it bigger than a California King size? Maybe it was a Pierre Prince. Was a Pierre Prince more important than a California King? Who knew? There was room for all of Coxey's Army in there with her. She rolled over, ignoring the pain in her right hip. She looked at the clock on the bedside table. It was early yet. If she had been in Florida she'd be about to begin the schlep along the beachfront with Sylvia. She smiled. Today, instead, she'd bundle up, walk along Fifth Avenue and look in all the store windows to see the Christmas displays before everybody else was up and out. She'd wrap herself warmly and she'd wear the new brown leather gloves she'd managed to buy herself at Bergdorf's. But first, maybe, she'd just pull up the blanket and sleep for a minute . . .

When the buzzer rang, Phyllis sat up. Who could that be? The chambermaid never came this early. And certainly the children wouldn't be up yet. She'd already learned that New York was a late-rising town on the weekends. Phyllis gingerly swiveled her legs out of bed, grabbed the robe that the hotel had thoughtfully spread across the foot of the bed, and moved toward the door of the suite. The bell rang again before she could get to it, then there was a knocking. Forgetting to even look through the peephole, Phyllis threw the door open angrily. "What! What?" she asked, and then, as the door swung back she saw a huge bunch of flowers, taller than most bridal *chuppahs,* with Sylvia Katz standing behind them, in the hallway of the Pierre, dressed in a wrinkled green polyester jogging suit. The jacket was half unzipped and Phyllis could see part of the "I Love New York" logo on Sylvia's T-shirt.

"You up yet?" Sylvia asked.

"I don't think so," Phyllis told her. "I think I'm having a bad dream."

"Very nice. No 'hello' *and* you call me a nightmare," Sylvia said, unperturbed, as she stepped in past Phyllis. She was carrying her patent leather purse and an Eckerd's shopping bag.

Sylvia left the flowers in the hall, but she set the bag down on the coffee table, appropriated a silk-covered club chair, and sat in it, her purse primly perched on her lap. "There," she said.

Phyllis carried in the flowers and turned to her friend. "When did you get here?" Phyllis asked. "How did you get here so early?"

"I took the last plane last night. I got in at eleven forty-five, but I didn't want to bother you."

"So where did you go?"

"I didn't go, I stayed. I stayed at the airport."

"At the airport motel? At La Guardia?" Phyllis was shocked. Sylvia didn't spend money like that.

"No. What motel? At the airport. I had a chair."

"You spent all night sitting up in a chair at the airport?"

Sylvia Katz shrugged. Phyllis thought, with something close to a pang of guilt, of her huge comfortable bed. "You should have called," she said.

"I did. You were out. So I stayed at the airport. It was fine."

"But what are you doing here?"

"I had to get away," Sylvia said.

"Away? Away from what?"

"I couldn't stand the pressure I was getting."

"What pressure? Who was bothering you?"

"Ira. Your husband. You know how he can be sometimes. All I would hear him say when I'd visit was, 'Sylvia, New York is a lonely and dangerous place.'"

"Ira can't talk. He's dead."

Sylvia waved her hand. "You know what I mean."

"I'm not in any danger and I'm not exactly alone."

Sylvia rose from the chair, as if it was the webbed aluminum one at the Pinehearst. She walked slowly toward the bedroom door. She motioned with her head to the partially opened bedroom door. "Don't tell me you're . . . you know."

"Of course not. Not yet anyway."

"Are you even thinking about it? Feh!"

"I'm thinking about it."

"Feh." Sylvia repeated and then looked around the suite. "This is some place," she said.

Phyllis nodded, as if she were used to it. "The kids insisted," she said. "You want a tour?"

"I wouldn't say no," Sylvia told her.

Phyllis opened the door to the bedroom, showed Sylvia the gorgeous bed, the huge closets, the four telephones, and the palatial marble and mirrored bath. "So why are you really here?" Phyllis asked as Sylvia rummaged through the bath products and shampoos on the vanity.

Sylvia looked into the mirror and then down at her T-shirt, protruding stomach, and the sandals she was still wearing (though now they were complemented—if that was the right word—by a pair of thick red socks). "I didn't want to spend the holiday alone," Sylvia admitted very quietly. "Not again."

"But I thought the children were coming in from Cincinnati?"

"They were. Then they weren't. My daughter-in-law got sick."

"Hah! If you believe that, I have a dental bridge I want to sell you."

"You having dental problems again?" the literal Sylvia asked with concern.

Poor Sylvia, Phyllis thought. Her daughter-in-law hated her and her son allowed it.

"Should I go back?" Sylvia asked in a small voice. "I don't want to horn in."

"Of course not. You're welcome. The children will love to see you." Hoo-haa! Now there was a fib of significant proportions, Phyllis thought, but no one should have to spend the holidays alone. "Sylvia, come out of the bathroom. Sit on the couch, or maybe you want to lie down in bed." Sylvia shook her head and went to the straight-backed chair that flanked the tea table.

"This is fine," she said, sitting down stiffly.

"You want some breakfast?"

"No. I had a bagel at the airport. I don't want to be any trouble to you, Phyllis. I could go stay someplace else."

"Where?" Phyllis asked. "At a hotel? You know how expensive New York hotels are? Anyway, everything's booked for Christmas." Sylvia must be truly desperate if she was actually offering to spend money. "Look," Phyllis said. "I'm calling room service. I'm getting myself some French toast and I'm getting you some, too. Plus coffee and fresh-squeezed grapefruit juice. It's better here than in Florida. I don't know how they do it." Phyllis picked up the phone.

"Can I help you, Mrs. Geronomous?" a voice asked. It was amazing how the hotel staff knew her name and everything about her. She'd only been there for five days.

"Breakfast for two," Phyllis said, a little self-consciously. As if she had something to hide. As if . . . "My *girl*friend came to visit," she explained. The room-service clerk made no comment.

"Isn't that expensive?" Sylvia asked. "Room service and all? At Howard Johnson's they charge you an extra $2.50. Just to take it up the elevator."

Phyllis merely shook her head. "They don't charge that here," she said. No, they didn't charge extra because the prices were already astronomical. She would pay for this herself. Susan didn't have to pay for everything. But for the moment, looking at Sylvia's glum but gallant face, Phyllis didn't care if she spent her whole month's check. "Sylvia, sometimes life needs some embellishment," Phyllis said. "After all, this is your first trip to

Manhattan in years, isn't it?" she asked. Sylvia had lived in Queens, but she wasn't much of a cosmopolitan. "You never came into the city, did you?"

"Yes," Sylvia said. "I was here with my sister right after the war."

For Sylvia there was only one war: World War II. Forget Korea or Vietnam or even Desert Storm. "Well, things have changed a little since then. The war is over," Phyllis told her and picked up the phone again.

"Yes, Mrs. Geronomous?" the kind voice asked. "Is there something else?"

"Please," Phyllis said. "A bottle of champagne. We're having a party."

twelve

Date: December 9, 1996
From: Sharon@missioncontrol.com
Subject: Operation Geezer Quest
To: Sig <Sis@sigmonde.com>
Sig, I haven't finished all the backup, but
Montague Dunleathe was listed as one of the
ten richest men in Great Britain, according to
Forbes International 1981 Yearbook. Born in
Glasgow in 1921. A canny Scot. He made most
of his money in airlines back in the seventies.
He owns most of Montana. He was married for
twenty-six years to one of the Guinness
heiresses, but she died in '89. No children . . .

The E-mail message went on, but Sig didn't need to. It was unbelievable. Somehow, Phyllis had managed to meet and attract a rich geezer. Sig shrugged. Go know.

Sig had been feeling grim this Monday morning, as she had most Monday mornings the last few months. The market was jumpy, and so was she. One of the guys in the cage had bitten her head off, and she'd found that a restricted security had been accidentally (and illegally) transferred out of one of her clients' positions. It would take her and a clerk an entire morning to straighten that out with a net gain of zero, but here, here on her terminal screen was the first really Merry Christmas greeting she'd received this season. She turned away from the screen and punched Bruce's number into her speakerphone. "Houston?" she asked when he picked up. "We have liftoff."

"Have you been having another one of those private Tom Hanks film festivals, sister mine?" Bruce asked. "He's happily married, Siggy. Forget *Apollo 13*." Bruce groaned. "God, I should have known better than to trust Sharon. Do you know how many hours I spent trying to pull Mom together for that ball on Saturday night? And then Bernard just wanted to try on her dress. Do you know the crazy old queen has called me three times since last night?"

"Forget Bernard. We've got a hot one."

"I know he's hot, but he's hot for me! And I'm not into older men."

"Bruce, I'm talking about Montague Dunleathe. He's richer than God and he's going out with Mom."

"You're kidding me. Well, it won't do any good. She'll wreck it."

"I'm going to double with her."

"You're *what*?"

"I'm going to double with her. That way I can try to control her—well, at least as much as I can."

"Ha! Good luck. Control a tsunami, why don't you."

"What the hell is a tsunami?"

"A Japanese tidal wave, Sig. Amazing! You *don't* know everything." He paused. "All right. I'll come up to the hotel early. And you can try your double-date control. But it's hopeless. Anyway, I'm glad I'm the one with the easy job; you know, turning a sow's ear . . . "

"Bruce! She is your mother."

"I mean it in the nicest possible way." A thought occurred to him. "Anyway, who are you going to bring? You haven't had a date since Bob Dole was in puberty."

Sig decided to take the high road and ignore the comment. "I'm going with Phillip," she told her brother. She'd broken it off with Phillip when he'd told her that they had no future. It would be a blow to her pride to ask him to see her, but she needed an escort and she had no one else.

"Dead man walking."

"Bruce, just button it and be at the Pierre by three."

∞

It was a quarter to eight and the Pierre suite looked like a tsunami had hit it: the bedroom was a beach strewn with the flotsam and jetsam of rejected wardrobe items. The bathroom was an impressionist painting, one makeup color melding into another all over the vanity and onto the floor. Sig, dressed in a severe navy sheath, was busy trying to straighten out the living room and simultaneously listen to her brother and her mother fighting in the bathroom. "I'm *not* putting on those goddamn Barbara Bush pearls again," Phyllis was saying. "I'll look like Nathan Lane in *Birdcage*."

"As long as you don't look like Gene Hackman, you're ahead of the game," Bruce told her.

Sig tried to clean up around Mrs. Katz, who sat placidly while she did so. What was the old bird thinking of? How long did she plan to hang around? "This must be Susan, and that must be Bruce," she had said, looking at Todd, who was more effeminate. "And that, of course, is Sharon," she said.

"The fat one," Sharon responded glumly.

Sig was spending almost a king's ransom—and the room looked worse than an adolescent's dorm. Sig kicked a Bergdorf's bag under the sofa with a vicious swipe. The afternoon had been three hours of constant argument. First Phyllis had wanted to go as she was; then she'd agreed to get dressed up, but she wouldn't double with Sig. Finally Sig had prevailed, but *then* Phyllis wouldn't let Bruce renovate her face and hair. "He met me plain, on the plane," she said. "He likes me like that." Bruce had finally ended the discussion by threatening to jump out the window. Sig picked up half an armful of newspapers, opened a closet, and chucked them inside violently. Then she threw her mother's schlep bag, pilled cardigan, and assorted debris behind the floor-length curtain. Nothing with Phyllis was ever normal, easy, or painless.

Even this stroke of luck with Montague Dunleathe seemed about to go down the drain. They had to make Phyllis appear financially secure, attractive, and at least minimally pleasant. An impossible task, Sig realized. Bruce wasn't negative, he was realistic.

Sig looked around at the suite. The hundred-and-sixty-dollar flower arrangement from Renny was breathtaking. Sig added more water and picked up the card. "*You fascinated me. I'd like to get to know you better. Paul Cushing.*" Her mother fascinated a man like Paul Cushing? Sig opened her eyes wider, moved past the arrangement to the sofa, and plumped up the pillows. Then she pulled magazines out of her bag. *Town & Country*, *Forbes*, *Fortune*, and the British *Country Life*. She arranged them casually on the coffee table and lowboy. Then she took out a copy of the *Wall Street Journal*, folded it to the NASDAQ page, and left it lying over the arm of a club chair.

At last everything looked perfect, including Phyllis. She entered the room, arrayed in a silvery beige St. Laurent pantsuit, a Hermés scarf tucked in at the throat of the jacket. Sig nearly shuddered thinking of what all *that* had cost her, but she had to admit her mother looked casually elegant. It was Bruce who looked like the wreck of the Hesperus, or whatever the hell the boat was that Phyllis always talked about.

"Is she soup yet?" Bruce asked. Sig nodded. "Thank God," Bruce said, and fell back into the bedroom, sprawling across the bed. "Bring me a blood transfusion."

"Mom, I have to talk to you," Sig said brusquely. Sig took her mother into the bathroom, now filled with Phyllis's new wardrobe and a few of Mrs. Katz's *shmatas*. "Enough is enough. She's not supposed to stay here," Sig was telling her mother.

"What do you mean 'supposed to'? She's staying. She doesn't have any other place in New York to stay."

"Mom, New York is full of hotels."

"I have a perfectly good room here."

Sig tried to restrain the overwhelming urge to kickbox her mother in the spleen. She was edgy, no doubt about it. The clock was ticking and, though things looked promising with Monty, Sig would not be able to front this gig for much longer. To have Mrs. Katz here, always sitting calmly on a straight-backed chair in the living room, her purse on her lap as if she were riding the bus, was not conducive to romance. Her mother needed a duenna like Sig needed a credit check. Sig took a deep breath. "The room here is for you," she explained as if she were talking to someone significantly younger than Jessie.

"Oh, the bed is enormous. I wouldn't even know she was there, if it wasn't for her snoring."

"She's sleeping in the same bed with you?" Sig asked, her voice betraying the horror of it all. All that old female flesh, the fallen rumps, the veined and knobbied legs, the arthritic hands. Sig shuddered. Someday she would . . . "Mom, tell her to get her own hotel room. If you're going to sleep with anyone here it should be a man. This is a love nest, not an old age home."

"Oh, excuse me, Miss Schprintz. Just because you're paying the bill you'll decide who can come and who can go? Sylvia may not set the world on fire, but she's the only friend I had who doesn't get offended by my jokes. She always included me in everything, even though nobody wanted me and I didn't want to go. She's a good friend. You have no right . . . "

Sigourney was doing a quick mental calculation. If she didn't have to give her mother much walking-around money, she might be able to float this thing until the new year. She'd go back to the Sylvia Katz issue later.

"How's Monty?" she asked, her voice as casual as she could manage. How do you question your mother about the seriousness of her intentions? Did he get to first base? Second? Sig shuddered again. The idea of the two physical ruins uniting was more nightmarish than Sylvia Katz beside her mother in bed. Perhaps, Sig thought, it would be better if people just expired at fifty—no muss, no fuss, no bother. The bottom line was Monty certainly wasn't going to get too far with Sylvia Katz snoring in the bedroom.

"Look," Sig said, "this isn't Mrs. Katz's home. It's not even your home. For God's sake, it's not my home. This is a place that we're using to . . . "

"Oh, Susan, Susan, Susan. What am I going to do with you? Life needs a little embellishment sometimes. Think of Mrs. Katz as that. How could I tell Sylvia to go stay in some motel on West Fifty-fifth Street? She's my friend, Susan. And she's not messing up my chances with Monty, believe me." Phyllis stood up, went to the dresser, and consulted the mirror above it. "He knew what I looked like before my makeover. He likes me as I am, warts, perm, friends, and all.

"Anyway, I'm doing my part: I've seen Monty twice since the ball. We had brunch and we've gone Christmas shopping." Phyllis looked at Sig. "We got something for you," she said. Phyllis needed to show that Monty was going to be a good father to Sig.

"I don't need a present, except a proposal for you from Monty," Sig snapped.

"Look, I don't see men asking you to marry them," Phyllis said sharply. "I'm doing the best I can. I'm always the one who has to do everything." Phyllis sat down and crossed her legs. For a moment Sig had a feeling that Mendel may have been right: Phyllis sounded exactly like her and she could hear it.

"I'll go out with Monty because I like him, not just for you. But he'd be a good influence. He knows his business and responsibility." She stood up. "I need to get my bag," she said and turned and walked into the bedroom.

The buzzer rang and Sig closed the door on her brother. "I'll get it," Sig said. Phyllis nodded and moved toward the couch.

"Don't sit down!" yelled Bruce from the bedroom. "You'll wrinkle the pants!"

"Such a nag," Phyllis said.

"Look who's talking!" Bruce yelled.

"Stop it, both of you," Sig told them, feeling, as usual, like the only adult in the room. Sig glanced at herself in the mirror and straightened the back of her hair where the cowlick pushed it up. Then she opened the door.

Montague Dunleathe stood before her, rising on the balls of his feet. He put out his hand and shook hers heartily. "Hello, hello," he said, his accent thick but charming.

Sig invited him in and hoped he noticed the room and all the trouble she'd gone to. But it seemed that Montague Dunleathe only had eyes for her mother. "Phyllis, you look good enough to eat."

"Please. Let's not get into that kind of talk so early," Phyllis told him. Sig wondered if she was going to faint or, alternatively, strangle her mother. She could hear a smothered whoop from Bruce in the bedroom. She'd strangle him too while she was at it. But Monty seemed delighted by Phyllis's ridiculous humor. He sat down and chuckled.

"That reminds me," he said, "what's old and wrinkled and smells like ginger?" He waited, and when neither of the women answered, he laughed. "Fred Astaire's face," he told them, and he literally slapped his own knee.

Sig heard another smothered whoop from the bedroom and thought again of fratricide. She was grateful when the buzzer rang again. She ushered Phillip into the room. He was a tall, thin man with a sharp suit and a dull sense of humor. "This is Phillip Norman," she said, introducing him to Monty.

"My name's *not* Norman," Monty said.

Phillip didn't smile at the lame joke. "No," he began to explain. "Norman is my surname."

"So, you've been knighted. It's Sir Norman?" Monty asked.

"No," Phillip began, "it's just Phillip Norman."

"My name's not Norman," Monty repeated, and this time Phyllis cackled. So did Bruce in the bedroom.

Phillip looked toward the door. "That's just Mrs. Rochester," said Sig. "We keep her in the other wing with Jane Eyre. Pay no attention." Sig looked at her watch. "We're going to be late if we don't leave now. And this being the holiday season and the city is jammed, we'll lose it if we don't show up on time," she told them and led her party out into the night.

❦

"Why would you bury all the lawyers a thousand feet underground?" Monty was asking.

Phyllis leaned closer to him. "Why?" she asked.

"Because underneath it all, they're nice guys."

Phillip Norman, who was a corporate lawyer at AT&T,

attempted a smile. "Who are you with again?" Monty asked, grinning wickedly. "Wasn't it Dewey, Cheetem, and Howe?"

Phyllis barked a laugh. "No, I think it was Pipedown & Beenice."

Monty roared. "How about some more champagne?" he asked.

They were on the West Side, at Cafe Luxembourg, which was a little bit noisier and a little more raucous than Sig was used to. But she had to admit, it had its advantages. The first was that she wasn't totally embarrassed by the conversation of her mother and Monty, and the second was that if Phillip decided to talk, no one could hear him. Lastly, no one she knew would see her here with him, and that was salving to her pride. Dinner was almost done, coffee had been served, and Sig was getting to feel as if the whole charade might be worth it.

"No more for me," Sig said as Monty tried to pour the last of the champagne. "Some of us have to work in the morning." She could hardly believe it, but her mother and Monty seemed to be getting on like an asylum on fire. In a way it made sense. They were equally bizarre.

"None for me," Phyllis agreed. "I'll have a terrible headache in the morning."

"It's not the champagne that'll give you the headache. It's the lack of sexual release," Monty told her.

"Somehow I don't think that's one of my problems," Phyllis said, but she had a gleam in her eye that made Sig nervous and Monty bold.

"Not to put too fine a point on it, the solution to your problems is in my pants," he told Phyllis.

"Listen, honey, I may need love, but I don't need a laugh," Phyllis replied with restraint. "Why do men think *anyone* cares about their penises besides their urologist?"

"I rest my confidence on public opinion," Monty leered. "Do you know what a rattlesnake and a two-inch willy have in common?"

Phyllis shrugged.

"Nobody wants to fuck with them," Monty said and laughed uproariously again.

Phyllis couldn't help laughing back, but then she composed herself and compressed her lips. "Personally, I have no further interest in ever seeing any man's three-piece set again."

But the rejection only seemed to incite Monty. "No one has said no to me in almost thirty years," he admitted.

"Get used to it," Phyllis told him, but Sig could tell that Phyllis was actually rather charmed by this crass, wild Scot.

Sig wondered how long their luck would hold.

thirteen

The first night of Hanukkah had come and gone. Since they were young, the Sibs hadn't paid much attention to the holiday, but now that Travis and Jessie were around they'd gone back to buying gifts. It was too bad, Sig thought, that Hanukkah, which came on different dates each year, never came *after* Christmas—when Sig could take advantage of the marked-down prices. Tonight, she'd decided she was going to show her apartment to Cornelia Warren, a broker, then do some shopping for modest gifts, check in on her mother, and finally wind up at her firm's despised-but-necessary-to-attend Christmas dinner party. It was always an endurance test, but this year guaranteed to be a trial by fire. As usual, it was held downtown at one of those wood-lined, steak-serving, Dewar's-scotch kind of places—the places that Sig detested.

She left work early, rushed home, showered, dressed, and blow-dried her hair. Then she got three hundred dollars from the cash machine near her corner and went out into the December twilight with the determination to get things done.

Forty minutes later Sig weaved out of FAO Schwarz, empty-handed and more than a little bit queasy. She'd seen a basket filled with a momma cat and three kittens and very nearly bought it for Travis, until she looked at the price tag and realized it was two hundred and seventy dollars! Jessie was into Barbies, but she already had so many of them that the only one Sig was sure might fill the bill was the special edition Holiday Barbie. Sig wasn't spending a hundred and twenty-five dollars on a plastic doll. Who had this kind of money? Who were these people? The store was full and Sig, a delicate tinge of green highlighting her complexion, left with her three hundred dollars intact but her pride in tatters.

Somehow it seemed natural to walk the two blocks to the Pierre. Just to check on her mother, she told herself. But she knew she herself needed comfort and reassurance as much as she needed to suss out the situation. Her mother wasn't a warm, cuddling type, but she was rock solid, and right now Sig needed something solid. She had calmed herself down by the time she got up to the suite. It was just as well, because Phyllis—as usual—was too self-absorbed to notice much.

"What are you doing tonight?" Sig asked, perhaps a little wistfully.

"Oh, Monty's coming over. Maybe we'll go out to dinner, or maybe we'll call down for something."

Sig hoped they went out; room-service dinners at the Pierre could easily hit three hundred bucks, and that was without wine. "So what are *you* doing?" Sig asked Mrs. Katz pointedly.

"Oh, I guess I'll just stay in, too. I have some reading to do." The old woman pulled a rolled-up copy of *Modern Maturity* from out of her sweater pocket. For the second time in less than a minute, Sig seriously considered the option of strangling a postmenopausal woman to death.

Christ, she should have invited Mrs. Katz to her firm's dinner as her escort, just to get her out of the way! How on earth was Monty supposed to get close to Mom with Sylvia Katz always underfoot? Didn't Sylvia have *any* tact at all? "Perhaps we could meet downstairs for drinks later?" Sig hinted to her mother. If she could get Monty and her mother into the bar, things might happen. And in the meantime maybe Mrs. Katz would go to bed and leave the coast clear.

"I don't usually drink that late," Mrs. Katz told Sig. She lowered her voice, "If I do I have to get up in the middle of the night. Or *you* know."

Sig didn't want to know. Sig didn't even want to think about it. When would she hit the adult-diaper phase of life? God, she was getting morbid. It was the holidays; they always did this to her. She glanced at her watch. Now she was almost late for the damned dinner. "I won't be out late. Enjoy your evening with Monty," she said pointedly to her mom.

"We will," Mrs. Katz sang out.

∞

Sig had tried, successfully, to avoid her boss all night, but that was only half of her challenge. If she gave Bill a chance, he'd give her another talk about how she wasn't pitching, how she hadn't ACATed an account in four months, and how, in the end, there would be no Christmas bonus this year. Sig couldn't bear to hear it. But now, alternatively, she was having to sit and listen to the braggadocio of the other brokers at her table. Brokers were a lot like fishermen: they always had to tell how big their catch was. And they all had a tendency to lie. The lie served two purposes: it made these guys feel better about themselves in this bad year and it made the other guy feel worse.

Sig knew for a fact most of them were lying. The wire operators posted all new accounts and Sig checked them weekly. Sig knew she wasn't the only one not pulling her weight, but for her—older than many of the others, the only woman, and one who had always been a real rainmaker—there seemed to be a lot more at stake.

She managed to get through most of the meal by talking animatedly to some sales assistant from Staten Island and smiling widely around the table from time to time. She hoped to give the impression that she was just too happy to pay any attention to anyone else. She sighed with relief when dessert was served and she made an immediate exit.

In the taxi she could relax and drop the act. She couldn't help but wonder what her mother was doing right at that moment. It *had* to be better than her evening.

∞

Sig arrived at the Pierre after fighting the post-theater traffic. She walked through the beautiful rotunda and proceeded into the Café bar. She looked at her watch. With the long cab ride uptown it was already half past eleven. Probably too late to call upstairs, but Sig thought perhaps she'd try. It was ridiculous, but Sig wanted, longed for, the comfort of . . .

"Hello. What are you doing here?" Sig looked up into the very blue eyes of an older man. It took her only a moment to recognize him—it was Mr. Cushing from the Winter Wonderland Ball.

"What are *you* doing here?" Sig asked.

"Chaperoning Wendy," Paul said. "But you didn't answer my question."

Sig laughed. "Well, I'm sort of chaperoning my mother. I think she told you she's staying here," she explained. She thought of the flowers he had sent. "But I guess you knew that." Somehow, looking at Paul Cushing she thought, for a moment, she could tell at least a small part of the truth. "I'm a little concerned about that character she met at the party the other night."

Paul smiled again. "You can't be too careful nowadays," he agreed. "Mothers and granddaughters need to be protected." He lowered his voice. "Would you like me to check him out for you? I have a service that does that."

"Really?" Sig asked. "Is that a bit paranoid of you?"

Paul shrugged. "Perhaps," he said. "But when my son and daughter-in-law died, I was left with no one but Wendy. I'm probably overprotective, but she is an heiress, and it isn't easy for anyone raising a teenager nowadays."

Sig nodded. "I don't think it was ever easy. Not that that's a comfort to you." She paused. "I'm sorry to hear about your son and daughter-in-law."

Paul shrugged. "He drank and drove. I'll always feel guilty that I couldn't ever stop him." He shrugged again. "I'm grateful Wendy survived." They both fell silent. "Hey, how about a drink?" he asked.

He was a nice man, Sig thought. If he wasn't so old she'd even . . . but actually he was a perfect father figure. "Would you like to come upstairs for that drink?" Sig asked on the spur of the moment. If Phyllis had antagonized him, he seemed to like that—or be amused by it. Maybe he was bored—or a masochist. Hey, you never know.

"I'd like that," he said. "I have to admit I really admire the closeness of your family. It's rare to see people who enjoy being together the way you all do."

Sig just smiled. "Oh yes," she said, and reminded herself that discretion was the better part of valor. Then inspiration hit. "How would you like to come to my mother's birthday party the day after tomorrow?"

"Certainly. Can I bring Wendy? I like her to see families together."

"Of course."

He handed her his card. Sig and Paul Cushing strode over to the elevator and Sig pressed the button. The doors immediately rolled open and they went up to the suite. She had taken out her key and was as quiet as she could be in opening the door. She didn't need to disturb her mother if Monty had already gone home. But from the foyer she saw a light on. Sig could hear voices coming from the living room. As she came closer to the doorway she heard her mother's voice. "Oh, nice meld. It's a natural."

"You said it was possible with a hand and foot," added a husky voice.

"Yeah, but you could get minimum points if it's concealed," she heard Mrs. Katz say.

Sig tiptoed into the living room, Paul Cushing following. Then she froze. "You can't do that. The frozen discard pile has a wild card," a voice rebuked Mrs. Katz. There, at the table where room service usually lay its tray, sat her mother, Monty, Bernard Krinz, and Mrs. Katz. The scary part was that in the middle of the table lay a pile of garments and shoes, while Monty was naked from the waist up. It took Sig another moment to realize that Mrs. Katz was worse than naked: she had taken off her own shoes and stockings, which lay on the table, along with her lumpy sweater, her glasses, and her dress. She sat there in a voluminous nylon slip and you could see that she was buckled into some kind of frightening foundation garment under that. Sig averted her eyes from the straps and zippers and screamed. "It isn't just the cards that are wild in this room," she yelled.

"Oh my God!" Mrs. Katz said, her hand fluttering to her huge and sagging chest. "You scared me."

"What in the world are you doing?" Sig demanded of the four miscreants.

"We're playing strip canasta," Monty explained pleasantly. "I've lost my shirt to your mother."

Sig looked past Monty's chest, matted with white hair, and over to her mother, who sat coolly with her cards arrayed in front of her. She hadn't even lost an earring. None of the garments and accessories on the table belonged to her. Thank God! But what did Paul Cushing think? The idea of these superannuated delinquents misbehaving made Sig feel crazy. She wasn't sure if she should laugh or cry, but whichever she chose, she knew she didn't like it. "Who started this?" she asked accusingly.

Mrs. Katz looked up at her calmly. She actually seemed to have *more* clothes on rather than less, now that her heavy corset and long-line brassiere with all their structural underpinnings showed. No wonder her husband Sid left her: she seemed to have as much metal supporting her as the Tappan Zee Bridge. "It was *my* idea to play canasta," Mrs. Katz said modestly, as if she should get credit instead of blame. "We needed a fourth, so we called Bernard." She hiccuped. There were three empty whisky sour glasses in front of her. Had she been drinking?

"And who suggested this gambling part?" Sig asked.

"Well," her mother said calmly, "Sylvia never likes to gamble for money, so Monty suggested we play it like strip poker. Since he's never played canasta before and he doesn't wear jewelry, we gave him a handicap."

"I've got my Cartier cuff links riding on this hand," Bernard said, with more enthusiasm than he'd shown during the whole Winter Wonderland evening. "I haven't played canasta since my mother died."

Sig turned to Monty. "You talked them into playing strip canasta?" she asked, her voice rising in disbelief. "What's next? Spin the bottle? Truth or dare?"

"How do you play those?" Monty asked, obviously interested. "I don't think we had them in Glasgow." Sig averted her eyes from Monty's chest. His neck hung like a wattle from under his chin and joined his chest at some place that she didn't care to see. His jowls were imperfectly shaved, his eyebrows wilder than Brooke Shields's in a twister. Growing old was a terrible thing. It was a disgusting disintegration, a humiliation of the flesh.

Sig promised herself she would double up on her aerobics and lose three pounds. She would not ever let her flesh sag, her skin bag, her step drag. She would rather die first. She looked across at her mother.

"How was *your* evening?" Phyllis asked.

fourteen

Sylvia Katz lay mounded on the Chesterfield sofa, nursing a glass of Maalox and holding a plastic bag of ice against her forehead. Phyllis couldn't help but smile, though she tried to suppress it. The wages of sin were costly for Sylvia, but the improvement to her personality that alcohol brought was, at least from Phyllis's point of view, well worth it. Sylvia had shown another side of herself the night before and Phyllis had certainly enjoyed it. She suspected that Monty and Bernard Krinz had enjoyed it even more. "You better think of getting up soon. Sig and Sharon are coming over to pick you up for the birthday party preparations. They want to make a big deal out of it." Sylvia slid the ice back onto her forehead. "So," Phyllis asked, a wicked grin beginning to spread across her face, "would you like some scrambled eggs and cheese for lunch? Or maybe some eggs benedict. The hollandaise is delicious."

"*Oy gevalt.* I must be coming down with the flu," Sylvia said. "Even toast would . . . " She shuddered.

"Maybe it's morning sickness," Phyllis laughed.

"Such a joker."

"Who's joking? That was some night you had last night. Three whisky sours."

"I don't remember everything, but I think Monty and I were losing."

"I think the two of you melded," Phyllis said.

"Don't be disgusting. Anyway, he's *your* boyfriend."

Phyllis shrugged. It was odd: Monty was bald and unattractive. He certainly drank too much, and his nose was veined with blood vessels to prove it. He was short and had a potbelly. But when he had taken off his shirt, Phyllis had felt a certain . . . Well, she couldn't exactly put a name on it, not even for herself. His chest was furred with grizzled white hair. His breasts were almost the size of hers. Yet Phyllis hadn't been able to stop thinking of what it might feel like to have her own torso pressed against his.

"Excuse me. It's none of my business, but . . . "

Whenever Sylvia was about to make something her business, something which she had no business to make her business, she prefaced it with those words. Phyllis smiled. Amazing how she could be endlessly patient with the bluntness and stupidity of Sylvia, yet totally intolerant of even the slightest dumbness from Susan or Sharon. Why was that?

Sylvia cleared her throat with a noise that sounded like the one her dishwasher used to make, just before it went on the fritz. "If you keep seeing him, this Monty, especially only late at night, do you know what he's going to think?"

"That I'm a vampire?" Phyllis asked.

"Joking. Always joking. Well, I want to tell you this, and I mean it: he's going to start to think that you're asking for it, and then you'll be sorry. It'll end in tears."

"Asking for it?" Phyllis wondered if Sylvia had somehow overheard the children's plans for Monty. "Asking for what?" Phyllis asked.

"You know," Sylvia lowered her voice. "S, E, X," she spelled.

"Yeah, and then what?" Phyllis asked.

"Then what? Then he might want you to do it. You know,

Oscar Bernstein wanted Natalie Schwartz to do it with him after they went out the first month. She told me. She was horrified. First he stuck his tongue in her mouth. Then he asked her to . . . " Sylvia lowered her voice again and leaned forward. She had to sip her Maalox again to gather strength. "He wanted her to kiss his dickie bird," she whispered. Sylvia let herself fall back on the sofa. "Ecch!" she gargled.

"Listen, Sylvia, Monty's already stuck his tongue in my mouth."

"See! See how I knew about this! Oh my God! You have to stop it now. He's not like Bernard. Bernard is a perfect gentleman. But that Monty . . . I think he spiked our drinks."

"Really?" Phyllis asked.

But Sylvia was really taking this seriously. "It's not too late. Nip it in the bud." Sylvia straightened up, clutching her purse to her bosom. "Lunches. Daytime. Nothing in the dark. Otherwise they get ideas, these men."

Phyllis shook her head. "I'm the one with ideas, Sylvia. I *liked* it when he kissed me."

"With a tongue? He kissed you with a tongue and you *liked* it? Come on. Don't be crazy. Do you eat snails, and other *traif*, too? I'm warning you, Phyllis, you're playing with matches! What are you going to do when he wants to go to bed with you?"

"Go to bed?" Phyllis laughed. "I should live so long. Sylvia, I *want* to have sex with him. I like him." As she said it, Phyllis realized it was true.

"I liked Sid," Sylvia admitted. "That didn't mean I enjoyed . . . you know."

Phyllis paused again. She knew she wasn't like a lot of women she had known, but now, here, with Sylvia Katz, the gap widened into a chasm. "So what exactly are you telling me? That you didn't like sex with your husband?"

"Who could like it? His thing—it was purple. And the rest of it was wrinkled and it hung and shook like President Nixon's jowls." Sylvia shuddered and finished the Maalox. "Remember how his jowls would tremble when he talked? Just for that they should have impeached him. Every time I looked at the president I thought of Sid and his . . . " Sylvia winced. "Why would a man want to show that to anyone? There's a reason they call them private parts."

Phyllis thought about Monty and the way he put his hands on her shoulder and her back when he moved her around the dance floor. He was a very good dancer. She'd always felt that that was an indication of . . . possibilities. Not that she'd ever tested her theory. She'd never slept with anyone except Ira. But the thought had entered her mind. Not often. But once, when they had vacationed with Kitty and Norman Steinberg and she'd thought Norman was . . . well, interested.

Ira had never been a good dancer, but he'd stopped dancing altogether long before his heart disease. And once he got the diagnosis, there was no more hanky-panky. When had he been diagnosed? Phyllis wondered, for a moment, when the last time she'd had intercourse with Ira had been. Certainly not in this decade. She wasn't sure if it had been in the eighties, either.

As best as she could figure, it would have been in Lake George the summer of 1979. If she had known it would be the last time, she would have paid more attention. Phyllis sighed, remembering the sun coming in the hotel window, Ira on top of her. She used to like it when Ira would hold her breasts. By then they were already sagging, but he didn't seem to mind. His touch had always been very gentle, tender. When she was younger she'd worn her hair long, and Ira would take out the pins slowly so that her hair fell down to her waist. If he wasn't very imaginative or creative he had at least been affectionate.

Phyllis shook her head. Now her breasts were down to her waist and her hair was short. She wondered what Monty, no pinup himself, would think about her body. And what she'd think of his. She knew what she looked like, and the news wasn't good. But somehow, when she'd seen his hairy chest and when he'd held her up against him, when his hand on her lower back moved her commandingly around the dance floor, she felt a shiver in the old places. Phyllis blushed. She was about to turn seventy. It was ridiculous to think this way, to feel this way at her age, she told herself. But it felt very good.

Phyllis looked at her friend Sylvia across a divide almost as wide as death itself. She knew it was laughable for her to have these feelings, but the tips of her breasts tingled in a way she hadn't even wanted to remember. And down there, there . . . well, she felt alive again. Maybe it was the old way and she just didn't remember. Like riding a bicycle, it seemed, you never forgot. Then the fact that she'd never learned to ride a bike occurred to her and she smiled. She liked the feeling she had, and it was sad that Sylvia didn't. After all, what were these areas of feeling on her body but life itself, concentrated into three intense points?

Sylvia was talking again. Phyllis forced herself to focus. Sylvia was in the middle of a lecture. "Not only that, but you know it isn't safe anymore," Mrs. Katz said. "You have to worry about what could happen."

"What's going to happen? Morning sickness like you've got? I'm going to get pregnant?"

"Very funny," Sylvia snapped. "No. I mean you could get the AIDS. You could die."

Phyllis looked directly into Sylvia's eyes. "I'm about to turn seventy. I'm going to do that anyway, Sylvia," she said. "But I think I'd like to live a little more first."

Sharon and Sig arrived at the Pierre to pick Mrs. Katz up and take her over to Sig's apartment to help with setting up for tomorrow. This way Sig could be certain that Mrs. Katz was safely out of the way later, and with any luck Sig could convince the elderly woman to stay over, giving Phyllis and Monty some much needed privacy. She had volunteered to bake one of her special angel food birthday cakes, and Sig had accepted the offer. It wasn't that she didn't want to spend the money on a professional cake, and she did want to break in her oven, since she had never used it. Sharon was her stolid self, only waiting to see if she could get through Hanukkah and Christmas without disappointing the children too badly, or throwing Barney out of her house.

"Ready to go?" Sig asked. Monty was due to arrive and take Phyllis out yet again.

"Pssstt," Mrs. Katz said as she was putting on her coat in the suite foyer. "He's not a nice man. He tried to get fresh with your mother," she whispered. "It was a good thing I was here."

"What do you mean, fresh?" Sig asked, with her heart lifting but her stomach churning.

"I heard a noise. I was almost sleeping, but I heard a noise. So I came out of the bedroom and they were here on the sofa and he was trying to . . . " Mrs. Katz stopped. "He was getting fresh," she reiterated.

At that moment Phyllis stepped into the foyer dressed in a knit suit and matching toque. Sig raised her eyebrows. "I know," Phyllis said with a shrug. "The hat. Bruce made me." Sig wondered how much the hat cost and wondered if it would look equally good on her. "Bruce insisted. And Monty said he likes hats."

He was fresh with her mother *and* her mother wanted to please him? This *did* sound promising, Sig thought.

"It's adorable," Mrs. Katz said about the hat. "So are you."

"You see why I keep her around?" Phyllis asked.

Just then there was a knock at the door. "He's early," Sig said, "that's a good sign."

"It can't be Monty. He didn't ring up. It must be one of the chambermaids."

When Sig went to the door and opened it, she found her brother, Todd, and Bernard Krinz before her. For a moment Sig was disoriented. Bruce hadn't seen Krinz since the benefit fiasco, had he? And what was Krinz doing here now? Todd seemed to wonder too, because he was holding on to Bruce in a possessive way. Bruce smiled and pecked him on the cheek.

"Hi," Bruce said casually, walking passed Sigourney, with both Todd and Bernard in tow. "Hello, Sylvia. Hi, Mom," Bruce said. "Tilt the hat." He approached his mother, kissed her on the cheek, and then angled the toque so that it was the perfect enhancement. The foyer was getting crowded. Bruce breezed into the living room. Once he sat down, they'd never get out. Then he threw himself onto the sofa.

What the fuck was going on? Sig wondered. "Bruce, could I talk to you for a moment?" she asked as she glided toward the bedroom door.

"Oh God. I can't get up now. I'm exhausted."

"*Now*," Sig said in the voice she used to use to wake him up on schooldays—the voice she used before she got the pot of cold water. Her glare levitated him off the couch. When the door was closed between them and the living room Sig started in. "What the hell is going on? What did you bring *him* over here for?"

"Oh, he called. He invited me to a book signing he was doing and I bought one and invited him over for a drink."

"Are you insane?" Sig asked. "Monty is due here in ten minutes and you're bringing Bernard back? I'm trying to get a proposal out of Monty, not another old-age orgy."

"Lighten up. Lighten up, Sig." Bruce threw himself onto the bed. "This is not brain surgery here. It's only dating. Anyway, the guy says he might want to get into my card company."

"What else of yours might he want to get into?" Sig asked. "You are incorrigible. You are such a little flirt. There's no excuse for your behavior. Jeopardizing this whole thing for . . . "

"Hey Sig, we're not talking about a cancer cure. It's not like *you* need the money." Sig felt like strangling him right there on the bed. "Anyway, *I* need the money. And Krinz isn't such a bad guy, for an old pooftah." Too furious to talk, Sig turned and stomped into the living room where she found her mother being helped into her coat by Monty.

"*Tempus fugit,*" he was saying. "I'm taking your mom to a little concert."

"The opera?" Bernard asked longingly.

"No."

"The San Francisco Orchestra at Carnegie Hall?" Bernard asked.

"No. Warren Zevon down in the Village."

"Have a good time," Sylvia said brightly.

Monty raised his eyebrows and leered at her. "You have a good time, too," he said. "Who sleeps with cats?" he asked in a teasing voice, obviously repeating a joke between them.

"Mrs. Katz," Sylvia giggled.

"And sometimes Mrs. Nussbaum," Monty reminded her and laughed.

Bruce had joined them. "Monty, you got tickets to the Warren Zevon concert?" he asked in disbelief. "They're almost impossible to buy."

"It's a little prebirthday present." Monty put his hands on Phyllis's shoulders. "I understand tomorrow is your mother's natal day." He smiled at her. "You're adorable in that hat. Very Betty Bacall." He picked Phyllis up and spun her around the room while Bernard, Sig, Bruce, and Sylvia looked on, stunned.

"I guess he's just an excitable boy," Bruce said, and they watched their mother and Montague Dunleathe leave for a night of rock and roll.

fifteen

Sharon, Barney, Jessie, and Travis were gathered in Sig's apartment. Sharon and Sig were busy putting out the final touches for the big do. Todd was in a napkin-folding frenzy, ready to perform origami miracles of the season. He seemed to be in some kind of a snit. Well, why not? Sig was. It was Phyllis's birthday—her seventieth, though she kept insisting she was only sixty-nine. In previous years Sig would have sent her mom a check and a card, but since she was here in New York and since her romance with Monty had blossomed, Sig and Bruce and Sharon were hoping that a family gathering might force Monty's hand, while getting a ring on their mother's.

Despite the bustle, Sig became aware that it was unusually quiet. Where were the kids? "Who's watching your children?" she asked Barney. Mrs. Katz was still diddling with the birthday cake and Barney seemed totally uninvolved. Sig pushed past them.

"Oh my God! They're throwing things over the railing." Sig imagined poor Travis making a very quick trip down thirty-two stories. Sig brushed against her sister on her way by, strode across the festive dining room, through the immaculate living room, and out onto the tiny terrace. Travis had just launched a linen cocktail napkin out into space and Jessie was about to pitch a crystal champagne flute.

"Freeze," Sig told the two children in a voice that stopped both of them dead. "Give me back that glass, Jessie," Sig told her niece.

Mutely, Jessie shook her head and clasped the flute behind her.

"Jessie," Sig asked in her sweetest voice, "have you ever been spanked so very hard that your tushie turned red?"

Jessie shook her head again.

"Today might be the day. Now give the glass to your Auntie Sig."

Jessie thrust the Baccarat crystal at Sig, who smiled and took it gently from her hand. "Good choice, Jessie," Sig said approvingly. "Your tushie is safe for one more day. Now go inside and behave or you and your brother won't get your Hanukkah presents from Auntie." The two kids preceded her into the apartment. "Barney, where are you?" Sig yelled. Barney came out of the kitchen, an olive martini in one hand and a clutch of hors d'oeuvres in the other. "Everything under control?" Sig asked him in a pleasant voice.

Barney nodded. That morning Sharon had told Sig that a bank was going to foreclose on their home next month if they couldn't raise some money. Barney didn't seem concerned. Sig leaned close to him, despite his intoxicating aroma. "Keep one eye on the children, Barney, or I'll pluck out your other one and put it in your goddamn martini. Next to the olive."

Sig pushed past Barney into the kitchen. Mrs. Katz was putting the final touches on her angel food cake, a fantasy complete with a portrait of Phyllis, "Happy Birthday," and a wreath of pastry posies encircling it all. Monty seemed to dote on Phyllis and, with any luck, this family gathering would be the opportunity to show off their loving family and put the pressure on him to make the move. More problematic was Phyllis. Despite the grand inquisition that the Sibs continually attempted, Phyllis hadn't told them anything about the way *she* felt. But what else was new? Who knew what she would do in the face of a proposal? There was no doubt she enjoyed Monty, but she still persisted in doing nothing but wisecracking at him and ducking all their questions.

"Please, Mrs. Katz," Sig begged. "Please finish that up."

"Good doesn't mean fast," Mrs. Katz said.

Sig was called out to the dining room, where Sharon was overseeing the table and deeply confused. "How many for dinner?" she asked. It had been hard to find anyone appropriate to invite. Phyllis had been feuding with her sister for thirty-five years, so their aunt and uncle were out of the question. She'd *never* spoken to her in-laws, Ira's side of the family. Sig had resorted to inviting Phillip Norman. She'd also invited Bernard Krinz. What the hell. And then Sig had remembered Paul Cushing and her invitation to him and his granddaughter. To her delight, he'd accepted. With a little luck, he might also be attentive to Phyllis and push Monty over the edge into a proposal. It seemed that Bernard's presence had some kind of effect like that on Todd, who was more attentive to Bruce than Sig had ever seen. Anyway, if Cushing didn't work as a ploy, Monty could be dumped, and Paul Cushing looked like a very good next candidate.

∞

Bruce was helping his mother prepare for the festivities. Preparing her toilette wasn't getting any easier. "So? How's it going with Todd?" she asked as she twitched and fidgeted while he attempted to do her makeup.

Bruce sighed. "It isn't easy being gay in the nineties."

"Hey, it's easier than being gay in the fifties. And you think straight people don't also have problems? You think Monty is perfect? Do you think I should tell him I'm really going to be seventy? I mean . . . "

"No, he's not perfect. Definitely don't tell him your true age. I never tell anyone mine. I don't think it matters to him. But don't take chances. He's very rich."

"Rich, schmitch. Brucie, he's nice to me. He makes me laugh. He's kind. Okay, he wouldn't know a kreplach from a doorknob, but he's a good person."

"So? Will you marry him?"

"He hasn't asked me," Phyllis said coyly.

"But if he does?"

"Well, I think he loves me . . . "

"Nobody loves me that I love back," Bruce admitted. "Not even you."

"Bruce Geronomous! How can you say that? Don't you know that I love you? Of course I do. You think I put on control top pantyhose just to get a rich husband? I did it to please *you*."

"You did?"

"Yes. Because you've always liked slim. Audrey Hepburn. You with those movies. How many times did you watch Audrey Hepburn in *Charade*? Let's face it, you liked her better than me."

Bruce nodded. "I loved her. She would have been perfect for me if she was a guy."

Phyllis took Bruce's face in her hands. "Honey, nobody is perfect for anybody. Not Ira. Not Monty. Not this Todd. Not even Audrey Hepburn, she should rest in peace."

"So you won't marry Monty? You don't believe in true love?"

"No, Bruce. I believe in true compromise. Be nice to Todd. Don't tease him. It sounds like he's nice to you."

The party was in full swing. Well, perhaps it would be more accurate to say half swing, but it was as swinging as it was going to get, Sig realized. Phyllis had sung her favorite song while doing an imitation of Bea Lillie. One of the problems was that virtually nobody remembered Bea Lillie, so even a good imitation—which Phyllis's probably was—was wasted. But the song, "There Are Fairies at the Bottom of the Garden" went over really well with Todd, Bruce, Bernard, and the children. And Monty, as he always did, laughed hard and smacked his thighs.

Monty had convinced Mrs. Katz to have another lethal whisky sour and she'd become as frisky as a mating whale. "And who are you?" Sylvia Katz asked, turning to Paul Cushing. "Do you come down to Florida much?" Paul admitted that he didn't. "Where's your wife?" Sylvia asked archly.

"Sylvia, forget about it." Phyllis told her, taking her by the arm and pulling her back into Monty's presence.

Sylvia put out her hand. "You know, the birthday girl is quite a catch. The men in Florida were crazy about Phyllis," she said. "They couldn't get their wheelchairs over to her fast enough."

Monty laughed, though Sylvia was serious. "I have no need of a chair, you'll see. But I do have a need for Phyllis." He took Phyllis's arm, tucked it under his own and looked at the three Sibs. "There's a poem I'd like to recite," he began. Bruce visibly restrained Todd from getting up from their seat on Sig's white divan to take another photo. Monty stood and, like a schoolboy back in Glasgow, put his hands straight at his sides, ready to declaim to Phyllis. He began Andrew Marvell's poem, "To His Coy Mistress":

> *"Had we but world enough, and time,*
> *This coyness, lady, were no crime."*

"Oh, Jesus, Sig," Bruce whispered. "He called Mom a lady. Do you think she's going to go ballistic?"

"Shut up, I think this is the big moment," Sig told him.

Monty continued.

> *"I would*
>
> *Love you ten years before the Flood,*
>
> *And you should, if you please, refuse*
>
> *Till the conversion of the Jews.*
>
> *My vegetable love should grow*
>
> *Vaster than empires, and more slow."*

"What's he talking about?" Sharon whispered. "Does he want her to change her religion?"

"What's vegetable love?" Barney asked. "Is the guy drunk or perverted?"

"Shh." Sig silenced them.

> *"But at my back I always hear*
>
> *Time's winged chariot hurrying near;*
>
> *And yonder all before us lie*
>
> *Deserts of vast eternity."*

"Nice and cheerful," Bruce said. But Sig looked over and noticed that Phyllis looked enraptured.

> *"Then worms shall try*
>
> *That long preserved virginity,*
>
> *And your quaint honor turn to dust,*

And into ashes all my lust.
The grave's a fine and private place,
But none, I think, do there embrace."

Monty ended with a flourish.

"Really cheerful," Todd commented. "Did he write that?"

"What did they teach you in high school?" Bruce asked Todd.

Todd shrugged. "I must have been out that day," he said.

Sylvia was wiping her eyes with a Kleenex. Monty turned to Phyllis and took her hand. Then he turned back to her children. "I'd like to ask for your permission to marry your mother," he said. "I won't do it if you have any objections—out of respect for your father and all. I'd understand, but I love Phyllis and at our age, we don't have time to waste. I have no family; I wasn't lucky enough to have children, but I've always felt family is the most important thing." He got misty-eyed. "I like you all and I'd be very gratified if you could think of me as part of this family."

"He wants dysfunction?" Bruce whispered, but Sig ignored him. She held her breath and looked at her mother.

"We would like that very much, Monty," Sig said. "But of course, it's up to Mom."

Monty turned back to Phyllis and pulled out a blue velvet box. He popped the lid and even from across the room the Sibs could see the sparkle of a huge centered diamond and large triangular baguettes at the side. Phyllis looked at the ring and looked back at Monty. For a moment, Sig's stomach lurched and she thought Phyllis was going to crack wise and reject Monty's offer. Then—miracle of miracles—Phyllis stood and began to recite herself.

"As my son, the compromiser, would put it:

> *"Roses are red,*
> *Kids like a toy,*
> *I'm saying, 'Yes.'*
> *I'll marry the goy."*

Sig let out her breath. Bruce, Todd, and Sharon cheered. Barney raised his glass and Paul Cushing clapped. Sylvia began, again, to cry. It was a beautiful thing, Sig thought—by tomorrow she might be able to tell the hotel that her mother was leaving.

Phyllis slid the ring onto her finger. It was enormous. She held her hand out and grinned. "It's bigger than my knuckles are," she said. "And they get bigger every year."

Monty kissed her and it was a real wet one. "I'll replace it as often as necessary with one even bigger," Monty told her. His affection was obvious. For some reasons tears welled up in Sig's eyes.

At that moment, she caught sight of Paul Cushing, who was looking at her from across the room. He nodded and smiled. And he lifted his glass to her. "May I propose a toast?" he asked. And everybody turned to him. "To Phyllis and Monty. When you love somebody, anything is possible." He winked at Sig, but in the moment before he did, Sig had seen something in Paul's blue eyes: sympathy, affection, or perhaps pity. Sig shuddered before she lifted her glass with all the others.

sixteen

D o you think he'll want a prenup?" Sig asked her brother. She was on her headset phone from work, but it was just after four P.M.—when everyone on Wall Street turned into dinosaurs. She herself felt like chopped liver—but she had just enough energy left to discuss the possibility that her mother was actually going to marry a very wealthy man.

"You know, our plan worked," Bruce said, as if reading her mind. "I bet we could do anything if we worked together."

"Yeah, but it isn't going to happen overnight and we still have to survive." Because she was using her headset phone her hands were free. Sig stretched out her hand. She stared at her emerald ring. She thought of her mother's huge diamond, the new one that Monty had given her. Sig sighed. She'd feel naked and vulnerable without it, but it was her only valuable piece. It could pay for the Pierre and Mom's clothes and maybe even her back mortgage payments. "So? You think he'll want a prenup?" she repeated.

"I don't think Monty's that kind of guy," Bruce said. "He's old-fashioned. I mean, the Scots aren't known for their open-handed generosity, but they don't like to go to lawyers the way we do."

"We have to tell Mom not to sign anything."

"Oh yeah. Like she takes direction well!" Bruce laughed.

Sig laughed, or approximated one. She looked down at the comforting green depths of her ring. "Look, whatever happens that way, the whole thing is a miracle."

"Yeah," Bruce agreed, "Plus, I'm starting to get emergency reorders. The cards are selling. I was right. I feel so light I'm walking *en pointe*. I look like the goddamned sugar plum fairy."

"Well, you're *my* goddamned sugar plum fairy, and I love you," Sig told him, feeling a flood of affection for her kooky brother.

"Oh, I bet you say that to all your queer brothers," Bruce replied, but he sounded pleased. "Anyway, gotta go. I'm meeting with Bernard Krinz. I actually think he's going to invest some money in the business. I need it to deliver the new orders fast. Not to mention that Bernard's made Todd sit up and take notice of me. It's a beautiful thing. I figure I can be profitable again by gay Valentine's Day."

"Great," Sig told him. "Good luck with Bernard and Todd," and disconnected the phone, but it rang again almost immediately and Sig, her headset still on, hit the connect button. It was probably the cage, confirming some of her sales. It had been a very busy day.

"So, you won't believe this," Sharon's voice brayed into Sig's ear. "I just got a call from Mr. Moneybags and he and Mom are planning to come up and spend the day."

"Oh, that's nice."

"Huh? It's a lot nicer than *nice*," Sharon said vehemently. "Monty suggested that we go over to tour Jessie's school. He said he'd heard I could use some help with the school fees. He says he wants to endow the place."

"That's wild," Sig said. The guy must *really* like her mother, she thought, then felt a pang. No one, no man, had tried to please her that way in a long, long time. "When you asked him, he just said yes?" she inquired.

"I didn't ask. He just offered." Sharon sounded wheezy with delight. "That's not all. He also says he wants to talk to Barney about a job in his company."

"This is a Christmas miracle," Sig breathed.

"Speaking of Christmas, are you going to come up here tonight for Jessie and Travis's Hanukkah party? It *is* the last night of Hanukkah. You know they'll want their Aunt Sig here. *And* I'm making latkes."

Sig nearly groaned aloud. Fried potato pancakes were just what Sharri needed more of, Sig thought. "Is Bruce coming?" she asked, hedging for time.

"Yeah. He's promised her the new Barbie."

"What Barbie is left?" Sig asked. "Bisexual Barbie? She comes with both Skipper and Ken?"

"Don't be disgusting," Sharon said. "I don't know, but Jessie's so excited she threw up this morning."

That's always the omen of a good time to come, Sig thought. At least the party wasn't going to be held on her carpet. "Okay," she said wearily, "I'll come."

"Great. Barney will pick you up at five."

Sig had just taken off her headset when the phone rang again. If it was an order, no matter what the size, she'd tell them to call back Monday. She placed the gear on her head and pressed the connect button. The voice on the other end was deep.

"Sigourney? Is that you?"

"Yes."

"This is Paul Cushing. I need to talk to you."

"Now is fine."

"No. I need to see you in person."

Sig thought of the latke party and her shopping. "How about Monday?" she asked.

"Why don't I drop by your apartment Monday night?" he

said. "It's important." What was that about? she wondered, but she had too much to do.

Sig spent the rest of the time making calls to her mortgage broker, the co-op board, and the loan officer at Citibank. It took her more than three hours, but before she was done she had managed to talk everybody into believing she'd get current in her payments within two weeks. She'd made her decision: she'd have to sell the ring, and then the apartment, but she'd do what she had to do and a Merry Christmas to all.

There was one more call she had to make, though she couldn't bear it. She lifted the phone and dialed Sotheby's and asked for Mr. Grenville. She was put on hold. The telephone music was playing "We Wish You a Merry Christmas" and it was just ending. Then, to Sig's despair, she heard the drum intro for "The Little Drummer Boy." Sig immediately covered the earpiece so she wouldn't have to be tortured any further. When Mr. Grenville was put through, Sig released her hand and began by reintroducing herself. Hesitantly, she said, "I think I would consider selling the emerald now."

"Ah. A fine stone. And our pre-Christmas sale would be the time to sell it. But you'll have to hurry. It's too late to be in the catalog."

Sig looked down at her finger. It's only a little piece of colored glass, she tried to tell herself, then sighed. No man had ever given her a ring, and now she had to give up the one she'd given herself. "I'd like to put it in the auction," Sig said.

With some money in sight she took a cab uptown to Takashimaya, the chic Japanese department store on Fifth Avenue. The tearoom on the lower ground floor was the only place Sig could go to during this season and have a guarantee she wouldn't be accosted with *any* version of "The Little Drummer Boy."

After a snack, Sig needed to focus on her holiday gift shopping. She'd do it all there. She still had most of the cash she'd taken out, and she'd use her credit cards if she had to. She had decided on a beautifully packaged box of green teas for Barney, who, as far as she knew, didn't drink tea; an Italian silk scarf for Sharon, since scarves came in only one size; a long, hand-knit muffler for Bruce in an absolutely killing smoky color; and finally, resentfully, a cleverly designed pair of rubbers for Mrs. Katz. Sig hoped they would fit over the socks and sandals.

That left only her mother and, exhausted and fighting the holiday crowd, Sig made her way up Fifth Avenue, past Bendel's, Doubleday's, and Trump Tower. She easily passed up Tiffany's. After all, with that doorknob that Monty had given her mother, it looked like Phyllis wouldn't need any jewelry. Sig sighed, looked at her own ring, and got as far as Bergdorf Goodman. She decided to step in. There had to be *something* marvelous there for her mother, the woman who was about to have everything.

Sig entered through the Fifty-seventh Street revolving door but found herself awash in a tide of purposeful shoppers. She passed through the accessory department, passed the leather goods, and lingered only a moment in the perfume hall before taking the elevator upstairs. She walked around the third floor, where the crowd was thinned out by the prices and the intimidating help, until she found herself in the back corner, where luxe carpeting and two antique fauteuils sat invitingly. "Bridal Salon" said the sign, and Sig found herself walking into the hushed holy of holies. There, a mannequin stood in a satin and tulle fairy-tale creation. Sig stopped and stared, her breath caught, her eyes devouring the beautiful dress. She'd never worn one, but if she ever had, she wished it had been this one. "Can I help you?" the heavy, middle-aged saleswoman asked.

Sig jumped and turned to face her. "Are you looking for a mother-of-the-bride dress?" the woman asked politely.

All at once Sig felt both a thousand years old and as vulnerable as an infant. "No," she said. "I'm the daughter of the bride," and then surprised herself and the saleswoman by bursting into noisy tears.

∞

Phyllis and Sylvia, bundled up tightly against the December chill, were walking up Madison Avenue. "This," Phyllis said, "is where the really rich people shop."

"Not Fifth Avenue?" Sylvia asked.

"Nah," Phyllis told her as she took her friend's arm and helped her avoid a fast-strutting matron holding a Yorkie under her arm. "This is the place. And it's the last day of Hanukkah. I'm going to get myself a present—a trousseau."

Phyllis had always kept a little money aside. It had been her habit from the very earliest days of marriage to Ira. Though she'd worked with him all those years, he'd never paid her a salary. She had merely asked for the housekeeping money and managed to put a little bit of it away. Over forty-seven years it had added up. Of course she'd had to use it from time to time, but only bits, and only for things like gifts for the children or a surprise trip with Ira. She was frugal. Even now, when she had just a modest amount coming in, she managed always to put aside a little bit at the end of each month. She'd been afraid she might have to use the money for private nursing, or that the government would get it if she had some catastrophic illness. Now, instead of waiting for a rainy day Phyllis was going to spend it—well, maybe not all of it, but plenty, and she was going to spend it on a trousseau. She and Ira had gotten married right after the war when there was still a shortage of lots of things, especially money. She had never had a trousseau, but she was determined to come to Monty, her fiancé, her lover-to-be, with all the accoutrements a bride should have with her.

Sylvia looked around at the fur-clad holiday shoppers. "I think we could do better at the Saw Grass Mall."

Phyllis laughed. She'd learned a few things watching her son make her over. "Natural fabrics, Sylvia," she said. "And we're starting from the panties out. Monty's seen your underwear, but he hasn't seen mine."

"Bernard saw mine, too," Sylvia said with a dreamy smile.

When they passed the window full of negligees, Phyllis stopped in her tracks. Silk with the iridescence of butterfly wings was mated with lace as frothy as sea foam. Sylvia followed her friend's eyes. "Do you think it's machine washable?" she asked. But without even answering, Phyllis moved toward the door like a somnambulist.

She bought it all. All of it and a silk bathrobe in a pinky champagne color that made her look sixty again. She didn't question the outrageous prices, she didn't look at the sale rack. She did none of her usual moves. She merely pointed at the most beautiful things, had them wrapped, and paid for them. And the adventure of it all was heightened by the idea that only Monty would see her in this new garb.

"Spending money is exhausting," Sylvia Katz said as she took a booth seat at Three Guys coffee shop on Madison.

"How would *you* know?" Phyllis asked as she slid into the seat opposite.

Phyllis herself had bought three pairs of extraordinary lace undies, two matching bras, and the most beautiful nightgown she'd ever seen. They had cost her almost a thousand dollars, but she hadn't winced. Instead, she'd imagined the look on Monty's face when she stood before him. Her only regret was that she hadn't ever felt this way before, and that the body under the fabrics would not be nearly as silky as the garments themselves. She sighed.

"Phyllis, are you having regrets?" Sylvia asked, and then, before Phyllis could explain, ordered an egg salad sandwich from the harried waitress.

Phyllis herself ordered a BLT without mayo. "I'm going to get myself a new coat and a hat to match," she announced to her friend. "And maybe a bag." She looked across the table at the huge, battered, ugly purse that Sylvia, as always, was schlepping. "I'll buy one for you, too," Phyllis said. What the hell, she was spending this much, she might as well spend a little more.

"Oh, no," Sylvia protested. "When Sid left me, this is all he left me with." Sylvia paused. "Do you think this Monty will be nice to you? I mean, really nice?"

"I think so," Phyllis said. "It's very odd. It seems to me like Ira loved me, and put up with who I was because of it. But Monty loves me *because* of who I am. Does that make any sense to you?"

"No," Sylvia admitted and reached for the egg salad sandwich plate that the waitress was handing off.

For a moment, Phyllis was flooded with pity for her friend. Loving Monty had given her more compassion and more generosity. "Hey, you want some dessert?" she asked. "Lunch is on me. I'll blow ya."

❧

"Delicious," Monty exclaimed, and gave a pat to his mustache where singed bits of potato pancake still hung. The holiday meal had been hideous, the latkes inedible and the salad sandy, and all of the embarrassment complicated by the fabulous gifts Monty had dispensed to the whole company, putting Sig's in the shade. Then there was the endless stream of apologies from Sharon, who absolutely demanded insincere but constant reassuring response.

"I think I'll slit my throat," Sig whispered to Bruce.

"Before you wear that Hermés scarf?" Bruce asked. He was distractedly stroking the suede jacket he'd been given.

"All right. I'll wear it tonight going home. *Then* I'll slit my throat."

Bruce nodded. "When *I* go home, I'm going to have seventeen hysterical messages from Todd, who is convinced that I'm having an affair with Bernard."

"Well, are you?"

"Don't be ridiculous. I'm not that kind of a boy. I always go for looks over money. It's my curse."

"Speaking of looks over money, I think things are looking good between Monty and Mom."

"I sure hope so. I wouldn't eat one of Sharon's latkes for less than the opportunity to inherit a million dollars."

At that moment, Monty cleared his throat. "Well," he said. "It was a wonderful meal." He rose from the table. "Thank you, mine host." He smiled at Barney. "And now, if you'll step into the living room, I have a little proposal I'd like to discuss with you, son. I think you need to keep busy."

Bruce and Sig exchanged looks. "Son?" Bruce asked.

"Oh my God," Sig said. "He *is* going to offer Barney a job."

"Pur-rump-a-pum-pum," Bruce said.

seventeen

When Monty arrived at the Pierre after the latke party, he was dressed in his evening wear, except for the Murray's Space Shoes on his feet. "Well, you look snazzy," Phyllis said, and realized how out of date the word was. For the first time in close to fifty years she felt as self-conscious as an adolescent. "Have you got special plans?" she asked.

"I do," Monty told her and leered at her in a most attractive way. Though he was bald, and more overweight than he should be for his health, Monty exuded a kind of self-possession that made him attractive, even sexy.

There was a knock at the suite door, though Phyllis wasn't expecting anyone. "May I?" Monty asked and went through the foyer and opened the door to reveal Bernard Krinz.

The architect actually entered the room smiling, then scanned it. For once his handshake didn't feel like that of a used car salesman hoping to close a deal. He seemed, instead, enthusiastic—even impatient. For a panicky moment Phyllis thought Bernie was looking for her, but then Mrs. Katz came out of the bedroom, out of her lumpy sweater and in a beaded dress. Monty put his hand on Krinz's shoulder and gave it a hearty squeeze.

"Well," he said, "Metropolitan Opera opening night, the best box in the house, and a lovely woman to enjoy it with. Wagner isn't my favorite, but I'm sure you'll enjoy it."

Phyllis turned to Sylvia in complete bewilderment, but Sylvia seemed dressed and ready, as if she knew all about it. Bernard helped her on with her voluminous coat and her ever-present purse. It wasn't until they had gone that Monty turned to Phyllis and smiled. "More costly than buying off my little brother with a chocolate bar, but it is a guaranteed five hours of absence and privacy." Then he leaned toward Phyllis and put one hand over her shoulder and against the wall, so she was imprisoned between his bulk and the window at her right. She knew he was about to kiss her—a real kiss, a kiss that mattered and might lead to other things, and she felt a flutter in her chest that wasn't angina. It had been a long time since she'd been really kissed, and she wasn't sure how she would react.

At that moment the suite bell rang again. Monty raised his brows, smiled, and answered it. This time three waiters, one with a wheeled table, one with champagne (two bottles) and ice buckets, and the last with a tray of savories paraded into the room. "I thought we might dine in," Monty said. The head-waiter set up the table and, with a flourish, was about to lay the pink linen napkin on Phyllis's lap when Monty stopped him. "Thank you, but no. I'll take care of her," he said, dismissing all the staff. "If we need you, we'll call."

Monty had ordered everything. Oysters for himself, her favorite melon for starters. The fruit tasted wonderful with the champagne Monty fed her. Phyllis had never been babied in this way. When there was any taking care of to be done, she took care of it. She took care of the children when they were little, she took care of the business and Ira when he was sick, and she took care of all the extended family members when they were grieving. Now there was someone who had ordered her dinner, down to her favorite salad, and had even noticed the salad dressing she preferred. Monty was a man who paid attention. "I'm not used to this," Phyllis admitted.

"Well, you better get used to it," Monty said and spooned the last one of his oysters into her mouth. "It's fun to treat you really well." He smiled a wicked grin. "I have an idea." He stood up, leaving the rest of dinner and the unused cups and the silver coffeepot which was being kept warm by a Sterno can. "I don't think we need more food now," he said. "I think all we need is time."

He took her hand and Phyllis felt a tingle, a buzz so electric that she almost giggled aloud. The man was seventy-four years old and totally mad, but she responded. Yet at the same time as she felt his heat for her rising and being matched by her own, she felt a certain reluctance. It was shyness, and even a little fear.

As if he sensed her hanging back, Monty encircled her in his arms. " 'We are old, Father William,' " he said, misquoting some ancient poem Phyllis could barely remember. "I don't want to rush you, but I *do* want you."

"You do?" Phyllis asked, both shy and coy. She liked to hear him say it. She liked everything about this old man.

"I want you to sleep with me," Monty said, nuzzling her ear. "My performance may not be what it once was, but every now and then . . . " His voice was husky. "I don't believe in long engagements, do you?" Phyllis nodded and let Monty lead her slowly into the bedroom.

He kissed her at the threshold and then led her to the bed, laid her down, and gently took off her shoes. "I'm a little nervous," Phyllis admitted.

"Only a little?" Monty asked and laughed. "At our ages the tables have turned. You can't lose your virginity, but I can easily lose my pride." He bent over and kissed Phyllis, just a brief kiss, but he still tasted of oysters, champagne, and something else. Then, matter-of-factly, he sat down on the side of the bed. He took Phyllis's hand in his own. "Do you know what I've learned in the last five decades about sex?" he asked. Phyllis, still self-conscious, shook her head.

"What I've learned is that there's a lot that goes into loving a woman that most men are too impatient to bother with. Age has stolen a lot from me, Phyllis my dear. But it's granted me patience." He bent over and kissed her again, this time deeply. "I can promise you two things: that you have nothing to be embarrassed about and that, in the end, you're going to have a very, very good time with me."

And he was right.

∞

It was only two mornings later that Sig was awakened by wild knocking on her door, interspersed with equally wild buzzing of her buzzer. No one gets up this early on Sundays in New York. "What? What?" she mumbled grumpily and managed to wrap a mohair shawl around herself to get to the relentless noise of the door. Only nine shopping days 'til Christmas and she had to be bothered with this?

Sharon, panting, her face red, stood beside Bruce, who was as deadly pale as an Irishman's ass. "What's going on?" she asked. "Is Mom all right?"

"No," Sharon said.

"Oh my God, is she . . . "

"It's not that," Bruce rapped out. "She hasn't had a stroke. *I'm* going to. Monty's checks have bounced, both for my business *and* for the school contribution."

"What?" Sig croaked. "That's impossible. What about Montana? What about the airline? What about the Guinness heiress?"

"Fake. All fake," Bruce told her. "Except the heiress. He married *her* and bled her dry. He's a fortune hunter. He met Mom on the flight from Florida in first class. He must have been trolling for a rich widow."

"Mom flew first class?" Sig asked. She put her hand up to her head. The three of them were still standing in her doorway. Sig bent down to pick up the Sunday *Times* from the doorstep. She'd have to check to be sure her ad for the apartment was listed. "Come in," she said. "Come in." Bruce and Sharon filed past her, Sharon's shoulders hunched. They sat down in the living room. "Okay," Sig said, feeling more tired than she ever had in her life. "Start from the beginning."

"The statistical genius over here got it wrong. Her data, as they say in the market research business, was severely compromised," Bruce grimaced. "Monty is penniless. He invested his wife's money in his airline. It went bankrupt more than a decade ago. He's been living on credit and loans ever since. Copernicus, here, had the numbers wrong."

"But it wasn't my fault," Sharon cried. "Mom picked him out, not me."

"Where *is* Mom?" Sig asked and she felt both a fluttering in her stomach and the beginning of that feeling she got when her throat closed.

"I guess she's still at the Pierre," Bruce said.

Sig groaned and visibly shuddered. What was the bill there going to be? She'd dropped off her ring for auction, but now, even with its sale, her prospects of keeping her home and straightening out her life were worse than ever. She couldn't stave off the despair. "Okay," she said with a studied air of calmness she didn't feel. "I have a plan: first we kill Monty. Then Bruce, you kill Sharon while I kill myself."

"And nobody kills Mom? What kind of plan is that?" Sharon

bleated. "It was *her* fault. This Monty was *hers*," Sharon said.

Bruce ignored his suburban sister. "It just might work," Bruce told Sig, then patted her now bare hand comfortably. "Sharon, if you want to, you can kill Mom before I kill you."

Sharon began to cry. "It wasn't my fault," she repeated.

"Oh, shut up," Bruce told her. "Everything's always been your fault."

"It is not. It wasn't my fault Barney turned down the job with Monty."

"He turned down the job?" Sig asked. "Is he crazy?" Bruce looked at her. "Rhetorical question," she assured him. "Did he really turn down the job?"

"He said it was beneath him. It was only middle management, something in the marketing department. He said he wouldn't lower himself to less than vice president."

"My God! He's been downsized and out of work for close to two years and he turns *anything* down?" Sigourney asked.

Bruce shrugged. "Just as well. It was a fake, I'm sure."

Before this grousing degenerated into a full frontal attack, Sig pulled herself up. "Enough," she said. "I'll be dressed in four and a half minutes."

"What are we doing?" Sharon asked.

"We're going to the Pierre to have a little heart-to-heart with Mom."

∞

The dark, glossy door to the Pierre suite looked solid as a castle portcullis. They'd rung the bell three times and now banged on the door. "I feel like Westley rescuing Buttercup in *The Princess Bride*," Bruce said.

Sig looked at him grimly. "You're the only princess around here," she snapped. "No time for your movieolas now. And

Westley would have had the door down by now."

"*We'll* have to call security." Bruce shrugged.

"Excellent plan. I need some security," Sig murmured. Then they heard a rustling, and the peephole eye was filled. The door swung open and Mrs. Katz stood there, clad in a fluffy Pierre robe. "So early?" Mrs. Katz asked. She cleared her throat. "Maybe you should come back later."

Sig pushed the door open all the way and strode past Mrs. Katz, the useless freeloader. How much had her visit cost Sig? The other two Sibs followed. Sig got as far as the living room, which was disordered by newspapers, a blanket on the sofa, and the remains of a small room service repast, when Mrs. Katz caught up with her. "Where are you going?" she asked.

Sig gave her one of her looks and walked on to the bedroom door. Her hand was on the doorknob. "Don't you believe in privacy?" Mrs. Katz asked protectively.

"Don't *you*?" Sig retorted. "You came up here and moved in on my mother. You've stuck to her like glue. What privacy did you give her?"

Mrs. Katz raised her brows in hurt surprise. Then, "Plenty," she said, shrugged and turned her back. "*You'll* see."

Sig threw the bedroom door open. Bruce and Sharri were right behind her. Before her their mother, her hair disordered but her face composed, lay in the crook of Montague Dunleathe's hairy old arm. "Oh my God!" Sharri said and threw her hands up over her eyes.

Monty, his bald head shining but his side hair awry, opened his own eyes and sat up. His chest was as hairy as his arm. His breasts sagged onto his belly. Sig almost closed her own eyes. Somehow she hadn't imagined this. "Oh my God!" was all she could say, a hollow echo of her sister.

"What are you doing to my mother?" Bruce demanded.

"I think it's known as 'the traditional.' Or do you in the States call it 'the missionary'?" Monty asked.

Phyllis opened her eyes. "Well, that's what you *started* with . . . " she began.

Sharon threw both her hands up as if to ward off a blow. "More information than we require," she cried out and shuddered.

"So who asked you to ask?" Phyllis wanted to know. She started to sit up until it became clear that she, too, was naked. Sig couldn't help but notice the pile of frothy silk thrown on the floor beside the bed.

Bruce averted his eyes and made a strangled noise. "God! Who would think Mom was . . . was . . . like Louise Brooks in *Pandora's Box!*" Sig snatched up a terry robe from the bedside chair and threw it at Monty while her mother fumbled to pull the sheet up under her armpits. Sig actually felt sick, but she had to persevere. She walked across the Axminster rug to the nightstand. She picked up the engagement ring that was lying there and held it up to her eye. It sparkled, without doubt, but now, looking closely she could easily see the colors were wrong—instead of the white brilliance of a perfect stone, the marquis cut reflected all the colors of the room. "Cubic zirconium," she yelled and flung the ring as hard as she could toward the window. "You fake," she cried. "You total fake!"

"Susan, get control of yourself," Phyllis rapped out. "What do you think you're doing?"

"What do *you* think you're doing?" Sigourney asked. "You just met this guy. You don't even know him, and you're in bed with him?"

"I'm engaged to him, Susan. And you *wanted* me engaged to him." Phyllis shrugged. "Me, I figure marriage, schmarriage. But Monty is old-fashioned." She looked up at him with a look on her face that Sig had never seen there before. It confused and upset her. It made her feel excluded, and even . . . resentful. She looked at Monty.

He was not just old-fashioned but *old*. Sig couldn't help but stare at the mound of aged flesh that confronted her, his mottled skin and the hair thrusting itself out of his ears, matched by the horrible web of wrinkles across the top of her mother's sagging chest. It was bad enough, Sig thought, that *she'd* had to suck in her stomach whenever she'd slept with Phillip Norman. At least she was toned, while Phillip's flesh was firm and smooth and tanned. He'd known how it pleased her in bed, and he was athletic in showing it. Why, then, did she have the feeling that Monty gave her mother something else, something more? She put the thought from her mind. "Get out!" she told him. "Leave my mother alone."

Monty raised his bushy brow, then shook his head. "You forget. We're betrothed."

Sig could barely contain her rage. Her hands were shaking and she felt the trembling go up her arms and into her body. Everything had gone wrong. There wasn't going to be any rescue, not for her, not for her mother. Her ring—her real one—was gone now and forever, and so was her mother's. This fake, this charlatan, had ruined everything. She'd lose her co-op, she'd give up on her job, and she'd wind up in Forest Hills, or Park Slope, or Riverdale, in some crummy rental apartment with her mother in the guest room—if there *was* a guest room. They'd split the rent, using some of Phyllis's Social Security check to make ends meet. It was she, Sig, the unmarried daughter, who would wind up taking care of their mother until her own breasts were down to her waist. "Get out!" she yelled again, but this time her voice was very close to tears.

"Excuse me?" Phyllis said. "Exactly who do you think you are?" She looked from Sig to Bruce and Sharon. "What are the three of you doing here, anyway? This is *my* life and you have no right to interfere like this."

Sig rolled her eyes. If she'd had a gun . . .

"Mom," Bruce began to explain, "the man is a liar. He's a con artist. He's . . . he's like Eli Kotch in *Dead Heat on a Merry-Go-Round*. Except not as good-looking as James Coburn. The guy is broke."

"Hey," Phyllis yelled, "I wasn't going to marry him for his *money*. Monty's seventy-four years old and he can still get a boner. Plus, he knows what to do with it!"

"And this from a woman who swore off genitalia," Monty said proudly, reaching with one arm to embrace her and with the other for the cigar at the side of the bed.

"Mom, get out of that bed," Sig snarled. Phyllis shrugged and obeyed, naked though she was. All three of her children screamed simultaneously and turned away in horror. Sig managed to pick up the lacy silk gown from off the floor and throw it at her mother, who calmly started to put it on.

"What's the problem here?" Phyllis asked as she smoothed the crumpled gossamer around her thickened waist. "He had money. Now he doesn't have money. Maybe he'll have some money again. Anyway, in the meantime, I promise you he's not stealing your inheritance." She paused and smiled wickedly. "And he wasn't stealing my virtue, either." Phyllis looked over at Sig. "If we're in the truth-telling mode, you don't have anything to be so proud about, Susan. If you think he was trying to con you, you were trying to con him with all of this." She gestured at the room, the new clothes, the fresh flowers.

Sigourney stared at Monty. "She has no money. Do you understand? She doesn't have a dime, except her pension check. There is no portfolio. The jewelry was costume. She has no prospects of getting any more money, either, unless you consider the pathetic cost-of-living adjustment to her Social Security payments. There is no house in Palm Beach. *I'm* paying for this suite. And I've run out of money. You're bankrupt, and I'm about to go under, too."

There, she'd said it. Now they'd finally understand—know all about the foreclosure, her failure, everything. But she'd still protect her mother. "You picked the wrong horse," she told Monty. "Get up and go away and leave my mother alone. You were in it for the money and there is none."

"It's time to beat it," Bruce said angrily.

"That," Monty said, "has become abundantly clear." And he calmly got out of bed, slipped his trousers on, and did so.

eighteen

You're *not* seeing him. Forget about it."

"What does that mean? What does that mean, 'forget about it'?" Phyllis asked.

"It means what I said," Sig repeated. "He doesn't like you. He wanted your money. Which, I might remind you, you have none of. Mom, he married an heiress before and squandered all *her* money. He just thought he was doing it again." It was black Monday, and what with the Monty fiasco and work about to begin, Sig was morose.

"Don't be ridiculous. How could I be an heiress?" Phyllis asked her daughter, who was tearing into her clothes.

"The portfolio. First-class flying. The clothes," Bruce explained. Sig had asked him over to keep all eyes on their mother while she was at work.

"The guy is a con man," Sig repeated. "Probably a thief. Didn't you ever hear of Sunny von Bulow? No way you're going to see him again."

They had stayed at the Pierre yesterday only long enough to morosely pack up Phyllis's belongings and for Sig to hyperventilate and sign the American Express bill. Now they'd adjourned, along with the adhesive Mrs. Katz, to Sig's apartment.

"I can't believe the tuition check bounced," Sharon whined.

Sig had called her in to also guard their mom. "I'm so embarrassed. How can I show my face at Jessie's school?"

"Nothing stopped you before," Bruce spat. "Barney's checks used to bounce like a spaldeen." He paused. "What about me, Sharon? I just put in an emergency reprinting order that I can't pay for. I could have had a deal with Bernard, but Monty offered me an interest-free loan. I can't believe I was so stupid. This is the most important season of the year in my business. I was operating on paper, but at least I was on *good* paper. Now I've sent *bad* checks to my suppliers. How am I going to explain *that*? I was hanging on by a thread, but Monty's ruined it all. I'd like to strangle the Scottish son of a bitch."

"A nice way to talk in front of your mother," Phyllis said, crossing her arms. She paused, thinking it over. "He *did* like me. I know he did. And I don't care if he doesn't have any money."

There was a flutter at the other side of the room. Sig couldn't help but notice Mrs. Katz, sitting prim and proper on the edge of the chair clutching her purse with both hands. What is it with her, Sig thought? Mrs. Katz shook her head, as if she had palsy, or wanted attention. Probably both, Sig decided. She took a deep breath. It was either out of annoyance or to calm herself. "That's not the point, Mom. He's clearly a sociopath. I know. I've dated a dozen of them. No normal man throws checks around like that. Not when he knows they're going to bounce like rubber. Forget about Monty," Sig told her, exasperated. "No more Montague nonsense."

"Who are you? Mrs. Fucking Capulet?" Phyllis asked.

Sig took a deep breath. "Mom, we need you to marry a rich man. If you don't, the two of you will be living in the Bronx on food stamps faster than I can say 'cost of living cut,'" Sig warned. "Anyway, Monty thinks you're rich. He got out of your bed and walked away. Once he found out you weren't, he left you. You wouldn't have had enough money left over each month to buy a subway token to visit us with."

Phyllis shook her head. "You know what's wrong with you, Susan? You're too responsible. What's all this to you? So I'll live in the Bronx. That's where I came from. You're not my mother."

"Mom, I don't want to hurt your feelings, but you were hustled."

"Hustled? Me! Monty couldn't even beat me at canasta!"

"Or he didn't want to," Sig told her. "That's the way a hustle works."

"Well, I'm not even going to *touch* just any old geezer," Phyllis told her. "Florida was full of *them*. That's why I got out."

Phyllis sat very still for a moment. Sig wondered if she saw her mother's lips tremble. Sig lowered her voice and put her hand on her mother's shoulder. "I'm sorry, Mom. You deserve better. You really do."

Phyllis looked up at Sig. "So do you, Susan." She shook her head and lowered herself into a chair. "So. What next?" she asked.

Sig sat down next to Sharon on the sofa, distracted again by Mrs. Katz, who was holding her purse by the strap and methodically spinning it 180 degrees. Sig snapped herself out of the trance. "Well, next is bankruptcy for me. And I guess I leave Wall Street. And I suppose I have to find another job—which is really easy for a woman my age at my level," Sig snorted. "I'm completely tapped out."

"Oh, come on, Sig," Bruce shrugged. "You're always poor-mouthing. You did that last routine to unload Monty, right? I'm the one about to lose my business, and I've got nothing else. What's the portfolio really like? It ain't as light as Mom's," Bruce said.

Sig stared at him. It was always easy, she thought bitterly, for her family to think she could do anything, that she could pay for anything, and that she had everything under control. "I'm sorry to disillusion you, Bruce, but I'm not *talking* poor. I'm not even *acting* poor. I'm broke. There is no portfolio anymore. I've been selling off stock for the last two years. *And* taking a loss. Have you ever heard of downsizing, Mr. Entrepreneur? Mr. Economic Miracle?" She shot a look at Sharon. "Even Barney has heard of downsizing."

"We're going to have to take the kids out of private school," Sharon mourned. "They told us they couldn't come back after the Christmas break if we didn't pay up."

"Swell. So we're all sunk," Sig said. "I'm a senior broker who isn't delivering. All my corporate lawyer and marketing and real estate clients have dried up. *They've* been downsized. I have no commissions coming in. How much longer do you think they'll allow me that big corner office? I've been warned twice, so it's not much longer. And I'm not going back to the bull pen." She shook her head. "I'd rather wait tables."

"You mean it, Sig?" Sharon asked with disbelief. "Fired? Like Barney? You really mean it?"

Sig, tears of humiliation choking her throat, merely waved her hand and nodded. Her sister's empathy touched her.

"Oh my God," Sharon said and began to cry. "You're going to lose the apartment? This will be so hard for Jessie and Travis."

"Yeah. And it might be a little tough for Sig herself," Bruce added. "Same old Sharon." He went over to Sig and took her hand. "Why didn't you tell me?" he asked.

She shrugged. "What good would it have done?" she asked. "*You* couldn't help me."

Bruce squeezed her hand, looked down at it for a long time, and then nodded. "So I guess a small no-interest loan is out of the question right now?" he asked.

"Always with the jokes," Phyllis said. She stood up. "Sig, I have a little money put aside. You think it would be enough . . . ?"

Sig just shook her head. "Mom, my mortgage payment is thirty-eight hundred dollars a month. My maintenance is twenty-two hundred and I haven't made a payment on either for almost nine months." She paused, letting the numbers sink in. "This place is now owned by the bank. They'll probably foreclose in the next month or so."

"You're really going to lose the apartment?" Bruce asked.

"Unless someone buys it fast and I get out some equity," Sig sighed. "I waited too long. I've put an ad in the *Times* and I've gotten a few calls and I've also sent around the particulars to residential real estate agents, but I've only had a nibble or two and neither of them were serious." Now tears rose in Sig's own eyes. "An agent is coming this afternoon with the first prospect. Maybe something will happen. Other than that, I'm lost."

She sat down, exhausted. "And even if I get a quick sale, once I pay the mortgage, the second mortgage, back maintenance, the commission to the broker, and all the rest of it, I may have just enough money for a studio apartment in Bensonhurst." Sig was heartbroken to have to give up her home. What had she worked so hard for all her life? What else did she have? Now what would she have to show for it? "Something went wrong with this country," Sig said. "Nobody has any money."

"I do," said Sylvia Katz. "I have plenty. You want some?"

The three siblings looked at her with impatience, while Phyllis took the time to move next to her friend and pat her on the arm. "Thank you, Sylvia. But we're not talking about small change. Sig needs close to a hundred thousand dollars."

"I got that," Mrs. Katz said calmly. "I got a lot more than that." Phyllis rolled her eyes and patted Sylvia's shoulder again, though she felt like she wanted to strangle her instead. Her daughter's life had completely fallen apart—no husband, no children, no money, no job, and no home. Meanwhile, her best friend had finally gone *meshuga*.

"Sha. Sha, Sylvia," Phyllis said dismissively.

"I have it right here in my purse," Mrs. Katz said, and finally opened the huge black patent leather monstrosity on her lap.

Phyllis, standing beside her seated friend, couldn't help but see that the large purse was indeed stuffed with neatly stacked and freshly strapped parcels of money. Each bundle—and there seemed to be scores of them—said $10,000. "Oh my God," was all she could say.

Bruce also looked down at the purse. He made a noise like the one old Jews made at the synagogue before they began to pray—a sort of half sigh, half groan. "Where did you get all that?" he asked, his voice hushed.

"Is it real?" Sharon breathed, looking over his shoulder.

"I got it when my husband left me. He had to pay a lot. A lot. My lawyer, Diana LaGravennes, was very good. She made Sid pay. I didn't know what to do with it, so I kept it. I didn't like to spend it."

Bruce whistled. "What has four legs and runs after cats?" he said. No one responded. "Mrs. Katz and her lawyer," he said, but no one laughed.

"You've carried that around with you all this time?" Phyllis asked, utterly astonished. It didn't matter if she lived another seventy years, she realized, she would never know the boundaries of human peculiarities or the interior of human hearts.

"Well, I didn't know what else to do with it," Sylvia admitted. "Sid took care of the banks and other things. Before he left me he'd always paid the utility and phone bills. I never even had a checking account. Anyway, what should I do with so much money? I never even wrote a check. I'm always reading about old women getting swindled by banks and brokers." She looked up at Sig. "Nothing personal, darling. Present company excluded." She shrugged. "So I just kept it. It seemed safest."

"It seemed *safest*?" Phyllis asked, her voice rising. "You walked The Broadwalk with a hundred thousand dollars in your purse?"

"No," Sylvia explained. "It's two million two hundred thousand."

"Two million two hundred thousand dollars?!" Sharon and Bruce echoed at once.

"Well, plus my change purse. I keep my change and my Social Security money in this." She pulled out a silver mesh bag.

Phyllis began to laugh. Once she began she couldn't stop until tears rose in her eyes. "You wouldn't spring for a motel when you flew up here! You had over two million dollars in your purse and you sat up all night at La Guardia? For six years in Florida you had to get up at four A.M. so you could breakfast by five so you could eat lunch by ten so you could eat dinner at three-thirty and save four dollars on early bird specials. You took home the extra rolls. You stole the Sweet'n Low packets from every diner we ever went to. You slept on my sofa here in New York. And the whole time you had more than two million dollars in your purse? In your purse! *In your purse?* Are you crazy? Did you ever hear of purse snatchers?"

"I hold on very tight," Sylvia said.

Phyllis laughed again until it hurt and then just shook her head. "You betcha," she said. Then the fatigue swept over her and she had to sit down. What now? For the first time in her life she was speechless.

Sig, who had been very quiet watching the two older women friends, came to join her siblings to peek into the money bag.

"So how much do you need, Susan?" Mrs. Katz asked, and

pulled out a packet of bills. It was a big packet, all fresh, with a $10,000 unbroken brown band around it. Mrs. Katz began to take out more of them, stacking them like children's bricks on the table.

"Oh, I couldn't . . . " Sig said. "I don't know when I could repay—"

"Borrow the money," Phyllis rapped out at Sig. She turned to Sylvia. "Thank you, Sylvia," she said. "I never loved you for your money, but it doesn't hurt." She looked back at Sig. "I didn't realize how things were with you. I came up here to be a good mother to you, not to be selfish. I want to help. Call one of your other candidates. I'll see him." Then, with dignity she sat herself down, alone, at the other end of the room.

Meanwhile, like a snake fighting a snake charmer, Sharon managed to tear her eyes away from the contents of Mrs. Katz's purse. "I'll go back through the files," she said. "We made a mistake with the first, but we'll do it right this time. I can find the right guy."

Bruce looked over at Sharon. "Not a bad idea," he said. He looked over at Mrs. Katz. "Maybe you could help us with this project," he said. "*Then* we'll pay you back."

Sig crossed the room to her mother. She thought of how content her mother had looked in Monty's arms, though the man was a liar and crook. "You mean it, Mom?" Sig asked, her voice low.

Phyllis merely sat there, her head down. "If that's what I have to do, I'll do it."

∞

Sig was back home from work, exhausted and drained. Her mother, Mrs. Katz, and all their possessions had been transplanted from the Pierre to Sig's library, which now looked like some bizarre cross between a college dorm and a convalescent home. Sig had taken one look at the pill and medicine bottles, Mrs. Katz's denture holder, the damp socks over the radiator, the prunes in a plastic jar on the bureau, along with all the other detritus of the two old women's lives and simply closed the folding doors on the whole thing.

Sig's buzzer rang. She shut the door on the room with the intention of not showing it at all. Sharon had gone home to her still unemployed husband, promising to dig out the files for new marital candidates, and Bruce had dropped her at the train on his way to Chelsea. Sig was on watch. Their mother and Mrs. Katz were lying down in her spare bedroom, but Sig was still awake, finishing the little touches to the apartment that she'd been told would help make it sell quickly. She had straightened the pillows, put out flowers, and scented the air with two bowls of Floris potpourri. If she knew how, she'd bake a cake, just so that the welcoming smell of sweet batter rising would entice a buyer. She was still in shock over Mrs. Katz and her incredible bag. It couldn't save her, but it could buy her some time so she could save herself. For the first time in weeks Sig found herself humming: when she realized she was humming the theme to *Felix the Cat* she had to smile. "Whenever he got in a fix, he reaches into his bag of tricks."

Sig went to the door to meet Cornelia, the agent from Stirling & Ross, the primo residential brokers in New York. She knew it was best not to be in when people came to look, but since there was no place else to stash her mother and Mrs. Katz, this time there really was no alternative. She may as well be here, sitting nonchalantly in the library, while some witch who'd married money criticized her bathroom wallpaper. Sig took a deep breath and opened the door. Cornelia was there, another one of those residential-broker-ladies-of-a-certain-age who invariably wore important earrings and a belt with a gold-tone buckle. Cornelia swept in, her smile tight. "Well, hello," she said, simultaneously raising her brows, looking around, and immediately flicking on the lamp in the foyer. "You've done a lovely job with this place," Cornelia said. "It'll sell quickly." Goddamn it, Sig thought, she'd forgotten to turn on the lamps, which was the number one broker trick. But the rest of her rooms were really light, it was only the foyer that was windowless.

She looked up over Cornelia's shoulder and started with surprise.

"Paul Cushing," Sig said and put her hand out to him. She experienced that moment of dislocation when she met someone she knew from another setting—like the time she bumped into her gynecologist's nurse in Bloomingdale's. She had completely forgotten about his promised visit and the news he couldn't tell her over the phone.

"Is this a bad time?" he asked.

"No. Not really. I'm just letting this broker take a look at my place. I'm thinking of buying another one . . . " Sig tried not to blush. How embarrassing, for Paul Cushing to show up when Cornelia did and to know she was selling her apartment. Sig was acquainted with Cornelia well enough to know that to make a sale Cornelia would definitely tell a prospect—or even a stranger—when a property was distressed.

He smiled warmly. "It's so nice to see you again, Sigourney. I had no idea you were even considering selling your place." He looked around. "So many of these New York apartments don't seem very warm. But you've made a home here." He looked directly at her. His eyes were very blue. "Why don't you show us both around? I didn't get a complete tour when I was here for your mother's birthday."

Cornelia smiled brightly. It was clear to Sig that the woman wasn't going to lose an opportunity here. "Well, let me begin by pointing out the two foyer closets . . . "

"Oh, don't bother," Paul Cushing told her politely but firmly, and Cornelia wilted. "Sig knows what I like. *She'll* show me around." Then, to take out the sting, Paul Cushing smiled at Cornelia. His smile was really devastating for an old guy's, Sig thought. Cornelia, an old babe, recovered and actually fluttered her lashes at him. So *that's* how it is, Sig thought, as Paul took her elbow and allowed her to lead him into the living room.

"I know you've been here, but I don't think you saw the view, Cornelia." Sig took them to the window and pulled aside the Scalamandre curtains. She looked out at the view she loved. "You can see three bridges from here," she told them, staring at the river. "The bridges themselves are easier to see at night, but the park is best in the daytime." She looked up—he was tall—to find that he wasn't looking at the view.

"How's your mother, Sig?" Paul asked. "I have something I want to tell her."

"Oh, she's just fine," Sig said brightly. Maybe he'd do for Mom, she thought. "Actually she's here. She got tired of the hotel. She's resting now." Sig pictured what her mother looked like without three hours of Bruce's prep time and thought it best that she and Paul didn't run into each other. Not right now. She'd show him the guest room later—on another visit. She'd make *sure* there was another visit. Was this more than some kind of coincidence? Was it some kind of holiday gift? Sig looked at Paul. He was much better looking than Monty, and Sig knew that he was legitimate—how many millions had Sharon said he was worth? Maybe Sharon didn't have to go back to the files after all. Perhaps they had somebody right here.

"What is it that you need to tell my mother?" Sig asked.

"I looked up background information on Montague Dunleathe as I told you I could. I hate to say anything bad about a man, but he might not be as he seems." He paused. "I say this to protect you and your mother. Like I protect Wendy."

"That's very considerate of you. I appreciate it." His timing couldn't have been better, Sig thought. He didn't know the half of it.

"I wouldn't like to see your mother hurt."

Sig smiled up at Paul Cushing. "Step into my parlor," she told him.

nineteen

he Rainbow Room? On Christmas week? It will be a mob scene, nobody goes to the Rainbow Room," Sig was saying to her mother.

"How can it be a mob scene if nobody goes there?" Phyllis asked.

"Nobody who's anybody," Sigourney said.

"Well, we are. For dinner. All four of us," Phyllis told her daughter. Sig shrugged.

"Look, you don't have to go if you don't want to," Phyllis told Sig. "*I* don't want to go."

Sig narrowed her eyes. "No. You're going. You're going and you're going to enjoy it. If you could like Monty, you'll *love* Paul Cushing."

"Nah. He's not *my* type. He's more . . . "

"More what? More classy? More rich? More sincere? He's certainly more attractive. He's very, very attractive."

"Oh, you think so?" Phyllis asked. She half closed her already hooded eyes. "What do *you* think, Sylvia?"

Sylvia, sitting in the club chair as usual, shrugged. "I prefer Monty," she said in a dreamy voice. "But maybe that's because he played canasta with me."

Sig shook her head. She was surrounded by senile dementia.

Well, she supposed things could be worse. Sylvia Katz could be her mother.

So far, Sig the big Wall Street investment broker hadn't been able to convince Mrs. Katz even to put her money in a bank, much less invest in even the most secure stocks and bonds. Mrs. Katz, plain and simple, was having none of it. Sig had even given up trying to explain about interest. Mrs. Katz didn't care about interest. "I know from interest. When you have money everyone has interest in you." All Sylvia Katz wanted was to keep hold of the contents of her patent leather purse, which she would never spend, not even to save her modesty in a game of strip canasta. "Don't be mad, Susan," Mrs. Katz said now. "Mr. Cushing is very nice, but I'm like your mother. Except for the S, E, X part. I prefer Monty."

"Montague Dunleathe is a crook," Sig said, totally exasperated.

"He played a good game of canasta," Mrs. Katz said nostalgically. Then she pulled herself together and looked back at Sig. "He didn't try a thing," she assured her. "Not with me, anyway. It was just a friendly game."

Sig merely rolled her eyes. The junk from their room had spread into the living room and was now threatening even her foyer. Mrs. Katz's shapeless sweater hung over a doorknob in the hall. Someone's reading glasses, the earpiece held onto the frame by a safety pin, were lying on the lowboy. The Halls Mentho-lyptus lozenges (which Mrs. Katz perpetually sucked on) were on one sofa table. On the other was an equally fetid collection of objects: Phyllis's brand of lozenges—billed as "curiously strong peppermints"—were spread beside their tin box. There was also an old Chap Stick, a stack of dimes— which Phyllis still collected, though telephones no longer used dimes —some coupons torn out of a magazine or newspaper or both, a pencil stub, a half-filled-in crossword puzzle, and two more pairs of reading glasses, one with a neck chain and one without.

Sig thought she might go mad, but with some luck Paul Cushing would take Mom off her hands, while Mrs. Katz would eventually be weaned into a place of her own—or at least make a home with Phyllis.

It seemed to Sig that—God knows why—Paul had been doing his best to woo Phyllis. He had taken both her mom and Mrs. Katz out for dinner yesterday, then he'd taken Sig, Wendy, and Phyllis to the Radio City Christmas show today. Sig had called in sick, and, anyway, nothing was happening these days right before the holiday.

Of course, Phyllis had almost blown that for them by talking throughout the entire picture, but her comments were a lot funnier than the film, anyway. And it seemed that Paul Cushing could live with it because he'd given them this invitation. At least that's what Mrs. Katz had told them after she took the call. Paul Cushing didn't seem to Sig like the Rainbow Room type. He was much smoother, more sophisticated than that. Still, Sig had called up Bruce to do a job on Mom and now they were ready to go.

"Paul's very nice," Sig said to her mom, fishing.

"Very nice," Phyllis agreed. "But he doesn't like me."

"Of course he does. He likes you very much."

"Not in that way," Phyllis said. She looked Sig over. "Very nice," she said approvingly. "But you should wear a shorter skirt."

Bruce stood over Mom, spraying in the last few touches to her hairstyle with a fixative strong enough to bond frogs to steel girders. "There," he said, and gave the front of her hair a tug. "One final fillip."

"Speaking of Phillips . . . " Sig began and took a look in the mirror. "He should be here any moment." She'd lowered herself again, but she had to. "I won't see him after this," she said aloud.

"Well, thank God. Progress is being made," Phyllis said. "Now, if you'd only open your eyes and date a real man, not a corporate clone too scared to commit or have kids."

"Mother, most men don't want me. They say I'm too much to handle."

Phyllis smiled nostalgically. "Your father used to say that to me." She lowered her eyes and her voice. "Monty said it, too," she murmured.

৩৫

The Rainbow Room was crowded, but when they got off the private elevator and were greeted by the obsequious maître d' they were immediately ushered to a desirable table for four right beside the dance floor. Paul Cushing obviously had clout. And they'd arrived just in the nick of time, because as they took their seats the lights dimmed, the small orchestra played an anticipatory drum riff, and then, one by one, Rockettes appeared at the top of the curved miniature staircase. The women tap-danced symmetrically and beautifully down the stairs, one more perfect than the next, one leg more shapely than the one beside it, until they were all on the dance floor and moved into high gear. They dazzled the crowd, not only with their tapping and kicks but with the mechanical perfection they performed in.

Sig, however, was bored. She looked across the table. Phillip was looking on, also blasé and certainly bland, but Paul's eyes sparkled and he led the applause. There was something about Paul—even though he was so old—that seemed always to find new pleasure in life. When he bent to his left and said something to her mother that Sig couldn't hear, she wished she knew what it was.

After the performance, once the applause calmed down, the band began to play "Night and Day." When Phillip asked her to dance, Sig was surprised but pleased, at least until she got onto the dance floor. Sig could dance, but not with Phillip. He made her feel awkward. He couldn't lead, and she actually found herself stepping on his foot. Each time she did, he apologized. Phillip was, without a doubt, the worst dancer north of the Mason-Dixon line. Probably south, too. Sig was very grateful when Paul Cushing tapped Phillip on the shoulder and cut in.

"Thank God," she breathed. Phillip relinquished her with only a slightly hurt backward glance.

"It looked like you needed rescuing," Paul said, "but I wasn't sure." Then he took command. He stepped back from her a bit and looked at her. "Nice dress. Very festive. Red is your color." Sig blushed. "Did you like the flowers?" he asked.

"They were lovely," Sig said warmly. Then Paul pulled her closer. His hand on the small of her back, asserting a gentle pressure, felt delicious. "My mother was very touched." Sig found it effortless to match her steps to his, to anticipate his moves and to relax. She hadn't done that the first time they danced, at the Winter Wonderland Ball. Younger men didn't know how to dance, but dancing became almost a participatory sport with Paul. They moved through the rest of "Night and Day," and they continued moving together to "I've Got You Under My Skin." Sigourney relaxed, and leaned a little closer to him. Then she remembered her mother, and the whole point of the exercise.

This is bizarre, Sig thought. I'm having a better time with Paul than I am with my date. Then again, Phillip was only nominally Sig's date, or anything to Sig. "We have to go back to the table," Sig said reluctantly as the band began to play "Just in Time." "This has been fun, though."

Paul smiled at her, took her elbow, and began to lead her off the floor. It felt good to have him take charge and move them between the dancing couples. But the good time evaporated right at that second. Because just before they reached their table, Sig looked up and saw her mother dancing with Monty— Montague Dunleathe—halfway across the room. "Oh my God!" Sig said and dropped Paul's hand, stepping away from him.

"What is it?"

Sig could say nothing. She merely pointed. He followed her gaze and raised his eyebrows.

"Your mother?" Paul asked. "Is she all right?"

Sig shook her head. Then she got very, very angry. What was going on here? She'd been duped. Surely this wasn't merely coincidence! "How did he know we were going to be here?" she demanded of Paul.

"I haven't a clue," he admitted.

Sig didn't know whether she should believe him or not. She was filled with a furious energy. She'd been had, and she knew it. Paul Cushing had, most likely, been dancing with her merely to distract her. He must be plotting on Mom's behalf, along with her other friends. "You picked this place," Sig said accusingly.

"*Me*? I didn't pick it. I thought it was for you. Why would *I* want to come here?"

"So *that* could happen," she said, pointing. "Otherwise it's because you like the Rockettes and enjoy being surrounded by people with bad haircuts. I don't know. I just know that Mrs. Katz said that *you* had made the reservations. Did Monty ask you to do it?"

"Mrs. Katz told me your mother wanted to come." He paused. "Wait a second," Paul's face, when he concentrated, looked all of his seventy-one years. "No, actually, I think she said *you* wanted to come." He grinned. "Frankly, I was surprised. Then I hoped it was for the dancing. You're a great dancer, Sig."

Sig didn't have time for any more talk. She had to figure out what the hell was going on with her mother. She strode across the dance floor and reached Monty and her mom. They had just executed a complicated-looking but graceful dip. Monty looked up. "Oh, cheerio," he said, as if being there in his ratty old dinner jacket, her mother wrapped in his arms, was the most natural thing in the world.

"What do you think you're doing?" Sig asked, outraged. The last time she'd seen them together they were in bed, naked. Somehow, in public and clothed, this looked almost as intimate. Montague Dunleathe, still holding her mother, stopped and looked up at Sigourney.

"You look very elegant tonight," Montague said.

"Stop with the con, Monty. It doesn't work on me. And let go of my mother." Sig looked down at her mom. "It's time to go," she said stiffly.

"But we just got here," Phyllis almost whined. Ah, Sig thought, that's where Sharri got the whine from.

"Just in Time" was about to end. Monty pulled Phyllis out of her dance swoon and they stared into each other's eyes. They were standing altogether too close.

"Excuse me," Sig said. "I'd like to cut in." She tapped Montague Dunleathe on the shoulder.

"I'm not leaving," Phyllis said.

Sig looked at her mother. "You promised not to do this," she reminded her.

Phyllis shrugged. "I didn't do anything."

"I believe the expression here is 'It's a free country,'" Monty said to Sig.

"Only for people who don't pay their taxes," Sig spat.

Sig reached out her hand and took her mother's. "Who helped you? You should be ashamed of yourself. What did you do, make secret phone calls?"

"No. Sylvia made the calls," Phyllis pointed out.

"Oh, great. You've turned Mrs. Katz into the nurse in *Romeo and Juliet*. She's your go-between now?" Sig stepped between them and looked at Montague boldly. "Stay away from my mother," she said. "I don't want to see or hear from you. I don't want you to speak to me, my mother, or Mrs. Katz. You're a user, and a fortune hunter, a hurtful cad, and worse than all of that together. If you have any further questions about your character, you can reach me at my office."

By now, quite a little crowd had gathered around them. Paul Cushing stood to the side, as did the useless Phillip, but Sig didn't care. She took Phyllis by the arm and, turning her back on all the people in the room, led her mother to the elevator.

In it, on the way down sixty-six floors, the elevator music played five verses of "The Little Drummer Boy."

∞

Mrs. Katz confessed. It wasn't hard to wring the truth out of her: Monty had secretly been calling for days and Mrs. Katz, who thought it was romantic, had passed messages on to Phyllis.

"What do you think you were doing, Mom?" Sig asked furiously.

"How could you do this?" Sharon wheezed at her mother.

Bruce just glared at his mother. No words were needed.

Phyllis sat up in the chair. "Okay, I see where you're going with this line of questioning. I'll do it your way."

"Good," the Sibs chimed in unison.

Sig called Paul Cushing and did a lot of apologizing about the Rainbow Room fiasco. He seemed perfectly comfortable with everything she said and proposed. He came over and took her mother and Wendy out in a carriage ride through Central Park on Wednesday night. Had dinner with Sig, Phyllis, and Mrs. Katz on Thursday. Then the four of them went to see *Showboat* on Friday and Paul even got an extra ticket for Mrs. Katz. Things had progressed so well that they actually spent Saturday evening with Sharon, Barney, Jessie, and Travis. They took a stretch limo down Fifth Avenue so that the kids could look at all the Christmas lights in the store windows. Wendy loved Jessie, and the feeling seemed mutual. Things were moving quickly and Sig felt as if her plan was working. So why did she feel so unhappy? It was an odd sensation, almost dreamlike, as if everything she cared about was slipping from her grasp.

twenty

Sig wriggled out of the red slacks and decided she'd wear a black skirt and dark pantyhose instead. It was only once she had dressed that she remembered that Paul had admired the red dress she'd worn earlier in the week at the Rainbow Room. Oh well. It wasn't she who had to please him. She didn't want to look too dressed up, so she put on boots rather than shoes. She threw open the door to her beautifully designed closet and picked not the short black boots nor the knee-high black boots but the ankle-high black ones with the turnover cuff. She actually had four pairs of black boots, she realized, as well as three pairs of brown, six pairs of brown shoes, eleven pairs of black ones, and then, of course, there were all the other, less basic colored shoes. My God, Sig thought, looking at it all. There wasn't a pair that cost less than $200. How much money have I wasted over the years?

She sighed. Even with the temporary loan from Mrs. Katz there would be no more shoe buying, no more custom closets. Sig pushed the door shut with a bang and surveyed herself in the three-way mirror, though why she cared she couldn't fathom. It was just another date night for Mom, and all Sig was doing was serving eggnog and Christmas cookies before seeing Mom off at the door. She gave a last look over her shoulder at the fit of her skirt. Was it a little tight across the back? She'd have to double up on her sessions at the gym after the holidays were over—at least until her membership ran out. There would be no more private workouts at David Barton's, the best gym with the best personal trainers in town. Sig sighed again and went out to the living room.

There Mrs. Katz was glued to the love seat. It irritated Sig to see that lately she always selected that spot, when it would fit her mother and Paul cozily. Instead, they'd be forced to sit on a larger sofa, or even across from each other. Mrs. Katz was so out of it. Sig immediately felt guilty for thinking that way, especially after Mrs. Katz's generosity. But the woman *was* human Super Glue, and Sig literally had to tell her to vacate the room so that Paul Cushing had some privacy when he escorted Mom home. Not that he lingered.

It was an odd thing, and it worried Sig, but Paul Cushing didn't seem to be at all physical with Phyllis. In some way she hated to admit, Sig was also relieved by that, perhaps because of the incident with Monty. Or maybe she was uncomfortable with her mother's sexuality. Or in the sexuality of anyone old. It was just that otherwise Paul seemed so warm. Sig worried that perhaps it meant he wasn't as serious about Phyllis as she and Bruce and Sharri hoped he was. Well, she should be grateful. At least with Paul, she wouldn't have to worry about barging into a bedroom and finding him naked and in bed with her mother. Sig shuddered at the thought.

"Are you cold, darling?" Mrs. Katz asked. "Maybe you should put on a sweater."

"I'm fine," Sig said. She looked over at the placid Mrs. Katz, sitting there with her black bag on her knees. In a way, Sig was envious of her. She didn't read anything. She didn't knit or do crosswords. She didn't even watch TV. She just *sat*. She simply was, and it seemed enough for perfect contentment, if not a perfect house guest.

"Are you going out tonight?" Sig asked hopefully.

"It's possible. Bernard is coming by."

"Bernard? Bernard Krinz?" Sig repeated.

"Yes. We were going to talk more about my investments."

"Investments?" Sig asked. "What do you mean? The only thing you put money into is your purse."

"Oh no. Bernard has called up almost every day. He tells me about his market positions. I love his putz and calls."

"That's 'puts,' " Sig corrected. "*Puts* and calls."

Now what was up? Was *Krinz* pulling a con? No. He was a reputable world-respected architect. Still, if anyone was going to invest Mrs. Katz's money Sig would be dipped in yogurt before she'd let it be anyone but her! She was about to investigate further when she was interrupted by the doorbell. She checked her makeup on the way past the foyer mirror and took a moment to refresh her lipstick with the tube she kept in the hall console drawer.

She opened the door. Paul Cushing was standing there. A sprinkling of snow, complementing the white hair at his temples, nestled on the broad shoulders of his blue cashmere overcoat. Despite his age he was still a very handsome man. He looked down at her. "Oh, black is your color, too," he said, as if he remembered his compliment from the Rainbow Room.

She began to help him off with his coat when she got an almost irresistible desire to brush the snow from his hair. She put her hand up, only to pull it away in time. *What am I thinking of.* "Is the snow sticking?" she managed to ask.

He turned and smiled at her, nodded and then looked down her legs. "You might need boots more practical than those," he said, and grinned the lopsided way that he had when he was teasing. "Though it would be a pity to take those off since they look so nice on you," he added.

Sig looked down and actually felt herself blush. Maybe her mother was right—she *did* need a father, even at this late date, to notice and approve of her. Paul's compliment made her feel girlish and squirmy, as if she was about to toe the floor with one boot, her hands twisting behind her back. Instead, she forced herself to calmly hang up his coat. Then she noticed he was carrying a small, light blue bag—Sig's favorite color and the color of her kitchen ceiling glaze: Tiffany blue. Her heart began to beat faster in her chest. Had he brought a ring for Mom? Was he ready to propose? It was odd, Sig thought, how her relief was mixed with something else. What was it? Regret? Disappointment? Envy?

God, she really was getting crazy! It must be the holidays. All the sappy music, all the Capra movies on TV. She was glad she wasn't going to see Phillip, but she'd have to try to start seeing somebody as soon as she could, before her Electra complex got the better of her. If she could afford it, she'd start up some sessions with Dr. Lefer, her old shrink.

"My mother is not quite ready," she said. "Why don't you come into the living room?"

Paul grinned. "Is the duenna there?" he asked.

"Mrs. Katz?" Sig grinned back. " 'Fraid so."

"Who sleeps with cats?" Paul asked.

"Mrs. Katz. And sometimes Mrs. Nussbaum," Sig told him, echoing Monty's old joke. They entered the living room and Paul, to her dismay, took a seat not on the sofa but on one of the leather Barcelona chairs. Sig was about to sit down on the sofa herself when the doorbell rang again.

This time it was Bruce and Todd, again along with Bernard Krinz. "Happy holidays," Bruce said. The three men were coated with snow—the weather was getting worse. So was Todd. He looked absolutely mournful. What was it with Bruce? Was he going for an old geezer just for the money? It made Sig's skin crawl. What was it doing to Todd?

Whatever it was, they were very festive. Bernard had a sprig of holly pinned to his conservative lapel, Todd had on a red and green sweater, while Bruce was wearing the scarf that Sig had given him for Hanukkah and was carrying wrapped boxes. "Merry Christmas," he said. He kissed Sig on the cheek and she felt the coldness of the air outside still clinging to him.

"Bruce, you shouldn't have."

"I should and I did," Bruce said. "The orders have been rolling in. I'm having the best Christmas ever. Queer Santa came through for me in the end. Once I receive payments, I'll be in the black again. And Bernard gave me a bridge loan to tide me over!"

Bernard Krinz smiled. He looked at Sig and her brother. "Black's a very good color for both of you," he said. Sig tried to smile at the oily old toad, failed, and led the three of them into the living room. Bernard went directly over to Mrs. Katz and sat next to her on the love seat, while Bruce and Todd went to shake hands with Paul Cushing.

"Merry Christmas to all, and to all a good night," Bruce sang out and handed a wrapped box to Paul. Then he gave another to Mrs. Katz, this one a larger parcel. He gave a small gift to Bernard Krinz, another to Todd, and then handed the last box to Sig. "I've got something for Mom in my pocket," he added proudly, before throwing himself onto the sofa, disarranging all of Sig's carefully placed pillows. He grinned, clearly very satisfied with himself.

"Should we open them now?" Mrs. Katz asked.

"Why not?" Bruce responded. "Jews always open their Christmas gifts early."

Mrs. Katz went first and cheerfully pulled the paper off her large box, opened the glossy cover, and looked in.

"Oh, my goodness!" she said, and lifted out a beautiful Fendi leather bag.

"I thought you might like that one," Bruce smiled. "I think it's the right size. And the catch on *this* one works."

"Oh, my goodness," Mrs. Katz repeated. "I'm speechless."

"Just as well," Bruce murmured. Meanwhile, Bernard Krinz had carefully unwrapped the package he'd been given, saving both the ribbon and the gift wrap, to reveal a Rizzoli volume of immense proportion.

"Oh, Bruce, you shouldn't have," Bernard said.

"I should and I did," Bruce said again. He looked over at Sig and Paul. "It's the International Architecture Association's award-winning buildings. Todd took the photos. Bernard has three of his buildings in the book."

Bruce smiled over at Paul. "And yours?" he asked. Paul looked at Sig.

"Ladies first," he told her.

Sig picked up her small box and tore off the paper. Aside from her home and a job that made some money, she couldn't think of anything she wanted or needed, except, possibly . . . she looked up. "I haven't a clue," she said to Bruce. Then she opened the box and there lay her emerald ring, protected by the white cotton batting stuffed beneath it. "Oh, Bruce," she said. "Oh, Bruce." Her eyes filled with tears. "How did you get it?" she asked. "Oh, Bruce, you shouldn't have."

"I should and I did," Bruce repeated one more time, but this time he wasn't so flippant. "Don't get me wrong, I didn't buy it at the auction. I just stopped Sotheby's from selling it. I had to forge your name on the release, but . . . anyway, I also have a check for you, and it'll equal what the ring would have brought in, less commissions and tax. At least I think so. Consider it a loan."

"Oh, Bruce," Sig breathed, and ran to kiss her brother.

"Enough, enough," he said, standing up. "I better see what's keeping Mom. She probably needs me to put on her mascara."

"Well, wait a minute," Paul Cushing said and opened his little blue Tiffany bag. "I have something for you all as well." He handed Bruce a wrapped box, then handed one to Mrs. Katz. "I didn't know you would be here," he said apologetically to Bernard. "But I did *get* the Whetherall board to accept your proposal for the new headquarters."

"A very nice gift, indeed," Bernard said.

Then Paul turned to Sig. He took a small box out and handed it to her. Sig smiled at him. He was so kind, so generous. "This is for your mother," he said and Sig felt disappointment well up in her chest. It must be the engagement ring. Well, why feel badly? Wasn't this what she wanted?

Sig handed the package to Bruce. "How about you take it in to her?" Sig asked. Then, sotto voce, she added, "Ixfay her ace-fay while you're at it."

"Sure," Bruce said, winking at her. "You open your present, Paul, and I'll get Mom for hers."

Paul tore the paper off the box that Bruce had handed him and pulled out a silvery fringed scarf. It was beautiful, and when he slid it around his neck it set off his high color and the gray of his hair.

Sig, admiring it, saw Bruce come out of the bedroom and go into the kitchen. She watched out of the corner of her eyes as he came out of there and went into the powder room. Then, just a moment later, she saw him move through the hallway into the library. Sig got up and started to follow him, but she met up with him in the foyer. "What's going on?" she asked. "What are you doing?"

"Looking for Mom."

"What do you mean, looking for Mom? She's in my room."

"No she isn't. She isn't anywhere in this apartment."

"That's impossible, Bruce. I've been here all day and she didn't go out."

"Well then, Miss Smarty Pants, you find her."

Sig spun around and started toward her bedroom. As Sig passed the living room, Mrs. Katz asked, "Did you lose something, dear?"

Sig ignored her and continued through the room. She pushed open her bedroom door and stepped into the room. Nothing. She checked out the step-in closet and then walked into her bathroom. Nothing. As she turned to leave, she saw a paper taped onto the vanity mirror. Sig picked up the note and saw that it was in Phyllis's handwriting.

Dear Sigourney,

Sharon will always be a mess, but Bruce is finally settling down. Todd will appreciate him now and be perfect for him. I worry about you, though. You don't know what's important, Sig, or where to find it. Somehow, you thought you were responsible for me, for Daddy, for your brother and sister. Maybe you even think you're responsible for the hole in the ozone layer. Get a grip. You gotta stop bailing out your family—including me—and instead take care of yourself. Notice who your real friends are. We'll all be fine. Will you?

My advice is, be a little more patient and wear shorter skirts.

Meanwhile, I've left with Monty. Don't be angry or worried and don't look for me. I'll be fine, I promise. I love him, and he loves me. I'm happy, Sig. You should be so lucky.

Sig came out to the living room, opened her mouth to say something, then crumpled the note and began to cry.

"What is it?" Paul asked, rising and coming to her. "Sig, what's wrong?" She looked up at him.

"My mother ran off with Monty the fortune hunter. And she has no fortune." Sig sobbed. They were loud, embarrassing noises, but she kept sobbing as if her heart would break. Paul put his arms around her.

"What do you mean, she's gone?" Bruce asked. Sig handed him the crushed note. Bruce read it quickly. "Come on, Sylvia. She's probably just downstairs in the lobby, talking with Laslow the doorman. Let's go get her." Reluctantly, Mrs. Katz stood up and, with purse in hand, went out with Bruce.

Paul released Sig and she went into the kitchen to get a tissue to wipe her eyes and to collect herself. Maybe Mom had just been bluffing. Sig was leaning up against the counter, trying to get control of herself when Paul came in quietly and stood in front of her. "Are you okay?" he asked. He was very close. She could smell the scent of a mild soap, and something else equally good.

"I'll be fine," Sig told him, but then burst into tears again and, almost automatically, stepped forward and buried her face again into his shoulder. This time Paul put his arms around her more tightly and held her, patting her lightly on the back.

"This is all my fault," he said. "I told you I had heard some scuttlebutt about Dunleathe. I should have done more. I could have . . . "

"You knew what he was up to?"

"No. Certainly not. But I knew that she was having a hard time after he left. That's why I wanted to keep her busy."

Sig lifted her head from his shoulder and looked up at him. Paul bent to her face and started to kiss her, and—for a moment—the shock of electricity from his lips to hers overwhelmed her senses and blotted out thought. It had been a long time since she'd been kissed like this—or maybe she never had. Paul's lips were surprisingly soft, yet he kissed her with a firmness backed up by his left hand, with which he cupped her cheek and held her mouth to his. Without thinking, Sig raised her hand to his and covered his fingers with her own.

Then she realized what she was doing. She was kissing her mother's rejected boyfriend, and she was liking it! Sig pulled her mouth away, then pushed Paul back. Hard.

"What are you doing?" Sig asked.

"Seems obvious," Paul shrugged. He reached for her hand. "And I'd like to do it again. I think I could improve on the original."

"But . . . "

He took out a handkerchief and began carefully, tenderly, to wipe Sig's streaming eyes. "You're very beautiful, Sig," Paul said. "And you're very smart. But you're also a very dopey girl."

"I'm not a girl . . . "

"To me you are. Remember, I'm older. A lot older." Paul smiled, but there was a wistfulness around his eyes. "I hope I'm not too old. That's for you to judge." He finished wiping her eyes and cheeks and shook his head. "This wasn't in my plans. Not at all. Anyway, you're a very dopey girl, *and* a woman to me." He paused. "Lucky for you I like dopey girls. *And* real women." He reached for her shoulder, but, despite the flush of heat his touch sent down her neck and back, Sig pulled away.

"My mother," she croaked. "You're dating my mother."

"See what I mean?" Paul said, and smiled again. "Your mother was never interested in me. She told me all about this Monty guy and how much she liked him. I, on the other hand, was always interested in *you*."

"What?" Sig simultaneously heard the declaration and the past tense. One filled her with a strange yearning, the other with pain. "Were?" she repeated. "You *were* interested?"

Paul reached out to her again and pulled her gently to his chest. This time she let him. "See how dopey you are?" he asked in an indulgent voice. "Remember those flowers I sent to the Pierre? They were for *you*. When you ignored them, I just figured you thought I was too old."

"You were interested in me?" she asked again, hardly daring to believe. "I mean, you are?"

"Yes, I *was* interested in you. And I *am* interested in you. And I *always will be* interested in you. Anyone could see that but you. So now the basic question that remains is: could you possibly be interested in a geezer like me?"

Sig colored yet again. Did Paul know about Operation Geezer Quest? He looked down at her. His eyes were very serious as well as very blue, his hair more white than pepper and salt. The soft suede of his jacket—very soft—felt so good under Sig's cheek. She rubbed against his shoulder until he lifted her face to his again. Then he kissed her, this time in a long, lingering way.

Totally shocked, she not only found that she liked it, but kissed him back. Deeply. At last, to her regret, Paul took his mouth off hers. "Sigourney, I've been coming around because of you. Since we met. I was at the Pierre that night with Wendy, but I was hoping to meet you. It's not that I didn't sincerely *like* your mother," he said. "I do. She's so much like you. Sharp, no bullshit, a real challenge. But I can't help it, Sig."

"Help what?" She felt as if she were melting, as if she was in some dream.

"I can't help wanting to love you. The first time I saw you, Sig, across that charity dinner table, I thought how absolutely open your face was. How smart, how mischievous, and how bold. Your face said, 'Hey, you'd be a real mensch if you could take me on.' I don't see that much. Not the fun, or your feisty joy." His face got very serious. "I've taken a lot of losses, Sig. Life doesn't play fair or last long. I'm in it for the joy, Sig. Not everyone is capable of it. Your mom is, and you are, too."

"Feisty joy?" Sig asked, but her own face had softened. She felt transformed by Paul's praise. Something *had* happened, something more than the kiss.

"I'm crazy about your mom, Sig. I'll help you find her, I promise. But it's you I love. No matter what length your skirts are." Sig found she couldn't breathe. "I'm an old-fashioned guy, Sig. Old, and old-fashioned. But all my parts still work. I don't have much time, so I'm impatient. And I don't sleep around. So you don't have to decide now, but do you think that you might marry me, Sigourney?"

Sig *did* feel flooded with joy. "I don't know," Sig said. "I mean . . . " She paused. "I think so. Uh . . . yes. I think so." She paused again. "But first you have to do something for me."

"Anything. Slay a dragon? Kill Monty Dunleathe? Engineer a hostile takeover?"

"No. Nothing like that. First I want you to kiss me again a few times."

Paul smiled his devastating smile. "It would be my pleasure," he said. "And yours too, if I do it right." He paused. "What else?"

Sig stopped smiling. "Help me find my mother. That's what I want for Christmas."

twenty-one

*P*hyllis stretched and opened her eyes. One of the disadvantages of old age was that she had become a very light sleeper. But now she had found an advantage even to that: she and Monty had spent the night dozing and each time one of them shifted or woke, the other would also rise and they would hug and change positions before falling back to sleep. Phyllis smiled. It had been a wonderful night. She was no spring chicken, but she was proud of herself.

Monty wasn't much to look at, and his belly sagged almost as much as her breasts did, but he was a true romantic. Once they had met at the airport he had taken her hand and he hadn't let go. The whole flight to the Caymans and the taxi ride to the hotel he had kept hold of her. "I'm not going to take a chance on losing you again," he said. "They didn't make two of you."

Phyllis couldn't argue with that.

∞

The Cayman Islands, though tropical and in the Gulf Stream, were certainly not Florida. Nothing like it. This was a place she could *like*, Phyllis thought. The beaches were perfect white windswept sand and dozens and dozens of waving, clacking palm trees. There wasn't a Broadwalk in sight, and while there were plenty of older people, there were young people too and they all seemed to be active and more alive than the parade that had dragged themselves along the Florida Broadwalk every morning. There were young and old playing tennis on the lit courts, riding bicycles, and playing on the many golf courses. The kids would like this place.

When they pulled up to the hotel—a gorgeous white building decorated only with flowering plants at each balcony—Phyllis was impressed. It didn't look like Dania, Florida. And there were no French Canadians.

"You like it?" Monty asked.

"It's very nice," Phyllis said. "Do we have a room or a suite?" she teased. Now that she had stayed at the Pierre suite, she knew the difference between the two. And though Monty had explained a great deal about his financial position to her on the flight—about how his competitors had used illegal means to force him out of business and discredit him, how he wasn't as rich as he'd once been nor as poor as she'd thought—Phyllis didn't care. She wanted to see not how much he had, but how much he spent.

"You can have whatever kind of room you want," Monty told her. "I own the hotel."

Phyllis laughed. Then she realized that, for once, he wasn't joking. "I used to think that life could use a little embellishment," she said. "Somehow I think I'm changing my mind."

That wasn't the only surprise: there was a Hanukkah menorah and a Christmas tree, both decorated with bougainvillea, and then more surprises within the hotel: his real engagement ring, this one a huge sapphire, and a necklace to match. Then they were served a candlelit dinner on the balcony, overlooking the pool and the ocean, and then bed.

It amazed Phyllis, in a way, that she felt so much passion. She smiled again this morning, pulling the sheet up over her shoulder. It had been so long that she *had* forgotten. It was *not* like riding a bicycle. And, to be honest, Ira had never been, well, an artist. He'd been a meat-and-potatoes kind of man when it came to bed. But Monty! Monty was caviar and peaches. She was proud of herself. You *could* teach an old dog some new tricks, because Monty had already taught her a couple.

And then there was the cuddling. Ira used to fall right to sleep, but Monty . . . he seemed to actually enjoy hugging. She turned her head on the pillow to look at him. Well, he was nothing special to look at. Ira had been a good-looking man. Monty was not, and it didn't help that he was sleeping with his mouth slightly open. And could he snore! But then, he said she did too.

Monty slept on, but Phyllis wanted his company. She elbowed him in his breadbasket. After all, how much time did they have? The knowledge that this relationship could not last for forty years gave Phyllis a bittersweet feeling. Every moment must be lived, used, remembered. "Monty," she whispered. "Wake up."

He didn't open his eyes, but he smiled. "So it wasn't a dream," he said. "You're here, my love." And, eyes closed, he reached out and pulled Phyllis to him.

∞

Sig stretched and opened her eyes. For a moment, she became frightened. What if it wasn't true? What if she turned her head and Paul *wasn't* there? Sigourney had been through a lot— some bad relationships, a difficult fight to the top at her brokerage firm, her brother's near-bankruptcy, her father's death, her sister's . . . everything—and she had survived it all. But, after last night, after the tenderness and heat of last night, she didn't think she could bear it if Paul wasn't there beside her. It would truly break her heart if she'd dreamed it or if he really wasn't going to stay with her. Because, despite his age, despite both of their imperfections, it had never been like that, it had never been like last night.

There was an advantage to older men, Sig found. They took their time, they knew their moves, and they seemed to know what worked for women. At least Paul did. He was sure of himself and he wasn't afraid to show what he felt. That was more erotic than the flattest abs could ever be. Phillip had been so clinical. Sig knew that, but hadn't known men could be so emotional. Paul had actually had tears in his eyes and she liked it. While he had been holding her, loving her, he had looked at her with such a melting passion that when she thought of Phillip Norman and their athletic but empty nights she was embarrassed and almost ashamed. *This* was the way it was supposed to be: she'd realized that and would not forget.

Now that she'd experienced it, Sig knew she'd never settle for less. No more Phillip Normans. She wanted Paul Cushing, she wanted him for the rest of her life, and she'd do anything to ensure that. But when she opened her eyes and turned over she found that Paul was gone. The bed was empty.

"I didn't know how you take your coffee, but I hope it's black. You don't have any milk," Paul said from the doorway.

She spun around, tangling her legs in the blankets. He was wearing her chenille robe, which looked adorably peculiar on him, but Sig was so happy to see him that she wasn't going to waste feelings on details. Paul was carrying a tray with two cups of coffee, two glasses of juice, and a plate covered with a napkin. He walked to her side of the bed, put the tray on her lap and then walked around to the other side. "Do you like my peignoir?" he asked, and slipped out of it. Despite the age spots on his hands, his grizzled chest hair, and the rest of the signs of living, he was long and lean and beautiful to Sig. "Mrs. Katz seemed impressed by it. I bumped into her in the kitchen. She didn't have her glasses on and she thought I was you until I spoke."

Sig laughed, jostling the coffee. "Hey," Paul said. "Be careful with that! I don't cook breakfast that often." His face got serious for a moment. Sig could always tell because the parentheses deepened on either side of his mouth. "Not cooking is one of my shortcomings. Although for you I could try." He kissed her, then paused. "I've been thinking of other things, though. I already called my office. They traced your mother to the airport. She met Monty there. She didn't take a flight to a U.S. destination. We think she left the country with Monty, but it's going to take me a little while beyond there. Sometimes the FAA can be difficult." He took her hand.

Sig nodded.

"We'll find her, Sig."

She had no doubt Paul would. He'd deal with all that later. But right now, all she wanted to do was kiss him over and over for the rest of her life. He was right: she was dopey. Instead of kisses, she handed him his cup of coffee. "Sorry about the milk," she said. "Is that the way *you* drink it?"

Paul shook his head. "I like it with cream, Sig. Cream and no sugar," he smiled. "Why does that remind me of you?" He reached out and rubbed the back of her neck. She wanted to purr. "Probably because everything does." He put down the coffee mug on her bedside table. "Move that tray over," he told her. "I have something I want to share with you."

Sig giggled and put the tray on the floor.

"Will you marry me today?" Paul asked as he wrapped his arms and legs around her. "I'm an old-fashioned guy, Sig. None of these tawdry affairs. I want to marry you. I want you to be my wife. I want you to have my ring on your finger and my name at the end of your name. I'm sure it's politically incorrect, but it's a strong urge, Sig. One of two strong urges I'm having right now." He pulled her to him more closely and Sig found it difficult to catch her breath.

"I want to keep my own name," Sig said. She paused. "And I want something else."

"Okay," Paul breathed in her ear. "Anything you want. But I want you."

Sig felt her toes curl. She also never knew there was such a direct connection between the inside of her ear and her other canal. Her breath became even more difficult to catch until she heard herself begin to pant. "Oh, Paul," she moaned. She felt his tongue just touch her ear and at almost the same time his teeth gently bit her earlobe. The dress—the wedding dress at Bergdorf's had popped into her mind. She pulled away. She had to tell him. "I saw a special gown. It's silly, but I want to be a bride for you."

"It isn't silly," he told her. "It's sweet. It's the way it should be. Of course you'll have a gown. And a veil, if you want it," Paul said. "Marry me," he whispered, "or I'll never lick your ear again. Will you?"

"Yes," Sig said. "Yes, yes, yes."

∽

"We're in the Caymans. The Islands. We were married two days ago," Phyllis was shouting into the phone, as if she had to physically bridge the gap between the Caribbean and New York. "Monty is really very wealthy, but he didn't want to be loved for his money. When he lost everything, back in 1984, he learned who his real friends were. And who they weren't— which was almost everyone. Then he made another fortune, starting from scratch," Phyllis yelled proudly. "He just tested us with that bounced-check stuff. I told him it wasn't nice to test people and he's apologized. He won't do it again. He has a nice little gift for you and Bruce and Sharon to make up for it."

"Mom, I'm getting married."

"No, Susan, I'm *already* married," Phyllis shouted. "Monty and I already got married."

"Congratulations. But I'm not talking about you! I'm talking about me! I'm marrying Paul Cushing on Christmas Eve Day."

For a moment, only silence and static hummed along the line. Then Phyllis began talking again, this time in a normal volume. "Thank God. So you finally woke up and smelled the orange blossoms," she told her daughter approvingly.

"You're not surprised?"

"Don't be ridiculous. He was interested in you from the beginning."

"You knew?"

"Knew? I tried to tell you, but you couldn't see it. *Mazel tov.* Now we both will have mixed marriages," Phyllis laughed. "Well, better than no marriages at all."

"Mom, I really love him. I mean . . . I mean, I *really* love him," Sig said.

"I knew that, too. I was just waiting for your brain to catch up with your heart. So, did he give you a ring? Is it a sapphire like mine?"

"No," Sigourney admitted.

"Well, don't worry, he will." And then either Phyllis laughed or there was a burst of static, but whatever the noise was, when it was over the phone lines were dead.

∽

"I heard from Mom," Sig announced to Sharon and Bruce after plugging them into a conference call from her office. Might as well talk. Sig hadn't been able to do any work; her head was too full of plans and her heart too full of hope. Corny Sigourney, she thought to herself.

"Where is she?" Sharon asked.

"Where's Monty?" Bruce wanted to know. "I'm going to find him and choke him."

"Forget about it," Sig said, "he's your stepfather now and he's loaded. Offshore accounts on the Cayman Islands. His reputation may be no good here, but apparently he's a really wealthy man." Sig giggled. "Anyway, that's not the important news."

"*That's* not the important news?" Bruce asked.

"So what is?" Sharri wanted to know.

"Well, I'm inviting you to a little gathering tomorrow."

"Oh no. Is this the C-list brunch? Another goddamned Christmas party," Bruce moaned.

"No. It's just my wedding."

Sharon laughed. "I thought you said 'just your wedding,'" she giggled.

"She did," Bruce said calmly. "So Paul Cushing got up his nerve and asked you and you said yes?"

"How did you know?" Sig and Sharri asked simultaneously.

"Because I'm truly sensitive to nuance," Bruce said. "Marriage must be in the air, along with Taiwan flu virus. Anyway, Todd and I have been thinking about it, too."

"You're kidding!" Sharri and Sig exclaimed together.

"No, it seems to be the season for it. You know what the song says: ''Tis the Season to Be Married.'"

"Not for me," Sharon said darkly.

"Well," Sig said. "I'm happy for Mom and I'm happy for Monty. I'm happy for you and Todd. So will you come tomorrow? Paul and I are just going to do the ceremony at City Hall."

"Fabu," Bruce said.

"I'll be there," Sharri responded. "With the kids. A flower girl and a ring-bearer. Did he give you a big ring?"

"God! You sound just like Mom!" Sig told her sister.

"Nah. Could never happen. Not with any of us," Bruce told them. "Oh, and Sig? Do you need any help with your hair?"

Sig laughed and put the phone down. There was so much to do: paperwork, phone calls, and the wedding preparations. While all of this had been happening she also had seen an almost overnight turnaround in her business. Monty had asked her to manage some investments for him, while, oddly, both Bernard Krinz and Mrs. Katz had decided to put their money in her hands. As if that wasn't enough, Paul had put Wendy's very significant trust fund under her supervision. But that would all have to wait until the new year. Sig stood up and turned off her Quotron. She was leaving early to prepare for her wedding and then she and Paul would spend the next week together on their honeymoon.

twenty-two

For a change, Bruce was not hovering around Phyllis. Instead he was hovering around Sigourney, and as he took a step backwards he breathed a sigh of complete contentment. "God! This is just like *Peau d'Âne* when Jean Marais has to find a woman more beautiful than his dead wife. And the only one he can find is his daughter!" Bruce was a little hyper, but Sig loved him and knew he was happy for her. Instead of dissing him she kissed her eccentric brother. "Are we in a French movie?" he continued. "Sig, are you Catherine Deneuve?" He didn't pause for breath. "You *are* absolutely ravishing," he said, and Sig smiled, believing him. "But let me fix your lipstick. And don't kiss anyone else."

Sig was wearing the Bergdorf's satin wedding gown and strangely enough didn't feel the slightest bit ridiculous. That was because she was wearing it for Paul, and as he had said to her, "When you love someone, anything is possible."

Sig had even opted for the veil. She definitely didn't feel like the mother of the bride now. Paul—older, more experienced, and so loving—made her feel young. She didn't feel too old, too overdressed, too dramatic, or too anything. What she felt was beautiful—her most beautiful self.

So she wasn't surprised that when she looked into the mirror she saw that Bruce was right. Her eyes sparkled, her hair was lustrous, and the satin of the dress glimmered. She didn't care that they were only marrying at City Hall, or that they had no guests other than Bruce, Todd, Sharon, Barney, her niece and nephew, Wendy, and Mrs. Katz. When she thought about it, those were the people she needed to have around her—them and Paul.

And her mother, of course. She would like it if her mother and Monty could have been there. But now she understood: if her mother had felt like this, did feel this way about Monty, Sig had been very, very wrong to stand in her way. Sig truly believed that if Paul didn't have a penny she'd still be on her way downtown. She looked forward to all of the small things in their future life together—cooking dinner, helping to raise Wendy, seeing movies together, and just talking. Corny Sigourney. Corny or not, she hoped her mother felt half as besotted with Monty as she did with Paul. And she hoped that her mother's honeymoon in the Caymans would be half as nice as their honeymoon, which they were going to spend here, in Sig's apartment, which Paul had bought and put in both of their names. Sig was about to have her cake and eat it too, and she only hoped that her mother was enjoying more than just crumbs.

It was getting late. Paul was not, of course, supposed to see her arrayed like this, so he would meet them downtown. But he was sending a limo for them. Anyway, Sig felt that if he did see her it wouldn't bring bad luck. She'd already had all of that that she'd ever need. Now she had nothing to worry about. If anyone was willing, had experience or the knowledge of how to make a marriage work, it was Paul. He'd loved his late wife, he'd loved their son, and he loved his granddaughter. He knew how to be married, and in case she didn't, he'd show her.

The buzzer rang, and the doorman announced that the limo

was waiting. Bruce and Sig took the elevator down to the street level, where they were greeted by Jessie and her brother, both in white velvet outfits trimmed with bunny fur. As Sig and Bruce stepped out through the door, the children threw handfuls of spangles, rice, and confetti at her. "Not yet, not yet!" Sharon yelled. "You throw it *after* Auntie Sig gets married."

"That's right," Uncle Bruce told them. "Don't mess up her outfit." He brushed some of the sparkles off Sig's shoulder, then turned and looked at Sharon, who was wearing a shapeless blue velvet shift. "Where's Barney?" he asked.

"I've left him," Sharon said.

Sig and Bruce stood there in the cold, stock-still. "You're kidding!" Sig finally exclaimed.

"Hey, one out of every three American marriages ends in divorce," Sharon said, always ready with research. "I figured I'd carry the brunt of it and let you off the hook. It leaves you safe with Paul and Mom fine with Monty."

"Come on, Sharri. Seriously. What's up?"

"Get in the car, kids," Sharon told the children, who did. Then she exploded. "Oh, Sig, Barney's not just a failure. I could take that. It's that he's so comfortable failing. It was too much! Imagine turning down a job when Jessie and Travis have no lunch money! When *you* were paying his kids' tuition. It was enough."

"Another Christmas miracle," Bruce exclaimed, looking up to the ominous sky. It looked like a white Christmas was on its way. He put his hand on Sharon's arm. "I'll support you any way I can," he said, his voice solemn. "Except, of course, financially." They all laughed.

"Congratulations," Sig said in a serious voice. "You deserve better, Sharri."

"Hey, even alone is better than Barney," Sharon said.

"Time to go," Mrs. Katz called from the car. "You don't want to make a man wait. The groom could get cold feet." She actually sounded nervous.

"You could get cold everything out here," Bruce said.

Sharon, Bruce, and, lastly, Sig got into the long black stretch limo. A word to the driver and they moved off toward City Hall.

∞

Downtown, despite the tacky surroundings, Sig didn't mind that she'd spent so much on her wedding dress. She swanned through the long, high-ceilinged corridor, as near to perfection as she would ever be. "To the Marriage Bureau," said an ancient sign painted in gilt. It looked as if it was older than City Hall itself. How many brides-to-be had looked at it? Had they all been as happy, as hopeful as she was? Sig wondered. They trailed down the long hallway of the huge municipal building, following the faded signs until they at last reached the right office. A none-too-clean waiting room with assorted odd chairs and even odder people awaited them. The holidays clearly made for some strange bedfellows. Mrs. Katz held open the door as Sig, in her forty-eight-hundred-dollar gown, swept into the room. With her entrance, the dirt, the very, very pregnant bride-to-be sitting beside her nervous groom, the couple getting married with their two children along with them, the bored clerk at the desk—all of it—seemed to fade away. All Sig saw was Paul Cushing, who was standing beside Wendy, his granddaughter. With him there the room was transformed: the pregnant girl in her cheap polyester gown was beautiful. When Paul turned and looked at Sig, when she saw the joy and affection—the love—in his eyes, the room became beautiful, just as she did. The rest of the room felt it too, and it seemed as if there was a deep breath, a collective sigh. Today Sig was a princess, not a businesswoman: a princess, and beautiful enough so that all of them were transformed. Paul Cushing smiled and walked across the room toward her.

"The judge will be ready to see us in a minute," he said, taking her arm.

"Hey, hold on there," Bruce said. "This part is my job. *I'm* giving her away." Bruce appropriated his sister. "She's not quite yours yet."

"Smile pretty," Todd told them as he focused the lens and took a picture.

Mrs. Katz held out the box she was carrying. "Don't forget this," she said, and Sig opened it. She found two beautiful bouquets. In the frenzy of planning, she'd left out flowers! "Oh. Thank you," she said. "But why two?" Then she looked at what else was included. There was a blue handkerchief and a tiny locket.

"Something old, something new. You know . . . " Mrs. Katz said. Sig smiled and reached into the box. "And then you'll lend them to me. Okay?" Mrs. Katz asked. "That will be the borrowed part. The locket is old, the flowers are new, and the handkerchief . . . "

"But why the two bouquets?" Sig repeated.

"One's for me," Mrs. Katz admitted. "I'm going to be like your mother." She lowered her voice. "Except for the S, E, X."

"Don't tell me *you're* running off with Monty," Bruce joked.

"No, no. Don't be silly," Mrs. Katz said, the joke going right over her badly permed hair. "I'm getting married here after you do. I hope you don't mind."

Sig couldn't imagine what delusion this was, or who on earth Mrs. Katz could think she was getting married *to*. She never left the apartment, and when she did, she'd always been with Phyllis. The only male other than Monty, Todd, or Bruce that Sig had ever seen Mrs. Katz talking with was—"Bernard! You're marrying Bernard?" Sig quickly looked around the room. And there he was, sitting in a chair in the corner. "Don't you know that he's . . . "

"He's perfect for me." Mrs. Katz said. She lowered her voice again. "I don't have to change the monogram on my towels. Plus he promised to take care of my money. And no . . . "

"I know. No S, E, X," Sig laughed and then bent down and hugged Mrs. Katz. Oh, why not? Krinz was no crook. He'd been married before. And a lot stranger marriages had worked.

"Hold that pose," Todd exclaimed, tearing up. "This is so beautiful."

"Get out of here with that thing, will you?" Bruce told him. "We've got to get this show on the road." He paused. "It's not a show. It's a Frank Capra movie. *It's a Wonderful Life.* God, how did this happen? It's the holidays and *I'm* in a Frank Capra movie!"

Sig had to agree, finally, with Bruce's endless movie references. It *was* a wonderful life, or she expected it to be. The ceremony was both enormously quick and exceedingly slow to Sig. She felt her hands actually shaking under the flowers she clutched. It happened so quickly, and she had waited so long. Had she made a mistake? All the time that the judge spoke words over them she looked only at Paul's face. He was not a young man and she hadn't known him more than a month, but already he was very, very dear to her. How would it feel, now that she had found him, to have to live life without him? How many years did he have left with her?

At that moment, the judge asked for the ring. Bernard, serving as Paul's best man, collected it from Travis and handed it over. How morbid I am, Sig thought. Nobody knows what's going to happen, ever. At any minute something could go wrong, something could happen; a test result could come back positive, or a random incident of violence could strike.

As if in response to that thought, the door was thrown open and Montague Dunleathe stuck his head into the room. "We're not too late! We're not too late!" he exulted and stepped aside so that Phyllis could walk in. She looked exactly the same as always, except that she was tanned, well dressed, and for some reason Sig immediately focused on the fingers of her left hand. There *was* an enormous sapphire solitaire, along with a diamond-studded wedding band. So it was all true.

"I couldn't let my eldest daughter get married without me," Phyllis said, smiling at the crowd. "So . . ." she paused, obviously pleased with her dramatic entrance. "Don't let me interrupt anything."

Sig looked at Bruce. They both rolled their eyes. Their mother was an act of God, a freak of nature, a pain in the ass. But they loved her.

They began Sigourney and Paul's wedding all over again.

It didn't take long for the ceremony to end and then they all waited while Mrs. Katz—now Mrs. Krinz—married Bernard. "My dress wasn't as nice as yours," Phyllis whispered to Sig during the second wedding, "but Monty gave me a lovely gift for a wedding present." She leaned closer to Sig. "A million dollars. It's in my name in a bank in the Caymans. And *that* check didn't bounce." She looked down at her sapphire ring, not quite as big as the perfect diamond that Paul had just given Sig, but quite big enough.

"He's got a condo in the Caymans as a present for you two."

"We don't need any gifts," Sig said.

"Speak for yourself," Bruce told her. "Todd and I could use it."

"Yeah," Sharon added. "I got a job, but I'll take all the help I can get."

"*You* got a job?" Sig asked, taken aback. Todd clicked his camera; Sig could imagine the look on her face.

"On your own?" Bruce added. Todd took his picture, too.

"Shut up, Bruce," Phyllis admonished. "Be nice." She looked at Sharon. "*You* got a job, on your own?" she asked. Todd completed the trio with a shot of Phyllis.

"Just a little something for the wedding album," Todd chimed in and went on to his next victims, the newlywed Krinzes.

"I'm going to be research librarian at Stirling Corporate Headquarters," she admitted, shyly.

Bruce, Sig, and Phyllis burst into applause. "Well done," Monty said. "Have you heard the one about . . . "

"Well," Paul said, interrupting the family conference. "We have quite a bit to celebrate. Let's go." They got into the waiting cars, drove past the busy last-minute Christmas shoppers and finally reached the Carlyle, where Paul had kept a pied-à-terre for years. He had a light dinner waiting and he was about to break out the Veuve Clicquot. "Here's to all the newlyweds—all six of us."

"Well, eight actually," Bruce added. He turned and looked at Todd. "We've gotten married," he said. "Or its equivalent in this state." Shyly, he held up a beringed hand.

"Oh, Bruce!" Phyllis cried. "I'm so proud of you." She turned to Todd. "I couldn't like you better, even if you were a doctor." She kissed him on the cheek. Todd actually blushed, then raised his camera and took a picture of them all.

"Congratulations, or best wishes, or whatever," Sig said to Todd and hugged him. Then she turned to Bruce. "Best wishes to you," she said and the two of them embraced.

"Love is a beautiful thing," Mrs. Krinz told them all, Bernard Krinz at her elbow.

I guess she's not Mrs. Katz anymore, Sig thought with a pang. No more cats jokes. But, she thought, there'd be plenty of Krinz jokes. As if he heard her thought, Bruce leaned over to her. "Doesn't she make you Krinz?" he asked.

"No, he made *her* Krinz," Paul said. "But I couldn't make your sister into a Cushing." Sigourney had kept her own name.

"No," Bruce agreed. "You could only make her into a really happy woman." He looked around the room. "What a long strange trip it's been," he said.

"Yes," Mrs. Krinz agreed. "The municipal building was *way* downtown."

Sig laughed, and Phyllis joined her. Paul filled all of their glasses. Sig looked at him in that way that couples exchange glances. Meanwhile, Phyllis winked at Monty and Bruce and Todd both cracked up.

"Happy holidays to everyone," Phyllis said, raising her glass.

"*And* a dysfunctional new year," Bruce added.

"It's a sure thing," Sig told him and smiled at her family.

OLIVIA GOLDSMITH

FASHIONABLY LATE

ACKNOWLEDGMENTS

I would like to thank Nancy Lee Robinson for the honor and privilege of working with her on this book. No better secretary, editorial aide, and friend exists anywhere. Plus, she laughs at my jokes *and* can reload the printer!

I would also like to thank Jean Merrill Balderston for her invaluable championing of the right choices and her positive and creative suggestions. Her sensitive and generous reading of all my work meant more than I could say. Thanks also to the kind readers of my previous books who sent kind messages. They were greatly appreciated. Paul Mahon was supportive, funny, and contributed some of the best chapter titles: his humor and wit are both deeply appreciated. Diana Hellinger was kind and patient enough to read draft after draft and in some magical way known only to her friends, her enthusiasm never faltered. Ruth Bekker was insightful as only she can be. Thanks also to Linda Fontaine Grady, one of the most stylish women I know, for her views into retailing and fashion. Curtis Laupheimer and Justine Kryven were wonderful, as always. Also in the "wonderful as always" department is Paul Eugene Smith. I hope I never take his contribution for granted and he never gets tired of being acknowledged. Lastly, I would like to thank Jim and Christopher Robinson for doing without their Nancy when I could not. Now, if they'd just shovel their driveway!

Finally, I would like to thank George Craig, Eddie Bell, Jack McKeown, Susan Moldow, Joseph Montebello, Larry Ashmead, and Charlotte Abbott of HarperCollins for the TLC and author care they lavished on me.

PART ONE
DESIGNER GENES

---

*He who only sees fashion
in fashion is nothing but a fool.*

—Honoré de Balzac

1

REAPING WHAT YOU SEW

Fashionably late, Karen Kahn and her husband, Jeffrey, walked past the flash of photographers' lights and into the Waldorf Astoria Hotel on Park Avenue. Karen felt, for that moment, that she had it all. Tonight was the annual award party and benefit held by the Oakley Foundation, and Karen was about to be honored with their Thirty-eighth Annual American Fashion Achievement Award. If she couldn't arrive fashionably late here, where could she?

Stepping through the lobby and into the deco brass elevator, alone together for the last moment before the crush began, Karen looked at Jeffrey and couldn't repress a grin. Soon, she'd be among the crème-de-la-crème of fashion designers, fashion press, and the wealthy society women who actually *wore* the fashions. Despite all of her hard work, despite dreaming that this could happen, Karen could hardly believe that *she* was the woman of the moment.

"It's taken me almost twenty years to become an overnight success," she wisecracked to Jeffrey, and he smiled down at her. Unlike Karen, who knew she was no more than ordinary-looking, Jeffrey was handsome. Karen was aware that tuxedos make even plain men good-looking, but she was still taken aback by how much they did for a looker like Jeffrey, who was both sexy *and* distinguished in his formal clothes. A lethal combo. The gleam of the black satin of his peaked lapels set off his thick pepper-and-salt hair. He was wearing the cabochon sapphire shirt studs and cuff links she had given him the night before. They perfectly matched the washed-denim blue of his eyes, as she knew they would.

"Not a moment too soon," he said. "It's important to schedule your Life-time Achievement Award before your first face-lift."

She laughed. "I didn't know that. Lucky it turned out that way. Although if I *had* the lift first, I might still be considered a girl genius."

"You're still *my* girl genius," Jeffrey told her, and gave her arm a squeeze. "Just remember, I knew you when." The elevator reached their floor. "And now, see how it feels to *really* hit the big time," Jeffrey told her.

Before the stainless and brass art deco doors opened, he bent down and kissed her cheek, careful not to spoil her *maquillage.* How lucky she was to have the kind of man who understood when a kiss was welcome but smeared makeup was not! Yes, she was very lucky, and very happy, she thought. Everything in her life was as perfect as it could be, except for her condition. But maybe Dr. Goldman would have news that would . . . she stopped herself. No sense thinking about what Jeffrey called "her obsession" now. She'd promised herself and her husband that tonight was one night she'd enjoy to the utmost.

As the elevator doors rolled aside, Karen looked up to see Nan Kempner and Mrs. Gordon Getty, fashion *machers* and society fund-raisers, standing side by side, both of them in Yves Saint Laurent. "You'd think they could have put on one of *my* little numbers," Karen hissed to Jeffrey, while she kept the smile firmly planted on her face.

"Honey, you've never done glitz like Saint Laurent does," Jeffrey reminded her, and, comforted, she sailed out and air-kissed the two women. One was in an oyster white satin floor-length sheath with gold braid and a tasseled belt— a lot like curtain trimming, Karen thought. Perhaps Scarlett O'Hara had been at the portieres again. The other was in black lace shot with what looked like silver, though, since it was on Mrs. Getty, it must be *platinum,* Karen joked to herself. Both women took their fashion seriously: Nan Kempner had once admitted in an interview that as a girl she had "cried and cried" at Saint Lau-rent's when she saw a white mink-trimmed suit too expensive for her allowance. The legend was that Yves himself had come down to meet the girl who cried so hard.

The foyer was already crowded with the usual backdrop of men in exquisite black wool and women in every sort of fabric and color. Funny how men always clung to a uniform. Only the Duke of Windsor had the fashion nerve to wear colored formal wear; midnight blue rather than black. But if men didn't display much overt fashion, they certainly controlled this world. Despite her success, and the success of a few other women designers, Karen knew that the business was owned and controlled by men. And most of those in control were here tonight.

In addition, tonight there was a larger-than-usual gaggle of paparazzi. Fashion seems to have become the new entertainment, Karen thought, not for the first time, but it still surprised her. There was rarely a fashion event that didn't draw a wild mix of society, Hollywood, and the rock world. She controlled herself and didn't do a Brooklyn double take as she was pushed against Sly Stallone, who was there with his latest model. Paulina the Gorgeous stood beside her husband, Ric Ocasek. Clint Eastwood stood beside Frances Fisher, who looked great for a woman who'd just dropped a baby. The Elle Halle camera crew was also there, apparently busy trying to get a shot of Christie Brinkley. Billy Joel didn't seem to be with her, but David Bowie was there, with Iman. And that, Karen thought, was only in the *foyer*.

An enormous noise came from the ballroom itself, which was where Karen and Jeffrey were headed. In a matter of moments, Karen greeted Harold Koda from the Metropolitan Museum of Art Costume Institute, Enid Haupt, one of the wealthiest and most charitable of the New York *doyennes,* Georgina Von Etzdorf, another designer, and bald-headed Beppe Modenese, who worked to polish the Italian fashion industry's image in the United States. They passed Gianni Versace, standing next to his sister and muse, the impossibly blonde Donetella. And still Jeffrey and Karen hadn't yet made it to the ballroom. This event was definitely going to be a success, Karen thought, and she was happy not only for herself but for the fashion business in general.

"Well, the gang's all here," Karen smiled. "At least they didn't give a party for me where nobody came."

Before she had a chance to exult, they were interrupted: "Oh my, if it isn't Kubla Kahn," said a waspish voice behind them. Karen winced, turned around, and was staring into the wizened face of Tony de Freise, another Seventh Avenue designer, but one whose star was fading.

"It's *Karen* Kahn," Jeffrey corrected.

"Yeah, and it's a hell of a pleasure dome she's decreed," Tony sneered. Looking around, he paused, and his mouth tightened. "They did this for me once. Don't let it go to your head. They just build you up to tear you down." He shrugged and turned away. "See you on the slopes."

Karen sighed, but tried to keep her smile visible. There was professional jealousy in every business, but there seemed to be a little more jealousy in fashion. Karen wasn't sure why that was. Belle, her mother, had once described politics back in the teacher's room at grammar school by saying, "The fighting is so dirty because the stakes are so low." Perhaps the fighting in the fashion world had become so dirty because the stakes were so high. In the eighties, fashion had become global; the take was bigger than ever before, and it seemed as if the knives had been sharpened.

"Well, *that* was a pleasant omen," Karen whispered. "I feel like Sleeping Beauty at the banquet when the Bad Fairy appeared."

"Oh, forget the Bad Fairy," Jeffrey told her. "No one pays attention to Tony anymore."

"Yeah. That was his point."

Karen realized all at once that this new visability would also make her more vulnerable. Other designers could take shots at her now. There *were* those rare few who continued to go their own way. Bill Blass, probably richer than any other American designer (with the exception of Ralph Lauren), was always friendly, open, and noncompetitive. He'd been one of the first of the established fashion moguls to be nice to Karen. If his talent wasn't huge and his clothes were sometimes uninspired, he'd be the least offended to hear it. Geoffrey Beene, a true original, was another who went his own way. His clothes *were* inspired, an example of true artistry, and perhaps that was one of the reasons he was an iconoclast and always above the fashion fray. In school, Karen had learned a lot by simply *looking* at Geoffrey Beene's designs.

Karen smiled and decided to shrug off the de Freise incident. Now she'd have to face the rest of the mob. She and Jeffrey walked into the ballroom and were engulfed by their competitors and co-workers. There *are* nice people here, Karen reassured herself. Then she saw Norris Cleveland.

Karen tried to spend most of her time and energy in the workroom, out of the gossip and back-biting arena. She also tried not to compare herself or her work to anyone else. But if there was one woman in the business she disliked, it was the one approaching her right now. Norris Cleveland was, in Karen's opinion, worse than a bad designer. She was the kind of designer who gave fashion artists a bad name. She was lazy and derivative; the worst of her clothes were either dull or unwearable, *but* . . . The "but" was that Norris had a genius for having friends in the right places and getting her parties, quips, nights on the town, *and* her newest line placed in all the right newspapers, magazines, and television shows. Of course, calling them *her* clothes was an act of charity: Norris stole a little from here and a little from there. Lately, it seemed Cleveland had been imitating Karen's style. The worst part was that she even copied badly! But Karen was determined not to let anything or anyone spoil the night. She smiled at Norris, or at least she bared her teeth.

Norris was as bad at business as she was at design, but a few years ago she had married Wall Street Money and her company had been saved by a new inflow of cash. If the word on the Avenue was true—that Norris's husband was getting tired both of writing checks and of being referred to as "Mr. Cleveland"—it did not seem to have dimmed Norris's smile tonight. She came at Karen with her arms open, revealing her painfully thin body encased in a sheath of yellow jersey. Now, as Norris made a kissing noise at each ear, Karen heard cameras begin to click. Somehow cameras *always* followed Norris Cleveland. Karen wondered if they were real press, or simply ringers on the society designer's payroll.

"Congratulations, darling," Norris said, in that breathy, exclusive-girls'-school monotone that was so prevalent among the ladies who lunched—a sort of Jackie Kennedy Onassis with emphysema. Norris had always been pleasant to Karen, but on some deeper level, she could feel the woman's envy and distaste. After all, Karen was nothing but an upstart. "I'm *so* pleased for you." Yeah, right. Norris then turned to Jeffrey and put her hand on his arm. "You must be *very* proud," she said to Jeffrey, and for some reason, when Norris said it, it sounded like an insult. Cameras flashed again, and Karen wondered if she'd be cropped out of the picture when it ran in *Town and Country*.

Jeffrey just laughed. "Norris! What a dress!" was all he said.

She kept smiling. "Well, you're not the only ones celebrating tonight. Have you heard? *I'm* about to launch my perfume."

God, how much money did her husband have to throw away? Karen wondered. A perfume could not be launched for less than ten or fifteen million dollars. A good launch cost triple that. And only the good ones lasted.

Karen *hated* the perfume business. It was a cash cow for a lot of the fashion merchants, and had been since Coco Chanel invented the deal, but it was well known that it had brought only money and pain to Coco. Still, it would be perfect for Norris. Without feeling a moment's guilt, she could sell packaging with her name on it to desperate people who vainly hoped for romance.

"Best of luck," Karen murmured, and was delighted when Jeffrey moved her forward. "I hate her," Karen told her husband out of the corner of her mouth.

"She knows that," he answered.

Karen and Jeffrey moved smoothly through the crowd. It was wonderful, even hard to believe. *Everyone* said hello to her. She was definitely the Cinderella at *this* ball. And if she had spent most of her life on her knees in her workroom, tonight was the reward, the recognition for all that work.

"Serious Money ahead," Jeffrey whispered, and nudged her. "A pillar of the community."

Bobby Pillar, the guy who had singlehandedly created a new television network and was now launching his own shopping channel, was moving toward them. Karen had met him once or twice before, but now, beaming, he approached her, his hand outstretched. "The It Girl!" he cried, and instead of shaking her hand, he hugged her close. She was surprised, but after all, he *was* Hollywood. Always trendsetters, they'd given up air-kissing in the nineties—it was replaced with full frontal assault. Now Bobby surveyed her proudly, as if she was an invention of his own. "So? When are you going to create a line for *me?*"

Karen shrugged, but smiled. There was something *hamishe* about Bobby. He was warm, familiar, and very, very Brooklyn. "Not tonight," she told him.

Bobby laughed. "We ought to talk," he said. "You ought to see the kind of numbers I'm talking about."

Jeffrey said his hello, someone else greeted Bobby, and then Karen and Jeffrey were free to wander off. When they were out of earshot, Jeffrey turned to look back at Bobby. "Can you imagine?" he said, outraged. "The guy is selling schlock jewelry and polyester pull-on pants. I don't care if he's *desperate* to upgrade, he's not dragging *your* name down. Look what happened to Cher, and she just did an infomercial."

Karen shrugged. "Still, it's nice to be asked." *She* certainly didn't consider the attention an insult. Her husband was a cutie, but he was also a snob. Of course, he could afford to be—his family was wealthy, German Jews with more than enough money in Manhattan real estate. He'd gone to private schools and had always been part of a more glittering world than she had. He'd always been sought after while Karen was just a girl from Brooklyn.

She wasn't interested in socialites. The people in the room tonight—the ones who actually attracted her, who fascinated her—were the other *designers*. She wanted to talk with them. Yet those she respected always made her feel shy. And although tonight she was being recognized by them, there was not a lot of camaraderie in the fashion world. While she admired Valentino's gowns, and sometimes appreciated the exuberance of Karl Lagerfeld, she couldn't imagine hanging out with them. They spoke at least four languages, knew all the best restaurants in all the best cities, owned palazzi and villas, and went to the opera for *fun*. Karen couldn't imagine them seeking out her company to split a Diet Coke and a rice cake.

Three of the fashion "walkers" congregated against the doorway. John Richardson, Ashton Hawkins, and Charles Ryskamp were successful in their fields. Cultured, attractive bachelors, they accompanied society women to events like this when their own husbands were too busy or too tired or too dead. No matter what their age, it seemed that society women required events to go to, escorts to take them, and dresses to wear. Sometimes Karen wondered at it, but it did sell gowns.

Slowly she and Jeffrey continued to make their way through the crowd to their table, where Defina Pompey was standing, tall and majestic as an ebony column. Karen and Defina had worked together for more than a decade. Fifteen years ago Defina had been the hottest runway model of the season and now, even with Linda Evangelista standing not too far behind her, Karen could see why. Her friend was still gorgeous, more beautiful than Beverly Johnson or Naomi Campbell on their best days. Today, when it was truly unchic to do a show without several black models, it was hard to remember that it was this woman who had broken ground for all women of color. Defina was deep in conversation with a painfully skinny, intense young woman dressed in black and an elegant Italian-looking man—Defina had a gift for languages and spoke flawless Spanish, Italian, and French, but she still knew how to communicate with the homeboys.

Defina looked across the table and flashed a smile at Karen. She was wearing a white silk jersey gown that Karen had designed for her. With it, Defina wore the wrap jacket that did great things for any woman who wanted to camouflage a thickening middle. Defina, in the days since she'd left modeling, had broadened and matured in all senses of the words.

"May I introduce you to someone who would like to meet you?" Defina asked smoothly. She turned to the Italian and dismissed him with a *"ciao"* and a gracious smile. Then she sidled over to Karen, the little black fashion wraith fighting the crowd behind her. "This one is so green she actually thinks Calvin and Anne Klein are related. Should we tell her they're married, and Kevin is their son?" Defina suggested, *sotto voce*. The wraith got closer, extended a skeletal arm, and put out her bony hand. "Karen, meet Jenna Nuborg. She's a freelance fashion writer who would like an interview. I told her you'd *love* to."

Defina had put a little too much emphasis on the word *love* though only Karen would pick it up. Defina knew how much Karen hated to be bothered by the fashion reportorial tyros. God, they could be stupid *and* annoying. As if that wasn't enough, they were most often oversensitive and quick to take offense. But Karen had no illusions: it was the fashion press who had put Karen here tonight. After years of effort, Karen had managed to survive in the cut-throat world of haute couture, but it wasn't until Jeffrey had insisted on hiring Mercedes Bernard to do their public relations work that Karen had really broken from the pack and become a national, and perhaps almost an international, name.

"Do you mind if I ask you some questions?" the Nuborg woman asked. Her voice was as thin as her arms. This was no time for an interview, but before Karen could think of a pleasant way to put the woman off, the girl continued. "What, in your opinion, is the sexiest part of the female body?" she asked. Defina, standing behind the reporter and towering almost a foot over the Nuborg's head, smirked at Karen.

"Her mind?" Karen asked, as if the question had been a riddle.

The girl didn't smile. Too intense for that! "What is your biggest unful-filled desire?" she asked relentlessly.

Karen's smile faded. Without thinking, she moved her hand to cover her stomach, as if to shield her empty womb. She remembered Dr. Goldman tomorrow. She blinked, paused, and told herself to get a grip.

Before Karen could begin to answer or make an excuse, tall, pale Mer-cedes Bernard floated over. "Jenna. It is Jenna, isn't it?" the PR woman was a genius at remembering names, and while the pre-party arrival noise crescen-doed around them, there in the glittering ballroom of the Waldorf, Mercedes began to detach the Nuborg mollusk from Karen's side. "Perhaps later would be a better time for this," Mercedes was saying, her cool but pleasant smile already in place. Mercedes projected an aura of *noblesse oblige*. Though she spent her business life trying to cadge publicity and snag the best coverage from a host of egomaniacal fashion editors and journalists, she managed somehow to retain her dignity. The industry "poop" on her was that "Mer-cedes bends but never stoops."

The Nuborg turned once more to Karen. "Which is better: elegance with-out sex appeal or sex appeal without elegance?" Karen opened her mouth, but Mercedes's long white hand took the reporter by her bony, black-clad shoul-der and firmly turned her away. Karen sighed with relief. She knew that some day she would have to sit down and pretend an interest in those clichéd ques-tions, but at least she didn't have to do it right now. Later, she would kill Defina—but she'd be careful not to spoil the white dress.

"Where do they get those questions from?" Defina asked innocently, wrinkling her brow. She looked over at Karen. Then she got serious. "I'm sorry," she said. "I was just fooling around. I didn't know she would . . ."

"That's okay. It's nothing," Karen told her.

Defina widened her eyes. "Smile pretty at Nuclear Wintour," Defina told her, and Karen flashed a grin at Anna Wintour, arguably the most powerful woman in fashion publishing. Anna was shrewd and tough and glamorous and difficult. She had a lot of nicknames, but Mercedes, the most literate among them, always called her "The Wintour of our Discontent." Needless to say, Mercedes only said it *behind* Anna's bony back.

At the next table, Karen could see Doris and Donald Fisher. He had started The Gap stores, and he, along with Peter Haas Senior of the Levi Strauss family, probably pushed more denim than anyone else in the world. With them was Bill Wolper of NormCo, the fashion conglomerate that was more successful than anyone else in the market. Everyone knew that big-time fashion wealth had come from the mass market. The real money had never been on Seventh Avenue. As Jeffrey reminded her over and over, "Henry Ford got rich making Fords, not Lincolns." It was only in the last dozen or so years that top-of-the-market Seventh Avenue American designers—who made Lincolns—had built enormous empires. And they had done it by moving out and down. Lincolns had been downgraded to Fords—bridge lines—for the malls. People like Ralph Lauren, Calvin Klein, and a half dozen others had created fashion empires larger than any that had come before. Now Karen stood on the brink of an opportunity potentially as vast. And sometimes it frightened her.

But the faces around her table were all supportive ones. Aside from Jeffrey and Defina, she could smile at Mercedes, who had brought an obviously gay male friend. Mercedes came from the generation that always had male escorts for social events. Everyone knew Bernard was a lesbian (though no one ever mentioned it). Only Defina had the nerve to once refer to the woman as a "Mercedes diesel."

Casey Robinson, their vice-president of marketing, sat next to Mercedes and he was with his gay companion Ray. Karen sighed again and had a flash of gratitude that she had met and married Jeffrey early on in her career. So many women in her business bemoaned the lack of heterosexual men in the industry.

Karen smiled at Casey, Mercedes, Defina, and the others. All of the people at the table tonight had helped her get here. When she learned she'd earned the Oakley Award, Karen had decided to have these people surround her and share in her success. She had not invited her family. They hadn't contributed in the same way, and somehow their presence always complicated things. Just this once, Karen had decided to keep the night for herself, to share the event with her mother and sister only *after* the fact. She felt a little guilty about it, but as her friend Carl had explained, "The choice is between inviting them and spoiling your evening, or not inviting them and having a great night but feeling guilty. I say go with the guilt! Guilt is like a muscle. Learn to *use* it."

As if the thought of Carl had conjured him up, Karen saw her tall, fat, balding friend making his way toward her. The table wouldn't be complete without Carl. Since the days at South Side High School, back in Rockville Centre, Long Island—which both she and Carl still called "Lawn Guylind"— he had been her biggest cheerleader. Actually, her *only* cheerleader. Certainly, neither her mother nor her younger sister were supporters of Karen's dream to make beautiful, fabulous, comfortable clothes. Belle was too practical, too critical for dreams, and poor Lisa, younger than Karen, needed support and couldn't give any. Only Carl, with his crazy optimism, his sense of humor, and his mother's sewing machine, had supported Karen's ideas. He was her earliest fabricator and ally. Now his bulk crossed the last part of the Waldorf dance floor and he enveloped her in his big embrace.

"Brava, brava, brava!" he boomed, and smacked kisses on both her cheeks.

"*Grazia,*" Karen responded, exhausting all of her Italian vocabulary with that single word. It had been agony for her to learn French, which Jeffrey had insisted she do for her career. Karen was no Defina when it came to languages. She still spoke English with the heavy, adenoidal tones of Nostrand Avenue (where her family lived before her father could afford Rockville Centre).

"So how did you achieve this enormous success?" Carl asked in a mock announcer voice, holding up a butter knife from the table setting as a faux microphone.

"I guess I just kept my nose to the grindstone for a long time," she answered, too modestly and sweetly.

"Oh, is *that* what made your nose look like that?" he asked. "Let's get a picture of it." Carl popped out a tiny camera. He handed it to Jeffrey. "Yo, Defina. Get over here! I want a picture with the stars of the evening."

Defina smiled and obliged, but Karen saw Jeffrey's expression tighten. Why hadn't Carl asked her husband too? Sometimes Carl could be incredibly undiplomatic. Karen was always aware that Jeffrey could be made to feel like an appendage, when the truth was he had made all her success possible. But to Jeffrey's credit he obligingly held up the camera and squinted.

"The Three Musketeers and their mid-life crisis," he said as he flashed the picture.

"Isn't that a book by Dumas?" Carl cracked.

"I think so," Defina said. "But I can never remember if it's Dumas *père*, Dumas *fils*, or Dumas the Holy Ghost."

"Hey, guys, you're confused," Karen explained. "Even *I* know that it's *Casper* the Holy Ghost."

Jeffrey shook his head at their foolishness. "Could you behave like celebrities instead of tourists for just one evening?" he asked.

"Speaking of celebrities, I saw John Kennedy Junior in the lobby," Carl whispered. "I nearly passed out. I swear, he is a real and present danger to the gay community. The boy could cause cardiac arrest." Carl began breathing hard with actual or feigned excitement. It was difficult to tell with Carl. "Oh, to be Daryl Hannah for just one night!" he cried.

Karen rolled her eyes at him. "Behave," she warned. Carl was obsessed with the Kennedys, or pretended to be. He was probably the only person in the country who could name *all* the Kennedy cousins of this generation. It was a parlor trick he did, kind of like naming the wives of Henry the Eighth or the seven dwarves, except it took a lot longer.

By now most of the people in the ballroom had taken their seats, and Carl joined the Karen Kahn team at the table. He picked up a glass and when one of the waiters brought champagne, he cleared his throat and got serious. "Let us all toast this year's winner of the coveted Oakley Award," he saluted. Karen was touched. Then, on cue, everyone at the table pulled out a slice of toast and lobbed them across the table at her—even the sedate Mercedes. Then they all collapsed in giggles. All except Jeffrey.

"Jesus Christ!" he said. He obviously hadn't been privy to the gag. "A food fight at the Waldorf Astoria?" He shook his head while Karen couldn't stop laughing. Tears came to her eyes and she had to use a napkin to make sure she didn't blot her mascara.

Suddenly the mistress of ceremonies, Leila Worth, began speaking from the podium set at the corner of the stage. "If I may ask for your attention," she cooed over a sound system that had to be set on supermax to be heard over the braying and whinnying of the *mavins* of couture. The fashion crowd was a loud one. At last they settled down.

The next part of the evening was a blur to Karen. There were the inedible couple of courses of food and the blah, blah, blah of several speakers who talked about the Oakley Awards and the industry and fund-raising. There was the buzz of conversation that rose to an almost unbearable din between each speaker, and the predictable music—some Lester Lannin knock-off band. Then the lights dimmed and Leila Worth got back behind the podium.

"Tonight we are gathered to honor an American fashion great." Goose pimples ran up Karen's arms and down her back. Was that her? She looked down at her plate of untouched chicken divan and wild rice. *She* was a fashion great? She didn't know if she was thrilled, embarrassed, or upset. Maybe all three. Did Coco Chanel, Karen's idol, feel ambivalent when *she* was feted? Probably not, but then Chanel *was* a fashion great. Karen sat there feeling like both Miss America and an imposter. She tried to focus again on Leila's words. After all, you didn't get a Life Achievement Award every day.

"In the last twenty years, American fashion has become the fashion of the world," Leila was saying. Karen wondered how the French and Italian designers in the room felt about hearing that! If it wasn't completely true, it was more true than it had ever been before. America *was* the place that had created a system that could move a designer's vision out to virtually every corner of the world. It had taken three decades, but the Oakley Awards had been one of the mechanisms that had focused the attention of the fashion magazines and buyers on American designers. Leila could be excused the hyperbole.

"Nobody represents American fashion, nobody knows American women, better than the designer we are here to honor tonight. In the last decade, the continuous flow of beautiful, luxurious, and wearable clothes has never stopped coming. No one has a greater mastery of form, a deeper understanding of the subtleties of color, and no one has been more industrious or creative in her search for the right material, the unique material, the original material, as Karen Kahn. Here are some examples."

The spot focusing on Leila went black, and from out of the wings the parade of tall, gorgeous women began. Leila's disembodied voice continued, describing some of the designs and their importance or originality. Now, in the semi-darkness, Karen knew what to do with her eyes. She drank in the spectacle—a collection of the work she had done in the last decade. Karen nodded at the big-shouldered sheath dress and matching knit jacket, the unconstructed blazer and sleek cropped pants, even the bias-cut silk knit evening gown, though evening wear had never been her strongest suit. The clothes on the models moved, they reflected the light, and they seemed both a decoration and an organic part of the beautiful bodies they draped. That was the trick, the riddle, that Karen was always trying to solve—how to conceal, reveal, and yet also be a natural extension of a woman's body.

With most of these clothes, she thought, she *had* succeeded, and just for once, for this delicious moment, she could sit there and be happy with her work. She was no *wunderkind*—hell, she was hitting middle age—but if she felt that she'd been overlooked for years, now that she was finally being recognized she'd just consider it fashionably late. Karen could sense that the audience felt her vision, and when the last number—the previous season's rich cocoa cardigan and legging outfit in wool with a simple chiffon undertunic—swirled off Leila called out her name. Karen rose effortlessly and walked across the gleaming empty dance floor to the stage.

The ovation sounded thunderous, but so was the sound of her own heartbeat in her ears. She hoped her hair looked all right; she knew that the satin pants and cashmere jacket she was wearing, the latter trimmed in satin banding, would catch the light and throw it back to the audience. She ascended the steps and turned toward the audience. The spots blinded her, but she was prepared and tried to look out at the darkness behind them without wincing. Leila hugged her, and the applause surrounded the two of them, a clichéd tableaux from every award ceremony that had ever come before. Karen looked over the room full of everyone who was anyone in the fashion world.

"Thanks, friends," she began.

Jeffrey and she were getting ready to leave when Willie Artech approached their table. Willie was another designer, slightly younger than Karen, who also had been juggling an emerging Seventh Avenue business. About five years before he had been the hot guy, but underfinancing and missed delivery dates—an absolute mortal sin in the rag trade—had taken the luster off his name. So had AIDS. He stood there now, alone, in a tuxedo that was far too big for his wasted frame.

"Congratulations, Karen," he said. He raised a glass unsteadily. "We who are about to die salute you."

Everyone at the table, most of them in the process of gathering their things, stopped.

"I'd hoped to get the award tonight, but homosexuality isn't as fashionable as it once was." He shrugged. "*Res ipsa loquitur.* That's Latin for 'the facts speak for themselves.' " Willie grinned, his head skull-like. "Pretty appropriate, don't you think? A dead man speaking a dead language." His voice dropped, and he bent his head. "This was a hard night. I'd hoped to win. I don't have any children. I would have liked to leave behind something that would make sure I'm remembered," he whispered.

"I'm sorry, Willie," Karen murmured.

Carl stood up. His lover had died just two years ago. "Let's go, Karen," he said. Jeffrey, who had been off to fetch coats, returned and helped Karen into hers. The table broke up, leaving Willie standing unsteadily alone.

Defina took Karen's arm. "Don't take it personally," she whispered. "You know how it is with gay men designers: it's always '*chere, chere la mere.*' And tonight you got hit with his mother stuff."

Despite Defina's attempt at comfort, it was an unpleasant ending to a wonderful night and Karen felt an immediate stab of guilt. Somehow she knew how Willie Artech, the spectre at the table, felt.

"Jesus," Carl said as they exited the room. "In the face of eternity, who could care so much about an award?"

But Karen, clutching the Oakley plaque, her hand once again protectively over her belly, could understand how someone might.

2

BARREN KAREN

The day after she received the Oakley Award, Karen sat numbly in Dr. Goldman's waiting room, trying to cope with his verdict. Irreparably infertile.

Somehow, she'd known all along. From the first, through all the tests, all the drugs, all the examinations, despite Jeffrey's own doubts and his regimen of doctors, she'd known it was her and she'd known her condition was irrevocable.

It was odd, but the moment the doctor gave her the official news, Karen flashed on the idea of finding her real mother. But perhaps that wasn't odd. Perhaps that was typical of barren female adult adoptees, she thought. How would she know? How many of us are there, she wondered? Are we a significant enough demographic lump to be charted as some baby-boomer subset? Have we already appeared on Oprah? Is there a twelve-step program or a support group for us?

She felt right now as if she could use some support. This was the punishment she got for being so happy only the night before. The Oakley Award, the glittering crowd, the happiness, all receded until it seemed as if it had happened some other year, or some other lifetime. It was dangerous to have been that happy. Here was the final proof.

After almost thirty months of trying, of unspontaneous, prescribed sex, painful, humiliating tests, medical specialists, and counseling, it had long been clear that something serious was wrong. Nothing to be so surprised about, she told herself. This was not unexpected. Here, at last, was the final

verdict: *irreparably infertile.* No more searches for specialists, vaginal thermometers, doctor's appointments in the middle of the day just at the exact
moment she was ovulating. No more pain, expense, and bother. No more
hope.

It stunned her.

Was it the hopelessness that put the idea of finding her real mother into
her head? Karen didn't know where the longing came from—this craving to
feel whole that now a baby would clearly never satisfy. She hadn't thought
much about her real mother before—but now the need to search for her hit
Karen in the stomach with a force that was almost nauseating.

She thought of Willie Artech—from all the events of last night, only his
image didn't seem to recede. Didn't Jeffrey often accuse her of focusing on the
bad things? Well, she couldn't help what she focused on. Right now it was
Willie Artech, dying, and wishing for children to make sure he was remembered.

But she didn't want a child in order to be remembered—not exactly. It
was more to connect her to the thread of life, to transform her and Jeffrey
from a couple to a family. Well, for whatever reason she wanted a child, it
wasn't going to happen. Perhaps that was why, instead, she wanted her
mother. Her real mother.

So here she sat in the ever-so-tastefully-decorated Park Avenue fertility
clinic beside four women, all but one mirroring the pain and fear in her own
eyes. Funny how they called the place a fertility clinic when only the sterile
ones come here, she thought bitterly. Sterile and rich ones, she reminded herself. Dr. Goldman had already cost what? Six or seven thousand? And this was
how it ended. She winced. Money couldn't cushion this blow, except to give
you a glove-leather Barcelona chair to sit in while you tried not to lose your
composure and your lunch right there, all over the Axminster carpet.

She felt like a completely different woman than the one who had been on
the stage at the Waldorf only fifteen hours before. What had all of *that* meant?
No memory of glory could lessen this pain.

She knew that she couldn't tell her mother. Not either fact: that a baby
was out of the question or that she wanted to search for her own natural
mother. As always, Belle's feelings came first. Belle was the punch line of that
old mother-daughter joke: when the mother finds her daughter dead on the
floor, a suicide, she cries out, "How could she do this to *me?*" Oh yes, Belle
would make a pity party out of this one. Belle only wanted to hear about
Oakley Awards. She was comfortable around achievement, not failure.

Worse yet, Belle had been urging Karen and Jeffrey to have children for
more years than Karen liked to remember. It would be awful now to have to

admit that Belle was right. We *should* have tried to have a baby sooner, Karen thought. But I've been so wrapped up in my career. Carving out a place in the fashion world had been no day at the beach. And then, once I got a foot in the door, how could I not follow through? When my stuff really took off, with all the work, the success, and the travel, there just hadn't been time. Babies, I figured, could always come later.

Except now they never would. Karen felt a stab of pain somewhere around her nonfunctioning female parts. Guilt? Phantom ovulation? She reminded herself that the doctor today had said that her infertility was not wholly age-related. "It's quite possible that you'd never have been able to bear a child, although your condition is aggravated by age." Perhaps my guilt at waiting so long to try to conceive is misplaced, she told herself, and tried to believe it.

Not that her mother would ever believe that. Her mother would be more than eager to tell her not only that it was all her own fault but also that Belle had warned her. Belle wasn't *always* right, but she was right often enough and vocal enough about it so that she seemed unassailable. Belle was a smart mother, but not a comforting one. Karen felt tears rise in her eyes, although she never cried. Instead, she took a steadying deep breath and blinked. At her age she was experienced enough to know that very few people had anything close to a good relationship with their parents, but at this moment she longed for a bosom she could weep on without constraint, blame, or guilt. No wonder men came to women for comfort: the lure of the breast was powerful. Yet Karen would never go to Belle for solace. Maybe it was no accident that Belle was so flat-chested. No lure there, Karen thought. Well, if men go to women for comfort, where do women go?

To their girlfriends. Karen had three: Lisa, her sister; Defina; and Carl, who was not anatomically female but could certainly pass for one in almost every other way. But Defina was still celebrating last night; Carl, though always ready to listen, was all the way over in Brooklyn; while at this moment Lisa was out on Long Island with Belle, waiting for Karen's arrival. Karen sighed. Her stomach still felt as if it were to heave. There would be no comfort until she got home to Jeffrey late tonight. And maybe not then. Because while he always reassured her on other issues, this was one he was too intimately involved in to be counted on. Their shared baby-making odyssey had tried his patience to the breaking point and put more of a strain on their marriage than she'd like to admit.

"Mrs. Kahn?" there was a question in the nurse's voice, and Karen knew she'd have to act as if the room wasn't spinning around her. But could she get up from the damn chair without blowing chunks across the glossy magazines on the coffee table? Maybe it would pass for morning sickness. More like mourning sickness, Karen realized. The woman sitting beside her, the only one not appearing frightened, the one who was very obviously pregnant, turned her blonde head and raised her almost transparent eyebrows. She was reading the style section of the *New York Times*, which carried a long report on the Oakley Award. Yes, she was putting it together, Karen could see. Yes, I am Karen Kahn. *That* Mrs. Kahn. Great, Karen thought. Now she'd get to read about this visit in tomorrow's Liz Smith column. She could just picture the item: "What top Seventh Avenue designer was seen at New York's chicest infertility clinic?"

She looked back at the pregnant woman beside her. There ought to be a law that infertility clinics sent their success stories elsewhere instead of flaunting them in front of us, the barren ones, Karen thought. There also ought to be a law that famous people, or even semi-famous ones, could not be stared at when they were in moments of extreme pain. Karen sighed. Yeah, and while she was at it, why not pass a law against childhood leukemia and racial cleansing? This was the downside of celebrity, Karen. Live with it.

Get up, she told herself. Don't puke, don't trip, and don't give this albino breeding bitch a chance to ask if you can get maternity clothes for her at wholesale. Somehow Karen's knees found the strength to propel her upward and she crossed the room in three long strides. Karen was a big girl, tall, with long legs, and—despite constant dieting attempts—she was far from thin. That was why she knew how to design clothes that minimized thighs and camouflaged waistlines. Now, she clutched her layered cashmere sweaters and matching shawl around her as if they were armor.

"Yes?" she asked the nurse who gave her a professionally bright smile as if it didn't matter that this was the worst day of Karen's life. The best night, followed by the worst day. Twenty-four rocky hours. "That will be seven hundred and forty-three dollars," the woman said pleasantly, without shame. Karen unzipped her De Vecchi bag and pulled out her checkbook. She fumbled for her Mont Blanc but couldn't find it. The nurse, still smiling brightly, slipped her a Bic. Karen noticed her own hands were shaking. She tried to write out "7" on the amount line and it looked more like a snake that had been mashed on the roadway than a number. It was hopeless. She tore the check out and into two pieces, threw the cheap pen on the desk, and chucked the pigskin checkbook back into her bag.

"Bill me," she said, and her anger gave her enough energy to make it through the door to the elevator and down into the lobby of the building. How could they make you pay to get this news? Her lip trembled, but she wouldn't cry. She never cried. She walked out of the building and onto Park

Avenue. The awning over the door was flapping in the wind and a fine rain had begun to spray everything the brown-gray color, like wet wood smoke, that painted New York on its bad rainy afternoons.

Perfect, she thought. I'll never get a cab to Penn Station in this. I should have taken a limo, just like Jeffrey had suggested. But Karen hated to keep the driver waiting. It wasn't that she was cheap—it was simply an embarrassment to her. The idea of a bus or, worse yet, the subway, made her so dizzy she thought she might fall onto the wet concrete. New York is unlivable, she thought, and every place else is worse. I should have gotten the limo and taken it. Not just to here and the station, but all the way to Long Island. What the hell is wrong with me? I can't give myself a break. Karen Kahn, woman of the people. That's my father's influence. Karen felt a wave of self-pity wash over her, and with it all her reserve of strength was gone. "Please," she said aloud. "Please."

And her prayer was answered. A taxi pulled up to the canopy and two men stepped out, leaving it vacant for her. She got into it gratefully and took a deep breath. "Penn Station," she told the driver, who was dressed in the native garb of some Third World country that she would not be able to identify on a map. He nodded and she hoped he had a clue how to find their destination.

She leaned back into the impossibly uncomfortable seat. What an irony it was that her one prayer had been for a taxi. Just my luck, she thought. Major unanswered wishes in my life and *that's* the one I make when the Wish Fairy is feeling generous. Too bad I hadn't wished for a baby.

She glanced at her wristwatch, a chunky antique gold man's Rolex—the only thing that made her big wrist look small. The cab was crawling through the usual midtown war zone. She'd never make the 4:07. She would be late.

Well, what else was new? She habitually ran late. Fashionably late. Jeffrey always told her she tried to do too much. But after all these years, Belle still got in a frenzy whenever Karen was tardy. That's what Belle called it and through pursed lips expostulated: "There is no need for tardiness." Sometimes Belle sounded exactly like a second-grade teacher, which was exactly what she had been when she first met her husband. But once they adopted Karen, Belle had never taught again, at least not professionally. She had taught Karen how to dress; how to make hospital corners on sheets ("Fitted sheets are for lazy women"); how to properly polish good leather shoes; how to wax her legs; how to set a table; how to write a thank-you note; how to correctly sew on a button; and a million other small but unforgettable life lessons. In some ways, Belle was born to teach.

Maybe that was her problem as a mother, Karen thought. Belle only had the two of us to work on. It got too concentrated, too intense. She should have spread it around among a class of thirty children every year. It certainly would have taken some of the pressure off Karen and her younger sister, Lisa. But if Belle had worked, would Lisa have been conceived at all?

Karen stopped herself. There I go, blaming my job for my infertility. Karen reminded herself again that the doctor had said the problem was not entirely age-based; that it was probably congenital. How had he put it? That "it was aggravated by age." Well, she was aggravated, all right. Karen couldn't put the idea out of her mind that if only she and Jeffrey had tried earlier, if they had put just a little of their effort into reproduction instead of into the business, that they might have succeeded. She was famous—infamous really—for never taking "no" for an answer. "If you don't take no, you've got to get a yes," she often told her staff. But she'd have to take a "no" on this.

Of course, they could try to go the petri dish route. But Karen knew that Jeffrey would be opposed, and she was herself. After all, with all the unwanted babies, all the hungry and homeless in the world, how could she justify spending thousands just to try to perpetuate her genes. Somehow, it didn't work for her. Not that there were any guarantees, any way.

If only I'd tried earlier, Karen thought. If only I'd . . .

That's crazy, she told herself. That's the backlash of guilt women feel if they can't do everything perfectly. Look at Connie Chung. Is she busy hating herself this afternoon? You'll drive yourself *meshuggah* with this, so stop it.

The taxi jerked to a halt behind a bus that was belching black smoke and also had one of those annoying John Weitz ads staring at her. The cab was still three long blocks from Penn Station and they were the three cross-town blocks of Thirty-Third Street that would be hell on a rainy Friday. Fuck it, Karen murmured to herself, and leaned forward, putting her face close to the hole in the bullet-proof plexiglass partition that separated her from the driver. "How much to drive to Long Island?" she asked.

"JFK?" he questioned with a voice that rose in a hopeful Pakistani-like lilt.

"No. Rockville Centre. On Long Island. Only a little further than JFK," she lied. But she was desperate. Still, she wondered if she had enough cash. One of the perks of success: Karen hadn't been in a bank in years. Her secretary got her cash, but Karen perennially ran short of it. She'd made a habit of tucking folded hundred-dollar bills into the zipper compartments of all her purses. Emergency money. She opened this one and, sure enough, there was the hundred. She took it out, unfolded the crisp creases, and showed it to the driver, slipping part of it into the little scoop for the fare. He eyed it hungrily and turned off the meter.

"How we go?" he asked. The accent didn't really sound Pakistani. And that odd bolero jacket he was wearing was interesting. If it was done in a faille. . . . Anyway, he wasn't Pakistani. Maybe Afghan. They drove camels, not Buicks, didn't they?

"Through the midtown tunnel, then the L.I.E. Not too far," she lied again. Well, it would probably take less time to get to Rockville Centre than it would to get across Manhattan. And she just might, with luck (and if they beat the traffic even by only a few minutes), make it to Belle's house in time for dinner.

To her relief, the driver agreed. Karen directed him to turn east instead of west and leaned back on the thinly cushioned plastic seat, clutching her hands over her perpetually empty womb. It will be okay, she told herself. Jeffrey will understand. He won't be too disappointed and we can start to talk about adoption. We may be a little old for the Spence-Chapin agency's standards but Sid could probably arrange a private adoption, or know lawyers who do. Money would be no object and they would have their baby. It will be all right, Karen told herself. She wouldn't take "no" for an answer.

The approach to the Midtown tunnel was utter chaos—Karen imagined it looked like the final evacuation of Saigon. The cabbie lurched behind a huge eighteen-wheeler and jockeyed into position. The fumes were unbearable. Karen watched as all that metal tried to insert itself into the narrow tunnel opening. It was a lot like the medical procedures she'd been through lately, she thought with pain. Not that they'd done any good. She sighed. As the taxi began to inch its way into the mouth of the tunnel, the radio with its ghastly music cut off. Karen, grateful, closed her eyes against the glare of the tunnel lights and waited while the double-lane procession of vehicles made their escape from New York.

At last the cab surged out of the Midtown tunnel toward the L.I.E. The misty rain was turning to a deluge, and in less than twenty minutes Karen knew that the VanWyck Expressway would be flooded, as would the B.Q.E. The infrastructure of the city was falling to shit. "Hurry," she told the driver, trying to beat both the rain and the rush hour. "Hurry," she said aloud again, and tried to believe that once she got to her mother's it would all be all right.

3

CUT FROM A DIFFERENT CLOTH

Karen Kahn, nee Lipsky, had been adopted by Belle and Arnold Lipsky when she was already three-and-a-half years old. That was late for an adoption. She had very few memories of her early childhood and none of that time before she lived at 42–33 Ocean Avenue in Brooklyn with Belle and Arnold. She wasn't sure if that was normal or not, but she figured that the trauma of leaving one home for another would be enough to produce early amnesia in any child. She knew, vaguely, that she'd been fostered out, but her real memories began with Belle: Belle pushing her down Ocean Avenue toward Prospect Park in a stroller. At almost four years old, Karen must have been too big for one, but perhaps Belle had wanted to pretend that Karen was still a baby. Perhaps Karen herself had wanted to pretend it.

What she could remember clearly was the stroller, its blue and white stripes and the silly bobble fringe on the sunroof. With it, she remembered the bells of the Bungalow Bar ice cream man, and the fascinating little house—complete with shingled roof—on the back of his truck. She remembered her mother handing her that first creamsicle, and the pleasure she got not just from the taste but from the contrast of the bright orange ice and soft, white creamy center.

From around that time she could also remember an early morning visit to the Botanical Gardens: the lilacs had just come into flower and she had darted among several enormous bushes, delighted by the smell of the flowers and the exquisite colors that the purple fountain of blossoms made against the satiny green leaves. She had laughed and run from bush to bush—until she glanced around and noticed that Belle was nowhere to be seen. Alone, Karen remembered how the bushes took on an ominous look, hunching over her menacingly, and she had begun to cry. When Belle found her, she had scolded Karen both for running ahead *and* for crying.

Belle Lipsky was not, perhaps, the ideal maternal figure. Small-boned and thin, she was always immaculately groomed and dressed in coordinated ensembles. She wasn't pretty—her features were too sharp, too pinched—but she was what people back then called "well put together." Karen had always been proud of how Belle looked, her attitude. Karen particularly remembered Belle's hats—already *de trop* back in the fifties, Belle had been loathe to give them up, and Karen, back then, had thought they were the height of elegance. But the hats, like all of Belle's clothes, were "for looking, not for touching." From her earliest years, Karen knew that she was expected to keep Belle's and her own clothes clean and her room neat. Belle was a neatness fanatic and their Brooklyn apartment had been as sterile as Belle's reproductive system was.

Belle and Arnold had been married for only a year when they adopted Karen. It had always been odd and embarrassing to Karen that she was older in years than her parents' marriage, but they seemed not to discuss it, and so neither did she. Once Belle had joked that Karen had just come into the family fashionably late. Karen knew better than to ask questions. In fact, she had been taught to discuss nothing unpleasant or upsetting. Questions about her adoption were discouraged. Growing up had been all about keeping still, keeping clean, and keeping quiet. Arnold was himself a very quiet man and both he and Karen knew that if there was any talking that was going to be done it would be done by Belle.

Belle was not, by any means, a neglectful mother. It was just that there were certain areas she had interest in and others that left her cold. There was much they did together. She read aloud to Karen. (After all, she *had* been a school teacher.) They took walks together, and shopped for clothes. Karen was always dressed to perfection, at least until she began to assert a taste very different from Belle's. But up to the time she was eleven or twelve, she and her mother made weekly forays to downtown Brooklyn and ransacked Abraham & Strauss. More exciting to Karen were the special Saturdays when they went into Manhattan. Then they tore through S. Klein, Altman's, Orbach's, and Lord & Taylor's before stopping for lunch at the Fifth Avenue Schraft's, where Belle always ordered a celebratory Shirley Temple for Karen and a whisky sour for herself. They had been good companions on those trips and Karen had learned not only to wait patiently while Belle tried on a myriad of outfits, but also to critically appraise them at Belle's request. Sometimes she wondered if that's where her interest in clothes began. Had she always had a talent for fashion? Or had Belle developed it? Because, back then, Belle had always listened soberly to Karen's assessment.

If Belle was obsessed with shopping, Karen became equally engrossed in fashion. She collected dozens of paper dolls, and designed clothes for all of them, but paper wasn't real, wasn't sensual. She loved the feel of real fabrics and the numberless combinations of colors and textures. To this day, Karen believed that fashion began with the cloth, that within the fabric was the center from which she spun every outfit. Unlike Belle, she didn't want to own clothes; she just liked looking at them and being around them. Karen felt as if she had grown up with her head tucked under a rack of clothing, surrounded by Belle's rejects and selections, and that from her earliest times nothing had interested her more than the drape of a fabric, the contrast of piping, and the way a seam was cut.

Back on Ocean Avenue, Karen had longed for access to Belle's closet, a walk-in that was off-limits to her. In it, Belle arranged every garment based on its color, style, and use. Not all blouses hung together; the ones that were made to go with suits hung with their matching jackets. But all skirts were separated, for some reason only known to Belle, from the rest of their ensemble and lined up along one rod, all on their own. It was an arrangement as inflexible and confusing to Karen as the Dewey Decimal System at the Brooklyn Public Library. Belle's shoes, scarves, belts, and stockings were all arranged in meticulous order. Her mother would have known in a moment if Karen had touched anything. Belle never wore slacks—she was too short for them, she said—but she had dozens of silk dresses that Karen longed to touch and play with. Not to mention the hats. The closet was a place of wonders. But though mother and daughter shared shopping jaunts, they had never played dress-up. Belle wasn't a playful woman.

The taxi was approaching the Rockville Centre exit. The driver was talking to himself under his breath. Karen prayed that he wasn't outraged enough by the length of the trip to dump her there, at the side of the Expressway. The rain had turned into a downpour. Karen felt as fragile as Tennessee Williams' Blanche DuBois; and like Blanche, at that moment Karen was dependent on the kindness of strangers.

She directed the muttering driver the rest of the way and at last the taxi pulled up to the brick house with the carefully pruned hedges. Karen gave the guy the hundred and pointed the way back. She got out of the cab with relief and turned toward the house. Through the darkness, the lights of the living room chandelier glimmered. Her mother and her sister were waiting for her.

Karen sighed. Even if Belle was undemonstrative and almost anally neat, she had at least shared *something* with Karen. Their interest in clothes had been a bond—if only for a time. And if it wasn't quite twenty-four-karat unconditional mother love, at least it had stood them in good stead for many years.

All that, of course, had changed when Lisa was born.

Karen's sister, Lisa, looked nothing like her. Well, of course she wouldn't. I was adopted, Karen reminded herself, but it still sometimes surprised her to see Lisa after a long absence. They were so very different. Now Lisa, tiny and petite as ever, stood in their mother's living room. She was one of those small-boned, taut, thin Jewish women—if Jewish-American princess was listed in the dictionary, they'd use Lisa's picture to illustrate it. In fact, Lisa looked a lot like their mother who, at sixty-four, still had the slender figure of a girl and the nervous energy that kept her movements youthful.

Lisa looked across the overdone, mirrored living room and smiled. "Look who's here!" she cried. She was pretty, and sometimes Karen wondered if all of her own designs, which did so much for tall women and so little for petite ones, were not an unconscious hostile response to Lisa's looks. Karen loved her sister, but Lisa had always had it easy. Six years younger than Karen, she had been an unexpected surprise to her parents, who had long before accepted their barren marriage and compromised with Karen's adoption. Lisa's appearance had been an incredible renewal, a vindication of Belle's femaleness just at the time when other women were starting to contemplate menopause. The pregnancy had given Belle not only a glow, but also a perfect little baby to dress up, play with, and show off. Just at the time when Karen was moving into her gawky stubborn stage, Belle was rewarded and distracted with an easy baby.

Lisa had accepted all the bows and frills that Karen had already begun to reject. She still wore them. Lisa went along with all of her mother's sugges-tions and seemed always to do things the easy way: she got B's in school, went to Hofstra University for only a year, and her "career" had been running her own small boutique. She married Leonard when he was out of medical school and retired early to have her daughters, just like her mother. And she was clearly her mother's favorite.

At least that was the way Karen saw it. Lisa, she knew, felt that *Karen* had always been favored. That it was *Karen*, as eldest, who got most of the atten-tion, was considered the smart, the talented, the successful one. My mother has a political gift, Karen thought, and had to smile: Belle could simultane-ously make her two daughters feel the other had most-favored-nation status. But maybe that wasn't just Belle. Maybe it had more to do with us as sisters.

Older versus younger. Adopted verses natural. Perhaps sisters *never* worked this shit out, Karen reflected as she smiled back at Lisa. Underneath all of it, Karen knew she loved Lisa dearly. She had loved her and taken care of her from the first time she saw her, a tiny infant.

"How was your day?" Belle asked.

Karen thought of the abortion of a fitting session she'd struggled through with Elise Elliot, her most important new client, an argument with Jeffrey, and the horror at the clinic, but she managed a smile. "Great," she said, because from long experience she knew that was the only answer Belle was equipped to deal with. "How was yours?"

"Great," Belle answered brightly. "We went all the way over to Neiman-Marcus. Lisa bought me a great outfit. She *insisted.*"

"It was on sale," Lisa said, and shrugged as if to say it wasn't a big deal.

Still crazy after all these years. Karen couldn't get over their insatiable need to shop. Karen shrugged. Before she was a name, she had made the effort to get the two of them into most of the Seventh Avenue showrooms, despite the trouble and ill-will it often caused. Like the notorious Gabor sisters, her mother and sister had developed a reputation for returning more stuff than they bought. But Karen at last had come to understand that shopping for them, as for so many women, was a highly developed bonding activity. It was like men with sports: a father could be completely out of touch with his son's internal life but they could always manage a conversation about those Mets. Lisa and Belle bonded by shopping. It was unfortunate that Karen and her mother, as adults, had no longer been able to do that shopping gig. Since Karen's interest in design had deepened, Karen had become, in Belle's words, "too particular." And "too dull. You need some color." Color to Belle meant red and aqua and royal blue. Even now, when women paid thousands of dollars for Karen's unique vision, her exquisitely modulated color sense, Belle had never really acknowledged that Karen's taste had been anything but difficult to understand.

She managed to smile at her mother. "Where's Dad?" Karen asked.

"Oh, you know your father. Working late on somebody's stinking case." After more than forty years of marriage Belle had still not forgiven Arnold for only being a labor lawyer, "not a *real* lawyer," as Belle often pointed out. He'd never joined a Park Avenue firm and done lucrative corporate work. He'd formed his own labor practice and, worse, did a lot of pro bono. "A Harvard lawyer! He could have made millions," Belle always said regretfully.

"So, are we eating?" Belle asked them now. She moved through the arch to the dining room, where three places were set on the mahogany Sheraton-style table. The china was lovely—Royal Doulton—and the crystal gleamed. A tiny cachepot of violets sat at each place. Belle set a pretty table but she was less than a wiz in the kitchen. Food represented mess and bother: she'd discovered frozen entrées long before anyone else and served what Karen always thought of as "hospital meals": the portions were small but no one complained because the food was so bland. And there were *never* any leftovers. Arnold didn't seem to mind—aside from his work, Karen's father noticed few details and often ate out. She'd been left on her own to Belle's culinary torture.

As a kid in Brooklyn, Karen had made a habit of hoarding chocolate and Bit-O-Honey bars from the neighborhood candy store. That way she always had something to eat when faced with Belle's empty refrigerator. Karen had relied on the sugar. When they had moved to Rockville Centre, in the sixties, it had been harder to get a fix. There were no stores within easy walking distance of their new suburban house and kids were not allowed to leave the junior high school during the day. Karen had gone into acute sugar withdrawal and lost a few pounds—to her mother's delight—before she found a fat friend, Carl, who kept her supplied. Carl's dad owned a deli/butcher shop and Carl could take anything he wanted from the shelves. A friend with greed was a friend indeed.

Karen was still what her mother called "a big girl." At five ten, she towered over Belle and Lisa. Though she had slimmed down a lot, she still wasn't thin and had accepted that she never would be. Yet even now, the two small, dark, thin women made her feel out of scale. She felt better when they all sat down.

There were so many, many evenings when they had sat down to a dinner like this: "the three girls" as Belle had called them. It was funny, Karen thought, how often Belle spoke in the third person or indirectly. "The three girls are going shopping," she would say as they drove to Alexander's or Loehman's. If she swerved in traffic, Belle would say, "She better watch where she's going" or "She better keep her eyes on the road." Belle was, no doubt about it, as distant from herself as she was from her daughters. Karen sighed. She would have liked to see her dad tonight. They didn't talk very much, except about work, but Arnold had a solid presence, a calmness and comforting size that Belle lacked. Tonight, after the horrible news from the clinic and the cold, rainy ride, her father's empty place at the table reflected his absence from her life so much of the time; it felt achingly familiar. It wasn't that he didn't love her, she supposed. It was just that he was never around. No wonder she had always been so pathetically grateful for attention from men.

But it wasn't just that. She couldn't blame Arnold. Lisa had always been able to play hard to get and she had never had attention from their father either. Was it genetic, or just her good looks? Even now, with Lisa's fine skin beginning to show those tiny wrinkles at the eyes and the slightest beginnings of puckering around the mouth, Lisa was still attractive enough to turn any man's head. Even so, it was Lisa's elder daughter—who had not just her face but also Arnold's tall, lanky body—who was going to be the real beauty of the family.

As if she was reading Karen's mind, Lisa looked up and smiled. "I can't tell you how thrilled Stephanie is about her intern job." Stephie—who wasn't doing well in high school—had opted for a work study program. She was to work part-time at Karen's.

"Isn't it dangerous, her going into the city like that alone every day?" Belle asked. Still rooted in Long Island, Lisa and her family lived in Inwood.

"Oh, Ma. She's almost seventeen. She'll be a senior in high school next year. All the kids in her class have jobs. But they're stuck at Burger Kings and J.C. Penney's. I think she can negotiate the four blocks from Penn Station to Karen's showroom."

"Oh, don't tell me. A *schvartzer* could grab her at any minute."

"Mother! Not '*schvartzer.*' 'Black.' You can't call black people 'schvartzers' anymore."

"Why not?" asked Belle. "It means the same thing."

Karen shook her head. How had Arnold put up with Belle for all those years? Karen knew there was no sense talking to her mother. She may as well talk to her own ovaries. Nothing would change. And technically Belle was right, *schvartzer* did mean "black" in Yiddish, but the connotation was all wrong and completely different. Belle was an expert in the letter-of-the-law arguments: as a kid, Karen nearly had apoplexy trying to get Belle to admit to hypocrisy or unfairness in her positions. Belle couldn't or wouldn't acknowledge them. She spoke, for instance, about how the family had left Brooklyn because of "the element." Belle would have been shocked and disgusted by anyone who said "nigger," but wasn't her code just an epithet by another name? Belle never specified exactly what "the element" was, just that "the element" had changed. When Karen had studied high school chemistry and gotten to the periodic table, she had asked her mother which of the elements on it they had been escaping from. Belle hadn't seen the humor. Humor was never Belle's strong suit.

Karen looked over at the woman and suddenly wondered if her real mother was so . . . so Belle-ish. It wasn't that Karen didn't love and appreciate Belle. She was grateful. After all, Belle had taken her in and cared for her and educated her and taught her so many things. Despite Belle's prejudices and her third-person disembodiment, Belle was a careful, involved mother. Sometimes *too* involved. Karen felt guilty for being critical of Belle in any way. But wasn't that the unnatural inheritance of an adopted child: we couldn't afford to reject a mother when we had already been rejected by one.

Now Belle picked up the salad plates and compulsively wiped up a miniscule spot of salad dressing beside Karen's place. It was a silent rebuke. Then Belle went out to the kitchen for the next equally small course.

Lisa looked across the table at Karen and shrugged. They understood that there was no changing Belle. Lisa lowered her voice. "Are you all right?" she asked. Karen shook her head. "What?" Lisa's face tightened with concern. "The doctor?"

"Not now," Karen told her, and jerked her chin toward Belle in the kitchen. "Talk about something else."

Lisa nodded and raised her voice to a normal level. "I really mean it about the job for Stephanie. She needs something like this and I won't lie. The money will come in handy."

Lisa was always short of money. It confused Karen. Leonard had to be doing very well, but somehow it seemed that Lisa was always in some sort of trouble with her Bendel's account or her Bloomingdale's card or her other bills. Still, she kept on spending. Karen knew that long ago Lisa had begun smuggling in any new clothing purchases and hiding them around the house. She'd told Karen that since she had no money of her own, she had to beg Leonard for cash. Karen almost visibly shuddered when she thought of living like that, but Lisa seemed to prefer to have too little money and too much time on her hands than to go out and get a job. Since closing her little boutique—more a hobby than a business—she had not worked. The idea of working seemed to fill her with horror. Karen had to smile. My sister Lisa: a Jewish, female, Maynard G. Krebbs.

Belle returned with the inevitable plates of desiccated chicken. Beside the flat, white breast there was some punished broccoli. Belle believed that nothing should be cooked *al dente* except perhaps her Jell-O, which was frighteningly chewable. To this day Karen didn't know her mother's secret for creating that leathery skin on a gelatin cup.

"I'm looking forward to spending more time with Stephanie," Karen said aloud. Actually, she had some reservations about hiring her niece as an intern. And Jeffrey was furious about it. "The girls in the showroom are competitive and jealous already," he had said to her. "We don't need this." He was probably right, but Jeffrey had never really liked Lisa or Leonard. He considered them both too provincial and too materialistic, and he thought their kids were spoiled. "Plus, it certainly won't help Tiffany's self-image," he had added as an afterthought, referring to Lisa's other daughter. Karen had to agree with that.

"How's Tiff?" Karen asked now. Tiffany was Lisa's younger daughter, her fat one. Built kind of like Karen, the girl was already at thirteen almost as tall as her sister, Stephanie, and had to be double Stephanie's weight. There was no doubt that Tiff was bright, and she did well academically, but there was no denying she was troubled. Except, of course, by Belle, who insisted Tiff's weight was simply a question of lack of willpower and spite.

"She's fine," Lisa said, but her voice tightened.

"She's *fat* is what she is," Belle said, and stabbed at the dried-out piece of chicken on her plate. "Fat and cranky."

For a moment, Karen felt dizzy—almost as if she might faint. She'd heard this, just this and just like this, before. This is *déjà vu,* she thought. Or perhaps it had actually happened. Then it came to her. She had sat there so many evenings when she herself had been a teenager and Belle had called her fat and cranky in exactly that same dismissive tone of voice.

When Lisa had been no more than a toddler and Karen had started the rocky preteen years, she and Belle had begun to disagree for the first time. Most kids had fights over clothes with their parents but with Belle and Karen fights took on epic proportions. Arnold, predictably, refused to participate. A labor lawyer and negotiator, he refused to negotiate at home. His abstention meant, for all intents and purposes, that Belle had the field all to herself. The battles were all about appearances and control. Belle had threatened, cajoled, ridiculed and then gone back to threatening, all to get Karen to "dress properly," to diet. And to give up the idea of Pratt and go for one of the Seven Sisters colleges. But, along with some of her baby fat and her status as an only child, in her teen years Karen had lost her eagerness to please. She was a rock, and when she started wearing thrift shop looks, Belle went ballistic. Remembering it now, Karen shook her head. There had been so much animosity over what had only amounted to a normal passing phase.

Mrs. Watson had saved Karen. A WASP, one of the few left in the suburban town, Ann Watson had lived in the only old house on the street—a white-pillar Georgian that was as disheveled as its owner—a birdlike older woman who drank most of her days away. Once the land the Lipskys' house sat on had been part of the Watson estate. Now Mrs. Watson's lawn was weedy and smaller in size than the other plots, sold off one by one. But Mrs. Watson had taught Karen to play bridge, taught her about couture, about why the tatty Aubusson rugs on *her* floors were better than Belle's spotless wall-to-wall, and she had given Karen her cast-off Chanel jackets (the skirts were too small), which Karen had worn with work shirts and jeans. Mrs. Watson had approved. "You," she'd said, squinting at Karen over the top of her daiquiri glass, "*you* have a gift. Natural style." Mrs. Watson had been a refuge.

And Mrs. Watson had given Karen a major gift: a window to view her own future. Mrs. Watson told Karen about Coco Chanel, and Karen—not a great reader—went to the library and read everything she could about the design great. Gabrielle Chanel became Karen's idol, her avatar. All the paper doll drawings, all the looking at clothes and fabrics came together and made sense. Mrs. Watson was the compass who showed Karen her true direction. Karen saw that there was a job she could do, a thing she could be that she *wanted*.

Of course, Belle had never approved of Mrs. Watson. *"Alte goyem,"* she'd said. Whenever the woman's name was mentioned, Belle made the same face, one of distaste, that she was making now about Tiffany.

"Fat and cranky," Belle repeated. Both of her daughters ignored her.

"So when do you leave for Paris?" Lisa asked. She, too, wanted the focus of the conversation to change.

"Not until the end of the month, and not then if things continue this way. I can't seem to pull the line together this season. Wouldn't you know this is the year we pick to do our first show in Paris. Home of Coco Chanel and Worth, and I'm going to show them some *farshlugginer* wrap dress." Karen thought of the Oakley Award night—less than twenty-four hours before, back in the Mesozoic period—and sighed. What had happened to her enthusiasm? Her confidence? Had it drained out somewhere in Dr. Goldman's office? "A designer is only as good as her latest line," she said.

"Oh, you say that every season," Lisa tut-tutted.

"Maybe you're *not* ready," Belle opined.

Karen shook her head and wondered how it could be that both her sister's unquestioning faith in her *and* her mother's lack of same offended. I must be unreasonable in my expectations, she told herself. And today has certainly not been a good day. But it seemed as if, after all this time, Lisa still expected Karen to be able to do anything effortlessly and Belle still assumed Karen was the toddler lost in the lilac bushes. Karen sighed. Well, she reminded herself, you're not the only one from a dysfunctional family. Ask John Bradshaw.

She thought again for a moment about her real mother and wondered if at this very moment the woman was harping at her own daughter, the one she had not given away to strangers. Karen remembered—or thought she did—cuddling up to a neck she'd once held and the smell of powder on her real mother's skin. She remembered a green toy frog. Maybe, just maybe, she remembered the yellow and white alternating bars of a crib, and her hand extended through them to the big warm hand of her real mother. Had that really happened? What is she doing now, Karen wondered, and then forced herself to look up and join the conversation.

"I wish *I* could go to Paris," Lisa was saying. "We haven't been since our honeymoon. But Leonard says that with this *bat mitzvah* expense there's no way we're taking a vacation this year." Karen wondered if she was supposed to chime in with an invitation to France, but before she had a chance to think about it further . . .

"You're spending too much on this, anyway. What do you need buses for?"

"Buses?" Karen asked.

"To take people from the synagogue to the affair," Lisa explained.

Belle tsked and moved them back to Tiffany. "What is she wearing for the ceremony?" she was asking. "Not that green taffeta, I hope."

"Mother, she *likes* it."

"She looks terrible in it, and she'll have those pictures the rest of her life. She'll resent you for not telling her. Her children will ask her how her mother let her wear that dress."

"It's a Ralph Lauren."

"Yes, and it's designed for a little Christmas *shiksa*. Who can wear plaid, especially a green and red taffeta plaid?" Belle turned to Karen. "Am I right?"

"I haven't seen the dress," Karen said, and heard Arnold's old tone of neutrality in her own voice. Like Switzerland and Arnold, Karen didn't want to be dragged into a World War.

"Come and look at what *I'm* going to wear," Belle said, and she and Lisa immediately stood up. There was never a regret about leaving Belle's table. Slowly, Karen followed the two women as they trooped down the hall, through the master bedroom, to that holy of holies, Belle's closet. Since Brooklyn, it had grown and was now an entire guest room that adjoined the master suite. In it were custom-made shelves for each pair of Belle's shoes, all of which were kept immaculately on shoe trees and wrapped in clear plastic shoe bags. There were custom-made drawers: wide flat ones that held Belle's scarves and narrower, deep ones for her sweaters. She had one wall sectioned off into cubicles, each of which held a purse and matching gloves. There was even a shelf across the top of one wall that had hat stands attached at the base, so that Belle's few remaining hats were displayed, although each was only marginally visible, swathed in polyethylene film.

This closet had once been Karen's bedroom. Lisa's old room held Belle's coats and jackets. Belle had not yet sprung for a moving rack, like they had at the dry-cleaners, but Karen knew her mother had been thinking about it. The most amazing thing to Karen was that Belle still knew every item in the closet, when she had last worn it, where, and with whom. No wonder she had quit teaching school so long ago. Belle's closet was a full-time job.

Karen remembered reading that in later life Coco Chanel had moved into the Ritz Hotel but that she kept all but a few of her clothes across the street in an apartment at 31 Rue Cambon. But Coco's life had been the *creation* of those clothes—she had no daughters, no husband, no family. Yet Belle's clothes filled all the space left when Karen and Lisa moved out. Sometimes Karen wondered if Belle eventually would fill the whole house with her wardrobe and buy the old Watson place to live in.

"Hallo. Hallo." Arnold's yodel came down the hallway, followed by Arnold himself. Karen's adoptive father was a big man—more than six two—but he slumped so much that it was hard to know just how tall he was. He wore suits that must have been unrumpled at one time but not in the last decade. Even Belle, with her compulsive neatness, couldn't keep Arnold looking tidy. Now he came in, his battered briefcase under one arm, two wrinkled newspapers under the other. "I should have known you'd be in here," Arnold said and smiled. He looked tired. When he bent down to kiss Karen, she saw the darkness under his eyes.

He was a good man. When she was young, in her grammar school years, Karen would sometimes go with Arnold on the weekends to his office. He would take time out on those days to explain about the rights of workers and the power of unions. She still remembered the poem he had mounted on the back of his office door. It was by Margaret Widdemer, written back in 1915, around the time of the Triangle fire. Karen couldn't remember all of it, but two lines were still clear: *I have shut my little sister in from life and light/ (For a rose, for a ribbon, for a wreath across my hair).* Long ago, Karen had seen the irony in the fact that Arnold had spent his life trying to protect garment workers, while Belle kept shopping for a deal that had to be based on their exploitation.

"You're home?" Belle asked, unnecessarily. "There's chicken," she added as an afterthought.

"I ate," Arnold told her. "Hi, honey," he said to Lisa, who had popped her head out of the closet to peck his cheek. Karen noticed that he didn't kiss Belle and Belle didn't make a move toward him. She was, after all, immersed in her Closetworld.

"I have work," Arnold said, turning his back on them.

"What else is new?" Belle murmured.

For a moment Karen wondered if the three of them—women together— had bewildered him and driven Arnold away, or whether he had simply learned to fill up the empty spaces. He was a nice man. She watched as his stooped and rumpled back departed down the hallway. Then Belle spoke up.

"*Now* she's going to show you something," Belle said, and both of her daughters knew that she was referring to herself. Lisa looked on attentively, but Karen sighed and backed out to the bedroom and sat down on the loveseat. There, on the lower shelf of the coffee table, as always, sat the leather-bound photograph album from the early days in Brooklyn. Belle wasn't proud of it and rarely took it out. Karen noticed it as if for the first time.

"So, what do you think?" Belle asked, and held up a David Hayes-like dress and jacket ensemble. Very Queen Elizabeth. Belle was nothing if not predictable. "Look at this," she said and showed them the jacket lining, a turquoise-on-black reversal of the black-on-turquoise pattern of the dress. Karen nodded, bored, but Lisa actually cooed encouragement.

"It's great."

Belle ducked her head back into the closet. In the moment they had alone, Lisa looked at Karen. "Call me tonight at home. Tell me what's up." Mutely, Karen nodded.

"And what do you think she found to go with it?" Belle asked, and Karen watched the two of them disappear into the closet again. In their absence, quick as a snake, Karen pulled out the old brown photo album and set it on her knees. She flipped it open to the first page, where four aging photographs showed Belle and Arnold on their wedding day. Karen had perused it all before, so she turned now to the manila envelope glued to the front inside cover. In it were loose pictures that Belle had never mounted but had also not been able to throw away. Karen heard her mother and sister exclaiming over something. In just a moment they would be expecting her to join in.

She put her hand into the envelope and pulled out a handful of black and white photos. Quickly, she fanned them out on her lap. There were two she was looking for. The first she found immediately: a picture of herself as a baby, two or perhaps a little younger. Belle must have gotten the photos from Karen's real mother. In one Karen was lying on her back in a crib and beside her was a rubber frog. The frog she remembered. Despite the black and white photograph, she knew it was dark green, the color of lilac leaves, except for the belly, which was a chartreuse, and the tongue, which was a bright, cherry red. She *remembered* that frog.

It took her longer to find the other photo. She was perhaps a little older in it, dressed in a snowsuit and standing in front of a doorway. It was a black and white photo, but Karen knew the snowsuit was royal blue. How old was she then? You could clearly see the brickwork of the wall and she was only six courses of brick high. On the door—a plain, black-painted, wooden one— were the numbers 2881. Karen grabbed the two photos, stuffed the rest of them back in the envelope, and had just managed to slip the album into its usual place when Belle and Lisa came out, her mother brandishing a turquoise suede clutch bag as if it were the Holy Grail.

"Look what she found!" Belle caroled, referring to herself and the bag.

Karen tapped the photos, safely tucked in her pocket. "Look what she found!" Belle repeated, and Karen nodded, wondering what she, herself had found.

4

THE CUTTING EDGE

The Lincoln Town Car pulled up to her West End Avenue apartment. Karen had called ahead from her mother's to have the car meet her at the L.I.R.R. station. She jumped out before the driver could run around and open the door for her. It was funny: Jeffrey insisted on a limo and never would open the door himself but Karen was equally insistent on the service sending nothing more than a black sedan. And she *never* let the drivers help her out. Arnold's influence? Maybe that was the difference between growing up with inherited wealth and growing up middle class: inherited wealth didn't mind letting other people do the work for them. Karen knew her biggest problem was what an expensive business consultant had called "her failure to delegate." But she just couldn't help it. She did the job better or faster or both if she did it herself, and at least that way she was certain it would get done. So why the hell should she be imprisoned in the goddamn Lincoln while Joey or Tim or Mohammad ran around to her door?

She stepped under the British racing green canopy of the co-op that she and Jeffrey lived in and, as always, got to the door before George the doorman opened it. Maybe, she reflected, it wasn't her failure to delegate but it was other people's incompetence that created her problems.

"Good evening, Mrs. Kahn!" George called out cheerfully, turning from the magazine she knew he had secreted in the credenza drawer, though he was strictly forbidden to read while on lobby duty.

The West Side had gentrified over the last decade, but plenty of homeless and the occasional junkie still wandered the streets. In New York City the doormen were required to be vigilant. She should report him for the clandestine magazine but she wouldn't. "Hello, George," Karen sighed and hit the elevator button just before he scuttled across the black and white marble tiled floor to it. She put her hand in her raincoat pocket and felt the crackle of the two old photos that were nestled there. They comforted her, a sort of psychological hand-warmer. The elevator door drew open and she stepped into the mahogany box while George pressed the seventh floor button for her with his white-gloved finger. "Thank you, George," she sighed and, mercifully, the elevator door rolled shut.

Karen had lived in the building since she and Jeffrey were first married. It was a huge step up from the Amsterdam Avenue walk-up she'd rented before. The down payment on the co-op had been the wedding gift of Jeffrey's parents, who had disapproved of Karen, the apartment, the neighborhood, and—most of all—the West Side address. "What's so wrong with Fifth Avenue?" Jeffrey's mother, Sylvia, had asked. "Or Park? We saw a lovely little three-bedroom that was reasonable. And you'll need the space once you start a family." But Karen had insisted on this West End Avenue apartment and Jeffrey had supported her. But then, Jeffrey had always liked the role of iconoclast.

It was more of a loft or *atelier* than a regular apartment, and Karen had loved it for its inconveniences as much as for its spectacular space. Who needed an eat-in kitchen? She never cooked. She had hundreds, maybe thousands, of books in the apartment but not a single cookbook. Instead, she had a loose-leaf binder with a take-out menu from every restaurant in New York City that delivered. They were arranged by country—Thai, Chinese, Mexican, etc. The apartment's tiny kitchen was just fine. A phone was the only kitchen appliance she needed.

She adored the place the first moment she'd seen it and still did. Sort of like her feelings for Jeffrey. Karen might be accused of making snap judgments, but no one could say she wasn't loyal. Now that they could afford something much more expensive, she regularly fought with Jeffrey, insisting on staying here. It was her haven.

She stepped out of the elevator into the tiny private foyer they shared only with old Mrs. Katz in the north-facing apartment. Karen put her key in the lock of 7S and opened the door. Before her was a thirty-foot expanse of parquet floor and a row of seven windows, each one tall enough to be a door. In fact, two of them in the center were French doors that, when opened, let out to a tiny Juliet balcony that looked down onto the tops of the ginko trees seven floors below. The doors were shuttered on the outside. She'd had them painted Charleston green—eight parts black and one part green, simultaneously chic and practical in dirty New York City. Window boxes of trailing white geraniums and ivy gave the place a park-like touch. On bright days sunlight poured through the windows and across the floor in a wonderful chiaroscuro.

The room was also graced with a soaring ceiling and served as both a living room and library. The north wall behind her was lined, floor to ceiling, with glass-fronted bookcases that were filled almost to overflowing. Two paintings—an early one of Jeffrey's and one by their friend Perry Silverman—hung on the white walls. Karen adored the Silverman for its wonderful depth of color. Other than that, the furnishings were spare indeed. There was a Donghia sofa that Karen's colleague Angelo had done for her back in the days when they were both young, struggling designers, before there were things like AIDS and infertility to worry about. The sofa was upholstered in a simple white linen but had a sinuous curve across its back that was almost female.

Along the right-hand wall there was a twelve-foot-long refectory table that she and Jeffrey had bought in France. Its top was made from three ancient, wide cherry boards that had been polished for two hundred years by French nuns who knew all that beeswax and elbow grease could accomplish. The lines of the table were simple yet elegant in the way that only the French achieved. The table was surrounded by a dozen white upholstered Parsons chairs. It was a bitch to keep the linen white on a New York dining room chair, but after every dinner party Karen did an inspection with club soda and Ivory Liquid in hand. And the trouble was worth it, because the crispness of the white cloth against the patina of the tabletop was magical.

The only other piece in the room was an incredibly ornate demilune console table situated against the left wall. Karen had fought for days with Jeffrey until he finally allowed her to buy it at the Christie's East auction. He had called it "campy" and "nellie" and "overdone." Everything but what he actually meant, which was "too Jewish." Jeffrey and his parents had what Karen thought of as Ralph Lauren Syndrome: the unbearable longing to be understated gentiles. In her opinion, it was a problem all too common among wealthy New York Jews.

It was the first time in their then-new marriage that they had had a big disagreement and it was the first time Jeffrey had fixed it by coming up with a Real Deal. From then on, whenever they made major compromises they always called them Real Deals. It was a serious kind of game they played throughout their marriage, a kind of formalized tit-for-tat. She could have this if he could have that. Jeffrey had given up his painting to manage her business but she had to give him free financial reign. She had agreed to build the

Westport house if he allowed her to keep their apartment. The demilune table was the first one of their compromises and in return for buying it she had to let him hang his friend Perry's painting, even though she didn't like it.

She'd gone to the auction without him, but once she got the crazy gilded thing into the apartment and put an enormous vase filled with white cala lilies and blue delphinium spikes in place, he had admitted that it was just the *outré* touch needed. And Karen smiled every time she looked at the grinning carved dolphins that supported the base of the zany piece. After a while she also found herself smiling at Perry's painting. She'd come to love it. In fact, though it made her feel guilty, she now liked it more than Jeffrey's painting, which she had tired of in time.

Off the apartment's living room there were two hallways: one led to the tiny windowless kitchen that had caused her mother-in-law such grief. The other led to an enfilade of doors, where the three bedrooms and a tiny maid's room were located. Karen used the maid's room as her at-home studio and simply kept the door closed on the chaos of fabrics, sketches, and trims that always littered the place. But both their bedroom and one of the guest rooms, which they used as a sitting room, were always immaculate. Her husband was *very* neat. Sometimes she thought she had married her mother. But didn't everybody?

"Jeffrey?" she called and he shouted out from down the hall. She took off her raincoat, her mushroom-colored cashmere jacket and shawl, and threw them on one of the dining room chairs. Then she threw herself onto the plump, down-filled cushions of the sofa, kicking off her suede wedgies before she put her feet up.

"You're home early," Jeffrey said from the doorway. "I just got in from work." He paused and looked at her. "Dinner go poorly? Lisa already called and said she wanted to talk to you. Didn't you talk over dinner?" He crossed the room and picked up her coat. Wordlessly he walked to the closet hidden behind the bookshelves and hung the jacket up. She felt the reproach. Never marry a man more fastidious than you are, she would advise a daughter, if she ever had one. Karen sighed.

"I couldn't take it anymore," she said. "Belle drives me crazy."

"Belle drives *everybody* crazy. It goes without saying."

She nodded. "How was work?" she asked him. Jeffrey had spent the morning taping his portion of Elle Halle's television program—they were both doing the interview—and the rest of the day away from his office, meeting with the NormCo people. The NormCo situation was one she'd rather not think about.

"Fine. Progress on all fronts."

"Did you say nice things about me to the television guys?"

"Well, I told them you were lousy in bed but a great cook."

"Two lies!" she cried and tried to take a swipe at him. She wondered what he *had* said to the TV cameras but knew she wouldn't get it out of him. He was a tease.

"How did the work on the Elliot fitting go?"

"That was lousy too." But not as lousy as going to the doctor, she thought. She didn't mention Goldman now. "Elise wasn't happy. Nothing is coming together for the collection. *And* Tangela was impossible."

"I don't know why you don't fire her."

"Well, for one thing, she's Defina's daughter. For another, when she's good, she's great. And she's no worse than any other fitting model. Anyway, we'd been at it for six hours."

"No, *you'd* been at it for six hours. *She* was just standing there."

Karen sighed again. She supposed it was better to have a husband who hated the admittedly difficult and temperamental models than one who fucked them. But it was always tiresome to listen to his complaints, and she was already bone weary. Plus, they had the rest of the evening ahead of them and this was the only real opportunity she would get to talk to him until next week, what with the presentation to NormCo, the final preparations for the Elliot wedding, and the three charity events they were scheduled to attend in the evenings. The two of them had become a very social couple lately.

"What did Ernesta leave you for dinner?"

"What does she always leave? Chicken. Steamed vegetables. Salad. Diet fucking Jell-O with razor-thin sliced strawberries in it. Total calorie count of sixty-three and a half."

"You want to order out?"

"Nah. Too much trouble. I'll just eat it and bitch," he smiled at her. "You want to eat again? I know how those meals of Belle's can be." He really had the most devastating smile. No matter what bratty behavior he was up to, he could almost always charm her out of her rancor with that adorable grin.

Marrying your idol is a great coup for a woman, but it leaves you always at a disadvantage. Karen had adored Jeffrey from the first moment she saw him. He was everything she was not. He came from money. He had real class. He was very attractive. He was well-educated: a graduate of the Yale fine arts program, no less. They had met when he was slumming in Brooklyn, studying and teaching design at Pratt. He had glanced at the little garmento wannabe that she was and looked right through her. But Karen had been riveted and she still was, by his astonishing good looks and his wit and his style. She'd always feel that he was the catch and that she'd done the catching.

"So, I've put together the numbers for NormCo," Jeffrey told her. "With a little jiggling and a little juggling, we look pretty good. Of course, I overvalued the inventory by about two hundred percent, but I'll let their accountants try and work that out. They can't actually accuse us of dishonesty. All they can do is feel we're unrealistically optimistic." He got up and moved out toward the kitchen.

"So, what kind of money will you ask for?"

"The trick is *not* to ask. The trick is getting *them* to make the first offer. I just hope they're talking Serious Money. I'd like us to be comfortable."

Karen smiled. She thought of the joke about the old Jewish man who gets knocked down in a car accident. People rush to help him, cover him with a blanket, and call for an ambulance. "Are you comfortable?" a man asks. "Well, I make a living," the victim says. Wealthy Jews, she had learned, had a code about their net worth: to Karen, she and Jeffrey were already rich. To Jeffrey, it would take another few million at least before they were "comfortable."

Now, working together, they quickly set the table. Even when they ate alone, Jeffrey insisted on real china and damask napkins. They always used the real silver, despite Ernesta's mild grumbling over the polishing she had to constantly do. Alone, Karen would eat out of the pan standing over the sink or lying in bed. But Jeffrey was a grown-up who ate at the dining table. Karen took a deep breath. She hated to bring this up over a meal, but now was the only chance Karen would get to talk with him.

"I saw Dr. Goldman today," she said, biting her lip.

Jeffrey's smile disappeared. "What's it going to be now?" he asked, and the bitterness in his voice made her wince. "Hot wine enemas? Coca-Cola douches? Oh, Karen."

She tried to smile. "Well, the good news is, we don't have to try anything. The bad news is, that's because nothing will work."

The little vertical wrinkle he got between his eyebrows, the only noticeable age sign on his tanned and handsome face, appeared. He ran his hand through his thick salt-and-pepper hair. His eyes, such a beautiful, clear light blue, clouded over. "I'm so sorry," he said. He reached across the glossy tabletop and took her hand. "I'm so sorry," he repeated. Then he looked down at his plate and they both sat there for several moments in silence.

While they'd been going through this process, they'd long ago made a Real Deal on it: if either Karen couldn't conceive, or if Jeffrey's sperm was weak, they wouldn't try in vitro or donor insemination. Both of them agreed that it was immoral, not to mention painful and humiliating, to spend that kind of money and effort to make their own genetic product when the world was filled with unwanted babies. Now, looking at Jeffrey's bowed head, knowing it was her fault that they couldn't have a child, she wondered if he regretted the deal.

"Are you still hungry?" she finally asked him.

"Only for you," he said. And, taking her hand, he walked her away from the table, across the gleaming, empty floor, and down the hall to their bedroom. The light in there was dim and the bed—a simple Shaker pencil-post—was made up in her favorite Frette sheets. Jeffrey drew her to it. He stopped and wrapped his arms around her. Then he nuzzled her neck and began whispering, his voice husky.

"Oh, baby, it will be all right. Look at the up side: no more thermometers, no more calendars, no turkey basters, no more wasted sperm samples." He kissed her on the nape of her neck and she felt a shiver run down her back. "All my sperm for you, now," he told her. His arms were so long, and they felt so good wrapped around her. He was a big man, and one of the things she had loved about him was how he managed to make her feel small. She leaned her body into his. "I love you, you know," he told her.

"Prove your love," Karen said, and they fell onto the bed, hungry for one another.

Afterward, as she lay in his arms, the beautiful sheets rucked up and wrinkled around her, she turned to look at his profile. It was perfect, and if she cast it in gold it would pass for the head of an emperor on a Roman coin. Karen ran her hand along Jeffrey's sternum and down the thin, soft line of hair that ran from his chest over his stomach to his groin. It was so sweet. *He* was so sweet.

"I was thinking of looking for my mother," she murmured.

He turned over, ready to go to sleep. "Didn't you have enough of her tonight?" he asked.

"No, I mean my real mother."

He was silent for a few minutes. Karen almost thought he had fallen asleep. "What for?" he said. And she heard him sigh.

"I don't know. I just feel like I want to."

He turned over again, this time on his back so he could see her. "Why open a new can of worms?" he asked. "Don't we have enough to deal with at the moment?" He put his left arm out so she could lie against his side. She felt comforted by his warmth.

"Jeffrey, you honestly don't mind? About the baby, I mean."

He hugged her closer. "Karen, I think I gave up a long time ago. We're so lucky already. Why should we have everything? It would only tempt the gods."

"Don't be superstitious," she told him, though she was herself. "Anyway, we *can* have everything. I'm going to call Sid tomorrow and get him working on an adoption. I was talking to Joyce and she said they have a very good contact in Texas."

Jeffrey rolled onto his side, away from her, and cradled his head in the crook of his elbow. "What are you talking about?" he asked.

"A private adoption, Jeffrey. It's more expensive but a lot easier than going through the state. We might be too old for that already. And apparently there are a lot of babies available in Texas."

"You know what's wrong with you? It's not a problem with your ovaries. It's a problem with your head. You're obsessed. It runs in your family."

"What?"

"Your mother is an obsessive, your sister is an obsessive, and your nieces are obsessives. You are obsessed with this baby thing."

Karen didn't think it was the time to mention that if obsession ran in her family she hadn't inherited it genetically. "What's so obsessive? Don't *you* want a baby?"

"Karen, I don't want some stranger's baby, especially one from Texas. I'm a New York Jew. What would I do with a little cowboy?"

"Love it," she said.

Jeffrey pulled away from her and sat up. "Wait a minute." His voice sounded flat. "*I* always felt we could live without a baby. *You* were the one all gung-ho. I did my part. Now it appears that we can't have one of our own. Okay. Okay. I accept that. But I don't want to raise somebody else's."

Karen felt her stomach tighten and the flesh went clammy on her back and thighs. She sat up, too, and looked across the bed at her husband. He looked back at her.

"Come on Karen! Not 'the look'; I don't want 'the look.' You can't expect me to go for this. We *never* discussed it. It was not plan B. Adoption was not plan B. You never know what you are getting in a deal like that."

"I never knew you were so opposed to adoption."

"You never asked. You wanted your own baby. That's what we discussed. I wasn't wild about the idea but I don't think men usually are. It's a natural thing. But this isn't natural. And look what happens. Look at the Woody Allen thing. And Burt Reynolds and Loni Anderson. When celebrities adopt, there's always trouble. And then there's all the heartbreak when a birth mother reneges. Not to mention the genetic roulette that you're playing. Wasn't Son of Sam adopted? And that serial killer in Long Island? Like I said, you never know what you're getting in a deal like this."

"But Jeffrey, *I'm* adopted."

"Yeah, but not by *me*. I knew you were adopted, but I also knew who you were and how you had turned out. That's different than nurturing some illiterate, promiscuous, white-trash, trailer-park scum's offspring. Who knows how *they'd* turn out?"

"I can't believe you're saying this." Was that why he'd been so cool to the idea of her searching out her birth mother? Karen put her hand out, touching his shoulder. Did he think *she* was the offspring of some promiscuous, white-trash, trailer-park scum? And *was* she? She realized she didn't have the courage to ask him. "Please, Jeffrey," was all she said.

Jeffrey shrugged her hand off his shoulder. "I can't believe you're asking this," he said. He threw his feet over the side of the bed and walked across the room. The light from the window hit him across the shoulders and down one long, lean flank.

"Where are you going?" she asked.

"I'm hitting the shower," he said.

To Karen it sounded like he wanted to hit her.

5

HARD LABOR

Karen never did get to call Lisa the night before and left way too early to do it the next morning. Karen got to her office by half past seven, but that was nothing new: ever since she'd had a single employee—Mrs. Cruz from Corona, Queens—she'd gotten in early. All these years later Mrs. Cruz was still with her, now one of her two chief pattern-makers, supervising a workroom that held over two hundred employees. Mrs. Cruz had two long subway rides to get to 550 Seventh Avenue. Still, almost every morning, including this one, Karen met Mrs. Cruz there, outside the legendary building that now housed KKInc, and they rode the elevator up to the ninth floor together where both of them had keys to open up the floor. On the way up, they passed the showrooms and offices of Ralph Lauren, Oscar de la Renta, Donna Karan, and Bill Blass. All of the foreign fashion world was there, too: Karl Lagerfeld and Hanae Mori. Five fifty was the temple of high fashion in the United States. Karen still couldn't get over the thrill of seeing her name on the elevator directory along with those others.

But Karen knew what a slippery ride it could be. Back in January 1985, way before she had moved in, the Halston Originals showroom at 550 Seventh Avenue was dismantled. Whatever fixtures and furnishings that hadn't already been carted away were sold to the next tenant, a newcomer in the fashion business named Donna Karan.

No one thought of Halston anymore. He wasn't just dead, he was forgotten. He had been the first American designer to sell his name, and in his case it had meant his destruction. A corporate entity licensed Halston everythings, while poor Roy Halston Froleich had been legally stopped from using "Halston" ever again. He'd been well-paid but robbed of his work and identity. Karen thought of poor sick Willie Artech. What would happen to *his* work and his name? She shivered, and turned to the dark woman beside her.

"Good morning, Mrs. Cruz," Karen said, and smiled at the short, stout co-worker whose black, glossy hair showed an inch of steel gray at the roots. Karen looked at Mrs. Cruz's face and realized that the woman had had both children and grandchildren over the years they'd worked together, while Karen had remained childless. "How's the new grandson?" she asked.

"Fat as a little piglet. How are *you* this morning, Karen?" Mrs. Cruz inquired. She nodded to a brown bag she held. "Would you like some fresh *pan de manteca?*"

"Oh, Mrs. Cruz. You're killing me. *I'll* wind up fat as a little piglet. I swore I was starting my diet this morning."

Mrs. Cruz shrugged. "You're thin enough. Coffee?"

Karen couldn't resist either the Cuban coffee Mrs. Cruz carried in a big, shiny metal thermos or the freshly baked bread. "Yes, please. And a *thin* slice of *pan de manteca.*"

Mrs. Cruz smiled, pleased. They arrived on nine to find the door already opened. That was unusual. Was a thief loose on the floor or was some competitor going through her designs? Karen had heard of a hundred tricks that magazines and competitors used to snoop, to spy, to get a fashion scoop. One magazine regularly sent pretty girls to apply as fitting models to all the designers, including KKInc. Just last month Defina had caught one sketching a design. Once a sketcher had dressed up as a florist's assistant, complete with a smock, and delivered a huge bouquet personally to Karen while they were doing a final run-through of the line. He had been sent by a competitor, but they'd never been able to prove it was Norris Cleveland. Now, as word leaked out that she was doing the Elise Elliot wedding, someone could be snooping. Or had NormCo sent a due diligence team over to do a little unauthorized auditing? Or even worse: Did the camera crew that had been working on Elle Halle's show decide to do a surprise morning visit? Karen wondered for a moment if she had time to put a little blush on before she got ambushed. She decided she didn't, but she winced at her blurry reflection in the stainless steel elevator walls. The two women shrugged at one another and stepped out onto the floor. The only entrance was here, through the showroom.

The lights were on and Defina Pompey was standing at a pipe rack of clothes, flicking through each one and rattling the hangers as she moved along. Defina was never there until ten—and sometimes a little later. It had always been a bone of contention between them, but the few times Defina *had* shown up at nine had convinced Karen she didn't want Defina earlier. Defina was a night person, and stayed to all hours cheerfully. It was just in the mornings that she was dangerous.

"*Aye. Caramba!*" Mrs. Cruz muttered and scuttled across the beige carpeting to the door of the workrooms. The Cuban *pollo*. Defina confused Mrs. Cruz in a number of ways and the Cuban was scared of her. For one thing, Defina spoke Spanish with a perfect upper-class Madrid lisp. Mrs. Cruz could barely understand it. Why should an American black woman from Harlem be able to speak like that? Plus, all the workroom said Defina knew some strong Santeria magic. Mrs. Cruz avoided Defina whenever she could.

Now Karen smiled cautiously at Defina. The big woman scowled back.

"You're in trouble, girlfriend," Defina growled.

"Tell me something I don't know," Karen sighed and walked past Defina to her office suite at the corner of the floor. Defina followed her. "What's up? How come you're in so early?"

"I must have been thinking about the collection for Paris while I was sleeping. It woke me up."

"Now I know I'm *really* in trouble. Nuclear holocaust wouldn't wake you."

"Well. It wasn't just the collection," Defina admitted. "Tangela came in at six this morning and made so much goddamn noise I couldn't get back to sleep." More beautiful even than Defina had been, Tangela was giving both of them a lot of trouble. Karen sighed. If Tangela had been out all night it wouldn't be a good afternoon in the fitting rooms.

Mrs. Cruz scurried in with two cups, steaming full of *cafe Cubano*. Silently she put them down on Karen's work table and scurried out. Karen sank into the glove-leather swivel chair behind her work table and sighed again.

She had hired Defina just a few months after she'd hired Mrs. Cruz, more than a dozen years ago. Defina had been tall, black, beautiful, and hungry. She was still all four, but had put on forty or fifty pounds since then. Naomi Sims had made the cover of *Fashions of the Times* back in 1967 but it had taken a lot longer for women of color to be accepted on the runways. Out of desperation, when she was broke, Karen had employed Defina as a runway model in her first show, and she'd been the first Seventh Avenue designer to use a black model. Both the clothes and Defina had been a sensation, and they'd worked together ever since: through Karen's marriage, Defina's various affairs, through the birth of Defina's daughter—Tangela was Karen's godchild—and on and on. Defina ran the showroom and modeling staff now, handling the sales force and sometimes even taking orders. Karen and Defina were more than close: they were a living diary for one another. They remembered the small day-to-day memories of more than a decade of working together, often for ten or twelve or fifteen hours a day.

"Listen, there were plenty of times *you* stayed out all night back when you were eighteen," Karen reminded her. "That's what you do when you're young."

"Yeah, but I didn't let no guy start fucking me on the kitchen table and wake up my mama." Defina shook her head. "He had her panties off and her bare black ass was pressed down against my white marble-topped table like dough on a pie tin. He'd climbed up onto the table and had his Johnson out when I walked in." She shook her head.

"What did you do?"

"I threw his sorry ass out of my house! That's *my* house, *my* kitchen, and *my* goddamn table. I don't need to sponge up no funky pubic hairs of his off of it." Defina was a big woman—close to six foot tall—and Karen knew she was quite capable of throwing a man out of her elegant townhouse on East 138th Street. She'd done it many times before.

Now Defina crossed her arms, turned away, and stared out the window. "You know the saddest thing? I stopped myself—for only a minute—and wondered if I wasn't just a little bit jealous. I mean, I know the man is worthless dogmeat, but I doubted myself for a moment. You know, it's been almost half a year since I got any. Probably be more than that till I do get any." Defina shook her head.

Karen patted her shoulder. "Hey, just remember. It isn't you. It's New York in the nineties. None of my single girlfriends can find a decent man. If I wasn't with Jeffrey, I'd kill myself."

"Well, just try being single, almost forty, *and* a black woman. Forget it! There ain't no one out there for me. Any black man with a brain, a job, and a Johnson that's working is chained down by the bitch he's already with." Defina shook her head.

She dropped the street argot. Sometimes Karen felt Dee used it to protect herself. Defina sighed. "I don't have to tell you how hard it is. I get lonely but I don't want to settle. And I don't want a white man. Not that I've had too many offers lately." She shook her head. "But what kind of example is that for Tangela? I chose to raise her in Harlem. I wanted her to be black, to be proud. But I also wanted her to be educated, to know all three Mets: the opera, the museum of art, and the baseball team. Maybe I've pushed her too hard. I knew it would be confusing for her, make her exceptional, but in her generation there *are* other educated, cultured blacks. Doctors' sons. Lawyers' sons. They're going to be good men. That's why it's so important that Tangela meets a good man now, not some drug-dealing trash like this poor excuse for a pecker."

Karen patted Defina again, then walked across the room to her chair. The big black woman turned to her and brightened. "I know what I'll do," she said, going back to street talk. "I'm gonna put a hex on him," Defina said. "Gonna see Madame Renault and put a hex on him."

Karen never knew whether Defina was serious or not when she talked about hexing. She knew that Defina did visit Madame Renault often and wasn't sure whether the woman was a palm reader, a voodooer, or something worse. Karen didn't like to inquire.

"What did you say to Tangela?"

"Don't matter what I *said*. Matters what she *heard*. Which was nothing. Purely nothing. She was passed right out. Couldn't rouse her. Left her there, bare-assed, on the cold marble. She'll have a hell of a backache when she comes to." Defina shook her head. "Doesn't the girl have any shame?" she asked. Her pink lower lip trembled.

Karen got up from her chair and crossed the room. She put her arms around Defina—no easy trick. Karen held Dee for a moment until Defina hugged her back. "Oh, Dee, she'll be okay. It's just a phase. She's a good girl."

Defina wiped her eyes. "She's been a bitch to raise. I never counted on her being so good-looking. It's a curse for a black woman. It draws trouble to us. She's too pretty for her own damn good."

Karen laughed. "That's what your grandma said about *you*. You sound just like her." Defina had been raised by her paternal grandma after her own mother died of a drug overdose.

"Well," Defina said, brightening, "that's the truth. And I didn't turn out *too* bad."

Karen laughed. "Oh, you're bad all right. I saw you flirting with that photographer at the Oakley Awards. Was he drinking age?"

"*C'est pour moi de savoir et pour vous à découvrir.*"

Karen made a face. "It sounds fancy in French but it's still just fourth grade 'That's for me to know and you to find out.' You're a baby. And you still don't know how to dress. Take that turban thing off, why don't you? And lose the beads." Defina wore most of Karen's line and looked ravishing in it. The beiges, creams, and soft browns that Karen favored worked to perfection against Defina's deep brown skin. Defina was *very* black; the darkest mahogany with only the slightest red undertone. And the layers of silk, cashmere, chiffon, cotton, and linen suited her down to her undergarments. But to Karen's complete frustration, Defina insisted on adding enough jewelry, chains, beads, amulets, and charms to open a botanica. And this didn't include the scarves, the clacking bangle bracelets, or the batik turban.

Now Karen shook her head. "Jesus, you have everything hanging off your neck but the kitchen sink. You're a woman, not a store window! What is all that stuff? Why don't you just stick your IUD on a chain and wear it around your neck?"

"There's an idea," Defina mused. "But I don't use an IUD anymore, and I don't think punching a hole through my diaphragm would be good for my uterus. Not that it gets much use." Defina paused then to consider. "Maybe I still *do* have my old copper T somewhere. I like copper jewelry." Karen shuddered. Sometimes she couldn't tell when Defina was putting her on. "So, speaking of the uterus, how did it go yesterday with the doctor of all doctors?" Defina asked.

Karen turned her head, just a bit, away from Defina and toward the windows that looked south.

"Okay," she said, but she knew she wouldn't get away with it.

"Yeah. And I'm first cousin to the Duchess of Kent. What's with you, girlfriend? Still trying to keep secrets from old Defina?"

"No. Well . . . Look, I don't want to talk about it."

"Honey, I told you over and over again: you want babies, you come with me to my herb woman and . . ."

"Defina, would you stop it? You're a Columbia University graduate and I am not going in for Santeria. No chicken's blood will be shed in my name. I know you don't really believe in that voodoo."

"It isn't voodoo, and it isn't Santeria, either. I wouldn't have anything to do with that tacky, country thing. But Madame Renault has *powers*."

Defina's father was Haitian, though her mother had been from South Carolina. Raised in Harlem by her father's mother, old Madame Pompey, Defina was into some weird stuff. For two years now, she'd been begging Karen to consult with Madame Renault on fertility, and had even gone so far as bringing Karen a little velvet bag, sewn closed, to sleep with. Only God and Madame Renault knew what was inside it. Defina had cautioned Karen not to open it, and Karen hadn't been tempted. It was a measure of her desperation that she had actually put the bag under her pillow for a few nights, until Ernesta found it and threw it away. Anyway, it hadn't worked.

"Well, I can see when a subject is closed. So, listen: I'm concerned about the Paris show. I really am."

"Great. Like I'm not already frantic. Can't you undermine my self-confidence a little more? You want me to jump out the window?"

Defina laughed. "Knowing you, on the way down you'll be yelling out that you want me to cut velvet."

Karen had to laugh. It was the oldest joke in the rag trade: the dress manufacturer at the end of a bad season who didn't know what to do next. In despair, he throws himself out the window, but on the way down he sees what his competitors are doing and yells up to his partner, "Sam! Cut vel-v-e-t!" Karen knew that the business was in her blood that deep.

But the pressure felt more intense than ever. Maybe it was the Oakley Award that had heated everything up. But along with the rest of the stuff she had on her mind, Karen had decided that this was the season she would finally show in Paris—and she was petrified. Her fear wasn't helping the collection. Defina's comments weren't helping either. "This stuff has got to be really good. It's got to be great. I'm not going to get away with a little deconstruction or grunge."

Defina pursed her lips and stuck out her tongue. It was very, very pink against her smooth black face. "Grunge," she spat dismissively. "The lambada of style." Dee's face turned serious. "Look, you've always been different from the other designers."

"Yeah. For one thing all of them are gay and male."

Defina shrugged. "Honey, saying 'gay male fashion designer' is like saying 'white Caucasian.' It's redundant. Anyway, they're going to be showing all kinds of wild stuff. This line can't compete. The thing is, Karen, that none of the collection is bad. It just ain't good."

"Oh, great. *There's* a comfort. I've finally lived up to my ambition: to achieve mediocrity. And just in time for the *pret*. What should I do? Copy myself? You know what Chanel used to say? 'When I can no longer create anything, I'll be done for.' "

"Hey, Karen, don't take it so personally. It's a *business*. I figure as long as you don't copy out of the Koran you'll be okay. That nearly ended Claudia Schiffer's *and* the Kaiser's careers." Defina raised her already arched eyebrows. "And also try to remember that sarcasm is the devil's weapon. *I'm* just trying to help."

"Well, you *ain't* helping this morning. Do me a favor and don't come in early again. In fact, if I see you in the office before ten A.M. ever again, you're fired!"

Defina stuck out her pink tongue again and turned and walked out of the office. Now she'd avoid Karen. But she'd already had her say.

And Defina was right. Karen *shouldn't* take it all so personally. Fashion was a funny thing—it was creative but it was so grounded in reality that its very limitations were its opportunities. And everything started with the body. Karen looked down at her own and sighed. She was herself a part of the baby-boomer generation that was now aging and needed forgiving clothes.

Young bodies, beautiful bodies, were the ones that didn't need the disguise of clothes to cover a sagging line, rounding shoulders, or a thickening trunk. Young bodies could look great in a thirty-eight-dollar sweater dress from The Gap. It was older women who needed artifice. But the irony was that only young bodies modeled the clothes. Few girls would actually be able to afford Karen's clothing. Karen knew her clientele: women her age and older who—no matter how thin—felt they had to camouflage their bellies or their thighs—or sometimes both. Like Defina, they'd put on weight. Or the few who hadn't still had necks and elbows and upper arms that weren't what they had been.

Karen's job was to help them look great. She'd created a code for her goals. She called it "the three esses and the two cees": soft, sensual, and sexy; comfortable and classy. To do it, she herself had to concentrate. She certainly hadn't achieved it in the new collection. Now, she lined up three sketch pads on the big table in front of her. For some unknown reason, most women designers worked with the cloth on the model, while most men worked in sketches. Karen did both. She wondered, for a minute, if that made her bisexual. She grinned at her own joke, but the blank pads wiped the smile off her face. It was always hard to get started. When sketching, she worked quickly, using the three at once, so if she got stuck on something she moved to another pad before she got cold. She had already opened her drawer and pulled out a number six pencil—she felt like she needed the freedom a number six would give her—when she was interrupted. She looked up, annoyed.

"Yes, Mrs. Cruz?" Very unusual for Mrs. Cruz to come to the front offices again. What was up?

"You want more coffee?"

"No. Thanks anyway." She looked guiltily at her cup. She'd been so involved with Defina she'd forgotten to drink up. Now it was cold. "That's okay."

Without a word, Mrs. Cruz picked up the cup, poured off the cold coffee into a jar, and refilled Karen's mug with fresh, steaming *cafe Cubano*. Karen picked it up and smiled for the first time that morning. It felt so good to be taken care of.

"Karen, I was going to talk to you when we first came up the elevator. But then we ran into Defina. Still, I should say something. There is talk among the girls in the back. I tell them to be quiet. But they still talk. About being sold. About being fired. It isn't good for the work. What should I say? Or maybe *you* should say something."

Karen looked over her cup at Mrs. Cruz. The negotiations with NormCo were top secret—no one should know about them, but somehow rumors always spread. Well, Karen couldn't blame the workroom women. Garment workers had always been exploited, and just because she had tried to do things differently was no reason for them not to fear for their jobs.

Despite being the owner of the company, Karen had been raised by Arnold to consider herself part of labor. She'd taken in his passion for fairness, what Belle called his "pinko socialism," from the time she was little. Arnold wasn't great with kids, but in his own way he'd been sweet to Karen. He'd sit in his little study and explain some complicated issue—why the farm workers were striking, for instance, and why the Lipskys shouldn't eat grapes from California—and Karen would listen soberly. She'd sooner cut her throat than cross a picket line, even today. So she understood the fears of the women workers.

Still, today it felt like just one more thing to deal with. And Karen wished that once, just once, someone would give her the benefit of the doubt. To believe that since she'd *always* hired union and paid well and fairly, that she'd continue to. That since she'd *always* pulled the collection together in time, that she'd manage to do it again. That since she'd *always* kept Jeffrey happy, that she'd still manage to, even with a child. Karen sighed and put down the empty cup. Like Bill Blass, she used workers on Eighth and Ninth Avenues, not in Hong Kong. And she'd always been union.

"Mrs. Cruz, I guarantee nobody's job is in jeopardy. You have my promise. Can you tell everyone that?"

Mrs. Cruz smiled and nodded. She had a sweet smile, with tiny irregular teeth, like biwa pearls. "I *already* tell them. But I tell them again. Stronger." She made a motion to refill Karen's cup but Karen waved her away.

"No more. I've got enough *shpilkiss* already." Mrs. Cruz had hung around the garment center long enough to know the Yiddish word for "restlessness." She nodded and left.

There was a knock, although the door was open, and Karen looked up to see a hand extended and fisted, ready to knock again. "Yeah?" Who the hell was this? No one had appointments this early. Even Janet, Karen's secretary, wasn't in yet.

"Hell-ow!"

Oh, God! Karen could tell by the accent that it was Basil Reed, the Brit consultant that NormCo had sent in to do a once-over. She had found him as condescending and as annoying as was humanly possible, but she'd managed to answer most of his questions and then stay out of his way. He'd finished his "fact-finding mission" and submitted his report. What the hell was he doing here now?

"I know the hours you keep, so I suspected you'd be in. Hope you don't mind me knocking you up like this, but I just had another question or two to complete my due diligence. I came in from London yesterday, so my timing is still all balled up. Thought this might work for both of us."

Karen blinked. Had he just said something about knocking her up? Not fucking likely with her ovaries! His accent was so "uppah clahss" he was almost impossible to understand. Something about him made her want to be her most vulgar and Brooklyn. Mayfair meets Bensonhurst. A new sitcom maybe?

Basil had poked through all of her private business. He had insisted on knowing exactly who owned KKInc stock. It had embarrassed Karen and made her feel, somehow, vulnerable. The fact was that she alone owned fifty percent. The rest was divided between Jeffrey, who had close to thirty percent, and other members of the family. When Jeffrey's father had put up the investment capital, he had insisted on the thirty percent with another ten reserved for his wife and daughters. When he died, the thirty percent had gone to Jeffrey. But it was Arnold who had insisted that fifty percent belong to Karen. He had incorporated them, and drawn up the papers. In lieu of fees, he and Belle and Lisa and Leonard split the remaining ten percent. She hadn't liked Basil Reed learning all that.

"Come in," she said now. "Take a seat." It was the last thing *she* wanted, but she knew Jeffrey wanted her to make nice.

"I've only one question, really. What are you going to cover in your presentation to NormCo?"

Oh, God! They were all going to drive her crazy with this NormCo meeting! Did Basil expect her to go over cash flow, inventory, sales and marketing costs right now? "I thought I'd just review the line," she said.

"The lion?" he asked.

"Yeah. The new line."

"Is this some company logo you are considering? Hasn't one already been used? I'm afraid I don't know anything about a lion."

"You saw it. Remember?" Jesus, these money men! They irritated Karen so much. All they thought about was numbers and had completely negated the actual product from whence the numbers came. "The line," she repeated.

"I'm afraid I don't remember. Is it an actual wild animal, or are you talking about photos or graphic design?"

"A wild animal?" Karen was completely confused. What the hell drug was he on?

"The lion. Is it tame, then?"

Then she got it. "Not a lion. A *line*. The clothes we're showing this season." He was a twit, but Karen had to admit that with her Brooklyn accent she did pronounce the word with two syllables a lot like the way he pronounced the animal name.

"Oh. Yes. Of course. How very stupid of me." But Basil didn't sound as if he was apologizing, nor as if he thought it was *he* who was "stew-pit." Jeffrey must be right about how bad I sound, Karen thought. She thought of her speech at the Oakley Awards and nearly blushed. Had she sounded awful? Jeffrey had asked her twice to have diction lessons but she'd refused. "I yam who I yam," she'd told him, doing a pretty good Popeye imitation to cover her hurt feelings. Maybe she should reconsider.

Basil Reed stood up. "Well. Very good, then. Splendid. I'm sure Bill will be riveted." Karen thought that if rivets should go into anyone she would like to see them through Basil Reed's own forehead. "Well, I'm off then. See you Monday next."

"Yeah. Monday next," she said, and gratefully watched the twit leave her office. But before she could get back to work, the phone rang. It was her private line. Otherwise, she'd ignore it. But maybe it was Jeffrey, wanting to make up. She lifted the phone.

"Karen, what was that you were wearing at the Waldorf?"

God, it was Belle. Karen wished she could just put the receiver down quietly and pretend this call was not going to happen. Oh well. Too late now. What in the world was her mother talking about? Belle hadn't been to the Oakley Awards. "Did you see *Newsday*? The picture is terrible. You look big as a house. But what are you *wearing*? It's all wrinkled."

Karen hadn't seen the papers but she knew that Mercedes spent a lot of time placing pictures from all of the social events that Karen and Jeffrey attended. And of course she'd push the Oakley Awards. Karen had started to get used to seeing her picture in the paper, and it was all for business. But she wasn't used to Belle's Monday morning quarterbacking. "It was satin, Ma. Satin wrinkles."

"But for pictures! For *pictures*, Karen. And why were you looking down? It makes you look like you have three chins."

How could she explain to Belle what it was like to be barraged by paparazzi popping shots at you? Why, even the Queen of England had been caught once with a gloved finger up her nose! How could Karen explain to Belle that she had no choice over which angle of her was shot and that it was an honor for a picture—any picture—to get into the columns. After all, she had hired Mercedes Bernard to spend all of her time doing nothing but wooing the press to get this very result. But, of course, Belle hadn't just called to harp. She'd want to stay on the line until the unspoken question was answered: why Belle had not been there. "Mother, I'll call you back," Karen promised.

"*Jeffrey* looks very nice," her mother said, and Karen almost laughed out loud. It was the same old Belle tactic: "Lisa calls me every day. Why can't you?" Karen shook her head.

"I'll talk to you later," Karen said, and hung up the phone. It rang again.

"Karen?" It was the unbearably nasal whine of Lenny, their accountant. "Look, I'm sorry to bother you," he began apologetically—Lenny always sounded apologetic—"but KKInc is going to be late paying its federal withholding tax. After last time, you made me promise to tell you if it happened again. So now you know. Don't tell Jeffrey I told you."

"How much do we owe?"

"Not a lot. About twenty-four thousand."

"So why don't we pay it?"

"Jeffrey says he needs to pay the factor."

"Goddamnit, Lenny! We owe it to our staff to make their tax contribution first. Plus, now we'll have to pay penalties." She heard her voice rise. Well, it was no use blaming Lenny. He just did what he was told and at least he called her and warned her this time. "Thanks, Lenny," she sighed. "I'll take care of it."

Finally left alone, Karen closed her eyes and tried to regroup. She looked up to the framed Chanel quote she had over her office door. "Fashion is architecture: it is a matter of proportion." She usually spent the two quiet hours of her morning here, in her corner office, working on sketches. Without this time, how and what would she do with the fit models this afternoon?

She picked up the pencil. What was wrong with her? Why was she so blocked? She thought of poor Halston again: once he sold out, his first season's line had succeeded, but after that all the rest had flopped. Was that what was bothering her? Well, she wouldn't let it. Quickly, deftly, she threw a half-dozen lines on the page. A sleeve, a shoulder, and then the flowing line of a smock. No, she would make it a dress. She moved to the next pad and repeated the sleeve, narrowing it a bit, then sketched the shoulder and now a longer smock-like line. Not right. It looked like Kamali on a bad day. Karen swiveled her chair just a little bit to the left, starting this time with a simple rounded neckline, then the shoulders, and then the smock-like swirl. She put the pencil down and looked at the three pads. Jesus Christ. She'd just done her first maternity collection! Karen looked at the three attempted sketches, the obvious belly bulge below the breast line. She bit her lip. Was Jeffrey right? Was she obsessed? She would have sworn that she was not thinking, at least not consciously, about the visit to Dr. Goldman. But her left brain clearly knew what her right brain was doing. Well, she wouldn't need any clothes like these. She picked up the number six pencil and scribbled across all three pads. Goddamnit! The pencil point broke, and the pencil folded under the pressure of her hand and cracked in half.

Karen stood up and threw the broken pencil into the trash. She went to her purse and took out the two photos that she'd secreted in the side pocket. She stared at the sober little girl in the pictures. Then she put them away. Perhaps Jeffrey was right. Maybe searching for the mother of this little girl would open a can of worms.

Well, she would never get anything done this morning. Now it was not a question of discipline. From long experience Karen had developed her creativity muscle and had learned how to force herself to keep her ass in the chair until something developed. But she also had learned from long experience when nothing was going to happen. This, she could tell, was one of those times. Her confidence was shaken. Let's face it, she told herself. You need to do some really good work and you're not in any shape to do it.

"Aunt Karen?" Karen looked up, glad of an interruption now. Her niece, Lisa's oldest daughter, stuck her head in around the corner of the door.

"Stephanie! Hooray! You made it into the city in one piece! All ready for work?" Karen smiled at her niece despite her panic. Oh, God! How could she have forgotten? Today was Stephanie's first day in her internship, but neither Jeffrey nor Casey had been able to come up with something for her to do. Karen could just have her help out Janet, but photocopying would be such a drag. Karen had meant to do something about this before, but with all the other worries she hadn't gotten to it.

She looked at her niece. The girl really was adorable. She had that lovely fresh coloring that couldn't be faked later either with makeup or lighting. Only youth and health brought that. And she had a perfect size-eight body. Karen considered for a moment. Was she a perfect size eight? Maybe Stephanie could fill in as a fitting model. Tangela was sometimes such a pain. In the Seventh Avenue world there were two very different kinds of models: fitting and runway. Fitting models didn't have to be young or beautiful (though it didn't hurt), but their bodies had to be perfectly proportioned. They were used as mannequins and from the original—cut to their measurements—all sizes were made simply by adding or subtracting inches. Since fit was all important, a good fitting model, one with the right proportion, could work steadily and earn a lot of money. The wrong fitting model could ruin a whole line. In his early days, Ralph Lauren had designed with his wife, Ricky, in mind. He used Buffy Birrittella, a petite girl like Ricky, as a fitting model for all his shirts. Even when they were sized up, the shirts never fit any woman who wasn't proportioned like Buffy. Meanwhile, Susan Jordan, easily over forty, was still used by three of the designers in 550, and her opinion about what felt right and what didn't could make or break a design.

Yet you never saw poor Susan in a show. She just didn't have the look and never had. Poor Tangela had perfect proportions but lacked the look. She could make a good living as a fitting model, but she wanted more.

Runway models (who sometimes were also used in showrooms) didn't have to have quite so perfect proportions, but they had to be attractive, young, and with a look or attitude that put them across. Karen had learned from shows how important it was to have the right girls. The right girls could make magic—they could make bad designs look good and old things look new. That's why the hot models could get the money they asked for.

Karen looked at her niece appraisingly. Maybe she'd do as a fitting model. She'd have Mrs. Cruz measure her. Stephanie had no confidence, no attitude, but she might make a good fitting model. Maybe it wasn't just guilt, charity, and nepotism that had brought Karen to hire her: the girl might be useful. But what in the world would Karen do with her *now*? On her first morning, shouldn't her aunt take Stephanie out for breakfast or, at the very least, give her a tour? But Karen simply didn't have the time. She looked at her watch. She'd already lost more than an hour of prime design time. She paused. Maybe Janet was in. She buzzed her secretary and gratefully smiled when Janet's thick, nasal voice came in over the intercom. "Could you come in here?" she asked, and smiled up at Stephanie.

Janet came in behind the girl.

"Stephie, you know Janet, don't you? Janet, schedule half an hour with Stephie for later in the morning. Could you take her now and show her around? Then bring her in to Mrs. Cruz to have her measurements taken." Very casually, Karen added, "Maybe you'll help out in the fitting room. Is that okay, Stephie?"

The girl nodded, her eyes big. Karen smiled. "You'll just spend the morning in the showroom and the afternoon watching me work with Tangela. She'll explain a lot about what we do. Okay?" Stephanie nodded her head again and Janet ushered her out.

Now, Karen stared at the ruined pages on the pads in front of her. She tore them off, threw them away, and closed her eyes for a moment. She picked up the pencil and stared at the pads again. She knew it. Nothing. She waited. Still nothing came.

She had developed, over the years, a handful of tricks to corral inspiration. She'd thumb through fashion books or collections of paintings. (She'd used lots of Renaissance dress ideas.) Or she'd walk—sometimes for dozens and dozens of blocks—and stare at what people wore and how they wore it. (The awful was sometimes more inspiring than the good. People's mistakes were interesting to Karen.) Or she'd go to her exercise class—somehow when she got her body moving she'd connect with a different part of her brain and images simply formed. Or she'd go to her own closet. Not to see what she had, but to see what she lacked. It was difficult, of course, to fill in the negative space. To imagine what she needed rather than what she had. She'd found that was the key to an important piece of clothing: The long jean skirt that she had created five years ago came from her staring into the closet and it had become a classic. So had the tent dress with the matching ten-pocket vest. And all her signature stuff in sweatshirt material. If all else failed, sometimes she'd go on shopping jaunts with Defina. They'd do a lot of looking, a lot of talking to sales clerks, and a lot of watching the other shoppers.

Maybe that's what she could use today to get a kick start on her creativity. She hadn't slept for hours after the argument with Jeffrey, and she already felt tired, as if the day was almost over. She couldn't just drag herself through it, either. She had the meeting with NormCo to prepare for, and the ever-present pressure of the new collection and the Paris show. *Plus* a trunk show coming up in Chicago and dinner this week with a reporter from *Women's Wear*. Worst of all was the major interview on the television show. That Elle Halle thing. Karen had already sweated out a segment on a Barbara Walter's special, but this was an hour-long show! It was Mercedes's idea of following up on the Oakley Award. *Oy vey!*

Janet, who was young and still in awe of Karen, was bustling around outside her door. Now the girl knocked and stuck her head in.

"I just wanted to remind you that Mrs. Paradise and Elise Elliot are coming in again today."

Shit! Elise Elliot, a great star during the Audrey Hepburn era, had made a huge comeback in the critically acclaimed work of director Larry Cochran. Now they were to be married. That he was almost thirty years younger than the bride caused a great deal of talk both in Hollywood and in New York, towns that had seen everything. Now, after years of living and working together, Larry had joshed that he was going to make an honest woman out of Elise. She—a newsmaker for two generations—knew the event would be a circus for every photographer and cameraman that could crawl out of the woodwork.

She had come to Karen for help and it wasn't easy to give. Elise Elliot knew all there was to know about clothes and was used to getting her way. Though wealthy, she still watched every penny. And she, as all great beauties, mourned the fading of her looks, the softening of her face, and was attempting perfection one last time. She'd been driving Karen crazy with the fittings.

"Oh, Jesus!" Every time Karen used any expletive, Janet—a nice Catholic girl from the Bronx—cringed. But the other inheritance from Janet's parochial school upbringing was that she was the only kid under thirty who could spell—the nuns were good for teaching something other than guilt. They had also instilled in Janet the ability to cope with Karen's ever-changing schedule. Yes, the sisters at Our Lady of the Bleeding Ulcers had prepared Janet well. They'd prepared Janet to take aggravation.

"Do you want me to reschedule?" Janet asked. "I told them it was tentative. They said they were flexible."

That was a lie. Elise Elliot was as flexible as a cement block. A sophisticated, charming, slim, and beautiful cement block, but a cement block all the same. "No," Karen told Janet. After all, you couldn't reschedule a legend: Elise Elliot had been a movie star for close to thirty years. Karen's designs would get great coverage, guaranteed to make "Star Tracks" in *People* magazine, but the whole thing had become a pain in Karen's ass, and if Annie Paradise, the writer, hadn't asked, Karen would never have done it. But Annie had recommended Ernesta to her, and Karen was so grateful, she'd do almost anything to oblige.

"You know that the camera crew is coming in this afternoon."

It was too much! Jesus, when did it start to get easy? "No. I didn't know that. I thought they finished up everything but my interview with Elle Halle. I thought yesterday's taping of Jeffrey was the end of that."

"They say they just want some background. You know, the showroom and the workroom. Maybe one more fitting."

"Goddamnit!" Karen couldn't tell *them* no, either. Why was it that the bigger she got the less control she seemed to have? "Tell Mercedes to handle them. They always create chaos. Tell them *I* am not available."

"Okay. Okay." Janet backed away.

She had to get out of the office, Karen decided. She would clear her desk, then hope that Defina got into a better mood, and the two of them could *schlep* around to Saks or maybe they'd call a car and go all the way to Paramus. Karen preferred to shop the suburban malls than the less reality-based New York stores. She got more ideas there, somehow. For now, she'd give up on ideas. Karen gathered the pads together and was just dumping them into the wide, flat drawer where she stored them when Jeffrey walked into the room. "Hi, honey," he greeted her cheerfully.

Karen blinked in surprise. Men killed her. They really did. Didn't he have a clue? She was still upset by their talk last night. Hurt and disappointed. And she was angry about this withholding tax business. She'd *told* him not to do that again. Jeffrey had pushed her to expand the company, but he'd assured her they'd have enough backing to do it. This was one more thing to make her crazy, but if she got into it now they'd have another fight and she hadn't gotten over last night yet.

How come he was acting as if nothing had happened? Didn't he understand what last night had meant to her? Didn't it hurt him too? Or was he just being brazen and trying to "tough it out"? Sometimes, when Jeffrey knew he was in the doghouse, he did use that tactic. It always left her feeling confused and vulnerable. Should *she* act as if nothing had happened? Should she pitch a fit? Or should she be cold and risk being accused of being overly sensitive or bitchy? Not knowing what to do, Karen figured she'd go for the tax stuff. It was easier than the baby stuff.

"Jeffrey, what about withholding? Are we in trouble again?"

Jeffrey blinked. It was the only sign he ever gave of being surprised. "No, we're not in trouble."

"Has it been paid?"

"Not yet."

"Why not? Isn't it due?"

"Karen, why don't you let me run the business? You knew that if we tried to do the bridge line that we wouldn't be able to repay our loans unless we managed to get through a couple of good seasons. Well, we've got the orders, but we don't have the cash flow, and the factors are giving me a little trouble. I'm just trying to finance the piece goods you're buying like a mad woman and pay the manufacturers enough to keep them shipping. We knew the loan was going to go up before it came down, but we didn't know it was going to go up this much, or that our receivables would get paid on a ninety-day cycle. So if I have to borrow from Peter to pay Paul, it's only temporary. We have to keep the factors happy and confident. The IRS is never happy, so what's the difference?"

"The difference is, that's not our money. The staff already earned it. You said you wouldn't do this again."

"Well, I am. Don't look at me like I'm a criminal; I'm doing it for you. Look on it as a temporary loan from your beloved staff, negotiated by your beloved husband." He kissed her on the cheek. "I'd like to start to go over the numbers with you before the NormCo presentation," Jeffrey said pleasantly. "Then you'll understand this better. We could go over it this weekend, but you're doing that stupid brunch." Karen had invited both his family and her own out to their house in Westport. She had to do it: she hadn't invited them to the Oakley Awards and hadn't had any of them over in months. With her niece's *bat mitzvah* coming up, she felt obligated to do some family thing before that extravaganza. Jeffrey looked down at his sheaf of papers. "I know you don't enjoy going over these numbers."

Now she'd never get to work, Karen thought with a pang. "That's okay," she said.

"This afternoon looks good for me," he said. "It's important that you understand all the figures, just in case you're asked. It would hurt our credibility if you wound up looking like window dressing." The man was incredible. Business as usual. Last night had never happened, or meant nothing.

"Jeffrey, I'm not an idiot and I'm not window dressing," she snapped.

He waved his hand. "Oh, you know what I mean. I don't want them to think that you don't have a clue about the business end and are just some flighty designer."

She looked at him steadily. "Why should they think that?" she asked. "Is that what *you* think?"

"Of course not. I know it."

She didn't like his joke. "I've got work to do," she said coldly and buzzed for Janet. "Send Defina in," she told Janet. "I'm ready for her."

Jeffrey knew he'd been dismissed and he didn't like it. "Just be ready for me at noon," Jeffrey told her. "We have a lot to go through." He turned and tried to slam the door, but wisely, years before, Karen had put an air compressor on the hinge. No one was going to slam the door on her, in her office, she figured. She could just see Jeffrey stalking past Defina in the hallway. He ignored her.

"Spread the joy," Defina cried out to him as she hustled into Karen's office. "Glad I'm not married, when I take a look at you two this morning," she said cheerfully. "What's coming down?"

"Men. You can't live with 'em . . . "

"And you can't live with 'em," Defina finished for her. "So, what's next?"

"When the going gets tough . . . " Karen began.

"The tough go shopping!" Defina exclaimed, finishing Karen's sentence again. Defina grinned and waited while Karen grabbed her purse and put on her lipstick.

"One thing I *know*," Karen said. "I'm not going to be back here to see him at noon." At Janet's desk, Karen paused for a moment. "Cancel the models, see if you can move Miss Elliot's fitting to tomorrow, and tell my husband he can forget about the NormCo presentation rehearsal. I'm out of the box until three." She walked down the hall with long strides, Defina at her side.

"Girlfriend," Defina said approvingly, "you are every husband's nightmare: a wife with her own Gold Card."

At the elevator, the new receptionist called out to her. "It's your sister," she said. "Will you take the call?"

Oh shit! Karen realized that she *still* hadn't called Lisa. One more thing she had to do. "Tell her I'll call her from the car phone," Karen barked, and she and Defina stepped into the steel box of the elevator.

6

FASHION CENTS

Lisa closed the front door and breathed a sigh of relief. The abortion of the
morning was, at last, over. It hadn't been worse than usual—it was just that
the usual was bad enough. She had managed to ignore the absolutely inde-
cent shortness of Stephanie's skirt and the positively gross broadness of
Tiffany's ass while stopping the two of them from squabbling any worse than
they absolutely *had* to in front of their father. She had managed to get Leonard
out the door and even weedled a couple hundred bucks out of him by telling
him she was having the Mercedes lubed. Fuck the Mercedes; she would
spend the money on her own maintenance. Not that two hundred bucks
would do much, but she was always short of cash and at least now she could
carry something in her pocketbook.

Lisa turned and walked down the hallway of their four-bedroom colonial-
style house, pausing at the door of the breakfast room. She surveyed the
remains of the meal. Stephanie, as usual, had eaten nothing, while Tiff, also as
usual, had cleaned not only her own plate but her sister's and her father's. Lisa
had seen her do it in the reflection of the glass-paned doors. She hadn't said
anything. She couldn't take another traumatic scene. She shook her head. The
kid was already a size fourteen and she wasn't even thirteen years old. She
would look like shit at the *bat mitzvah*.

Lisa winced, imagining the satisfaction the bitches at the Inwood Jewish
Center would have over that. And there was no way Lisa could control it or
do anything about it. Both she and Leonard would be humiliated, but she

knew from experience that diets and trying to force or reward Tiff were useless. They had already sent her to weight-loss camp two years in a row now
and Tiff had managed to *gain* weight at both of them. Had she gnawed tree
bark, and was tree bark fattening? Lisa still didn't know how her daughter
had done it. Neither did the last camp director, who had "suggested" to Lisa
that she should try counseling for Tiff and not return her to camp this year.

Lisa turned away from the table. Camille, her housekeeper, would be in
at nine and she could clean up the mess. The sight of the congealed egg yolks
drying on the plates made Lisa feel sick and out of control. Well, so what? So
she couldn't control her preteen daughter. So sue me, she thought. But Lisa
could control how *she* looked and she knew that she was going to look better
than anyone else at the *bat mitzvah*. It would be an opportunity to shine. One
of the problems in her life, she admitted to herself, was that while she had
wonderful clothes, she didn't have enough fabulous places to wear them. The
affair would be an occasion where she could really show herself at her best.

Today she had to find shoes. While she had promised herself that her last
pair of Walter Steigers would be her absolute *final* shoe purchase, she had
been lucky enough to find a Donna Karan pants suit on sale at Neiman-
Marcus when she'd shopped there with Belle. It was fifty percent off, God's
way of saying she was meant to have it. It was a fabulous color for her—a sort
of soft wine shade in a heavy silk broadcloth. With her dark hair and the gold
buttons of the suit as contrast, the color gave her a fabulous glow, and Lisa
already had the exact shade of lipstick to wear with it. The only problem was
the shoes.

She did already have a maroon pair of suede Manolo Blahniks, but the
heels were a little too high for a pant suit—she hated that tarty spike-heels-
with-slacks look—and, anyway, the maroon didn't have the soft mauviness
that the Donna Karan suit had. It would be a push to wear them together and
Lisa despised that kind of dressing. The "well-it-almost-goes-so-what-the-
hell-look," she called it. It would be better to wear black shoes than the
maroon ones. But Lisa had tried the suit on with the three different pair of
black shoes she had—a snake skin, a silk faille, and a patent leather pair—
and none of them really worked. So today Lisa planned to find the right pair
of shoes.

She dressed carefully. It was important to look good when you shopped,
she thought. Because if not, you wound up buying anything out of desperation to change how bad you looked, and that was when you made mistakes.
Over time Lisa had learned to dress properly for her various shopping expedi-
tions: to wear pantyhose and heels if she was going to shop for a dress, not to
have complicated belts and waistbands if she was going to be doing a lot of

trying on, and to be sure to put on enough makeup so that the horror-lighting in the try-on rooms didn't make her feel suicidal. If there was advice Lisa could give to every woman in America it would be, "Wear a good foundation if you're going into a mall."

After she showered and rolled up her hair, Lisa carefully applied her makeup and then went to her closet. It wasn't as extensive as her mother's because Lisa simply didn't have the room. And Lisa's closet was as chaotic as Belle's was anally neat. But Lisa followed a different fashion method anyway: she, unlike Belle, didn't wear the same style year in and year out. She didn't save things for ten seasons. She didn't take up hems and then take them down again. Lisa was constantly adding to and discarding from her closet and at any given time her style could change dramatically. And it did.

It was a funny thing: just when she would feel that she had what she needed and was comfortable or satisfied with her wardrobe, she would open a magazine and see a whole new look. Sometimes she'd simply throw the *Vogue* or *Elle* aside, but the image would stick with her and eventually she would find herself nervously going through her clothes: silk sweaters sliding off their hangers, trousers with and without cuffs, suede jackets, tweed blazers, tube skirts, knit dresses—a riot of colors and textures and styles. But her things would seem dated, old, dull. They just would have lost their stylishness, as if it had evaporated overnight, the way an expensive perfume would if left uncapped. All the lovely silks and wools and linens would seem obsolete— the colors too strong, or the pastels too washed out, the silhouette too wide, or perhaps too tailored. The new pictures from the magazines would work their seductive magic on her. She *had* to have those clothes. Nothing else appealed.

Lisa would fight the feeling, sometimes for a week, sometimes for longer, but getting dressed every day would become torture. She would feel archaic—like one of those scary old women she would see from time to time, the type who were all dressed up in the hairstyle and clothes of some bygone era, some time, perhaps, when they were loved. God, Lisa hated their dated, pathetic look! And then Lisa would eventually be forced into the mall, where she would just pick up one or two outfits of the new style, promising herself they were all she was going to buy.

But when she would get home and stuff the new purchases next to the other clothes in her brimming closet, she would see just how impossible the old stuff really was. Sometimes she wondered if she didn't have that multiple personality syndrome—had Sybil bought some of these clothes? Lisa just couldn't live with the old stuff. It was awful. So she'd begin buying again, upgrading everything. It seemed as if it were a never-ending process.

Leonard had lost patience years ago. He said, "Fashion is just a racket to sell clothes to women." Like most men, he didn't understand. To be honest, he simply wasn't making the kind of income he once had, but then who was in the nineties? Still, even if his patient load had dropped a bit and even if payers were slow, he was cheap at heart. And, Lisa thought, maybe a little bit envious. Since they'd married he'd lost most of his hair and gained a bit of a paunch. She hadn't varied from her size six. She wasn't sure Leonard wanted her looking too good. And he certainly didn't want to see her look good if it cost him more than a dollar.

If she had known that he was going to behave that way, she never would have married him. But she comforted herself with the thought that she'd done as well as she could for a brunette. Her mistake was that she hadn't traded up a decade ago, the way some of the women she knew had. So here she was, still stuck in Inwood with a dermatologist, when it could have been Park Avenue and a thoracic surgeon. Lisa sighed.

If she just had more money, she could live decently. But how could she make money? She was not like her sister. Karen was good at making money and Lisa was good at spending it. Of course, she did own some stock in Karen's company, but Leonard had explained to her over and over again that she couldn't sell it because the company was privately held. Lisa didn't know why that should make a difference, but apparently it did. So now she just regarded the stock as worthless paper, and when she got desperate for money, she cleaned out her closet and dragged a pile of stuff down to the resale shop. One month she got a check for seven hundred and fifty-nine dollars that way. Of course, the stuff she had sold had cost her ten times that, but she wouldn't wear it again, anyway. And she had bought a great alligator purse with the money. It wasn't exactly the purse she had wanted—it was a compromise, even at seven hundred dollars.

It felt as if everything in her life had been a compromise since her marriage. Lisa had been the prettiest girl in her high school and she had longed to get out of Rockville Centre, a town without any distinction, and move to one of the Five Towns. Her insistence meant that she and Leonard had started in a garden apartment in Inwood and, when the time came to upgrade to a house, Leonard had insisted on staying there to continue establishing his practice. But Inwood was the least exclusive (which to her made it the least attractive) of the Five Towns. She might as well be living in Siberia. Lisa hated that moment when, in talking to another woman or buying something in Saks, she had to give her address and hear the pause that lasted for just a fraction of a moment. Then they'd say, "Oh. Inwood." She didn't dress or look like a woman from Inwood. She looked like a woman from Lawrence, whose husband was a surgeon. She could feel herself being demoted. Among the descending class order of Lawrence, Woodmere, Cedarhurst, Hewlett, and Inwood, Lisa still longed for the exclusivity of Lawrence with the passion she reserved for a Calvin Klein dress.

Now, with a sigh, she turned from the rainbow collection in her closet to the phone beside the queen-size bed she still shared with Leonard. She hated to sit on a dirty, unmade bed. She lifted the phone and stood next to the bedside table. Karen had looked awful last night, her face puffy and her skin pasty. Lisa was concerned. Karen had promised to call. Why hadn't she? Lisa would just give her another quick call.

She dialed Karen's office main number—she could never remember extensions, even Leonard's private line. She asked for Karen, and the girl at the desk recognized her voice. "Is this her sister?" she asked. Lisa, pleased, told her she was. "Well, she's on her way out the door, but I'll stop her for *you*." Lisa didn't bother to say thank you; she knew the kid was just trying to rack up a few brownie points with both of them. Lisa tapped her foot and waited until Karen came on the line. Lisa loved her sister but sometimes, without even trying, Karen made Lisa feel as if she had disappeared. Like by not calling her back last night. Or by letting her eyes glaze over at dinner when Lisa told her about the details for the *bat mitzvah*. Waiting for her sister now, Lisa got that feeling, the bad one, as if she was turning transparent. For a moment, she flashed on Marty McFly in *Back to the Future* and the way he had begun to disappear when it looked like history would change and he would never be born. He'd been playing the guitar when his hand dissolved. She looked down at her own hand holding onto the phone. It was solid. She was here; she did exist. And, in a minute, Karen would be talking to her.

But the voice that came on was only the secretary. "She says she'll call you from the car," the girl told her.

Lisa put her tongue between her teeth and bit the tip, though not hard enough to really hurt. "Fine," she said, and hung up the phone. It was okay, she told herself. Karen was busy. She had a big business to run. But Lisa felt her energy drain out of her, like dirty water down a bath drain.

Sometimes she felt as if other people's lives were much more real than her own. Enervated, she turned back to the arduous task of getting dressed.

Who would she be today?

"Is everything organized for the trunk show?" Karen asked Defina once they were in the limo.

"Funny you should say that. I got the list right here with me." Defina pulled a printout from her huge Bottega Veneta purse. Like most women in New York, Karen and Defina carried what Karen called "*schlep* bags," either huge sack-like purses or a shopping bag that was made out of leather or canvas and carried along with a purse. Someday, Karen thought, she'd like to design a perfect *schlep* bag that would have enough room to hold all the crap that women carted around with them, yet would not ruin the line of their clothes.

"Where are we going?" the driver asked.

"Good question." Defina turned to Karen. "Where we going?" she echoed.

Back in time, Karen wanted to answer, to the seventies, when women still shopped in what the fashion world called the B-hive—Bonwit's, Bendel's, Bergdorf's, and Bloomingdale's. Back when my ovaries still worked, when my job thrilled me, when I had the choice about having a baby. But Bonwit's had closed, Bloomingdale's had been sold, Bendel's had relocated, and several of the stores had been found guilty of price fixing and had to pay off consumers from a class action suit. Nothing was what it had been. There was no sense looking backward. "Let's do the new Barney's," Karen exclaimed. "Madison and Sixty-First Street please."

In the seventies, Barney's had still been Barney's Boys Town, a huge retailer specializing in men and boys' suits and owned by the Pressman family. It was still owned by the Pressmans, but Barney had retired long ago and Fred, his son, had passed the baton on to his sons Gene and Bob. Only last year they had made the gigantic move from their Chelsea neighborhood to the Madison Avenue venue they held now: at the northernmost end of the department store archipelago and at the delta to the river of boutiques that flowed up Madison Avenue along with the one-way traffic. Barney's was the hot spot to shop. "Let's watch the women in Barney's and then do Madison Avenue."

"Can we have lunch at Bice?" Defina asked. The restaurant—pronounced "Bee-chay"—was *the* hot spot right now among the fashion crowd, but Karen hated the loud room, despite the great food.

"God, it's only ten after ten. How can you be thinking of lunch already?"

"I like to plan ahead," Defina said. "That is my job. So? How about Bice?"

"Okay," Karen agreed.

The limo made a left onto Thirty-Fourth Street and began driving east toward Madison. Karen leaned back and looked out through the protection of her dark glasses and the tinted windows of the car. Despite the double-dip of tinting, the people in the street looked mostly hideous. There were as usual both ends of the New York street fashion spectrum: there were the women who believed somehow they were invisible on the street and could dress in torn sweats, hair clips, and last night's makeup. What did they do if they ran into a friend? Karen wondered. At the other end of the scale were those who seemed to dress for the street as if it were their theater. There weren't many of them out there. Thirty-Fourth Street was where New York City's middle-class, or what was left of it, shopped. But the days of glory, when Gimbel's didn't tell Macy's, and Orbach's sent secret sketchers to the Paris collections so that they could have line-for-line knock-offs faster than anyone else, were long over. Gimbel's was closed, Orbach's was gone, and even the grand old dowager B. Altman's had disappeared. Now only Macy's held the neighborhood together. Karen watched as streams of people in brightly colored, badly fitting coats and jackets pushed their way in through the revolving doors at the Herald Square entrance. Karen got an idea.

"Stop the car," she said.

"Shit. I *knew* it! There goes Bice."

"Can you keep the car here and wait for us?" Karen asked the driver, ignoring Defina's grumbling.

"Lady, Jesus himself couldn't park on Thirty-Fourth Street. And if I circle, it might take me forty-five minutes to get around the block."

"Okay," she told him. "This is it then. We'll take a taxi from here." She opened the door before he could get out.

"That's gotta be the shortest limo ride in history," Defina grumbled. "Karen, Macy's is two blocks from our office."

"I didn't know we were coming to Macy's," Karen told her.

"Yeah, and I wish we weren't," Defina looked around and shook her head. Karen had to admit that the homeless scattered along the railings of the little park and the newspapers and litter blowing across the wide street didn't make the area look attractive. "Honey, you sure you didn't get Madison Avenue confused with Madison Square Garden? One is a beautiful street full of things you *got* to have and the other is the place where honky Long Island hockey fans beat each other to shit. We are near the latter, not the former."

Karen ignored Defina and started walking toward the north entrance to Macy's. "I want to see how the other half lives," she said aloud.

"Well, sheesh, honey, if you take me out to lunch at Bice I'll bring you up to Harlem." Karen gave Defina a look and the two of them pushed their way into the department store.

Macy's was a bazaar, a souk, an agora. Ever since there had been marketplaces, humankind had been working itself up to the diversity and complexity of Macy's Thirty-Fourth Street. Karen turned to Defina. "Real people shop here," she said, and headed toward the escalators.

The main floor, where space was most costly and traffic densest, was a confusion of accessories, specials, and the small, high-markup items: makeup, jewelry, and the like. Karen walked past two long counters of mid-priced purses. The selection was staggering, but unimpressive. She stopped for a moment and picked up a black leather purse. It was a nice envelope shape but someone had killed it by tacking fringe along the bottom. She flicked the fringe with her finger and turned to Defina. "Why?" she asked. Defina shrugged. They walked on and took the escalator. As they moved up toward the second floor, Karen could get a panoramic view. The place was enormous and there had to be hundreds of people engaged in the business of buying and selling. They were mostly women and they were on the neverending quest of looking good.

Karen's eyes moved toward the down escalator and the endless descending parade of people facing her as she and Defina moved upward. As always, she was entranced by the way women had put themselves—or had failed to put themselves—together. There was a young businesswoman wearing a bright green suit, a color that only a key lime pie should wear, and a teenager in an interesting combination of plaids and denim. Karen learned a lot simply by trolling the malls and keeping her eyes and ears open. Now, at ten-oh-seven in the morning, the women shoppers already moving through Macy's had the desperate eyes of early-morning drunks. An elderly woman in a bone-colored Adolfo knit reached out to a mark-down rack. Her nails were three-inch talons, painted a color that could only be called "traffic-cone orange." She wore lipstick to match. Karen nudged Defina.

"You know what you have to give me if I get like that?" she reminded Defina.

"A total makeover?"

"No. A bullet to the brain."

"Honey, you wind up lookin' like that, you too pitiful to shoot."

Then Karen saw her: a woman standing alone, no one ahead or behind her for a dozen escalator steps. She was well past middle-age, stooped but still a big woman. She carried a battered shopping bag in one hand—obviously not a purchase she had made that day. But as Karen ascended and the woman was brought down by the moving stairs, Karen focused on the woman's face. It was Karen's own face, or what her face might be like in twenty years. It was the same square-ish head, the same big but undefined nose, and the same wide mouth. Karen bit her lip and felt her hand bite into Defina's upper arm. "Look at her," she hissed to Defina, but by the time Defina turned her head, the woman had moved passed them. Karen turned, craning her neck, but all she could see was the blue sweater and gray hair of the woman. "She looked like my mother," Karen cried.

"You crazy? Your mother's half the size of that old thing. And she wouldn't be caught dead in a rat-bag outfit like that one," Defina said.

Karen realized that she wasn't making sense—at least not to Defina. *Am I losing it?* she wondered. *I spend the morning drawing maternity clothes and then I imagine seeing my real mother on the escalator at Macy's. Get a grip, Karen!*

"You all right?" Defina asked.

"Sure. Peachy keen."

At the second floor Karen took a quick detour through a row of dozens of nightgowns. All of them had been mucked up with cheap lace or embroidery or acetate satin ribbon. Karen sighed. In a week, after one washing, once the sizing was gone, these would look like rags. Karen knew that at the bottom end of the market, low-quality garments were splashed with cheap orna-ments. Ruffles, polyester lace, fake silk flowers distracted from the skimpy fabric and lousy design. But why wasn't there even *one* simply constructed Egyptian cotton nightie? Okay, it didn't have to be *Egyptian* cotton. Sea Island would be good. Or even just plain cambric would do, and be so superior to this polyester-blend junk. Karen knew from her old fashion history days at Pratt that cambric had originally been made of linen in a French city called Cambri. She sighed, looking at the shoddy nightgowns. Why did Americans get fooled? A French woman wouldn't be caught dead in this crap. Karen shook her head.

"Oh Lord, spare me another one of Karen's why-can't-they-just-keep-it-sim-ple-so-that-the-poor-folks-can-get-some-quality speech." Dee hadn't understood Karen about the mother business, but she did know what Karen was thinking about ninety percent of the time.

Karen took one more look at the cheap nightgowns. The bows and ruffles that would look awful after one washing added what the industry called "hanger appeal." Did poor people really think they got more with ugly design? Even paper towels were ruined with patterns of unicorns or pilgrim fathers. Karen believed, deep in her heart, the way other people believed in flossing or the Bible, that form should follow function. But if it was her reli-gion, she was clearly alone in practicing it. "Let's go to designer stuff and then up to budget sportswear," she said to Defina, who shrugged agreement.

"You're the boss. But why you wanta see fat women trying on rayon pants is beyond me."

"Bitterness is unattractive in the young," Karen reminded her.

"Who's young?" Defina asked.

They checked out the KKInc boutique. It seemed as if the designer floor was bigger and more crowded than ever. How long would it take to look through everything? Hours and hours. Karen got tired just thinking about it. Macy's gave them a lot of floor space but that was because Macy's *had* a lot of floor space. Always, in department stores, it was a fight for exposure. If customers didn't see your stuff how could they buy it? Among better designers Ralph Lauren, Donna Karan, and Armani battled for the most space. In the bridge lines it changed from day to day but in more moderate-priced sportswear, Liz Claiborne had won hands down.

"Let's check out Norris Cleveland," Karen said.

There wasn't much there, except for a line-for-line copy of a box-pleat skirt that Karen had done three seasons ago. Except Karen's didn't pull across the belly the way this one would because Karen hadn't bias cut the fabric. "You'd have to be a size four *with* a tummy tuck to look good in that." Defina shook her head and snickered. Then she lifted the price tag and raised her eyebrows. "She's asking eight hundred bucks for this!"

Karen shook her head. "Something is wrong when shopping becomes an experience that requires the help of a personal trainer for stamina, a psychotherapist for self-esteem, *and* a financial adviser who figures out if you can afford to make that eight hundred dollar investment in a *skirt*."

As always, once they got up to the moderate-priced sportswear, Defina started paying attention. First they went through the racks to look at the merchandise. Nothing with nothing, as Belle would say. Not much design talent here. People who didn't know the industry thought of designers as dictators, but Karen knew she was more like an incumbent office holder who needed to keep in touch with public opinion. She liked to see what trends moved down from haute couture to the masses, and which sold. They looked at merchandise for a while. Liz Claiborne might have more selling space than anyone, but it was a lackluster showing. No one else looked too good, either. Then, before they began to watch shoppers, Karen suggested they check out the stuff made by NormCo. She knew they produced the Bette Mayer mass market line. A salesgirl said they'd find it on the fourth floor.

The floor was enormous, without many salespeople. They looked for more than ten minutes for the Bette Mayer department and found it, at last, after being misdirected twice. (Of all department stores, only Nordstrom's still really trained their staff to help.) Karen sighed and finally found the Mayer stuff. Bette was an uninspired designer who had made her name by being the first to bring stonewashed silk to the masses. But her silhouettes were predictable and boring: the same old blazers and coordinates with the only change the size of the lapels or the padding in the shoulders. Karen hadn't bothered to look at it in years, and only did it now because she wanted to see what NormCo produced. Back to back against two racks she and Defina began snapping hangers and moving through the clothing. "Eeuw!" Defina said as she lifted up a jacket. "Look at the interfacing on this."

The jacket was a mess. The lining of the sleeve clearly bagged out below the cuff and the interfacing at the chest was already bubbled. Paco Rabanne had once said, "Architecture and fashion have the same function. Now I am an architect of women." Well, the house that Bette built wouldn't shelter any female! Karen reached for the price tag. Ninety-nine bucks! But even for less than a hundred dollars, the jacket was no buy. After one trip to the dry-cleaner it would decompose.

"Look at this," she said, holding up a scoop-neck blouse. It was coordinated tonally to the blazer, a bright green against the blazer's darker green. There was a lot of labor in it: there were sleeve plackets, two back pleats at the shoulder line, and the buttons were self-covered and fastened with loops. But it was made of some polyester-based blend that had a ghastly feel. What had happened to Bette's stonewashed silk? This would be hot to wear in warm weather and chilly in cold. "Eeuw. Sleazy."

"Creepy," Defina agreed, touching the goods.

"Flimsy."

"Sleazy, Creepy, and Flimsy. Weren't they three of the seven dwarves?"

Karen didn't bother to respond. She thought of Chanel, who had said, "You know you're a success, in fashion, if certain things are unbearable." *This* was unbearable. Would NormCo try to do this to her stuff? Karen picked up the price tag instead. Twenty-nine bucks. Jesus, how could they do it for that price? "Where was it made?" Karen asked Defina, indicating the blazer with her chin. While Defina looked for the jacket label, Karen found the origins of the blouse.

"Made in the USA," she said, surprised. At least Arnold would be proud if she did a deal with NormCo. He was all pro-U.S. workers. But could *she* be proud of an association with Wolper, NormCo's CEO? She'd have to insist on an anti-schlock provision. Did Robert-the-lawyer have one in boilerplate?

"This piece of crap is from here, too," Defina said. "I thought everything in this price range had moved offshore."

"Well, no labor costs abroad. My dad says they just chain people to their sewing machines and throw them a little raw meat once in a while. Of course he's a well-known pinko." But, as they went through the racks, they found that most of the Bette Mayer clothes, though a combination of cheap and shoddy, as well as impractical, were made in the U.S.A. "How can they do it so cheap?" Karen asked.

"Beats me."

Karen had been wrestling with the reality of the couture business since she opened her doors: the vastly expensive custom-made ensembles for the very rich are not the profit-making end of the business. It is hard to believe that a twelve-thousand-dollar evening gown in *peau de soie* is a money-loser. But it is usually true. The wealthy women who shopped for custom-made clothes actually *cost* the designers money. Karen was only going to make money the way the other designers did: by selling cheaper goods to the mass market. It seemed like one of those nasty ironies of life: it was the middle class that was soaked for profits and that actually underwrote *haute couture*. As Arnold's daughter, Karen had never felt comfortable with the deal. But she loved her work.

Now she looked at the shoddy clothes. "Who's designing this shit?" Karen asked rhetorically.

"Well, I can see it ain't you, baby. I wonder if Bette even *looks* at it? Even she isn't this bad."

Karen shrugged. There were fewer and fewer designers who understood how to cut. It was all about perfection of line and of material. The trick was to tame it but keep it alive. This stuff wasn't just dead, it had never lived. God, she'd hate to have her name on something so disgusting. "What else does NormCo do?" she asked.

"Don't they do Happening?"

"Yeah, I think so. Let's go check it out." Happening was a fairly new line of jeans and casual wear. For two years it had flown out of the stores, then NormCo had bought it last season.

They wandered around the sixth floor. Karen was starting to feel hungry, but it was way too early to think of lunch. Maybe brunch. That reminded her of Westport. "Hey, Dee . . . "

"Hey, yourself."

"Want to come out to Westport for brunch this Sunday? Bring Tangela?"

"I was wondering when you'd get around to asking me out to see Jeffrey's house. But to eat?" She paused to consider. "Karen, I love you but you're a cripple in the kitchen."

Karen frowned. "Don't mock the afflicted. Just say, I'm culinarily impaired. Anyway, don't worry. I'm bringing it all in from the city."

"Honey, in that case, it's definite." Defina gave Karen a big smile.

It took them another ten minutes to find Happening and ten more to go through the racks. The news wasn't good.

"Well," Defina said, "what they lack in design they make up for with lousy goods. What's happened to them?"

"NormCo?" Karen asked. She knew that at the low end the basic rule of business was to try to do what the others in your price bracket were doing—

only a little bit sooner, better, and cheaper. Happening had done it in the past but the line didn't look like it was happening anymore.

"Is it selling?" Karen wondered aloud.

"Let's go ask a sales clerk."

"If we can *find* one."

Because Karen was becoming too well known she always hung back on this part of their forays. She got herself busy near the try-on room while Defina went in search of sales information. While Karen waited outside a fitting room a woman walked by with her four-year-old daughter. The woman picked up a cheap cotton knit top. "What do you think of this color, Maggie?" the woman asked the little girl.

"No!" she said. Karen was surprised at the child's vehemence.

"I guess it's not your color," Karen said to the little girl and smiled at the woman, who was dressed in a pair of Gap jeans and a nondescript turtleneck.

The woman smiled back. "Oh, Maggie has always had really strong ideas about clothes," she said, and smiled down affectionately at her daughter. She took the child's hand and the two of them walked away. Karen could see the crease of fat on Maggie's arm at the elbow and the way her hair swung back and forth, neatly, as if it was cut from a single piece of cloth. From this angle Karen could just see a part of the child's cheek, smooth as a plum and as delicious-looking.

Karen, who never cried, was blinking back tears when Defina returned to make her report. "Flew out of the store last season, grew roots this one," she told Karen.

"Oh, great. Let's let NormCo ruin our product line."

"You're talking like you don't have a choice. Do like Nancy Reagan said: 'Just say no.' "

Karen lifted her head to try and see the mother and daughter as they consulted over another possible purchase. "Nothing is that easy," she told Defina.

They spent a couple more hours in the market and wound up having a late lunch at Mad 61, the other hot restaurant in the basement of Barney's. Karen was depressed, and Defina, as always, sensed her mood.

"Best shoes," Defina demanded.

It was an old game that they had been playing for years. It needed no introduction.

"Roger Vivier's."

Defina raised her head, paused only a moment, and nodded. Sometimes it wasn't so easy, and they argued for days. "Best florist," Karen popped back.

"Renny," Defina answered with a shrug, as if *everyone* knew that. "Best knock-offs."

"For bags? Or dresses? Or what?"

"Gowns."

"Victor Costa. Give me one that's hard."

"Bags."

"José Suárez."

Defina shook her head. "Those aren't knock-offs. They don't have the labels but they're the exact same bag made by the same manufacturer. Except for Hermès."

"They're still knock-offs. If they don't have the label, then they're not originals."

"If a tree falls in a forest . . . " Karen had to smile. With her nonsense, Defina had lifted her mood. She didn't even call Jeffrey to cancel, and she forgot—once again—to call Lisa.

7

CUT AND DRIED

For weeks Karen's already frantic life had been interrupted by the camera crew from Elle Halle's show. Richard, the director, had told her to ignore them, to go on with life as she usually lived it. But of course that was impossible. For one thing, she had to worry about how she looked all the time they were around. What would it do for her image if she looked like ca-ca on toast? Karen knew that in person she had the energy and style to carry herself pretty well, but the camera was *not* her friend. Despite her talent and her energy, the camera wasn't fooled. It simply reported the facts. Karen knew she wasn't very pretty, that she wasn't thin enough, and that she wasn't young anymore. The camera reduced her to her minimum. This wasn't paranoia: Janet had a whole shelf of scrapbooks with clippings and pictures in them and Karen didn't look really good in any of them. But Jeffrey and Mercedes had insisted that KKInc jump at the opportunity to be featured in one of Elle Halle's classy, hour-long "Looks." And now, all that was left to complete "Elle Halle Looks at Karen Kahn" was the interview with Elle Halle herself.

Karen was dreading it. They were going to shoot it this afternoon and Karen felt as if she were going in for double root canal. Given the choice, she'd prefer the dental work. Because she had no illusions: despite her smile and her soft voice, Elle Halle liked to do extractions and *she* never used anesthetic. Her forte was getting hold of some decaying psyche part and tugging until her victim gave it up, showing the rotten root and all. Gently elicited confessions and tears were what spiced up an interview. Although Elle seemed empathic and warm to the television audience that loved her and loyally tuned her in, Karen had to wonder about a woman whose life work it was to expose the pain of another on national television.

Karen had already met Elle twice. Both times the woman, tall, blonde, smooth, and commanding, had seemed pleasant. But that was what everyone said about Belle—if they didn't know her. "Oh, come on," Mercedes said as Karen got ready to leave for the studio. "It's not *that* bad."

"Didn't someone say that to Marie Antionette right before the blade hit?"

Mercedes raised her eyebrows. "Have you talked to a doctor about this martyr issue?" she asked dryly. She looked at her wristwatch. "Come *on*. Let's go. You don't want to piss *these* people off by being fashionably late."

"Where is Jeffrey?" Karen asked as she picked up her coat.

"He's in with Casey and the financial guys." Mercedes raised her eyebrows. That must mean NormCo people. She paused. "He's not going to come."

"What do you mean?" Karen felt her face go pale, the blood draining down to her heart, which began thumping uncomfortably. "He *has* to come," she said. "I can't do this alone."

"You're not alone, Karen." Mercedes reminded her. "*I'm* coming with you."

Karen didn't bother to be polite. She shook her head. To manage this she needed someone she *liked* to be with her. "Defina," she said. "We have to get Defina." God, this would be too much to do alone. She couldn't face the ordeal of selling herself, of being herself, and talking not about her clothes but about her life to twenty million people without some support. Why did people care about a designer's personal life anyway? Didn't her clothes speak for her?

Janet looked up from her desk and smelled crisis in the air. "Defina hasn't come in yet," she told her boss.

Karen felt her hands begin to shake. She would go into Jeffrey's office. She would stop the meeting. Whatever it was, this was more important. She couldn't go over there, do this big deal, be examined under Elle Halle's microscope, without knowing that Jeffrey was rooting for her.

From the beginning, it was Jeffrey who had believed that there was not only more recognition due to her but also more money to be had in the recognition.

He'd been a graduate student studying painting when she was at design school. She was so inexperienced, so very green. She'd never dated in high school—she'd gone to the prom with Carl. She'd been slow to mature. She hadn't even gotten her period until she was fourteen! So of course Jeffrey had dazzled her. So much so that she had virtually followed him around, doing errands for him and picking his stuff up, a sort of human golden retriever to his elegant Afghan hound. And he *was* a hound. Jeffrey had liked her and had bedded her, but she had known there was no commitment there. He slept with a lot of girls at school. All the pretty ones, and Karen. Jeffrey had made it clear that she amused him and that they were friends, but there was nothing more forthcoming. Though she adored him, she was smart enough not to ever tell him so and she never expected anything more.

Once she'd graduated, it was only through her efforts that they had kept in touch. He'd never called her, but he seemed pleased to hear from her. When she'd gotten out of school, she'd been lucky enough to snag a job working for Liz Rubin, who was a legend, the first woman sportswear designer to have her own Seventh Avenue company. Karen had started as just one of a half-dozen assistants, but within six months she'd been moved up to Liz's special assistant. They worked together according to Liz's hours: sometimes Karen would get a call at eleven-thirty at night and she and the tiny older woman would work until dawn. Karen suspected that sometimes Liz—like Karen's idol, Coco Chanel—called not because she was inspired but because she was lonely. But if that were the case, the other woman had never opened up. Always distant, always authoritarian, always in control, Liz had taught Karen more in the sixteen months that they worked together than Karen had learned in all of her years of design study. Soon only work and Liz made up Karen's life. It was a busy time, and Karen wasn't unhappy. Because, though Liz never spoke about her feelings for Karen, Karen felt they were there.

Naturally, during that busy time, Karen had lost touch with Jeffrey. In fact, she'd lost touch with almost all her friends, except Carl. For her there had only been work. One of the reasons Liz had chosen her, Karen always believed, was because no matter what demands Liz put on her, Karen had never said no. She'd always been a hard and willing worker and, as her reward, Liz gave her more and more work to do.

And she hadn't minded that she got no credit. The idea of her own name on a label had simply not occurred to Karen. After all, she was only twenty-two. She just wanted to do her garments her own way. But that became the rub. Because after the first few months of working closely with Liz, Karen hadn't been able to stop herself from voicing her opinions. Once she'd gotten over her awe of Liz Rubin, she'd said what she felt, and sometimes her opinions seemed to have gone right for the jugular. "That's boring, Liz," she would say, and make a suggestion or sketch an alternative. They'd argue. Karen always figured Liz liked her *because* of opinions. She'd been wrong. She remembered the last fight: it had been over button placement on a jacket. Liz, never one to hide her light under a bushel, had altered a design of Karen's and screamed at her when Karen insisted that the buttons be again placed asymmetrically. "It's just a gimmick," Liz had cried. "The jacket is a classic. At Liz Rubin, we do *classics*." Karen had looked at her fiercely. "Well, *I* do what's right. And these buttons, on *my* jacket, have to slant across the front."

Funny that a few buttons could cause so much trouble. They changed Karen's whole life. Liz had fired her.

Karen hadn't been able to believe it. Because she *knew* she'd been right. To her it seemed simple—anyone should see it. Especially Liz. Karen just hadn't thought of the politics and ego involved. She knew the news of her leaving would cause rejoicing among the other assistants, the ones she had bypassed. But it wasn't just her pride that was hurt. Cold as she was, Liz Rubin had represented something more to Karen than just a job or a paycheck. Liz was like Karen and it was the first time that Karen had ever met anyone like that. Liz had shown her what she could be and it hurt Karen to be discarded that way.

Karen had sat alone in her apartment crying for two days. She had no one to talk to, nothing to do. (There was a limit to how much she could lean on Carl.) She realized then that she had no life, aside from work. She called home, but Belle was no help and Lisa was still just a kid in school who worshiped her older sister. So, in desperation, Karen called Jeffrey, who was sharing a ratty, lower Broadway loft with Perry Silverman. (Jeffrey's parents had offered him a pied-à-terre on Sutton Place but he felt it was too bourgeois.) Perry and Jeffrey invited her over and had taken her out, gotten her drunk, and comforted her. She was sure they probably also privately laughed at her naive misery. "It's just a *job*," Jeffrey had said. And Karen had tried, despite a tongue made less articulate than ever by all the bourbon, to explain that it was more than that.

"Why would she fire me?" Karen cried over and over again. "Why?"

Jeffrey had listened and then had laughed. He laughed! But somehow, this comforted her. "She was jealous," he said, "because you were right. She does 'classics.' *You* do originals. And you had the nerve to tell her."

"Is *that* what I did?" Karen had asked, amazed.

"Of course," Jeffrey said, as if anyone would know that. As if Karen should have. "And she resented you for it," he added. "She used you, but she resented you." He put his arm around Karen while she cried some more on his shoulder. Then he took her to bed.

After that night, Karen had not cried again. She spent more than a month looking for a job by day and sleeping with Jeffrey most nights. In some strange way, the loss of Liz was made up for by having Jeffrey in her life again.

She told him each evening about her day's adventures and interviews. She was thrilled when she at last got not one but two offers. She asked him which she should take, then she was shocked when he encouraged her to turn them both down. "C'mon," he told her, "you don't want to be some no-name house designer. Look what you've done already. *You* did most of Liz Rubin's fall line. You don't have to prove yourself to anyone. You just need an opportunity to shine. You need someone to believe in you."

It was then she had gotten the offer from Blithe Spirits to do her own line of sportswear. Moderate priced, but a little higher-quality than most. It wasn't Seventh Avenue, but it would have her name on it. Karen Lipsky for Blithe Spirits. Jeffrey's advice had been right, and she'd gotten the chance because she'd listened to him. It was an unbelievable opportunity for a girl only two years out of school, but before she had a chance to jump at it, she'd gotten more good advice from Jeffrey. "Turn *them* down," he said. "Tell them that you've gotten an offer for twice as much money."

"But I haven't," she cried.

Jeffrey had laughed. "So?"

"I should lie?" she asked. Neither Belle nor Arnold had taught her that. But Jeffrey had nodded. "What if they find out I'm lying? What if they tell me to take the other job?"

"They won't," Jeffrey laughed. And he ruffled her hair as if she were a puppy. "Try it tomorrow. You'll see I'm right."

And he was. She'd been petrified, as frightened then as she was of Elle Halle now. But she'd bluffed, hands wet with sweat. And, at last, she'd gotten the job at quadruple the pay she'd been making with Liz. She had, for the first time, more money than she had time to spend. Not that the money was so great, but she had no free time at all—she'd had an unbelievably hectic schedule putting a line together alone.

Just when it was about to be shown, she'd called Jeffrey. They'd been seeing a lot less of each other because of her crazy work schedule. "Can I come over?" she had asked, the way she always did. "I'm scared that the whole thing is a mistake. Can I stay over tonight?" The silence at the other end of the phone had been ominous. What was wrong? Something had changed. She'd been too busy with the work to have noticed anything before.

"Karen," Jeffrey had told her gently. "You know how much I like you. But you have to know this: I'm engaged to be married."

Devastated, she'd gone to Carl, of course. "I should have told him I loved him," she wept. "I should have kept calling."

"No, you shouldn't have. He'd have dropped you quicker. At least now you have your pride."

"I don't want my *pride*. I want Jeffrey!" she'd wailed like a child. And so then Carl had explained everything about men, just the way Jeffrey had explained everything about work. "He *likes* you Karen. Of course he *likes* you. You're fun, you're funny, you're smart. And you're sexy. I can tell, even though I'm gay. But the Jeffreys of the world are always going to pick beauty and class and clout over funny and smart. He comes from money. She comes from more money. You're better, but June Jarrick is the niece of a senator. It isn't fair, but that's the way it is."

She saw the announcement of their engagement in the *Times*. Even today, ready to go downstairs to get the limo to Elle's studio, Karen could still remember the pain of that moment and the emptiness that followed.

Her new line had been a huge success and had flown out of the stores. She'd gotten the first personal publicity she'd ever had in magazines and the fashion press. But she'd been miserable. This time work wasn't enough. And other men were like ghosts compared to Jeffrey's warm flesh. She got a calendar and obsessively crossed off each empty day until the black date of Jeffrey's wedding. And then, out of nowhere, she'd gotten the call from Liz Rubin.

"I want to see you, Karen," Liz had said. "Can you come over now?"

As always, Karen had. And she'd been shocked by Liz's appearance. If she'd been thin before, she was skeletal now. Karen's eyes had grown big, but she hadn't said anything. Neither did Liz. She didn't have to. "I saw your Blithe Spirits line. It was very good," she told Karen. It was the first and last praise Liz ever gave her. "Come back. Work here. I'll need someone to take over. The doctors give me six months. I want you to do the spring collection."

Other girls might have said no, but Karen had come back, and Liz had died on Mother's Day that year. At twenty-five, Karen was the heiress to the throne. The press, always suckers for sentimental stories, had gone nuts over both the Liz Rubin spring collection and Karen's rags-to-riches story. She was called the "Crown Princess of Fashion." Carrie Donovan did a profile of her for the *Times* Magazine Section and she was on the cover of *"W"*. And even though her name wasn't on the label, Karen didn't mind because it was her homage to Liz. A memorial.

Plus, the work had also saved her from thinking about Jeffrey. She had, instead, a couple of brief affairs but always knew how many months, weeks, and days until the big social wedding. She kept the clipping announcing the engagement. She often stared at the picture of June Jarrick. Perfect June, in her simple linen dress and her double strand of real pearls. From time to time, because she couldn't resist, Karen had drinks with Perry, obstensibly for fun but really to pump him for news. "Leave it, Karen," Carl warned her, but she picked at the wound despite the pain.

Jeffrey was set to marry in another six weeks when he had sent her a note and asked to meet.

She knew she should say no, but she hadn't, and they'd gone out for drinks. Drinks led to dinner, which led to more drinks, which led—inevitably—to bed. They'd always been good in bed.

Karen hadn't asked any questions. They'd spent the first night making love for hours. Jeffrey had clung to her like a drowning man and she had accepted his desperation as a tribute, of sorts. The next morning she'd left early, going to work without waking him or leaving a note. He'd called her at the office an hour later. It was the first time he'd called her.

Karen wouldn't let herself think about the fact that he was cheating on his fiancée with her, or that Jeffrey had earlier "cheated" on her with his fiancée. She couldn't think at all. She only felt that she couldn't live without the comfort of his body and she knew without asking that he felt the same way. He came to her apartment every evening, sometimes as late as midnight, and she never questioned where he'd come from. She always let him in. She didn't even tell Carl, because she knew he would go batshit on her. Twenty-one days before his wedding to June, Jeffrey asked Karen to marry him. "You're going to be rich and famous," he said. "Karen Kahn sounds a lot better than Karen Lipsky." If it was an unromantic proposal, and if it came a little bit late, she comforted herself by thinking of it as fashionably late. Any guilt that she felt was smothered in the overwhelming tide of gladness. She had nothing to do with his predicament, she told herself, or the pain he was about to cause June. After all, she had known him and loved him long before.

Karen had never asked Jeffrey what he had said to June or his family, but months later, when she was at last introduced to the Kahns, she felt the blame there. It didn't go away when June married Perry on the rebound. If anything, it intensified. Still, she was so wrapped up in her joy of conquest, of her possession of him, that it didn't matter. Jeffrey was and would always be her dream prince, her first love. When he told her that he was going to help her with her career, she was thrilled. When he created a business plan for her own company, she was touched. As a thirtieth birthday present he created her КК logo. When he raised money to get her started, she was ecstatic, and when he told her he was giving up his own career to manage her business, she felt as if no one had loved her and taken care of her as he did. So she had left Liz Rubin and they had launched ККInc at what appeared now, in retrospect, to be the perfect time: yuppies were in full flower and disposable income was boundless. In the closing years of the eighties, Karen had established herself and her name. Now that money was tighter and the consumer more demanding, discerning women still chose her because—expensive as she was—she gave good value. And all because of Jeffrey.

She had never taken him for granted, just as she had never taken anything she had worked for and won for granted. This was her strength and her weakness. She always lived with the fear that she could lose it—the business, the money, the man. Now, at a moment when she could be consolidating everything, she felt more unsure than ever.

Mercedes was staring at her. For all of her sophistication, Mercedes might as well have been singing "Baby, baby, stick your head in gravy." Mercedes licked her thin lips and turned to Janet. "We'll send the car back for Jeffrey. Send him over as soon as he's done." She turned to Karen. "It will take you an hour to get made up and miked. I'm sure he'll be there by then."

Karen nodded and moved down the hall, through the showroom and to the elevator, but her heart kept beating hard and she wished she could hide in the workroom with Mrs. Cruz. Jesus, wasn't this supposed to be the fun stuff? she asked herself.

Then she thought of the photos—the pictures of herself that she had taken from Belle's house. She would take them with her. Somehow, they seemed like a talisman. She would be safer if she had them with her. She ran back to her office, got them, and slipped them into her coat pocket.

The studio was over on West Fifty-Seventh Street, where half a dozen talk shows originated. Karen was hustled down a long green hallway and met by Paul Swift, the producer of the segment. He, in turn, introduced her to an assistant who led her through a maze of rooms to the makeup artist. Karen had already done her makeup, but the tall redhead looked at her critically. "I think we should start over," she suggested blandly. "The lights will wash you out. I'm going to start with a darker base, then I'm going to shade your neck and throat, get rid of the puffiness, and narrow your nose a little."

"Will it hurt?" Karen asked. The girl didn't laugh.

The redhead tucked paper towels into Karen's collar and threw a plastic smock over the rest of her. For a while she swabbed at Karen's face in silence. Karen used the time to get even more nervous. What would Elle want to know? Would she ask about why Karen and Jeffrey were childless? Had she found out about the NormCo deal and would she blow their secrecy on national TV? God, had they found out about Dr. Goldman? Did they know she was adopted? Would they talk to Belle or Lisa? So far they hadn't contacted either one, at least as far as Karen knew. But maybe Elle would pull a "This Is Your Life."

Karen's heart began to beat much faster and she found it hard to breathe. What if Elle Halle had found out about her adoption? What if someone on their research team had discovered her real mother, living in poverty some-where in the Pacific Northwest? Karen Kahn, the famous designer, and her mother in rags. Wasn't that the kind of thing that made Elle the success she was? Karen couldn't get any air deep into her lungs. She yawned.

"Need a bag?" the redhead makeup artist asked.

"What?"

"You're hyperventilating. Lots of people do it before the show. Need a bag? If you breathe into it you can balance your carbon dioxide. Or we can get you a Xanax. Amy Fisher had a panic attack right before *she* went on."

What a comfort. Karen couldn't decide if the woman was a moron or a sadist. "I'll be all right," Karen told the girl, but she wasn't so sure.

The redhead had finished the base coat and Karen was painted an even orange. With her round cheeks and soft chin she looked a lot like a pumpkin. The redhead began painting brown stripes alongside her nose and under her chin, then blended them with a sponge. Karen closed her eyes. She decided she would kill Mercedes, then fire her.

The girl pulled off the plastic smock at last and Karen looked into the big mirror. Actually, she didn't look so bad. She looked rather technicolor, like herself only more so. "There you go," said the redhead.

"Thanks," Karen said, and was about to compliment the job when the segment producer showed up again. He wanted her safely back in the green room. They were walking down the hall when a familiar short broad bulk approached.

"Hey, Karen. Lookin' good," Bobby Pillar said.

"You ought to know. You own a network," Karen smiled. "But not this one. What are you doin' here?"

"A little of this, a little of that. And maybe watching you. I have a feeling you'd just be a natural on television."

"A natural disaster," Karen croaked. "I'm afraid I'm going to wet my pants."

"So what if you do? That they'll edit out," he laughed. "Why don't we do lunch some time?" he asked.

"Sure," she said, but was relieved when her minder cleared his throat and gave her a not-so-gentle little push toward the green room. A technician came to her with a tiny mike on a thin black cord. "Could you snake this up your sweater?" he asked. She nodded and pulled the end out of the turtleneck. "Now could you take this end and clip it somewhere?" he asked. The lower end of the cord had a black box about the size of a Walkman attached to it. Karen wondered if it would spoil the line of her sweater.

The sound man, meanwhile, was fiddling with the mike. "You know," he said, "this sweater collar is really going to make a problem for us. I think it will rub against the microphone. Could you put on something else? I could call wardrobe."

She looked at him as if he was crazy. She had thought for weeks about what she was going to wear and had decided on this tunic and leggings as both comfortable and becoming. Now, at the last minute, he wanted her to put on something else? Something not designed by her? "Get Mercedes," she told the guy.

She sat down on the Herculon-covered sofa that was the major piece in the green room. For some reason, green rooms, the holding pen for the talk show cattle, were never green. This one was beige, and the walls were smudged. Probably with the tears of other guests who went out there and ruined their lives, Karen thought. Then Mercedes walked in. She'd already been told the problem.

"Defina's on her way over," Mercedes told her in a don't-you-dare-panic voice. "She's bringing a few pieces so you can choose whatever you want."

It took twenty minutes, but Karen saw Defina's face behind the rack of stuff being pushed into the room and took the first deep breath she had taken—for what seemed like hours. "Starting another fire?" Defina asked. "Never fear." She plucked a taupe jacket off the wheeled rack. "The producer says this will only be shot from the waist up. You can leave on the leggings, so how about this? Or, if you want to go real casual, how about this boatneck sweater?"

Karen turned to Mercedes. "Which would work better?" she asked.

"You won't see the mike if you wear the jacket but I like the casualness of the sweater better."

"Me, too," Defina agreed.

˒ Karen nodded. She peeled off the turtleneck and reached out for the sweater. Defina shook her head. "You need another quart of makeup, pale face," she said, pointing to the line that ended halfway down Karen's neck. This time the redhead came to Karen. So did the producer and the director. Apparently they were behind schedule.

"Elle is waiting," Paul Swift whined, and the redhead slapped the makeup on faster. At last, Karen was ready for her clothes. Carefully, Defina and Mercedes lowered the sweater over her painted shoulders. Then they snaked up the mike and this time it was clipped easily. It felt pretty comfortable, but Karen felt a little bulge just below the elbow seam. She reached up and closed her hand over something. It was a sachet or something like it, pinned on with a gold safety pin.

"Leave it," Defina told her. "Madame Renault sent it. It'll help."

And, for once, Karen felt she needed all the help she could get. What the hell, she told herself. Was the magic of Madame Renault any more superstitious than her own magic photographs?

"So what do you think clothes *should* do for a woman?" Elle was asking.

"They should compliment her, and they should be comfortable. And they should protect her," Karen said. She'd gotten used to the lights and felt as if she had managed to be both entertaining and sincere. Elle Halle moved in a little closer, crouching forward on her elegant white wing chair.

"Who do you feel deserves success in the fashion world?"

"Well, I think it comes to those who best reconcile a woman's external reality with her internal dream." Karen wondered if she sounded pretentious. It *was* what she believed.

"So what do you think about the clothes by Christian Lacroix? Or some of the other designers of excess?"

Lacroix was the first new French couturier to set up shop in twenty years. After a couple of seasons of huge publicity, he'd sunk in acclaim. The word was his backers had lost millions. This was one of the pitfalls that Karen had been afraid of. She knew Elle was hoping she would rip into some of the other designers. If Karen took the bait, she'd create a lot of bad feeling. If she didn't, she'd look like a goodie-goodie, and maybe commit the greatest television sin of all: she'd bore her audience.

Now she looked over at Elle. The woman was perfectly groomed. She was wearing an Ungaro. Her hair was a smooth helmet of dozens of blonde-colored strands. Not one was out of place, but Karen had noticed there were two people who ministered to the helmet every time there was even the slightest pause in taping. Karen also couldn't help but notice that no one had fixed her own hair since she had sat down. She wondered if her scalp was sweating from the lights, and if her hair was lank.

"I think diversity is wonderful," Karen said. "I think men and women should have all the choices they want. But for me, I don't want to dress in a costume, no matter how lovely." That should take care of Lacroix et al.

"So, are you calling Lacroix a costume-maker?" Elle asked brightly. She hadn't let Karen slip away gracefully.

No, Karen thought. I'm calling you a bitch. But she kept her face friendly. In fact, she laughed. "Wait a minute," she said. "*You're* the one who said that." Where had that come from? She'd turned things around neatly. Karen felt the little sachet bump against her elbow. Thank you, Madame Renault.

"There's a lot of stealing that goes on in your business, isn't there? For instance, a lot of people say that when you look at Norris Cleveland's designs this year, you're looking at Karen Kahn's from last year. How do you feel about that?"

Karen laughed uncomfortably. "You know what people also say? That there's nothing new under the sun. We all get our inspiration from all over. If I've inspired anything I feel flattered if it's well done and depressed if it isn't. Norrell was a great designer, and he said he just reinterpreted Chanel for his whole career."

Elle dropped the line of questioning, but immediately screwed that look of concern onto her face that the audience knew meant a real killer was coming. Karen braced herself.

"Women like you because you represent success in business. You have done so well in a man's world. So how do you think your husband feels, being second-in-command?" Elle asked. "Has it made problems in your marriage? It isn't easy for any man to take a back seat to his wife, and your husband is, if I may say, a very dynamic guy."

Jesus Christ! What had Jeffrey said in *his* interview?

"Jeffrey doesn't take a back seat to me," Karen said. "He's in charge of all the business decisions. He's always been the driving force behind me."

"So, you agree that he's behind, rather than leading the way. That you're the creative one."

"No. That's *not* what I said." Exasperated, Karen looked away from the camera, away from Elle. "We don't have a competitive relationship," she said. "We compliment each other. I structure the clothes. He structures our company. We *both* create."

"But *you* got the Oakley Award," Elle said sweetly.

"Yes, and Jeffrey was very proud."

"That's very modern," Elle said. "Does he mind that you have controlling interest in the company? You *do* own the vast majority of the stock?"

Holy shit! Where did *that* come from? Surely Jeffrey hadn't mentioned that. And the company was privately held, so how had Elle's researchers dug that up? If Karen denied it, she'd be lying, and if she confirmed it, wouldn't she be humiliating Jeffrey? Karen felt the seconds stretch out. She had to say something. "I don't have a vast majority," she said. "Both of us are happy with the way our business has developed," she added. "Don't you think we ought to be?"

Elle didn't answer. "Would you ever sell it?" she asked.

Karen took a deep breath. "I can't see it happening," she said. "But I suppose that anything is possible."

Karen felt sweat beading on her upper lip. She wished they could take a break, that she could get a glass of water and ask Defina how she was doing. She wondered if Jeffrey was there, behind the lights or in the green room. Was he groaning over her responses? Was she allowed to interrupt so she could regroup?

It wasn't necessary. Because just then Elle reached over and touched Karen's hand. "Thank you so much for coming here today," Elle said. As Karen opened her mouth to say "You're welcome," Elle had already tossed her perfect head and turned to look past the lights to the director. "Do we need any reaction shots?" she asked the darkness, and Karen sat and waited for the answer.

It was over at last, and Karen expected to feel a swell of relief. She'd gotten through it, come off pretty well, and hadn't been confronted with anything scandalous or shameful. Elle hadn't paraded her real mother in front of her.

It was strange, then, that she felt disappointed.

8

EVERYONE HAS ONE

Karen didn't like the country.

When she was going on seven years old her mother and father thought it best to get her out of Brooklyn for the summer. They rented a bungalow in Freehold, New Jersey. Belle was heavily pregnant with Lisa and the city heat was too much for her. But so was the Jersey heat, and because of it Belle spent her days enervated, lying on a webbed plastic and aluminum folding chaise. Karen had spent their first few hot summer days alone, wandering the country lanes. When she found a bank along the roadside where wild strawberries grew, she had picked and eaten dozens of them without noticing they grew amidst poison ivy. Who knew from poison ivy in Brooklyn? She'd come down with a terrible case—all over her hands, her face, and the inside of her mouth. It had been torture.

She spent two weeks in bed while Belle slapped calamine lotion on her and yelled every time Karen scratched herself. "You'll get scars!" Belle warned. As it happened, Karen's only scars from the experience were emotional: she still saw the country as truly dangerous. City danger was visible and largely avoidable—cross the street to prevent problems with an approaching gang of pubescent boys, avoid both cats and men nicknamed "Slasher," and don't get into taxis driven by Asians. But in the country, danger lurked in even the most innocent-looking flowers. The woods were filled with men with guns, rabid animals, dangerous ankle-breaking sinkholes, and worse. People could disappear into the woods and never be heard from again.

That was one of the reasons why Karen was unenthusiastic when Jeffrey had proposed building the house in the country. Of course, Westport, Connecticut, was hardly the country—it was more like an extension of New York's Upper East Side with lawns. Karen didn't need it. With all the trouble she had with her work schedule and in keeping their New York household organized, she felt that another domestic responsibility was not at the top of her hit parade. But when Jeffrey had been insistent, she'd agreed to make a Real Deal: they kept the New York apartment instead of upgrading to a better address, but they built the house in Westport.

She had to admit that it was actually a beautiful house. And Jeffrey had done it all. Valentino had his interiors done by Peter Marino. Versace used the Italian Mongiardino. Yves Saint Laurent had Jacques Grange and Oscar de la Renta used three: Fourcade, Despont, and that American *doyenne* Sister Parrish. So you had to give Jeffrey credit. Artificially weathered to a dove-soft gray, it was one of those modern shingled jobs that had all the charm of an old house with all the conveniences of a new one. It was Jeffrey's masterpiece. It sat well back from the road, shaded by two enormous maple trees, and the back had six hundred feet of river frontage.

Karen had to admit that the spacious white rooms with the oversized furniture (all with white linen slipcovers) were spectacular, but she didn't revel in the place the way Jeffrey did. He had suggested that Elle Halle's film crew come up and tape them walking there among the trees. That had been a few weeks ago, and Karen had ruined a pair of boots *schlepping* along the muddy river edge. If God had meant people to walk in the country, he would have made sidewalks. But what else but walking was there to do in the country? No movies, no shopping, no taxis, and you had to drive for miles to get anywhere. Somehow, sitting on the fieldstone terrace and slapping at mosquitoes wasn't Karen's idea of heaven. And who needed five bedrooms and four baths? Especially now, when they'd never be filled with children.

Ernesta refused to make the trip out to Westport, so on the weekends when Karen was there she depended on help from a local housekeeper. But Mrs. Frampton was almost more trouble than she was worth. Karen had to explain everything to her so often and in such detail she simply found it easier to do most of it herself. This morning, a sunny Sunday, she was trying to get the woman to help her organize the brunch.

Brunch was the only meal that Karen trusted herself with when she was entertaining people. She'd never have people over for dinner without a caterer or Ernesta's help. But brunch was relatively easy—a few bagels, some fruits and cheeses from Stew Leonard's, a little smoked fish brought up from the city, and she was home free. Even Jeffrey, a stickler for those kinds of details, admired her brunches.

Today, however, it wasn't coming together, but then, nothing had this weekend. Jeffrey had been insistent on making her go over all the stats again and again with Robert-the-lawyer laboriously reviewing the endless financials for the NormCo meeting. It wasn't until Saturday night, when they were expected for dinner at some friends in Weston, that she had felt even close to human. She'd put on the new brown faille tunic she was experimenting with and a pair of darker brown knit linen leggings. Very Medieval. She was always conscious of what she wore on evenings out. People expected her to dress well, and even though she'd like to live in sweat pants, she had to oblige. So she strove to come up with weekend wear that looked great but felt as comfy as sweats. And she did look great. Jeffrey had—as always—looked ravishing, his gray tweed linen Armani jacket setting off his hair perfectly. And he told half a dozen funny stories over dinner. She had remembered why she loved him. They came back to the house and the warming effects of a bottle of Bordeaux had helped them begin lovemaking, though it had prevented Jeffrey from finishing.

This morning the glow had faded and Karen was faced with the reality of more than a dozen guests and their imminent arrival. She had brought bagels from H & H and Ernesta had prepared and wrapped two trays of Nova and assorted cream cheeses from Barney Greengrass, The Sturgeon King. The stuff cost a fortune; sometimes all the money that she made and spent made Karen feel guilty. (She coped by donating a lot to charities and by rationalizing how her spending helped the economy. Jeffrey called her "a conscience with a Gold Card.") The sides of the sliver-thin salmon already looked hard and darkened and Karen wondered if the twenty-nine-dollar-a-pound lox would be tough. It looked like pink leather. Oh well.

"Mrs. Frampton, have you sliced the bagels?"

"No, Mrs. Kahn."

The woman didn't make a move. "Well, could you slice them *now?*" Karen asked. She never knew if Mrs. Frampton was passive-aggressive or simply stupid. And she didn't know which was worse. Of course, it could simply be hostility: after all, Karen was a New York weekender with lots of money while Mrs. Frampton had lived in this town all her life and had next to none. Mrs. Frampton's son was a local cop who lived with his parents plus his wife and two kids because he couldn't afford to buy a house in Westport. Between her church friends, other cleaning women, and the gossip she got from her son, Mrs. Frampton knew everything that happened in the whole township. And probably told everything she knew about Karen to anyone who'd listen. That was another reason why Karen hated the country. She was a native New Yorker and she looked with contempt at the out-of-towners, both the tourists or the bridge-and-tunnel crowd. They didn't know where to buy good Nova, or the best bagels, or where they could get their down comforter refurbished. They couldn't have played "the best" game with Defina. They were interlopers. Here *she* was an interloper, and people like Mrs. Frampton, George Hazen who cut the lawn, and Bill Mackley at the hardware store made her feel like a stranger in a strange land. She assumed they were anti-Semites and doubted their good intentions. But Jeffrey loved them. He called her paranoid and them "salt of the earth." He spent hours bullshitting with the locals: go figure.

Karen surveyed the living room making sure all was ready. It was an enormous space with a beamed barn-like ceiling. Aside from the two groupings of sofas and chairs, there was only a big glass dining table surrounded by a dozen bleached Windsor chairs. On the wall behind the sofas and the dining table hung a triptych in soft, almost no-color colors painted by Jeffrey's old roomate, Perry Silverman. The only other hues in the room came from the two magnificent Kerman rugs on the floor. They were all in the softest tints. Because they were silk mixed with wool, the colors changed as you walked on them and moved the nap. There was nothing in the house that Karen loved except for the Silverman painting and the rugs. The painting had been a wedding gift, but the rugs had cost her way over thirty thousand dollars each— and that was *wholesale*, through a decorator friend of Carl's. But they were worth every penny to her. They made the room.

Mrs. Frampton had finished with the bagels and stood, blankly, beside the counter. "Could you put those on a platter?" Karen asked. "I think the blue oval one would be best." Mrs. Frampton nodded and crouched before the kitchen cabinets searching for the tray. The kitchen was a kind of *haute*-suburban fantasy: there were dozens of cabinets, all white wood and glass-fronted (which meant that everything inside them had to be meticulously arranged). There was a triple porcelain sink, complete with not only two porcelain faucets and a spray attachment but also an instant hot water faucet *and* a pump to dispense detergent. There was a dishwasher with a front that looked like the rest of the wooden cabinets and a Subzero refrigerator large enough to hold a side of beef. It was also decked out to continue the cottage look. In the few months they'd been in the house, Karen had yet to turn on the oven and had only used the halogen Corning stovetop to heat water for her tea. That reminded her.

"Have you started the coffee?" she asked Mrs. Frampton.

"No, Mrs. Kahn."

"Well, could you start it now? Fill it to the brim. We'll need at least twelve cups. And when you see it getting low, could you make another potful? And could you grind fresh beans? Jeffrey likes the hazelnut blend."

She left Mrs. Frampton in the kitchen coping with the scream of the electric coffee grinder and carried the platter with the toughening lox out to the buffet. Meanwhile, the florist had delivered an absólutely impossible arrangement—it was rubrum lilies and tuberoses. She must have been showering when it came. Karen rolled her eyes. Only in the suburbs. Already the room smelled like a funeral parlor. No one would be able to eat with that perfume! Oh God. She put her hand to her forehead and rubbed both her temples.

All she wanted was to throw a nice little party, to get through the morning and early afternoon without hurt feelings, without an argument, and with a little bit of fun. This was a kind of obligatory gathering, but weren't they all? Belle had reminded her more than once that she hadn't entertained her family or Jeffrey's in months, so she was paying off all her social debts in one swell foop. Guilt, Karen figured, was definitely hereditary—you got it from your mother. The erstwhile occasion was her niece's upcoming *bat mitzvah*, but this was also a way to see all the family and friends she and Jeffrey were too busy to see very often. Still, even if she had been busy, she loved both her nieces and she wanted Tiff, especially, to feel special.

She also wanted everyone to get along. Stephanie would be meeting Tangela outside of work for the first time and she hoped the two of them might like one another. And if she wasn't going to have or adopt children, and this was the only family she would get, she hoped that for once Belle would get along with Sylvia, Jeffrey's mom, and that she, Karen, wouldn't feel uncomfortable with Jeffrey's two sisters.

Yeah. Don't bet the farm.

She lifted the vase of heavily scented flowers and carried them out the back door. The grass was almost up to her calves: they'd fought the lawn and the lawn won. Jeffrey thought it looked more natural and less suburban this way, but Karen knew their neighbors did not approve. She looked around her. White lilacs grew alongside of the slate terrace, and if she denuded the garden, she could replace the offensive blooms in the flower arrangement with the milder lilacs. They wouldn't give any color to the room but at least they wouldn't make anyone nauseous. Karen walked to the side door of the garden shed, found secateurs, and quickly cut two dozen branches of flowers. She did the best she could in pulling out the seventy bucks worth of lilies and rearranging the greens and the lilacs. They looked boring—really second rate. Then she noticed a couple of dead branches on the bushes next to the forsythia. She cut them off and added them to the arrangement. They gave the flowers a kind of off-center balance, a starkness of death to contrast the rich pearly droop of the lilac bunches. She brought the vase into the dining room just in time to hear the front doorbell ring. Jeffrey had put a Mozart CD on—he always preferred classical music on the weekends, although she'd rather listen to the Spin Doctors, or even old Stones tapes—and apparently Jeffrey couldn't hear the chimes. Karen hustled to the front door.

Defina stood there, holding a foil-covered dish, accompanied by Tangela. "Well, I'm glad it's you," Karen said with relief. "I could use some help and I'm not ready for criticism yet."

"Baby, I'm glad it's *you*. I swear, if we had knocked on another door by mistake, we would have been arrested, or maybe sent to the back entrance. Are black folk *allowed* in this town?"

"If they can afford it," Jeffrey said dryly and walked down the rest of the stairs into the foyer. Karen could tell he was already annoyed—he hated entertaining the family. Oh, great. So much for their rapprochement. "Let me help you with your coats." Karen took the dish out of Defina's hands while the woman shrugged out of her full-length Luneraine mink. Karen didn't like to touch it. She never wore furs, but she knew the coat was Defina's pride. It was a bit too late in the season for fur, but hey, who'd complain? Tangela was also wearing a floor-length mink—Defina's old white coat—and Karen had to admit that on her it looked good.

"I didn't know what you were serving but I thought cornbread goes with everything!"

"I've never tried it with pickled herring, but it *could* just be the next culinary craze," Karen told her. "Minsk soul food."

"I *said* not to bring it," Tangela complained, "but she don't listen. Everything has to be *her* way." Tangela turned to Jeffrey, who helped her with her coat, and gave him not only a big smile but raised eyebrows and a come-hither look to boot. "Thank you," she breathed.

Jeffrey raised his own brows, shot a look to Karen, and disappeared to hang the coats. Defina followed Karen into the kitchen. "What can I do?" she asked.

"Find yourself a seat," Karen said. "I'm just going to pop these croissants and the *pain au chocolat* into the oven." She laid out a dozen flaky crescents on the cookie tin and slid them into the stove. Was Mrs. Frampton eyeing Defina with disapproval or was that her imagination?

There was a knock from the brass doorknocker and Jeffrey led in Perry Silverman. Perry was still Jeffrey's best friend—one of the few that Karen sincerely liked. Perry, unlike Jeffrey, was still a painter, and if his career lately wasn't brilliant, his paintings were—or had been. He was successful enough to still own the SoHo loft he and Jeffrey had once shared, paint full-time, and get a show mounted every couple of years.

Karen had invited him for a lot of reasons, one of which was guilt. Perry's nine-year-old daughter Lottie had come down with a particularly virulent strain of leukemia and wasted away quickly, despite state-of-the-art treatment at Sloan Kettering. Since then, Perry's marriage to June, his wife of eleven years, had failed. Perry was a mess—just recently he'd canceled his last one-man show. Aside from poker with Jeffrey, Perry seemed to go nowhere and do nothing. Karen felt honor-bound to invite him, but she was surprised he'd accepted.

Perry kissed both her cheeks—not the New York social air-kiss but real smackers. She hugged him.

"Mmm, feels good," he said. Then he greeted Defina and Tangela and looked around. He shook his head. "Connecticut," he said grimly, "where the charm is strictly enforced."

"Along with the racial segregation," Defina cracked.

Karen rolled her eyes. Great. The two of them could bond in their negativity. And simultaneously piss Jeffrey off. Swell start to the brunch. "Come on, let me show you the house," Karen said. They walked through the swinging kitchen doors into the living room.

"Mother of God!" Defina exclaimed. "It's as big as a church."

"Mother," Tangela whined, correctively. Tangela looked at Jeffrey, who was already playing bartender, handing her a goblet of orange juice. "I think it's beautiful," she simpered. Jeffrey ignored her.

"What are you drinking, Defina?" he asked briskly. The doorbell chimed and Karen went to get it. Sylvia and Jeffrey's two sisters stood outside. Since Jeffrey's father had died, Sylvia spent most of her time with Sooky and Buff, her two married daughters. Sooky—Susan—was married to Robert, an attorney who handled KKInc's legal work, but Buff—Barbara—was divorced from *her* Robert, an investment banker. Both sisters were the kind of wealthy Jewish girls who had made Karen feel insecure all during high school. They were smart, verbal, and caustic and neither one of them ever let herself outgrow her size six wardrobe.

Sylvia had a new hairstyle. It was now more white than anything else, but there was still some pepper-and-salt, like Jeffrey's. It looked simple and chic. Her mother-in-law was wearing a Sonia Rykiel sweater outfit. Sylvia was one of the "Sisters of Sonia" cult and had been buying seriously from Rykiel for years. And Karen knew that when a wealthy woman did that she was not simply buying clothes but defining herself and her stake in a society that wore them. Karen didn't know if she should take it as an insult that Sylvia never wore her designs, or if Sylvia simply didn't think about things like that. But she suspected Sylvia did. "Come in," she said with the best smile she could manage, and the three women, followed by Robert-the-lawyer, did.

Robert-the-lawyer himself specialized in acquisitions, but his firm had represented June in her and Perry's divorce. June had come from some big family money and Robert-the-lawyer's firm had made sure she kept it. Not that Perry seemed to have been particularly interested in it: he had taken Lottie's death even harder than June. He didn't seem to have any interests right now. Karen had been afraid he might feel ill-will toward Robert, but he just looked up at the arriving group and managed a nod. He'd known them all since he was roommates with Jeffrey at school.

Belle arrived late, with an excuse from Karen's father and a long story about how he almost came with her but then canceled, about how he changed his mind and was going to come later. It made Karen tired to hear even a part of it. Before Belle was done, Lisa, Leonard, and the girls arrived and the party was complete.

Karen spent the first half-hour or so exclaiming over clothes, getting drinks, and looking for Mrs. Frampton. The guests seemed busy with the food and one another, but there were definitely three camps: the Kahns; Belle and her descendants; and the outcasts—Perry, Defina, and Tangela. Karen kept trying to get them to mix. It wasn't easy. It was just as well that Carl hadn't been able to come since he wouldn't have made it any easier. It took a little while for her to have enough time to get a breather. Finally, she had a moment and stood at the kitchen door looking across the room at the assembly. It was funny to think that the room held all of the stockholders of KKInc. In a way, they were all her business partners. They looked pleasant, affluent, and as if they were enjoying themselves.

But all at once, Karen was swept with a terrible sense of separation. All of these people seemed like actors, strangers. What did they have to do with her? What struck her most was the difference between her mother and Jeffrey's. Jeffrey's mother somehow looked both younger and older than Belle. Her style was more natural, more casual, and a lot smarter, which gave her—from a distance—the appearance of a woman of forty. Yet her hair color and her face with its subdued makeup showed her age, simply and without artifice. About Belle, people said, "She looks good for her age." About Sylvia, people simply said, "She looks good."

Belle looked forced. With her pleated dresses and fitted jackets she reminded Karen of a Jewish Nancy Reagan—all gold buttons and overstyled hair. Adolfo meets Rockville Centre. Poor Belle. She tried too hard. Karen felt a wave of pity for her. Once, in an interview, a stern Russian journalist had said to her that she didn't like people who dress too well because she was suspicious that they thought of nothing else. That was Belle. Yet despite the care she took with her lacquered shell, Belle's fear that she didn't quite fit in the world she wanted so desperately to belong to—Sylvia's world—was well founded. Belle couldn't quite penetrate the world of wealthy, educated, informed Jewish women.

Sylvia, on the other hand, seemed oblivious to everything but Jeffrey. How she loved her son! She found every excuse to tap him, to pat him, to stroke his cheek or ruffle his hair. And Jeffrey accepted her adoration as if it was his due. He wasn't a Jewish prince to his mother, he was a Jewish deity. Karen understood. She felt almost the same way about Jeffrey herself. It reminded her of the joke about Jesus: "How do you know Jesus was a Jew? Because he lived at home until he was thirty-three, because he went into his father's business, and because his mother thought he was God." Karen smiled. Jeffrey had always been close to his mother.

Jeffrey's dad had wanted him to join the family real estate business, but with Sylvia's help, Jeffrey had resisted, gone to art school, and become a painter. Karen knew what a sacrifice it had been to give it up in order to manage her business and still felt both guilty and grateful. It was good that now, after more than a decade, he was beginning to paint again. Of course he wanted out from under, wanted the NormCo deal to set him free. He deserved it, she reminded herself. She'd have to try to be more supportive.

"Come and see, if you want to," Jeffrey was saying now, and opened the door that led out to his studio. Since they'd built the Westport property, he'd designed a studio and had been working in it. Though he'd been very private about it, now it appeared he was willing to show his work to his mother and anyone else who chose to come along.

Just then Arnold arrived. Karen greeted her father, got him coffee, and settled him on a sofa while Sylvia, Sooky, Robert-the-lawyer, Buff, Belle, Lisa, Tangela, and Stephanie followed Jeffrey. Lumpy Tiff stood at the sideboard, waffling down yet another bagel. God, she looked awful. Karen felt her heart go out to the girl—Karen herself had been lumpy as a teenager and she hadn't had a gorgeous older sister to compete with. Now Karen tried to seem casual as she crossed the room to the girl. "Tiff, don't you want to see Uncle Jeffrey's paintings?"

"No," Tiff said calmly, and picked up another bagel. Was it her third or her fourth?

"I don't want to see Uncle Jeffrey's paintings either," Perry volunteered. "If I do, he'll want me to tell him what I think of them."

To be honest, Karen herself was not actually thrilled with Jeffrey's work. But what did she know about fine art? To her, the nudes seemed, somehow, too glossy, too obvious, rather *louche*. More *Penthouse* than *Art News*. Did Perry mean that he didn't like them either? She respected Perry's opinion and had come to love his subtle canvases. She looked at him. Had he been drinking? Enough to be drunk? At noon? Not that she'd blame him. If she was in pain over not conceiving a child, what must his loss feel like? Lottie had been an adorable little girl. When Karen imagined losing a child that way, she thought perhaps she was better off infertile.

Perry was a good-looking man, with long narrow eyes and a longer nose. His mouth was generous. If he wasn't quite so short and balding he'd be a real dish, Karen thought, surprising herself. She didn't remember the last time she'd noticed what Perry looked like. Had she only noticed now because this was the first time she'd seen him at a party without June?

"So, Jeffrey told me about the 'Elle Halle Show.' How did it go?"

"Like a swim with a barracuda."

"When is it on?"

"They're saying the week after next. But you never know for sure."

"So is she a babe, or what?"

"A babe?" Karen laughed, remembering Elle Halle's cold eye. "You're asking if Elle Halle is a *babe?* I can think of another 'b' word, but if this is remotely connected to some pathetic fantasy of yours, you're way out of your league. This woman eats network vice-presidents for brunch. If you're thinking of dating, why not just go for a black widow spider and be safer?"

"I asked a few out, but they all said they had to wash their webs that night. Too bad. It would have been an easy death." He grinned in a kind of cute, lopsided way.

He was serious, under the smile. "Is it rough?" she asked him.

"That's not quite the word I would choose," he told her. "*Agonizing* is a start in the direction of accuracy."

"Do you blame June? For the split-up, I mean."

"God, no. You must know the difficulties in living with a creative person: the mood swings, the hypersensitivity, and the introspection."

"Yeah. Jeffrey can be difficult."

For a moment Perry's face remained blank, until his eyebrows raised in an expressive are-you-stupid look. Then he barked a laugh. "You're a riot, Alice," he said, in a not-bad Ralph Kramden imitation. She was about to ask what the joke was when the swinging door opened.

"I think something's not right in the kitchen," Defina interrupted. Karen sniffed, and the bitter smell of burnt bread wafted to her.

"Oh, shit!" She hustled across the living room, into the kitchen. It was empty except for the smoke. Goddamnit, where was Mrs. Frampton? She pulled out the blackened croissants.

"Bread Branch Davidian style?" Defina asked her.

"Jesus! See if I have a couple more packages in the freezer, will ya? And turn on the vent fan. Maybe I can air the place out before they get back from the studio."

"No such luck."

As if to prove that, Belle joined them. "You didn't put the timer on?" she asked. "It's easy enough to put the timer on."

"I don't know how the goddamn thing works," Karen told her mother.

"In her own kitchen, she knows how things work," Belle said, confusing Defina, but Karen knew it was Belle's third person way of saying *she* knew better. Karen sighed.

The kitchen door opened again and now Sylvia stuck her head in. "Is everything all right?" she asked, her face all innocent concern. Why did Karen just know Sylvia was glad there was a problem?

Defina spoke up. "Yeah. The blackened catfish will be ready in a minute. You want your collards well-done or rare?"

"Uh, well-done please," Sylvia murmured and backed out of the room. So, for that matter, did Belle.

"Well-done collard greens?" Karen asked, and burst out laughing. "Come on. *You* don't even like collard greens."

"Oh shit. She don't know that. She didn't have a clue, and it got them both out of here, didn't it?" Defina opened the freezer door. "Hey, the bad news is there aren't any more croissants, but you do have three boxes of frozen sticky buns. Throw out that pan and just put some foil across the oven rack." The two friends got busy and soon the buns were in the oven. The thought made Karen wince. She still hadn't told Defina about Doctor Goldman's results. Well, there was a lifetime for that.

"What do you think of Perry?" Karen asked instead.

"Seems nice." Defina had taken the emptied bun boxes and thrown them into the garbage.

"Nice enough to date? He was married to Jeffrey's ex-fiancée, June. They're divorced and he's available."

Defina stopped what she was doing and put her hands on her hips. "For one thing, the man is in shock. For another, he's white and I done that thing. It don't work for me anymore. In the end, I feel too lonesome. And it certainly is no favor to my daughter, who's still trying to figure out if she's black or white. Lastly, he's only up to my waist, which, I admit, could come in handy sexually, but I'd just as soon get a tall one and teach him to kneel. Plus, even if I *did* have an interest, which I *don't*, your sister-in-law is all over that little white boy. Now hand me the oven rack."

Unobtrusively, during Defina's rant, Arnold had entered the room. Karen looked up and her father was there, leaning against a wall.

"Want more coffee?" Karen asked.

Arnold shook his head. "But maybe, if you have it, a Pepto?"

"Are you okay?" Karen asked. He didn't look well. Had she poisoned everyone with the fish?

"It's nothing," he assured her. "Just my usual." She got him a couple of pink tablets and he wandered off.

Karen and Defina had gotten things reorganized just as Mrs. Frampton returned to the room. Where had she been? "Get these baked. They take ten minutes. Then bring them out on a tray," Karen said curtly. She didn't mention the burned croissants. Mrs. Frampton looked at her impassively. Defina opened the door, took Karen's arm, and led her back to the guests, who were still talking about Jeffrey's work.

"They were wonderful. Weren't the paintings fabulous, Leonard?" Lisa asked her husband. He nodded glumly. "Well, weren't they?"

"Yes," he said. Lisa sighed.

Sylvia was, as usual, standing beside Jeffrey, her arm entwined in his. "Have *you* seen his paintings?" she asked Karen. "Aren't they wonderful? So . . . so . . . evocative."

The nudes Jeffrey was painting were anything but evocative. He was calling them studies, and he told Karen he was doing them merely to get back into the flow. But they weren't tentative or rough as studies usually were. They were direct and in-your-face. Evocative! Karen smiled at her mother-in-law. A man's most positive art critic was his mother. How come a woman's wasn't? Jeffrey was beaming. But Karen couldn't help but notice that Perry was scowling. Well, since he had stopped painting it couldn't be easy to listen to or see anyone else's work being fawned over.

"They are tremulous," said Buff. "Don't you think so, Perry?" Defina was right, Karen thought with surprise. Buff *was* coming on to Perry.

"Tremulous?" Perry asked Buff. "In the sense of shaky?" Buff turned to him and was about to answer when Tangela interrupted.

"Who do you use for a model?" Tangela asked provocatively.

Karen nearly laughed. It looked like *all* the women were busy running at the men. But Defina's brow lowered. "Who you thinkin' your boss's husband *should* be usin' as a model?" Defina hissed at her daughter. She took Tangela by the arm and led her over to a corner. Jeffrey just shrugged.

Karen smiled at him, just as Belle and Robert-the-lawyer joined their group. "Tell us about Elise Elliot," Belle asked. "Is she nice?"

Sylvia finally managed a smile at Karen. "Now there is a woman who is aging gracefully," Sylvia said approvingly. "What a lady."

Karen thought of the hell that Elise had been putting the workroom through, shot a look at Jeffrey, and smiled. "Yes, she's just a lovely person," Karen agreed.

"Has she had surgery?" Buff asked. "I mean, have you seen the scars?"

Karen shook her head. If she had, she wouldn't tell.

"So when's the date?" Robert-the-lawyer asked.

"Are you invited?" Belle wanted to know.

"Of course we're invited," Jeffrey said, offended. He wasn't merely a purveyor to the wealthy and famous.

"So, Belle," said Robert-the-lawyer, "it sounds like your daughter is going to be in the big time."

"She's already in the big time," Belle corrected.

"Nonsense, I'm talking Big Time here. This NormCo acquisition looks like the real thing."

There had been several other firms that had nosed around KKInc before, but it had taken this long for a company with the kind of money that NormCo had to get deeply interested. Karen had asked Robert to keep the offer quiet. Belle and Lisa owned stock in her company and she didn't want them to get their hopes up. Robert-the-lawyer was such an asshole.

"Who needs big business?" Arnold asked as he shuffled over. "My girl is doing just fine on her own."

"Hey, come on. Launching the bridge line cost a lot of money. Servicing the debt isn't easy. They need this deal."

Arnold turned to Karen. "Do you think so?" he asked. "Wolper stinks. He broke two unions, Karen. Never get into bed with a partner who stinks."

Oh, God, Karen thought. There's going to be a brawl. She loved Arnold but he had to get over his prejudice against every corporation in America. After all, she was a corporation now. "It's just a preliminary meeting," she told her dad, and felt guilty at the fib.

"So, tomorrow is the big day," Robert-the-lawyer said, helping himself to more at the buffet. "You think you're ready for it, Karen?"

"I think I can handle it, Bob." She liked calling him Bob. It was a kind of stupid name and he had so much pomposity that it felt good to deflate him. Why did he talk to her as if she were a nitwit? Did she act like one? Or had Jeffrey influenced him and made him believe that Karen was incompetent? Karen still resented that Jeffrey had made them give up Sid, a lawyer friend of her father's, and move to Robert's fancy firm. But Jeffrey had insisted and—after all—*he* handled the business.

Early on, the two of them had begun to play at roles: She was the creative designer and he was the guy in charge of the "guy things." Karen acquiesced because he seemed to gain some dignity from the division of labor. And she had benefited because she hadn't been hassled with the tedious taxes, cash flow, union negotiations, accounts receivables, and all the rest of it. But at times like this, she felt her role chafe. After all, they weren't just talking about hiring a new PR firm or selling remaindered bolts of fabric. They were talking about selling *her*. And sometimes the idea of losing control tormented her.

Rather than discuss it anymore, she turned and joined Tiff, who was sitting alone on the sofa. On the coffee table before the girl there was a plate piled high with three sticky buns that Mrs. Frampton had succeeded in heating. As Karen sat down beside her niece, the girl picked up the top bun and greedily bit into it. Karen could see the steam rising from the soft dough, but despite the obvious heat, Tiff kept chewing, sucking air in through her teeth to cool the hot mouthful.

"So, are you excited about the *bat mitzvah*?"

"No," Tiff grunted.

"Have you memorized your Haftorah?" The Haftorah was the section of the Torah that Tiff would have to read, in Hebrew, to the congregation. "*I* couldn't do it. I never even went to Hebrew school, you know," Karen told the girl.

"You were lucky."

"What are you going to wear?" Karen asked.

"What difference does it make, when she looks like a pig?" Belle asked the room loudly. Tiff shot a murderous look at her grandmother and picked up the next sticky bun.

"Put that down," Belle told her.

"Make me," Tiff said, her mouth full.

"Look how she gets talked to by her own grandchild! Don't talk when you eat," Belle exclaimed.

"Suits me fine," Tiff said, and took another bite. The room was silent. All conversation had stopped. Lisa joined them. Karen looked up at her. Lisa, as a compliment to Karen, was wearing one of the sweater-and-matching-leggings outfits Karen had done last year. But Lisa had glitzed it up with a Chanel belt that had about a hundred Karl Lagerfeld studs. Karen knew that finding a style that worked wasn't easy: look at Ivana Trump. Karen knew Ivana had once paid thirty-seven thousand dollars for a beaded jacket from Christian Lacroix. Of course, that was *before* the divorce. Lisa didn't spend that much, but she spent enough and still hadn't come up with a style, or if this was it, it didn't suit her. And she should lose the snakeskin boots. Karen loved her sister, but she knew that Lisa lacked two things: an eye and a spine. Karen gave Lisa a look, the look that meant "intervene with Belle." Not that Lisa ever did.

"Mother, please," Lisa pleaded ineffectually.

"Don't 'mother please' me. The girl has no self-control. Look at her! She's going to make a spectacle of herself. She eats like a horse and her sister eats like a bird! Fat and skinny had a race, all around the pillowcase." Belle ran her hands nervously down the flat front of her jacket and across her skirt as if she was brushing away nonexistent crumbs. Arnold joined them and in a quiet voice murmured something to his wife. "Don't start with me, Arnold," Belle said resentfully. But when he took her arm, she followed him out to the terrace.

Stephanie came over and sat beside her aunt. Like her mother, she was a peace-maker. "When are you going to be on TV?" she asked. "I just love Elle Halle," she added.

"Yeah. She's a real babe," Karen agreed, and flashed a grin at Perry. "I think the show is airing in two weeks."

"It's so exciting," Lisa said. "We're all going to watch it together. Do you want to come over?" she asked Karen.

For some reason, the idea gave Karen the willies, so she only smiled non-committally. "Maybe," she said. She loved Lisa, but somehow spending time with her had become more and more difficult. Lisa was jobless, Karen was childless, and perhaps they envied one another a little. Karen didn't know why but it seemed as if Lisa was on a whole different track, living in some other universe that wasn't even parallel. It made Karen feel both guilty and alone.

It was funny: she didn't give a rat's ass about either Elle Halle or Elise Elliot but everyone else was impressed with that. She *did* care about the Oakley Award, but no one here had even mentioned it. Karen sighed.

"I'm really excited about my job with you," Stephanie said. Karen patted her leg.

"Me too, Stephie." Karen looked over at Tiff and watched the girl slowly chew the third sticky bun, while a tear dripped down her cheek. Karen felt a wave of compassion for her. Karen patted Tiff's thick thigh as well. "Do you know what I've gotten you for your *bat mitzvah?*" she asked Tiff.

"A Kevorkian machine?" Tiff asked.

Karen laughed in surprise. The kid was really funny. Maybe Tiff would be all right. She was smart and had a sense of humor. She'd come through this awkwardness. After all, her aunt had. Karen smiled at the girl. "No. I got you pearls. You know what your grandmother always says."

"Yeah. That I'm a fat pig."

Karen winced. "She says, 'Every woman should have a triple strand of pearls.' So here's what I'm doing: I'm giving you one strand now, another on your sweet sixteen, and a third one when you're twenty-one."

"*Really?*"

For the first time that morning Karen saw Tiff's face light up with a smile. It was odd, but for a moment Tiff actually looked a little bit like Karen. Karen bent over and kissed the girl on her soft, plump cheek. "Do you want them now?" she asked, "so you can wear them to the ceremony?"

"Yes," breathed her niece, so Karen took her by the hand and led her toward the bedroom.

"Can I come too?" Stephanie asked.

"No," Karen told her gently. "You can see them in a minute."

When she and Tiff came back and joined the others, Tangela and Stephanie crowded around the younger girl. Karen realized it was the first time she'd seen the two young women together all afternoon. Didn't they like each other? "Ooooh, they're beautiful!" Tangela cried, fingering the necklace.

"How come you never got *me* pearls?" Stephanie asked Karen.

Were all sisters doomed to envy one another? "*You* never got *bat mitzvahed*, and you got diamond earrings for your sixteenth birthday. I think you're in good shape," Karen smiled stiffly and got up. She made her way over to the table. She felt drained, exhausted. She'd like to go up to her bedroom and lock the door, lock all of these difficult, troubling, annoying people out. She wondered, for a crazy minute, what would happen if her real mother walked in right now and joined these people. How would the stranger behave? It couldn't be worse than this. Karen felt so disappointed in everyone. She looked down at the table. She realized she was starving. Well, that's how she usually reacted to disappointment: by eating. She picked up a bagel and slathered on some cream cheese with chives.

"At the risk of sounding like your mother, you don't need that on your thighs," Defina told her.

"Isn't that the pot calling the kettle black?" Karen asked, and took a big bite.

Defina patted her belly. "This pot don't have to show *her* collection in Paris at the end of the month. And nobody around here better be calling nobody black, except me." Defina picked up the last of the sticky buns in one hand, took a bite, and lifted the empty plate in the other. "Let's get this shit cleaned up," she suggested.

Karen joined Defina in the kitchen. She rolled her eyes.

"I tell myself that all families are dysfunctional . . ." Karen began.

"Honey, some are more dysfunctional than others. No wonder white people been so mean to blacks. We shouldn't take it personal. They been mean to each other, too. I guess it's just natural." She began to hand the dirty coffee cups to Karen. "Your mother-in-law keeps confusing me with the help," she said. "Should I tell her she doesn't have the butt to wear the Rykiel?"

"I think not," Karen laughed, lining the cups up along the sink. Speaking of help, where the fuck *was* Mrs. Frampton? Karen would have to fire her. "I'm not sure I can go back out there," Karen said. Her lip trembled. "I had really wanted this to go well."

"Yeah, and I wanted Tangela to become an architect. The secret to happiness is a combination of low expectations and insensitivity. I just *know* you can manage both if you try harder."

"You know the saddest thing? I can't stand the way Jeffrey's mother dotes on him. Isn't that bitchy? But she just drives me crazy."

"Girlfriend, that's just natural. Remember what Princess Di learned. If you have to live with his mother, even four hundred rooms ain't enough."

"I guess it's a mother-in-law kind of thing."

"You know what Carl would say if he was here?" Defina changed her voice to a good imitation of his confidential whisper. "They say that Jackie didn't get along with Rose, either."

Karen laughed. "If only I knew who I disliked the worst: Robert-the-lawyer, Sylvia, my sisters-in-law, or my own mother."

"Go for your mother," Defina advised. "What the hell. My daughter always does." She sighed. Through their pain the two women smiled at one another. Then, in a perfect Yiddish accent Defina asked, "You want I should poison them?" Karen had to laugh. Dee dropped into Harlem street talk. "Madame Renault's recipe. It ain't too late. They still be eating."

Karen never knew what to think when Defina brought up the fortune-teller. "Tempting, but not today," she told her friend. "Let's just hope the herring does the job."

Lisa stuck her head in. "Oh, here you are," she said. "Listen, Karen, I'm worried about you. Could we talk?"

"Not right this minute," Karen told her. God, she still hadn't had a chance to really sit down and talk with Lisa. And when was the last time she'd called her? Karen felt another stab of guilt. She hadn't even told her sister about Goldman.

"I'll just excuse myself," Defina said discreetly.

"Oh. Great." Lisa smiled. "Hey. You've got lipstick on your teeth," she told Defina.

"Really?" Karen knew what was coming, but Lisa's eyes popped open when Defina reached up and removed her upper bridge, wiping it on a paper napkin. Then she popped the false teeth back in. "Thanks," she said, smiling broadly, and turned to go back into the fray.

9

DRESSED FOR SUCCESS

In the insane world of fashion if something happens once it's a trend, if it happens twice it's a fad, and if it happens three times it's a classic. Then, the next day, it becomes old. Right now, Karen knew she was hot. NormCo knew it too. But who knows? Maybe next year, maybe even next season, she'd be as cold as Tony de Freise. Karen had read in *WWD* that Tony had just declared bankruptcy. It could happen to her. But how could you prepare for that?

She was as prepared as she could be for the meeting with NormCo except for this—what would she wear?

Like her mother, Karen was obsessed with her closet, but in a completely different way. She had three closets, actually. One at her apartment, one at the office, and one at their house in Westport. And she had virtually the same spare collection of clothes in each. Coco Chanel, Karen's idol, kept only a few suits and a pair of trousers in her suite at the Paris Ritz. Karen identified. Unlike Belle or Lisa, Karen kept subtracting, not adding, to her closet.

Karen was commited to easy dressing. Her catchword in fashion was *wearability*. She knew that most women had too many clothes, were confused by fashion, and didn't know how to put things together. Or they picked the wrong look for themselves to begin with. For thirty years Karen had been making over strangers in her head. All the days she rode the New York subway to work, she never got over her disbelief of how women put themselves together. Had that blonde *really* put on the salmon ruffled blouse along with the red dirndl skirt and said to herself, "Yes! This is how I want to present myself to the world." Even among her wealthy clients, it was rare that Karen saw a woman who looked pulled together.

Karen had formulated a few theories about why it was so hard for women to look comfortable and stylish. American women didn't know how to dress partly because they had too much. She remembered a French woman who had once visited Belle. Chic, elegant, and a Parisian attorney's wife, the woman had looked in Belle's closet with horror and asked: "But how can you dress well? You have too much to choose from!" As the brilliant shoe designer Manolo Blahnik had said, "It's all a question of selection, to choose less. That is something Americans do not understand. They think more is better."

Karen had observed that French women, even the middle-class ones, wore expensive clothes, but they had far fewer things than Americans and formulated their ensembles much more carefully. Of course, they learned the hard way not to make mistakes: it was next to impossible to return merchandise in Paris. Can you imagine the attitude?

Karen's ambition was to take the chic style of the French and blend it with the greater casualness of Americans. And to a great extent she'd succeeded. What she was aiming for was foolproof dressing, so that American women could have the best of both worlds—the pulled-together chic of the French *and* the freedom of American coordinates. They should have choice, but not be drowned in fifty different looks and styles, the way her sister Lisa was. Or frozen in time as Belle was. Or married to a single designer, as Sylvia was.

Almost all the clothes Karen designed were in neutrals—wheat, greige, ivory, bone, gray, brown—colors that were natural, casual, *and* elegant. Colors that all worked together. Again, Karen thought of Chanel, who said she mistrusted colors not in nature, the colors of "bad taste." Coco took refuge in beige because it was natural, not dyed. And red, because it was the color of blood. Coco had said, "We've so much inside us it's only right to show a little outside." Karen had adopted a lot of those theories, although she no longer used red. She'd gotten sick of it during the Nancy Reagan years, and anyway, she wondered if Chanel had preferred it simply because it suited *her* so well.

That, of course, was always the argument: that women designers weren't as good as men because, inevitably, they designed for themselves. Karen knew it was partly true about her. But didn't male designers design for their mannequins: an impossibly perfect ideal that also didn't serve the average woman very well.

It wasn't just colors, of course. The silhouettes, though they changed, had to be comfortable, had to flow, and yet had to work well with previous collections.

The problem was, she'd done it all at high-end prices, nothing that the average American woman could afford. Even a bridge line, though cheaper, was still expensive. Karen shook her head at the confusing terms of the garment industry. "Bridge sportswear" wasn't worn for sports: it was the jackets and blouses and skirts and slacks that yuppies wore to work. And "moderate sportswear" was the code name for the cheaper stuff for the mass market. Bosses wore "bridge," while their secretaries wore "moderate." Karen would like to see all the working women given a better choice.

Now, the NormCo deal would allow her to open a more moderately priced line to go up against the Liz Claibornes and the lousy stuff of a Bette Mayer. In fact, that was what NormCo specialized in. Karen knew the secrets of her cut and style could be adapted for a larger market in less luxurious but still sensual fabrics. That was what the NormCo deal was all about; still, with licensing you lost so much control. She tried to imagine what it would feel like, okaying a collection and then seeing something with her name on it that she'd never designed. She'd have cardiac arrest. Bill Blass had once been asked to put his name on a designer coffin! Karen laughed and shuddered every time she thought about it.

The other danger was overexposure. Cardin and Halston had licensed so many products that their names lost luster. The fashion world was a fickle one, and very few designers had managed to maintain their cachet as Chanel had done. But then, nothing of Chanel's was *ever* licensed. During her lifetime she controlled it all, and the Wertheimers controlled it all since her death. Few had that luxury. You constantly had to walk the line between obscurity and overexposure.

On the other hand, Karen knew she couldn't manage to do much more than she was doing now without losing control anyway. She couldn't grow quickly without a lot of outside money. And if she tried it more slowly with their own money and it failed, well, that was simply a stupid risk she was not prepared to take. The best, as Jeffrey always said, was OPM: Other People's Money. In this case, the Other Person was Bill Wolper of NormCo.

Karen looked through her closet again. For once, she wished for something in black. If she wore the silk knit, would she look too casual? She'd almost feel safest in one of her signature wrap cashmere sweater sets: her basic dress with matching jacket or shawl, but that was surely too sporty. And maybe too warm. Still, she *was* the creative one and she wasn't going to put on a stiff little suit for Bill Wolper or anyone else. Karen believed a suit only looked good on a woman when she seemed naked underneath it. The fact was, she didn't even *own* a stiff little suit. Her claim to fame was that she had gotten successful business women *out* of them.

It seemed that Bill Wolper had gotten a lot of successful business women out of their suits, too. He'd slept with everyone. At least that was the word on the Avenue. Karen had never met him, but she'd seen pictures of the guy and had been unimpressed. The only attraction she could imagine he had was the size of his checkbook.

She had shared the elevator with one of the staff of Oscar de la Renta who had filled her ears with gossip about Wolper. But maybe that was simply to turn her off. Maybe he'd heard word of the possible deal. There was a certain amount of envy in the rag trade and right now she knew she was the girl of the moment. Not because of anything so new, but mostly because of her high profile in the press.

And PR was almost as important in her business as Karen's designs were. She'd hated to admit to that, but after years of struggling to get exposure, she'd let Jeffrey hire Mercedes Bernard. Karen knew she and Jeffrey had been lucky to woo her away from the magazine. They got her at the right moment: Mercedes was tired of years of high status and low pay. She wanted a score before retirement, and Jeffrey had promised her stock. In the sixteen months since Mercedes had arrived, Karen had been the subject of a major article in *Vanity Fair*, both *New Woman* and *New York* magazine had done a cover story on her, the fashion books had given her a lot more editorial coverage, she'd been interviewed by Charlie Rose and Barbara Walters, and had been on CNN half a dozen times. She and Elsa Klensch were bosom buddies.

If Karen resented the fact that the journalists seemed focused on her and her life more than her designs, she knew that she simply had to live with it. America was the center of the cult of celebrity and name recognition was everything. Fashion designers used to be almost laughable, like hairdressers. But now they seemed to be regarded more as movie stars, and people pranced around them. So Karen played the game because she knew that her high profile was one of the things that made her desirable to NormCo.

The telephone rang. Karen didn't have time to answer it, but she couldn't help listening as the message was taken by her machine. "Karen? It's Lisa. I tried you at the office but there was no answer. I'm so sorry about the brunch. I know it wasn't great. I hope you're not mad. Let's talk." There was a brief pause but Karen could hear that her sister hadn't hung up. "I miss you, Karen," Lisa said, and then, after a moment, there was the buzz of the dial tone followed by the click of the machine turning itself off. Karen felt yet another wave of guilt. She should have talked to Lisa. How long had she been putting her off? But it was harder and harder to. As Karen's life expanded, Lisa's had contracted. How could she explain without sounding as if she were bragging?

Now Karen reached up and took down the stone-color silk knit button-less cardigan and the matching dress. She put on a new pair of Fogal panty-hose. At twenty-six dollars they were a ridiculous luxury and they snagged if you even sneezed, but for absolute sensuousness and for subtlety of color there was nothing that could touch them—including her own fingernails. Karen usually couldn't be bothered to put on the little cotton gloves Fogal sold to help you get safely into your hose, but today she did, and slipped into them with only the smallest undignified wriggle at the thigh. They had a con-trol top that compressed her line down to the knee. The tricks a middle-aged woman had to resort to underneath a dress to get it to move well!

Why was it that every woman in America over the age of consent hated her thighs, Karen wondered, and not for the first time. It was, in fact, a preoc-cupation of her life and one of the keys to her success. Knowing how women, all women, hated their thighs or their bellies, Karen designed virtually every bit of clothing around that fact. Now she lifted her arms and slithered into the silk knit, wrapping the sleeves of the cardigan around the waist. The cardigan could actually be worn as a sweater, but neither she nor any of the people who worked for her had ever done it. All of them, and most of her clients, used the matching sweater to camouflage their waists and thighs and hips. At eight hundred and sixty dollars retail, they made expensive belts, but they did the job. It looked casual, comfortable, but great. And it felt great, too. Clothes *had* to feel good against the skin. Karen would never do a blouse or dress in Lurex—it would scratch. Now she pulled out the pair of kid-leather shoes that were toned to the Fogal stockings and slipped into the stacked-heel pumps. Then she strode to the mirror.

It was great. It was better than great. It was *right*. Simple, but simple wasn't easy. Karen knew just how far the right clothing went to not just dress one but to protect one as well. What were all those fucking power suits that men put on for the boardroom about? Armor, twentieth-century style.

She looked at her reflection. The color was good for her—it enlivened the dishwater brown of her hair. She picked up an envelope purse in just the same tone and slipped her notes into it. Then, as an afterthought, she added the two photos of herself as a child. They had become like her American Express card—she didn't leave home without them. She looked back at her-self. The bag looked nice, and the luster of the silk gave the dress a lot of energy, while the sweater camouflaged any weakness she might have. She had to stop for a moment and almost sighed aloud. Funny that her weakness—well, the nonfunctioning part of her person—was actually housed there, somewhere under the belt-tied arms of the sweater. Still, glancing at herself in the mirror, she didn't *look* like an unfertile woman. She looked sexy and sophisticated, yet at ease, successful and secure, without being flashy or dowdy. Karen wasn't young anymore, but she wasn't quite middle-aged. At least she didn't feel as if she were. Yet she never wanted to dress too youthfully—she hated that look of desperation. Her clothes reflected that philosophy and she knew her clientele could sense that. After all, they were rarely young girls.

Now, the next big question: Accessories! Karen moved to the bureau. She rejected the idea of a scarf as too fussy. She designed them but she rarely wore them. At least not as scarves. She wrapped them as belts, tied them around her hair, knotted them around purse straps. Still, something across the expanse of shoulder and neckline, something to break the line and draw attention to her face, would be nice. Jewelry, perhaps?

She turned to the miniature chest of drawers that sat on the bureau and it housed her entire collection of jewelry. She didn't have much real stuff, mostly because she didn't like it. The only designer whose gold and precious stones she adored was Angela Cummings, but Karen was too practical to spend ten thousand dollars for an inlaid gold cuff bracelet that got in her way when she sketched. Mostly she wore the costume stuff that she herself designed. Now, she took out a six-strand necklace of irregularly shaped gold beads. It had a kind of Cleopatra-in-the-Year-Two-Thousand feel to it, and she clipped it around her neck. Yes, the gold set off the sheen of the silk knit and Karen liked the feel of the heavy beads on her chest. Dressing *was* a kind of armor. She was girded for battle.

By the time she was ready, Jeffrey was already waiting for her in the limo downstairs. The presentation was going to be held at the NormCo headquarters on Park Avenue at Fiftieth Street. Defina, Robert-the-lawyer, and a couple of key staff members would meet them in the lobby. The moment she stepped into the car, Jeffrey handed her a folder. "You want to go through these numbers again?" he asked.

"No," she said, and he was smart enough to desist.

She was nervous. This wasn't like a trunk show, where she knew the kinds of questions she'd be asked and knew the line she was selling. This felt more like an eleventh-grade algebra test, something she had never been able to adequately prepare for. She had a sinking feeling now, as then, that when she was asked, "What is the value of x," she would answer wrong.

As if he was reading her mind, Jeffrey said, "Remember, if they ask you what value we place on KKInc, you can't give them a number."

She nodded, tensely. Christ! It was as she suspected all along: *any* answer she gave for the value of x would be incorrect.

And what was x, exactly? What were they selling today, if they could sell anything at all? Her name? Her freedom? Her staff? Karen considered herself a good merchant, but despite her sales ability she felt out of her league. And confused. This was a male transaction, all about stock shares and cross-collateralizing and ROIs and net profit margins. She looked over at Jeffrey. He understood all those pages of printouts. But did he understand how she felt? Was he trying to sell *her* to NormCo today? Weren't there names for men who sold their women?

She thought again of Coco Chanel. Coco's friend Madame de Chevigne had given her one warning: "My child, all men are pimps." Coco had never forgotten it.

Now Karen took a deep breath. I'm going crazy, she thought. It's just nerves. I always get like this before a really important meeting. Paranoid, almost. I was like this when we met with Jeffrey's father, back when we first expanded the company. And when we met with the factors to borrow money so we could do the bridge line.

They had needed too much money to go to the family. And they weren't established enough to get it from a bank. So in the garment center, you went to a factor. Factors sometimes loan money without receiving any receivables as collateral. The loans are called "unsecured" loans, and they make lenders very nervous. Well, they made Karen feel pretty unsecure herself. But she had managed to present herself well, show all the orders on the books, and get the money that had, so far, allowed them to deliver on those orders.

But somehow this was different. Karen tried to focus. The difference here was that she wasn't sure if she actually *wanted* to get to the difficult goal they were trying to reach. It had all become too hard, too big, and too complicated. She shook her head. Somehow she had always imagined that things got easier as you moved up the ladder. She had hated working for another designer so much that she had gone out on her own. But being her own boss had presented a whole set of different difficulties. Financial ones. Emotional ones. And it was so stressful. Being the boss of others seemed almost worse than being an employee. It was lonely. Only Jeffrey kept her balanced.

Now Jeffrey put his hand on her thigh. Even through the two layers of silk knit, she could feel his hand was cool, even cold. Was *he* frightened? "You'll be great," he said. "You'll knock 'em dead." Despite its coolness, his hand on her leg sent a small electrical charge through her. When was the last time they had really made love? The night she had come back from Dr. Goldman's, the night he had said no to adoption.

The limo pulled to a stop in front of the Park Avenue NormCo building. A statue of a business-suited man with his arm extended stood there. It was titled "Taxi!" and was, she supposed, meant to be a whimsical bronze reminder of what "the suits" look like at rush hour. But it gave her the creeps. She felt better when she saw Defina's black face peeping over the arm of the statue. "The only guy in New York who can keep it up," Defina laughed, patting the uplifted bronze arm. Karen laughed too and slid out of the car, careful not to snag her hose on the limo door. She moved up the wide granite steps with Jeffrey behind her. She walked briskly, her carriage self-assured.

"You don't fool me," Defina whispered. "I can tell you feel like shit. But *they* can't. You look great."

"Thanks, you witch."

"Sure you don't want to replace that 'w' with a 'b'?" Defina asked and grinned. "Sometimes I'm *so* glad I'm not a white girl. At least *I* don't go pale when I'm scared."

Karen grinned back at her. "A little more blush needed, perhaps?" she asked.

"That, or a higher profitability picture," Defina cracked.

Karen rummaged through her lizard skin envelope bag and pulled out a compact. "Blusher is easier," she said with a sigh.

They were joined by Robert-the-lawyer, Casey Robinson, Mercedes Bernard, and some people from Robert-the-lawyer's office. Robert-the-lawyer didn't just look pale—he also had a sheen of perspiration on him.

Karen coolly handed him a handkerchief. "Never let 'em see ya sweat," she told him, quoting Donna Karan, and then led the way across the marble lobby to the bank of elevators marked with the NormCo logo. She announced herself at the security desk, and when the elevator arrived, she turned to them all, managed a big smile, and repeated the line that Shirley Temple's mother was supposed to have told Shirley before each movie take: "Sparkle, Shirley, sparkle!" Then they boarded the elevator in silence.

Bill Wolper's office was, of course, on the executive floor at the top of the elevator bank. Jeffrey took her arm as they stepped out of the elevator and into the hushed, enormous, and very bland reception area that greeted NormCo visitors. Karen couldn't help but contrast it with their own tumultuous offices. As if reading her mind, Defina gave one look to the gray plush carpet, black upholstered chairs, and granite reception desk and turned to Karen. "Who died?" she asked, *sotto voce*. The calla lilies in the four-foot vase were the last funereal touch. Well, Karen thought, at least form did follow function here. The place was a mausoleum filled with nothing but stiffs.

"This is definitely grown-up," said Casey Robinson. "And very butch, I might add."

"Enough, Casey," Jeffrey told their VP of merchandising. "Remember that you're hetero today."

If the office was austere to the point of sterility, the panorama was spectacular: south down Park Avenue with a perfect view of the top of the Chrysler building, and all of mid-Manhattan spread out in a glistening loop. Forty stories down and twenty blocks south there were raucous sweatshops filled with hungry immigrants working—probably for subsidiaries of NormCo—at starvation wages. But here, all was quiet and plentiful.

Jeffrey kept his hand on Karen's elbow and moved them smoothly to the reception desk, announcing them to the soigné middle-aged woman who looked up attentively. The little group clustered together with Karen at the center, rather like a herd of plains creatures protecting their young from wolf attack. Except, of course, that she was no longer young, she thought wryly. Maybe it's more like the way priests prepared the sacrificial lamb. But at my age I'm mutton dressed as lamb, she told herself, and looked down at her outfit to be sure it wasn't too young for her. No, she looked right.

Herb Becker walked out of an unobtrusive door and approached them, his hand extended in peace (or to show he held no weapon). Becker was NormCo's financial guy, a *real* stiff, who had already spent a lot of time with Jeffrey and Lenny, the KKInc accountant. Karen had met him only once before. Now he took her hand and swung it up and down as if she were a slot machine about to deliver the jackpot.

"Welcome to NormCo. Bill has been expecting you." There was a way they all said that name that made it sound like it was more formal than "Mr. Wolper," or even "His Majesty." The Englishman, Basil Reed, said it that way, too. How do they do that, she wondered.

"I'm looking forward to meeting Bill," she said, perhaps a little too sweetly. She felt Jeffrey's hand tighten on her elbow. She smiled at him. "Shall we?" she asked. The group moved forward as one, and for a terrible moment she thought they might all get knocked over as they tried to clear the unobtrusive door. But they thinned out to single file, although Jeffrey kept his hand on her elbow, walking slightly behind her. It began to annoy her. If he was her umbilical cord to the mysteries of the financial mother-ship, what was she? A baby? A fetus? Or was *she* perhaps the mother lode herself? What she knew she *wasn't* was a child or anybody's property. Even Jeffrey's. Was he holding on to her to comfort her, control her, or show his ownership? Whatever it was, it was time to let go, and as they approached the conference room Karen smoothly but firmly pulled her arm away.

The conference room, like everything else at NormCo except their profits, was understated. Recessed spots in the ceiling around the edges of the room made the conference table seem suspended in an oval of light. There was a silver coffee service, surrounded by white porcelain cups, sitting on a sleek laquered credenza. Alongside the coffee was a neat pile of the kind of tiny pastries that melted in your mouth and left no crumbs. In fact, Karen was sure there wasn't a crumb in the room, unless you counted Bill Wolper himself.

He stood at the far end of the table and, while he wasn't a tall man, she was surprised by the big impression he made. He was beefy, though not fat, and his head was large and rather blockish. But in person he was surprisingly attractive. In his late fifties, he still had dark glossy hair and wonderful skin. It glowed in a rosy way. He probably was simply a victim of high blood pressure, Karen told herself, but she had to admit on him it looked good. He put out a big, square hand to her but she noticed that he didn't move from his place at the head of the table. The mountain would have to come to Mohammed. She walked smoothly down the aisle behind the row of conference chairs and extended her own hand. He took it, and she was surprised once again, this time by its warmth. Why had she imagined that he was some kind of cold-blooded creature—a lizard, or serpent, perhaps?

"Bill," she said and tried to make it sound like a name, not a title.

"Karen Kahn," he responded, and he made hers sound like an accolade. "Oakley Award winner," he added. It was odd, how he'd picked the thing she was most proud of. They looked at each other for a moment, their eyes locked. His were a deep brown, and his lashes were almost as thick and dark as the hair on his head. He had two lines that ran from somewhere beside his nose to each corner of his mouth, sort of like parentheses. When he smiled, he had a dimple.

What's with me, she wondered? I actually think Bill Wolper is attractive. As if that's relevant. You're looking at him as if this is a blind date instead of an arranged marriage. What's going on?

She rarely noticed men in that way. She was perfectly happy—more than happy—with Jeffrey, despite their problems lately. But hadn't she done the same thing at the brunch with Perry Silverman? God, she was going crazy! She had to refocus her attention on the financial facts that she and her team were about to present, and she had to be able to assess the package that Wolper's team would be laying before them. She took back her hand. Had she let him hold it too long? Jeffrey extended his own and gave Bill's a hearty shake. Then introductions were made to the rest of the staff: Casey, Defina, Robert-the-lawyer, and Mercedes Bernard on her side; Basil, Herb Becker, and a few anonymous suits on theirs. They lined up at opposite sides of the table, Karen to the immediate right of Wolper. For a moment Karen wondered if chess tables might not be provided for them all so that pawns would begin to be moved around. Oh, Karen, get serious, she told herself, as everybody took a seat.

Another well-dressed, middle-aged woman appeared and asked Defina how she took her coffee.

"Black, of course," Defina said, and smiled at the woman innocently. As usual, Defina was the only black at the meeting. Still, she was graceful about it. But when the woman asked Mercedes for her order, Mercedes stood up. "You don't have to get it for me. I'll get mine myself," she said crisply. Her feminist disapproval didn't seem to cause even a ripple among the suits, but Karen could feel Jeffrey squirm. Bill Wolper simply observed, neutral.

"Well, shall we begin?" Jeffrey asked and pulled a folder out of his attaché.

Folders for everyone were distributed around the table—the glossy gray and black ones of NormCo and the beige, textured KKInc ones. There was also an engraved card that welcomed KKInc to NormCo's worldwide headquarters. Karen ran her fingers over the letters. How much had that touch cost, she wondered. Bill Wolper cleared his throat. "Let me start by saying what a real pleasure it is to sit down to this meeting. I know that many of you have done a lot of work to bring us to this point and, whatever happens, I want you to know how much I appreciate it." He looked back at Karen. "I have a feeling this was meant to be," he said. "*Kismet.*"

"*Bashert*," she replied. It was Yiddish for "fated," but she bet that Bill Wolper didn't know that. She hadn't even remembered that she knew the word, although Belle or Arnold must have used it from time to time. God, what was there in her that made her so contrary? She refused her Jewishness to Belle, who prized it, and then she threw it in the face of Bill Wolper, who must despise it. Karen heard Jeffrey sigh beside her. Well, he was probably beside himself, as well.

Herb Becker began the meeting with an overview of NormCo and all its subsidiaries. Karen looked at the spidery org chart and sighed. She hadn't seen anything as complicated since the printouts of her last ultrasound scan. She hoped that NormCo wasn't as dysfunctional as her reproductive system. Out of nowhere, she thought of the mother and little girl she had seen in Macy's—the delicious crease of the child's elbow and the satin smoothness of her chipmunk cheek. What, she wondered, would it feel like to have a little girl like that? Remembering the child, she missed part of Herb's boring explanation of NormCo's retailing arm. She glanced over at Bill Wolper and realized that he had his eyes on her. Was he looking at her as if she were some toothy subsidiary to acquire, or was it more personal? She felt her color rise.

"Karen, it's time for your delivery," Jeffrey said. She stood up and walked to the screen that had been revealed when a wall smoothly disappeared into the floor. Everything here was smooth, except her. Karen took a steadying breath. "Look, here's the thing: ΚKInc isn't like other companies. I know everybody must say that about their company, but in this case it's true. In each of the last five years, we have had between two hundred and three hundred percent increases in our volume. Annually. And I don't believe it's just good luck. It's not even good merchandising." She turned to Casey. "Not that we don't *have* good merchandising," she nodded to him. "It's because we know what women want and what women need. We understand today's woman. Because we *are* her."

"Well, some of us are today's woman," Jeffrey said with a smile.

"And some of us just want to be," Casey murmured to Defina. Jeffrey gave him a look.

Karen smiled at them all. "See, the thing is, it's all based on design. And in fashion, we have the endless excitement of designing for the body; deciding what should be revealed and what should be masked. Some people believe that the heart of fashion is sex. That's partly true. But I believe that women who follow fashion aren't doing it to please men. They do it to please themselves. It's one of the few means of self-expression left. It has also been said that clothes are a necessity, but fashion is a luxury. So, the women who buy our particular designs are buying them not only to express their personality. They also buy for the luxury of owning because owning this luxury also allows a woman to feel her place in society. People don't buy our clothes because we advertise them well or because we merchandise them well or because we get great publicity, although we do all of those things. They buy them because once they get into them, they can't *not* buy them. We *design* them that well, and either you believe that and we make a deal because that's what you believe in, or else we shouldn't be talking. Because if you're just looking for a name to buy, buy another name. We're proud of our name, but we're proud of it because it stands behind our designs." She looked directly at Bill. "Know what I mean?" she asked.

He looked straight at her and nodded, his face serious. The man hadn't taken his eyes off her since she'd entered the room. Was he flirting, bullshitting her, or was he serious business? Did he *understand*?

"Let me show you," she said, and nodded so that the first slide appeared.

From then on it was easy. She showed them the line and explained the thought behind it. Then she sat down. Defina took over and covered the licensing operations, Casey went through their merchandising, and Jeffrey presented the numbers. That brought up a few tough questions from Herb and Basil about the phenomenal growth and the decreasing profitability, about servicing the debt the bridge-line borrowing had created, but Jeffrey took the rap on it and admitted the problems they had had with interest payments and cost control. "It was," he said smoothly, "one of the reasons we were so interested in NormCo." He went on to say that he felt the strength of NormCo's buying power could help them reduce those costs.

Herb then made his pitch. He showed them the ideas for licensing that his group had prepared, along with mockups of the KKInc moderate sportswear line, children's clothes, home products, and leather goods. Most of the prototype stuff was ghastly, emblazoned all over with Karen's initials. Hadn't anyone told them that logos were over? Karen thought. Who had designed this stuff and how could she break their pencil so they could never draw again? Herb, unaware, smiled proudly. "We can roll you out in all these areas quickly and smoothly," he promised. It made Karen feel like a piece of dough. "Of course, these are only prototypes. But we can get you into mass market faster than anyone else could. And we see other ways we could help," Herb told them. "Our knowledge of offshore production might be useful. We have the contacts, worldwide."

Before Karen had a chance to talk about her feelings regarding the exploitation of Third World workers, Bill turned to her, touching her arm through the silk knit of her sleeve. She could feel his warmth. "But why are *you* interested in NormCo, Karen?" he asked.

There was a silence at the table. And the silence stretched on and on.

"I want to do more," she said, at last. "I want to be able to get my ideas out to more women. In a way, it's just ego—but not because I want to see my name in the paper or because I like picking up awards from the design groups. In a way it's bigger ego than that. I believe my stuff is really good. And that, given the opportunity, more women—not just the rich ones—will recognize that it is. I want them to be comfortable *and* look good *and* feel better because of me." She paused. "It isn't easy being a woman today. You work three shifts: you have a job, you've got a home and kids, and you have to maintain yourself and your appearance to keep looking attractive. If you let down at any of the shifts, you feel like a failure. I want to help make that third one easier. And I want to be recognized for doing it. It's my contribution." She paused again. "Look, I know it's not curing cancer, but it's what I can do. We have always believed that we could make it in a really difficult business with two simple watchwords: 'underpromise' and 'overdeliver.' It's the opposite of what most guys in the fashion industry do, but so far it's worked for us."

It was almost one o'clock and Bill Wolper stood up. "This has been a very interesting few hours. I want to thank everybody for their contributions and insights." Basil, Herb, and the other staff members stood up. So did Jeffrey and the rest of the KKInc staff. But Karen sat there for another moment. Was that it? Was that the only reward she got for spilling her guts? She felt flat, as if she'd let everyone down. Bill turned to her, leaned over, and took her hand. "I have an engagement for lunch, I'm afraid. But I hope you'll let me take you out another time."

She looked up at him. "We'd love to," Jeffrey said, and Karen rose.

Somehow, they all got down the hall and out of the building without saying a word or breaking what Casey would call their "grown-up style." But once they got out of the building and onto Park Avenue, Jeffrey let out a war whoop. "Yes!" he yelled. "*Yes!* We got 'em. I know we got 'em."

"Did we?" Karen asked.

"Absolutely. They're salivating. Couldn't you tell? We got 'em!"

"But do we want 'em?" Casey asked. "Jesus! That Basil and Herb Show was too much. Don't they sound like some new salad dressing?"

"Just doing their job," Jeffrey said. "We handled them."

"Well, I wouldn't want them to be doing a job on *me*," Casey sniped. "But Karen, *you* were terrific. Some delivery."

Karen blinked at the word. What was this, a conspiracy to make her sad? She was selling her company, her baby, *and* being reminded she'd never have a real one.

"Yeah, baby, you were wonderful," Defina agreed.

Well, anyway, she'd read the whole thing wrong. She'd done good.

"You were great!" Jeffrey told her.

"So were you. All of you were," Karen managed.

"We are going to get one helluva offer from these guys," Robert-the-lawyer predicted. "I'd say more than we expected." Karen could almost see him working out his percentage.

"I say twenty. Twenty million dollars," Jeffrey predicted.

"It doesn't mean we'll *accept* their offer," Karen said. She thought about Bill Wolper and was surprised all over again. She thought she was going to have to sell herself and instead she felt as if she'd been seduced. She turned to Defina. "What do you think, Dee?"

"Honey, I don't know about the money, but I saw way too many double K's to be comfortable. Call me oversensitive, but if there was just one *triple* K I would have run screaming from the room."

"They're saving the KKK line for the south," Casey cracked. "There's a guaranteed brand recognition factor there."

"ЖKInc. Where race is always an issue, gender is interchangeable, and reality is an option," Jeffrey snapped, then shook his head. "You know what we're called in the industry? 'ЖKInc-y.' I swear to God, if NormCo gets just one tiny whiff of that, you can forget this deal or any other."

"You mean I have to give up my satin pumps?" Casey asked.

Defina raised her eyebrows. "I think they like us *because* we're a little left of center. Come on, this is the fashion business."

Karen tried to intervene. "Oh, come on, Jeffrey! You think Bill Wolper hasn't heard rumors that Halston was a little light in his loafers? Or that he thinks Willie Smith's early demise was from a heart attack? Jeffrey, we are not Midwest Corporate America. We're not even Wall Street. We're the garmentos—the crazy gays and ethnics that dress America. Surely even the great, white Bill Wolper has a clue."

Jeffrey turned to face her, his expression almost savage. He'd gone livid—his face was almost the gray of his hair. "Goddamnit!" he cried. "Goddamnit!" And Karen was shocked to see tears—real tears—on his long, dark lashes. "You're the ones without a clue. Robert and I have spent months setting this up and making this happen. Do you know how we've been sweating out the debt load we're carrying? This deal would put all of us—all of us—into the Bentley Turbo R category. And instead of thanking me, you're sniping at the opportunity of a lifetime as if they're lying dozens deep on the ground. Do you know that right now if our creditors insisted on immediate payment, we'd be forced into bankruptcy? And if Munchin or Genesco or any of the manufacturers decide not to ship our product until their invoices are paid we won't have any receivables next season? There won't be a next season. I'm doing a high-wire act here and I don't have a net. Jesus! You're all a bunch of imbeciles! No! *Worse* than imbeciles. Children. You're a fucking bunch of children." He turned his back and strode alone down Fiftieth Street toward Lexington Avenue. The group stood there in silence for a moment. Then, predictably, Robert ran after Jeffrey.

"Jeffrey, wait!" he yelled.

The rest of them just stood there at the corner, paralyzed. At last, Casey broke the silence. "What the fuck is a Bentley Turbo R?" he asked. No one answered.

At last Defina spoke. "I never knew Jeffrey thought children were even worse than imbeciles," she said.

10

OUT OF THE CLOSET

Karen felt as if she'd never been so tired. But she'd promised Carl she'd come, and she'd hardly seen him except at the Oakley show, which wasn't the same as spending time alone together. She was always so busy. She dozed in the limo to Brooklyn and now awoke as it stopped in front of Carl's Curl Up and Dye on Montague Street. The salon was on the ground floor of a brownstone that Carl owned and lived in. It was the trendiest place for haircuts in Brooklyn Heights, but in the fashion scheme of things that was only about half a step higher than being the coolest person in Piscataway, New Jersey. The driver held the limo door open for Karen as she stepped onto the cracked sidewalk of the quaint street. Brooklyn Heights reminded her of Georgetown, which reminded her of Cambridge, which reminded her of . . . well, of all those trendy-but-still-just-so-slightly-suburban locales.

"I'll be a couple of hours. Maybe you'll want to have dinner next door," she told the driver. "My treat." Capulet's on Montague was a sort of yuppie fern bar restaurant. She'd had drinks with Carl in there many times, but the food was mediocre at best. Anyway, the driver shook his head.

"I'll be fine, Mrs. Kahn," he told her, so she turned and walked toward the lighted window of Curl Up and Dye. What would it be like, she wondered, if your job were to sit in the deepening twilight and wait. She knew she wouldn't be able to do it. But maybe it's very restful, she told herself. Why are you always assuming that other people's lives are unsatisfactory and other people's style or job or deportment or accent needs to be improved? Why?

Because I'm crazy, she answered herself, and she rattled the locked door of the salon.

Carl heard her, stopped sweeping, and came to the door. He was wearing black jeans, black Doc Martins, and a white and black T-shirt that said, "I CROSS-DRESS MY KEN DOLL." "There you are," he sang out. "Hey, you look a lot like the Oakley Lifetime Achievement Award winner."

"What a coincidence," she managed to smile.

He put the broom aside, with a shake of his big head. "Life," he said. "One night I'm in the ballroom of the Waldorf and the next I'm sweeping up a stranger's hair off the linoleum. Cinderella in reverse." He sighed. "If you want anything done right, you have to do it yourself."

"Tell me about it," she agreed.

Carl looked at her in the harsh light of the overhead fluorescents. "Talk about Curl Up and Dye," he said. "You look like what the pussy dragged in."

"Well, at least I've come to the right place."

"Not for pussy, honey," he smirked, flipped off the light, tapped in his code on the burglar alarm, and put his arm around her. "We're outta here, Mary," he said. He reached down and picked up a flashlight. He flipped it on but nothing happened. He sighed deeply. "A flashlight is something I carry dead batteries in," he said. "Well, at least it's heavy. There was a homeless guy crouched on my upstairs landing yesterday. Scared the shit out of me. He was harmless, but you never know." He hefted the flashlight and took her through the side door and into the little hallway that led upstairs. He groaned as he began pulling his overweight body up each step. "Ooh, Mary! My dogs are barking. This is an overrated job for an overweight guy over forty. It sure takes it outta you."

They came to the landing and he pulled out a key to get them inside his apartment. Like any time she was stressed out, Karen was starving. She was grateful to smell something already cooking. In the bay window a small round table and two comfortable chairs were set, the candles already lit.

Carl's apartment was an almost perfect approximation of a tatty English country house, from the faded cabbage rose chintz slipcovers to the sisal that covered the floors. Old landscapes and botanical prints and heavily varnished dog paintings hung on the walls while the Empire striped wallpaper had faded around them. Everything had a used but homey patina. In the twenty-eight years she had known him, Carl never bought anything new. It wasn't out of cheapness: it was his form of creativity. He was always finding a vase that could be rewired into a lamp, which then required a lampshade, that then had to be lined with a particular pink silk, not to mention being fringed with the fringe that came off a bedspread he had bought second hand in some nameless thrift shop. He had created a fussy, charming little nest and he had shared it with Thomas, until Thomas died two years ago. Now, looking around, Karen noticed for the first time that somehow the place seemed faded in a tired, not-so-charming way. "Sit, sit," Carl told her and, with relief, she sank into one of the armchairs pulled up to the table. There was a tree-level view of Montague Street, the streetlights just turned on, shedding pools of yellow light in the deepening twilight.

"What have you been up to?" he asked. "Win any other lifetime awards this week?"

"No. I just had to do the Elle Halle interview and meet Bill Wolper."

"Well, ex-cuuuuse me. Did you have dinner with the Queen as well?"

"No. I'm doing that tonight."

"Oooh, Mary. She's so nasty! Someday I'm going to regret sitting next to you in Home Ec class." Carl was the only boy in Rockville Centre High who refused to take shop.

"We met in Drama Club," Karen corrected. She herself had never taken Home Ec. This was a fight they'd been having for almost two decades.

"Wasn't Rockville Centre High's Drama Club a kind of head-start program for homos?" Carl asked.

"If it was, what was I doing there?" Karen asked.

"Oh, you know my theory: you're a gay man trapped in a woman's body. That's why you're such a great designer."

Despite their joking, Carl heard the deadness in her tone of voice. He looked at her more closely. "So, how bad is it?" he wanted to know. That was the nice thing about Carl: he always knew her temperature. It was so relaxing, not having to explain or pretend.

"Not so great. There's a cash flow problem, and maybe an offer to buy us out, and Jeffrey's all bent out of shape and my mother is crazy. And I'm so tired. I feel like everything's going too fast and going wrong, even when it's going right. What would you call that?"

"Fear of success?"

"Feels more like fear of failure. Actually, I feel like my heart is breaking. Any suggestions?" She felt her nose begin to run. She sniffed.

Carl bent toward her with concern. "Read nonfiction," he advised.

She blinked. "What?" She wiped her nose with the back of her hand.

"What are you reading?"

"Uh. Anita Brookner. The new one."

"No. Stop *immediately*. Try *Money and Class in America*. Lewis Lapham. Arnold would approve. Very good. Or Naomi Wolf's new one."

"Carl, what are you talking about? I'm falling into a suicidal depression and you're doing Men on Books?"

"Look, baby, I hate to pull rank, but I've had my heart broken more often and by more guys than *you* ever will. Take my advice: now is *not* the time to be reading *The Bell Jar.*"

She began to laugh. She always laughed with Carl. Since the time they were teenagers—both of them too big, too fat, too plain, and too smart to fit in Rockville Centre—they had always been able to laugh at whatever their problems were.

Carl nodded. "Maybe some food will help your broken heart," he said. He disappeared into the kitchen and came out bearing a tray. "Make woojums eat nice hommy. Woojums feel all better," he said in baby talk and set the tray on a stand beside the window, using it as a sideboard. "So how much are they offering?" he asked.

"Who?" Karen asked, but she knew what he was talking about and couldn't help but smile. That was Carl: from baby talk to Wall Street in the blink of an eye. "We don't know yet. But Jeffrey thinks upward of twenty million." Karen almost giggled with the ridiculousness, the unreality of the number.

Carl turned and then froze, the platter of biryani in his hands. "Upward of twenty million *dollars*? And you're heartbroken? Honey, you *do* have a problem." He put the platter down on the table, brought out a few other dishes, and sat down in the chair opposite her. He reached out for a serving spoon and ladled a portion onto her plate. "Eat," he said. "You'll have to keep up your strength to carry all that money to the bank."

"But I don't think I want to sell," Karen told him. "I mean, we're having a little trouble servicing our debt, but that's just cash flow. And I really can't think of what I'd do with the money, except maybe put more in our pension fund. I already have two houses. It's not like I'm hungry or I don't have a place to live, or we need shoes for the baby."

Carl's eyes lit up. "What baby?"

"Forget it. I was just speaking generally. No baby. Definitely no baby. The latest hot flash, you should excuse the expression: I can't conceive, I can't carry it, and Jeffrey won't talk about adoption." She took a breath and told Carl all about Dr. Goldman. "Anyway, no baby. So why sell the business?"

"Excuse me for mentioning this, but I don't see the intimate connection between the two. Except that you're in disagreement with Jeffrey on both."

She sighed. As always, Carl got it. "Exactly. He wants to sell, I don't. I want a baby, he doesn't. And if those weren't bad enough pressures, Belle is driving me crazy, both of my nieces are acting up, and I keep noticing inappropriate men as possible sex partners."

"Well, in that last category you're not alone," Carl assured her.

"Maybe I'm just overworked," she said. "God, Carl, it's hard to believe that I've actually gotten even busier than I used to be. I've got a design team working on the bridge line, but it's killing me. Plus I'm doing the Paris show and I've just finished the dresses for Elise Elliot's wedding. It seems like the harder I work the more behind I get."

"These all sound like classy problems to me. A lot of pressure, but classy problems. All except the baby, and Jeffrey." He paused then and brightened. "Did you meet Elise Elliot yet?" he asked. "What is she *really* like?"

Karen rolled her eyes. "She's like a very rich, very beautiful client. How do I know what she's like? You want to know her inseam? I can tell you that."

"Your life is so glamorous," Carl said. "Karen Kahn: tape measure to the stars. Are you going to the wedding?" Karen nodded. "Do you think Jackie Onassis will be there?"

Karen took a deep breath. If Carl went off on a Kennedy tangent she'd run screaming down Montague Street. "I think I'm going crazy," Karen said. "I don't even know why I do most of the things I am doing." She took another deep breath. "You know what I've thought of?" she asked. He shrugged. She told him about the urge to find her real mother, the way it simply wouldn't go away. She talked, Carl ate. It was comforting. It was the only thing that hadn't changed since she was sixteen years old.

"You know the saddest thing?" she asked finally. He shook his head. "I'm really sad about the baby thing and I keep getting sadder. I mean, I don't figure my Oakley Award will keep me company in the nursing home. I'd love a kid. I think about all the things I'll never get to do, like buying a first pair of shoes, or the first party dress. And you know, I'm really sad that I'll never get to wear a bed jacket."

"A what?" Carl asked, his mouth full.

"A bed jacket. You know, those quilted satin things that women in old movies wore in the hospital after they gave birth. I don't even know if anyone makes them anymore. And what the hell do you wear under them, anyway? You think all those women were naked from the waist down? Anyway, I don't know why it bothers me so much, but I guess I always wanted to wear one. It just seems an important part of the female experience."

"Yeah, like leg waxing."

Karen smiled, but her smile was watery. "It's hard to give up that bed jacket."

Carl nodded.

"So, what do you think?" she asked, as she always did.

Carl finished chewing and daintily wiped his mouth. "Honey, I think what I always have thought: you're overworked. You don't have time to know what you feel about anything. Meanwhile, I think you're going through a rough patch in your marriage, but hey, who doesn't? I love you, and I'll support you in whatever you decide, but Karen, sweety, with this last thing, what do you expect to find?"

"My real mother," she told Carl.

"And how will that help? How will that change anything? Don't get me wrong—I think you should go for it. Finding one's roots—except, of course, those in our hair—is very popular nowadays. People seem to want to do it. Although for me, knowing mine is more than a little dispiriting." Carl had grown up over the Rockville Centre butcher shop that his father ran. Pfaff's Pork Store. The kids, inevitably, had called him Porky Pig. He was still living over the store, and still kind of porky, but he no longer saw his family and he was now a strict vegetarian. Some things *had* changed.

Carl looked at Karen and raised his eyebrows. "What if you find out your real mother is working behind the counter in Pfaff's Pork Store? Or a rummy living on welfare in an SRO hotel in Queens? Look at all the blood relations that the Kennedys have. It hasn't made any of them happy. Think of all that tragedy. I mean, who buys into this crap that blood is thicker than water? And what's so great about being thick anyway? Mud is thick. My mother is thick as a plank, but that doesn't help me." He lowered his eyebrows and his voice and reached out and took Karen's hand. "Honey, you don't think that you're going to find a pot of love at the end of the rainbow, do you?"

Karen shook her head. "I honestly don't think so. I was just thinking about it, that's all." She sighed. "Oh, who knows?" She looked at his pink round face, a face that showed true concern.

Carl rolled his eyes. "So, on a happier note, how's your sex life?"

Karen snorted. "What sex life? We never see each other, and when we do, we're exhausted. I don't know. Maybe it was all those special practices we had to get into when I was trying to conceive. You know, standing on my head, waiting for the little sperm to find my ovum. It wasn't very spontaneous or attractive. Maybe it turned Jeffrey off me completely."

"Or maybe he's angry. I always held out on Thomas when I was mad at him. Famous passive-aggressive strategy."

"What would Jeffrey be angry about?"

"Oh, Karen, gimme a break. He could be mad because you don't cook. He could be mad because you haven't given him a son. He could be mad because his father didn't love him. He could be mad because you're the boss and he's not."

"But he *is* the boss. He makes all the financial decisions. He always has."

"Come off it; it's a bone. The company is *Karen* Kahn, not Jeffrey Kahn, and *you* are it."

"Kahn is his name too. Come on, Carl. He adjusted to all this a long time ago."

"Sez you." Carl paused. "Look, what do I know? Once I didn't speak to Thomas for a whole weekend because he bought Miracle Whip instead of Hellmann's Mayo. I thought if he really loved me he'd remember that I hated Miracle Whip." Carl turned his head toward the window. The streetlight shadowed his eyes. "I'd give anything to get a do-over on *that* weekend."

Karen nodded. Poor Thomas. Poor Carl. What would it be like to have to go back to living alone? Karen wondered and shivered at the thought. She felt so much sympathy for Carl. He'd lost so much of his life, so much of his history, when he'd lost Thomas.

What would I do without Jeffrey? she thought, and though it was warm, she shivered again. There had really never been any other man for her. Her life had been school, Jeffrey, then work, and Jeffrey. She'd grown up with him. She acted independently, she traveled alone, she had her own friends and her own life, but knowing that she always went home to Jeffrey made all the difference. Going home to emptiness was unimaginable. Poor Carl. Karen felt a stab of guilt. After all, Carl was right. She and Jeffrey were healthy, they were still married, and their worst-case scenario was that they would get a lot of millions of dollars. Carl was the one who had lost big time, yet she was the one doing the complaining. "I'm sorry, Carl," she murmured.

He turned back to her. "Oh, hey. No sweat." He shrugged, looked back at her. "So, you're not getting any lately. Well, sex is nice, but just remember that it doesn't beat the real thing."

Karen had to laugh. Carl winked at her. Then his face got serious. "You know, neither of us is getting any younger. I hate to mention it, but we're middle-aged. And since Thomas died I *feel* middle-aged. Old even. It seems like it isn't the years that age me, it's all the disappointments. When you're young you can carry them or shake them off. But they start to accumulate— all the losses, all the hassles, all the disappointments. And the cumulative weight starts to crush out hope. I can't tell you how many memorial services I've attended. I'm bummed out. It's hard to live without hope that tomorrow will be better. I think middle age begins when you start to fear that tomorrow might be worse."

Karen nodded. "Has that happened for you?" she asked.

"I'm on the cusp," he smiled, but his smile looked tired.

"Maybe you need a vacation, Carl."

"Oh, yeah. With Thomas gone, who is gonna watch the store? Can you spell 'steal,' boys and girls? I'll come back and find we did two weeks of Visa charges and not a single cash transaction. Anyway, you were the one who needed advice." He smiled at her. "Listen, honey, I know you love Jeffrey and the two of you will work this stuff out," he sighed. "I'm doing heads in Brooklyn while you're giving head to the best-looking man in Manhattan. How could my life go so wrong?"

"Is that what you'd like? To be in Manhattan?"

"I should have been there from the beginning. But Thomas and I were afraid. And it's too late now."

"Maybe not. No one cuts hair like you do. You've got the talent."

Carl shrugged. "Maybe," he said. "But I certainly don't have the money to start up a business on Madison Avenue. And I'm not willing to travel with my scissors in a bag and do heads in people's apartments."

"How much would it cost to set yourself up? You know, with this deal, we could easily afford to back you."

Carl smiled at her. "Karen, sometimes it's hard to be your friend. You've always been so talented and so competent and so brave. I knew it back in Rockville Centre. You were going to break out. I didn't have the drive or the talent. I was scared and I played it safe. I wouldn't borrow money to get a business going in Manhattan. So I'm stuck teasing blue hair. I was like Jeffrey. I was afraid I might fail, so I hitched my wagon to your star."

Karen stiffened. "Jeffrey wasn't afraid. He gave up his career to help me. I couldn't have made it without his help. And without the money from his parents. They lifted the burden off my shoulders. If Jeffrey resents me, it's because he gave up his career as an artist for me."

Carl leaned back in his chair. "Umm-hmm," he said.

"Oh, you're impossible! You always take my side."

"I'll be on your side forever more. That's what friends are for," Carl hummed. "So sue me. But Karen, you are wildly mistaken if you think that you didn't do this on your own. The problem with you is that you never think in black and white. Everything with you is always shades of gray. Honey, I tell you, nothing could be more black and white then this: *you're* the one with the talent. It might make you feel lonely to know it, but you would've done this somehow, anyhow. Nobody gave you anything, and you deserve everything you've gotten. Don't sell your business if you don't want to. It's *yours*. *You* did it. And anyone who tells you otherwise is a liar. Or trying to manipulate you." Carl pushed himself up heavily and collected her plate along with his own. "Let's talk about something more important," he suggested. "Like how about dessert?"

"Nothing for me," she sighed.

Carl carried out the tray and waltzed back in with a teapot, a pair of cups and saucers, and a plate heaped with Kron chocolate-covered strawberries. "You sure about that no dessert rule?" he asked, tempting her. "Fruits don't count," he added, smiling. "Take it from one who knows."

Karen smiled, shook her head, and with a sigh of surrender, reached for the luscious-looking plate.

11

MARRIAGE A LA MODE

New York society meets Seventh Avenue at weddings. After weeks of design discussion and fittings, the wedding party for Elise Elliot's marriage to Larry Cochran was about to take place at Saint Thomas's Episcopal Church on Fifth Avenue. It was one of the two or three society churches in New York, rivaled only by Saint James on Madison Avenue, a slightly more chic address. But for sheer beauty, Karen knew it was hard to beat Saint Thomas's incredible stone frieze that rose thirty feet behind the altar, carved in faux-medieval bas-relief.

The church made Karen the slightest bit uncomfortable, but these goyim knew it all when it came to class. She wondered if any of the other Seventh Avenue designers, now a part of the larger social world, also felt uncomfortable staring at a crucifix. Of course, in his home, Calvin Klein had a collection of crosses and Donna Karan had done a whole line of jewelry using them. Ever since Madonna, religion had become a designer accessory.

She doubted that any of them would have been invited a generation ago. Designers used to be seen as nothing but tradesmen. Now they were hip. It was funny though how many Jews had made it by purveying fashion and style to the old-money WASPs. In some ways, fashion was like Hollywood. In both fields Jews had become major movers and shakers, the trendsetters. But in Hollywood and on Seventh Avenue no one did it by being too visibly Jewish. In fact, most of them seemed to be drawn to a WASP ideal. Jewish men married blonde shiksas with names like Kelly and Buff. So many in the fashion industry had changed or disguised their names. Ralph Lauren had, of course, been Ralph Lifshitz. Arnold Scaasi had reversed the spelling of his last name so he was no longer an Isaacs. The great Norrell had been Norman Levinson. The late Anne Klein had started life as Hannah Golofsky. What if she hadn't married Ben Klein?

Of course, Karen knew how important a name was in this business. Clothes, perfume, an entire line of goods was sold based on name recognition and the images that name conjured up. Karen had not kept her name, but then there was a certain alliteration to "Karen Kahn." Would Karen Lipsky's gowns be walking down the aisle here at Saint Thomas's? Would women be turning up for her trunk shows?

The organ began to play. Karen had to admit that it was also hard to beat the Episcopalian music. This was no "Hava Nagila." Saint Thomas's was the American equivalent to Saint Martin's-in-the-Field, a London church where the choir and the ecclesiastical songs of praise were as important as the stonework. But today, Karen thought, the beauty of both would take a back seat to the beauty of the congregation gathered to see this unlikely but terribly romantic union take place.

Karen had come into the church several times while she worked on the wedding outfit designs. After all, a costume ought to be appropriate in its setting. Elise Elliot had actually made the suggestion, and she had been right.

Elise was one of the last great movie stars; she was from a time when studios not only ruled but *orchestrated* actors lives. Those days long gone, she had the personal wealth and professional savvy to create and oversee this event for herself, trying to achieve the almost impossible: to maximize the publicity while retaining her dignity and some of the privacy of the moment. Though Elise had been demanding, even obsessive, about the dresses, Karen admired her. She was a woman with great presence who had been dressed by the very best couturiers for three decades or more. Few women really understood clothes and what worked for them and what didn't. Elise knew, and demanded what was needed.

But Karen also recognized that under the cool, knowing, and beautiful exterior, Elise was a woman terrified of looking foolish. She was mortally afraid that her age would show and that in pictures published all around the world she would be observed, judged, and laughed at. Karen took on the job to make sure that didn't happen.

It was a difficult job. From what Karen could see, Elise loved Larry as passionately as Karen still loved Jeffrey. So Elise deserved a celebratory dress. Also, a bride should look new and fresh. But how could Elise look fresh *and* her age at the same time? If that conundrum wasn't enough, Elise had two matrons of honor: tiny, bird-like Annie Paradise and corpulent Brenda Cushman. They could not possibly be dressed similarly with any hope of success, yet Elise had insisted that their costumes be coordinated, and she had asked Karen to create a look that was both female and sophisticated.

Elise, not only an actress but an heiress, was paying for everything, but while money wasn't an issue, her perfectionism and the difficulty of the assignment was. Vera Wang and Carolina Herrera did the gowns for ninety percent of society weddings, and while it was an honor that Karen had been asked, it was eating up her time. Jeffrey, who was waiting for the offer from NormCo and would be tense until he got it, complained bitterly. Karen knew that because of the investment of time she would never make any money on the deal, but she also knew that her designs would be seen worldwide, and if they looked good she could prove in a single stroke that she could dress *any* woman beautifully: tall, regal, but aging Elise; short, thin, Annie; and big, round Brenda. It would be quite a coup, but it was no easy trick. And, in a way, it would enhance KKInc's value to NormCo. But only if the dresses worked.

Just when they'd finished making up the dresses, Elise, who always kept herself in the same perfect shape, had lost weight in the last two weeks before the wedding. Hysterical, Karen and Mrs. Cruz had to spend an emergency evening taking in the bridal dress. Karen didn't trust anyone else to do it. Meanwhile, Annie Paradise had been on a book tour and missed two fittings, while fat Brenda had dieted off quite a bit of weight, only to rebound at the last minute. It was all enough to make Karen, Elise, and all the women in the workroom absolutely crazy. But they had persevered and now Karen sat in the ninth pew, along with Jeffrey, like everyone else waiting for the processional march to begin and hoping for the gasp that accompanied the entrance of a successfully dressed bride.

Karen watched while the final guests continued to flow in. There were people from the New York society world, designers that Elise had been a client of for years, titled Europeans, young models, plus a full measure of Hollywood royalty. Isaac Mizrahi, a great designer who hadn't yet managed to find the backing to expand from his couture work, arrived with Sandra Bernheart. Christy Turlington and Amber Valletta, two of the hottest mannequins, arrived almost at the same time. That seemed a new trend—top models as best pals. Ralph and Ricky Lauren sat with their two sons, David and Andrew. Donna Karan was seated with her husband, Stephan Weiss, both all in black. And while Calvin Klein didn't seem to come, his wife, Kelly, and her stepdaughter, Marci, were there to represent him. Kelly was wearing her famous pearl necklace—Calvin had bought it for her from the Duchess of Windsor's estate. There were a lot of jokes about Kelly in the fashion business. The marriage was once rumored as one of convenience, and a pun had been popular based on Kelly's maiden name, Rector. "Heard that Calvin married Kelly?" says the first guy. "Rector?" the second asked. The first raises his brows. "Wrecked her? He damn near killed her!"

Karen looked around. Jean Paul Gaultier showed up in an outfit that looked like prison stripes, and sat next to a very tightly-put-together Blaine Trump. In the mega-rich international contingent Karen could just see Gianni Agnelli, who, as always, had on a button-down shirt that was, as always, unbuttoned and, also as always, was wearing his watch on the *outside* of his cuff. Ann Bass who was once married to Sid, Mercedes Bass, who was now married to Sid, and Mica Ertegun, who had *never* been married to Sid, were all there. Beside them, Norris Cleveland sat, *sans* her husband. Karen wondered if the divorce rumors were true and if Norris had a sketch pad secreted in her Judith Leiber purse. Meanwhile, all the New York wives of the wealthy were wearing everything from tonal Armani to the rose-infested smocks of Anna Sui.

But it was Hollywood that, as always, went wild. Phoebe Van Gelder made an entrance in a leather Thierry Mugler that was slashed in a dozen places. "So appropriate for a house of God, don't you think?" Jeffrey asked. Dustin and Lisa Hoffman arrived, he in something nondescript, conservative, and she in a sort of monastic thing that might have been a Jil Sanders. Someone gorgeous that Karen didn't recognize—she didn't have time for much television—was wearing the most outrageous Ozbek—all clinging bronze lace, absolutely sheer, with bright orange satin tacked-on sleeves along with eggplant-colored tights and knee-high leather boots. "Who is she?" Karen whispered to Jeffrey.

"*What* is she?" he shot back. Jeffrey was a fashion conservative. "Her designer hates women."

Karen knew that not only Jeffrey but a lot of women and some of the media believed that most fashion designers hated women. They believed there exists some kind of twisted conspiracy among gay men designers to make women look ridiculous. Jeffrey called them "the gay mafia." But Karen didn't see it that way. Gay men seemed to like women, but wanted to dress only those women who were built in the gay man mode: long, tall, lean with broad shoulders. Their designers were often flamboyant, dramatic, silly. And mostly they came up with ideas for the sake of pleasing themselves. So you might say that gay men fashion designers dressed women to look attractive to gay men.

If there *was* a conspiracy, it was the conspiracy of the straight white males who actually owned the fashion business. The guys with the money, the guys like Bill Wolper who had an enormous investment in making sure that women were continually dissatisfied with the way they looked and were simultaneously being barraged with new images of how they *should* look instead. The conspiracy to create dissatisfaction and a constant search for the new was the *real* fashion merchandiser's tyranny.

Karen looked up in time to see New York's most beautiful couple, Cindy Crawford and Richard Gere, taking a seat together, holding hands. Karen knew, of course, the talk about them but they seemed a happy couple to her. Could people, actors and models, put on an act in public all the time? Michael and Diandra Douglas were, as always, beautifully dressed, but Al Pacino looked more like Al Capone in a pin stripe. Karen was surprised to see him arrive alone.

"Money and talent don't mean good taste," Jeffrey murmured. He himself was in the most quiet of dark suits. He despised eccentricity in men's fashion. Oddly enough, Karen liked that about him. Did she think fashion was too lightweight for a real man to care about?

She looked at his profile. She loved him very much. Even though they wouldn't have a child together, despite her disagreement on the NormCo deal, and even though he didn't understand or share her craving for a family, Karen knew that she loved him. And that he loved her. He was probably right about adoption, about her real mother, and mostly everything else. He had always believed in the best part of her, even when she didn't. When he told her she had talent she had believed him. What if he hadn't encouraged her? She reached her hand out and put it on the soft dark wool of his jacket. She could feel the firmness of his forearm beneath the suit sleeve and the silky cotton of his shirt. She thought of Carl, alone in Brooklyn Heights. Jeffrey was all she had, but he was enough. He was a lot more than enough.

She took a deep breath. The ceremony was about to begin. She was about to be judged by everyone. Her hands were cold. If *she* was this nervous, how did Elise feel right now? Elise was used to public appearances. Was it possible that Karen was more nervous than the bride? She felt the wings of butterflies in her stomach. She and Jeffrey had never had a proper wedding. After Jeffrey had backed out of his engagement to June and asked Karen to marry him, it had somehow seemed inappropriate for her to sashay down the aisle in a billowing white tulle victory gown. Even if she *had* felt victorious against great odds. Anyway, she wasn't the tulle type. They had, instead, gone down to the municipal building and had one of those three-minute city jobs. Karen had never planned on a big wedding, but she did regret the total lack of ceremony. On the other hand, she wasn't sure if she could stand to participate in something this choreographed. But Elise Elliot, after all, was an actress *and* from a generation of debutantes that had "come out." She must be used to playing a central role.

Karen just hoped she had gotten the costume right. Elise would never forget this dress. Well, what woman did forget her wedding gown? But, then, if there was more than one wedding, Karen wondered, did they remember *all* of their gowns? Could Liz Taylor remember what she'd had on when she married Mike Todd? Or John Warner? Or Burton for the second time? Calm yourself, girl, Karen told herself sternly. This is only a dress, not exploratory surgery. But she had broken out in a cold sweat. Surreptitiously, Karen wiped her damp palms on the side of her oyster boucle jacket. She felt the outline of the photos that she had taken for good luck. They comforted her.

And then the wedding march began. The amazing, triumphant sound of the massive organ reeds rose from the end of the nave. At the same moment, all heads peered toward the back of the church. The center aisle, carpeted in red, was illuminated by dozens of spots that were hidden in the deep gloom of the vast ceiling buttresses. And so the wedding began.

If she craned her head toward the altar, Karen could see Larry Cochran, lanky and blonde, step out from some side door to wait for his bride. With him was another young man, much shorter, wearing a less perfectly tailored morning jacket and tails. But Karen, like everyone else, didn't have much time for the groom. At weddings it was the women who held the spotlight. As the music continued to play, Brenda Cushman entered the center aisle and began the long walk to the front of the church.

She looked good, Karen could see, and she sighed with relief. Karen had put her in a simple dress, the shoulders built carefully to support the heavy swing of the silk broadcloth. The color was perfect for dark Brenda—it was neither pink nor gray but somewhere in between. It was shorter than you would expect, but the movement around the hemline drew attention to Brenda's terrific legs. To Karen, a garment was partly about movement. A woman with flaws especially needed the right energy and movement in her clothes. Brenda, carrying a handful of blush roses and freesia, moved confidently down the aisle.

Then Annie Paradise followed. Annie was built like Lisa, Karen's sister, petite and small-boned. Karen had used the same heavy silk broadcloth but a slightly less gray shade, just a shadow of a difference. She had cut the same asymmetrical square neck but the dress itself was a sheath, its simplicity almost oriental, showing off Annie's slim line. The richness of the fabric, the subtlety of the color, proved that, in the words of Chanel, "Simplicity doesn't mean poverty." Karen was pleased.

And then the organ announced the bride. Karen, like the rest of the congregation, turned her head but she could not even catch a glimpse of Elise. There was a moment's pause and then, as Elise stepped out of the shadows cast by the loft at the entrance to the church, the hush was replaced by that huge sigh, the offering made to great beauty.

She was walking on the arm of her uncle, a tiny elderly man, and she towered over him. But their proportion did not make them a joke. His shortness emphasized her stature. Beside him, she looked like a goddess. She too was dressed in the heavy silk broadcloth, but its color was two tones lighter. Karen had left the square neck, but had filled it in with a yoke and a high wimple out of magnificent lace dyed the exact same pink-white. It covered Elise's chest and neck up to her jaw line, an older woman's most vulnerable parts. And, as a continuation of that thought, Karen had created a veil that sat on an almost invisible headpiece, draping only the sides of Elise's face and then dropping in incredible folds down the back of her gown. The gown itself was almost severe, cut in a princess line straight to the hem, but the sleeves belled generously, exposing a clinging undersleeve of matching lace.

Elise was lovely. The color of the gown was almost exactly that of her pale skin, and though that had been a gamble, it had paid off. Even at this distance, Karen could see that rather than monochromatically washing Elise out, the color and sweep of the veil and gown had expanded her, perfected her. She did not look young, nor did she look old. She was ageless and, at that moment, more beautiful than anyone Karen had ever seen. Tears rose in Karen's eyes and she had to blink furiously. She didn't want to miss a second of this vision, this masterpiece that she, Karen, had created. For a moment everything came together in the way it could in only the most perfect of all possible worlds. Fashion, a minor creation always judged by the stage on which it was set, and by the woman who wore it, can sometimes transcend time and achieve art. Karen had accepted Elise's style, her age, her joy, and even her fears, and together they had transcended.

Jeffrey took Karen's hand. "My God," he whispered. Then he pulled his eyes off Elise and turned to Karen. "Congratulations," he said, and his pride in her completed Karen's joy.

Moving down the aisle, Elise Elliot passed Karen, her beautiful profile staring straight ahead, serene in the knowledge of her great beauty and dignity. Karen watched her pass, admiring the fall of the train and its overlay of veil. Over Elise's shoulder Karen could see Larry Cochran as he caught his first sight of Elise. His face was transfixed, with love and shock and perhaps some disbelief because his bride was moving toward him, an absolute embodiment of eternal beauty. The crowd, for once, was still, moved by the perfection and serenity that was Elise. It was only when she stopped at the altar that the spell was broken and the genteel buzz began.

"Unbelievable," Jeffrey told her. "I don't care what it cost us. It was worth it. This is going to make you bigger than the Oakley Award. Mercedes better make sure that she's got the releases out on this."

But for once Karen didn't care about the business. She heard the comments, the hum of approval and disbelief and yearning and envy, but for once none of it mattered. This wasn't a fashion show and she wasn't selling tickets. She had created something special, something wonderful, and it didn't matter right now what other people thought. She knew what a difficult job it had been, and she was satisfied. If it was the *succès d'estime* that Jeffrey now predicted, that was just icing on the cake. Karen leaned back against the pew and, as the bride and groom made their promises, she felt as if all was right with her world.

She leaned over to Jeffrey. "I don't care what NormCo offers," she said. "I don't want to sell."

He turned to her. "Karen, it might not be a question of choice. You know that if we don't expand we'll fold, so this may be our best option."

"Not after this. We'll be getting bigger orders from everyone. I just know it."

"Then we'll have bigger cash flow problems."

She looked at him, her mouth set as firmly as his own. "I won't sell, Jeffrey," she told him.

PART TWO
HEMMING AND WHORING

*Clothes are the fabric of history,
the texture of time.*

—JAY COX

12

FASHIONABLE COLLECTION

Lisa tried to remember how long it had been since she and Karen had really talked. Next to the phone was the new issue of *People* magazine, with Elise Elliot on the cover and the article about Karen inside. Well, from that alone Karen must be overwhelmed with calls. Lisa told herself she shouldn't feel resentment. But this time she had been determined to wait until Karen called *her*. It was becoming a long wait. And with little else to do, her boredom and resentment grew. She'd been bored for a long time now.

It hadn't always been so. In the days when Lisa owned a dress shop she'd been like a junkie who covered her own addiction by dealing. The shop had met all her needs. It gave her someplace to go every day to get away from the children. It allowed her to be the big fish—albeit in a pond as small as a boutique on Central Avenue in Lawrence. It gave her a reason to dress up, a way to legitimize her Manhattan shopping sprees, a feeling of importance when she was recognized as a buyer at the Broadway showrooms, and even a means to unload some of her personal fashion errors—Lisa had been known to put something she'd worn back on the rack with a fresh price tag. It had given her a sense of power: when an annoying customer hesitated over a purchase and left the shop, Lisa could tell if the woman would be back; then she'd remove the item and put it away out of spite. When the woman returned for it, Lisa would smile sweetly and tell her it had been sold. Lastly, it had given her a place to socialize—the acquaintances she had struck up with clients served her well. And she had managed to expand some of the acquaintanceships almost into friendships, partly by giving those women she courted special discounts on the clothes they liked. If it was buying friendship, Lisa didn't think about it. Lisa didn't like to think about anything unpleasant.

Her sister had run a small, exclusive manufacturing business. She'd run a small, exclusive shop. Things seemed just fine for a while. But the outcome of it all was predictable, even if she herself hadn't seen it coming. The one thing the store didn't do for her was make any money. At first it wasn't expected to. Then it had held its own for a few fat years in the mid-eighties. But with her discount policy for all the socialites of the Five Towns—even before Wall Street's Black Monday in October and the end of spending as a sport—the shop was a losing proposition.

Leonard had finally put his foot down. Since the shop had closed, Lisa had found her "friends" dropping away and her life reduced to an ever-narrowing circle. Boredom set in—Jesus, it was her daily companion. Meanwhile, her sister's business and life got bigger and bigger.

But now, at last, Lisa felt she had a way to fight back. Throwing her daughter's *bat mitzvah* was putting Lisa back into the spotlight again. If she couldn't be a successful businesswoman, she'd be a successful social hostess. This would be an affair to remember. She had begun drawing up lists over a year ago, combing through her files of old clients, her outdated address books, her clippings from *Newsday* and the local paper of attendees at charity events, the upper-echelon members of the temple and the one country club she and Leonard still belonged to. Though she had already thrown herself into charity work to try and keep herself afloat in the circles to which she aspired to belong, her inability to either donate largely or bring in big donors had relegated her to the scut work—addressing invitations, picking up circulars at the printer, and stuffing envelopes—definitely not what she'd had in mind. By now she'd quit most of the organizations. God, if she had wanted to be a secretary she'd have gotten a paying job in the first place.

This affair, she felt, was her last chance to pull together some semblance of the sparkling social life she had always imagined for herself but never quite managed to achieve. She still couldn't understand why: she knew so many women and she tried always to be nice, but somehow even when she managed to get an invitation out, she and Leonard seemed always to be on the fringe rather than the center of conversations. And they were rarely asked back.

Lisa blamed it on Leonard. After all, how interesting was the conversation of a suburban dermatologist? And even among suburban dermatologists, Leonard must rank in the bottom ten percent. It wasn't that he talked about embarrassing things, postules or *acne vulgaris*. It was rather that he talked about dull things or nothing at all. She should have married a real doctor. There were times when she wanted to kick Leonard and beg him to either shut up or to say something *interesting*. But most often he left the burden of social conversation to her, so she chattered on, always feeling nervous and inadequate. She couldn't really compete with the talk of trips to Monte Carlo or cruises up the Asawan Valley. And she had no glittering career. Talking about clothes had been appropriate when she ran a shop, but as she continued, in desperation, to talk about them—now that she was no longer in the business—she was sometimes afraid that she, too, had turned boring. Doctor and Mrs. Leonard Saperstein, town bores.

But how could that be? Clothes play such an important part in every woman's life. Unlike men, women had outfits that were markers, milestones in the progress of their existence, and they never forgot them. Every girl remembered exactly what dress she'd worn to the prom, and even if she didn't have a hundred photos documenting the event, successful or unsuccessful as the evening may have been, she could tell you exactly what she had worn. Just as every woman could describe her wedding gown, down to the smallest detail. Men, of course, couldn't describe their (usually) rented tuxedos and there was no need to. But imagine a woman renting a prom gown or a wedding dress! Lisa knew that Catholic women even remembered their First Communion dresses, just as Tiff would remember her *bat mitzvah* dress for as long as she lived. Clothing was *important*. That's why Lisa respected her sister so much, even if she didn't always "get" her sister's designs. Because to Lisa, Karen was doing something important. Creating clothes *and* magically making money at it, two important things that Lisa had failed to do. No wonder Karen had no time to call her. Lisa understood her sister's life was busier and better than her own. Karen was too busy being interviewed and getting even more famous and rich.

At this point, money was a central issue of Lisa's life, running like a warp thread through the fabric of her day-to-day existence. To be more accurate, it wasn't the money, but the lack of it, that had become such an issue. In the early days of her marriage, Leonard had just paid the bills and given her as much cash as she needed, but it had been years since that liberal policy had been in effect. Lisa sighed. One of the painful realities of her life now was that she had never appreciated how good it had been when it had been good. She had just assumed there would always be money for all the clothes and lunches and manicures and haircuts that she would ever need, or that her daughters ever needed. Now it was disorienting to find that those things she'd considered necessities were luxuries that she might actually have to do without. Lisa wasn't given to introspection, but in some numb way she wished that she had been able to savor all that she had back then, before she had lost it.

Now Leonard's constant refrain was that she had to "cut back." It was such a medical phrase. He made it sound like a surgical procedure. And Lisa felt it *was* a kind of amputation, because without her daily regimen of shopping, lunching, charity "work," and beauty treatments she was left with too much time on her hands. She'd idly thought of a job at Saks—maybe in a designer boutique—but the pocket money and discount wouldn't make up for the way her skin would crawl when she'd have to wait on some woman she knew. Lisa had never wanted a job, and even now the idea of showing up at an office to be under the rigid hand of some difficult boss while she was expected to perform monotonous routines was nightmarish. Yet there was something even worse looming on the horizon. Twice now, Leonard had suggested that she take over *his* office: in his constant cut-back monologue, this had been an option he pressed on her. Then he could save the salary he paid to Mrs. Beck. But being with Leonard all day, reduced to the cliché of the doctor-and-wife-suburban-practice-team, was more than she could bear. It actually made Lisa feel claustrophobic, as if she'd been buried alive. She had put her Joan-and-David-shod foot down.

Unfortunately Leonard had put his foot down, too. He couldn't *force* her to take Mrs. Beck's job, but there would be little of the luxury and display that Lisa had counted on at the *bat mitzvah*. Leonard had given her a clear choice: she could work with him and they could spend more on the affair or she could choose not to and they would spend a lot less. So Lisa had thrown all her creativity into making the most out of what she could, while retaining her empty freedom.

Sometimes she wondered why things had gone so wrong for her, and how Karen had managed to do so well. But, she reminded herself, Karen had always been the smart one. Karen's success didn't surprise Lisa at all. It just seemed to Lisa that things always came easily to her sister.

What *did* surprise her was Karen's marriage. After all, she, Lisa, was the pretty one and Karen probably wasn't very easy to live with. How she had managed to attract a man as good-looking, charming, and exciting as Jeffrey was the puzzle. But remembering their on-again, off-again courtship and how Jeffrey had kept Karen at a distance until her break-out year made it seem to Lisa that Jeffrey had only gotten serious once Karen had gotten a name. Lisa wondered, idly, whether Jeffrey ever cheated on Karen, but he didn't seem to, or if he did he was very careful. Karen would have told her if she suspected anything, and Karen never had. After all, even if they hadn't spoken much lately, they were still best friends, weren't they? But why, Lisa asked herself now, did her elder sister always get everything? Wasn't it the adopted one who was supposed to be messed up? Somehow Karen had managed to snag a great husband and a great career out of the air, while Lisa was losing her looks and her life was adding up to a big goose egg.

But now, each morning, she eagerly went to the mailbox to go through the RSVPs. She had a list that she had ranked by "Most Desirable," "Second Tier," "Family," and "Obligatory." There were many overlaps, of course (Karen, for example, was "Most Desirable" as well as "Family"), but Lisa was hoping that if she kept the proportions right and managed the party properly it would yield her another chance at making it in the Five Towns social scene. It gave her hope.

Today, though, the mail was a disappointment. There was a refusal from Marian Lasker and her husband, the developer. Along with it came acceptances from Leonard's cousin Morty, and a deadbeat of a patient, a chronic eczema-infected plumber who Leonard had insisted they put on the list. He and his whole flaky family were coming. Damn it, that meant four places gone! Disgusted, Lisa threw the RSVPs onto the table and got up to get dressed. But first she stopped in the bathroom to check herself out on Mr. Scale.

For years Lisa hadn't let her weight vary by more than three pounds. She did it through discipline and constant vigilance. Getting on Mr. Scale had become the one part of her day that allowed her to still feel in control, to give her pride and a sense of achievement. Along with brushing their teeth, she had taught the girls to weigh themselves daily and for years they had all talked to Mr. Scale. Even now, as she walked into the bathroom, Lisa superstitiously began her ritual in a baby-high voice. "Is Mr. Scale going to be nice today?" she asked aloud. "I was a very good girl, except for the soy sauce last night. But I didn't have much." It was a game she had played with Stephanie and Tiff, until Tiff had gotten mad at her and wouldn't play it anymore. Well, Tiff was mad most of the time now and she and her sister made Lisa's life miserable. It was obvious that Tiff was jealous of Stephanie. Lisa could understand it: Stephanie *was* perfect. It must be difficult to have a sister so impossible to compete with. Thank God Karen wasn't beautiful as well as successful, Lisa thought, and then immediately felt guilty. Now Mr. Scale would probably punish her for her bad thought by making her fat. Well, Lisa could see the problem Tiff had, but what Lisa could *not* understand was why Tiff didn't even *try*. Karen made the most of her looks. Tiff could do so much more with herself if only she would diet and accept some help from Lisa.

Lisa stepped on the scale and, sure enough, groaned to see the two pounds that had inflated her weight. At thirty-seven, she knew it was critical to keep her figure. She watched, terrified by what happened to women in their forties, and she was determined to keep her belly as flat and her flanks as lean as they had ever been. It was the goddamned soy sauce! It must be water weight from all that salt. Well, she'd have a fruit plate for lunch and dinner, and she'd do an extra class tomorrow at the gym. She looked in the mirror wall of the bathroom. Wasn't her belly pooching out? Miserable now, she stomped over to the closet to pick out something that wouldn't cling. The phone rang. She thought it might be Karen at last and went to it gratefully, but when she lifted it up she was greeted by a stranger's voice.

"Mrs. Saperstein?"

"Yes?"

"I am calling to talk to you about *House and Garden* magazine," the voice said breathlessly. "In the past, you've been a subscriber and we were wondering . . . " Shit! It was one of those interruptive, annoying, disappointing telephone salesmen. In one of his pointless cut-back moves Leonard had stopped all her magazine subscriptions. Now she just bought them at the inflated newsstand price behind his back. But Lisa would not let her exasperation show to the salesman on the phone.

"How nice of you to call," she said sweetly. "I can't tell you how interested in your magazine I am. I don't know how I let it lapse, but we have been *so* busy." She could feel the man's hope jump at the other end of the line.

"Well I would like to . . . "

"Before you say anything, would you mind holding on for a minute? I'm *so* interested but there is something here I just *have* to take care of." Without waiting for an answer, she laid the phone down. She went back to her closet and slowly began riffling through the clothes there. What would best cover her tummy? She began to hum Roy Orbison's "Pretty Woman." She'd been restored to her good mood and wondered, only for a moment, how long the idiot on the phone would hold. Well, she'd outwait him. It wasn't like she was expecting any important calls.

After a few minutes, she settled on cinnamon silk Perry Ellis slacks and a Michael Kors overshirt that Karen had given her. She rooted around at the bottom of her closet for the black platform Charles Jordan sandals she had bought at the beginning of the season. Lisa took a minute out to go back to the phone and picked it up to hear if the poor sucker was still waiting. The receiver was neither dead nor buzzing, so she laid it down again gently. She went into the bathroom and adjusted the water for her shower. Then she put her hair in a shower cap, and after clipping her toenails, checked the phone again. It *was* buzzing this time and she hung it up, turning on the answering machine so she could avoid the nincompoop's call if he should decide to ring back.

It was only when she had finished showering, shut the water off, and stepped out of the shower that she heard the click of the machine and a voice beginning to talk. "Ah, hello? Lisa, are you there?"

It sounded like Jeffrey, her brother-in-law, but what would *he* be doing, calling her? Jeffrey never called her. Wet and dripping, Lisa made a beeline for the phone and snatched it off the hook.

"Jeffrey?" she asked.

"Lisa. You *are* there. Great. I wanted to talk to you," he paused. Lisa waited. The pause lengthened.

"I'm right here," she said. "What's up?"

"Well, a little of this and a little of that. Part of it is business, but part is family stuff. I tell you, I'm kind of worried about your sister."

"Really?" Shit, he must be *very* worried to be calling me, Lisa thought. It wasn't that they didn't get along. It was more like she had always felt dismissed by Jeffrey, and his whole family. Even though the Kahns were actually from Westchester, it was typical Lawrence behavior. "What is it?" she asked now.

"Well, it's a lot to go into over the phone. I wondered . . . " he paused again and Lisa waited for him to speak. "I know it's a lot to ask, but could you possibly get free for lunch? I'd really like to talk to you."

Surprised and complimented, Lisa smiled and her voice reflected it. "Sure," she said. "I'll just have to make a few calls." Ha! Like there was a long list of people waiting to lunch with her.

"Great," Jeffrey said. "Meet me at the St. Regis at one. Can you make it in by then? You know where it is? Fifth Avenue and Fifty-Fifth."

"Ah, sure," she said brightly and thought that she'd have to reject the Perry Ellis slacks and upgrade to something a lot more St. Regis-ish. Too bad she still hadn't found the wine-colored shoes to go with the Donna Karan pantsuit. It would have been perfect. "I'll be there," she purred.

"Oh, and Lisa, could I ask another favor?"

"Sure."

"Don't mention this to Karen. Okay? It's in her own best interest, I promise you."

"Sure," Lisa repeated easily, and then set the receiver gently on its hook. She felt a flutter of excitement in her chest. At last, she thought, she had someplace worthwhile to dress up for.

While her mother was preparing for lunch with her uncle, Tiff Saperstein had skipped her afternoon classes and was spending time at the Roosevelt Field Mall. It wasn't one of the best malls, but it was big and far enough away from home so Tiff felt safe.

Trolling the mall was one of the few times that she felt it an advantage to be big and fat. She would be thirteen in just a few weeks, but because of her height and size she knew she looked a lot older. Not older and pretty, or older and sophisticated, the way Stephanie looked, but at least old enough so that no one would stop her and ask her why she was cutting school, or why she was there without parental supervision. Kids alone weren't allowed in the mall. But she didn't look like an average kid. She wasn't cute, or skinny, or dressed in bicycle shorts and a cut-off tee. She wore an oversized men's plaid shirt with a white T-shirt under it, baggy pants, and Converse sneakers. She knew she was invisible, and although she resented it a lot of the time, in places like this she had to admit it was very convenient.

She still had twenty-seven dollars left from her saved allowance, plus the extra ten-dollar bill she had taken from her father's wallet this morning. If he ever noticed any money missing, Tiff knew he would blame her mother, not her. He'd never think of her. Nobody did.

Tiff put her hand up to her neck and, through the flannel, fingered the pearl necklace that her aunt had given her. Well, Tiff had to admit, Aunt Karen *did* think of her, but now Aunt Karen had given Stephie-the-bitch a job. It wasn't so much that her sister had a job while she didn't. Steph was really stupid—the work study program was one step away from Vo Tech. What bothered Tiff was the fact that Stephie would get to spend time with Aunt Karen every day. Tiff dropped her hand away from the necklace and strode across the tile floor of the mall to the Mrs. Field's Cookie store. The first thing she'd do was spend five dollars on macadamia white chocolate chip cookies. Then she'd go into the stores.

Tiff despised the casual specialty stores. The Limited. Bennetton. Ann Taylor. None of their stuff was any good. She also hated the middle-market department stores. As far as Tiff was concerned, all that crap was for the birds. She knew what she liked and it wasn't any cheesy Macy's Own label. So, with a warm cookie stuffed in her mouth and the others melting in the bag, Tiff headed for Saks and the designer floor. She knew just what she liked and just where to find it. Because, when it came to shoplifting, why settle for anything less than the best?

About the time that Tiff was gobbling down the Mrs. Field's cookies, Stephanie sat in the small white room reserved for coffee drinking and ЖKInc employee lunches, gazing across the wide expanse of two white Formica tables at Tangela. Tangela was talking to her mother, or rather Defina was talking at her. Defina was keeping her voice low but Stephanie knew that angry-mother noise and could recognize it anywhere.

"Have you punched more holes in your earlobes?" Defina was asking. Tangela said something Steph couldn't hear, and then asked for a loan.

"What do you need to borrow money for?" Defina asked.

"A Hermès bag," her daughter said in a bored voice.

"Tangela," her mother said with a sigh, "the 'H' in 'Hermès' is silent. It's pronounced 'ermez.' "

"Why?"

"Because it's French."

"We ain't French."

"No, but that's the classy way to say it."

Tangela shrugged. "White people."

Just then Karen walked in, overheard Tangela and laughed. "It's actually worse than that," Karen said. "The dropped 'h' in French is classy, but if the English drop an 'h' it's trashy. Go figure." Karen left with a cup of coffee, and though Steph couldn't overhear exactly what Defina was finishing up with, after an elegant shrug from Tangela, Defina raised her voice. "You may think you're too good to be a fitting model. If that's so, then don't take the booking. If you show up here, I want you ready to work, just like the other girls." Tangela shrugged again, and Defina just shook her head and strode out of the room.

Stephie had thought she herself was pretty, and she had also thought she was thin, but that was before she'd met Tangela. Tangela had given Stephie a whole new definition of both pretty *and* thin. Tangela's skin was the light brown color of some really creamy ice cream flavor and her nose was more refined than Stephanie's own. Now, looking covertly at her, Stephanie watched as Tangela read something in a fashion magazine and flared her beautiful nostrils in contempt or disgust. Tangela hadn't really spoken to her here at the office or at her aunt's brunch, nor did she seem to want to become more friendly. Tangela wouldn't ignore her if she was thinner and prettier. The older girl must just figure I'm a school kid, a stupid baby, Stephie thought, a nerd whose aunt was only doing her a favor by letting her model. Tangela didn't notice when Stephie walked into a room, and she didn't seem to have anything to say to her when they worked together. But Stephanie was fascinated by the older girl. Now, screwing up all her courage, Stephanie picked up her egg salad sandwich and her diet Pepsi and walked over to the table where Tangela sat alone.

"Want half my sandwich?" Stephie offered, as boldly as she dared. Tangela flared her nostrils again and looked across at her as if she were some kind of insect.

"Why don't you ask if I want flabby thighs?" Tangela sneered.

"It's diet bread," Stephanie hastened to explain. After all, she'd been watching her weight and dieting since she was nine. "The mayonnaise is fat-free," she added.

"Then it's about the only fat-free thing you got," Tangela said. She waited while the words sank in. "Listen up. Just because you're Karen's niece don't mean I got to crib with you," Tangela told her. "You're no model. You're just a rich kid from the suburbs, playin' at this job. Play by yourself." Tangela stood, picked up her enormous black shoulder bag, and walked from the room.

Stephanie sat there for a moment, stunned. She hadn't been put down like that since Jennifer Barton had been mean to her back in the third grade at Inwood Elementary. She blinked back tears and looked around to make sure nobody else had witnessed her humiliation. But the other women, mostly finishers from the sample room, were busy talking to one another. Stephanie hung her head. The egg salad sandwich sat there like a judgment. The smell of it suddenly made her feel sick. In a single motion, she stood and crumpled the sandwich into the napkin that had been under it. Then she threw it into the garbage. She would skip lunch. And maybe she would skip dinner. In fact, she felt like she might never eat again.

Like her daughter, Lisa had barely eaten any lunch. It was that thrilling being in Manhattan, dressed up, lunching with a fabulous-looking man at one of *the* best places.

One of Lisa's preoccupations was what she thought of as The Game. Always attractive and, under Belle's tutelage, always carefully dressed, she had become more and more interested in the impact she made on other people. Back in high school and in her one year at college she had focused on the impression she made on young men. But in the last decade and a half, that interest faded. Like the majority of women, Lisa dressed to impress other women.

Of course, it wasn't just *any* other women. Lisa didn't care what her cleaning lady thought of her wardrobe. In fact, she didn't care about what anyone in all of Inwood thought. Lisa played for bigger stakes than that. She dressed to impress the most fashionable and chic women she could find.

The problem was they were a bit thin on the ground in her neck of the woods. So Lisa spent a lot of time getting herself dressed and accessorized and then going to places where what passed for the fashion *cognoscenti* of Long Island congregated. There were a couple of department stores and the restaurants that catered to women shoppers. Lisa also frequented one of the tonier malls. But the problem with all of those was that women actually involved in shopping rarely noticed other women, and women eating lunch might admire the clothing of a stranger, but would always feel superior to see that stranger dining alone. Because what Lisa actually sought was not just the admiration but the envy of those women. She knew the appraising look they gave, often hidden behind oversized sunglasses or an averted face because, if you were dressed really well, another well-dressed woman couldn't resist at least one appraising look. For Lisa, The Game was to elicit that look and also to catch the woman in the act of awarding it. When she did that, Lisa's own reward was to flash the loser a quick but superior smile. Because, over lunch in Lisa's world, you were not what you ate, you were what you wore.

She'd become expert in The Game. She could dress not just in the latest style but always with a new twist. She'd add an accessory, or an unusual leather, or an antique scarf or pin that could not be duplicated. Once, in the Tea Room on the third floor of Manhattan's Bendel's, a woman had stared at her purse throughout all of lunch. At the end of the meal, the stranger couldn't stop herself from approaching Lisa and asking where she had gotten it. "I had it made for me in Italy," Lisa had lied coldly. It actually hadn't counted as a point in The Game, because by breaking that invisible boundary and speaking to her, the woman had revealed herself as unworthy. She lacked control and class, so besting her gave Lisa no satisfaction.

Manhattan was *the* place to play The Game. It was a tough crowd. Today she had finally gotten it right. She had strolled through the lobby of the St. Regis and easily gotten two businessmen to turn their heads. A good sign, but one that didn't really matter. She had arrived at the restaurant and the maître d' had given her that approving look that gave her the tiny extra bit of confidence one needed. Then she got to walk across the floor of the beautifully appointed room to the corner table where Jeffrey had stood up to greet her. He was the perfect accessory, the last touch she needed to appear as if she had a charmed life. Two women, lunching together, had tried hard to keep their eyes averted. They had failed. Lisa had preened herself, like a raptor after a kill.

She and Jeffrey had greeted each other, ordered a drink, and then Lisa didn't know what to say. But she knew she wanted this moment to last. What was going on in Karen's life right now? "Have you met Elle Halle yet?" she asked. She raised her voice a bit, hoping the other women would overhear.

"Met her? I feel as if she moved in! I had to spend *hours* with her," Jeffrey complained.

Lisa was too excited to eat or even to think too much about the conversation. Jeffrey talked for a little while about Stephanie and the internship and went on for a long time about business affairs. Lisa never understood why men did this. Leonard was never more boring than when he talked about the practice, but for Jeffrey, Lisa smiled and nodded and tried to respond vivaciously so that everyone could see what a good time she was having. So when Jeffrey leaned over and took her hand, she was surprised—almost shocked. She, like her mother, wasn't a physical person. For a moment, she wondered if he might not attempt a pass at her. It was a horrible thought, but she was relieved to see not a lustful but a worried look on his face. Still, he seemed to want something from her. She focused again on the conversation.

"You can see why I'm concerned," he was saying. "I just don't feel as if I can keep the ball in play much longer."

Lisa blinked. When had he moved from business and begun talking about sports?

"And she doesn't know how stressed out she is. Sometimes I'm afraid she'll work herself to death."

Lisa knew then who they were talking about. She nodded, putting an understanding look on her face.

"You know, a while ago she said the strangest thing. She said she wanted to find her real mother. That isn't normal, is it? Out of the blue like that, I mean, it has to come from stress."

Jeffrey had gotten her attention. "Karen wanted to do *what?*" she asked. In all the years of growing up, in all the time they'd spent together, neither of the sisters had ever mentioned that Karen was adopted. No one in the family did. Somehow, it didn't seem nice.

"That's what I said. But that's not the worst. She also has started this thing about adopting a baby. Can you imagine?"

Lisa opened her eyes wide. "So, you've given up on trying for a baby?"

Jeffrey paused. He looked uncomfortable. "She didn't tell you?" he asked.

"Tell me what?"

This time the pause was longer. "She finally went through the last stuff with Dr. Goldman. The news wasn't good. It's definite. She can't have children. No way. I think that's a big part of this. Honest to God, Lisa, she isn't acting rationally. That's why I want you to talk to her. Maybe she'll listen to you."

Lisa sat there, too stunned to feel complimented. Her sister hadn't even mentioned Dr. Goldman's results to her. Lisa couldn't believe it. Maybe Karen *had* been busy lately, but they had always confided in one another. Hurt and offended, Lisa tried not to show her surprise, but a bitter thought occurred: Why should Jeffrey think Karen would listen to *her?* Karen obviously didn't think Lisa was even important enough to tell this news to.

"Anyway, I know you don't own much stock in the company, but if we manage to get a twenty-five-million-dollar offer, after the conversion and taxes it would probably mean close to half a million dollars for you."

"What?" Jesus Christ! Had he said half a million dollars for *her*? What was he talking about? Something about an offer. About a conversion of stock. She should have been paying attention. *Half a million dollars for her*? She could buy a house in Lawrence. Maybe, with half a million dollars, she could even convince Leonard to move to Manhattan. Her whole life would change! What did Jeffrey want her to do? "How do we get the money?" she asked.

"Karen has to agree to sell to NormCo if we get a decent offer. I'm not supposed to tell you anything about it, nondisclosure and all that, but I'm sure Karen already has." Lisa nodded, although Karen hadn't said one word. "All I'm suggesting is that you have to find some way to talk to her. This sale is really in her best interests. We may lose the business if we don't sell out. And I'm afraid that after Robert made that little slip at the brunch, that Arnold might affect your sister's views."

"Arnold?" Lisa dismissed her father with the same shrug that Belle habitually used. "Are you going to tell Belle? You know, my mother and father could use the money, too."

Jeffrey shook his head. "Not right now," he said. "You know Arnold. He'll drag out six hundred reasons why NormCo is politically incorrect. If they *once* bought polyester that was made from nonunion petroleum by-products, he'll be calling them fascists and scabs. Karen doesn't need that right now."

Lisa blinked her eyes. She wondered if this was what they called "insider trading." But Karen hadn't told her about her sterility *or* about this offer. Lisa wondered if she could consider herself an insider in Karen's life anymore at all. Half a million dollars! How much money would *Karen* make in a deal like this, Lisa asked herself.

All at once it seemed so unfair. Karen had everything: a husband who wasn't only handsome but also concerned about her. She had that great apartment *and* the new house. Now, she was going to also be millions and millions of dollars richer. Lisa reminded herself that she loved her sister, but she also knew it just wasn't fair. Everything came easy to Karen. And she didn't even appreciate what she had.

Jeffrey stretched his hand across the table and took hers again. This time, Lisa was prepared. "Will you help me?" he asked. Lisa nodded and returned the gentle pressure of her brother-in-law's palm against hers.

13

HEMMING IT UP

"The Elle Halle Show," broadcast that night, conflicted with Jeffrey's poker game with Perry, Jordan, and Sam. The game was like a religion with the guys—uninterrupted since grad school—but when Jeffrey asked Karen if she would mind if he taped it and watched it with her later, Karen was shocked.

"Okay," she said, "but you're going to have to learn to program the machine," she joked, to cover her hurt feelings. She guessed it was stupid to care who she watched the program with but she had just assumed that she and Jeffrey would watch it together. Well, she had a lot of other invitations, and she guessed the best one was from Defina.

So Karen left the office at half-past seven and took a car all the way uptown to Striver's Row, the genteel part of Harlem, an oasis of upper-middle-class brownstones and trees. Black doctors, stockbrokers, ministers, and real estate developers lived there, alongside Defina. She had bought her brownstone with early modeling fees, and since then had poured a lot of money into making it the showplace it was. Turning down the row it was hard to believe the pretty street was in the midst of the blight that was Harlem, but the nervous driver had not forgotten where he was.

"Are you going to be long?" he asked. "Maybe it would be best if I drove downtown. You give me a call, and I'll be back up here in a couple of minutes," he promised. Karen got angry, and thought of all the times that Defina had trouble just getting a cab to take her home. Why was life so unfair and so complicated? On the other hand, she understood that the driver's entire business capital was tied up in his limo. Could he be blamed for being nervous?

"Please wait," she said. "It's a safe neighborhood. This was where Spike Lee filmed *Jungle Fever*."

Her reassurance didn't seem to work, but the driver didn't have a choice. And maybe he'd learn something. If the Huxtable family had lived in Manhattan, they would have lived on Striver's Row.

Defina had the door open before Karen had climbed the stairs to the front entrance. Dee was wearing a pair of palazzo pants and a kimono-style jacket that Karen had done years ago. "I can't believe you still have that," Karen cried, looking her over.

"You can't believe it still *fits*," Defina told her. "I just had new elastic put in the waist. I can get into it, but you don't want to see my butt without this jacket covering it."

"I don't want to see your butt at all," Karen told her, and walked into the hall.

The house was laid out like a typical brownstone, only nicer: there was an entry hall that ran along one side of the house and from which a beautifully curved walnut staircase climbed three floors. Defina had refinished the woodwork and stairs herself, and the dark wood gleamed against the black-and-white checked marble floor of the hall. A sliding double-pocket door was thrown open and the living room and connecting dining room behind it were open to view. Defina had painted both rooms a brilliant red lacquer, and with the dark wood floors and the shiny brass chandeliers, they had a wild elegance. Carved wooden masks were mounted between the panels of molding on the walls and Defina had also framed some African textiles that looked to Karen like a cross between modern art and something out of an Egyptian tomb. The furniture was fairly plain—comfortable pieces upholstered in mud cloth and a nicely oiled Danish modern table, surrounded by half a dozen rush-bottomed chairs; sort of an *Out of Africa* by way of Park Avenue look. In preparation for their evening, Defina had already rolled out the television to a central spot in the bay of the window. Karen looked over at the table and saw that there were only two place settings.

"Tangela isn't joining us?" she asked.

"Tangela isn't living here anymore," Defina told her.

"Oh, Dee, when did that happen?"

"Last week. I told her I wasn't running a hotel, and she told me she knew that because the laundry service sucked. I smacked her. She moved out before I could throw her out." Defina sighed. "Maybe it's for the best," she said. "But I can't help thinking that she's going to blow it." Defina paused. She seemed reluctant to speak. "Karen, let me ask you somethin'. Does Tangela seem different to you?"

"Different from the other girls?"

"No, I mean different from the way she used to be. She's still seein' that no good black-ass boy and I swear he's into drugs."

"What are you talking about, Dee? Some grass?"

"Grass? Weed? Shit, honey, I smoke weed. I'm talking about coke, or maybe even crack. She's thinner than ever, and I don't think even Tangela can have that much attitude without chemical assistance."

Before Karen could say anything, Defina had begun to move food from the sideboard to the table. Karen sat down. Who was she to give advice? After all, she was fated to be permanently excluded from the mother role. "It's hard to raise a kid."

"It's hard to raise a *black* kid," Defina agreed. "And then, she's not really black, is she? I mean, her father was white. Not that whites see her that way. And she doesn't fit in with blacks either." Defina sighed. "I tried to give her an identity. I probably did all the wrong things."

"How can you say that?" Karen asked. "You've tried so hard."

"Trying isn't enough," Defina said. "You got to succeed." She shook her head and spooned some rice onto Karen's plate. She handed her a dish of chicken. "I surely shouldn't have let her take the modeling work. It made us too competitive. And the money was too easy and too good. That much money is bad for a Harlem kid. When she dropped out of school I knew the kind of trouble we'd be getting into."

"Listen, Dee, maybe wanting a place of your own is just a normal part of growing up."

"Grow up yourself, Karen. Nothing about what Tangela is doing is normal. She's getting paid big buckets of money to stand around and look good. But she feels she don't look good *enough*. She's not black enough, and she's not white enough. She wants magazine work, and to strut the catwalks. But nowadays a girl has got to be more than beautiful—she's got to be perfect. This job has helped her *lose* self-confidence, not gain it. And she's getting paid a lot of attention by men. Of course, they're the wrong kind of men." Defina shook her head. "I'm just afraid she's going to make the kind of mistake that you can't recover from. But I guess there isn't anything more I can do." Dee bent her head, picked up her fork, and began to eat.

Karen sat silently for a few minutes, trying to choke down some of the dinner. Defina was upset, and all of this had been going on while Karen hadn't even noticed. She'd been too wrapped up in television shows, acquisition pitches, and celebrity weddings. How long had it been since the two of them had talked? She and Defina spent so much time together, but didn't have time for the stuff that counted. Their lives had become work. Karen put down her own fork. "For once, I'm not hungry," she said.

"Me neither," Defina agreed. "Let's just veg out and drink." She grabbed a bottle of French Merlot and handed a goblet to Karen. "Want some crackers or a piece of bread?"

"Best bread?" Karen asked.

Without losing a beat, Defina said, "Eli Zabar's."

"Wrong! Orwasher's."

"Get outta here!"

Before Defina could launch into an argument, Karen distracted her. "Best watch?"

"The gold Cartier Panther."

"Nah. Harry Winston's Ultimate Timepiece. *They* don't have logos." Both the women hated wearing anything splashed with someone else's initials. Defina shrugged.

"You got a point, but when the logo is Cartier I make an exception. Best pearls?"

"Helen Woodhull." Karen watched Defina nod her approval. "Best exercise coach?"

"Radu." Defina, along with another hundred dozen famous New York women, worshiped Radu Teodorescu.

Karen shook her head. "Lydia Bach," Karen said.

"Oh, *come on*." Karen decided not to fight that one out. Personal trainers were not something to argue about. New York women believed in them more than their religions.

They went over to the couch. Each one leaned their back against a sofa arm and drew their feet up, so they were facing each other, their soles almost touching. "It's funny, Karen. I always thought that the only thing I really wanted was a nice home, money in the bank, and my daughter. Ha! When I got the first two I tried for the third, and when I had Tangela, I found I also wanted a man. Listen: there's kids, a home, career, and marriage. They tell women we can have them all. I say if you're good, really, really good, you can manage to have two of the four. White men don't have the same problems. They can have it all if they get the right wife. Black men don't usually get any of it and they know it so they don't try. But for women, this is the bait and we keep running for it. Here's the reality, Karen: I've had a successful career and a nice house, but I haven't found a man and I've failed as a single mom. So what's it gonna be for you? 'Cause if you keep trying for all of them, I guarantee you're gonna fall apart. It seems like the best Life ever gives women is two out of four."

"How about one out of four?" Karen asked. "I wanted my career, my home, my marriage, *and* a baby. The doctor told me there isn't going to be any baby, NormCo may buy out my business and Jeffrey told me if I want to adopt there isn't going to be any marriage."

"Keep the husband, skip the kid. That's my advice," Defina said, pouring another glass of wine.

"Oh, come on, Dee. This is just a phase. Remember that time we made the skating skirts for you and Tangela? And you went to Radio City and skated with her while I clapped?"

"And we had hot choclate and cinnamon toast at Rumplemeyer's afterward," Defina remembered smiling.

"And remember for her birthday—when she was ten, or was it nine?—and she said she didn't want toys anymore, she wanted earrings? And we bought her all those stuffed animals at FAO and put earrings in all their ears? Remember her face?" Karen continued the remembrance: "Remember when you first started working for me and you brought her into the office every day? And she wanted a desk just like yours? We got that little one. And she'd sit down and try to do everything that you did?"

Defina's eyes filled with tears, but, like Karen, she wouldn't cry. "Yeah, I remember, and I wonder which one of those things were mistakes? You know, a mother and a daughter without a husband and father makes a kind of pressure-cooker. Tangela was *so* dependent on me that it was only natural she came to resent me. First she loved every single thing I did and said, and then she hated it. That's hard. And I expected so much from her. I wanted her to be black, but I wanted her to feel comfortable around whites. She had to be street smart, but she had to get good grades. I've been as hard on her as she is on me." She paused, her lip trembling. "But this new stuff is breaking my heart."

Karen felt at a loss. "Look," she said, "you'll see her at work. Maybe it's good for you to have some distance. Maybe that's all you need."

Defina shook her head. "Work was the problem. I should never have let her model. The game is different now. It's much tougher. Don't let your niece get any more involved. There's no room left to be real or imperfect. It used to be fun. But now it's turned into a really sick business. It's too much pressure for anyone."

"But Tangela's doing well. She's booking lots of work, and the agency likes her."

"Yeah, but she isn't the first black model like I was, and she's not gonna be more than second tier. And I think she knows it now. Even so, she can't give up fashion and go back to school. You know how it is: no one gives up the excitement for the grind. So she's stuck. Three years ago, when she quit school, she thought she was going to be a superstar. Now she knows she isn't, and it's killing her. She's seen her limits, and she's not even twenty-one. That isn't normal. And it doesn't help that I told her so."

Karen felt Defina's pain. God, how hard would it be to lose a daughter this way, to drugs and dangerous men? Was it worse than what Perry had gone through when his daughter died of cancer? Karen felt the hairs rise on her arms. Wouldn't it be better to be childless than to go through this kind of pain? Jeffrey thought so. But somehow, Karen still didn't.

"Maybe you can just take it easy on her, Dee. Maybe once things calm down you'll be able to work it out."

"Yeah, if she's not pregnant, dead, or married to some pimp by then." Defina shook her head. "Sorry to be so down. Enough of this kind of talk. Maybe you're right. It's a phase. It will pass." Dee picked up the wine bottle and filled both of their glasses. "Only two choices for a woman at a time like this: suicide or chocolate. I was going to put my head in the oven but the soufflé would have fallen. So let me get it and a couple of shovels to eat it with. Anyway, we ought to be drinking and celebrating. It's just that this mother-daughter stuff is real hard." Defina reached for another bottle of wine and pulled the cork.

"Tell me about it," Karen said. And then, as if her own cork had been popped, she told Defina all about Doctor Goldman, about her own longing for her birth mother. "And you know the craziest thing, Defina?" she asked, when she was just about done. "All the time I was doing the Elle Halle interview, I kept thinking she was going to bring my real mother out of some closet. I was petrified, but when it didn't happen, I wasn't relieved. I was disappointed. Isn't that crazy?"

Defina shook her head. "Not crazy to me. You know what I've always wondered? Where do you find comfort, Karen? Not from Belle. And it looks like Jeffrey isn't giving you any nurturing. Until last year, I had my grandmere. She was a rock. I can't tell you how I miss her. A woman can't make a whole life out of work. I know that for a fact. We got to have something, someone to love."

"That's why I would like to adopt a baby."

"Damn! And I just spent an hour telling you how lousy it is to have a kid."

"Don't worry about it. Jeffrey doesn't want to do it anyway."

Defina shook her head, rose and returned carrying her chocolate soufflé. "So, what are you going to do? Aside from eating half of this, of course."

Karen looked at her watch. "Well, right now I am going to join twenty million people who are about to watch me make an ass out of myself. So turn on that television. I don't want to miss this."

Defina looked at the time, whooped and scrambled off the couch to switch on the TV. The Elle Halle theme music was already playing and her introductory voice-over, the lead-in to all of her shows, had begun. "Tonight," she was saying in that perfect television tone, "we are going to take a look at a woman whose contribution in the fashion and business world has already been filled. But she is a woman poised on the threshold of much bigger things. Tonight I talk with Karen Kahn, mistress of the fashion world." The theme music swelled and a quick montage of pictures swirled across the screen: Karen at the office, on the telephone; Karen at the Oakley Awards; Karen on her knees beside Tangela, cutting fabric, her mouth holding pins; Karen beside Jeffrey, walking along the river in Westport. Then there was a dissolve to the commercial.

Defina whooped again. "Karen Kahn, mistress of fashion," she imitated. "Sounds like you're some kind of S & M freak. But girl, you looked *good*."

"I looked like shit in that shot with Tangela. God, am I that fat?"

"Oh, shut up. Have some more soufflé. I hope I got this VCR to record."

The hour-long show flew by. Karen couldn't believe how thick her accent was, or how big she looked next to Elle Halle, but she still watched, mesmerized. It was strange to see herself and it was stranger to think that so many others were watching her too. But, thank God, the coverage was really pretty favorable. The program showed her working, at some of the charity functions, and in meetings with Casey, her design staff, and Defina and Mercedes. Overall, the view was a good one: a hard-working girl who had pushed her way into the big leagues. There was a short segment where Jeffrey talked about the business, and another one where they showed the Westport house. There were also a few snooty shots of Karen getting in and out of limos, but altogether it wasn't too glitzy. It ended with her acceptance of the Oakley Award. It was good coverage. Karen spooned the soufflé into her mouth and wondered if the show would affect NormCo's offer. She thought she came off well, and Defina agreed.

"Well, there's nothing else on, unless you want to buy a genuine faux diamond in an actual gold-tone setting for the amazingly low price of . . . " Defina hit the remote and the shopping channel appeared. But it wasn't junk jewelry that was being sold. It was schlocky windbreakers with some kind of matching skirt.

"Who the hell would wear *that*?" Karen asked.

"I don't know, but a hell of a lot of people seem to buy this stuff. Duchess Diane and her wrap dresses have gotten a whole second wind."

"Yeah, but who the hell buys *her* stuff?" Karen asked. She stared at the screen and watched another outfit being offered. It was a woman's suit and it was awful.

"You know, Joan Rivers sold a hundred and twenty million dollars worth of jewelry last year," Defina said. "You're looking at the future, Karen. It's not going to be department stores; it's on that screen."

"Oh, come on, Dee. People like to touch the goods. Shopping is a tactile sport. Anyway, this doesn't have any class. Doing something like that could ruin my name. Look at what happened to Halston when his clothes showed up in J.C. Penney."

"That was then. This is now. Women don't have the time to shop, but they still have the urge. Television shopping offers instant gratification."

Karen shook her head. "Forget about it. Look, I hate to watch and run, but I got to go."

"One more drink."

Karen paused, got the vibrations, and then agreed. She could feel Defina's loneliness and it shocked her. Dee had always been so strong. They polished off the rest of the second bottle of Merlot between them, and only then did Karen get up. Defina walked her out to the waiting car that sat there, unmolested, and they hugged on the sidewalk.

Defina looked back at her house. It was lit, and from the street you could see the hallway and the inviting red rooms. But Defina looked away. "It's a funny thing," she said before she turned back, "I've almost paid off the mortgage. For years I thought that all I wanted was to own that house. But now, living in it alone is not exactly what I had in mind. I miss my grandmere. I miss Tangela—the little girl she was. And now I'm sorry I gave up all those men for her. I was trying to do what was best for her, but where has it left me?" Defina was definitely a little bit drunk. She looked at Karen. "The TV show was great," she said. "But you don't live on TV. You go see if you can find your mama. We need all the friends we can get."

As Karen walked into her dark apartment, the phone was ringing. She fumbled for the light switch and picked up the nearest extension. Lisa was talking before Karen even got the phone up to her ear.

"Oh, it was great! You looked *great!* Did you see the shot of Stephanie? In the background when you were in the hallway? She's just *thrilled.* We're *all* thrilled. We taped a copy. Do you want one?"

Lisa was always so generous, Karen thought. She waited while her sister went on for a little while longer; then there was the beep of call waiting. "Can you hold a minute?" Karen asked, and hit the button in the receiver.

"Karen?" her mother's voice asked. "Did you watch it?"

"Yes," Karen told Belle.

"What did you think?" Belle asked. Karen could hear the reservation in Belle's voice.

"I thought it was fine, Mom. What do *you* think?"

"Well, since you asked, I don't think you came off too well. You should have worn some color. And sometimes, like when you were talking on the phone, you seemed—well—pushy. You know what I mean?"

Karen sighed. "Mom, I have Lisa on the other line. Can I call you back?"

"Certainly. Your father says to tell you 'congratulations.' " Karen could tell her mother was pissed, but she'd run out of patience. She hit the button and got Lisa back.

"I have Mom on the other line," she lied. "Can I call you later?"

"Sure, but I really *got* to talk to you."

Karen could hear the disappointment in Lisa's voice, but she just couldn't cope right now. "Sure. Thanks for calling," she said. "We'll talk tomorrow."

Karen was in bed, exhausted and almost asleep, when Jeffrey got in from his poker game. He walked into the bedroom without greeting her and sat down at the edge of the bed, taking off his shoes. She could tell by his careful movements that he was a little bit drunk.

"Did you win?" she said. He didn't answer. "Did you lose?"

Slowly he turned to face her. "We didn't play. Perry turned on the god-damned television. We watched the show and then I drank."

She tried to ignore her disappointment, but after all hadn't he promised they were going to watch the show together? Wasn't that the deal? Anyway, this was all wrong. There was something in his tone, something odd. "Didn't you like it?" she asked.

"Like it! I saw forty-two minutes of you and three minutes of me. That left fifteen minutes for commercials. Seems a pretty unfair division for two partners, or don't you think so?"

Karen sat up, knocking over a pillow that fell to the floor. She didn't bother to reach for it. Now what? "But it was good coverage, Jeffrey."

"It made me look like a schmuck. *You* made me look like a schmuck."

"Jeffrey, I didn't want to *do* the show, and I didn't edit the show."

"No. You just said that you were the creative one. You just told them that I was the jerk with the pencils in the back room."

"Jeffrey, what are you *talking* about?" She tried to remember exactly what she had said, and exactly how the Elle Halle people had cut it. She and Defina had had some wine, but she hadn't been drunk. The show had seemed fine, and neither Jeffrey nor Karen had looked bad.

But Jeffrey stood up. He was so angry that his eyes had turned a steel gray. They narrowed and, unconsciously, Karen pulled the blanket up over her chest as if his gaze could harm her. "You made me look like a schmuck," he repeated. "Remember—I was the artist. Perry, Jordan, and Sam watched and I knew what they were thinking. That I live off of you. You didn't talk about how I got the seed money from my father. You didn't talk about how the business was my idea in the first place. But you did tell fifty million people that you own controlling stock. Why didn't you just castrate me?"

"That's not fair, Jeffrey. I *did* say all of the other stuff. They cut whatever they wanted to out."

"Sure. Like you cut me out. Out of the credit. We still haven't gotten the NormCo offer, and even if we don't take it, we need a good appraisal to raise a loan. You think this makes negotiating with them any easier?" He turned and, barefoot, began to pad out of the room.

"Where are you going?" she called.

"Out," he said.

"Barefoot?" she asked, but he didn't answer. She was so angry, she hoped he would go out without shoes. This was so unfair. And so unlike him. He had *never* been the kind of macho jerk who competed. Elle Halle had brought out the worst in him. Or had she merely seen it and focused on it when Karen hadn't—when Karen hadn't let herself?

Karen was sick and tired of it all, but she knew she wouldn't get to sleep tonight. And tomorrow she had to make some progress on the new collection. She simply *had* to. Otherwise what would they show in Paris? She reached into the bedside table drawer and pulled out the little plastic prescription bottle. Tonight was a two-Xanax night. Fuck Jeffrey, fuck her mother, fuck them all. She popped the two tiny pills into her mouth and washed them down with a glass of Evian water. She'd had enough for one day.

The Merlot and the pills began to kick in only minutes after she turned the light out. The last thought she had before she slept was of Jeffrey, barefoot on the West End Avenue sidewalk. She hoped it was raining.

Karen slept until Jeffrey came noisily back. She looked at the clock. It was four ten. She lay in bed, trying to force herself to sleep. It didn't work. Now she ought to go back to sleep. But she couldn't give it up. You need your sleep. But telling herself that didn't help. She lay there, as limp as the lox on the trays she had served at the stupid family brunch, only miserable, exhausted, and sleepless.

Karen wasn't a great thinker, and she knew it. It wasn't that she was dumb: over the years she had come to understand that straight cognitive thinking just wasn't her forte. She was more intuitive, more indirect and creative. She lived through her eyes—what she saw often told her what to think and even how to feel.

So now she closed her eyes, not to try to sleep but to see what was bothering her. Jeffrey, of course, but not just this silly anger. That would go away. It was something else. Something darker.

She closed her eyes, and the first image that came, unbidden, was the picture from the Westport brunch of Sylvia, beaming up at Jeffrey, her son. It was as clear as a photograph—clearer, because in her mind's eye Karen could move around them and look at the scene from all angles. She could see Sylvia's Sonia Rykiel from behind, and her hand lovingly placed on Jeffrey's back, her silver hair contrasting yet complimenting Jeffrey's. She could see them in profile, Sylvia's aristocratic nose arching in just the same way as her son's.

Was that it then, Karen wondered? What's bugging me? Am I longing for the son I'll never have? But she didn't feel that kind of longing. Anyway, she'd always felt she'd prefer a daughter. She kept her eyes closed and stayed with the image. What she felt, she realized, was jealousy.

Even there, in the dark, in bed, she felt herself flush with shame. Jealousy was such a dirty feeling, one Karen was lucky enough to rarely feel. But she knew it when she felt it, and now she was jealous. God, she couldn't believe that she was that covetous! Or that petty. Or that territorial. She was jealous and possessive of her husband.

Sometime past five, she at last fell into a troubled sleep. But she woke up in less than an hour from a graphic dream. She'd been tiny, and in some kind of small boat, almost a basket, being rocked on the swells of a white sea. At first it felt good, but after a time she was hungry, and when she sat up to look about, all she could see was the heaving ocean all around her and darkness above it. The ocean was milky white and luminous but she could feel it turn from warm to cold and she became very chilled. She was cold, and hungry. She began to cry, with an infant's mewling, until a wave broke over her, mixing its wet salt with the tears that were already on her cheeks.

She woke up with real tears on her lashes, and immediately thought two things. I've never dreamed in black and white before, was her first thought.

Her second realization was that she was not envious of Sylvia for having a son. She was envious of Jeffrey for having a mother.

14

DRESSING HER WOUNDS

Queasy as she was with a Merlot hangover, the next morning Karen decided to take action. The fight with Jeffrey, the disappointed feeling after Elle Halle's show, the dream she'd had, all came together. She'd try to find her mother. But how?

How do you go about hiring a competent private detective? For orthodontists, hairdressers, gynecologists—maybe even plastic surgeons— you could ask around. But for a detective? She couldn't talk to Jeffrey about this—he'd made it clear how he felt. Karen wondered if she should call June Silverman and ask her if she'd had Perry tailed before their divorce? Maybe she should just call Bill Wolper and ask him if he used some kind of service to check into the background of employees and acquisitions. And could she queer his offer on her company if she were so bold as to ask him?

Having no other recourse, Karen let her fingers do the walking and found that though there were dozens of services listed in the Manhattan yellow pages, most had their actual offices located in Brooklyn. She avoided the one called "AAAA Investigations" but selected a few others randomly and dialed the numbers. The first four had answering machines or services. Yeah, like she would leave her name, a brief message, and her home phone number. They all sounded totally sleazy. Then she dialed one more and the phone was picked up by an avuncular-sounding guy located on Jay Street in Brooklyn. Karen made an appointment with Mr. Centrillo, who assured her he could "manage to squeeze her in."

When they pulled up in front of the narrow doorway sandwiched between a cop-supply-and-uniform store and a third-tier jeweler, Karen smiled at the black man behind the wheel of the limousine. His name was Corman, and he'd driven her before. "I'm just going up for fifteen minutes," she told him. "A half hour at the most. If I'm gone longer than that, please come up to room 201 and knock on the door. I don't want to be late for my next appointment."

Corman nodded his head but knit his brow. "Might be hard to find a parking spot, and I don't like to leave the limo in a neighborhood like this. But I guess it will be all right."

"Thank you, Corman," she said, and she felt real gratitude.

The stairs to Centrillo's office were old, wooden, and trimmed on the risers with metal strips. They sagged in the middle as if they were very tired. Karen felt very tired herself, but she knew it wasn't physical. She wondered how many people's accumulated misery had worn down those steps, and she also wondered what that misery weighed. If you were afraid your partner was embezzling, was that a fifty-pound weight? If you suspected your wife was cheating on you, was that a heavier burden? If you were looking for a husband who had deserted you and the children, was that two tons? How much misery was she, herself, carrying up the steps to the kind-sounding Mr. Centrillo?

His office was one of only two on the second floor and, she noted with some relief, the hallway, just like the stairs, was very clean. She turned the knob of the thick oak door and entered a waiting room the size of a small vestibule. A pimply young girl with big hair looked up and smiled pleasantly. "Miz Cohen?" she asked. Karen remembered to nod. She certainly hadn't wanted to use her real name. But what happened if this young woman had seen "The Elle Halle Show"? She wasn't sure if any designer was big enough yet to be on the front page of the *National Enquirer* but she didn't want this to be a test case. SEEKING THE MOM WHO ABANDONED HER. OAKLEY AWARD–WINNING DESIGNER FEELS THE PAIN OF BEING UNWANTED: KAREN KAHN'S PERSONAL STORY. She shuddered. Mr. Centrillo's ad was the only one that had not mentioned "discretion." That was what had led her to call him. It was as if he assumed that went without saying. And, she hoped, maybe people in Brooklyn hadn't heard of her. The bridge-and-tunnel crowd wasn't so ready or able to drop three grand on a layered cashmere sweater outfit. And it wasn't like she appeared on TV *every* night. Did anyone on Jay Street read Suzy's column or subscribe to *W*?

She looked at the girl sitting behind the narrow counter. The blue and purple blouse was polyester, and fit like a feed bag. The darts were cut too high and unevenly as well. Could they have charged the girl more than

$19.99 for it? It looked like one of the blouses NormCo had produced for Bette Mayer. Karen could imagine the feel of the cheap cloth against skin on a humid day like this one: it wasn't a pretty feeling. Wouldn't a simple cotton camp shirt look so much better and cost the same? And those colors! They fought with each other and neither one dominated. They were deadly with the kid's hair and pale skin.

Karen sighed. She had to stop these mental makeovers before she drove herself crazy. Was Jeffrey right? Was it a control thing? Or was her college shrink right? Was it all simply a distraction, taking her away from the thoughts that were too painful for her to bear? Or both, as Defina almost always added.

"Have a seat. Mistah Centrillah will be right with yah." The girl's accent was pure Nostrand Avenue. God, Karen wondered, do I sound like that? If I hadn't been talented, would I have wound up behind a desk like this one, wearing a blouse like that one? She felt enormous compassion for the poor kid. Where did my talent come from? she wondered. She stared at the receptionist, full of pity. Then she told herself to calm down. It was probably arrogant of her to feel superior—after all, her life was so screwed up she was here as a potential client, not just an employee. Despite the bad skin and the rotten clothes, the girl behind the counter probably had working ovaries. What difference did a lousy blouse make in the bigger scheme of things?

The glass-paneled door behind the girl opened and a small gray-haired man scurried out. Yech! If that was Centrillo, Karen instantly decided she was outta here. But the little man pushed passed the counter and through the exit door without even looking up. In his place a short, broad, balding man stood, his feet planted as firmly on the ground as the smile was on his face. "Mrs. Cohen?" he asked. And it was the voice from over the phone, the voice that had drawn her to him. The voice she thought of as "the good daddy" voice.

She nodded, rose, and followed him. Good God, she thought. What am I going to say? Please find my mommy? She suddenly felt childish and unprepared. Centrillo's office was sunny, clean, and spare, with the old boxy oak furniture she hadn't seen since her days in South Side High School. Karen took one of the two unpadded wooden arm chairs before his desk and he slipped into the matching swivel chair behind it. All she needed was a paddle arm and she'd start to take down U.S. history notes.

"So?" He waited, his big, flat hands lying still on the big, flat desktop.

She found it hard to speak. The silence continued until it became equally hard not to speak. She realized that she had not really prepared for this. She could see dust motes floating in the shaft of sunlight that slanted through the clean window. "I want to find my mother," she finally managed to whisper.

"Has she disappeared? Run away? Is she senile?" he asked, his voice lowered but still comforting.

"No. I don't know. I mean it isn't what you think." She paused. "Not my mother. My *real* mother."

"Oh. You mean 'birth mother.' You're an adult adoptee?"

He had given her a name now, a category, probably a whole file drawer in which her case, like all the others, would comfortably fit.

"Yes."

"How long you been looking?" he asked.

Forever. Never before. She sighed. "I haven't. I don't know how. That's why I came to you."

"Sealed record?"

"I don't know."

"Private or state?"

"I don't know."

"Birth mother's name?"

"I don't know."

"It was here in New York?"

She could hardly believe how incompetent she was about this. She, Karen Kahn, who put together four collections a year, gave interviews to journalists, who knew how things worked and could make things happen, who could present herself to Bill Wolper and impress the son of a bitch, here she was, trying to solve her central puzzle without planning or research. What the hell was wrong with her? Not only could she not produce children, she couldn't produce answers. She knew she must look like a fool, a nitwit who expected some big man would help her. What had he just asked? Where had the adoption taken place? She was about to tell him that she didn't know that either when she remembered, out of the blue. Once, her father had mentioned Chicago and how he hated going there for business, except it was the town she, Karen, had come from. "I think Chicago," she said.

She took a deep breath. She knew the basics about adoptive children's rights, but it was only the stuff she'd read in newspapers and magazines. She'd followed Baby Jessica, just the way everyone else had. And the teenager in Florida who'd been given as an infant to the wrong family. She also knew that children almost always wanted to remain with their adoptive parents, but was that simply because those parents were familiar?

There was a movement among adult adopted children to get to unseal court adoption records as their birthright. But the movement was not popular among others. Only a few weeks ago, Karen had read an Ann Landers column where a letter had begged adoptive children not to upset the lives of their natural parents by seeking them out. And Ann had agreed, saying that "Adopted children have the right to the medical history of their parents, but beyond that, a sealed adoption should remain sealed. Period." The court didn't want to help, adoptive parents didn't want to help, Ann Landers didn't want to help, and now it looked as if Mr. Centrillo didn't want to help. Somehow, it didn't seem fair. Didn't she have a simple human right to know?

She opened her purse, and began to search through it for the two photographs, her talismans. But they weren't there. She felt the blood drain from her face. Had she lost them? She could swear she'd put them in here. She'd been carrying them with her everywhere, but lately she'd been so busy and so disorganized. Where had she last seen them? A fine sweat broke out on her forehead.

She looked up at the big man, stricken. "I might have some pictures. And I'm almost sure that I was from Chicago."

Mr. Centrillo nodded. "I'll have to look up the Illinois laws. You know, this all goes state by state. Mrs. Cohen, I think you can see there's a difficulty here. Assuming it *was* Chicago and that it *was* a state adoption, and assuming that the records are *not* sealed, without names and dates this is not something that can easily be unearthed. What is your maiden name?"

At last, she could give him an answer. "Lipsky," she said, and gave Arnold and Belle's names and dates of birth and the old address in Brooklyn. "Will that do it? Will their name help?"

But Centrillo just shook his head. "Even *with* names and dates it is often very difficult. May I ask you another question?"

She nodded her head. She felt as if she couldn't speak at all. Even one word and she would burst into tears. God, when was the last time she had cried? She couldn't remember. But she felt her lip tremble.

"I know this is sometimes an awkward thing, but could you possibly get this information from your adoptive mother? Could you talk to her?"

As if by magic, Karen's tears disappeared, and the trembly feeling dropped away. "Impossible," she said. The man nodded as if he was not surprised by that answer. He sighed. "Have you got a birth certificate?" he asked.

"Yes," she said, with so much enthusiasm she immediately felt stupid.

"May I see it?"

"I don't have it with me," she admitted.

The man sighed again. "Mrs. Cohen, I feel as if I have to ask you this: Have you really thought this out? Perhaps this is not a case for a private investigator. Maybe you need to talk to someone else. A rabbi or a counselor or a family therapist . . ."

She felt the blood rush to her face. He was telling her to get a shrink! As if she hadn't already been through three of them! Jesus Christ, she didn't need to *talk* any more about how she felt! She just wanted to find her goddamned mother, and if she was conflicted, or disorganized, or unprepared, well, fuck it! For once in her life she was feeling a little vulnerable and irrational. Yeah, this is what happens when a woman acts vulnerable and irrational: she's told to go get a shrink, she's told to go have her head examined. Now Karen's eyes *did* fill with tears, but she was angry as well as in pain.

"Look, Mr. Centrillo, I know I didn't prepare myself properly for this meeting and I apologize for that, but I've been very busy. If you can give me a list of what you need I'll try and get it. If I do, can you find my real mother?"

"Please, Mrs. Cohen. Don't be upset. I know this is a difficult thing for you to undertake. And who knows? Sometimes I go to the court house or the Bureau of Vital Records and hit, one, two, three. Sometimes I search for years and only turn up dead ends. Most women who gave up their babies aren't proud of it. They started new lives, they moved on, they died. Whatever happened to them, they do not necessarily want to be located. I take it that your birth mother never came looking for you?"

Karen sat back against the hard wood of the chair in surprise. It had simply never occurred to her that her mother might search for *her*.

"Is that possible?" she whispered.

"Well, it depends. In some cases, where the birth mother has much of the information from the time of the delivery, she can have an easier time of it. But she also can run into sealed records. In sixteen states, if the records are sealed, there is absolutely nothing that either you or your birth mother could do to contact one another. Even if you both want to."

Tears began to overflow Karen's eyes and run down her face. It seemed so very, v ' sad. She thought of all the separated mothers and daughters, searching in vain. Smoothly and simply, Mr. Centrillo opened a drawer of his desk and handed her a box of tissues. Just like a shrink. The tears kept on sliding out from under Karen's eyes. She cried for a long time. She'd been saving these tears up. Finally, she mopped her cheeks and managed a gasp. "That's so sad," she said. "That's just so sad." She blew her nose.

Mr. Centrillo reached across the desk, took a Kleenex out of the box, and blew his own nose. Then he sighed gustily. "It is," he agreed.

They both sat there quietly for a moment, bathed in the sun. After a time, Karen took a deep breath, reached into her bag, pulled out her File-o-Fax and Mont Blanc pen. "Okay," she said, "tell me what I need to help you do this."

After they discussed that and fees, Karen had fished around to find the envelope that contained the cash for his retainer. Carefully he wrote her out a receipt. Then Mr. Centrillo stood up and walked her to the door where he paused and, looking down at the clean wood floor, said gently, "Mrs. Cohen," he took her elbow, "there is one more thing I am going to ask you. Do you know what you are looking for? Because even if we find your birth mother, you may not get it."

She took his hand. How could she begin to explain all that was going on in her life right now? "A girl's gotta do what a girl's gotta do," was all she said.

Corman, her driver, stood waiting in the tiny reception area. "It was just half an hour," he said. "Should I have come in?" She shook her head and let him help her down the stairs and into the car. Defina, as usual, was right. Karen needed all the help she could get.

15

A FRIEND IN TWEED

The morning had been a flurry of phone calls and congratulations from the staff. Everyone who called said the same thing: they didn't usually watch TV but the other night, on their way out the door, they just happened to tune in to a few minutes of Elle Halle and. . . . Karen almost had to laugh. And it was almost as funny to see how Janet and all the other secretaries, Mrs. Cruz, and even Casey were looking at her with new respect. It was as if television had the power to leave a gloss on you after your appearance. Only Jeffrey and Belle seemed immune to television's cosmetic treatment.

She'd decided to ignore her husband until he gave her an apology. Despite the sick feeling their fight gave her, she was carrying on BAU. Business as usual. Which included pinning an uninspired wrap skirt around Tangela's slim waist while Stephie stood by, watching. Karen surreptitiously checked Tangela a few times to see if the girl seemed high, but she was no more sullen than usual. Karen was about to give her a break when the phone rang. "Who is it?" Karen said aloud, knowing that Janet had the intercom on.

"Please come ta thuh phone," Janet said, her Bronx accent heavy as a house.

On her knees, pins in her mouth, both hands fighting with the fabric from hell, Karen didn't feel like coming to the phone. Janet should know better than this. That's what she was paid for. *"Who is it?"* Karen asked again, annoyed.

"Please come ta thuh phone," Janet repeated, and—with a sigh of irritation that had to be audible over the intercom—Karen got up heavily and strode over to her work table.

She was getting too old to sit comfortably on the floor. God, she felt so tired! She snatched up the receiver. "Who the fuck is it?" she asked Janet.

"Bill Wolper. I thawt you wouldn't want anyone to, yuh know, get nervous aw anything, hearing his name."

"Oh. Yeah. Thanks. Put him through," Karen agreed, properly chastened. Then she tried to pull herself together enough to ensure her sparkle. After seeing the TV show, was he finally calling with an offer? But that didn't make sense—wouldn't he call Jeffrey? Or had NormCo decided to pass and he was merely calling her to be polite? She felt the emptiness of rejection hit her in the pit of her stomach. Just because she didn't want them didn't mean she wanted a rejection. Well, if they did pass, was she glad or disappointed? The phone clicked and she took a deep breath. "Hello," she said, packing as much positive energy and enthusiasm as could be put into a single word and pushed through the little holes in the telephone handset. "Bill! How nice of you to call."

"Please hold for Mr. Wolper," a curt secretarial voice demanded. Shit! Karen *hated* when that happened. She'd been outphoned. She tried to gather herself together.

"Karen?" It *was* Bill Wolper this time. "Hey, I was wondering. Are you free for lunch?"

"When?" she asked, thinking of her overbooked week and the Paris show. Plus, she was already so tired.

"Today. Right now. Say I have my car pick you up in twenty minutes?"

The man was crazy, plus he had a lot of balls. Wasn't this like calling a girl up on Friday night and asking her out for Saturday? In Rockville Centre that had been called an "A.T."—Automatic Turndown—because even if you had *nothing* to do, you wouldn't admit it. Only a desperate girl said yes.

"Yes." Karen said, and surprised herself. Would Coco Chanel say yes, she asked herself sternly. But hey, she was no Coco Chanel. She'd made a life out of saying "yes" when other women would have said "no." And vice versa. Karen wondered, but only for a nanosecond, if she should try to include Jeffrey, but she didn't know where to find him, and she knew without asking that wasn't part of the deal. Fuck 'im. Would he be angry to be left out? Would he be jealous or possessive? Suddenly, she didn't care.

She could hear Bill's approval in his voice. "My driver will be waiting for you at twelve thirty. Lutece suit you?"

"Just fine," she purred. It was only the best intimate restaurant in New York.

Without asking herself anything further, she turned to her niece and her goddaughter. "Show's over. I'm outta here." She reached across her work table and into her *schlep* bag. She pulled out a hundred-dollar bill and held it out to Tangela. She hadn't said a word to her about her fight with Defina, but she wanted to be as kind as possible. "Let me blow the two of ya to lunch," she said, and Stephie giggled, recognizing her aunt's imitation of Belle. Karen smiled at the sullen older girl. "Take her someplace nice," she said. Tangela just reached for the money. "C'mon," was all she mumbled, and Stephie followed Tangela out the door.

Alone now, Karen pulled out a mirror to survey herself. The news from the front was not good. Her face, rather like a potato to begin with, could look acceptable when gilded with a good moisturizer, a transparent foundation, and a burnish of Guerlaine bronzing powder. Her eyes were bloodshot, plus she was having a catastrophic hair day, or CHD, as they all called it around the office. Karen shook her head, not that *that* would bring any fullness to the lank, no-haircut haircut that Jean-Pierre had given her. She'd have to lose that guy and go back to Carl. He understood her hair and was worth the *schlep* to Brooklyn. And maybe cutting her hair would cheer him up. She had to think of a way to do that. She looked into the mirror.

Karen had never felt really attractive. And she certainly had never been seductive. She was too direct and too embarrassed to act coy, to flirt. But maybe I'm just too insecure, she thought. Maybe my fascination with clothes all comes from that. Clothes could be a distraction from the imperfect face, the flawed body. But *why* did she feel so unattractive?

Karen thought of Belle. Was it a mother's job to initiate her daughter into the world of seductiveness and flirtation? Was a mother supposed to teach her daughter how to be female? Belle had certainly focused attention on how Karen looked and how to dress and makeup "properly," but the attention had been mostly negative. Karen remembered that, like Tiff, she had been humiliated by Belle's criticism. Was that why she never felt really comfortable as a vamp or successful as a seductress?

But everybody blamed their mother for everything. Maybe it was *Arnold's* failure that Karen felt. Wasn't it a father's job to help his daughter feel attractive? Unlike Belle, Arnold had never criticized. He'd simply not noticed Karen, at least not in any way that recognized her femininity. Whether he meant to or not, he'd helped to teach her that if she wanted to be noticed she had to work for it. That, along with his own workaholism, helped to make her what she was today.

Karen shrugged. Would her real parents have done a better job? If Mr. Centrillo found them, she'd be able to answer that question. Would she be a different woman if she had been raised by the unwed teenage mom who probably was her natural mother and abandoned by the kid who was her father? Karen told herself she probably would have been worse off and tried to believe it. They'd given her this face and body and she'd have to like it or lump it.

Anyway, now she had to take whatever emergency measures she could to look her best. And if the idea of flirtation made her nervous as hell, she'd have to try not to show it.

Fifteen minutes later, she strode out of the lobby of 550 Seventh Avenue to Bill Wolper's waiting stretch Mercedes limo, carrying a small batch of mail and memos to assuage her guilt at running off. Her skin was appropriately glossy, as were her lips, though the gloss *did* stop at her hairline. The hair was at least brushed, but otherwise unsalvageable. There was a limit to what a girl could do in a quarter of an hour when she was on the wrong side of forty. Still, the wheat-colored cotton knit tunic and short skirt she was wearing pulled her together and gave her a nice cleavage, and the wrap jacket in a soft waffle-weave cotton and linen knit was a great texture and forgivingly covered her belly.

Not surprisingly, Wolper's car was divine. Karen leaned back into the supple and supportive gray leather seat. It was pure luxury. The raucous noise from the street was completely blocked by the tinted windows and the liquid of the Mozart concerto playing on the sound system. For the first time in weeks, Karen tried to relax. This was a hundred times better than the rented limos Karen took. How did I get here, she wondered? I'm just a nice Jewish girl from Brooklyn and I'm sitting in one of the world's most luxurious cars being driven to one of the city's most luxurious restaurants. Karen shook her head to clear it. So far, despite the high profile she'd gotten in the last couple of years, despite the Oakley Award, or how often she saw her fashions featured in the glossy magazines, she never seemed to take what she had earned for granted. It seemed to her that though the climb had been long and hard and not without pain, despite all the press she'd gotten lately, she was still more the young hopeful than she was the established star. To Karen, the luxury of not having to look at the prices on the right-hand side of the menu, of being able to buy any piece of jewelry she wanted, of never having to go to the bank but always having a five-figure balance in her checking account when she inserted her cash card, all of it was something she didn't expect.

But what if this is it? Karen asked herself. What if this is the pinnacle and from here on it's all a slip down hill. She thought of Tony de Freise at the Oakley Awards. What had he said? "See you on the slopes." I would hate to have arrived and never even known that I had gotten there before it was over.

Karen thought. Do you only know you've reached the top when you look up at it from the decline? All at once she felt chilled, and asked the driver to turn down the air conditioning. I shouldn't be going out to lunch, she realized with a shiver. I should be working on the Paris collection. If I blow that, I blow everything.

She sighed. In this business you were only as good as your last collection. Karen's work had gotten nowhere this morning and she knew that so far this collection wasn't exciting. When she'd gotten into the business she'd made herself two promises: that she'd dress women beautifully but comfortably, never putting them in ridiculous, clownish, or restrictive clothes, and that she'd make sure her line was simple, so that all of her pieces worked with each other.

It wasn't easy then and it was getting harder. Elegant simplicity isn't easy. Most of her art was in knowing how fabrics—beautiful, sensuous, tactile fabrics—draped and flowed. She was always on the lookout for a great new fabric—just as when Lastex first came out in 1934, Chanel showed amazing new clothes in it.

But the structure of Karen's clothes was her other secret. They were unique because the simplicity of line belied the strength of the cut and seams. A cashmere swing jacket seemed to hang effortlessly from the shoulders, but what work had gone into the bias cut of that swing and the sewing of those shoulders! Her little linen tank tops fit so beautifully because of the almost invisible darts she knew, from years of experience, how and where to stitch. But the same darts had to be cut differently and higher on the silk shantung tank tops. And her slacks! They were famous. Women would kill to get them. Karen knew how to cut the leg, how to seam the crotch, how to make sure the rise was just right so they never pulled, never pinched, but so they also minimized the belly and thigh, and elongated the leg. Simple, yes; easy, no.

After years of learning, after years of trying what worked and what didn't, after moving up through the jungle of the garment center, after fighting for press coverage, for recognition, for sales, she'd finally made it. And now here she was, riding in this limousine, successful because of what she'd done but confronted with the challenge of the endless yearning for the new. Because in fashion it wasn't enough to be good, to be flattering, to be stylish. You also had to look new. Karen had to face it. Her women clients didn't buy clothes because they needed them. They bought the thrill of the new.

And if her clothes were classics, if they were timeless, if they transcended the rules, if they fit and flattered and worked, but if they weren't *new*, they failed.

Karen had come, over the years, to resent that last demand. She was inventive, but though she rose to the challenge time and time again, season after season, it had begun to feel like a bad parlor trick. Novelty, unlike the other demands of fashion, had no intrinsic value. Functionality and aesthetics were valid, but why did women—and the press—clamor for novelty?

Last season she'd done a good collection, sold well, and gotten generally good reviews. But *Women's Wear* had written up her show and called it "just a bit tired," and accused her of "recycling." One bad season, two at the most, could put her out of business, Jeffrey said. Always the press's darling, she'd resented their accusation and the resentment lingered. But now she was established, and just as they had built her, they would now undermine. It was the way of the industry. The Oakley Awards would only make her a more visible target for potshots. If she did sell to NormCo, she wouldn't have to worry so much about all this, but would they want her if she didn't do well in Paris? She shivered at the thought.

For a moment she wished she'd never come. She longed to be back at her workroom. She *needed* to be back at her workroom. If she didn't concentrate on the collection . . . To distract herself from that thought and to justify her existence, she turned to the pile of mail she had brought with her. It was a funny thing: when they had first opened the company, Karen had wandered around the office early in the morning, opening *all* the mail. It seemed a natural thing to do—after all, it all had her name on it. Now Janet opened, sorted, and distributed most of the mail before Karen even saw it. Despite that, there was still too big a volume to keep up with. Now, in her lap amid the in-house memos and other usual stuff, there were two envelopes of interest. The first was a heavy pasteboard card. Janet had slit open the envelope for her, so Karen only had to slip out the note.

It was written in an elegant script on embossed stock.

> Dearest Karen,
>
> I'm sure you must be pleased about the coverage that your wonderful clothes got, but you can't be nearly as happy as I am. I know I asked for a lot. No one could have done it but you. What an amazing talent you have and what hard work you back it up with. I think you know how very much my wedding meant to me, and with your help I looked as beautiful to Larry as I wanted to. I will always be in your debt.
>
> Deepest thanks,
>
> Elise Elliot

Karen blinked. It wasn't often that she was thanked, and thanked by the likes of Elise Elliot, who had been dressed by Givenchy, Mainbocher, and Marc Bohan of Dior. She'd taken time from her honeymoon to write. Cool as she was, demanding as she had been, the woman had a kind of patrician class. Karen was touched. The little pasteboard square had given her the answer to the question she'd asked herself. She was here in this car on her way to lunch because of her talent and hard work. The card was an omen that had come when she needed it most. She patted the card and slipped it in her purse. It wasn't quite as good as the Oakley Award, but it came close.

The second envelope was not as gratifying. Norris Cleveland, third-rate designer, was inviting her to the introduction of her new perfume. Of course, it was called "Norris!" Norris's new collection had looked almost exactly like one of Karen's old collections. Except the colors were lousy. Karen shook her head. Somehow it continued to bug her that she, Karen, had to struggle for everything she got and that Norris did it effortlessly. Why didn't Norris have to sell herself to the highest bidder? Well, perhaps she had. Karen crumpled the invitation into her *schlep* bag. She was sure it would be a beautiful party with beautiful people, but she doubted the perfume would be a Number Five or an Opium or an Obsession. Somehow Norris always managed the trappings without any of the content. Karen wouldn't even be surprised if the bottles of perfume were empty! Norris's success proved that talent wasn't necessary. So maybe Karen's own success was just a fluke.

She looked out the window of the limousine. A crowd of motley pedestrians at the curb were trying to peek in and see who was moving through the traffic in such an elegant way. The tint protected Karen from their peeking. She could have been one of them, dressed in off-the-rack polyester, wearing shoes from Fayva. Why had *she* wound up in here, looking out at them? Why did she deserve this? And how long would it last?

Of course, in spite of what an ass he'd been last night, Karen knew Jeffrey had helped her achieve it all, and he was right about almost everything. He was right when he told her that Ford got rich making Fords, not Lincolns. There was no real money in American couture. Perhaps that was why only Jimmy Galanos on the West Coast and maybe Scassi actually practiced it. Even high-end ready-to-wear, the next tier down, was precarious. "Designer" clothes cost a lot, but they also cost a lot to make. The sales volume wasn't high and the profit margin was small. One bad line and you could be wiped out. Designers like Ralph Lauren, Donna Karan, Anne Klein, and the rest who had "graduated" made their money in the lower-priced bridge lines and in the licensing business. None of them manufactured their own mass market lines. Ralph used Bidermann Industries to manufacture his women's wear, and they produced over fifty thousand styles a year! No wonder financing the bridge line without a partner and no real capital was eating ЖKInc up. It was hard to find a company that could produce her line, that would deliver it on time, that would keep up the quality, and that would wait to get paid. Unless she, Karen, wanted to sink to the Better Sportswear level of Liz Claiborne or Jones New York, she had better figure out a way to continue to finance the bridge line, or do this deal with NormCo and spread herself from designer wear all the way down to "moderate"—the level of Chaus and Tapemeasure.

The driver maneuvered the car past the pedestrian throng and through the brutal midtown traffic, over to the more residential East Fifties. That was where the townhouse that was the home to New York's finest French restaurant nestled beside other, more private, brownstones. In the slow crawl through midtown traffic Karen had had plenty of time to notice both the car and its appointments. There are limos and there are limos, she thought, noticing the perfection of the burled wood interior, the pewter alpaca lap robe with the "WW" monogram, crystal decanters in the silver holders screwed to the privacy panel, and the silver vase (also monogrammed and screwed to the wall) that held a trembling spray of dendrobium orchids.

What did Bill have to tell her? She was nervous. Her fight with Jeffrey had unnerved her. She hated to be at odds with him. She felt jeopardized now. She felt like a package being delivered. The silence was getting to her. "Bill seems to like to brand things and screw them to the wall," Karen commented aloud to the driver. The moment she said it, she could have bitten her tongue. But in the rearview mirror, the driver's eyes didn't even blink.

"We'll be there in a moment," was all he said. "Mr. Wolper will be waiting for you." The driver pulled to the curb, was out, and had the door opened before Karen had time to realize she'd been politely chastised. But when she herself got out of the car she did take a moment to look over the driver's well-cut gray suit and cap to see if it, too, bore the brand of the double "W". It didn't, but that didn't reassure her.

She straightened her skirt and at the same time tried to surreptitiously wipe her damp palms. What have I got to be so scared about? she asked herself, and walked down the two shallow steps to the restaurant door, where she was greeted by Andre and ushered through the chic and tiny dining room hung with a priceless Gobelin tapestry to the less formal glass-roofed garden in the back. She smiled at Sherry Lansing, the head of Paramount Pictures and a client for many years, who was lunching with Demi Moore, not a client. Karen also recognized one of the Kaufman brothers, a real estate billionaire and friend of the Kahn family. This was clearly a power lunch place, though Karen had only been here for dinner.

Bill Wolper was already sitting at a corner table waiting for her. He rose as she approached, although she noticed that he didn't move to help her into her chair; he let Andre do that. She also noted that he sat in the corner while she had to have her own back to the rest of the room. Was that the done thing? She began to be sure that she didn't like him. But then Bill smiled at her. "Thank you for coming at such short notice," he said, and sounded so sincere that she felt as if he might actually be apologizing. He turned to Andre and raised his bushy eyebrows. "Do you know Karen Kahn?" he asked. "She was on "The Elle Halle Show" this week." Then he turned to Karen. "I suggest we put ourselves in Andre's capable hands."

Andre glowed. "May I suggest the *homard?* We only have a few and I am serving them cold, in halves, as a salad to begin."

Bill looked over at her. "Would you like the lobster?" he asked, as if she might need translation. She couldn't decide if it was protective or condescending.

"Je voudrais le homard, mais pas maintenant, merci. Une salade verte seulement, et après la salade, le homard, s'il vous plaît." She smiled at both Andre and Bill Wolper. *"Je n'ai pas faim d'habitude au déjeuner,"* she lied. *"Jamais."* Actually, she was starving, but it was best to keep it light.

"Je comprends, Madame. Moi aussi." Andre agreed. He turned to Bill. *"Et pour vous?"*

Bill Wolper cleared his throat, perhaps a bit discomfited. Good. Karen suppressed a grin.

"I'll have the same," Bill Wolper said. He looked at Karen. "A Chardonnay?"

Karen thought of Defina's Merlot and her subsequent hangover. God, she didn't need any wine today, and the thought of a white wine made her ill. "I know it isn't done, but I prefer a red, even with lobster."

"Nous avons un Bordeaux supérieur," Andre suggested to her.

But, "Why don't we start with the Chardonnay?" Bill said smoothly, and Andre, remembering himself, nodded quickly and departed.

Karen blinked. The guy was clearly a control freak. She wondered, for a brief moment, whether she should insist on the Bordeaux but decided against it. First she'd wait and see what kind of an offer—if any—was forthcoming. She felt flutters in her stomach and tried to look calmly across the table, though she was made very uncomfortable by having her broad back exposed to the rest of the room. She wondered how often Bill might have brought women here and sequestered them in this way. And how many patrons were noticing who Bill Wolper was lunching with?

" 'The Elle Halle Show' was terrific," Bill said. "And you got great coverage for the Elise Elliot wedding," he added approvingly. "It must be great to see your ideas perform."

Karen blinked. He was right, and he'd put it well. It *had* been great. "Did you like her dress?"

"I like the *coverage*. Nowadays a designer *has* to be linked with celebrities. Most of them just have some movie star show up at one of their shows. You know, they hire a model to get her boyfriend to show. Big deal. What you did was a stroke of genius. Elise Elliot! She's popular with older women but she's also seen as hip. Younger women admire her. She's got class and cash and cachet. She could be to you what Audrey Hepburn was to Givenchy. How did you engineer it?" he asked.

Karen wondered if she should try to pretend it had been masterminded for months, but couldn't pull it off. "She just asked me to do it," she shrugged. "It was a risk, but the dresses all came out well."

"You got a *People* cover! I'd say that was 'coming out well,' " Wolper laughed. "I saw it and I wondered if you did it simply to drive our price up."

Karen smiled at him. Was he kidding? She didn't know what to say, so she said nothing. That seemed to be fine with Wolper, who continued. "A funny thing about being involved with fashion in business. It's made me have to learn to understand women." He grinned. "It isn't easy," he said. "I liked a lot of what you said in our office last week, but I didn't agree with you. I know all about that stuff—how women want comfortable, wearable clothes. But I don't think that is what women want. At least that's not what they're looking for when they go shopping." He paused. "You know what they're looking for?" He leaned forward and looked deep into Karen's eyes. Mesmerized by his concentration, she shook her head. "They're looking for adventure," he said. "They're looking for hope. They're looking for escape."

"I didn't know the mall was that exciting," Karen wisecracked, uncomfortable, but Bill didn't laugh.

"You think I'm joking?" he asked. "I'm not talking about your private clients. The Elise Elliots have other outlets. But think about most women's lives. Helping the kids get dressed. Packing school lunches, dropping two off at the school bus and one at day care. Getting in to the bank or the insurance office to spend a day over a word processor or a computer terminal or a file drawer. Trying not to think about how old she's getting, how disappointed she is in her husband, how long it's been since anyone looked at her legs, or looked in her eyes. Avoiding the home truth that no one may ever look into her eyes again. Then stopping at the convenience store, picking up one of the kids, dropping off another, getting dinner on the table while she throws a wash into the machine. Eating in silence with her husband while the kids talk about their day. Maybe a quick vacuum after dinner and an hour of TV once the kids are asleep. Routine sex, or, most likely, no sex at all. And trying not to worry about the Mastercard bill. Trying not to mind her husband, sleeping in the same undershirt for the second night in a row, and snoring. You know why that woman shops? You know what she is looking for?"

Still mesmerized, Karen shook her head.

"Hope. The hope that a pair of blue snakeskin pumps will change her life. The hope that a rayon dress might fix something that's gone wrong for her, or at least make her feel better for a few minutes when she first slips it on. The dream that the name on a label conjures up: that if she buys a Karen Kahn she'll *be* like Karen Kahn, have a life like Karen Kahn's."

Uncomfortable, Karen barked out a laugh. All her visits to Macy's, her time in the malls of America, made her believe that Bill might be at least partially right. But the idea made her uncomfortable. "My life's not that great," she said.

"It is to the readers of *People* magazine. That woman I'm talking about will feel guilty for doing it, but she'll spend thirty-nine dollars for a bottle of *eau de perfum* with the right name on it, and she'll rub that toilette water on as if it were going to do magic."

"But what happens when it doesn't do magic?" Karen asked. "What happens when it doesn't change her life?"

"That's the beauty part: she buys another brand. Better than giving up hope." Bill laughed.

Karen felt a little dizzy. But then she remembered Casey's market research. "Most perfume is bought by men as gifts for women," she said. "Two-thirds of it is sold at Christmas."

"You're a smart girl. But it doesn't change my position at all. That poor woman's husband doesn't know who she is or what she wants. But he can guess who she would like to be. So *he* buys the dream in a bottle. Same difference."

The sommelier returned with the Chardonnay and poured a bit into Bill's glass. He picked it up, sipped, and approved. Karen's own glass was then filled but she stubbornly didn't make a move toward it. Passive resistance. The hell with him and his theories about women and his wine bullying. She was fascinated by him, but repelled. He was smart and powerful and maybe even right, but it didn't make her like him.

Left to themselves again, Bill continued. "You are perfectly positioned to sell that dream, Karen. Your name, your image, has got a huge recognition factor, and the consumer associates it with class, with a toughness that's down to earth yet has urban glamour, with savvy. It's a uniquely nineties positioning. You're growing like crazy, but in a small, undercapitalized company, growth can be dangerous. You know what I mean: more sales means more piece goods, more piece goods means more debt, more debt means more interest, more interest means less profits. Or even *no* profits. You know, Karen, any schmuck can run a small company, but it takes real balls and talent to turn a small company into a big one. There's almost no room for error." Bill Wolper leaned forward to her. "Karen, I think you and I are the same kind of people. We've got balls *and* talent. So let me tell you what I think. I know I'm long overdue in getting our offer to you, but it wasn't out of lack of interest. I hope it wasn't interpreted that way."

Karen shook her head, as if Jeffrey hadn't been getting bleeding ulcers over it. As if they weren't going to run to the bank with the offer and try to raise more cash. Was Bill talking about Jeffrey when he said any schmuck could run a small company?

"I took a long and careful look both at your husband's numbers and at the report Herb put together with Basil's help." Bill paused.

Oh God, she thought, she was getting busted. She should have brought Jeffrey. Was Wolper going to reject her right here, right now? Well, then the whole thing would be over. It would be a relief in a way, but she was glad there would be no witnesses to this. She tried to smile, though her lips were dry and her upper one stuck to her front tooth. Still, she was determined not to drink the Chardonnay. "So?"

"So, I'm prepared to make you an offer, but I want you to understand that I'm making it only to you. Because you're the heart of this deal, Karen. NormCo would like to purchase you for fifty million dollars."

Karen felt the blood leave her face while her stomach seemed to simultaneously both cramp and float into her chest. Had she heard him right? Fifty million! That was more than twice what Jeffrey had first guessed. My God! How much money *was* that? Had she heard right? What was wrong with this picture? She grabbed the stem of the Chardonnay glass and took three big gulps. "I see," was all she managed. She wished she had played cards all those years with Perry, Jeffrey, and their gang, so she could be assured of a poker face right now. Instead she merely nodded.

"I want you to understand that we've been through all your numbers with a fine-toothed comb, and I've discounted the bullshit inventory. In fact, I've discounted mostly everything. Your people overestimated or overvalued it all—except the goodwill. And *that* they undervalued. Big time." He waited, as if he wanted that news to sink in. "Karen, I'm being blunt, but I believe if we're going to get into bed together we have to begin honestly. I need you personally to understand that I'm not paying fifty million dollars for your organization or for your PR or your sales projections or your overvalued, mostly worthless inventory. I'm paying it for *you*."

What the hell did that *mean*? she wondered. Was he making a pass at her? Was that part of the deal? She was speechless. Well, she hadn't worked with stupid but successful models all these years for nothing. She knew how to look good and keep her mouth shut. Karen took another sip of Chardonnay and then put the glass down firmly. Pull yourself together, she then told herself. This is no time for booze. What, exactly, was going on?

"I think we both know where you overvalued your company, but let me tell you specifically where you undervalued it. I don't think that even *you* have any idea of your potential. Potential, Karen. What excites me is potential. And talent. Talent and vision. Well, potential, talent, vision, *and* discipline." Bill laughed. "Quite a list, really. Qualities that are hard to find individually and almost impossible to find in a single package. You have all four, and I can see that. What *I* can do is give you the keys to the kingdom. I am the gatekeeper to what will become your empire. I can envision it, and I know that you can."

Well, she understood that. Thank God, Wolper was strictly business. But then he reached out and put his hand over hers, which was still cold from the chilled Chardonnay. His was warm, radiating heat. "You're someone I can really move fast with. I've been looking for you for some time," Bill told her.

Was there a *double entendre* here, Karen wondered. Now she *had* to say something, but in the back of her head it seemed as if there was a chorus of a hundred thousand little children dancing up and down singing, "Fifty million dollars! Fifty million dollars!" They sounded a lot like the Small World dolls she'd once taken Tiff to see in Disney World. Despite the mental noise, Karen managed to top his hand with her own. "I want to say how complimented I am by your faith in me," she told him. "Thank you for that. I'm really touched." And she was. Maybe this was just Bill Wolper bullshit but it sure seemed to work. He wasn't simply offering to buy her out. He was talking about creating something together. She felt dizzy as a wave of gratitude washed over her. This man was mega-powerful, it seemed as if he really believed in her, and he was willing to put his money where his mouth was.

The waiter returned with their green salads and Wolper freed his hand to pick up a fork. In her whole life, Karen had never felt less like eating. Perhaps this was the secret to successful dieting: just get offered fifty million bucks before each meal. Simple but effective. She looked down at the plate of greens in front of her. It would be impossible to get them into her mouth, chew them, and then swallow. She could as easily throw her legs up onto the table and give birth. God, she was giddy. Was it the wine or the money?

She knew she didn't want to sell her company, but it was surprisingly nice to be asked. And to find she was so highly valued.

Then she realized with a jolt that there was no way Jeffrey would let her turn down this offer. The singing in her head abruptly stopped. She'd been firm that she wasn't selling, knowing that an offer did not necessitate a sale. But she'd *have* to take Jeffrey's advice now. He had made this happen. It was more money then either of them had dreamed of, and he had engineered it.

Still, how on top of things had her husband really been? Bill was saying that Jeffrey had undervalued their worth by more than a hundred percent. Hadn't Wolper seen through Jeffrey's tricks and just told her what a bad team she had? How they didn't see or value the real asset—*her*? And so what good was her husband and Robert-the-lawyer at this game? Jeffrey, in his defense, had never sold a business before, but shouldn't Robert have prepared both of them for this?

Well, there were no free lunches. She knew that. She'd played with fire and now she'd be burned. Fifty million dollars was an offer she couldn't refuse. But what exactly would she have to give up? How much autonomy? What would change with the buyout? "How do you see us working together?" she asked.

"Very closely," Bill told her.

Karen wondered exactly what he meant. "You know, I'm not really very egocentric. Do you believe me?"

"Yes. It's one of your strengths. But you *are* very ambitious," Wolper smiled. "I understand the difference. I know a lot about you."

Just then the waiter brought the lobster halves, complete with beautiful homemade mayonnaise that bore no resemblance to the stuff in the Hellmann's jar. Karen picked up a piece of the lobster, dipped it in the mayo, and swallowed a bite. She didn't taste a thing. "It's an exciting idea," she said. "So let me ask you a question. You see what our profit picture looks like. You must have known we would take a lot less. Why the fifty-million-dollar offer?"

Bill was as direct as she was. "I'm not a charity," he said, "but an acquisition like this is like a marriage. You'll be useless to me if you're unhappy, if you don't or can't deliver, if you feel sulky or cheated or depressed. Cynics will say I'm just buying your name, but if that were true, I would have given you a low-ball offer. I want *you*," he said. "And that means an exclusive contract for twelve years. You work for me or no one." He paused. "By the way, don't think we'll pay a penny more. We won't. Now Herb will negotiate the shit out of your husband and the rest of your team. They'll ask for more. We'll refuse. We'll ask for a lot, and then back off on a few points. But it's all smoke:

it's just your exclusivity that isn't negotiable. I wanted you to know that. The bait is all that cash and stock up front. That, and your belief that I share your vision. Then you have to accept the exclusivity contract. Those are the terms."

Never good at math, it took her a minute to do the arithmetic. Twelve years! She'd be forty-three in a few months. A twelve-year contract would mean she'd be fifty-five by the time it ran out. Fifty-five! She felt the lobster turn uncomfortably about in her contracting stomach. She wished again that she hadn't gulped down that Chardonnay.

A little wave, more like a ripple, of nausea ran through her. Well, hadn't she been afraid of what just one bad collection could do to her business? Wouldn't this save her, make her financially secure forever? But what would it be like, having other people do work with her name on it? Or not being allowed to use her name on her own work? And God, the burden of supervising and controlling it all! If she was already overworked, what would this do to her? Bill looked over at her. "Karen, I'm sure you know about the fiascoes in this business. I don't want you warring with me the way Chanel did with the Wertheimers."

Karen smiled in spite of herself. Did Bill know how she worshiped Chanel? Did *he* have a Centrillo who investigated that stuff? Or was this synchronicity? In 1924 Chanel had been her own worst enemy. She'd signed away all her rights to her perfume for only ten percent of the partnership. For fifty years, despite constant suits and legal maneuvers, the Wertheimers had kept ninety percent. After Chanel died, they got it all. The Wertheimers were still one of the most powerful groups in fashion.

"So, you're giving me more than ten percent?" Karen asked.

"Yes, but I'm asking a lot. I want you to think it over and tell me that, in all good conscience, you're willing and able to deliver. That you're stable, that you're energized, that you're ready to give more and do more than you have before. I don't want to buy a neurotic or a bum out. That's my condition."

Karen's smile disappeared. How could she work harder than she already was? God, she already felt tired! Somehow, she'd begun exploring this deal thinking that selling the business might give her *more* free time. Still, the little voices kept singing: "Fifty million dollars!" She shook her head. "I'm going to have to think about all this," she said.

"I expect so. Listen, you don't even have to tell the rest of your team about it, yet. No point in getting them excited if you're going to back off. I'll hold this completely between us until I hear from you. And if you say 'no,' I'll just never make the offer."

Karen smiled her gratitude. That was thoughtful of him. It gave her an out and just might save her marriage. He was a smart, shrewd man. "One more thing, Bill. If I do this deal I need your guarantee that you won't lay off any of my staff. I'm going to distribute some shares of the company among them, but I don't want that to wind up being severance pay."

"Hey, we're going to have to hire help, not fire it," Bill said. "But I'm not sure I like this stock distribution. I want you to get the lion's share."

'Some of them have been with me since the beginning. If I do this deal, that's the way it's got to be," Karen said.

Bill thought it over. "Okay," he shrugged. "But I doubt they'll appreciate it."

Karen looked at him with gratitude. Was she losing it, or was he really an understanding person? Whatever he was, he certainly wasn't what she had expected. What would she do? Would she tell the gang about the offer or would she wait until she had first decided for herself? Bill had given her the choice. She looked across the table at his ruddy, attractive face. "Thank you," she said, and she meant it sincerely.

"Consider it my gift to you," he smiled.

Bill had insisted that she take his limo back after he had exited at Fiftieth and Park. But she had an appointment to meet Mr. Centrillo at the Soup Burger on Lexington and Eightieth Street and she certainly didn't want the driver to report *that* back to Bill Wolper. It seemed he knew enough about her without any extra help. So she had the driver bring her to the New York Society Library on Seventy-Ninth Street and, once she was sure he was gone, she walked over to Lex and the Soup Burger. With every step the little chorus kept time, singing the fifty-million-dollar song. She didn't know exactly how she felt—after all, she had no experience with this. Of course, she and Jeffrey would only get a portion of the money. With lawyer's fees, bonuses, and stock she would distribute, along with the shares already owned by her family and Jeffrey's, it would be a lot less. And there would be taxes to be paid. Still, it would be a lot of money. More than she knew what to do with. It wasn't like she wanted another house or a bigger car. Aside from a baby there wasn't anything she could think of that she really wanted. She longed to ask someone's advice but she could predict what each of her friends and family would tell her: Belle would tell her she'd be crazy not to take it, with an implication that they were crazy to offer it; Defina would tell her to follow her instincts; Mercedes would get excited but be shifty-eyed, pretending not to push for the sale while she busily calculated her potential share; Casey would get even more nervous; and Carl would tell her she was worth more. It wasn't them that she worried about, though. It was Jeffrey.

At the Soup Burger she smiled with relief to see Mr. Centrillo's broad face.

He was wearing a summer-weight hat, a cross between a Fedora and a Panama. He patted the empty place next to him. The restaurant was tiny—just a griddle, a counter, and a dozen stools running around the walls. She sat down gratefully. She felt dizzy, as if she had already spun around and around on the swivel seat of the red-leatherette-and-chrome stool.

"So, Mrs. Cohen, what's new?"

Well, I've just been offered a large fortune, she thought. But to get it I have to give up my freedom. And maybe sleep with the boss. Somehow, she didn't think it was the kind of thing to say to Mr. Centrillo. He seemed even more anchored to the earth than he had in his little Brooklyn office. She tried to focus. "Uhm, actually I'm a little anxious. Trouble with work. But I'm very concerned about you. What have you got to report?" She was on complete overload. What would she do right now if he told her he had met her real mother?

And then she realized that that was the person she wanted to tell her news to: her real mother. Not Belle, not even Carl, and certainly not Jeffrey. She wanted to brag about how she was worth fifty million dollars to the woman who had discarded her.

But Centrillo only shook his head. "I'm so sorry. My report is only that I've got nothing to report. Without any more data, it's going to take a while. I haven't run through every alternative yet, but so far nothing but brick walls. I'm sorry," he repeated.

Well, what had she expected? Karen asked herself. She had always been a fanciful child. She was being fanciful now. There was no mother at the end of the rainbow. She'd been as silly and as hopeful and as vulnerable as the little bird in the *Are You My Mother?* book that she used to read to Stephie. Why didn't she just walk out onto Lexington Avenue and ask lampposts and pigeons if they had conceived her?

"Do you have anything else that you could give me?" Centrillo asked. And then she remembered the pictures. Karen nodded mutely and searched through her bag for the two photos she had found at last, left in the pocket of the jacket she'd worn to Elise Elliot's wedding. "Here," she said, and passed them across to him. "I don't know where they were taken, or when, but that is me."

"Cute," he said. "Very cute." He sounded as if he really meant it. He turned them over but there was no identifying mark or scar. "Listen," he said, "have you had a chance to bring this up to your father?" Mutely, she shook her head. "Well, consider it. Even a few facts would help. Location and date would be a good start. A name would be even better." Centrillo looked at her kindly. "I know it's hard, but I think it's your only chance."

Karen sighed. She could hardly imagine bringing it up to Arnold. How could she be so brave in some things and so afraid to ask a simple question? Maybe that was the inheritance of every adopted child—an insecurity so deep that they couldn't bear to question the parents who had taken them in. But maybe she would have to. Would he tell her? And could she ask him to keep it from Belle? How much would it bother him?

"Mrs. Cohen, I don't think I can do any more until you get some more info."

"I'll talk to him," she promised.

She gave Centrillo her private office line; only she answered it. She'd have to remember not to announce herself with her name. The two of them left the tiny restaurant. The man walked off down Lexington Avenue to the IRT subway and Karen stood there and watched him go. Her chest felt tight. The voices had stopped singing in her head and she realized she'd never been so tired in her whole life. She couldn't tell Jeffrey about any of this, and she still had the unfinished, mediocre Paris collection waiting for her back at the office. She felt as if she might fly apart, right there on the corner.

If Bill Wolper knew how she really felt, he wouldn't have offered her a dime.

16

WHAT'S MY LINE?

Karen went home early, slept late, took the next morning off, and went to the Metropolitan Museum of Art. She avoided the Costume Institute, and instead spent an hour in the Annenberg Galleries, soaking up the colors of Manet, Fantin-Latour, and some of her other favorite painters.

It was funny, but she didn't really care for the most popular painters of that period: Monet was brilliant, but somehow too easy, and Renoir actually upset her—all that flesh that looked as soft as a rotten peach! Karen averted her eyes, and drank up only what pleased her: a still life of pansies in a clay pot and a portrait of a woman in a dark dress. On her way out, she passed a strange little painting. It was mostly in grays and black, a study of a boat. It looked like a Courbet. She stared at it. It reminded her of something—something she had seen in a movie or a dream. But she couldn't capture the memory, though it remained at the edge of her consciousness.

She left the museum by eleven and walked across Fifth Avenue in the drizzle. She headed east on Eightieth Street, past townhouses, Park Avenue, and the Junior League, the club where many of her wealthy women clients still congregated. Looking down, Karen noticed the sidewalk cement had taken perfect imprints of the ginko leaves that must have fallen some earlier autumn when the concrete had been poured. Three perfect little fans were left as impressions in the gray sidewalk, though the leaves themselves were long gone. They were New York fossils, and more graceful and delicate than any anti-deluvian crustacean that Karen had seen in a museum. They were perfect and beautiful, the ghost of leaves that had been. She wondered if any of the women from the League ever noticed them.

And what, she thought, will *I* leave behind? A big fortune that my nieces and their children could spend? Some sketches that Pratt might put in their archives? A mention in the fashion history books? Karen realized that she couldn't remember the last time she felt good. She felt tired, drained, and something else. Sad, maybe. She was old enough and, she supposed, wise enough to understand that pleasure in life, real joy, usually came at unexpected times: for a moment as the sunlight glanced off the Hudson when she strolled by the Seventy-Ninth Street boat basin; or, now and then, when Jeffrey had looked at her, or when she had caught an unexpected sight of him in a crowd, or stretched across the sofa asleep.

Joy couldn't be cornered but only courted—quiet moments, usually alone, were when she seemed to experience it. One wet afternoon after a rain when she saw real ginko leaves, brightest yellow, on the dull sidewalk, making perfect oriental patterns. And once when the evening light, slanting into the apartment windows, had made perfect golden shafts across the whole room. They'd reflected off the waxed floor onto the French tulips that drooped in a vase on the table. It had sent a deep thrill down her spine; it was a feeling she lived for. But how long had it been gone?

The offer from NormCo, which could make her richer than she had ever imagined, certainly wasn't bringing her any joy. Instead, since her meeting twenty-four hours before, she felt more conflicted and confused then ever. She'd been glad that Jeffrey had worked late and come in after she'd gone to bed. He'd slept in the guest room and left before she got up.

She hadn't told him anything about her meeting with Bill Wolper. She wanted to be sure of how she felt first. What would the money buy her? She didn't want another house and she hated driving so it wasn't a car she wanted. Money, in large amounts, was good to buy freedom with, but she was selling her freedom. Twelve years of it. It wasn't as if the NormCo offer would make her life any easier. If anything, it already had made her life more complex. Could she accept the offer and have time for a child? Even if Jeffrey relented and allowed adoption. And if she was working even harder, how could she make time for a child?

She was uncomfortable living with a secret, and, if and when she let the secret break, she would have to also cope with the expectations, fears, and hopes of everybody else: Casey, who was against the deal; Mrs. Cruz and most of the other production staff, who were afraid of it; Mercedes, who was so hungry for her share of the profits that she could hardly contain herself; and Jeffrey, who couldn't contain himself. Karen felt the pressure from every direction and at this point it felt that the deal might as well be just another distraction that was stopping her from being able to put the Paris collection together.

Only Defina, good old Defina, stayed unflappable and neutral about the deal. So, when Karen finally got to the office, she had had to tell her about her lunch with Bill and the offer. Defina listened to it all in silence.

"Fifty million, huh? Well, the guy knows how to bait a hook," Defina admitted.

"But what should I do?" Karen asked. "I don't know what to do."

"You'll know what to do," Defina told her. "Just don't make a move until you know what *you* want."

Just what Karen had predicted she'd say.

Karen worked hard all that day to make up for her absence. Now it was late—past ten o'clock. Defina was still there, buzzing around the office, singing some lame old Michael Jackson song. Karen by now had more than fifty new sketches arrayed before her, taped to the wall.

"Would you stop with that song?" she called out, irritated. Defina had the worst singing voice Karen had ever heard.

"Is it my voice? Or is it Memorex?"

"It's that stupid song." Karen stood up and stretched, then rubbed her eyes. God, she was tired! She walked to the window and looked out at the ribbon of lights that the cars and trucks made as they roared up Seventh Avenue. The Jackson song was bad enough. Thank God the triple-paned windows stopped traffic noise! Karen needed some silence.

Defina, for once, didn't seem to notice her mood. She wanted to talk, and since Dee had listened to Karen's whole rant about the Wolper offer, Karen couldn't quite manage to tell the woman to shut up.

"So, you think using Stephie as a fit model is working out?"

"Why? Is she giving you trouble?"

"No. She's a good girl." Dee shook her head. "I should have known better than to ask you. You don't notice anything you don't want to notice. I s'pose you haven't noticed how much weight your niece has lost."

"Stephie?"

"Well, I sure don't mean Tiff."

Karen thought about it. Stephanie's face did seem more drawn lately, but had she lost a lot of weight? She didn't have a lot to lose and she seemed in good spirits, if a little overwhelmed. "I think she's fine," Karen said, and turned back to her work.

"Who are you thinking of for Paris?"

Without further explaining, Karen knew what Defina meant. They had always talked in shorthand, knew what one another was thinking. But something a lot more important than who would model in Paris was troubling Karen. She was scared. It wasn't *who* would be modeling, but *what* they would be modeling. And who would come to see her collection, and what would they say?

"I don't know. How about Tangela?" Karen went back to the sketches on the wall and pulled two down, crushing them and discarding them.

"You don't mean it?"

"Sure I do. Maybe it would make her feel better about herself."

"Well, don't do it for me. It probably wouldn't help. Anyway she ain't ready for Europe."

It was getting late to book girls for Paris. All of the best ones, the most expensive ones, were booked well in advance. But Karen didn't have a super-model budget anyway. They would have to get younger girls, ones who would be thrilled just to walk down a Paris catwalk. Of course, using them was risky. They got stage fright, couldn't put the clothes across. Luckily, Karen had a secret weapon—Defina. She could teach anyone how to take a runway, with the possible exception of Tangela, who wouldn't learn anything from her mother. Karen turned to Dee. "Well, why don't you round up the usual gang of suspects?" she asked. Karen turned her back on the wall, rubbing her eyes again. The collection wasn't working. She felt another lurch of fear. It just wasn't coming together.

"How about Melody Craig?" Defina asked idly.

"Yeah. Okay. But she's so white bread. Let's keep it mostly young, American ethnics. How about Maria Lopez?"

"For heaven's sake, don't bring Maria. She's a Hispaniel."

"Stop it, Defina! No ethnic slurs."

"Hey, she's a Latino *bitch*. It ain't her race, it's her attitude I object to. And I swear she's into drugs. All South Americans are."

"Yeah, and all blacks got rhythm. Except maybe you. C'mon, Dee! Enough with the stereotypes."

"Girlfriend, some stereotypes are *true*. And I do got rhythm. I just can't sing." In spite, Defina began humming the Michael Jackson song again.

Karen thought for a moment. Well, if she couldn't get the clothes right, at least maybe she could get the models right. They could do a lot for a show. "I'm bringing Maria. *And* Tangela. And Armie. And Lucinda. I want a real American look, and they all know how to wear my clothes."

"Armie is too expensive now; and anyway she's probably booked. Don't look at me like that! You the one who made her popular. And Lucinda can't do runway. She's just a fit model. She can't walk."

"Then show her how."

"It ain't that easy. You know that."

"Oh, for God's sake, Defina. It isn't rocket science. It's only modeling."

"*You* try hauling *your* ass down a runway in front of a thousand pair of critical eyes. See how easy it is."

"I know it takes a special talent. But I think Lucinda has it. And I like her look. That's why I hired her."

Defina shook her head. "Any more fires you want to start tonight?" she asked. She waltzed out of the room, once again singing the annoying Michael Jackson tune.

For over a dozen years now, Defina had called Karen a fire starter. "You just set 'em and expect all of us—me, Jeffrey, Casey, Mercedes, all of us—to be your fire department," Defina grumbled. And Karen had to admit that Defina was right—and that she, Karen, was happy with the arrangement. A good, creative idea was like a spark, and it did start a fire. Whether it was a new kind of button she had to find or quick money from a factor needed to buy the extra luxe fabric she'd fallen in love with, Karen felt it was her *job* to coax and nurse and cajole and snatch her ideas out of the ether or wherever they came from. And it was her staff's job to make those ideas a reality. It took teamwork, and she, Karen, had put together a good—no, a great—team of firefighters. Too bad she was going to fail them now. Too bad she was going to put together a mediocre show, lose her rep *and* her sales figures. What did Chanel use to say? Something like, "You can't abandon a collection unless it abandons you." Well, Karen felt pretty abandoned. She sighed. Maybe she *should* sell out to NormCo before it was too late. The dispiriting sketches on the wall seemed to push her toward a sale, now, before she was crucified in Paris. She just couldn't concentrate. She closed her eyes, and the painting she had seen at the Metropolitan came back to her.

For some reason, Carl's words over dinner also came back to her then, too. What had he said exactly? That she was the talented one? Well, that wasn't true, but he had said something else: that she never thought in black and white. Black and white. That was the tune Defina was singing.

Karen stared at the sketches. The silhouettes were good. So were the fabric swatches. The collection was balanced. But it wasn't *new*.

She put down her pencil. Now Defina was humming the morphing part of the music from Michael Jackson's video. "Don't matter if you're black or white," she warbled. The images of the morphed heads came back to Karen. "Don't matter if you're black or white." Karen thought of the Courbet at the Met again. She knew now what it had brought up. It reminded her of her black and white dream. The dream had been so intense, both so visual and so deeply felt that if she closed her eyes she could almost reexperience it now. How could she have forgotten it?

Well, there was no time for dreaming now. She had to concentrate. Karen felt the hair on the back of her neck rise. She was getting an idea. A vision. Yes. *Yes!* She turned to Defina, who'd just come back into the room.

"Okay. Here's the scoop. We do two shows at the same time."

"What?"

"We do *two* Paris shows," Karen said excitedly. "Two. Simultaneously."

"Karen, honey. You've lost it. It's hard enough with all the competition to get them to come to *one* show."

"Exactly. That's why we do two at once. They can't possibly come to both. See? *We* know that. It gives us the upper hand. And one show is all black— the entire line in black."

"You *never* do black."

"I do now. I do *all* black at one show and the whole line in white at the other. Exactly the same clothes. In the same order. But one collection in black, the other white."

Defina blinked. "A bunch of nuns? Penguin shit?" she asked. "Girlfriend, you *are* changing your habits—you should pardon the pun."

Karen began to laugh. Dee would catch on. Karen wouldn't just be proving to Carl that she could think in black and white. This was more than a private joke. The fashion press, the important buyers, and key clients rush all over Paris during the week of the shows in what *Elle* magazine called "a single, monolithic unit." Every designer sweats out where to show his line, what time, who'll show before him, who after.

Now, she'd change all that. What if she threw a party and nobody came? No good. She'd sweated over it. Here in the U.S. she was a big deal, but in Paris, who'd care? Who'd come to see her? So, what if she threw *two* parties so nobody could come to both of them! Great!

Of course, it would cause a sensation. It had never been done. And she had never done black. It was *the* color, the darling of New York fashion mavins—everyone from Tina Brown to Grace Mirabella wore little black outfits all the time. But Karen, partly in rebellion, had never used it. Clients begged for it. The retailers screamed for it. But she'd resisted. It was as if, all along, she were saving it for now. Karen felt her heart beating, felt her face flush.

"This is a hell of a fire you're starting," Defina said, but she was beginning to grin. "Booking another location, more models, more invitations, and that's not to mention getting the clothes, the line ready . . . "

"Black-on-white invitations to one show, white-on-black to the other," Karen told her. "We do one show on the left bank, the other on the right. We play Michael Jackson. *Ebony and Ivory.* And the one you're humming. And we don't tell *anyone* in advance. We let them figure it out." Karen laughed. "We have *two* wedding dresses for the end." Paris shows traditionally ended with wedding dresses. "At the white show we have a white wedding gown and at the black show we have a black one."

Defina looked at Karen. "I like it," she said slowly. "It's got wit. And it's good marketing. The buyers *love* black. I just wish you had thought of it about a month and a half ago."

"Yeah, and I wish they'd stop fighting in Serbia. You can't always get what you want, Dee." She took a couple of Mick Jagger steps across the office. "You can't always get what you want," she sang.

"You can't always get what you want," Defina sang back. "But if you try sometime, you just might find, you get what you *need*. Uh-huh!" The two of them danced around the room singing the boop-da-boop boop-da-boop background vocals to the Stones song.

"I knew you were one smart white girl," Defina said approvingly.

"Hey! Stick with me and you'll be farting through silk," Karen promised.

Defina laughed. "I already am," she admitted.

"Eeuw! Dee! Gross!"

And right then, there in her messy office late in the evening, Karen felt such joy that for a moment she was struck almost breathless. She saw everything, each sketch, every swatch of fabric, the sheen on Defina's cheek, the ring of coffee on her Formica worktable, all of it with such a clarity and affection that it almost took her breath away. Even as Karen experienced it, she knew it couldn't last and the knowledge had such a bittersweet tinge that she felt as if her heart might break.

"This will knock 'em dead in Paree," Defina promised.

"Who needs NormCo?" Karen cried.

Defina looked at Karen, her face intense. "Well, who *does* need NormCo?" she asked seriously. Before Karen could answer, the phone rang. She turned and went to her desk, lifting the handset.

"Look out the window," the man's voice at the other end of the line told her. For a spooky moment Karen thought it might be Centrillo, and that maybe he stood outside, nine floors below, with her real mother handcuffed to his thick wrist. But it wasn't Centrillo's warm, comforting voice. "Can you see me?" the voice said, and she realized it was Perry Silverman's.

"Where are you, Perry?"

"Outside. On the corner. In the phone booth on the east side of Thirty-Seventh Street." Karen looked out the window. "See me?" Perry asked. "I'm waving."

She could see him, or someone, waving like a signalman, or more like

Gilligan, stranded on his island, waving for rescue. Was Perry drunk? Was the pope Polish? "I see you, Perry."

"So, will you sleep with me?"

"I think you missed a couple of steps."

"Oh, yeah. How about a drink first?"

"I think you already had one. Right?"

"You are one smart Jewish girl."

Hadn't Defina just said something like that? Karen looked over at Dee and shrugged. Defina pointed to herself and gave Karen the umpire's thumb. She was outta there. Karen nodded. It was time for her to go home, too. "What do you want, Perry?"

"Beam me up, Scotty."

"How about if I come down and take you home?"

"I haven't changed the sheets."

"You're skipping steps again, Perry." Karen could hear the automated operator's voice cut in to tell him his time was up. It sounded like the robot knew what she was talking about: Perry must be pretty close to the edge. "I'll be right down," Karen yelled over the operator's voice, hoped he heard her, and hung up the phone. She threw on her raincoat. "Would you lock up for me, Defina?" she called.

Perry was still standing in the phone booth when Karen got there. He was wearing what had once been an off-white Aquascutum. Now it was very, very off-white. Under it he had on paint-stained Levi's and a blue workshirt.

"Karen!" he cried out as he saw her, as if they were meeting here completely by chance. How drunk was he? Did he remember he had just called her or was he in a permanent blackout?

Perry walked out of the phone booth toward her. He didn't stagger, but there was a glazed, distant look to his eyes. He walked up to her, put an arm around her shoulder, his mouth against her ear. He was just her height, much shorter than Jeffrey. "Let's go make a baby," Perry whispered.

"Boy, have you got the wrong girl," Karen told him, and stuck her arm out, signaling to a taxi that was coming across the Thirty-Seventh Street intersection. "Get in the cab, Perry."

"Sure," he said cheerfully. "Where we going?"

"Spring Street and West Broadway," she told the driver.

"Great! I live right near there!"

"Really?" she said dryly. "What a coincidence."

He lost ground in the cab. His head lolled, and he might have fallen asleep for a minute. She had to help him out of the cab, and even with her help, he lurched and almost lost his footing. Only after he stumbled and regained his balance did he freeze, the way she and her friends used to, back when they played "statues" in Prospect Park. For a moment Karen thought he was going to be sick, but he just stood there, seemingly frozen. She had to look closely to see that his shoulders were shaking. Is he going to lose his cookies, she wondered, but then realized he was crying. She moved to his side and he lifted his face to her, the wetness of his tears catching the light from the bar at the corner. He looked over toward the blinking lights of the bar. "You know, I'm working as a bartender part-time again. Pretty pathetic, huh? I use to do it to make a few bucks when I was in college. Then, when I was painting full-time it was a way to break the loneliness, the isolation. But now it's just pitiful. I'm forty-six years old." He stared off into the darkness, then shrugged. "Well, I can always write my memoirs. I can call them *My Life Behind Bars*." He tried to laugh but it became a strangled noise.

"I can't paint anymore. I don't want to go on living without Lottie. She took all the light with her when she went."

Karen put her arm around him. He hugged her tight. "It's so dark. It's so dark," he whispered. She had nothing to say, no comfort to help with this, the greatest pain. So she just held him, the two of them standing in the gutter outside the Spring Street Bar.

"I didn't know I could love anyone so much," he wept. "Without my child alive, I don't see much of a point to living, either."

Right there, in the SoHo street, two thoughts came to Karen like blows. Would Belle have mourned this way for her if she had died? And how could she herself go on, without someone she loved as much as Perry loved Lottie?

For a week Karen and Jeffrey had been playing the who-can-come-home-last game. So when she got back to the apartment, totally exhausted, she was surprised to see him sprawled out on the living room sofa. From the foyer she couldn't see any more of him but feet and legs. She slipped off her shoes so that if he were sleeping she wouldn't disturb him. Also, she remembered to hang up her coat.

But he was awake. He had a pile of papers lying on his stomach and a glass with some clear liquid beside him on the floor.

"You're home early," she said.

"And you're home late."

"Was the game canceled?" He had been planning to take in a Knicks game, or at least that's the message he had given Janet.

"No, but Perry and Jordan didn't show, and the Knicks were so far behind that it was pointless. Sam and I called it quits early." He took a sip from his wine glass.

"Listen, Karen, I'm sorry if I acted like an asshole over the Elle Halle thing . . . "

Thank God, he was going to apologize! That was all she needed from him to drop her wall.

"Anyway, I may not have been such a good partner. I'm really down about NormCo. We still haven't gotten the offer, and maybe we'll never get it. I think they may have been turned off by the inventory valuation. It's my fault."

Karen looked away, guiltily. Here Jeffrey was afraid they wouldn't get an offer at all, while she knew they'd get an enormous one and hadn't told him. God, who should be apologizing to who? She walked toward him, but he backed away from her. She reached for his hand. "Jeffrey, please. Listen to me. I never meant to be a big business. I just wanted to do what I do. We're comfortable right now. We aren't poor. Business is better than ever. Don't worry so much. We'll service our debts. And I've just come up with a *great* collection for Paris. We've got nice places to live and money in the bank. Since we don't have any children what do we need all this money for, anyway?"

"Is that what this is about?" he asked, pulling his hand away. "Children? Goddamnit, Karen, how can you keep harping on that, even at a time like this? Don't you have any sense of proportion? This is a once-in-a-lifetime opportunity we're losing. This is important."

She thought of Perry, standing in the rain. "Proportion? It's not me who lacks a sense of proportion, Jeffrey! Having a *child* is a once-in-a-lifetime."

"So is selling a business."

"Well, nobody I ever heard of lay on their deathbed and said their biggest regret was not spending more time on business. Don't tell me *I've* got things out of proportion!" She wondered if she should bring up how wrong his own sense of the value of the business had been. Out of anger, she'd like to shock him, but she decided not to push that button. All at once, her anger left her, and she merely felt sorry for both of them. Jeffrey had never seemed so wrong, or so vulnerable. "Anyway, don't dare tell me this is an inappropriate time. We're talking about my future."

"Your future, your name. What about *my* future? It's my name, too. Just for once I'd like you to think about that." He spun around and by accident or on purpose let go of the wine glass, which flew across the room until it hit the dining table, where it smashed. The shards kept on moving all across the table's shiny surface until they flew off the end and onto the back of a white chair and across part of the white wall. The noise either didn't surprise or didn't stop Jeffrey, who strode over to one of the windows and threw it open. He stood there with his back to Karen while, in the silence, she could hear the spilled wine drip off the table. She didn't move. At that moment she pitied Jeffrey, and she despised him.

She could see Jeffrey taking a deep breath. It wasn't like him to try and control his temper, but he was definitely making the effort. He turned to her. "I wanted this deal, Karen."

"And I wanted a baby," she said. "But we can't always get what we want." Then she turned and left him standing there.

When she awoke the next morning, Jeffrey was placing a bed tray onto the tumbled coverlet. He had arranged a slice of melon, a croissant, a curl of butter, and some jelly along with the *Times*, *"W"*, and *Women's Wear Daily*. There was also a single white rose in a bud vase. Karen struggled up against the pillows.

"Who do I have to blow to get this kind of service?" she asked.

"Only me," he replied, and set the tray across her lap. He sat down at the foot of the bed and put his hand on her ankle. "I'm sorry about last night," he said. "I'm sorry about everything." Karen reached out for the coffee, picked up the cup, and nodded noncommittally. It wasn't going to be that easy.

Jeffrey was so good-looking, she always found it hard to resist him. There was no doubt he was spoiled—that he'd always been catered to by women from Sylvia on—but more than most men, he did make an effort to be adult. This breakfast was his apology. But did he think that he could buy what he wanted with a slice of cantaloupe? He sat now, his thick salt-and-pepper hair neatly brushed, the crisp white linen of his shirt almost luminous in the diffused morning light. His cheeks were freshly shaved. There was still a tiny bit of shaving cream left in one of his ears. On him it looked good.

She smiled at him. She couldn't help it. After all, he tried. In all the time they'd been married, whenever they'd had a big fight, he'd cool off and think it out. And then, later, he'd been willing to compromise. Which was more than most men were willing to do. Jeffrey always came back, and that, more than anything else, made her believe he loved her. She never considered that he might need her.

"Listen, I have an idea. A Real Deal," Jeffrey said now.

Karen put down the coffee cup she was sipping from. "A Real Deal?" she repeated. "Real Deals" were important. She looked over at him. "I'll take curtain Number Two, Monty," she joked. Then she got serious. "What do you have in mind?" she asked.

"I think I've come up with a way for both of us to compromise and get what we really want," he said. "How about this? When we get the official offer, if we get the offer, you agree to sell to NormCo and I agree to help you adopt a baby."

"A baby?" she asked. "We could adopt a baby?" He nodded. "But do you really want one?" she asked.

He tightened his grip around her ankle. "Look, Karen, I'm doing the best that I can. I know I've been making you miserable, but I didn't want to adopt, and I can't pretend to feel differently than I do. This sale is something that I really want and a baby is something *you* really want for the same reason. I can understand your feeling, even if I don't share it with the same enthusiasm. And you, I hope, can understand how I feel. I want you to be happy and I hope you want the same for me. So, what do you think? A Real Deal?"

She stared at him. Was he serious? And was it all right if he was? She felt her heart lurch in her chest. Was Defina wrong? Could she, Karen, have it all? "I don't know, Jeffrey. I don't know if I should have to bargain for this. I mean, you shouldn't be a grudging parent."

"Yeah, and you shouldn't begrudge selling KKInc, but if you *do* sell you'll have more time for a baby and so will I. Painting and a baby. Not bad for a nineties kind of guy, which we know I am. Somehow, it's the only way I can see it happening."

"You really mean it?" she asked. She looked at the wrinkled white bed-clothes. For the first time in weeks, her heart lifted, as if some burden she'd carried on her chest was gone. "I mean, we could have him crawling around right on this duvet."

"Yeah, and probably peeing on it. How do you get baby piss out of Porthault sheets?"

Karen laughed. "I don't know. I'll have to ask Ernesta." Then she stopped smiling. "What if we can't get a baby?"

"What if we don't get the deal? We do the best we can. We operate in good faith."

Karen blinked. If she made this deal, she'd have to call Bill Wolper right away and tell him to give them the offer. And when Jeffrey realized the actual offer price he'd be wild to do the deal. There'd be no way to stop him. Karen bit her lip. She sighed. Maybe she should level with Jeffrey now, tell him about her lunch with Bill. But it seemed that if she did that she'd not only look like a liar, she'd make Jeffrey look like a fool.

No, she'd wait. She'd contact a lawyer tomorrow and get the adoption moving. Then she'd give the word to Wolper. They could both have what they wanted.

Jeffrey got up and took her hand, then stooped to kiss her. "If it's what you really want, Karen," he said, "then I want it for you. I know I've been a prick lately, but I do want you to be happy." He bent to kiss her. Thrilled, she kissed him back. His hands moved to her shoulders and then lower. She pulled her lips away from his.

"Wait a minute," she said, and moved the breakfast tray onto the floor.

"Good idea," he agreed, and joined her in bed.

17

DOLLARS AND SCENTS

They arrived at the Norris Cleveland party fashionably late. Since they'd made the Real Deal, Karen's spirits had lifted. She was working with new energy, she felt good again, and waking up was no longer a burden. Jeffrey seemed happier, too. "Hail, hail, the gang's all here," Jeffrey sang as he and Karen sailed up the gang plank of the four-masted schooner that had been chartered for the "Norris!" perfume introduction. Leave it to Norris to drag everyone down to the seaport. Back in 1978, when Karen had just started working for Liz, Yves Saint Laurent had catered the Opium party on a boat as well. But his was a real Chinese junk. This one was only harbor junk. Perhaps Norris was just counting on the subliminal suggestion.

The Opium party had been the first fashion event Karen had ever been to and it had launched a perfume juggernaut. Opium was *still* selling—rare in the fickle world of fragrance—and it seemed to Karen that since 1978 the same people were showing up at all the perfume parties. Already Karen could see Robert Isabell, the New York *capo di tutti capi* of party planning, giving directions to staff. Last year Isabell had done Armani's fabulous Gio launch in the basement of a high rise.

Tonight there were no Chinese acrobats, as there had been at the Opium party. And there were no Moroccan tents and floor cushions as there had been for Armani. Instead, there were only wall-to-wall celebrities and photographers. Parties had gotten more and more like that—it seemed to Karen that the party was less important than the press it got. It was as if the middleman had been cut out: you could come, be seen, and be photographed, all without the bother of actually having a good time. Karen grinned to herself. It was *so* Norris Cleveland.

But everyone was there. Cher, who had been at both the Opium and the Gio party and had had a perfume of her own in between, had shown up. So had her old pal David Geffen, whose interest in fashion had become financial since he had bailed out his buddy Calvin Klein when Cal had run into financial trouble and almost gone under. But then, what was fifty million to David Geffen?

Amy Fine Collins, who wrote for *Vanity Fair and Harper's Bazaar,* glided by. She was not just intellectual, but the only fashion journalist who dressed with great style, eschewing the safe little black dress. Carrie Donovan, lately of the *Times*, and Suzy Mehle, the *grande dame* of the *Herald Tribune*, were also here. These guys were important. How does Norris get this kind of turnout, Karen wondered.

Jeffrey went off to get her a drink, and she stood alone for a moment before she felt the tap on her back. She turned and looked down into the beady but friendly brown eyes of Bobby Pillar. "I'd ask what a classy girl like you was doing in a place like this, but it might reflect badly on my own presence," Bobby said and laughed. Then he hugged her as if they had seen each other nightly since their chance meeting at Elle's studio. "You were wonderful on Elle's show," he said. "Didn't I tell you? You have an enormous warmth and naturalness. You know, that's a gift. People believe what you tell them." Bobby seemed full of enthusiasm. It shone off him. Even his bald head gleamed.

"Thanks, Bobby. I guess the show came off okay."

"So *did* you wet your pants? I looked, but I couldn't notice."

Karen had to laugh. He was outrageous, but down to earth. She actually liked him. "So, will you be selling Norris's perfume on TV?" she asked.

"That rat piss? She tried to hook me, but I didn't take the bait. Have you smelled it? Give me a break! The FCC would clap me in irons faster than the Cossacks joined pogroms. As if the authorities need an excuse to put a short Jew in jail." He laughed, and there was something so honest about him, so outrageously impolite but real that Karen had to join in. Maybe money did buy freedom, but Bobby had been this outspoken *before* he made his pile.

"So, *mammela,* are you going to talk to Uncle Bobby about doing a line for us on television?"

"I don't think so, Bobby. I'm just starting to think of mass market." Karen paused.

"Well, I hear you are talking to a little NormCo birdie. A vulture. Not such a great idea."

Karen stopped smiling. Before she could answer, before she could ask him how he had heard that rumor, Jeffrey returned. He and Bobby said hello and their conversation seemed to stop. It was clear they didn't like each other. She knew Jeffrey thought Bobby was vulgar. But that, of course, was part of Bobby's charm.

Bobby just smiled and lifted his hand in an exaggerated wave. "Call me some time, *mammela*," he said, and disappeared into the crowd, his short, broad body obscured by a group of tall, willowy models.

There was, of course, a full complement of models and ex-models. Lauren Hutton, as usual, was wearing Armani. The younger crowd included Linda Evangelista, Carla Bruni, Maria Lopez, Kristen McMenamy, and even Kate Moss. All of them were smoking. Karen wondered if Norris had to pay them to get them to attend. Karen also wondered which, if any of them, she could get to do her Paris show. Maria Lopez still looked good to her, despite what Defina said. Maria was less expensive than the others, and with Tangela and some decent blondes and brunettes they would have a real nice mix. Karen was really straining her budget with the two shows. Jeffrey was squealing, but she'd insisted and he had acquiesced—after all, they'd soon be rolling in the bucks. Still and all, they couldn't afford the supermodels. She had heard that Versace had spent a hundred thousand dollars to get four of them to do his show last year. A hundred thousand dollars just for models! That was half of Karen's whole Paris budget! So getting these girls to show up for a party was a major coup.

The habit that the supermodels had of hanging out together somehow added to their glamour although, having worked with them, Karen knew that there wasn't much glamour on the inside. That was really the problem with fashion. It was commerce. Fashion wasn't glamorous on the inside: it was all about production and a lot of hard work, kind of like a sausage factory. But it had to *look* glamorous, even if the designers didn't. If Gianfranco Ferrè was overweight, if Mary MacFadden was bizarrely pale, if Donna Karan was chunky, and Karl Lagerfeld was balding, they juiced up their image by using models who weren't.

The girls now stood preening, used to being the center of attention, and just before Karen turned away from them another tall, thin figure joined them. It was Tangela Pompey, and even from here, halfway across the long teak deck, Karen could see the glitter in the girl's eye and the outrageous way she was dressed. She had a blindingly purple mini-skirt on and a black bolero jacket as a blouse. The jacket barely covered her breasts and was held together with a single big safety pin. Tangela was all beautiful brown skin and desperation. Was it Karen's imagination that the other women seemed to disperse when she arrived? There was no doubt she was a beautiful girl, but she *wasn't* as beautiful as her mother had been, and she probably wasn't beautiful enough to make it much beyond where she was now. Karen knew Tangela could have a lucrative, long career as a fitting model—her proportions were perfect—but from what Defina said the girl wanted a whole lot more. Even now, when they worked together, Karen felt Tangela's lack of enthusiasm. Without an audience, the girl was dead.

Karen was about to turn away when she noticed the rest of Tangela's entourage. Aside from the Hispanic-looking guy—probably the boyfriend that Defina objected to—there was a minor rock musician, and another girl. Karen did a double take. The girl was Stephanie.

The latest bonding fashion was models and rock stars. Patti Hanson married Keith Richards. Rachel Hunter married Rod Stewart (both couples were in attendance tonight). Stephanie seemed to be following the crowd. Why else would she be hanging all over a scruffy-looking blonde who Karen recognized as the member of a rock band. Karen was just surprised—no, shocked—to see her niece. How had she gotten in? She was too young. Had Norris invited her? Had she crashed the party? Had Tangela brought her? Karen watched as Stephanie mimed a pout, walked a few steps away from her blonde Adonis, then, turning, ran back across the deck and threw herself at him. Karen saw the guy's hand squeeze Stephanie's ass. Stephanie just threw back her head and laughed.

What to do? Play the aunt and use the classic line, "Does your mother know you're here?" Act outraged and send the kid home? Ignore it and hope it's just what teenagers do? She turned to Jeffrey. "Look who's here," she said. He followed her gaze with his eyes, and they widened when they saw his niece. "Time for some divine intervention," Karen decided, and made her way through the crowd to Stephanie, who was being nuzzled by the unsavory rocker.

"Hi, Stephie," Karen smiled. She tried to act natural. Stephanie spun around. There already was a hickey on her long, swan neck. *Very* attractive. Karen didn't know people still *did* hickies. "Having fun?" she asked.

"Oh, hi. Yeah. Hi, Uncle Jeffrey." Before her niece could say anything more, a photographer began to shoot pictures while his aide asked for Stephanie's name. The rocker, Karen noticed, did his best to stay within the frame. Karen had to admit the guy was cute, if he'd wash his hair and lose the tattoos. "Isn't this the greatest party?" Stephanie asked as the camera flashed, her voice shrill.

"Just great," Jeffrey agreed. "Hasn't been one like this in close to three days." The sarcasm was lost on the girl.

"How are you getting home, Stephie?" Karen asked.

Her niece blinked. "I was going to stay over with Tangela," she said. Karen thought of Defina's stories about Tangela on the marble kitchen table. Forget about it!

"Gee, I don't think it's a good idea, honey. I really don't. Why don't you spend the night with us?"

Stephanie knew she'd been outmaneuvered. She threw a look of longing at the blonde guitar prince. Karen remembered when Stephie used to look at Malibu Barbies with that longing. She sighed. "Why don't you take a little time and say good-bye to your friend?" Karen smiled. "We'll be leaving in about fifteen minutes." The girl couldn't shoot heroin in a quarter of an hour, could she?

"What the hell is Lisa thinking of?" Jeffrey asked out loud as they walked away. It didn't help that Karen was thinking the same thought herself.

"Oh, you know how kids are. Stephie probably lied to Lisa. I lied to Belle. I'll talk to Lisa tomorrow. We've been here almost half an hour. Let's make our good-byes."

Karen knew she eventually would have to make her way over to Norris and congratulate her. With any luck, she and Jeffrey would have their picture taken for "W" and then they could go home. Karen moved among the beautiful crowd, Jeffrey at her side. It would have been unbearable to attend one of these functions without him. The press of the crowd was unbelievable. Was it safe, she wondered. Could the boat sink? She turned to Jeffrey. The two of them had been pushed against the rail of the boat, and the breeze from off the East River riffled his hair.

There, it seemed, they found a moment to be alone in the crowd. "You're a good aunt," Jeffrey said. "You'll be a good mother, too." He smiled approvingly at her and then looked uptown, toward the white necklace of lights that was the Brooklyn Bridge. For some reason, at that moment, for the first time in a long time, Karen filled with love. She loved Jeffrey again! It was such a relief! The water below them reflected splashes of light against Jeffrey's jaw, and the darkness shrouded the two of them as softly as a crepe de chine shawl. Karen felt, suddenly, happier than she ever had. Despite being at this silly party, despite the little scene with Tangela and Stephanie, she felt incredibly lucky, as if her own ship, despite a difficult and dangerous crossing, had safely come in to port at last. For a moment, she felt completely satisfied. Across the water, Brooklyn glittered in the night, looking more romantic than it had ever been when Karen lived there. She could hardly blame Stephanie for wanting to escape Long Island. Karen had not just crossed a river to arrive. She had crossed worlds to get here. She looked back at her husband.

"I've already looked into some of the adoption stuff," she said to him. "I think I found the right guy. Soon we'll be a daddy and a mommy," Karen added, a little self-conscious.

He smiled down at her. "Yeah, and then we'll be busting our own kid at parties." Darkness had fallen and, though the fairy lights that had been wound around the masts and stanchions were twinkling, it was dim on board. Just then, Anna Wintour drifted by, wearing the darkest of sunglasses. Karen didn't think she had ever seen Anna without them. Even in her *Vogue* office, Anna kept them on. How was she making it across the dark deck? Perhaps she was blind, Karen thought. Somehow, it would be a fitting irony if the queen of fashion coverage was sightless.

They had to say good-bye to Norris and collect Stephanie, but the crowd had its own ebb and flow. Susan Reliance walked by, her husband at her side. They were big money, oil money. And Susan's family was New York social since the days of the four hundred. Karen couldn't understand why people like her attended these soirees. Karen came because it was business, but what was a socialite's reason for coming? When she'd broken her leg Pat Buckley had *schlepped* around on crutches at parties for almost a year. Why? And why had Lauren Bacall come? Surely Norris didn't have dirt on *them* that forced them to show up. Maybe they just liked to stand in crowds and spill champagne on their shoes.

The boat shifted and a high-pitched murmur rose. Lucie de la Falaise lurched by, along with a woman in a Claude Montana that she should have been told wasn't for her. And then Norris appeared, wearing another of her creations, something in silk organza that would have made a good table drape. Because it was her party, and because Karen had good manners, she took a step forward and was about to greet Norris when she saw the man behind her. It was Bill Wolper.

As always at one of her events, photographers clustered around Norris, and Bill himself was being photographed from every possible direction. Karen hoped he didn't have a bad side, and that his mother wouldn't call *him* the next morning and ask why he looked so wrinkled. Karen stood frozen until Jeffrey noticed the direction she was staring in. "Well, well," he said, "no wonder we haven't gotten that offer yet. Maybe Bill is still shopping around. After all, if you can't get the original Karen Kahn, you could settle for a Norris Cleveland knock-off."

Karen felt a stab of guilt. She, not Norris, was the reason they had not received NormCo's offer. Somehow, after years of total honesty with her husband, Karen's new relationship with Bill had already filled her marriage with lies and omissions. Somehow, with her help, Bill had made Jeffrey look like a bit of a schmuck. Karen didn't like it. What if Jeffrey asked about all this? What if he looked dumb in front of Bill? Somehow, she wanted to protect him. "Shall we go say hello?" she asked. "But let's not mix business with pleasure."

"No fear. This is *all* business," Jeffrey complained.

The two of them moved toward Norris. Karen wondered if Norris wasn't having a flirtation of her own with Bill Wolper. He had even deeper pockets than Norris's Wall Street hubby.

Why should you care, Karen asked herself fiercely. But she found she *did* care. Could she lose this deal to Norris? Bill's hand on Norris's elbow didn't bother her as much as the thought of Bill praising Norris's talent. Could Bill tell the difference between a Norris Cleveland and a Karen Kahn? Was Norris his fallback position if she, Karen, turned him down? Before she could think about it, she and Jeffrey were greeting Norris. "It's all so wonderful," Karen said and smiled as sincerely as she could manage.

"Really distinctive. Just what I'd expect, Norris," Jeffrey said. Karen almost laughed out loud. Norris's party was as unoriginal as her fashions, and the perfume was a Gio knock-off. But if Norris knew that, it didn't seem to bother her. She flashed them her famous skeletal smile and turned to Bill.

"Do you know Karen Kahn?" she asked.

Bill looked at Karen directly for the first time. Karen was sure there was a message in his eyes, but she couldn't read it. Was it a challenge? Was it a warning? "If you don't say yes, someone else will"? Before she could decide, Bill held out his hand to Jeffrey. "I've met both of the Kahns," he said.

"Isn't it wonderful?" Norris asked. "We've already gotten a promise for a huge promotion at Bloomingdale's in New York. And Bernheart's in Chicago." Karen wondered about her use of "we." Were Bill and Norris *already* in bed together—at least in the business sense?

Karen shrugged. "That's just great," she said. "I'm thrilled for you. I wish you all the success you deserve."

As she and Jeffrey left them to collect Stephanie, Karen felt Bill's eyes follow her.

18

DIALING FOR DAUGHTERS

If Karen hadn't had a referral source for a private detective, she certainly didn't have that trouble in finding an adoption lawyer. In all the time she had spent sitting in fertility clinic waiting rooms, and with all the advice she'd been offered from other people's stories, one name kept coming up. Harvey Kramer was *the* guy to see. So on the morning after Norris's party, Karen brought Stephanie in to work, then closed the door of her office and called Kramer. Karen was shocked when she found out that she couldn't get an appointment for almost three months, but then she called Robert-the-lawyer and asked him to use some juice. His office got them an appointment for Thursday. Even in adoptions, it seemed, it was not what you knew but who you knew.

Kramer's office was busy and messy: after Robert's Park Avenue joint, this Riverdale house-converted-to-a-law-office seemed tacky and unprofessional. "Riverdale?" Jeffrey had asked. "Who the hell is in Riverdale?"

The answer was Harvey Kramer. Harvey Kramer and at least a dozen other couples as eager as she was to find a baby. In the somewhat gray zone of private adoption law, Harvey Kramer was it. Despite the juice from Robert-the-lawyer's office, they were still left waiting in the living-room-cum-reception area, parked on an old Danish Modern couch for almost half an hour, while Jeffrey alternately fumed and looked through two-year-old copies of *US News* and the *ABA Journal*. (As far as Karen could tell, no one read them even when they first came out.) At last Harvey, a fat man with dark hair and five o'clock shadow at nine-thirty in the morning, ushered them into his office.

"I saw you on 'The Elle Halle Show.' Very nice coverage," he said approvingly. "So, what can I do you for?" As if he didn't know.

Jeffrey kept silent. Karen, uncomfortable, mumbled something about wanting to adopt.

"You've had the home study? You registered anyplace?" Karen shook her head. "How many lawyers you been to?"

"None," Karen admitted.

Kramer rolled his eyes. "Virgins!" he said. He took a deep, belly-expanding breath. "Okay, let me explain the situation. Ya got two choices: state or private. But the state's only got little black crack babies or older kids who've been abused so bad they'll be wetting their beds until they're forty. Plus, there's something like a ten-year waiting list for white babies and none are available anyway. And no Jewish babies. None. Forget about it. Because in New York, Jewish girls in trouble go to clinics.

"So, that leaves private adoption, which is a tricky business. Ya gotta find a woman out-of-state who is about to give birth *and* willing to put her kid up for adoption. We know which are the good states, the one's with a lot of pregnant girls and no abortion clinics. The South and Midwest are best, but some states won't let ya advertise. Advertising is the way you hook 'em. Ya know what I mean?" It wasn't a question.

"Of course, ya gotta be careful about the bait: it's illegal to sell babies and in some states you can't pay for anything but medical bills. Ya gotta be *very* careful about that. Other states are more lenient, if you get my drift. Clothes, school tuition, rent. Sally, my associate, can help you with it all. We know where to run the ads and how to word 'em. Meanwhile, ya gotta get yourselves a separate, unlisted telephone line and a cellular phone so that ya can take their calls night or day. This isn't the kinda thing where they keep office hours or they'll call back later if they get a busy signal. Ya gotta be prepared for anything. Some will be legit and some won't. Your job is to get them to like ya, to make the human contact, ya know what I mean? But people in your position have ta be careful. You want to adopt the baby, not the mother. So when you've hooked her, then you refer her ta our office and Sally sends her all the forms. *If* the forms come back, and *if* we get a positive medical report, then I nail 'em with the preadoption agreement. Ya understand me so far?"

That *was* a question, so Karen nodded and looked over at Jeffrey, who was sitting absolutely still. Was he paralyzed with disgust or just getting ready to bolt out of here? Kramer didn't seem to notice one way or the other. Perhaps all his clients sat there, mute, like they'd been pole-axed.

"What ya really gotta understand is, it ain't over 'til it's over. Some of these girls will tell ya anything ta get a few bucks and a ticket out of Enid, Oklahoma. So just hang tough until we get 'em vetted. And even then, they'll turn around and decide ta keep their baby after you've nursed them through the last trimester *and* picked up all the bills. Each state has got a different rule: in Texas, once she signs the papers, that's it. Her rights are terminated immediately. The baby is yours. In California, on the other hand, they got a year ta change their mind. Totally flaky. So don't go thinking about California." He paused for a moment and shook his head. "The stories I could tell ya," he said.

"We handle all of the legal aspects, both here in New York and in the state where you find the baby. We need a retainer now. The fees'll be based on how much work is required in a particular state, and also on how many false starts ya get." His phone rang and, without excusing himself, he turned to pick it up. "Yeah?" he said. "Oh, *big* surprise. Like I didn't tell them she would go south. Okay, put him through." Kramer was silent for a few moments, listening. Karen was afraid to look at Jeffrey. Kramer began to talk again, nodding his head. "Yeah, I'm sure your wife's upset, but ya never should have sent the girl the money. We weren't even sure she was pregnant." He paused for a moment. "Hey, let me tell ya something: a month of phone conversations does *not* make a relationship. For all you know she's been pulling this scam on a dozen other couples." Karen closed her eyes. Her head was beginning to ache with a vicious pain right at her temples. Kramer continued. "Yeah. Okay. Well, next time refer her to our office *before* ya get that far, no matter *what* your wife says."

Kramer put down the phone and turned back to them without an apology. "My associate, Sally, will fill you in on the home visit. Ya gotta pay for a state-certified social worker to come in and check ya out. Sally's got the forms. We can't do anything until ya got your home visit. So, ya got any questions?"

Karen, in a state she might call shell-shocked if she had the wits to call it anything, just shook her head. This was the *best* guy in the business? She shook her head again. The pain in her head was exquisite. When Jeffrey stood up she managed to stand up beside him. Then it occurred to her.

"One thing," she asked. "Can the birth mother find the baby after the adoption?" For a crazy moment, she thought that maybe she should discuss her own adoption with Kramer. Maybe he would be better than Centrillo at this. Then she came out of her temporary insanity. Anyway, Jeffrey didn't even know about her search. She reminded herself she had to ask Belle or Arnold some tough questions. Meanwhile, here, she had to know about this. "Can the birth mother find the baby after the adoption?" she repeated.

"Not if ya do it right," Kramer explained. "Ya never give 'em your last name. Especially in your case. The records get sealed. Otherwise, before ya know it they'd be looking for discounts on your clothes. With celebrities, this stuff can be very tricky. If you knew the whole inside story on the Michelle Pfeiffer adoption, it would curl your hair. And the trouble I hear Tom Cruise and Nicole Kidman had! But, of course, they didn't use our office." Karen almost snorted with contempt. Name dropping! Was this guy just a liar, or did he know his business? "So that's why you need a new phone number," Kramer said. "And ya never give them your address. Why open yourself up ta blackmail? Some of my clients have had a romantic idea about sharin' the baby. Ya know, visits from the birth mother and all that. But either it starts them takin' legal actions to get the baby back, or they're pumping you for cash at every birthday. Forget about it!"

The irony of her life was not lost on Karen: she was paying one man to uncover an adoption and now would pay another to make sure this one could not be uncovered. I think all of this is making me mentally ill, she told herself. How can you be in two places at once when you're really nowhere at all?

Kramer stood up, too, and turned to the small, bird-like woman who had silently arrived in the doorway. "Sally. This is Karen and Jerry Kahn."

"Jeffrey," Jeffrey corrected. It was the first word her husband had spoken to the lawyer. Karen winced.

"Yeah. Whatever," Kramer said. "So set them up with a file and a home visit referral." He turned his back. "Oh, and they need to give you the retainer."

Karen wrote the check numbly. It was for four thousand dollars.

Karen sat with Carl at the middle of the refectory table that was now covered with dozens of crumpled sheets of paper.

"How about this?" Carl asked. "*Happy, healthy, home-loving couple want to kiss and cuddle your baby. My husband and I want to hear from you and we want to help. Call collect. 212 BABYNOW.*"

Karen made a face. "Sappy. I'm going to puke," she said.

"They're *supposed* to be sappy. They *like* sappy. This is the rainbows and unicorns crowd. The kind of girls that collect Precious Moments statuettes. Trust me, I know."

Karen sighed. The whole process was so bizarre, such a weird blend of Madison Avenue methods, telecommunications networks, and Victorian sentiment that she wasn't sure she could go through with it. Jeffrey had washed his hands of this part completely, which was just as well. She could imagine his reaction to this ad.

"How about this?" she proposed. *"Educated and warm, Jeffrey and I want to make a loving home for your child. We'll expose our baby to all that is best in life."* She looked at Carl.

"Forget it! It reeks of elitism. 'Expose our baby?' Are you exhibitionists? Plus, don't call it 'our baby'. It's still *her* baby."

"Well, you got a point there," Karen agreed. She threw the paper onto the floor, stood up, and stretched. "Maybe I should just go with Sally's version," she told Carl. Sally had been calm and helpful. She'd taken the check, given them a receipt, and provided Karen with a list of social workers and out-of-state newspapers, as well as notes on which ones accepted ads only from people whose home study had been completed.

Carl sat, doodling, while Karen began to pick up all the crumpled sheets. Maybe she could concentrate if there still wasn't so much to do for the Paris show. If it didn't go well, she wasn't sure the NormCo deal, even if she told Wolper she wanted it, would ever get signed. She sighed. Jeffrey was still in the dark, and she still hadn't called Wolper and given him the go ahead. She *had* to do it, but somehow she held back. She wondered why.

"I've got it," Carl said, interrupting her thoughts. *"Help us make our dream come true. Loving couple with fine home and fine values desperately seek a baby to share it all with. Can you help us?"*

"Not bad," Karen admitted. "Maybe we drop the desperate."

"Everyone's a critic," Carl grumbled, but they had their ad.

Karen and Carl had gone through the list Sally provided and picked all the newspapers in college towns. Then she and Carl and Defina spent three days calling classifieds in Mississippi and Tennessee and Georgia and Arkansas.

After fourteen hundred and twenty dollars worth of ads were placed, there was nothing to do but wait by the cellular. Karen got a new *schlep* bag with a special pocket for the phone and she wouldn't leave home without it. No one had the number except Janet, Defina, and Carl, but they weren't to use it except for the most dire emergency.

They didn't call, but neither did any one else. Carl and Defina tested it regularly from pay phones, since they figured that might be where girls would call from. But the phone was working. It was the ads that weren't. Karen called Sally, who suggested they try Ohio. "It seems to be happening right now," Sally told her, mildly. They placed four ads. Five days later, at a quarter to two in the morning, the phone rang. Karen, asleep in bed beside Jeffrey, awoke to the bird-like chirping of the cellular and it took her almost three rings before she could locate the phone in the dark beside her night table. She grabbed it at last and moved into the bathroom, closing the door behind her. She had to get on a plane in five hours and fly to Chicago for a trunk show. But she was happy to interrupt her sleep for this.

"Hello," she gasped, the sleep making her voice sound deep and heavy.

"Hello. I have a collect call from Carol. Will you accept charges?" Karen did, and tried to pull herself together enough to hook the girl.

"Hi, Carol."

A blurry voice at the other end of the phone mumbled "Hey."

"My name is Karen. Where are you calling from?"

"Across from the Pick-n-Pay. It's late isn't it? Is it late where you are?"

"It's late, but I'm glad you called." Karen felt herself begin to sweat. Was the call from Ohio? Were the new ads working? Was she talking to the mother of her baby? What the hell did you say now? Her mouth had never been so dry. Luckily, she didn't have to say anything. Carol was talking.

"Look, I got caught and I already got me one baby. You interested?"

It sounded to Karen as if the girl was drunk. What about fetal alcohol syndrome? How far along was she? "When's the baby due?" Karen asked. She tried to sound casual.

"I got three months to go. It's too late to do anything about it, isn't it?"

What was she talking about? Karen wondered. An abortion at six months? Oh, Jesus, I'm not equipped for this, she thought, and took a deep breath. "Have you got a pencil, Carol?" she asked as kindly as she could.

"No, but I got me a pen."

"Good. Good. A pen will do. Listen, I want you to write down this name. Harvey Kramer. I'm going to give you his phone number. He's our lawyer and he can help us sort all this out for you. I'll spell it for you. Are you ready?" Karen asked.

But the line was dead.

19

THE WAIST LAND

For designers, trunk shows are a little bit like book signings for authors. A lot of trouble, a bit of embarrassment, and only the possibility of increased sales. It was sort of risky—like throwing a party and having nobody come.

That's what Karen was thinking as she got on the American flight to Chicago, ready for the Bernheart's visit. Bernheart's was the best fashion merchandiser in Chicago. Karen hadn't slept after the call from Carol. Now she was tired and depressed. She took her usual seat—1D, bulkhead by the window—and waited for Defina to sit beside her. It was a luxury to fly first class, but one she felt she both deserved and appreciated. Karen had only recently begun to receive VIP treatment from the American Airlines Special Services staff. The *People* magazine article and the Barbara Walters and Elle Halle shows hadn't hurt. It was nice to wait in the private lounge and be served herbal tea in china cups until a staff member came to usher you to your gate. No plastic airport waiting room row seats, no staring vacantly at the IBM salesman sitting across from you, and no pushing toward the gate with the masses. Nowadays, Karen was ushered on before seating began and was greeted at the jetway door by name. Only after she had given her *schlep* bag to the flight attendant to stow overhead and taken her seat did she see the other passengers begin to be herded through the plane. Ah, she thought, success does have its privileges. She wasn't the type to enjoy being chauffeured around, but airports and flying were such an ordeal that she appreciated every bit of cushioning the airline could provide. Especially after last night. And she'd need to retain all her energy for the ordeal ahead.

Karen tried to perk up. After all, it was only one call. At least the ad had started to work. Eventually the call would come. Now, she had to concentrate on business.

Karen was always interested in what women wore when they traveled. It was hard to look good, be comfortable, and arrive unwrinkled. Mobile clothes, ones that packed well, that didn't cut or bind in an airplane seat, were difficult to design. Part of the secret was, as always, the fabric. Only a wonderful—and that usually meant an expensive—one would do the trick. Jersey was best, but there were some neat tricks that Beene did with mohair.

Now Karen watched the women who filed on. Older women wore polyester pull-on pants or jogging suits. Practical but hideous. Business-women were still wearing constructed suits. The synthetics didn't wrinkle but they looked cheap. The costly ones would fight their seams and the wearer's contours for the whole trip. Of all the passengers boarding, only one woman, in a long knit skirt and a simple silk overblouse, looked good.

Karen had never believed that there was a conspiracy of top designers whose styles held women hostage, but in the old days—the fifties and the six-ties—there was a general guide that designers had provided. Now, with fash-ion democratized, anyone could wear anything—and they often did. In a way, Karen thought this had made dressing more difficult for women. Without any boundaries at all, the choices seemed too confusing. At least these women looked confused.

Defina came on, looking good as always, pushing Tangela, Stephanie, and two other models ahead of her. Tangela plopped down in a seat across the aisle. "What do you think you're doing?" Defina asked her daughter. She handed her a ticket. "You're in the back," she said. "Behind the curtain, along with the others." Tangela stuck her lower lip out and Karen couldn't help but notice how much like Defina it made her look.

"Why can't I sit up here?" Tangela asked.

"When you do first-class work, you sit in first class," Defina told her.

Tangela grabbed at her ticket and flounced down the aisle. Two of the other models giggled and followed her. So did Stephanie, who seemed to Karen to be so excited that nothing could dim her enthusiasm. It would be her first model-ing in public. Karen wasn't sure she was up to it, and Defina had said she was certain that the girl wasn't, but Karen felt guilty about how little time she had spent with her niece and this was a way she could try and make it up to her.

"Hope this plane doesn't crash with the load of resentment it's got back in the tail," Defina said, indicating coach.

At last the plane was boarded and ready to move into the long line of flights waiting to take off from LaGuardia at 7 A.M. Insiders called the airport DelayGuardia. With the trunk show scheduled for eleven, and a two-hour flight in front of them, it didn't leave a lot of room for error, but with the hour time difference and with Casey Robinson as their advance man, Karen figured it would be all right.

Trunk shows were a lot of trouble. They were part celebrity press-the-flesh, part show-and-tell, and part sales pressure cooker. Karen had to charm her customers while selling the shit out of them. The ladies who lunched descended to a feeding frenzy. Department stores went to a lot of trouble and expense to publicize a trunk show; they advertised, set aside extra floor space, staff, and time, and sent personalized invitations to those clients they felt were most likely to appreciate and buy. They expected to see sales racked up.

And Karen was good at selling. She enjoyed it. And she was sincere. She never recommended stuff to women that didn't look good on them. Still, she sometimes wondered if part of what she was doing was immoral. Sometimes there was such a buzz surrounding a trunk show that she felt more like a drug pusher than a designer. Karen knew that fashion—shopping—was addictive to women. It was a healthy normal need that could become an unhealthy, frightening obsession. And after all, most women in America had addiction problems. Most women were addicted to food, and fashion was a little bit like that: overeaters always complained that their problems were harder to handle than alcoholism because, unlike drinking, you couldn't simply quit eating. You had to do some of it every day. And that was the problem with clothes. Women had to get dressed every day. And if they dressed badly, they had to live with the results all day long. Dressing badly in the morning felt a lot like overeating at breakfast—you were left with a load of self-hate that showed and that you had to carry all through the rest of the day.

Karen remembered the way Bill Wolper had described what she sold—hope, or the illusion of it. It made her skin crawl. Karen didn't want to sell hope, or a rotten perfume in a fancy bottle. She wanted to sell beautiful clothes to women who could enjoy them. There was no doubt that the shopping thing had gotten worse in the last decade. Of course, part of it was the eighties mentality of consumerism—shopping as a way of life. But Karen thought there was more to it than that. What had happened in the last ten or fifteen years was that most women had gone to work, and once they left home and were seen every day by others, the pressure to dress well intensified.

Back in the fifties, Karen imagined, women could stay at home and do their chores in housecoats. Hadn't Belle worn housecoats? What had happened to them? When women in the fifties went out, it became an event: they wore hats and gloves and high-heeled shoes. But the trouble that they took with their formal appearance was offset by being able to relax so much of the time at home. They didn't have to dress every morning in the rush before getting the kids off to school.

Today, there was no time for most women to relax at home. They were out there, in the business world, and—unlike men—they were being judged twofold all the time. They were being judged by their appropriateness and also for their attractiveness as women. Men could just put on another suit or sports coat, but women wanted more. They wanted to look appropriate *and* attractive and they had to do it every day. They had more at stake than ever and less chance of attaining their goals.

Because at the same time that women had gone to work, the look they aspired to was more difficult to achieve than ever. Models had gotten younger, taller, and thinner in the last few years than they had ever been before. The power of the fashion magazines had grown, the images were more unattainable, and as Karen had seen in the motley passengers getting on the plane, the average woman kept trying—and failing—to look good. Karen thought back to Bill Wolper's chilling description of the average woman's life. The women she would meet with today were more affluent than Bill's disappointed, trapped woman but as far as Karen could see her rich clientele were, in their own way, just as disappointed and trapped. Women spent money at trunk shows with a ferocity that was frightening.

Last season, a couple of her trunk shows in New York and Los Angeles had actually set records, but that didn't mean it would work in Chicago. An ever-more-sophisticated city, and one with a lot of wealth clustered along Lake Shore Drive and the Miracle Mile, it still had a patina of Midwestern conservatism: she couldn't always count on Chicago and the Midwest to understand her stuff. That's why it was so important now for them to get it. Because, in addition to the profit pressure on her and the expectation that Bernheart's had, if she ever expected to expand, it had to be out to the center from the two coasts. She was doing this show today partly to test market some of her new designs for Paris. She wanted to see if she'd get a reaction, and this was the only chance for a sneak preview that she'd get.

At last, the flight took off. Karen sat there, staring out the window at nothing, thinking about last night's call until the flight attendant offered her a mimosa. Who the fuck drank champagne in their orange juice at seven o'clock? she wondered. She shook her head, and the flight attendant served them breakfast.

Defina scowled at her. "What are you stewing over? Give it up, girlfriend," Defina said. "You are what you are and we got what we got and it's good enough. Nothing you can do about it now, anyway, so kick on back." She looked down at her plate. "Talk about happy meals! Eat your cheese omelet, but don't touch them little things they call sausages. Even in first class they look like cat turds to me."

"Eeuw. Dee!" Karen laughed and waved away all of her breakfast. She never had anything except a dry bagel anyway. She had one tucked in her *schlep* bag overhead, along with the baby phone. She wondered if it could get calls while they were in flight. Was she missing a chance right now? Well, if she thought about *that* she'd go crazy. She shook her head as if she could shake the thought of all that out of her mind.

She tried to focus on the day ahead of her. The Paris line had been developing well. The jackets, as always, were a big hit with the models already. Women, it seemed, could never have too many blazers, and it was true that hers were cut in such a way to hide a multitude of sins. Her slacks *always* sold and the new Japanese wool blends that she was trying—ungodly expensive at sixty dollars a yard wholesale—had been a great success so far. Although her clientele absolutely had to have natural fabric, this Japanese miracle stuff had the texture of wool but it didn't wrinkle. Great for travel. She'd used it for the first time in her last collection and they hadn't been able to keep the pants in the New York stores.

It was the dresses that she was more concerned about. She had taken a real chance with them. They were mostly long, almost calf-length, and in tussa silk or the lightest boucle. They had cap sleeves—no woman over eighteen should ever attempt a sleeveless dress. Karen followed Coco on that. After all, who wanted to stare at armpits all day? All of the dresses had optional jackets, and all of them buttoned down the front. Karen thought of them as a kind of thirties farm wife dress, but the long line was incredibly complimentary to most women. And they could go from the office to a dinner party. The best thing about them was that they were easy—no blouse to choose, no scarf to add. Slip into it, zip it up, and you were done. Thirty-second dressing.

The problem was that most women wouldn't try on dresses, so the pieces they had brought might just hang on the racks. Karen knew she was bucking her own image with something as different as the dress, but she was *sure* she could make women understand. All she needed was the opportunity to get with her audience.

That was the other thing that trunk shows did: they put her in intimate contact with the actual consumer. Karen knew that every designer is limited by the time in which she lives and the kind of women to whom she sells. She liked to watch normal women—not models or social ex-rays but normal, everyday women—try on, select, and discard her designs. Karen felt she needed to know exactly who it was who could afford to buy her nineteen-hundred-dollar jackets and her nine-hundred-and-eighty-dollar casual dresses. If she *didn't* know, how the hell would she be able to do the right thing by them? Were they working women? Were they young or old? There weren't many women under thirty-five who could afford to spend that kind of money. What was the price point beyond which they wouldn't go? Could they only justify the cost if it was a work costume or if it was a party dress? And most importantly of all, what was it that they felt they lacked? What was it that once they saw they would not be able to resist? Whatever she learned, Karen moved on and incorporated in the less expensive bridge line. And there wasn't a trunk show Karen hadn't learned from, although she had to admit that the lessons had sometimes been painful.

She had bet on the dresses now because they were both new and classic and because they were simple to wear—just slip it on with pantyhose and a pair of shoes and you were dressed. Simplicity and ease were her fashion religion. But this would be the acid test.

When they had landed, O'Hare was the usual hell, and it took them almost twenty minutes to find their limo. The driver should have been standing at the gate exits with Defina's name on a sign. Instead, he had waited at baggage claim, although they had no baggage. At last, seated in the automobile, they made the long drive on the JFK Expressway, which could more accurately have been called the JFK parking lot. The problem with the seven o'clock flight from LaGuardia was that it got you into Chicago just in time for the worst of the rush-hour traffic. But, at last, they pulled onto Michigan Avenue. It was nine-thirty and it gave the girls more than an hour to primp while Karen and Defina could use at least that much time to schmooze with management before they had to begin schmoozing the retail customers.

But when they arrived they were met by Ben Crosby, the vice president, who told them he'd already gotten a call from Mercedes Bernard. "She set up an interview with Mindy Trawler of the *Chicago Herald*. She's going to do the cover story in this week's style section. She's waiting upstairs."

Crosby, a small, round, very neat man, was obviously excited, but then he was new to the job. He was the type Defina would witheringly refer to as a *marchand de fromage*—a cheese seller. Karen felt like sighing but managed a smile. Christ! She needed some time to get ready. Karen's whole business depended on her relationship with the retailers. She was always fighting for floor space against the other designers. Ralph Lauren was virtually the only designer who didn't have to kiss retailing butt. With his sixty independently owned shops, and his twenty-four factory outlets, plus his New York Rhinelander Mansion, he could keep busy just filling up his own stores! Karen didn't have that luxury. No wonder all the other designers were jealous of Ralphie.

No matter how good Karen's clothes were, if they weren't displayed and promoted by the retailers, they wouldn't get bought. So she would do her best to make Crosby happy. And PR was important, but the interview should've been done over the phone and scheduled for a couple of days earlier so that it would run today and draw people to the store for the show.

Exposure—the right kind of exposure—was everything in her business, and there was no doubt Mercedes had helped buy it for her. Without good press and lots of it, even the best designers were crippled. Karen thought of Geoffrey Beene. Everyone in fashion knew he was the greatest fashion artist that America had produced but *Women's Wear Daily* hadn't covered a show of his in years, not since John Fairchild had begun feuding with Beene.

At the other extreme, Donna Karan had a talent for speaking to the press that was a true gift. She had a warmth that made even a stringer from a second-tier magazine feel as if Donna truly liked her. Who knows, Karen shrugged, maybe Donna actually did. But Karen did not, and it was hard for her to pretend.

She had other things to attend to, but Mindy Trawler would not wait. Oh, well. She guessed that some day the clipping from this interview would look good in her scrapbook, if she ever got around to pasting one up. And maybe Belle would get a copy sent to her from some Chicago friend. Hadn't Belle lived out here in her youth? Karen got a sick feeling all at once in her stomach. Had she, herself, lived somewhere around here? For all she knew, one of the women who turned up today might be a relative.

As she crossed the main floor, an odor wafted toward her. She looked up. Oh God! It was Norris Cleveland's goddamned perfume. The store was running a big promotion on it, and already there was a gaggle of demonstrators dressed in Norris Cleveland yellow, spraying the stuff into the air. A huge display had been set up, lit from above as if the bottles contained frankincense and myrrh. Well, at least Karen wasn't reduced to selling reek in a bottle. But it bothered her that both she and Norris were the blue-plate special today.

She didn't have time to brood about it. She turned to Defina. "You do the work and I get the glory," she said. "Can you get things organized while I do the interview?"

"I'd rather do ten shows than have to talk to one of them fashion bitches." Defina shook her head. The fashion press was notorious for being difficult and small-minded. Well, when one thought about it, what kind of person would dedicate their life to writing about a drop in hem lines or the new smock tops? Too often Karen had found they were envious people who had wanted a career in fashion but were too frightened or not talented enough to go for it. It was a variation on an old adage: those who can do, and those who can't write criticism. "Hope you got some freebies ready for the bitch," Defina added darkly. Fashion journalists were also notorious for taking everything they could, from free meals to fur coats. Karen shrugged.

"I'm sure we'll have something she likes," Karen purred.

"Yeah. Let's just hope it isn't one of the two-thousand-dollar jackets. You know, Karen, you can't do everything. Your plate's too full. One day you're going to try to fit in one little bit more and pop like a balloon. We'll be picking up shreds of you from down in the budget hosiery up to the bridal salon."

"It's okay. I've got key man insurance. You'll get a nice pension."

Defina rolled her eyes. "Well, I can't tell you what a comfort *that* is to me," she said. She turned to the models. "Let's go. We got an hour to turn you into good-looking women. I pray to God it's enough time." She trooped off with the four girls while Crosby ushered Karen upstairs to the buying office.

Mindy Trawler was in the stereotypical black dress that every fashion writer seemed to wear. Working at a second-tier paper in the second city would probably make her defensive, which would make for a difficult interview. Karen hadn't really liked a fashion reporter since Ben Brantley, but he was just a great journalist who had burnt out on fashion and now covered politics or something even dirtier. So Karen threw down her *schlep* bag and reached out to shake Mindy's hand. It was then, when the girl stood up, that Karen saw the big belly she was carrying. How pregnant was she? For a crazy moment Karen looked down at the girl's hands to check for a wedding ring. Yeah, right! Like I'm going to get to adopt *this* baby! She forced the smile to remain on her face. She was definitely going crazy, but knew that her irrelevant look for a wedding band had just been a way to avoid the sweep of envy that shook her now. Funny. Just a few minutes before Defina had been telling her how *these* women were always jealous of *her*. Well, this was a full turnabout. Karen knew she had to conceal her pain, but for a moment it was so real and so strong that she almost fell into the seat.

"When's the baby due?" she asked, trying to make her voice pleasant and casual-sounding.

"Next month, but it feels like I've been pregnant for a decade."

Karen nodded sympathetically, as if she had a clue. "This is so great!" she said. "I can't believe you've made time to interview me. Is there anything I can do to make it more comfortable for you? It can't be easy for you to be on your feet much right now. Do you want an ottoman while we do the interview?"

Mindy shook her head, as if she were annoyed by the attention. She got right to work. "So, let me ask you: A lot of designers feel Chicago is a second-class town from a fashion viewpoint. Do any of your favorite clients live here, or do you only like to dress the Elise Elliots of the world?"

Oh Jesus! Karen didn't need this! But she smiled. "Well, someone asked Chanel the exact same question," Karen said. "I'm no Chanel, but I'll tell you what she said. 'I like the ones who pay their bills. Keep your princesses and *comtesses* and pretenders to the throne. Such women are so impressed by their own nobility, to send a check is beneath them. Give me the chic, second wife of a rich businessman who cheats a little on his government contracts. Such a woman is too insecure to posture; such a woman pays her dressmaker.' "

"So, you like insecure women?"

Oh God. It was going to be one of these. "Not at all. I like all *my* clients," Karen said. She looked at her watch. "Do you have a lot more questions for the interview?"

"Well, actually, I didn't want to do an interview as much as follow you through the trunk show. Would that be all right?" Mindy smiled. "You know, a kind of backstage view for our readers."

Oh fuck, Karen thought. Just what she needed! A snoop behind the scenes catching every catty remark and each fumbled sale. Plus, she couldn't afford to have the press report on the Paris stuff beforehand. She could just imagine Defina's reaction. Here in the Midwest a trunk show was a way for the fashion addict to stay ahead of the curve. But that didn't mean Karen had to tip her hand to the press. Still, Karen smiled. This girl didn't look experienced enough to know what she was really looking at. "What a great idea," she said. "We'd just love it." And she considered the bullshit shoveling for the day officially begun.

Mrs. Montand stood in front of the three-way mirror looking at herself in one of the long silk dresses that Defina had brought in to her. "I can't, Karen. The dress is great, but it's not for me. I have no waist."

Karen looked at her critically. Mrs. Montand was a good customer, one who had been buying Karen's clothing almost from the beginning, but she was conservative and she knew what she wanted.

"She's right," Karen said quietly to Defina. "She *has* no waist."

Defina nodded. "But you've got great legs. Stick with the short skirts and the blazer jackets."

"Or how about the knit dresses?" Karen asked, hoping for a market test.

"With this ass?" Mrs. Montand raised her eyebrows.

"You'd be surprised." Karen turned around and displayed her own behind. "It works for me."

"Okay. I'll give one a try," Mrs. Montand agreed.

Karen had watched women trying on clothes all her life. It was funny: to wear clothes well you didn't have to be thin but you did have to have good shoulders and be long-waisted. Mrs. Montand's problem wasn't really her waistline—it was her short-waistedness. She'd look best in a tunic that disguised it.

It was amazing what clothes concealed as well as revealed. A tall, thin-appearing woman took off her tunic and it was clear that she was actually rather heavy. She was what the French called *fausse maigre* and could keep the illusion going with the help of the right clothing. Other women actually looked better when they took their clothes off. Those were the ones that needed help in selecting the right line.

Karen strode down the dressing room hallway and back out to the selling floor. It was funny that they called it that when most of the selling went on in the changing rooms. Not that Karen needed to push. Sometimes it actually frightened her to see how much and how compulsively these women spent their money. Karen often felt that lurking under the excitement of the purchase, under the thrill of the new, was a dark and lonely place. When women clients asked for one of everything, or for a particular design in every color, Karen felt their desperation. What kind of lives did they have? Did her clothes actually give them some comfort or was she nothing more than a Band-Aid, a Norris Cleveland on a hanger? Karen knew that some of the more extreme women didn't bother to unpack their purchases when they got home. They'd stick them in the closet like an alcoholic hiding an emergency bottle. It made her very sad. But she didn't like to question their motivation because she might have to examine her own.

As she worked the floor Karen kept hearing pops, like the sound of flash-bulbs or corks being opened. What the hell was it? She didn't have time to find out. More than two dozen women were already milling around going through the racks that KKInc had imported for the day. Defina kept her eye on the Paris numbers.

"Oh, God, I just love this jacket! And gray is *the* color this season," a big blonde matron told Karen. The jacket was a gray boucle wool. It would look like shit on her.

"It *is* great," Karen agreed. "But did you see this one?" She held up one of the navy double-breasted ones she'd done. "Navy isn't really a neutral, you know. Women think it is, but it's murder on most of them. You could wear it, though," she said, truthfully.

"Well, what's the best color this year?"

"The one that most becomes *you*," Karen told her, with a smile.

"Well," the woman admitted, "I don't really know so I mostly stick with black. Except you don't do it, so I get confused."

"Black is an unforgiving color for most blondes," Karen said.

Then she saw the woman register recognition. It was the old "Karen Kahn is talking to me" syndrome. Karen still wasn't used to it. The woman took the jacket and held it up. "I love the buttons," she said. Instead of the usual door knobs, Karen had done the jacket with self-covered buttons. It updated the look. She smiled at the big blonde.

"You might also want to try one of the long dresses. They'd be great on you." She took a size twelve off the rack and handed it to the woman. "What do you think?" she asked.

"I don't usually wear dresses, but it is nice." Then she looked at the size. "I'm a ten though."

Shit. If she was a ten, Karen was the tooth fairy. "They're running a little small," she said diplomatically. "Why don't you try both?"

Doubtfully, the woman took the two hangers and began to head toward the changing room. "I'm sure I'm a ten," she called back. Karen smiled and nodded, but she was ready to spit nickels. It was all that goddamned downsizing. Years ago, Albert Nipon had found that a lot of size-ten women would buy his dresses—if they could fit into a size six. So he just cut everything bigger. Loads had followed his lead. Most designers wouldn't admit they did it. It still amazed Karen that some women absolutely refused to buy clothing that fit them perfectly and looked great if it wasn't labeled with the size they wanted it to be. And so the industry had all begun downsizing. Of course, the very best couture houses kept true to size, but then *their* customers were the ones who were most figure-conscious and had the time and money to maintain their bodies. For the sportswear lines, downsizing had become just another marketing trick. Put a size-twelve butt into a size-twelve jean that was labeled a size eight and you racked up a sale. But where would it stop? Jeffrey, Casey, and even Defina had nagged her to do it, but somehow, up till now, she'd resisted. For one thing, it would give Mrs. Cruz a heart attack. Karen kept the smile plastered on her face and caught Defina's eye. "Get the blonde into the size-twelve dress," she said with clenched teeth. "Cut the size label out. It will look great on her." Defina nodded. She had a tiny, razor-sharp pocketknife on hand for just such operations. Karen looked up.

Mindy Trawler had her eye on the two of them. Karen smiled brightly, looking only at the girl's face and avoiding Mindy's bulging belly. She was immediately besieged by another two customers. They *had* to try the boucle. Karen had been at it for almost three hours now and it seemed to be the best show they'd done yet. Despite Mrs. Montand and her nonexistent waist, despite the blonde and her fixation with numbers, the dresses were a big hit and some of the other Paris designs were moving nicely. Karen felt justified but exhausted. Round little Mr. Crosby was almost dancing in the aisle. It was then that he turned and, with a flourish, announced that tea and champagne were about to be served.

Three carts were rolled up from a service elevator. The napery was a wonderful damask in one of Karen's signature wheat colors, with a vase of lilies in just the same shade. There was a huge silver tea service, gold-rimmed china cups and saucers, and a three-tiered silver server with wonderful miniscule cucumber sandwiches and tiny scones. They had really gone all out, and Karen was touched to see that the champagne in the silver coolers was Dom Perignon, not some domestic crap. It wasn't vintage, but it would do.

Dozens of the women customers, Tangela, Defina, and of course Mindy Trawler descended on the tables. But Karen needed a break from them more than she needed a drink.

She retired to their staging area and took a moment to glance at herself in the mirror. Jesus, she looked like shit! There were dark circles under her eyes that almost perfectly matched the mauve of her silk shirt. Well, at least she was color coordinated. She hadn't needed that 2 A.M. wakeup call last night. Despite the press of fans and customers, she'd have to take a break. She turned around and made her way back to the screened part of the staging area that Tangela and the other girls had been using as a dressing room. As she walked past the divider, Tangela strode in behind her, still wearing one of the brown farm wife dresses, nibbling on a sandwich. She looked spectacular. "Don't get anything on the dress," Karen warned her. Tangela scowled but nodded, turned, and left the room. It was only then that Karen saw Stephanie huddled in the corner, by a mirror, her back to the pipe rack of clothes and the rest of the room. Her back was bare and from where Karen stood it seemed as if her shoulders were shaking with sobs. Karen moved quickly to her side. Her niece *was* crying, her face running with the black tide of her eyeliner and mascara. She looked like a very young raccoon. Karen pulled a seat up next to her and put her hand on the girl's bare shoulder. "What's the matter?" she asked.

"I can't do this," Stephanie said.

"What do you mean? You're doing great."

"No. I know I'm not. I don't know what to say when the women talk to me, and nobody buys the things that I model."

"How would you know that?" Karen asked.

"Tangela told me."

Karen shook her head. Even *she* didn't know exactly what was selling—except for the French stuff—and wouldn't until there was a final count at the end of the day. This must just be a case of novice nerves. And Tangela's bitchiness. Well, Stephanie was entitled to be anxious. She had never really been exposed to anything like this before. Maybe it was too much for her. Karen felt guilty. She'd thought this would be fun, a sort of makeup for busting Stephie at the boat party. It hadn't occurred to Karen that it might be traumatic for her niece. She'd been too wrapped up in the adoption and NormCo and her marriage to give any more time or thought to poor Stephanie, and here the kid was feeling like a failure when she'd done a great job. Karen took a deep breath. How could she think about being a mother when she didn't even have time to be a good *aunt*?

"Stephanie, you're really doing great. You look fabulous in those slacks, and after you modeled the double-ply knit, three women tried it on. Don't worry. This is just new for you. Of course you're not used to it yet. But you will be."

"You're just saying that because you're my aunt," Stephanie cried, but after a few moments she did stop crying. She wiped her eyes and sniffed, leaving a ghastly smear of black across her face, her hand, and down her wrist. Lucky she was only wearing her underwear. "You're just saying it," Stephanie repeated.

"No I'm not," Karen told her. "I couldn't afford to take the chance of losing sales right now. Business is business, Stephanie. I could have left you back at the showroom today."

"Really? I'm really doing okay?"

"You're *gorgeous!* And you're doing a great job. Just don't get that shit on your face all over the cashmere or I'll kill you." Karen gave the girl a hug and reached over her for some Kleenex. God, Stephie's shoulders were bony! "So clean yourself up and get out there. I'll even let you have a glass of champagne." Karen smiled at her niece in the mirror and then saw Mindy Trawler reflected behind them. Shit. Just what she needed! How much of this little scene had the journalist witnessed? And how much would show up in print?

"The photographer is here," Mindy Trawler said coolly. "Is this a good time for you?" She was holding a champagne flute in one hand and a tea sandwich in the other. She wasn't drinking, was she? It must just be club soda, Karen told herself. "You could do a few pictures now?" Mindy asked. "Maybe the two of you?"

"Want to be in the newspaper?" Karen asked Stephie.

"Sure."

Karen smiled into the mirror. "Just give us a minute." She told Stephanie to wash up and meanwhile Karen reached into her *schlep* bag, pulled out some concealer, and blended it under her eyes. Then she took out the big travel blusher brush she carried and covered her whole face with a powdering of Guerlaine's terra-cotta. It gave the impression of a tan without any of the UVA violence to her skin. She put on a noncolor lipstick, but added a quick layer of gloss. Gloss reflected well in photos. Never a beauty, she looked in the mirror without much vanity. Well, it would have to do. She stood up. The fabulous Japanese fabric trousers she had on were worth every penny: there wasn't a wrinkle in them! Karen *hated* how most slacks got ICW—instant crotch wrinkle. No one appreciated fabrics like the Japanese.

She heard another of those popping noises. Was someone being shot downstairs? That would be an extreme response to a makeover. She took a look at her own makeover. Not too bad.

But she'd managed to smear some of the bronzer powder onto her jacket shoulder. Well, that was easy to remedy. She pulled off the jacket and threw it onto the counter, grabbing another one off the rack. She gave herself a quick final glance in the mirror. Her stuff worked. She walked out of the dressing room and onto the selling floor just in time to see Mindy Trawler pouring herself another glass of Dom Perignon. The stupid little bitch *was* drinking! Karen couldn't remember whether fetal alcohol syndrome was more likely in the first or last trimester. Without thinking she walked up to the girl.

"You don't really want that, do you?" she asked. "We have fresh orange juice and I think there's herbal tea."

"No thanks. This is great."

"But it's not really a good idea. I could send out for some other fresh fruit juice, if you like."

"I'm fine," Mindy Trawler said, and there was an edge to her voice that should have warned Karen to lay off. But she wasn't in a lay-off mode.

"I'm not thinking of you, I'm thinking of your baby."

By now, several of the women clustered around the table had turned and were watching the confrontation. "I'll take care of my own baby, thank you very much," Mindy said icily.

Mr. Crosby stepped forward and cleared his throat. He knew things had gone too far. "The photographer thought maybe you could stand over here, where we have your logo. It might be a good place for a shot," he said, and took Karen by the arm. Stephanie joined her. Defina, her eyebrows raised, followed the two of them.

"We gonna have to give her more than a two-thousand-dollar jacket if we want good press now," Defina warned Karen.

"Fuck her," Karen said, and hoped her voice was loud enough to carry. "Don't give her anything. She doesn't deserve to have a baby."

"Guess that isn't your call to make," Defina told her. "Anyway, what do you expect when a sick bitch whelps? Babies full of rabies. So what?" She patted Karen's arm. "Smile nice for the boys with the camera," she said. "I'll get the fire department together, go back to the Trawler, and try to put out *that* little blaze."

Karen spent an agonizing twenty minutes pretending to pin the hem on a dress that Stephanie modeled while the photographer and his assistant fiddled endlessly with the lights. She kept wanting to tell them that this wasn't some kind of Avedon art shot but just a crappy black and white for the newspapers. She was just getting up from her knees when she looked across the floor and saw Bill Wolper step off the escalator. She could hardly believe her eyes. What the hell was he doing here? He turned toward the show activity and she watched as his eyes perused the crowd. Then he saw her and smiled. She lifted her hand in greeting. It was funny, but at the same time she felt her heart flutter. But maybe it was only her stomach. After all, she'd skipped lunch. She walked toward him.

"I was in the neighborhood, so I thought I'd drop by," he said with a grin. His teeth weren't great, but she liked the fact that he'd resisted caps and that he had a dimple on one side of his mouth when he smiled. It was cute, just the one dimple. "How's it going?" he asked.

"It was going fine before I pissed off the reporter who's covering us. She'll probably pan me."

"The press," Bill said with a dismissive shrug. "One of my business associates came to me for advice: he couldn't decide if he should buy into a Nevada whorehouse or a newspaper. I told him I didn't know the difference."

Karen laughed. Bill smiled and showed that single dimple. "Well," he said, "now my day hasn't been completely wasted. At least I've made you laugh."

They stood there for a moment together. Karen was tired, but this was the best she had felt all day. "So," Bill said, "when do you knock off? Even *you* can't work all the time. Can I take you to dinner?"

Karen looked down at her watch. It was a quarter to five. They had at least an hour of packing up to do, then the *schlep* out to O'Hare for the flight back. But she could knock off right after the wrap, have dinner, and take a later flight. "The last O'Hare flight I can catch is at nine," she told Bill.

"Let's kill two birds with one stone. My 727 is at Midtown airport. It's a shorter commute and the food isn't bad. What do you say?"

Karen blinked. "Yes. I say yes," Karen said, and turned back to make the new arrangements.

When Karen told Defina how she was getting home, Dee had raised her brows again. Then, out of nowhere, she asked, "When's the last time you and Jeffrey did the thang?"

The truth was that Karen hadn't been able to remember. But they *were* busy. A lot was happening. "None of your business," she had said. "Why do you ask?"

Defina jerked her head in the direction of Bill Wolper. "I don't know what you're up to, but I know what *he's* up to," Defina had said. "And if it's the same thing, you're going to be doing it at thirty thousand feet."

"Come on, Dee, give me a break. I'm just hitching back a ride in a private jet. What's the big deal?" Karen had asked.

"The big deal is the big deal. That kind of man will mess with your body so he can mess with your mind. I mean it, Karen. Be careful," Defina warned. Karen promised to be careful. Then Defina grinned. "You hear those popping noises today?" she asked.

"Yeah," Karen said. "Were they serving champagne downstairs too?"

"Only in Norris Cleveland's dreams. It was her perfume bottles. They were exploding."

"What?" Karen asked.

"You heard me. Something was wrong with the packaging. Under the hot lights the perfume expanded. You can imagine the rest. Broken glass and stink all over everything. People were gagging. Next they'll be suing. They have to recall it all."

Karen began to laugh. "Oh Jesus! What a fiasco!"

"Couldn't have happened to a nicer girl," Defina said with a wicked grin.

Karen nodded. "There is a God," she said.

Now Karen sat at the cleared table of the NormCo 727. She lifted the little wooden stirrer that had crystalized sugar rocked around it and dipped it in her cappuccino. Dinner had been better than good, and Bill had been interesting, attentive, and a perfect gentleman. Karen wondered, just for an instant, if she was disappointed by that. The thought shocked her. If there was one thing she knew about herself, she knew she wasn't that kind of girl. She and Jeffrey had resolved their problems. Things were good again. So what was she thinking of?

"So, did you hear about the ruckus on the main floor?" Bill asked.

"No," Karen said innocently.

"It seems that your friend Norris's perfume was bottled when the liquid was cold."

"Is that a problem?" Karen asked.

"Didn't you take physics in high school?" Bill asked. "When molecules heat they expand. But there was no room to expand in those goddamned bottles."

"So it wasn't champagne that I heard."

Bill laughed. "No, it was the sound of a business failing. Norris won't be able to talk her way out of this."

Karen thought of the cynical remarks Bill had made at their last lunch. Karen was glad at least one perfume would fail and women wouldn't be sold false hope. Bill seemed pleased with Norris's failure, but wouldn't he be happy to sell junk if it increased NormCo's bottom line?

But she had to question her moral ground. Who was she to judge anyone? Hadn't she just spent the day selling very costly clothes to very wealthy women? Where was the glory in that? She hadn't even had a chance to check out the bridge line with its more modest prices.

The steward brought a salver of paper-thin mints and cookies, then discreetly withdrew. They drank their coffee in silence. Karen had stayed in some of the world's best hotels, and Jeffrey had introduced her to a level of elegant living she'd never known before, but Bill Wolper's totally understated and completely luxurious way of life was on a new level, and one that Karen could appreciate. The food had been perfectly prepared, the table had been perfectly laid, and the appointments in the plane seemed beautifully arranged. There wasn't a scratch or a mark or a stain on anything. She felt as if she were in a costly jewelry case, and the surroundings were the mounting for a precious gem. She smiled to herself. There I go, thinking about mountings again. She couldn't help wondering whether Wolper was one to show as much attention to detail in bed.

She wondered what he would think of her if she told him all the things that were really on her mind. If he knew that she was adopting a child—or trying to—would he be afraid she wasn't dedicated enough? If he knew about her search for her mother, would he think she was flaky? Whatever the answer was, she knew she couldn't take a chance.

"Would you like to see the rest of the plane?" he asked.

"Sure," she told him. Aside from the salon and the dining area, which doubled as a conference room, Bill showed her the office complete with word processors, fax machines, and a phone console more complex than the one at KKInc. There were two full bathrooms, and then Bill took her down a narrow central hallway toward the back of the plane. He opened a cabin door and there was a bedroom, complete with a pencil-post canopy bed! He opened another, smaller door and there was another bathroom, this one with a tub.

"I've never heard of a bathtub on a plane before," she said. "Does the FAA approve?"

"I had to have it," Bill explained. "It wasn't to show off. I just can't bear to shower. Never have. I'm a bath man. How about you?"

"I'm not a man at all," she said, and moved smoothly out of the bedroom and back down the hall. Bill followed her, and if he was disappointed or impatient he didn't show it.

"Let's sit down in the salon," he suggested. They moved past the steward who was clearing the table. The plane lurched as they got into the open area of the salon, but Bill steadied Karen and helped her to a seat on the suede sofa. "Something to drink?" he asked.

"No, thanks," she told him. She knew that now was the time for him to apply the pressure and, sure enough, he leaned forward with his elbows on his knees.

"You know, Karen, I don't want to rush you, but we can't stall your husband and my lawyers for much longer. I need your answer. Do you think I would make a good partner to you?"

Well, of course that was why he had shown up. Had she thought it was just to see her? Sometimes her own naiveté surprised her. And she owed him an answer. He'd been very patient. Of course, he had used *some* hardball tactics. His appearance with Norris Cleveland had certainly been a warning of sorts, hadn't it?

"We've been through your numbers with a fine-toothed spreadsheet program. You know, you've got a lot of problems. Basil figures you have three-quarters of a million dollars in receivables that are as good as uncollectible. You need cash bad, and instead you got returns up the ying-yang, about twelve percent. I know you're just start up, but the industry average is only three to six percent. I could help you with all of that."

She looked across at the man. She remembered Bobby Pillar's words of caution and she knew that Bill was called just about every name in the book. From Wall Street to the Ginza he was loathed and feared. But, stupid as it seemed, she liked him, and maybe she should trust him. Jeffrey thought so. Karen had started the adoption process. Tomorrow morning the home visit was taking place, and Kramer's office was already drawing up the intent-to-adopt papers. Surely a baby would be found. She'd made the deal with Jeffrey, and she'd have to stick to it.

Plus there was something about Bill that made her feel protected, cared for. He treated her with the kind of care that a bird might show its egg. Always considered a strong woman by Jeffrey and all the people she worked with, it was both novel and immensely comforting to be mothered this way.

"So, what do you say?" Bill asked.

Karen nodded her head. "Make us the offer," she told him.

That night, Jeffrey was already asleep when Karen got home. She was exhausted and getting into her nightgown when the baby phone rang. Karen decided not to mention her lawyer on the first call, despite Kramer's advice, so she took a deep breath and answered the phone. The woman—Louise—was married, had two children already, and explained she had been separated from her husband when she got pregnant with the third. Now she and Leon were back together, but Leon didn't want to raise another man's child. Tired as she was, Karen decided Louise sounded serious and sober, if not very bright. Karen couldn't help but wonder what kind of genetic stock she might be buying into, but she took Louise's number and promised to call her the next day.

20

WHIRLING DERVITZ

Sheila Dervitz must have been close to three hundred pounds. She was dressed in a sky blue sack-like suit and carried a large, cheap, navy blue leather briefcase. A hot pink and mustard scarf was draped around her neck. If fashion was a political barometer—and Karen believed it was—then Sheila Dervitz was still a part of the Rainbow Coalition. Karen tried not to wince when she looked at the woman, who was the social worker doing the home visit. It had been a bitch to steal away for the morning—there was so much to do—and then Sheila Dervitz had been late in showing up. She didn't apologize either. She just said she'd had a busy day yesterday. Karen wondered if Miss Dervitz had started off her yesterday at 5 A.M. and flown to Chicago and back.

"Let me get this straight," Defina had asked. "*You* pay her to tell the state that *you're* okay?" Karen had nodded. "Seems like a conflict of interests to me," Defina said, and Karen had to agree. "But why don't you just pay her twice as much and tell her to skip the visit?" Dee asked.

Now, Karen wished she could. She was exhausted, but faced the big blonde woman who sat on the sofa opposite her yet kept turning her head, this way and that, as if she saw rats in corners. Karen tried to appear relaxed. "I see you have a lot of books," Miss Dervitz commented. Karen turned and looked at the shelves behind her.

"Yes, we do," she agreed. Somehow, the way Miss Dervitz said it made it sound as if books were a bad thing.

"Are any of them inappropriate for children?"

"I'm sure a lot of them are," Karen said. Why hadn't she thought about the books?

"Do you mind if I take a look?"

"Not at all." Karen tried to say it as if she meant it. She looked around the living room. While she'd been in Chicago, Ernesta had outdone herself. There wasn't a mote of dust on anything. The windows, the mirror, and the glass in the bookshelves all gleamed. The floor had been freshly waxed and buffed. For the last two days Ernesta had insisted they all walk around in socks. Last night, after she got in from the airport, Karen herself had arranged the mauve spray roses in a vase on the demilune table, and this morning she and Ernesta, giggling, had made up the bed in the spare room with teddy bear sheets. Karen and Jeffrey had already gone through a painful first interview with Miss Dervitz in her office and now there was only this home visit before they were legally approved by the State of New York as potential adoptive parents. Had Belle and Arnold actually gone through this? Karen would have liked to have seen that home visit report! Would Belle have been intimidated the way Karen was? Karen doubted it. But the phone call from Louise meant Karen had a real baby on the line, if Miss Dervitz would let her keep it. Karen took a deep breath as the woman who would decide her future lumbered along the rows of books. Was she looking for pornography? Did the books of nudes from her life drawing classes at Pratt count? Oh, God, this was making her crazy!

"The cabinets lock," Karen told the woman. Then she felt as if that sounded as if they had something to hide. Miss Dervitz didn't say anything. She just spun around on her tippy toes, looking a lot like the hippo ballerinas in *Fantasia*. Why did Karen feel as if that meant she disapproved?

Karen felt powerless and Jeffrey certainly wasn't helping. So far he had not tried to make this interview pleasant. When Miss Dervitz had asked him if he felt he was capable of being a nurturing parent, he had shrugged. "Who knows for sure?" he asked. When she asked him if he had deep religious beliefs, he had told her he had deep *anti*-religious beliefs. Then he excused himself and went in to the office. Great!

Karen tried to be diplomatic, to explain and soften his answers and pick up the slack, but she felt that Miss Dervitz was busy comparing all that Karen had to her own life. The social worker asked a lot of questions about how frequently they went out, the kind of parties they attended, and gossipy questions about what restaurants they frequented and how much it cost to eat in them. Karen had tried to answer all Miss Dervitz's questions and charm her with glitz, but then was taken aback when the woman asked sternly the amount of time they really had to spend with a child. Karen had assured Miss Dervitz that she was not looking at this as a hobby. "I'm planning to cut back on my business commitments," she said. "Raising a baby would really be my first priority."

"You have a child selected?" Miss Dervitz asked. She made it sound like Karen had gone out shopping for socks.

"Well, there are a few mothers we have been talking with," Karen lied. She thought again of Louise. Would that amount to anything? Miss Dervitz grimly took some notes.

She wondered now if she should offer Miss Dervitz a visit to KKInc. Would it complicate things and make them worse? Should she offer Miss Dervitz some clothes at wholesale price? Would that seem like a bribe? Would a bribe work? And did she have anything that would possibly fit Miss Dervitz?

Now the social worker stopped and held up a book. It was Rushdie's *Satanic Verses*. "What's this?" she asked and did another pirouette.

"A novel." Didn't Miss Dervitz know that? Did the woman think Karen was a devil worshiper? "It's about the Islamic as opposed to the Christian view of the world."

"But you *are* Jews?" Miss Dervitz asked, spinning around again.

Karen nodded. Was *she* going crazy? Or was Miss Dervitz certifiable? Hadn't she heard about Salmon Rushdie? And if Karen told her about him would she sound condescending?

Miss Dervitz put the book away. Karen was about to say something when the phone rang. She moved to it and lifted the receiver, keeping an eye on the social worker. "Hello?" Who would be calling me here now? she wondered.

"Karen?" Lisa's voice was shriller than usual. "Are you sick?"

"No."

"So what are you doing home now?"

"Lisa, can I call you back?"

"You never call me back. Listen, I only need a minute of your time. The caterers just called me and they can't get black chintz for the table clothes. But I think taffeta is too wintery. What do you think?"

Karen didn't have a clue. What the hell was her sister talking about? Meanwhile, Miss Dervitz was disappearing down the hallway toward the bedrooms. Karen lowered her voice. "Lisa! I'm sorry I haven't called you back but I really can't talk to you now. I'm in the middle of something."

"Karen! Are you having an affair?"

Where the hell did *that* come from? No time to ask now. That was all she needed: talking about adultery while the social worker made a home visit. "I'll call you back," she told her sister and hung up the phone.

She found Miss Dervitz looking for dust balls under the bed in the spare room. Together they moved into the master bedroom. Karen couldn't believe it when Miss Dervitz began opening dresser drawers. Even if Karen *was* a devil-worshiping child pornographer, wouldn't she have the sense to get rid of all the evidence in preparation for the social worker's call? What in the world was the point of this? Karen held her tongue. Then Miss Dervitz went to her closet.

"Well, you certainly don't have much to wear, being a designer and all," she said brightly. She looked at the array of neutral-colored clothes hanging neatly on the rack. "Maybe you should think of spicing this up with some cheery colors," Miss Dervitz suggested. Karen told herself she was coming one step closer to making a home for Louise's baby. She tried to smile and nodded her head.

"What a good idea," she said.

That evening, and the next and the next, Karen spoke with Louise. Each call lasted over an hour. Karen felt Louise was developing trust in her. She brought up Harvey's name on the third night that they talked and Louise seemed comfortable with it. The next day, Monday, Harvey's office FedExed a package of legal, medical, and background forms to Louise. She filled them in and returned them within two days. Karen began to let herself get excited. This was her reward for moving forward with the Real Deal, for getting straight with Jeffrey. Everything would be all right. Before Louise called again, Karen showed all the information to Jeffrey and prepped him to speak with the woman. Jeffrey was nice to her, and when he handed the phone back to Karen, Louise had sighed. "He sounds so sweet," she said, and Karen could hear the wonder and the longing in Louise's voice. She wondered what Leon was like, and what price Louise had paid for her lapse.

Karen and Jeffrey paid for a sonogram for Louise and it looked like the baby was a girl. Karen began to think about how she would break the news to Belle and the rest of the family. So far this had been a secret along with the bad news from Dr. Goldman. But now, perhaps, it was time to share. Now that she didn't have only bad news to tell them. Falling asleep, after another marathon call with Louise, Karen had time to ask herself one question: Did she keep her bad news from her family to spare them pain or to spare herself?

21

TONGUE IN CHIC

Casey, some of his staff, Jeffrey, and Mercedes sat with Karen around the conference room table. They were going over weekly sales figures as well as the final tally of orders that the trunk show had garnered. The farm wife dress definitely had all the earmarks of being a runner—what they called a style that would be reordered over and over, as if it ran out of the store. In fact, it had all the earmarks of becoming a Ford—a design that would be copied by all the lower-priced knock-off artists in the business. It looked as if all the new designs that Karen had snuck in had done very well. It was, of course, no guarantee that the press or the Parisians would like them, but it gave all of them what Casey, in his best marketese, called a "positive indicator."

"We wrote orders till our hands hurt!" Casey told the group now, proud. "I'm telling you, these are the best sales figures ever!"

Jeffrey looked at him. "Those aren't sales figures," he said. "Those are orders. You know how many things can happen between getting that order and delivery five months from now? We have to get the orders booked and hope the goddamned factory will extend credit and make them. Then we got to hope they make them right. Then, if they sell in the store, if they don't get returned, we have to hope Chicago pays us before the interest eats up our profit or the factor shuts us down. You didn't make a *sale*. You only took an *order*. A *sale* is when a check comes in after an invoice has been sent."

"Jesus, Jeffrey! You know what I meant."

"Yeah, but do *you* know what *I* meant?"

Jeffrey had become more and more difficult. He jumped at everyone. Karen raised her brows at him and he calmed down but she knew what he was waiting for. The rest of the meeting was just routine—the usual reorders and sales volumes, problems with returns, and worse problems with receivables. Karen sighed. Because they had no track record with the big-volume manufacturers, they were having trouble getting delivery and the quality they wanted. Of all other designers, Karen envied Jil Sander most because Jil had grown slowly and had her own meticulous factory.

Karen shook her head. When business was so good, how could it also be so bad? She figured she could excuse herself. Jeffrey would have to sort it out. She simply had too much to do to waste time with this stuff. She'd be working through the weekend, and she had to take off time for Tiff's *bat mitzvah*. It left only six days until Paris. Not enough. Even cutting out all routine meetings, when she thought about the lineup for the next few weeks, she wasn't sure if she could make it.

The fashion world had two main seasons: Spring and Fall. The Spring line was shown in autumn and the Fall line was shown in early spring. Plus, there were two condensed lines for Summer and Winter. And there were also the less important holiday and resort lines each year. But the seasons were deceptive. There were actually two shows for each season: couture and ready-to-wear. And, if you were doing your collection internationally, you presented it first in Milano, then in Paris, and lastly, in New York. Not only that, but during those incredibly hectic Fashion Weeks you also tried to get a peek at other designers' collections, and showed the line again privately to buyers from all over the world. It was totally draining, and it was all about to start again. Karen would never forget coming through her first Fashion Week, exhausted and rung out, only to be called by an important editor the next Monday. "So, what's coming up for your next collection?" the journalist had asked. And she wasn't joking.

Since then, the things that had changed were only that Karen had gotten older and had more work to do. Year by year, it seemed, she loaded more tasks on her shoulders. The business had expanded from a small couture line twice a year to a big couture line five times a year, as well as a bridge line that did ten times the volume in sales. Karen had only done New York up to now, and showing the couture and bridge line here had been enough of a challenge.

In the fall of '93, American designers for the first time had gotten together and created Seventh on Sixth, a group of shows held not in individual showrooms, discos, hotel ballrooms, and the like, but in fashion tents in

Bryant Park, a block-long square on Sixth Avenue behind New York City's main library. Between the two hi-tech white tents that had been erected and the spaces that had been used in the library itself, Seventh Avenue had done a fairly good job of consolidating itself.

Karen had been one of the designers to lead the movement, and KKInc had gotten better coverage and more respect from the European press and more business from the buyers because of it. Now, though, thinking of the trial that Paris would be, only to be followed by the usual New York Fashion Week, Karen felt close to collapse. She just might not be able to do it. And there was no one who could do it for her.

Casey was droning on, when Jeffrey's secretary interrupted them and whispered something to Jeffrey. She handed him an envelope and Jeffrey began to tear the manila flap open even before she was finished whispering. He pulled out the substantial stack of papers, threw the envelope onto the table, and began riffling through the stapled pile. Karen saw that the envelope bore the NormCo logo.

Jeffrey's face lit up as he read the papers. Casey had stopped his report and Jeffrey stood up. "Ladies and gentleman, I have something to announce. This is it, folks. I've got the news we've all been waiting for. We have the NormCo offer here and it's for fifty million dollars! Fifty million. Can you read my lips?"

The whole room exploded into sound. Mercedes began to clap. One of the guys whooped like a sports fan after a touchdown. Casey began to ask questions, while Jeffrey, ignoring him, started to read part of the offer aloud. "And Bill Wolper himself plans to meet us in Paris to finalize the deal!" Jeffrey declared.

Jeffrey's secretary returned with several bottles of champagne. It was only eleven o'clock in the morning, but Jeffrey popped one open while the secretary distributed plastic glasses. He must have planned ahead. Staff had already gathered in the hallway, trying to poke their heads in to hear what all the noise was about. Someone thrust a plastic glass into Karen's hand. It was goblet-shaped, but no one had put the plastic base on it, so Karen couldn't lay it down. "To Karen," somebody shouted, and everybody raised their glasses. "To Karen," they all echoed, and Karen tried to smile though her stomach was knotted. Across the table, in the doorway, stood Defina. Karen's eyes met Dee's. Dee lifted her glass but she didn't smile either; she merely raised her brows and nodded her head.

Karen watched all the staff celebrate. Oh, what the hell! It wasn't every day a working girl got an offer worth millions. Jeffrey was right: she worried too much. She might as well relax and enjoy this, and if she had mixed feelings about giving up control of her company, she'd just have to learn to wince all the way to the bank.

Jeffrey had invited the core group out for a celebratory lunch. Mercedes, usually cool and pale, was actually flushed. Her eyes flickered a deeper green than ever. Karen wondered if it was the upcoming infusion of cash that had caused the color change.

They sat in the Pool Room of the Four Seasons. It was a wonderful space, one of the few truly elegant dining rooms in the city. At lunchtime the Grill Room was far more prestigious, but Karen had always preferred it here, with the ceiling almost as high as the room was wide. The center reflecting pool was as beautiful and understated as the rest of the room. The huge windows were uncurtained and draped with fine chains that rippled with the least breeze. The tables were widely separated by that greatest of all luxuries in New York: space. Karen had always felt that this was a sanctuary: nothing bad could happen to you at the Four Seasons.

Now the captain took their lunch orders. God! It immediately became a production. All of the women, with the exception of Karen and Defina, were fashion hounds who ate the way a thin New York woman ate: that is to say, next to nothing at all. Karen had always hated little fashion lunches with editors and buyers for that reason. There was a strange kind of reverse macho that went on. If men asserted their superiority by being able to outdrink one another, fashionable New York career women did it by undereating. Invariably, they looked at the intriguing menu and then ordered only a bottled water and an appetizer-sized portion of the tomato and basil salad as their main course. Then they'd tell the waiter to hold the oil. If you broke down and took a piece of the fabulous bread, they'd look at you, silent and shocked, as if you'd loudly farted. Karen's strategy was simple: she just ordered a Caesar salad and then went back to the office and ate later.

Mercedes told them all she was on a new diet. She explained it: "No starch. Not any. No pasta, no bread, no potatoes. Starch is the absolute killer." She was preaching like an evangelist, not that any of the men were interested. But all the skinny young girls from Casey's staff and the women from the showroom wanted the details.

"But can you have rice?" one of them asked.

"Never!" Mercedes almost shouted. "Rice is a sin. It's positively evil."

"Doesn't she sound like an evangelist?" Karen asked Defina.

"Un-uh, honey. That's worse than an evangelist. That's the Anti-Rice."

Karen snorted into her glass of mineral water. Finally, the lunch ordering was over, just in time for the drinking to begin. Karen had never seen the group as riotous, and for once even Jeffrey got into the act. They toasted and drank and laughed until way past three o'clock. Karen just went with the flow. After all, she told herself, once she got the money and her baby, all of these problems would be owned by Bill Wolper.

It was two nights later that Karen ran into trouble. Louise called, collect, as she always did at nine o'clock. Karen was ready for her. Louise had put her two kids to bed and was waiting for Leon to return from the night shift. Louise had signed the papers and returned them to Kramer's office. She'd accepted Karen's offer to pay the medical bills. She said her ankles were swollen, but that had happened in her first two pregnancies. Karen was sympathetic. They were having a hot spell in Arkansas and, despite Kramer's warnings, Karen wanted to send Louise an air conditioner. But when she offered, Louise turned her down. "It ain't Christmas," she said flatly. Then she paused. "What do you-all do for Christmas?" she asked. "Do you put up a tree?"

Without thinking, Karen answered her. "No," she said. "We're Jewish."

There was a pause. "What?" Louise asked. Her voice had changed completely. It was hard to believe so much shock and dismay could be packed into a single word. Karen felt her stomach lurch.

"We're Jewish," she repeated.

There was silence at the other end of the phone. Then Louise spoke, but her voice sounded different. "You didn't tell me that," she said. It sounded like an accusation.

"I'm sorry," Karen said. "I didn't think it was important."

Was that a gasp she heard at the other end of the phone? Karen bit her lip. "Please, Louise . . . " she began.

"We're God-fearing people," Louise said. Her voice, despite the softening of the Arkansas accent, sounded hard now. "You might not believe that, because of my situation and all. But just because I have to give my baby up doesn't mean I don't love it and Jesus." She stopped. "I love my baby, and I love Jesus, and there's no way I'm goin' to let my baby be raised by Jews." She hung up the phone.

Karen held on to the receiver. For a few minutes it was dead, but then it began to bleep in an unbearable tattoo. Karen had to move then, even if it was only to fold up the portable phone. But despite her movement, she felt paralyzed. Somehow, she knew it would do no good to call Louise back. She had just lost her baby, and she was about to sell her other one. Karen sat there, stunned.

The only thing she wanted was her mother. And her mother couldn't be found. She sat, paralyzed, for a long, long time.

Alone in the dark, Karen decided that, no matter what trouble it caused, she would ask Arnold or Belle or both of them for her birthright.

PART THREE
SLAVES TO FASHION

I have shut my little sister in from life and light
(For a rose, for a ribbon, for a wreath across my hair)
—Margaret Widdemer

22

AN AFFAIR TO REMEMBER

Lisa Saperstein looked into the full-length mirror as intently as if she were reading an eye chart. She was in the gray silk Thierry Mugler that she had overpaid for. But now that she looked most critically at herself, wasn't the gray bad for her coloring? Arrayed on the bed was the linen three-piece outfit that Karen had given her. Lisa didn't want to hurt Karen's feelings, but she knew she'd look like a wrinkled mess in ten minutes if she wore that. Her other choice was a melon-colored silk broadcloth dress, a Bill Blass, that she had picked up cheap at Loehman's. She'd been through all this a dozen times and had decided on the Mugler, but now, at the last minute, she wasn't sure. She struggled out of the Mugler and put the Blass on. Certainly, it looked the best, but it was also the most predictable. And it showed a lot of leg. Too much? She wasn't as young as she used to be. Her eyes rose from her hemline to her head. Oh, great! Now her hair was going flat. She knew she should have used more mousse. Well, she had a hat that matched the Blass. She pulled at her hair. She felt as if she was going crazy. Did she want to be a big-shouldered, avant-garde Thierry Mugler type, or a soft but not overly feminine Karen Kahn type, or a conservative but feline Bill Blass type? Why hadn't she made this decision before?

Lisa had always defined herself by what she put on. But she was never quite sure that she put on the right thing, until she saw other women's reactions. She had been mortified when neither Sooky nor Buff had noticed her outfit at Karen's brunch, just as she had been gratified at the St. Regis to see that two smartly dressed, obviously wealthy women, lunching together, had turned to check her out. It had been an accolade, most valuable because it was grudgingly given.

She thought for a moment of her lunch with Jeffrey. And the phone calls since then. It had felt good to be confided in and very good to go to public places with such a good-looking, interesting man. Because they had met several times now. But it definitely had not felt good to know that Karen had kept so much from her. She hadn't seen her sister since the Westport brunch, unless you counted seeing her on television. Why had her sister become so inaccessible and secretive? And when had she gotten the idea of looking for her other mother? Lisa, when she thought of that, felt sad. Didn't Karen want to be part of their family? Once they had been so close. Why hadn't Karen confided in her about the sale to NormCo and about Dr. Goldman? Lisa knew her sister must be taking that news hard, so why had she still not come to Lisa to be comforted and consoled? Why had she still not called?

Lisa thought about her own two girls. Sometimes she felt as if they were more trouble than they were worth. But what would her life be without them? She shrugged. Well, she wouldn't be going to this *bat mitzvah* today! And she knew other women envied her, having a daughter as beautiful as Stephanie. Surely, Karen must envy her. That gave her a moment of pleasure because she felt that so often she was the one being jealous. But if she could, would she trade her daughters for the excitement and importance of Karen's career? Lisa stopped looking in the mirror. She didn't know. But she *did* know that if Karen sold out, she, Lisa, could do a lot with the money. Why, they could move to Lawrence! She could completely rethink her wardrobe. She could get a really good fur coat. And trade the old diesel Mercedes in for a new convertible. Property values had fallen, and since the kids were going to be out of school soon, perhaps they could even afford to live in Manhattan. As soon as the *bat mitzvah* was over, she would *have* to talk to her sister and help Jeffrey convince Karen that selling the company was a good thing. What did Leonard know! That worthless stock wasn't worthless after all!

And then it occurred to her. If she had a million dollars, she would leave Leonard. What, after all, did she need him for?

She looked back at herself in the mirror. God, why was she thinking of divorce this morning of all mornings? Was it because Jeffrey had clearly found her attractive? Maybe some other man would. Who knows? Maybe today somebody would see her and think that she was much too young to be the mother of a *bat mitzvah* girl. Still, as Lisa struggled into her control-top pantyhose, she knew it wasn't the men she was dressing for.

Today she would be in front of a hundred and fifty pairs of eyes, more than half of which would be female. Of those, she really only cared about a dozen, the most successful, the most social of the group. She wanted them to accept her. It never occurred to Lisa that the girl in the prettiest dress was not the most popular.

Lisa had carefully culled the guest list, leavening the Five Towns' heavy hitters with the glitter that would attract them. Her sister, of course, was a drawing card. People always wanted to meet her, especially since the latest TV exposure. But Lisa had also dropped the word that June Silverman would be there. Since her divorce, June was always appearing in Manhattan gossip columns. And Lisa had also invited June's ex, the artist Perry. So people knew a semi-famous SoHo artist was coming, too. Lisa didn't really know them, but both had accepted. She hoped they were still cordial to one another. Well, she would seat them at separate tables. One of Lisa's girlfriends from college was now an actress on the soaps, and though Lisa hadn't seen her in years, she had called her specially and nearly begged her to come.

Of course, no one admitted to watching daytime TV, but since they all knew both her sister and the actress were coming to the party, at least half a dozen people had called Lisa to casually mention that as they were flipping through the channels they'd seen Karen on an "Elle Halle" or Susan on "The Gathering Storm." Lisa made sure the word got out that they were coming, knowing this would assure the best guests would RSVP affirmatively. And, in the end, they had.

She had worked hard on everything from the seating arrangements to the flowers to the band to the choreography of the candle-lighting ceremony. She'd actually written Tiff's speech for her on little three-by-five cards. She'd hired a great video guy and an even better still photographer. She'd forced Leonard to get a new tuxedo. For once, just for once, everything was going to be perfect.

At last, dressed and with the hat perched on her head, Lisa was ready. The family left together, Leonard driving, Stephanie sitting beside him, and Lisa and Tiff in the back seat of the old Mercedes. If Karen had made the deal already, I won't have to ride in a heap like this one, Lisa thought resentfully. She sat up very straight so she wouldn't wrinkle the Blass that she, in the end, had decided to wear, but Tiffany slumped and her taffeta would soon look as crumpled as gift wrap on the eighth night of Chanukah. "Sit up," Lisa told the child, but kept her voice low so that Leonard wouldn't hear. They had already argued this morning. Tiff ignored her mother, staring out the window as if Lisa and the rest of the family didn't exist. Her daughter had taken on the greenish tint of her dress, or was it just a reflection? For the first time, Lisa felt a tiny tremor of fear begin in her stomach and butterfly up to her chest. She had prepared for everything. But what if Tiffany hadn't prepared as well?

Karen spent her morning at the office, frantically tearing the collection apart. Since she and Jeffrey had made their Real Deal she had been filled with energy. Now, since Louise had refused to give them the baby, she felt drained, lost, and miserable, but she had to work on the collection and was operating on pure desperation. Her only comfort was that, despite the two false starts, Sally at Harvey Kramer's office had assured her that in the end this would work. "Those two didn't have the normal profile anyway," Sally had said. "To tell you the truth, I was never really comfortable with Louise. You're looking for a smarter-than-average young kid who's looking for a way out of trouble. And believe me, she's looking for you. It will come, I promise you." Karen carried the cellular phone with her this morning, but aside from a wrong number that almost made her heart stop, nothing materialized.

Meanwhile, the Paris deadline ticked like a bomb as she made her eleventh-hour changes. She always went through a crisis just before she did a show, but this was worse than usual. Paris had her jittery. She reminded herself of Chanel's motto: "Keep working till you hate the sight of it." So today, this morning before Tiff's *bat mitzvah*, she was working nonstop. She was grateful to everyone for coming in on the weekend, but her gratitude didn't stop her from feeling miserable and driving them crazy.

She had to leave at three, to everyone's relief. Karen and Jeffrey had been prepared to drive out to Inwood for the *bat mitzvah* ceremony and stay, of course, for the reception. But because of the two shows and last-minute problems, they were changing plans and going by limo. Then, immediately after the ceremony, Jeffrey would go to JFK and fly to Paris. He was playing advance man, trying to ease things through customs with a bundle of cash and firm up some of the final arrangements. Once he'd been dropped off, the limo would double back, pick up Karen from the party, and return her to the office for a midnight review. Karen knew that all afternoon and evening, while she attended the festivities, Mrs. Cruz and all of the staff would be working their brains out. It made her feel guilty, but there was no way she could miss Tiff's *bat mitzvah*. Despite the urgency of the Paris collection, for once Karen couldn't use work as an excuse. She'd been late for and missed too much other family business. Still, the timing was incredibly bad.

She ran home at the very last minute and tore into the shower, ready to get dressed. But even if *she* felt resentful, she didn't allow *Jeffrey* to react. He had been in a really upbeat mood since they'd gotten the offer, but now, he was cranky. "Who the hell ever heard of a black tie *bat mitzvah*? Beginning at five? I don't need this, Karen. Not with the week we've got ahead of us. And until the deal is signed and the NormCo check clears, anything could queer it." He looked at her with concern. "How's the finishing off? You don't have much time."

"I know that," she snapped.

"Why you had to pick this year to show in Paris is beyond me."

Karen glared at him. It had been a mutual decision, but now that fifty million hung in the balance it had become her fault. Typical. She decided just to let this one roll by, or else they would be in a fight that would wind up with him refusing to go this afternoon, and there was *no way* he was getting out of this.

As if he knew her thoughts, he looked up and grinned. "I don't want to have to do this," he admitted. "Christ, all I want to do is lock myself in the studio and paint. I don't need *any* of this. The whole ceremony is a trumped-up ridiculous thing in the first place. My sisters didn't get *bat mitzvahed. You* didn't get *bat mitzvahed.*" Karen just sighed. She could read him like a book. A children's book.

"Girls didn't get *bat mitzvahs* that often when we were thirteen," she reminded him.

"Exactly my point! Even the word is stupid. The Jewish tradition goes back five thousand years. Coming of age for a boy meant a *bar mitzvah.* That was it. So how long have they been doing *bat mitzvahs?*"

"Since women were aware enough to resent the daily prayer Jewish men are supposed to pray," Karen said. He looked at her blankly. "You know," she smiled sweetly, "the one that thanks God for not having created you a woman."

"Oh, come on. Nobody does that stuff anymore."

"Well, they still do *bar mitzvahs*, so they may as well do *bat mitzvahs.* Otherwise the message is that girls don't count."

"Yeah, right! Religion should be like the Little League."

"Well, why not? Tiff is the first girl in our family to ever be officially confirmed in the Jewish religion. When you think about it, that's something to celebrate."

"Oh, come on. When's the last time you set foot in a *shul?* Anyway, religion isn't about being politically correct. It's tradition, that's all. Look what happened to the Catholic Church after the pope did that Vatican II number. Meat on Fridays, and they went right down the tubes."

"Well, I'm proud of Tiff. This is really an accomplishment for her. She's doing this for all of us."

He gave her a look. "Tiffany Saperstein, Religious Role Model. I think she comes right after Joan of Arc in the Book of Martyrs. And can you tell me why Leonard and Lisa invited my mother and sisters?"

"Being polite, I guess."

"But they hardly *know* them. Do you know they asked June?"

Karen opened her eyes wide. Was Lisa nuts? Why would she invite Jeffrey's ex-fiancée, Perry's ex-wife? Karen wouldn't show her surprise to Jeffrey, though. He'd win extra points for Lisa's crassness. Karen would be loyal to her sister, even if Lisa did seem to be insensitive at best.

"Oh, stop it. You just don't want to be hassled with putting your studs in." Now, as he struggled to get his arm through the overstarched sleeve of his dress shirt, he managed to smile at her. He did like the sapphires. "Lighten up, would ya?" she asked him. "Just for me. Just as a favor." Then the doorman rang them. The car was already waiting. "Oh, God! Jeffrey, we can't be late."

"Hey, it's not me who has to blow-dry my hair."

It wasn't until they got downstairs and saw the limo that Jeffrey really lost it. "What the fuck is this?" he demanded. There was a twenty-two-foot-long, super-stretch, white Cadillac limousine waiting at the awning for them. George, the weekend doorman, was grinning.

"Jesus, Jeffrey," she said, "*I* didn't order it." The car was obscenely white. The driver got out. He, too, was all in white—a white three-piece suit, white dress shirt, and white cap. The Tom Wolfe of chauffeurs, Karen thought, but didn't dare say anything.

"Holy Christ, it's one of the Rockettes!" Jeffrey snapped. He turned to her. "Karen, I am *not* getting into that car. Pimps drive around in white Caddies. Nobody I know has *ever* been in anything but a black limo. Kahns don't do this. My mother would die first."

"Genghis Kahn, upholder of the family honor. Jeffrey, I have no time for this now. Janet called at the last minute when we decided not to take the Jag, and I forgot to tell her to specify that no Kahn ever rides in a *limo blanco*. The service probably sent this as a courtesy. Now shut up and get in. This is one time I can't afford to be fashionably late." Jeffrey shook his head with helplessness and disgust. He flapped his arms on either side and, in his formal wear, it came off as a fairly good imitation of an extremely tall, anguished penguin.

"Fine," he said, "but if this is how the party is starting, I don't want to think about the next four hours. *Excruciating* is a word I'd rather say than experience."

The driver had difficulty finding the temple, so Karen and Jeffrey arrived only moments before the service was scheduled to begin. They had no time to ditch it, so the ridiculous car pulled up right out front, where overdressed women were clustered at the door. All heads turned. Karen sighed. She had wanted this to be Lisa's moment, and Tiff's. She wanted—just for once—not to be noticed, not to be the famous older sister, but to let Lisa have this all to herself. The car halted.

"Don't get out here in front," Jeffrey commanded the driver. "We're enough of a spectacle as it is," he muttered to Karen. But it was too late. The driver hadn't heard Jeffrey or chose to ignore him. The guy was out and the door was opened with a flourish and the people were staring and there was nothing left to do but to step out onto the sidewalk, and simply be grateful that the driver hadn't unrolled a red carpet, or held aloft a glass slipper. They got out and joined the other guests.

Lisa, Tiff, and Leonard stood just inside the door, a tiny welcoming committee. Karen saw that Tiff was wearing the pearls, along with the ridiculous taffeta dress. She kissed her niece. "Neat car," Tiff said, stretching the two syllables out until they were almost a yodel.

Karen smiled. "Would you like me to take you to the reception in it?"

"Yes, please!" Tiff breathed, her eyes widening. Sometimes Karen forgot that despite her height her niece was still very young.

"She can't," Lisa said curtly. Karen noticed that her sister wasn't wearing either of the two outfits she'd sent over. Oh well. Instead Lisa had on something stiff, and with a matching hat! Lisa turned to her daughter. "We have the two buses coming to take the guests over to the reception. You have to be on the first bus." Tiff's face froze over in that look of mulish resentment it so often wore. Karen felt as if she could kick herself. She'd made a grand entrance *and* interfered in Lisa's plans. She hadn't taken a seat yet, and she had already fucked up twice. She kissed her sister's cheek. She'd wait 'til later to tell her that Jeffrey couldn't stay for the reception. There was so much that she hadn't spoken to Lisa about. But she had been so busy and Lisa had been inundated with a million details of the party. Still, Karen felt a small stab of guilt. Perhaps she didn't like telling good news to Lisa because she felt, sometimes, that it made Lisa feel as if her own life was insignificant. And she didn't like to tell bad news to Lisa because . . . well, she wasn't sure why, but somehow she hadn't wanted to talk to Lisa about Dr. Goldman or the horrible Harvey Kramer or Louise and the whole dialing for daughters episode. As she did so often, Karen suspected her own motivations. Was she protecting Lisa, or was she protecting herself?

She leaned forward and kissed Leonard. He looked grim and shook hands limply with Jeffrey. Karen heard the little whispers and saw the nudges that happened so often now when she appeared in a crowd. "Her sister," she heard somebody say. "Her sister." The whisper seemed to run like a sibilant wave through the knot of people at the door to the sanctuary. Belle and Arnold were standing there greeting friends. Karen kissed them, moving quickly, hoping to get through the door and take a seat, getting the attention off herself as soon as possible. This was Tiff and Lisa's day. But when Karen turned from her mother to kiss her father, she stopped dead for a moment. Speaking of dead, Arnold looked ghastly. How long had it been since she'd seen him? The brunch hadn't been that long ago. What was wrong with him? A big man, it looked as if he had shrunk, and certainly his face was ashen. "Daddy? Are you all right?" she asked. Arnold hugged her.

"I'm fine. You look wonderful. How are you, Jeffrey?" Despite his assurance, Karen stared at her father. He *didn't* look fine. His skin seemed too big for his head, hanging in jowls, yet it also seemed as if his skull had shrunken. His cheek bones jutted severely and his nose, always arched, now looked razor-sharp. The only softness to his face were the puffy bags under his eyes, and they seemed as big as satchels.

A crowd had gathered behind Karen, waiting to go in. Jeffrey nudged her and she walked through the sanctuary door, leaving her parents behind.

The room was enormous and modern, with some kind of horrible architecture that Karen imagined the inside of a nuclear reactor would look like. A vast sweep of cement up one side served as a decorative wall and the ceiling sloped down asymmetrically from there. In the front, an enormous glass window backed the dais and was interrupted only by the tabernacle housing and the small modern stone podium that served as a pulpit. The seats, movie-theater style, were upholstered in a hellacious orange plush. The windows had an ugly orange-stained glass motif and cast a pumpkin glow over everybody. Orange was Karen's least favorite color. Karen walked down the aisle and quickly took a seat. She looked around at the guests. Her mother had no siblings, but Arnold had four. Yet none of them had been invited, or if they had, they had chosen not to attend. In fact, there didn't seem to be anybody of Belle and Arnold's age, except Lisa's mother- and father-in-law. The group was mostly lots of young children and their young parents. Where were all of Tiff's friends? These events were usually filled with teens. Didn't they still line up and dance the Alley Cat at the reception? That's what had happened at the *bar mitzvahs* Karen had attended as a kid.

Karen covertly scanned the crowd again. Everyone was, in her opinion, overdressed, except for Sylvia, Sooky, and Buff, who waved from the other side of the aisle. As always, they looked understated. Well, perhaps for once a bit *too* understated. After all, this *was* black tie. Was it a sign of their contempt? But the quantity of glitz, sequins, and beading on the rest of the women was astonishing. Looking around, Karen realized she didn't recognize any other guests. Who were these people, Karen wondered?

Jeffrey looked at his watch. They were already late in starting. People were getting restive. At last, a cameraman walked down the aisle and made some minor adjustments. Then, from the back of the sanctuary, Tiff, Lisa, Leonard, Stephanie, and Belle and Arnold walked in. They were followed by the rabbi. Slowly, they walked down the entire aisle nodding to friends. Lisa's big straw hat was the exact melon color of her dress. What in the world was she doing? With her wide smile and her hat and her stiff-wristed waves at the audience, she looked like a Jewish Princess Di. At the first row of seats Belle, Arnold, and Stephanie stopped and sat down with the elder Sapersteins, but the rest of them continued up the three shallow steps to the dais. There, on either side of the tabernacle, modernistic stone chairs were arranged. Leonard, Lisa, and Tiff took seats while the rabbi began the service.

Karen had never gone to Hebrew school or even Sunday school. Arnold had always been a pinko agnostic and Belle could never be bothered. On High Holy Days, she had *schlepped* the girls to services but Karen had spent the time daydreaming. She hadn't gone to temple in years. She doubted that Belle had. Did Lisa and Leonard really care about all this? Karen had never heard them mention God.

Why do people turn to religion when they have kids, she wondered. It seemed a kind of automatic thing. Lisa had once said she wanted the girls to grow up with a sense of reverence, but when Karen asked her if their own pilgrimages with Belle at the holidays had given Lisa reverence, she had changed the subject and Karen dropped it. She hadn't wanted to sound critical.

Karen smiled grimly as she thought of the irony of losing the baby, Louise's baby, because she wasn't Christian. Well, she certainly wasn't a Jew, except in the birth sense. And then she stopped. For all she knew, she might not be a Jew by birth, either. Religion had been so unimportant to her, she had never considered that before. Who knows, maybe I'm Polish Catholic. But could I have told Louise anything different than what I did? Even if it meant I'd get to keep the child? Karen thought of the baby that she might have been given, and bit her lip. It seemed she was not Jewish enough to find comfort in this ceremony, but she *was* Jewish enough to be prevented from getting the child. It wasn't fair. Where would Louise place the child now?

I wanted that baby, I deserved that baby, and I would have been good for it. Better than its real mother. That thought made her pause. She was so confused. If she raised the child, would it be better off or would it always miss its birth mother, always feel uncomfortable, an outsider, as she did. That was not a heritage she would wish on a child. She herself would have been a lot happier if she could feel part of this or any group.

Now, as the cantor joined the rabbi and the service began, Karen had to admit that there was something moving about the tradition of gathering together to welcome a new generation into the fold. There was a child almost directly in front of her, perhaps seven or eight years old. The back of her neck was very white and her hair, pulled into a rhinestone clip, gleamed. Karen felt herself longing to stroke it. If she had a child would she and Jeffrey start attending temple? Would they sit together as a family at Park Avenue Synagogue? Would it feel good?

Would she ever have a child?

She looked over at Jeffrey sitting beside her. She couldn't imagine *him* up there on the dais, patiently going through the motions as Leonard seemed to be. Surprised at herself, Karen felt very moved by the little group on the stone chairs. It was a ceremony of passage, one that she had missed. Lisa, despite other problems she may have as a mother, had made this happen for Tiff. And maybe it would help Tiff feel as if she belonged. Belle had done nothing like this for either of her daughters. Karen looked over at her mother. Belle sat erectly, with a proprietary air. In fact, she looked as if *she* were responsible for the whole affair, although Karen knew she hadn't been involved at all.

What, Karen wondered, would her real mother have done for her? Would she have made a confirmation dress for me, or taken me to Bible school, or brought me in for Hebrew lessons? What was her real mother doing now, while Karen sat with all these people? And what did it matter? She's really nothing to me, Karen told herself. But if I'm not attached to my real mother, who am I attached to?

Truthfully, she guessed she was connected to the line of Sapersteins and Lipskys sitting in the orange light cast by the stained-glass windows. They had tried to be good to her, to love her as best they could. If it wasn't perfect, it would have to be enough. Karen looked up at Tiffany, nervously biting her lips. Karen was swept with a wave of pride, and she was grateful that her niece had put the pearls on. It made Karen feel more of a part of the experience, her tiny contribution. For a moment, Karen was overwhelmed with longing: to be connected, like a pearl on a string, in a line that moved from the past, through her, to the future. She looked again at Tiff and, despite her baby fat and her chipmunk cheeks, despite the rag of a dress she wore, Tiff seemed invested with the dignity of this moment. When the rabbi called her to the podium, Tiff stood up, and for once her height served her well. She was a big girl but in that enormous space she moved cleanly toward the rabbi.

The Paris show, the NormCo buyout, the disappointment of Louise, all disappeared into the background. Yes, Karen thought, if I had a baby I would want it to be a part of this tradition. Karen felt very proud.

It didn't last long.

Excruciating was the right word. Jeffrey's prediction had been correct. Karen sat in the orange velveteen upholstered seat of the tabernacle and tried not to squirm in discomfort, though everyone else already was. This was *tsouris*, the Yiddish word for trouble. Tiff was standing at the podium, the big scroll of the Torah spread out before her like an architectural plan. She might have had more success building it than reading it.

Tiff had started reciting in Hebrew calmly enough. Karen hadn't a clue what Tiff was saying and neither did most of the attendees, but Tiff seemed, at first, to be doing fine. Then the rabbi, a clean-shaven man who looked a lot like Mr. Rogers, had stopped her and made a small correction. Tiff had mumbled it and he had corrected her again. She'd repeated it properly and then continued for a moment, but he had again interrupted and corrected her.

Karen remembered hearing once that the Torah must be read perfectly. But surely there was a limit. Tiff had stopped then and for the first time the entire congregation had been silent. Not even the young children squirmed. The silence stretched out. When Tiff began again, not surprisingly, she had fumbled immediately and the rabbi had jumped to correct her once more. Tiff rolled her eyes. Karen had crossed her fingers and wondered if that was sacrilegious in a temple. At the next correction, Tiff shot the rabbi a murderous look and repeated the word. Then she stopped.

"*Chama*," the rabbi had prompted.

"*Chama*," Tiff had repeated, and stopped. Stopped cold. Then, for the last five excruciating minutes, he had read each word to her and she had echoed it like an automaton. The beautifully coiffed and magnificently overdressed congregation had moved from an embarrassed silence to rustling discontent. The rabbi prompted a word, Tiff repeated it, then stopped. Karen looked up at her sister, who sat beside the now-empty tabernacle, up there on the dias, her face frozen in a glassy smile. Beside her, Leonard was clearly boiling. It was then that Karen heard the first giggle. She thought it was Stephie's but she couldn't be sure. It was high-pitched and was immediately echoed by two or three and then a dozen more. Karen looked up at Tiff. Her face was flushing as dark as the red in the ugly taffeta plaid. Shushing began, and elbowing, and the giggles at last stopped. Oh God, Karen thought, what would they have to celebrate after this fiasco was over?

*   *   *

"Belle, if you say one word to Tiffany I'll strangle you." Arnold and Belle were sitting across from Karen and Jeffrey in the limo on the way from the temple to the reception.

"She's being threatened by her husband," Belle announced, as if they hadn't all heard him. Now they all looked as bad as Arnold. The ceremony had stretched out for over two hours. Jeffrey was consulting his watch every thirty seconds now.

"You'll make the plane," Karen hissed.

"What plane?" Belle asked. Usually she paid no attention to anybody else. Just my luck that now she listens to me, Karen thought. She'd have to tell Belle about Jeffrey's early departure before she told Lisa. Karen sighed. How had she ever managed to have a career *or* a marriage when handling her nuclear family was a full-time job?

"Jeffrey has to leave tonight for Paris. He's flying out of JFK."

"He's leaving after the reception?" Belle asked. "Do they have planes that late?"

"No. That's why he's leaving *before* the reception. He'll just congratulate them and go. It's very important. He has to get there by tomorrow."

"What's more important than his niece's *bat mitzvah?*"

Luckily, before Jeffrey could explain to Belle that the list was long and distinguished, Arnold interrupted again. "Leave it, Belle," he warned. It was unusual for him to interfere with her mother, but Karen quickly saw that its rarity apparently didn't give it any weight with Belle.

"How can you be leaving?" she asked Jeffrey directly. "Before the cake?"

"I don't eat dessert anyway," Jeffrey said.

"No, I mean . . ."

"Belle." Arnold's warning tone was almost a roar. Karen couldn't remember *ever* hearing Arnold raise his voice before. She looked over at her father. His face had taken on some color but it was probably an angry flush.

Belle was silent for a few moments as the limo drove through Inwood on its way to the reception in Lawrence. Hadn't they passed this once already? Was the driver lost? The streets here were confusing. One more thing to be anxious about, Karen thought. Then Belle spoke again.

"She told them that the dress would look ridiculous. She was right." She crossed her arms over her flat chest and brushed her shoulders with each hand, making a gesture that looked like a sparrow checking for dandruff. They looked at her mother, distant and self-satisfied. Didn't she have any compassion for her daughter and granddaughter? This must be the most humiliating day in their lives. Karen felt sick. They drove in silence for the rest of the ride.

They did get lost. The driver had to stop twice for directions. At the restaurant, the uniformed valets jumped to open the doors, but it didn't take four of them to do it, so the other three lined up while the Tom Wolfe driver also stood at attention. Karen looked around. "Are we the first to arrive?" she wondered out loud. The place looked deserted. "Didn't Lisa have two buses to bring people over?"

Belle shrugged. "Nobody wants my opinion," she said pointedly. "Where's the powder room?" All four of them walked in to the enormous foyer of the restaurant. It was clearly one of those places where catering for affairs like this was the only *specialité de la maison*. Two discreet chrome placards pointed in opposite directions. "Levine wedding" said the one pointing to the right, and "Saperstein *bat mitzvah*" said the other. They walked off in the direction indicated and, when they saw the ladies' room, Karen and her mother left the men in the hallway.

They were alone in there as well. "Where is everybody?" Belle asked.

"Maybe it took them a while to get boarded," Karen said, but she felt uneasy. What had it been like in those buses? The limo driver had gotten them lost and it had taken almost half an hour to get over here. Could the buses take that long? Surely *they* knew the way. Karen looked into the enormous mirror that was rimmed with light bulbs. She hadn't seen a fixture like that since the seventies. It was a kind of Hollywood disco style that had been out in Manhattan for a couple of decades. It cast a grim light on her and her mother.

Belle immediately began to unpack her purse on the vanity shelf, ready to make repairs. Karen looked at her own pale face. Her misery showed. She looked as if she'd recently lost a baby. Her face was colorless, her skin pasty. She'd eaten off all her lipstick in her nervousness at the ceremony and her hair had completely wilted. Nothing less than reconstructive surgery could save this face, she thought, as she reached for her makeup bag.

From the corner of her eyes, Karen looked over at Belle, who was applying mascara, her mouth half open in the expression Karen had learned to imitate when she put on her own mascara. For a crazy moment, Karen thought of asking about her adoption right then and there. There was so much she'd like to tell Belle, so much she'd like to share, if only Belle was open to it. But only Belle's mouth was open.

"Do you think Daddy looks okay?" Karen asked now.

"What do you mean? His suit? I told him . . . "

"No, no. I mean his health. Is he all right?"

"Oh, you know your father," Belle said, and shrugged. "Working all hours and eating *dreck*. What can I tell you?"

When they rejoined the men, after Belle's lengthy toilette, Jeffrey and Arnold were talking business. Not surprisingly, Jeffrey must have mentioned the goddamn NormCo deal. It was the only thing on his mind. Arnold, also in character, was launched into a complete labor review of NormCo's union policy. Didn't Jeffrey know better?

Karen felt the pressure mounting. The contract was moving toward her like a legal juggernaut and she would be crushed under it. Now she could identify with Indiana Jones, fleeing the rolling rocks. Yeah, here she was: Karen Kahn and the Temple of Doom. Actually, they had already left the temple. It was the Reception of Doom that she was at. Could it be worse than the temple?

And then she had a thought. The contract might be rolling her way but she still didn't have to sign it. What did she care about how much time Bill Wolper and his legal minions put into it? She didn't have to sign until she was certain that she would get what she wanted: a baby. Who was it who said, "It isn't over till it's over"? Well, whoever it was, they were right. She took a deep breath. She *wasn't* trapped. She *had* options. Now all she had to do was break up the fight between her husband and her father before it got violent.

"They've busted unions in all of their mills in the South," Arnold was saying. "They threaten to take production offshore, they bust the union, and then they take it offshore anyway. The domestic plants have been left with crumbs. Crumbs!"

"Arnold, you can't argue with their bottom line. They've been profitable for thirty-seven quarters. They must be doing something right."

"Only if you consider creating unemployment here and sweatshops in the Third World a moral victory."

"We're not talking *morality*, Arnold." Jeffrey's voice had assumed the edge that Karen knew led to an outburst. "We're not talking morality," Jeffrey repeated, "we're talking business."

"Aren't they related? Does morality stop where a P and L begins?"

Karen had heard this kind of argument between the two of them more than a dozen times, but it had never taken on such a personal tone. Well, of course, she'd never thought of selling out before. She took her father's arm with one hand and her husband's with the other. "This isn't a time to talk business," she said. "Let me buy you two handsome guys a drink." Propelling them by their elbows, she led them up the staircase to the reception. The place was still deserted, except for a single bartender who was standing with his back toward them, staring out the window. He turned as they approached the bar. "How about some champagne?" she asked.

"What kind are you pouring?" Jeffrey inquired.

The bartender picked up a bottle of some no-name California brand. Jeffrey shook his head. "Domestic champagne? Leonard strikes again," he said aloud. "Scotch rocks for me."

"Make that two," Arnold added.

"Arnold? You know what the doctor said," Belle warned.

What *did* the doctor say, Karen wondered. She'd just asked Belle about him and Belle hadn't mentioned a word about a doctor. Had Arnold been consulting a doctor? Why hadn't Belle told her that in the ladies' room?

"The doctor said I shouldn't be aggravated, Belle. Are you cooperating?" Arnold asked. Belle shrugged. She and Karen opted for white wine. The four of them stood there in the empty room, their glasses poised. What could they possibly drink to? Certainly not Tiffany's performance. They stood silent for a moment. Jeffrey looked at his watch.

"L'chiam," Arnold finally murmured, and all four of them gratefully gulped down some of their drink.

Forty-five minutes later the buses still hadn't arrived. After a brief argument, Jeffrey had left with the limo.

Now, at last, the two buses pulled up, followed by a line of other guests in cars. The caravan disgorged its wrinkled, irritated passengers. Lisa, at the head of the furious procession, marched up the stairs holding Tiff by Tiff's meaty upper arm. She might as well be pulled by her ear, Karen thought. Lisa was almost visibly fuming and Tiff had, contrarily, become virtually comatose. "The fucking assholes got lost," Lisa said by way of a greeting. "You hire the dickheads to get you from point A to point B and they can't even manage it! It wasn't like it was brain surgery. Or even dermatology," she said contemptuously, and looked darkly over at Leonard, who, with Stephanie, was helping guests off the other bus.

"She told you not to have buses," Belle reminded Lisa. To give her credit, Lisa didn't strike her mother.

Karen looked out the huge windows at the cranky crowd down below. Women were surveying their wrinkled gowns and angrily flapping them out, while men were running their index fingers around their wet collars. A line was already forming outside the ladies' room. "The air conditioning was shot in one of the buses. I'll sue the bastards, I swear to God!" Karen looked over at Tiff. The child's eyes had the glazed look of an accident victim.

"Let's start the fucking party," Lisa growled.

It took what seemed like hours for the ladies' room to empty out. Stephanie carefully checked under each stall to be certain she was the only one in the room. Then she entered the last one and was sure to lock the door behind her. She lifted the toilet seat. She had already eaten eleven cocktail franks and almost twenty shrimp. And that was just at the buffet, before the sit-down dinner. She had to get rid of it now, before any of those calories were absorbed. If I do this now, she promised herself, then I won't eat anything at dinner and I won't have to do it again. But the ceremony had made her so nervous and the party was going so badly that she couldn't control her eating. Well, at least she could control this. She stuck her middle finger as far down her throat as she could and began to gag. It took another moment but then the heaving started. She vomited once, and then, to be sure, she inserted her finger and heaved again. She was dizzy now and had to steady herself by holding on to the walls of the stall, staring down into the toilet below her. All of that disgusting food made her ready to retch again. How had it tempted her before? She was a pig to want to stuff herself full of that garbage! She reached for some toilet paper, carefully wiped her mouth, and dumped the paper into the commode. Then, with another scrap, she wiped the sweat from her upper lip and forehead. She flushed the toilet, turned around, and pulled open the stall door.

Her grandmother, hands on hips, stood there. "And what do you think you're doing?" Belle asked.

The party proceeded by fits and starts but it never congealed into anything remotely resembling a celebration. Sylvia and the Kahn girls seemed amused by it, and Karen avoided them. She was shocked when, out of the crowd, Perry Silverman came to sit beside her. "What are *you* doing here?" she asked. Jeffrey had told her that June was invited, but Perry too? Lisa had lost her mind. "I didn't see you at the synagogue."

"I was invited," he said. "But no booze there. So I figured I'd just do the reception. Free drinks. And I came to see you."

She wondered if he'd seen June yet. Karen didn't know what to say. "Lisa invited you? I didn't know you knew each other."

"We don't. Except for the time we met at your brunch." He took her hand. "Come on. Let's dance," he said.

He didn't seem to be drunk yet and so Karen acquiesced. He was so much smaller than Jeffrey that it felt odd when he held her around the waist and began to move her across the almost empty dance floor. To their right, two little girls were attempting to cha-cha to Cole Porter. Karen couldn't help smiling but didn't point them out. She knew one was about the age Lottie would be. Perry didn't seem to notice. He moved surprisingly well. He led with authority but without any undue force. Karen wondered if he remembered anything about the night he called her from the phone booth at her corner. He said nothing, simply directing her movements. After a few moments, she realized she danced better with him then she did with Jeffrey.

"My wife is here," Perry murmured to her. For a moment she thought he was warning her, as if they were doing something improper and might be caught. But then he glided them into a turn and she saw June, sitting across the room. June looked good, but a little heavier than her usual anorexic ninety pounds. "How did *she* get here?"

"By bus," Karen said, and snorted a laugh. "Do you mind?"

"Mind? If I knew she was coming I'd have maked a wake. But then, I guess I don't have to. This is a pretty good approximation of a wake, isn't it?" Karen didn't answer him but simply let him continue to smoothly move her through "Begin the Beguine."

But what *was* going on? Lisa had invited Karen's friends? How could she have invited both June *and* Perry? The bitterness between them was well known. And, oddest of all, why had June come? She must be interested in Perry. She didn't know Lisa at all, and Karen had never warmed up to Jeffrey's ex-fiancée. The whole thing was ridiculous. Karen watched the crowd. Although the first course had only just been served, she could see people had already begun leaving. God, Lisa must be dying. And Tiff looked as if she were already dead.

Just then, Belle dragged Stephanie across the dance floor toward Karen. Perry kept on dancing, his back to the two of them, but that didn't stop Belle.

"Do you know what she was doing?" she demanded of the two of them. "She was puking. She was puking in the bathroom." Perry stopped. He turned around. The four of them were in the center of the floor. "Puking up good food. I told her it was a sin. Children are starving, and she's puking up good food."

"I think I may do the same," Perry said. "Perhaps we could discuss this at another venue." He nodded to Belle formally. "So nice to see you again," he mumbled and, taking Karen's hand, he led her away. "Beware of consanguinity," he warned her.

Karen shook her head. "We're related by craziness, not by blood," she reminded him.

"Well, that's a relief." They were back at her table. "Hey. Where's Jeffrey?" Perry asked. "Not that I wouldn't be delighted to take his place." He sat down in Jeffrey's vacant seat.

Karen sighed. Perry had reminded her. Now she would have to tell Lisa that Jeffrey left. In the mêlée following the bus arrival, Lisa hadn't seemed to notice his absence, but Karen couldn't put it off any longer. It would probably offend Lisa, but now there was no alternative.

Before Karen could make a move, the bandleader spoke into the microphone. "And now, ladies and gentlemen, a moment I know you've been waiting for. Tiffany Saperstein's candle-lighting ceremony." The band played a tired fanfare, the lights flickered and then dimmed, and a cadre of waiters rushed across the floor with a wheeled table displaying an enormous pan cake. There was some scattered applause from the guests who remained and then a spotlight came on, illuminating the cake and a woebegone Tiffany standing behind it. She held a candle in one hand and a small deck of index cards in the other.

"For my first . . . " She was speaking right next to the microphone, and her voice came out in a breathy gabble impossible to hear or comprehend.

"Louder," someone yelled. She looked up for a moment, squinting against the light.

"For-my-first-candle-I-would-like-to-ask-my-grandmother-and-grandfa-ther-Saperstein-to-come-and-join-me," she said in a monotone. "I-have-spent-so-many-summer-vacations-at-their-house-and-have-enjoyed-all-my-visits." There wasn't a bit of emotion or even inflection to her reading of the card. There was more scattered clapping, the band began to play, and Leonard's parents rose, walked to the center of the room, kissed Tiffany, and lit a candle.

Then it dawned on Karen. Tiffany was surely going to call out her name and Jeffrey's. What would she do? A photographer was busily snapping pictures of the Saperstein grandparents beside Tiffany, immortalizing the moment, at least for as long as Kodak paper lasted. Oh my God, Karen thought, she had forgotten about this bit. She'd really screwed up royally.

Tiffany was equally impervious to the light bulbs and the cheek kissing. Before her grandparents were even finished lighting the candle, she moved on to the next card. "Now-I'd-like-to-ask-my-grandma-Belle-and-grandpa-Arnold-to-come-up. I-want-to-thank-them-for-all-the-love-and-support-they-have-given-me-over-the-years." The child's lack of affect was frightening. The entire room was silent, listening to her recite with a lot less liveliness than a Disney audio-animatronic.

Belle and Arnold made their way up to the enormous cake and kissed Tiffany. In the glare of the spotlight, Arnold looked worse than ever. He's getting old, Karen thought. Belle took the candle from Tiffany's hands and lit the second one on the cake. More pictures were taken and people clapped. Tiffany, emotionless, looked down at her cards. "Now-I'd-like-to-ask-my-sister-Stephanie-to-come-up-here. Sometimes-we-fight-like-cats-and-dogs-but-under-neath-it-we-really-love-each-other."

Stephanie moved easily into the spotlight. The girl was truly beautiful, tall and lithe and thin. Thinner than ever. Karen stared at her. Had she been throwing up on purpose? Was *that* what Belle had been trying to say? When the photographer started flashing, Stephanie came alive for him, throwing an arm around Tiffany and pouting for the camera. Tiffany ignored her and simply looked down at the next card.

"And-now-I'd-like-to-ask-my-Aunt-Karen-and-Uncle-Jeffrey-up-to-light-a-candle. They-are-always-very-good-to-me-and-even-if-I-don't-see-them-as-often-as-I-would-like-to-I-love-them-very-much."

Karen rose, sick at heart, and walked across the empty dance floor to the girl. She would have to explain about all this later. She took Tiffany's ice-cold hand in both of her own. "Are you all right?" she asked uselessly. Tiffany didn't even nod in response, but merely pushed the candle into Karen's hands. If Tiff noticed that her uncle wasn't there, she wasn't mentioning it. Karen could think of nothing to do but take the candle and move toward the cake.

"Where's Jeffrey?" Belle hissed in a stage whisper. "I *told* you about the cake."

Karen never got to light the candle. At that moment, Arnold crumpled, his left leg seeming to collapse under him. He fell, like an axed tree in an open field. And as he fell he clutched at the air desperately for a moment with his extended right hand. There was nothing for it to catch to stop his fall. But in the seconds before he hit the floor, he jerked his arm with enough strength to send the table, the cake, and all the candles flying.

23

BY A THREAD

Belle met Karen at the elevator on the seventh floor of the Harkness Pavilion of Columbia Presbyterian in northern Manhattan. She was still in her outfit from the *bat mitzvah,* and she looked as if *she* were having what the cardiologists were calling "an episode." "The doctor just left," she told Karen. "He said your father has stabilized."

"Well, that's good news, isn't it?" Karen looked at Belle's face. It didn't look like good news according to Belle.

"Of course it's good news. Apparently, it wasn't that serious to begin with. I just can't believe he had to pick right then to do it. He ruined the cake."

Karen sighed. "Mother, he didn't *choose* the time, it just happened."

"Well, I know *that,*" Belle snapped. They walked down the hall together toward Arnold's room. The hall was deserted. "Lisa and Leonard went home?"

"Yes. They left me alone about an hour ago."

"Oh, come on, Mother, I heard both of them offer to stay before I left and the doctors told you it was okay for you to go home to change. Let's not make this worse than it is." Why was it that though Arnold was the one lying on the bed with tubes in his nose, Belle acted as though she were the victim? Karen wondered if she could talk to the doctor by herself. Everything was distorted through Belle's perception. At one moment, Arnold was almost faking his illness, according to her, and at another she was virtually the bereaved widow. Karen needed to talk to somebody calming and competent. Where was Dr. Kropsey? "Am I allowed to go in to see Daddy?" she asked Belle.

"It's probably not a good idea. He's resting," Belle said.

But when they got to the door of his room, Karen couldn't resist peeking in to look at her father. Arnold was still hooked up to a lot of machines, but he had some of his color back and he was awake and alert. He lifted a hand and waved weakly to her.

"I'll go in and sit with him," she told her mother. It was a relief that only one visitor was allowed at a time.

"Fine. She knows when she's not wanted," Belle said, and Karen didn't bother to correct her but simply walked in and sat down beside her father's bed. Arnold still had the oxygen tubes up his nose, and Karen was shocked to see that the chest hair that escaped from the top of his hospital gown was totally white. Somehow, she had accepted the graying of the hair on his head, but his body had always been furry as a bear's. A brown bear's. When was the last time she had seen Arnold's chest hair? He was a modest man, and had always worn both pajamas and a robe around the house in the evenings, a fully buttoned shirt, tie, and jacket in the day—even on warm days. But had he aged slowly, while Karen hadn't noticed, or was this something new? Belle maintained herself so carefully that it seemed to Karen she hadn't changed in any way in decades. Like a fly in amber, her hairstyle, her makeup, and her wardrobe were immutable. Only Arnold aged.

Karen sat down beside him. She took his free hand, the one that didn't have the drip running into it. "You don't have to talk," she told Arnold.

"Who has the opportunity?" Arnold asked. "Your mother is here." Karen smiled. Arnold rarely made jokes at Belle's expense. His hand, still big, felt light and papery. She pressed it firmly between her own.

"Just rest, Dad," she said. He nodded, and closed his eyes for a few minutes. Karen wondered whether Arnold could go back to work. She suspected their financial position wasn't too good. Well, she could support them now. But would her dad consider any money from the deal as blood money? Arnold's eyelids fluttered. Then he opened them and looked directly at her.

"Could you do me a favor, Karen?" he asked. "Could you call a number for me?"

Business now? Was he crazy? Hadn't work driven him to this? "Can't it wait?" Karen asked.

"No. Do me a favor. Call Inez at 516-848-2306." Inez was her dad's legal secretary. "Tell her that I'm okay. Ask her not to visit. Tell her I said that, and that I said I was fine."

Karen reached into her *schlep* bag and pulled out a scrap of paper and a pen. After jotting down the number, she looked at her father. His gray eyes were rimmed with red, and his face, though not so pale as it had been, still looked puffy. Was his relationship with Inez more than professional? Inez was a middle-aged Puerto Rican woman who lived somewhere out on the island. She'd worked with Arnold for almost twenty years. "Sure, Dad. I'll call her," Karen promised, and jotted down the number.

Now it was Arnold's turn to pat her hand. "You're a good girl, Karen," he said. "I knew that the first time I saw you."

"Where was that?" she asked, before she had time to think about it. Then she blushed with embarrassment. God, was she going to use this opening to pump him?

But she didn't have to pump. Arnold seemed ready to reminisce. "Chicago. When we went to pick you up. Mrs. Talmidge was holding you and you put your arms right out to me. I'll never forget it." He patted her hand again. "You were always a good girl."

"Who was Mrs. Talmidge, Dad?" Karen asked, her heart beating so loudly she was sure all the machines surrounding them would pick up on it. You should be ashamed, she told herself.

"The woman from the Chicago Board of Child Guardians. She was a nice woman." He closed his eyes.

Karen sat there, his hand in hers. He had always been a good man. If he had been overwhelmed by Belle, how could she blame him? Who wouldn't be? And if he had sometimes escaped Belle and abandoned the two girls to her, wasn't that what all fathers had done back then in the days before paternal involvement? He had provided for Karen, raised her as his own, and he always approved of her and helped her in any way he could. Karen felt tears begin to film over her eyes, but she blinked them away. She turned as she heard the door open behind her and the doctor came in. He took Arnold's hand from hers and felt for his pulse. Then he motioned her out of the room, into the hallway.

"He's doing fine," the doctor told her when he joined her. "We may want to perform a catheterization, and there is definitely a problem with the valve, but that's nothing abnormal for a man his age. He's really stabilized. He's not in any danger. He's fine, Mrs. Kahn."

"What can I do?" she asked.

"Well, you could take your mother home. She is upsetting the nurses and keeping your father awake. She needs a rest herself," he said. "I could give you a prescription." Then he patted her shoulder. "Are *you* all right?"

Karen nodded. He looked like a nice man, only a little older than she was, and his eyes were warm. "Are you telling me the truth?" she asked. "He's not going to die?"

"Well, we're all going to die, but I don't think he's going to do it any time soon. It was actually fortuitous that he had this episode in a public place. It will give us a chance to diagnose and treat his condition before it becomes acute. But that's the thing to understand; this is chronic but not acute. With proper care he'll be just fine." Karen took a deep breath. She felt overwhelmed by the good news, and by the secret of Inez, and by the information her father had given her about her own background. Did things like her Paris show really matter compared to Arnold's life? What was she spending her time on?

"Thank you, doctor," she said, and turned to walk down the long hall to cope with Belle.

Every real New Yorker has a Greek joint they consider their own. The ubiquitous New York "coffee shop"—which usually serves lousy coffee—is the metropolitan equivalent of the American small-town diner. Seinfeld made Tom's Restaurant famous, but every metropolitan dweller claims a place that's a combination salon, kitchen extension, and waiting room. What the club is to the English gentleman, what the pub is to the English working class, what the café is to the French, that is what the Greek joint is to New Yorkers.

Karen's was the Nectar. It was no better or worse than the Athenian, the Three Guys, the Two Brothers, or the ten thousand other restaurants just like it. Like other New Yorkers, Karen chose it because of proximity, because of George, the owner, and because it had a good window booth.

Now, she sat with Defina in the booth she favored. They both had thick, white, china mugs before them. Karen's was filled with black coffee, Defina's with hot water and the herbs she had poured into it. Karen had also emptied two packets of Equal into her cup, despite head shaking from Defina. Defina was against chemicals, but the last thing Karen needed right now was nutritional guidance. She played with the empty sweetener packets, tracing patterns with their edges on the wet Formica tabletop.

Defina looked over the menu. "Greek cuisine," she said with contempt. "Since when do olives and feta cheese equal a cuisine? You gonna eat something?"

Karen shook her head. She had spent much of the night at Columbia Presbyterian, where she had insisted her father be sent once he had been diagnosed at the Great Neck hospital. "So it wasn't a real heart attack?" Defina asked.

"They don't think so. Anyway, they call them 'myocardial infarctions,' not heart attacks. They are calling what he had 'an episode.' But they think he has probably had a lot of them. They don't know how much damage has been done to the heart muscle but there's clearly some kind of valve problem."

"What does that mean, 'an episode'?" Defina asked scornfully. "Makes your daddy sound like a sitcom or something." Defina stretched her hand across the table and took Karen's. "He gonna be all right?" she asked.

"They think so. I mean, not all right like back-to-normal all right. All right like he-isn't-dead-so-he's-all-right kind of all right. He looks like death on a gurney. It was scary."

"I bet." The two of them sat there in silence, staring out the window. Amsterdam Avenue was just beginning to get busy, with a single early-morning yuppie carrying a briefcase, thrusting out his arm and running back and forth across the street trying to snag a cab. His unbuttoned coat flapped around his skinny body.

"He looks like a chicken."

Karen thought of the old chicken riddle. "Why did the man cross the road?" she asked, listlessly.

"Why do men do anything they do?" Defina responded with a shrug.

Karen watched the yuppie trying to get a taxi. Dozens of others struggled to the subway entrance. It tired Karen out just to look at them. "I don't know how people do it: get up every day, don't think about why they do what they do, commute like sleepwalkers, and show up at their job at Chemical Bank or Mobil Oil without questioning why. What's the point?"

"They're the lucky ones, Karen. The ones who *don't* think about it. The ones who just do it—they're the ones who are okay."

Karen wondered why she did what she did. All the fuss, all the deadlines, all the drama, to make a skirt for some woman to wear to a luncheon. Karen shook her head. "I don't understand anything," she said.

"*I* understand *everything*—except men," Defina said.

"You having trouble with Roi again?" Karen asked.

Roi Pompey was Defina's brother. Karen couldn't count all the times Defina had bailed him out of trouble.

"Nothin' worse than usual. Anyway, we talkin' about *you*."

"Oh, I can't stand talking about me anymore."

"Well, since you asked, I did get laid last night," Defina admitted.

"Defina? Are you still seeing Bradley?" Since Tangela had moved out, Defina had started to date, but her choice struck Karen as weird—or maybe irresponsible. Bradley was only twenty-three, just a couple of years older than Tangela. Bradley was unemployed, and weeks ago had stopped Dee outside her house on Striver's Row and asked Defina if she needed a handyman. It was how they had met, and, after cleaning out Defina's basement, the two of them had fallen into a carnal relationship. Karen had been shocked, not by the age difference as much as their difference in experience, education, and status. She'd been relieved when Defina—somewhat reluctantly—said she was giving Bradley up. Clearly, she'd changed her mind. Now, Karen lifted the cup of coffee to her lips. The thick crockery warmth of it was comforting. "But Defina, don't you want a man who's your equal?"

Defina reached over to the sugar holder and picked up a pink packet and a blue one. She threw the blue one onto the Formica and grinned. "Who needs Equal? I prefer Sweet and Low," she said, and laughed. Then the smile left her face. "So, what you gonna do about Paris? Do you need to stay here with your daddy?"

"I don't know," Karen said, exhausted. "I'm going up to the hospital in another hour or two and I'll talk to the cardiologist then. I should stay, but I know I also should do the show or God knows what will happen to the business, to the deal. Jesus, who knows?"

"Girl, I hear you 'shoulding' all over yourself. Give yourself a break. What does Jeffrey say?"

"I haven't been able to reach him, with the time difference and everything. Well, you know, he was just supposed to get off the plane and hit the ground running. I guess he did. I left word at the hotel."

Defina's eyes narrowed, but before she could say anything the cellular telephone rang. Karen's stomach lurched. Was it the hospital? She had reluctantly given her mother the cellular number. What the hell, she wasn't getting any baby calls anyway. Defina picked it up and sat there staring at Karen. Defina was nodding her head slightly and mumbling "uh-uhs." She hung up and shook her head. "If all that ain't bad enough, Casey just heard from Munchin and they refused to release two hundred dozen blazers from the bridge line until their invoices get paid."

Karen put down her cup with a loud bang. Coffee sloshed onto the Formica. Her stomach lurched with fear. Jeffrey usually wheedled the manufacturers to release goods, but he couldn't do it long distance from Paris. Lenny or Casey would have to handle it. God, did *anything* go right?

"One more thing," Defina said. "Our hairdresser just canceled for Paris."

Enough! That was it! Karen's fear turned to anger. "Great, the little prick! He's just mad 'cause I complained about my last haircut. Now what do we do?" She stopped for a moment. Where was her sense of priorities? Her father was just out of Critical Care at Columbia Presbyterian and she was worried about *hairdressers*? What was wrong with this picture? What was wrong with her life? She put her hands on her breastbone. Her heart was thumping in her chest. "Fuck!" she said. "Fuck, fuck, fuck!"

Defina looked at her. "Is this what they call 'an episode'?"

"Tell Casey to handle Munchin. Then call Carl. Tell him about my father.

Maybe he'll leave his shop, just this once, if he feels sorry for me. Ask him if he can come to Paris for the week. With or without my being there I'll feel safe if you go and Carl does the heads." She looked at Defina. "And you were overloaded before," she said guiltily. "I'm asking an awful lot of you Dee," she admitted. "I'm sorry, but I'm going to have to trust you to get it together for me. Can you do it?"

"Does the pope shit in the woods?" Defina asked.

Defina and Carl were waiting for Karen when she stepped out of the hospital's revolving door. Carl gave Karen a big hug. "So, is Arnold going to be all right?"

"So it would appear. That is if the doctors aren't lying and if nothing else happens in the next thirty minutes." Karen ran her fingers against her scalp. She'd gone home, napped, showered, and changed but hadn't bothered to blow-dry her hair. "It's unbelievable," she said. "Is there any other crisis that could develop in my life in the next twenty-four hours? Because if there is, I'm sure it will."

"I know what you need," Defina said. "You need Madame Renault."

"Yeah, great. Some mumbo-jumbo from a woman who's either deluded or a con artist. Come on, Dee. Don't start with me. You're an educated woman. You don't really believe in crystals, do you?"

"Crystals? They're bullshit. New age is all bullshit. *I'm* talking about the real thing."

"Well, even if she does have some kind of gift, how's she going to help? Is she a cardiologist? What I need is to get back to the office."

Defina raised her eyebrows and flared her nostrils. "Why do you think you're above help?" she asked Karen. "Wouldn't it be nice to know how the Paris show is going to go? And how your daddy is going to be?" Karen rolled her eyes but Carl nudged her.

"Oh, come on, Karen," he said. "Let's go." She climbed into the car, sank back into the seat between her two friends, and gave up. "Sure," she said. "I always go to a mystic after my niece is *bat mitzvahed* and my father has a heart attack."

"It was only 'an episode,' " Defina said. Then she gave a West One Hundred and Thirty-Fifth Street address and the driver, moving down Broadway, nodded. "At least it isn't out of the way," Karen joked.

"Girlfriend, there are people who come all the way from Europe to see Madame Renault."

The address turned out to be a fairly well-kept brownstone on a nondescript block, perhaps a little better than most of the Harlem streets. The three of them got out of the car and told the driver to wait. He didn't look comfortable, but he didn't say no. There was a tall stoop that led to a wooden double door, but Defina led them to a more discreet iron grating at the side of the stoop and rang a buzzer there. Through the crackly intercom, a voice asked who was there.

"Shouldn't she already know?" Carl asked, rolling his eyes.

Defina gave him a dirty look. "It's Defina Pompey," she said aloud. "It's an emergency." The buzzer squawked and they pulled open the grille, walking into the dark area under the stoop. Down two steps was an open door. They entered a vestibule with a green marble tile floor. The walls were painted a deep aubergine color. Well, at one time all of these homes had belonged to the prosperous middle class. This one had obviously been restored, or been carefully taken care of all along. Defina led them into a sort of waiting room, which was glazed a rich squash yellow. The floor was carpeted in a sea grass matting. There was no furniture at all except for three straight-backed chairs.

"See," Defina said. "She knew there would be three of us."

Carl rolled his eyes again. "It looks like the three bears' house," was all he said.

There was something weird about the room. Not just the lack of furniture, but the room itself, Karen thought. It was the color, the emptiness, and the way the light filtered in through the half-closed blinds. She didn't believe in auras or vibrations, but the room seemed powerful, as if it were held in readiness. She sat down in one of the chairs. Defina took another, but Carl stood leaning against a wall. "Can I come in too?" Carl asked.

"Of course not," Defina hissed. "This is very personal."

"Well, I *am* her best friend."

Defina looked at him. "Honey, you're confused. You're only her *oldest* friend," she said dryly. Then the door opened and Madame Renault stepped into the room.

Karen didn't know what she was expecting, but it certainly wasn't this: a tall, thin, elegant woman dressed in what must be an old Chanel suit. Madame Renault was black, her skin a deep red-tinged brown, and the jacket and skirt she wore was almost the exact shade of her skin. Her hair was the same color, but a shade darker, and pulled back in a dated but attractive chignon. The woman nodded to Defina and looked at Karen. "Come in," she said, her voice deep. There was a hint of an accent, but Karen couldn't tell exactly what kind. She also couldn't tell Madame Renault's age. The face was unlined except for around the eyes, but her hands, Karen noticed, were old—very old. Karen looked over at Defina who had stood up to greet her mentor. Defina gave Karen a little nudge. "Go on," she said. So Karen did.

The inner room was painted grass green and had a rack with herbs or wildflowers drying. The only other things in it were a table and two hard benches. A Keith Haring "Radiant Child" poster was hanging alone on the wall. Madame sat on one bench, so Karen took the other. The narrow table was between them. Karen was surprised at how nervous she was. How had this happened? How had she come to be alone in this room with this stranger? She didn't like it, and almost got up to go. But then Madame Renault spoke. Her voice, while not unpleasant, had an urgency that couldn't be ignored. "You are on a quest," Madame Renault said. Her face, so smooth, except around the brown-black eyes, showed nothing, but the eyes stared at Karen and for a moment Karen felt they looked into her own, deeper than anyone ever had. "You are searching, but you don't understand that you have already found what you're searching for."

Well, Karen thought, it's the same old mumbo-jumbo. She could be Glenda the Good Witch and I could be Dorothy. Make it general enough and use the old formulas and you couldn't go wrong. You'll meet a tall dark stranger, you will go on a long voyage, you are on a quest. Karen almost smiled. Next she'll tell me that the secret to life is chicken soup.

"You already know your real mother," Madame Renault said.

"What?" Karen whispered. Why had the woman said that? What had Defina told her? Madame Renault's face was blank as before, but her eyes as intense. She seemed to wait until Karen calmed herself enough to listen. "Your father is ill, but he isn't dying. But there will be a dying. A mother dying. And then there is someone else waiting for you. A child. A dark child."

Karen had broken out into a sweat and she looked across the table at Madame Renault, but now, at last, the woman's hooded eyes were downcast.

"Do I get the child?" Karen asked in a whisper.

"Oh, yes, but it will take a long trip." Madame Renault paused and then looked at Karen again. This time her eyes were filled with sympathy and pain. "Ah," she sighed. "You will have to give up something you love," she said.

She must mean the business, Karen thought. I have to give up the business to get the child. "So I have to sell my company?" Karen asked.

Madame Renault shook her head, but Karen wasn't sure if it meant no or if she was already onto something else. Then the woman reached out with one of her gnarled hands and held Karen around the wrist.

"You are like a spider. You have been weaving and weaving for a long, long time. Be careful. Your silk can run out. You may wind up empty. And the web that you weave may not be sound."

Karen remembered a poem that Belle had taught her: "Oh what a wicked web we weave when we first practice to deceive." Karen *had* been lying lately, and for the first time in her life. Now, she cast her eyes down. Madame Renault let go of Karen's hand.

"Don't worry, little spider. You will struggle out from the web of lies, but each thread you break will bleed. There is joy ahead of you, but first there will be much pain. I'm so sorry," the woman sighed. "It's the only way," she said, and rose. Without another word, she moved to the door and Karen was left alone at the table. Madame Renault opened the door and told Defina, "You can take your friend home now." By the time Karen turned around, Defina was at her side and Madame Renault was gone.

In the limo, going back to midtown, the episode seemed more and more like a dream: the gem-colored backdrops, the surreal rooms, the dramatic woman and her oracular statements seemed almost comic. But they weren't, Karen told herself. Even if it didn't make sense, something in Karen knew she had met the real thing.

"You were white as a sheet!" Carl said. "What did she say to you?"

Karen shook her head.

"None of your business," Defina told him. "I told you it's personal."

"Well, why couldn't she tell *my* future?"

"Your future is in Paris. That's as far ahead as *you* need to think. Anyway, she don't just take anybody."

"How much does she charge?"

Even though she was sitting down, Defina seemed to pull herself up to her full height. "She don't charge nothin'," Defina told him. "She says it's a gift and you can't charge money for a gift."

Karen wished they'd stop talking so she could remember exactly what Madame Renault *had* said. Karen remembered the woman's face when she told her that a child was waiting. Somehow, Karen didn't doubt her. She looked over at Defina. "Did you tell her anything about me?" she asked. Defina crossed her arms and turned her head to stare out the window. Her look of disgust was the only answer she gave Karen.

"What *did* she say?" Carl asked again. Karen wondered for a moment if she should tell about the prediction. Somehow, it felt too personal. But why not? He was her oldest friend.

"She said there was a baby waiting for me," Karen told him.

Back home, even when her regular phone rang, Karen jumped. For some reason now, the ads had started to work. So, if it wasn't some crazy girl calling from a pay phone about a baby, it would be the hospital calling her to say that they had been wrong about Arnold's condition and that he was really dead. But when Karen lifted the phone on her bedside table, it was only Lisa's voice that greeted her.

"Daddy's feeling much better," Lisa told her. "The doctors say he can probably come home the day after tomorrow."

"Great!" Karen said. Thank God he was all right. Then, though she hadn't thought of it since she left the hospital, her conversation with him came back to her. God, she had to call Centrillo and tell him about Chicago and the Board of Guardians! What was the name of the woman who Arnold had mentioned? Karen ran her hands through her hair. So much had already happened in the last forty-eight hours that she felt as if she was losing it. What *was* the woman's name?

Lisa's voice interrupted her thought. "We're not going back to the hospital," Lisa said. "Leonard is exhausted. And it's too long a drive. I don't know why you insisted on bringing him into Manhattan anyway. It wasn't that serious."

"We didn't know that then," Karen reminded her. God, what was the name of the social worker? She should have written it down. It was a thirties actress. Was it Norma Shearer? She couldn't remember, but she knew it began with an 'S'.

"Of course, the *bat mitzvah* was completely ruined," Lisa said. "Tiff has been crying since Saturday."

"I'm so sorry," Karen told her sister, though she knew as well as Lisa that Arnold's episode was merely the *coup de grace* in a series of mess-ups. She didn't need to mention it. The *bat mitzvah* had been dismal even before Arnold's half-gainer into the cake. Thank God Lisa hadn't asked her where Jeffrey had been. Karen felt awful for Lisa.

"Listen, why don't you come into Manhattan tomorrow and watch the run-through for Paris? I'll take you out to eat and we can both visit Daddy." It wasn't much, but it was all Karen had to offer right now.

"Sure," Lisa said. "I'll bring Belle."

Karen's stomach dropped. Then, "Talmidge!" Karen cried.

"What?" Lisa asked.

Embarrassed, Karen pretended to ignore Lisa's question, but pulled out a pencil and scribbled the name next to Centrillo's on her phone pad before she forgot it again. She was silent and so was Lisa. She cleared her throat. Lisa took the silence as a moment to change the subject.

"Listen," she said to Karen. "Jeffrey told me about the NormCo offer and I don't know if you're still unsure about it, but if you want my opinion, it sounds too good to pass up."

Where in the world did *that* come from? It was the first time that Karen could ever remember Lisa talking business. And now, out of the blue like this? What was up? When had Jeffrey had time to tell Lisa about the offer? They didn't speak at the *bat mitzvah*. And why had he? "When did he talk to you about it?" Karen asked, and tried to keep her voice neutral.

"Oh, at the reception."

Karen stopped fiddling with the pad and pencil and laid the pencil down. She felt a little chill run up the back of her neck and into her hair. Jeffrey had left the reception before Lisa had even arrived. Why would Lisa lie?

"Yeah," she said. "Well, it's not a final offer yet, so we'll have to see," she added vaguely.

"But you *are* thinking of taking it?" Lisa asked. She paused for a moment. "You know, Karen, if you had less stress, you might be able to conceive."

Karen was swept with anger so quickly and so fiercely that she nearly bit her tongue. "Lisa, I have to go. I'll see you at the run-through tomorrow," was all she said, and she hung up the phone.

24

RAGS TO BITCHES

Karen had another incredibly busy day in front of her, but after a quick morning visit to the hospital she got in to the office and at nine o'clock exactly she took the time out to call Mr. Centrillo and give him the new information. "Will that help?" she asked. "Is it enough?"

"I don't know, Mrs. Cohen. It may not be enough, but at least it's a start. I promise you, we'll do our best with it. I may have to try a few different avenues."

"Listen, I'll be going away on vacation for a little while." Karen didn't want him calling her private line while she was in Paris.

"Really? Where are you going?"

"Lake George." Where the hell had that come from, she wondered? She'd never been to Lake George in her life. She was going crazy. Should she tell Centrillo that she felt her mental health depended on him? Somehow, she felt he already believed that, so she simply said, "Thank you."

"You have a nice day," he said. "Try to take it easy."

Karen almost snorted. The day ahead of her seemed fifty hours long.

By lunchtime all of the ЖКInc staff were gathered in the showroom, which had been converted to a makeshift auditorium. Someone, probably Casey, had even brought in a lectern. Karen couldn't imagine standing behind it. It was too authoritative. Belle would like a lectern. In fact, now that Karen thought of it, Belle seemed to go through life with an imaginary lectern before her, giving all her pronouncements the added weight of a judgment from behind a podium.

Karen's hands were clammy, but she couldn't put this off any longer. She had agreed to go ahead with the sale, rumors were running like rabbits through the staff, and she was going to have to inform all of the employees what was going on. She had decided to bestow stock on everybody who had been with her for more than a year. She had, against the advice of Robert-the-lawyer and in the face of Jeffrey's disapproval, taken twenty percent of the company, a little less than half of her shares, and distributed it. That left her thirty percent, but with Jeffrey's thirty percent that was a safe majority—controlling interest for the short time until the actual transfer of stock to NormCo. Jeffrey and Robert-the-lawyer had had to accept her decision. She wouldn't do the deal any other way. If her conscience bothered her, if she worried, as Arnold's daughter, about some of NormCo's methods, she soothed herself by knowing she was making her workers well-off and that now, with Arnold's illness, he and Belle would need the money. Diluting her share was no big deal, really. How much money did she need? There would be enough for everyone. It meant that most of her staff would be receiving their choice of cash or NormCo stock at the buyout. So, she told herself, it was good news for everybody, especially senior staff, who would be making what Jeffrey kept resentfully calling "a bundle."

But Karen knew that most people resisted change and were afraid of it. So she wanted to make sure that she broke this news in the kindest, gentlest possible way. Jeffrey had planned to do it, but Paris had gotten in the way. She would speak instead, then Robert-the-lawyer would outline the buyout procedure, while Lenny, their accountant, would distribute folders to each of the employees that outlined their personal financial package. Karen wanted to make sure that everyone was as comfortable as they could be with the change, and assure them all that their jobs were secure. When Robert-the-lawyer stood up and asked for order, Karen managed to get to the front of the group without stumbling. But she couldn't get herself behind the lectern. Instead, she pulled over one of the showroom tables and perched on the edge of it.

"First of all, I would like to say that I'm sorry Jeffrey isn't here to share this news with you, but as you all know, he's in Paris getting things organized. He was the one responsible for making this happen." Was that true, she wondered, but didn't have time to consider it. She took a deep breath. "So, anyway, listen," she said, and then self-consciously thought: God, I sound so Brooklyn. Oh, well. I yam what I yam. "I know many of you have heard rumors, but I wanted to wait to talk to you until I knew for sure what was happening. We have been tendered an offer by NormCo to buy us out." She paused. There was a murmur from the back, where the sewing staff sat. "It doesn't mean that they would step in and manage our business or change it.

What it means is that we'd have a chance to expand our business in a lot of ways we never could before. For me, it means that things could be very exciting: I can do a lot of lower-priced clothes and a line of active sportswear that I've been dying to do. For you it will mean some extra money. Depending on how long you've worked here, it could mean a *lot* of extra money." There was another murmur, but this time a higher-pitched one. Karen saw Mercedes break into a rare smile. "And as far as your jobs are concerned, we would continue as we always have. I know that I couldn't have gotten where I am today without the help of all of you, and I hope that all of you like where we have gotten today." She paused to let that sink in. "I'm going to let Robert and Lenny explain the rest of this stuff, but I'm going to sit right here, and if anyone has any questions, feel free to ask."

Robert-the-lawyer stood up and walked to the lectern. A slide appeared on the unfurled screen behind him. He told the group a little about NormCo and a little about their offer. He explained the choice between cashing in and holding NormCo stock. He sounded competent and friendly. If he still harbored resentment over Karen's plan to give some of the money back to the staff, he certainly didn't show it. In fact, he almost made it seem as if it were his idea. There was enthusiastic applause when he finished. Then the packets were distributed with the formula for each employee. Lenny stood up amid the rustling of paper. Karen heard the gasps as people began to look through the packets and understood the only number that mattered to them in all of that photocopied, collated pile: their bottom line. By doing it this way she would be giving away millions of dollars, but wasn't that proportionately correct? After all, she and Jeffrey would become really wealthy. And, as she explained to Jeffrey and Robert-the-lawyer, she'd have to go on working with this staff. She couldn't bear to spend the next dozen years with resentful, unhappy people. Bill Wolper had said the same thing to her. And wasn't this the only thing that Arnold's daughter could do?

The rest of the meeting was brief. Lenny droned on about capital gains and tax liabilities for a little while. But once people had seen their package, the murmur among the staff couldn't be quieted. When Lenny finished, Karen stood up.

"So that's about it," she said. "Of course, it makes me a little nervous to try anything new, but I know most of you won't believe that." There was scattered laughter, especially from the women in the sample room, who had been forced to try new things over and over again. "Anyway, part of the deal is that I have to stay on for the next twelve years. So if you're sick of me now, it's a good time to bail out." There were more laughs and then Mrs. Cruz stood up. There were tears in her eyes.

"Thank you, Karen," she said, and she began to clap. The applause grew until the whole room was filled with it. One by one the other staff members stood up until everybody was standing, applauding Karen. She felt herself blush, and tears filmed her own eyes. Boy, she sure seemed to be doing a lot of crying lately, for a woman who never cried. So, maybe all of this was working out the way it should be. These people had depended on her and she'd come through for them. She thought of all the money she was keeping and hung her head in gratitude and shame.

Karen's announcement put everyone in a kind of hyper mood. People were happy, but their minds seemed to be elsewhere. It didn't help the work load. Everything that could go wrong did go wrong in the final prep for the Paris show.

Karen's only hope at the run-through was that the old show biz superstition about dress rehearsals was true for fashion shows: when dress rehearsals were fiascoes they guaranteed the success of the actual production. Now Karen stood amid the chaos "backstage" and was ready to pull her hair out. Or else she would pull out Tangela's hair. Or maybe Maria Lopez's. Defina had managed to book the extra girls they would need for the two shows. It had been last-minute, and they would take extra work to get into shape, but they'd be fresh and they looked right. Final alterations were being made on their ensembles. Ironically (or maybe predictably) it was the two most experienced models who were doing nothing but complaining: about the difficulty of the schedule, the music choice, about *everything,* and it was lousing up the timing as well as bringing down the spirits of everyone. Backstage was a shambles. The new clothes were strewn everywhere. Mrs. Cruz would have a fit. Defina was actually in charge of the show itself, but Karen always liked to be there to give the final adjustments to the way something draped and to add or—more often—remove an accessory or piece of jewelry. Now, though, after close to three hours of it, Defina had blood in her eye and told Karen to go sit out front.

"I'm only trying to help," Karen told her. "The show is running thirty-eight minutes too long already. I'm trying to help. You know what they say: designers solve other people's problems."

"Girlfriend, you're an artist. Artists *create* problems. And right now you're one of *my* problems. Get your ass out front and see what it looks like from the house."

Karen knew when it was best not to mess with Defina and this was clearly one of those times. Both of them were frazzled to the max and Karen decided not to push the envelope. She walked out in front of the makeshift wings that Casey had rigged and sat down beside her mother, Lisa, and Stephanie. Carl, who had come in to do hair, sat a few rows back, gossiping with Casey. There were another couple of dozen people watching the run-through, some of them taking notes and—at this point—most of them yawning from exhaustion. Many had been up all the night before, resewing hems and tearing out seams. Karen had insisted that they run the black and the white shows simultaneously, to make sure the models would mirror one another during the actual separate events. But she hadn't realized the difficulty in getting one girl to change her style to match another's. Tangela and Maria, who opened and closed the shows, seemed to insist on doing the opposite of one another. If one swooped, the other robot-walked. If one boogied, the other sashayed. An icy wind seemed to have surrounded the two of them and it was hard to see the fashion through the breeze.

Karen sat in silence beside her mother and sister. Tiff had refused to come. Arnold was resting easy and would be released tomorrow. He'd been quiet when Karen called him. She just wished her mother and sister would be as still. Since Lisa and Belle had heard about the deal and gotten their portfolios, both had developed an instant new interest in the business. Now they watched as three different numbers were modeled, each in both black and white. Squinting her eyes, moving her head, Karen actually liked what she saw, but the presentation was lackluster at best. Goddamnit! When she'd finally gotten the clothes right, the models and production were wrong. And the production had to be as good as the product. Because buyers and the fashion press were exhausted and overwhelmed by the dozens of shows they crammed in during fashion week. Most of them would have already spent a week in Milano, seeing Armani, Versace, and the other Italian giants. Paris had to be spectacular. The great shows were ones that created an excitement, a fairyland that even the most jaded of journalists, the most difficult of buyers, could not resist. This show was far from irresistible.

Vivienne Westwood's shows were magic. So were John Galliano's and sometimes Jean-Paul Gaultier's. That the clothes were often unwearable wasn't really the point. They were original, exciting, witty, and fun. Afterward, after the press had gone wild, the buyers usually found a very different collection in the showroom, clothes that their clientele would actually buy and wear. But at the shows it was attitude and choreography and some exaggeration that were so important. A mediocre collection could get rave reviews if the energy was high enough and the models pulled it together. To get the best from each girl, Karen never asked them to model anything they didn't like—somehow they would ruin the outfit otherwise. In the same way, she knew Mrs. Cruz distributed sewing the designs according to the seamstresses strengths—some preferred the simple lines, others pleats. Watching the collection now, Karen was sure that it worked—it might even be her best show ever—but no one would ever notice unless these girls got their shit together. Karen sighed.

Defina came out from the mayhem backstage to grab a glimpse of what the show looked like up front. She stood beside Karen's chair and watched glumly. Carl came up and sat behind them. One of the models appeared in the empire drawstring dress. The girl had a suburban teenage delinquent look on her face. It was a good dress, and she was built for it, but she stared down at her own feet, both sulky and awkward.

"Isn't she a bit much?" Carl asked the back of their heads. "You haven't decided to design for Amy Fisher have you?"

"Better than designing for Mary Jo Buttafuocco," Defina snapped. She pursed her mouth. "The amazing thing is that she was in love with Joey *before* she was shot in the head!" She turned toward Carl and lowered her voice. "Someone else may get shot in the head if they don't shut up. I don't think Karen needs any criticism right now."

"Who was criticizing?"

"I must be mistaken, because I thought it was you." She smiled at him, as if all had been forgiven. Then she turned back to the end of the sluggish parade of models. Her eyes never left them, but she spoke to break the tension. "Hey, Carl, speaking of Amy Fisher, what do you get when you cross Joey Buttafuocco with a Harvard graduate?" He shrugged innocently. "Ted Kennedy," Defina told him and got up and began to walk across the showroom to the stage. Carl paled.

"Hey, that's really unfair," he called out. "The Kennedys have been through enough tragedy without . . . "

"Spare me," Defina said, waving her arm and continuing to walk back to the girls.

Belle turned to Karen and patted her hand. "Well," Belle said, "it was the best you could do." Karen felt ready to explode.

Just what she needed right now: a critical pan from her mother. Why had Lisa brought Belle? Why had Karen invited Lisa? Because she felt sorry for her after the *bat mitzvah* fiasco. Why does everything go wrong for me? Karen asked herself. "Thanks, Mom." Karen choked on her own sarcasm. The sarcasm, of course, went right over Belle's head.

"Not much to it," Belle added.

"Sometimes, Mother, less is more."

"And sometimes less is less. Well, at least you picked pretty girls."

Karen's exasperation showed in her voice. "The problem *isn't* the clothes.

It's the girls. I mean the models," Karen told Belle, although why she was bothering to explain or defend herself was beyond her. The last number, the closing of the show, was due: the bridal gowns. And Maria and Tangela entered, Tangela in a gleaming white, Maria in the sister black gown. Both were as simple as monastic garb, done in the finest alpaca, but Karen had yards of tulle with an almost religious head dress on each of them. The tulle formed a halo around not only their heads but the entire outfits. The cost of it all had been worth it. It was a spectacular effect and, of course, the black wedding gown was a shocker, especially against Maria's pale skin and raven hair. Even Casey and Mercedes, fashion burnouts, let out a gasp when they saw the two models, and for once the two girls seemed to cooperate. They knew they were ravishing and they walked the makeshift runway together with verve. Defina could make the other models perform like this. She'd have to. Yes, Karen thought, it would all come together! Now, if they could only get all of these *schmates* sorted, packed, shipped, cleared through customs, pressed, and sorted again properly for the show, Karen knew she could manage to triumph.

"Is that it?" Belle asked. Karen looked at her but said nothing. "I thought you ended with bridal gowns?"

"Mother, those *were* bridal gowns," Lisa explained.

"Black? Black for a bride?"

"Truffaut did it years ago," Defina said.

"And who buys *his* clothes?" Belle asked.

Karen was about to answer, about to tell her mother that Truffaut was a director, not a designer, and Defina was talking about a movie, but she gave up. What was the use? Out of nowhere she remembered an incident from twenty years before: Belle had come back from a shopping trip bearing two blouses for Karen. That night at dinner, Karen wore one. When she sat down at the table, Belle had looked up and said, "What's the matter? Didn't you like the other one?"

Just then screaming erupted from behind the wings. Half of it sounded like Tangela's shrieking and the rest was Maria's machine-gun Spanish. In a heartbeat, Casey, Karen, and Mercedes were all up and running backstage, but it was too late. The two girls were actually slapping one another and, as Karen watched, Tangela tore the tulle headdress off Maria, shredding it. It looked as if some of Maria's hair came with it. The screams escalated to shrieks until Defina's bulk stepped between the two girls. Like some female Wrestlemaniac, Defina got each model into a hammerlock, their arms twisted like pretzels behind them. Karen thought she heard a seam rip. At least she hoped it was only a seam. At ninety-two bucks a yard, she didn't want any torn-up alpaca.

Or torn-up models, for that matter. Defina had managed to hold their bodies in check, but neither girl would hold her tongue.

"*Puta! Diabla!*" Maria was screaming. "You got three more passages than me! Because of your mother! Coke whore! And I don't tape my own shoes. I'm no department store mannequin." Apparently Maria objected to Tangela modeling more outfits; and Tangela obviously hassled Maria for not taping the bottoms of the borrowed shoes like the others so that they could be returned fresh to stock. Karen couldn't understand the rest of it but she could certainly understand Tangela's epithets.

"Spic cunt! You keep away from my man or I'll cut you! Filthy 'ho.' Mother-fucking-bitch!"

Defina let go of Maria, then slapped Tangela's face. Maria pulled what was left of the headdress from her hair, threw it on the floor, stepped on it, and spun away from the group. "You can forget about this," she said. "I'm out of here!" She looked at Tangela with disgust. "Like I want that coke hound of yours! I can't help it if you can't hold on to your dogs. And you'll be lucky if I don't sue you!" She turned to face Karen. "You can get yourself some other girl to do Paris for you. I don't work with trash." She flounced down the hall.

Shit! Karen looked at the yards of torn tulle, at the ruination. And Maria was the only runway model with Paris experience that they had! Mercedes ran after Maria, while Casey helped Defina restrain Tangela. It took the two of them to hold her. She was screaming at Maria at the top of her lungs. She was scary. She was a wild woman. Karen put her hands to her head. She remembered that it was rumored each year that Yves Saint Laurent had a nervous breakdown before his show. It seemed a perfectly sensible plan to Karen.

She looked at the mess of veils on the floor. She was almost ready to scream herself. How would she replace the black tulle? It had all been special ordered. And where would she get another model now? It wasn't the eleventh hour, it was eleven fifty-five. There were absolutely no decent experienced models available now. KKInc was already overbudget and out of time.

Just then Mercedes came walking back. "I lost her," she admitted. "I'll make sure she never works in this town again. But I have more bad news. Look what just came in." She handed Karen a copy of the Chicago paper.

Well, Mindy Trawler had stuck the knife in deep and hard. PUSHING CLOTHES AND PUSHY BROADS: KAREN KAHN'S TRUNK SHOW. The article twisted everything: it depicted Karen as a shameless saleswoman, forcing women to buy things they didn't want. Then, on top of it, Trawler showed how Karen was forcing her own niece, against her will, to model and push sales. Karen looked over at Mercedes, who rolled her eyes. "I knew I should have come to Chicago," Mercedes said. She sounded as if Karen had betrayed her on purpose. Karen decided not to bother to tell her about the little run-in with Trawler over the champagne. What difference did it make?

Karen wouldn't take it seriously. "Oh, come on. This is what happens. After you're the good news for a while you aren't news at all, not unless you become bad news. She had to have an angle, that's all." Karen shrugged. "It's not the end of the world. No one reads the fashion pieces. They look at the picture. And that's a good picture of Stephanie. The dress looks great."

"Let me see," Belle said, and grabbed the paper. Oh God, Karen thought, I don't need this now! But it was too late. Mercedes handed the copy over. Belle poured over the article, tisking and shaking her head.

Lisa and Stephanie read it too, standing silent beside Belle. Belle's mouth was pursed with disapproval, but what else was new? Karen looked over at Stephanie. Her eyes were big with excitement or shock. Even in the midst of this madness, Karen couldn't help but notice how very pretty her niece was. In the last few weeks she seemed to have matured somehow. Her cheekbones showed more and her face seemed better defined.

Karen thought of it at that moment. If Lisa came as a chaperone, could Stephanie fill in for Maria Lopez? The coverage in the Chicago paper had been bad but the photo had been great. Stephanie could do the black collection. With her dark hair, she'd look as good as Maria had. Still, Karen paused. She was worried about Stephanie. Karen had told Lisa about running into Stephie and rescuing her from the Norris Cleveland party, but Lisa had not seemed to react. Just as now she didn't seem worried about Tiff. Karen wasn't sure if Lisa's attitude was the right one or not, but she was certain that *she* would not have left Tiff at home alone right now or trust Stephanie alone at a party like Norris's. There was another option, however, and it would help cheer up Lisa while Karen could get over some of that guilt she always felt when she looked at her sister.

She walked over to the little family group. Her mother looked up at her. "You lie down with dogs, you get up with fleas," Belle said.

Once a bitch, always a bitch, Karen thought back, but restrained herself from saying anything. Instead she looked at her sister. "Have I got a deal for you," she said.

The arrangements were worked out. Stephanie would come to Paris to model, Lisa would chaperone, and Defina would work into the night with all the girls to give them some tips and more confidence. Finally Karen had time to sit down on one of the folding chairs at the back of the showroom. It was only then that she noticed Perry Silverman sitting quietly in the corner next to a pipe rack of discarded samples.

"How long have you been here?" she asked.

"Long enough. So now I know what you do. And you actually say that you *like* this line of work."

"I don't say that today," Karen sighed. He was drinking something from a Styrofoam cup. "Why do I suspect that isn't coffee?"

"Because you have the instinct of a private investigator," Perry told her, and extended the cup. "It's a martini, my own recipe. Hold the vermouth, hold the olive."

She took a swig of the straight gin and shivered. It was awful-tasting. "And you actually say that *you* like *this?*" she asked.

"I don't say that today," he smiled. "You know Karen, that was an extraordinary show you put on. I don't mean the cat fight. I mean the clothes. I'm no fashion *mavin*, but there is a sculptural quality to them. They're a kind of art . . ."

"Fashion isn't an art. Not really. It's a craft, but it's a very poetic craft."

"Nice work," Perry said.

"Thanks," she paused. "Hey, how did you get in, Perry? This is supposed to be top secret."

"I told them I was your lover," Perry said. "Wishful thinking."

"So much for my expensive security service. I wonder how many sketchers and competitors sat in. Heads will roll." She was actually too tired to yell at security. She'd let Casey or Janet do that. She reached out for another sip of the disgusting drink. There was only a little left. She raised her eyebrows, asking permission to finish it.

"Sure, go ahead. It's my last one anyway. I'm leaving New York for a little while, Karen. Twenty-eight days to be exact. I came to say goodbye."

"Rehab?" she asked.

"You're a regular Rhodes scholar. Minnesota, here I come. You figure the state *had* to become the alcoholism dryout capital of the world. The weather is so bad everyone there has to drink, and they certainly wouldn't make it on any other tourist business." He stopped smiling. "I never was that much of a drinker. Just since Lottie. I guess it crept up on me. So, I'm done with my self-pitying, self-medicating phase." He paused and his voice sank. "One night I caught myself thinking that if Lottie hadn't died, then I wouldn't have started drinking." He paused. "I probably would have been taller and have more hair, too." He tried for a little smile. It didn't quite come off. "I disgusted myself. I don't know who I'll be when I come back. Or where I'll live. Or what I'll do. I don't know if I'll be able to paint anymore, but since I can't paint now I guess it's not a key issue. I'll probably just be reduced to the three B's: bereaved, balding, and boring. But I'm not getting my hopes up. I might not even be that good sober."

Karen stood, moved toward him, and he rose from his chair. She put her arms around him. "Is there anything I can do?" she asked.

"This is good for starters. Want to try it lying down?"

"Men!" she said with mock horror. "They just want to have sex and kill things."

"The only one I've ever wanted to kill was myself," Perry said softly.

Karen hugged him again. "I'm glad you're doing this. I love you."

He looked down at his rumpled self. "Alcoholic artists who wear denim and the women who love them. Next on Oprah," he intoned. He fished keys out of his pocket. "To the loft," he said. "If it hadn't been for you and Jeffrey, I couldn't have afforded rehab."

Karen took the keys and said nothing. Jeffrey must have lent Perry money without telling her. Of course, she was glad that he had. "I'll be away too," she said. "But we'll take care of the place until you come back."

"Hey, mi casa, su casa," Perry said. "In this case, literally," he laughed, reached over, and kissed her once on the mouth. "The show is going to be great. You've got talent up the gazoo. Break a leg," he said, and he walked to the elevator, waved once before he stepped into it, and was gone.

25

PARIS WHEN IT SIZZLES

Fashion Week in Paris had become impossible more than a decade ago.
Because France took pride, as well as an investment position, in the business,
much of the cost of putting on dozens of shows for buyers from all over the
world was underwritten by the government, and everything was overseen by
the *Chambre Syndicale du Prêt-à-Porter des Couturiers et des Créateurs de Mode*.
However, French bureaucracy being what it was, it was no guarantee that
things ran smoothly.

The majority of shows had long been centralized in a complex in the gardens of the Louvre. Security and telecommunications were provided by the
state, but that didn't mean a ticket secured your entry, or that those without
tickets didn't get in. Seats were scalped, tickets were counterfeited, and at
least a couple of shows a year were near-riots when the doors were closed.
Fashion here was more than business; it was national pride and a way of life.

The paparazzi too were more violent and extreme here than they were in
the States, but here there was a lot more at stake. For over a hundred years,
Paris had ruled the world as the fashion center, and the first photos of any
major French collection sold to all the wire services and major newspapers
and magazines. Photographers would literally trample anyone in their way to
get a picture, and more than one buyer or hapless journalist had been injured
this year already.

It was hard to believe that clothes could generate such hysteria, but there
were, Karen reminded herself, fortunes hanging by a thread. Last season the

twenty-three couture houses had employed 2,424 people who had spent 273,416 hours working to produce 1,461 outfits. They estimated that they'd done a million and a half embroidery stitches at Lacroix, and used 350,000 sequins at Yves Saint Laurent. Maurizio Galante alone had used 9,000 pearls. When Karen looked at the beauty and the detail of the work, she felt as if she might swoon. You simply couldn't get that kind of quality back in New York, despite Mrs. Cruz.

Yes, Paris was more than art or craft. It was money. A lot of money. A major part of the French economy was based on fashion's hegemony. It wasn't just the couture houses, but the huge perfume empires that owned the fashion houses. One company, LVMH, owned not just Dior, but Lacroix, Givenchy, and Vuitton as well. And there were the enormous fabric mills that sold to high-fashion clients all over the world. They created and maintained the illusion of glamour that was published by the international fashion magazines and bought by women worldwide. No wonder that when Yves Saint Laurent was about to go under, the government bought him out. It was a matter of practicality. Saint Laurent had been the Chrysler of France.

Despite the government support, the French had lost ground to the Italians in recent years. Gianfranco Ferré had taken over Marc Bohan's job as head of Dior, Armani ruled women's wear, and much of French manufacturing had migrated to Italy. The French had never quite grasped the concept of working together in a factory—or anywhere else. The Italians were the masters. Twenty years ago, there wasn't even a word in Italian for *designer*. They were called *sartos*, which meant "tailor" and was a bit of an insult. Now, Armani, known as The Monk, ruled fashion worldwide, and the *beau monde* bought more high-style, high-priced clothes from Italians than from anyone else. But the Italians, though they could design and produce quality clothing, still didn't have the fantasy, the flair, the complete artistry of the French.

Americans were accused of lacking it all: no artistry, no flair, *and* no production. Karen's workrooms were a dying tradition. Only Jimmy Galanos still could produce that kind of quality. And when it came to bridge lines, well, Karen rolled her eyes at the problems she'd had. Everyone knew that in America production costs for fine garments were ridiculously high, and quality low. So here in Paris, Americans were seen as interlopers, nothing but merchandisers. Calvin Klein and Donna Karan were accused of being watered-down Armani, and de la Renta was scoffed at as a Romeo Gigli without balls. The French looked with disdain on anything American, except the dollar.

And dollars weren't enough. There wasn't a good hotel in Paris that wasn't completely booked during the shows, and it was impossible to reserve a table at any of the better restaurants: all were filled. Fashion was a cash cow, and it was milked by the French. Xenophobia aside, it was no wonder the French were not ready to welcome an American female interloper.

"Okay," Karen yelled as she strode out from the hotel and along the arcade of the Place des Vosges. "What's the *désastre du jour?*" In a hectic five days, Jeffrey had done wonders as an advance man. He'd made final arrangements for the show at the Grand Palais and also rented the space and arranged for tent rentals at the Place des Vosges. Defina, Jeffrey, Casey, Carl, and Jean-Baptiste, their French liaison, were standing in the courtyard of the Hotel Grenadine deep in conversation. Since New York, in three frantic days, her team had managed to pull everything back together. Defina had taken spare white tulle and dyed it black with indelible Waterman ink. Mrs. Cruz had laboriously re-created the headdress, and Stephanie had been rehearsed while Tangela had been threatened and tamed to a point of suspicious meekness. Lisa had immediately agreed to the Paris trip, and had barely bothered to ask Leonard's permission. She'd left Tiff behind—a punishment for her *bat mitzvah* performance—and come with a virtually empty suitcase to fill full of Paris clothes. Carl was planning on shopping as well. Meanwhile, he was doing some great hair things on the girls.

Now Karen walked into the tent and looked about at the vast white expanse. The tent was made from some kind of high-tech fabric, some form of plastic, and it had a tautness to it that gave it an almost architectural elegance, like a huge white cloth cathedral. Karen had checked it out the evening before, but overnight her elves had been busy. Now the place was decorated, no longer a pristine canvas.

Her name was on everything: across the entrance to the tent, on the label of all the clothes, on the invitations, the show programs neatly placed on the folding chairs, and in huge letters spread across the enormous arch behind the runway. She stared at it with satisfaction. But all at once, it didn't look to Karen like her name anymore. The writing seemed foreign, the combination all wrong. For an eerie moment she felt the way a stroke victim must feel, learning to re-identify once-familiar letters. That's my name, she told herself but, after all, the name wasn't only hers. It was Jeffrey's last name, not her own, and though she had never wanted to use Lipsky, she realized now that even *that* wouldn't be her real name. The letters danced before her eyes. She couldn't make sense of them.

Karen felt a stomach-lurching panic. She was about to take her biggest gamble and launch herself on the international fashion stage. Her name was worth millions to Bill Wolper, or even to Bobby Pillar, and she couldn't even recognize it. Was this what they called an identity crisis? Or maybe a panic attack?

It's nerves. Just nerves, she told herself. But anything could go wrong, and usually did. She thought of a fringe designer, Gregory Poe. He found fame by—among other things—creating purses that weren't just like the Pepto Bismol pink—they actually had Pepto Bismol between two layers of vinyl. Unfortunately, the vinyl and the Pepto Bismol didn't agree with each other. One bag exploded all over a *Vogue* editor's Balenciaga. This business was hard. Marc Bohan was dumped after more than thirty years at Dior. Tony de Freise had gone under. Norris Cleveland's perfume debacle was putting her into receivership. What will explode on me, Karen wondered. She averted her eyes from her name. She felt as if she might begin to laugh or cry, and that once she did, she wouldn't be able to stop. Tightening her hands into fists that were hidden in her pockets, she closed her eyes and counted her breaths. She got to ten, began again, and told herself this was all just the tension catching up with her. After a third series of breaths, she opened her eyes and—to her relief—instead of the dyslexic dancing letters, she saw her own familiar name once again.

The others joined her. Karen forced herself to look the facilities over. She calmed down. She didn't want to give herself a *kunna hora*—the Yiddish equivalent of a hex—but things seemed to be going smoothly. The invitations had all gone out and been received and now, as they all stood together in the white tent, Mercedes strode into the empty white space to join them.

"I think we're in very good shape," she said. "The problem with the shows so far this year is that there were only two kinds of things: things that are unwearable or things that everyone already has. People are either outraged or bored." She paused and allowed herself a small grin. "And the crowding at the Louvre was worse than ever." In fact, there had been an actual riot. Karen had heard some journalists say it was dangerous to go. "I think our two-show strategy is going to work," Mercedes continued. "We're the talk of the town. Enough people have told enough other people to have figured out the deal, but no one can figure out which is the A list and which is the B list. It's driving them all crazy."

Karen laughed. "That's because there is no A list and B list, thanks to you." It had been an all-night task for Mercedes to divide up the attendees so equally in status, wealth, and clout that no one would be able to decide if they'd been snubbed. Snubbing was death, and the French were notoriously difficult about seating and protocol. Karen remembered at one show last year the prime minister's wife refused to sit beside Princess Caroline of Monaco. But there would be no snubbing here. *Both* shows would be A-list shows.

Now, thinking of the confusion they'd caused, Defina giggled with Casey and even Jeffrey smiled. The strategy had also doubled the number of front-row seats, always most desirable and at a premium, though the people in them were stepped on by the photographers.

Still, at every show there were only forty front-row seats and eighty fashion heavies who felt they merited them. It was the first chakra on the way to fashion paranoia—had you been assigned a good enough seat? Now ҖKInc had twice as many good ones to dispense! The only question left was which show Karen would appear at and, after long consideration, she had come up with a solution. She was going to open the black show, although it was the tradition for the designer not to appear until the end. "But I'm breaking my tradition by doing black, so it makes sense. And anyway, if the black wedding dress on Stephanie does what I expect it to do, there will be pandemonium afterward. They won't need me. So I'll rush back over here and close the Place des Vosges white show."

Everyone approved, even Mercedes, who was the most worried about how all this would be taken. They certainly didn't want to alienate the French or the fashion press in their first Parisian outing. But Karen knew that there was no longer any choice at this point, and a calmness descended on her. Everyone knew their jobs and she would simply have to trust that they would do them. So when Lisa and Stephanie stepped out of the hotel doorway and onto the cobbles of the courtyard, Karen turned to smile at them. "If everything's under control, I'm going to take off for an hour with my sister," she told the group. "Casey, I'll meet you at the Grand Palais at noon." He nodded. He and Mercedes were going to handle the show there and Defina was doing the Place des Vosges. Karen turned to her. "Is Tangela all right?" she asked. Defina shrugged.

"She's broken up with her boyfriend. I don't know how she feels, but *I* feel great."

Karen smiled and patted her friend's shoulder. "Well, I'll be back to help you in an hour."

Le Marais had been a warren of tiny streets and ramshackle old buildings that had once been the equivalent of London's East End slums. But then the Pompidou Center and urban gentrification had kicked in, and in the last decade Le Marais had become the hippest and most charming *quartier* in Paris. The Place des Vosges, a perfectly preserved sixteenth-century square, was the centerpiece and around it were arrayed all the charming shops, fashionable bistros, adorable cafés, slick boutiques, and nouvelle restaurants that anyone could ask for. Karen could have stayed at the *haute* elegant Crillon, right on the Place de la Concorde, or the luxurious George V, off the Champs Elysées, but Le Marais was younger, hipper, and a lot less pretentious. If Karen was also a little intimidated by the grande hotels and established fashion houses in the tonier quarters, she wasn't admitting it.

Now, the three of them, Karen, Stephanie, and Lisa, took off, single file, along the narrow sidewalk. They passed a greengrocer, and an old-fashioned café that still had the tin-covered counter and unmatched battered chairs of a neighborhood gathering place. Everything seemed so charming, so pretty, in the watery morning sun. Colors looked different here in Paris light. Karen was glad she wasn't doing colors in her show. They wouldn't have translated well.

For her, this was more than a business gamble; it was a dream that she had made come true. She'd justified the expense to Jeffrey with the argument that this would put them in the big leagues, truly part of international fashion, but that wasn't her real reason for the show. For her, this was keeping a promise she'd made to teenaged Karen Lipsky back in Rockville Centre, Long Island—that some day she'd have a show in Paris, just like Coco Chanel. She smiled at everything around her. It was really happening.

The streets here were so much cleaner than in New York. One of the small Parisian street-cleaning machines trundled by, sucking up litter like a Zamboni with an eating disorder. A boulangerie displayed skinned rabbits in the window. Karen turned away from the dead *lapins* and to Stephanie. "Are you nervous?" she asked.

"Not really," Stephanie said. But she was pale and her eyes looked a little blank.

"Did the two of you have breakfast yet?" Karen asked. And when Lisa shook her head, Karen led them to a *pâtisserie* that had a dozen tiny tables. "The *pain au chocolat* is unbelievable," Karen told them. "And the croissants ain't bad either. What will ya have?"

"I'll try a real French croissant," Lisa said happily. "No Sara Lee."

"Nothing for me," Stephanie told them.

"Oh, Stephie. You have to have *something*. Aren't you starving? You didn't have anything on the plane."

"Well, plane food." Stephie waved her hand dismissively.

The girl was probably nervous, but she had to eat. Karen ordered an *infusion*, which always sounded so medical but was only a French herbal tea, along with three croissants. Stephanie and Lisa drank their *café au lait* but Stephanie barely touched the croissant that Karen insisted she order.

"This is so exciting," Lisa said. "I mean, it's so *French*."

Stephanie rolled her eyes and jerked her head, throwing her hair half over her face in embarrassment. "Well, it *is* Paris. Did you expect it would be Spanish?"

Karen smiled at her sister. "Did that sound stupid?" Lisa asked. "But you know what I mean," she said. Karen nodded understandingly. "Do you think I can get by, shopping without knowing any French?"

"They understand American Express," Karen told her. "Just wave your card and point. Most of them speak English anyway, though they don't always like to admit it. I confuse the hell out of them because my French is so good. Lucky they can't tell that my English is so bad! Once they realize I'm American, they respect me less, but by then it's harder for them to be snotty." Lisa laughed. Karen took another sip of her *infusion*. It felt good to share this time with her sister. It had been too long. Lisa seemed almost tipsy with pleasure. She seemed to have recovered without a scar from the *bat mitzvah* travesty. "Will Tiff be all right, without you this week?" Karen asked. "She could have come, too." Karen hadn't had time or courage to ask how Tiff had recuperated from the ordeal.

"Oh, she'll be fine with Belle," Lisa answered Karen.

"Why? We never were," Karen said. Lisa just laughed.

"I'm going to take Stephanie back to the hotel for a rest and then Mercedes is bringing her over to the Grand Palais. I'm just going to do a little window shopping and then I'll be there for the black show. I can't wait to see Stephie in that wedding dress." Lisa reached across the table and took Karen's hand. "Thank you," she said. "This is so exciting for both of us. I just can't thank you enough."

Stephanie jerked her head, tilting her hair over her face again. "Mother!" she said.

Lisa kept right on, despite her daughter's embarrassment. "And, Karen, you *are* going to accept the NormCo deal when you meet them over here? It's going to mean so much to me."

"Yeah. A new wardrobe," Stephanie muttered.

Karen sat back in her chair. "How did *you* know about the meeting?"

"Oh, I guess Jeffrey mentioned it."

Karen stared at her sister. Was Lisa blushing? Karen heard the irritation in her voice and saw her sister look away in embarrassment. To change the focus, Karen looked at her niece's untouched plate. "Are we finished?" she asked rhetorically. "Let's take a look around. Then I'll get you back to the hotel for your beauty rest."

*　　*　　*

Later, after it all, Karen couldn't believe it. In her wildest dreams, she couldn't have imagined the tumult, swarming press, the customers in a feeding frenzy. Maybe Defina was right, she thought. Low expectations *were* the secret to happiness. Because she had been so filled with apprehension about the show, because Paris had meant so much and seemed so unconquerable for a Jewish girl from Brooklyn, she was transported by the reaction the dual shows had generated. Everything had gone like clockwork, but it had been a jazzed-up, hip, hell of a clock. All the novice models had come alive on the runway. Their freshness had worked in her favor. But they hadn't looked like kids dressed up in women's clothes—except maybe for Stephie. Their simplicity had set off the sophistication of Karen's designs. The clothes had been successful beyond her expectations. She'd torn herself away from the black show at the Grand Palais and run by limo to the Place des Vosges in time to see the last quarter of the white show. Her only regret was that she missed the explosion when Stephanie had slouched down the Grand Palais runway in the black cloud of the closing wedding gown. Apparently the audience had gone berserk. Meanwhile, at the Place des Vosges, Karen had been dragged down the runway by Tangela and all the other young models at the close of the white show, where she'd been handed a fabulous bouquet of black tulips and white lilies by Carl. It was sincere, not orchestrated, and she really hadn't expected it, or the standing ovation that followed. Paris had cheered for her! Jeffrey had stood there too, his arms crossed, his smile a grin of approval that stretched from ear to ear. It had been wonderful. And Defina, behind her, had whispered in her ear. "It don't get any better than this." As usual, it seemed as if Defina was right.

But it turned out that Defina was wrong. Because back at the hotel, in Jeffrey's arms, it did get better. He fed her caviar wrapped in tiny crepes and held the champagne glass to her mouth. He babied her. "You did it!" he said, over and over. "You did it!"

He covered her face in kisses and then worked his way down. *Then* he gave her a back massage—a real four-star one. "Ouch! Not so hard!" she begged.

"What's the difference between light and hard?" he asked. She shrugged under his strong hands. "You can sleep with a light on," Jeffrey said, and she groaned at the silly joke and at the way his fingers were finding and unknotting the muscles in her neck. High on the massage, the excitement, the champagne, the success, and the relief, she felt that she could totally abandon herself to his love. And he was wild. Sex had always been good between them, but now, tonight, Karen felt his passion for her more than she ever had before. He seemed to want to possess every inch of her, to claim all of her as his own. And she let him, bathed in the luxury of complete approval. For once in her life, Karen felt perfectly loved.

Defina sashayed down the long promenade of the Plaza Athènèe Hotel to the *bergère* beside Karen's. As she sank into the armchair, she grinned. She knew that every woman's eye had been on her. There were no wives of *marchands de fromage* in this joint. "Still got what it takes, if I do say so myself. Maybe I should lose a few pounds and go back to the runway."

"Maybe you should sleep a few hours and get back to reality," Karen teased. "Want some tea?"

"Best tea sandwiches?" Defina asked.

"William Poll."

Defina nodded agreement. "Best tea?"

"In New York? The Stanhope. But in London, Claridge's."

Defina shook her head. "Nuh-uh. You ever had tea on the fourth floor of Harrod's? To die for."

One of the young, attractive waiters approached. Karen wondered if management selected them as a special treat for the women of a certain age who regularly took their tea at the Plaza Athènèe. The young men always seemed so proud to serve, as if it were an honor. She turned to Defina. "What will you have?" she asked.

Defina ordered Earl Grey and some sandwiches. *Le the Anglais* was always served in the afternoon at the Plaza. Once the waiter left with their order, Defina turned to Karen. "Well, girlfriend, you did it. Everybody, and I mean *everybody,* is talking about the show. *Tout* Paris. How does it feel to have a triumph like this?"

Karen grinned. "Pretty fucking good," she admitted. And after this tea, she was meeting Jeffrey back at the hotel for a good night's sleep, her first in weeks. No worrying about the deal, about the show, or about the baby phone. Karen felt most of the pressure drop from her shoulders. She took a deep breath and relaxed.

The waiter returned, an assistant behind him, carrying the tea service and all the little goodies that came with it. Karen leaned back, crossed her legs, and watched the rest of the room watch her and Defina. For this week, in Paris, Karen was a recognizable star. It was gratifying, but kind of silly too. I mean, when it comes right down to it, it's just *schmates,* Karen thought.

With that thought, somehow, all at once, despite the show, despite the good press, despite the orders, and despite Jeffrey's passion last night, Karen's giddy mood began to evaporate. She felt, suddenly, as flat as the champagne she and Jeffrey had left overnight on the bedside table. It's just *schmates*. Is that all she'd be left with in the end?

As if sensing her mood shift, Defina patted her hand. "Where's your husband?" she asked.

"Sleeping it off," Karen told her. "He put in quite a performance last night."

Defina pursed her lips. "Yeah, baby. Nothing like a little success to act as an aphrodisiac." She smiled, but Karen could see it was directed inward, at memories, not at her. "Nights after a big show, I coulda had any man I wanted." Defina laughed. "Well, I *did* have any man I wanted. But, of course, you couldn't keep them. Not usually."

"But Defina, they didn't leave you. You usually threw them out."

"Yeah. Because they couldn't give me what I wanted. Let's face it, girl-friend: most men want to find a mother. Well, *everyone* knows that, but the big secret is that it isn't just men who want mothers. We do, too. And there ain't no chance that we're gonna get 'em. Why do you think women always complain that men don't cuddle enough in bed? How come we're always dis-appointed? How come you live with any man long enough and you come to see him as weak? As a child? Because he ain't a mother to you! And the few men who could be are usually ignored by women because they're not what we see as attractive." Defina whooshed out a sigh from somewhere deep inside. She shook her head. "I could write a book," she said. "Sure was one thing my African ancestors got right: worship the fertility goddess, the mother. That's *all* anybody wants. A real mom."

"Well, I'm still looking for mine."

Defina raised her eyebrows. "Yeah, how's that going? And what has Belle said about it?" she asked.

Karen snorted. "I'm crazy, not stupid. I haven't told Belle. Nobody knows, not even Jeffrey. But the detective hasn't called. I guess he's only come up with dead ends. Do you think it's crazy?"

Defina looked at Karen, her black eyes warm with understanding. "Karen, I think you're a miracle girl. You keep spinning out designs and businesses and jobs and money for everybody. Sometimes I ask myself when the well is going to run dry." She reached out and took Karen's hand. "I just hope that this is something that will feed you. What did Madame Renault say?"

"Madame Renault said I already found my mother," Karen murmured. "She was wrong about that, but she also said I was in a web and would have to break strands and that each of them would bleed." Karen paused. "*And* that I have a child waiting. It doesn't seem like it. That's the only thing that really makes me sad."

"Madame knows a lot of things."

"But she also said I already had my mother."

"Well, you do."

"I don't know, Defina. Somehow this isn't enough. Maybe if Belle were different, if we were closer or if I was . . . well, anyway, I feel more connected to you and Carl than I do to my family. Maybe that's why I wanted a baby so much. To feel connected, to make Jeffrey and me into more than just a couple. I'm not related by blood to anyone I know. It makes me feel sometimes like I'm lost in space, in that big black nothingness. Sometimes I wake up at night with the sweats. I'm just connected to the mother-ship by a thin life line, and sometimes I feel it might snap."

Defina nodded. "Just like a spider with a line of silk! Did you ever see them throw themselves out into space to weave? They're taking a chance, every single time. They got to do it or else they'd never create anything. But I bet it don't feel good, even to a spider."

They were interrupted by a throat clearing, and looked up to see Carl towering over them. "Longer in tooth, perhaps, but more beautiful than ever," he said, and kissed each of them on both cheeks. Karen could see he was in new clothes from head to foot. "You look awfully grim for two girls who have just taken Paris by storm," Carl said. "Mind if I join the funeral? I see you got the best table in town. As well you should. Hey, did you check out the jewelry on some of these babes?"

Karen raised her eyebrows. "Carl, there isn't a babe in this entire hotel. Not at these prices."

"Well *excusez-moi*. You're absolutely right. I stand corrected. You can take the boy out of Lawn Guylind but you can't take Lawn Guylind out of the boy." He sat himself gingerly in a *fauteil* that a waiter had discreetly provided.

"Speaking of babes, what's the news on the baby front?" Carl asked.

Karen brought him and Defina up-to-date. Defina patted Karen's arm.

"You'll find your baby," Defina said. "You got any names ready for when you do?"

Karen smiled and shook her head. "I haven't thought that far ahead."

"Come on girl, you got to think positive. Want some suggestions?"

"Carl is nice for a boy," Carl said.

"Forget about it," Defina told him. It saved Karen the trouble.

"Yeah? Well, black people sure do weird names," Carl retorted. "Did you know that all four of George Foreman's sons are named George Edward? And a black woman in my building had triplet girls and she named them Latisha, Alisha, and Talisha."

"What's wrong with that?" Defina asked.

Carl crossed his arms and looked up toward the ceiling. "Exactly the kind of response I would expect from a woman who named *her* kid Tangela. Is that a girl or a fruit?"

Defina chose, regally, to ignore the obvious cheap shot and turned to Karen. "Do *you* think black names are weird?" she asked Karen.

"Some of them," Karen admitted.

"Like Tiffany Saperstein isn't." Defina sniffed. "Come to think of if, Defina is a very nice name."

Karen grinned. "Too many people have trouble pronouncing it. Is it a family name, Dee?"

"My mother made it up. You know, she was country folk. When she was carrying me she found out that another woman in town was carrying a baby she said was my father's. When we were born, my mother named me Defina because she said I was the finer one."

Karen laughed. She never knew when Dee was pulling her leg. "But you pronounce it 'Da-feen-ah.' "

"That's only since I moved to the city. You can imagine what happened when I got up north and found out that 'Defina' rhymed with 'vagina.' I only became 'Da-feen-ah' when I became a Yankee."

Carl looked around the elegant promenade. He leaned toward them and spoke in a confidential tone. "Isn't that the Duchess of Windsor at the table in the corner?"

"Carl, the Duchess of Windsor's been dead for more than ten years."

"That never stopped Bessie from attending a good party," Carl snapped. He raised his hand to signal a waiter. "Oh, *garçon!*" he called.

Both Karen and Defina winced. "Carl, you *never* call a waiter 'garçon.' It's very rude."

"Well, they *are* boys. And quite lovely ones at that." He turned to Defina. "But I promise I won't call any *black* ones 'garçon.' "

"My people thank you for that," Defina said sarcastically.

Then, as if to cap Carl's already high spirits, Lee Bouvier Radziwell Ross walked past them and took the back elevator. Like her sister Jackie, Lee never looked overdressed, though she did look underfed. "Oh my God!" Carl cried in a strangled whisper. "Did you see her?"

"She wasn't a ghost," Defina said.

"She looked gorgeous. Is Herb Ross here with her?" he asked.

"Lee didn't say," Karen told him dryly. Now Carl would be off on the Kennedys for hours, unless she got a hammer and stopped him.

"Did you ever notice how the Bouvier women always go for Jewish men in the end? I figure that's how you know they have good taste. They tried the rest and found the best. Jackie's with Maurice, Lee is with Herb, and Caroline's is with Ed." He turned to Karen. "Do you think she'll walk back this way?"

Karen just rolled her eyes and shook her head. Where was a hammer when you needed one? Carl knew when he had exhausted a subject, not to mention her patience. Then she did see a cool blonde walking toward them. But it wasn't Mrs. Ross. Still, she looked familiar. "Isn't that June Silverman?" Karen asked Carl.

"Where?" But when he had turned to look she was gone. Karen shrugged. At least it got Carl's mind off the Kennedys.

"So, how do you like my new outfit?" Carl asked. "Lanvin. Nice, huh?" It was nice. A blazer in a subtle black houndstooth on a buttery off-white ground. With it, Carl was wearing black pleated slacks, a butter yellow shirt, and a black silk foulard tie. "It all cost more than my Honda, but what the hell. You only live once."

"If you're lucky," Defina said, and sat back into her chair with a sigh.

A middle-aged woman walked by in a skirt that was not only far too short but also far too sheer. "Ah shall avert mah eyes," Defina said in a Blanche DuBois accent.

"She needs a slip," said Carl, master of the obvious.

"I think she's having one. But what kind is it?"

"How about a Freudian slip?" Defina asked, and paused. "Did the two of you ever hear the one about the two women psychiatrists?"

"No, but I think we're about to," Karen said.

Defina raised her brows and continued. "These two women psychiatrists would meet for lunch every week to discuss their cases and check in on each other's mental health. Anyway, one says to the other: 'I'm worried about myself. At breakfast this morning I had a little slip of the tongue in front of my husband and it's bothering me.' The other says: 'Tell me about it. Don't be ashamed. We ought to discuss these Freudian slips. They could give you an insight to your subconscious.' So the first woman explains: 'Well, I was eating breakfast and I looked over at my husband. I *meant* to say 'Please pass the buttered toast.' And instead, I said: 'You ruined my life, you fucking bastard.' "

Their laughter filled the tea room.

*　　*　　*

Karen slept for eleven hours. The next morning, she was awakened by the rolling cart that room service brought in. Along with dozens of flowers, what looked like fifty newspapers had arrived. They were arrayed across the bed. Jeffrey was already up, and when he saw her stretch he poured her coffee, then brought her juice. Fresh-squeezed orange juice was fourteen dollars a crystal goblet-full, but she didn't even feel guilty. While drinking it she looked through the photos in every paper. Jeffrey read her the coverage. Stephanie's picture, in Karen's black dress, seemed everywhere, and when Jeffrey snapped on the television they saw that it had even made the morning news show. "God! It's all great. But I hope Tangela isn't pissed," Karen said. It seemed that it wasn't only her collection but also her niece that was a big hit. Stephanie, in a terrible pun, was already being called "the waif of the future."

Jeffrey read her the faxed *Women's Wear* raves aloud. Then the *Tribune* and the *New York Times* arrived, and Karen had time to luxuriate in all the attention. Holly Brubach, a really smart fashion journalist, gave her a great write-up. They loved her. They all loved her! This was more than a success—it was a triumph! In fact, it was moving from what the French called a *succès fort* to a *succès fou*—total madness!

Then she saw the little box at the bottom of the big newspaper page. It was just a tiny squib: N.Y. DESIGNER DIES. She pulled the bottom of the page closer. "Willie Artech, well-known on Seventh Avenue, succumbed after a long battle with pneumonia. Staff announced his death in a release yesterday, but the future of his troubled fashion company remains unclear." That was all. Karen's hands went cold. She remembered him, standing alone at the Oakley Awards, and put the paper down. Poor Willie. She sat there and wondered if he had died alone. Then the phone rang.

"Don't answer that," Jeffrey told her with a leer. "I have other plans for you." Karen giggled but reached across the bed to the phone.

"*Les Etats Unis pour vous,*" the operator said.

Oh God, it must be Belle. Something wrong with Arnold. Karen knew she shouldn't have left him but what could she do? Karen clenched the phone, expecting the worst. But for once she was wrong.

"Hi, this is Sally." For a moment Karen listened to the voice and didn't have a clue as to who Sally was. Then she remembered: Harvey Kramer. Her life was moving too fast if she could forget her own adoption lawyer.

"Hi, Sally. What's up?" Karen felt her heart jump in her rib cage. Sally wouldn't call Paris if something important hadn't happened.

"I know how disappointed you were by Louise. I'm calling with some really good news. I have the perfect mother of the perfect baby-to-be," Sally said. "Another of our other clients had two mothers on the string. One just gave birth, so they've released the other girl to us. She's nineteen, in her sophomore year of college, and due in five weeks. She's all yours."

Karen lay there absolutely still. She could hardly believe it. She looked across the room at Jeffrey. "They have a baby for us," she told him.

"Well, we don't have a *baby* yet," Sally corrected. "We have a mother for you. With any luck at all, there'll be a baby."

"Can you tell me anything about the mother?"

"Yeah," Sally had said. "She's Catholic. First name is Cyndi. Keep it at first names, Karen. She can't raise a child right now, but she doesn't believe in abortions. She's studying accounting. A bright kid."

"What do we do now?"

The good news was that all of the paperwork, the medical history, the sonogram, and the other tests had already been completed. All Karen had to do was write a check to reimburse the couple who had previously paid for all this and to get on the phone with Cyndi and help her through her last month. Of course, it wouldn't be easy establishing contact long distance from Paris, but Karen knew she could manage. And then she'd be back in New York in just a few days. There was the madness of the New York shows, but after Paris, that would be child's play! Karen smiled. Child's play! Soon there'd be a child to play with!

Cyndi was in Bloomington, Indiana, and Karen immediately offered to pay for her next year of school. Sally said her office would check into the legality of it, and Karen only had to wait until this evening to talk to the girl. Sally said she had explained to Cyndi that Karen and Jeffrey were there on vacation, but that Cyndi shouldn't know anything further. Karen agreed, and Sally gave her the phone number.

Karen hung up and felt as if she was almost too happy. "Are you glad?" she asked Jeffrey. He smiled indulgently.

"I am for you," he said. "I guess it will take me a little longer to be happy for me."

"I want you to be happy for *us*," Karen said, and reached up to kiss him. He took her hand and kissed it. "Oh, *monsieur*!" Karen breathed.

"Is it a boy or a girl?" he asked.

"I don't know," Karen said with surprise. "I didn't remember to ask." Then she grinned and uttered the sentence uttered by all real mothers-to-be. "As long as it's healthy."

They both laughed, and Jeffrey insisted on ordering some celebratory champagne. "Let's just not mention this baby deal to anyone yet," he cautioned. "Not till we know," and she agreed. They breakfasted on toast and scrambled eggs and then they showered, made love again, and fell asleep in each other's arms. It was only a short nap, but when Karen awoke it was sometime past ten. She had just enough time to get ready for her eleven o'clock meeting. More than the press, more than the congratulations of her staff, more important even than the orders that were pouring in, was the fact that, for the first time, she had been approached by European mills to design fabrics for them. She had agreed to meet them. Afterward, she and Jeffrey had a lunch date with Bill Wolper. She lay still for a minute, savoring everything. For the first time in a long while she felt perfectly happy. She'd get her baby, she had her husband, and her career was better than ever. She would have it all! She left Jeffrey sleeping in the tousled sheets, a note on her pillow telling him she'd meet him back at the hotel at one.

It was every great designer's dream. Designing fabrics meant that she would not have to choose from other people's designs, but could create her own. Now there would be no limitations but her own on what she could create. Brocheir, the wonderful Lyons manufacturer, wanted her, and Darquer of Callais had also left a message to call. Their recognition meant more to her than even the Oakley Award. It was like giving an artist unlimited colors to work with, when before they could only use another's paint box. Karen was thrilled, and if Brocheir and Darquer had approached her, maybe Gandini and Taroni of Milan would follow.

But she didn't have time to gloat, because she had to come back to the room to call Bloomington, Indiana, for the first conversation with the mother of her child-to-be. She was still trembling with the excitement of the meeting with Brocheir representatives, and her nervousness now just increased the shaking in her hands. She decided to make the call alone, without Jeffrey. He would only increase her nervousness and this was a pitch more important to her than NormCo had been.

She called the hotel operator and gave her the U.S. number. Then she hung up and waited.

It was a long five minutes, and by the time the phone shrilled, Karen was trembling all over. She took a deep breath. If she was Catholic by birth, she would have liked to cross herself right now. Instead, she crossed her fingers and reached for the receiver.

"Hello," a voice was saying at the other end of the line. "Hello?"

"Hello," Karen answered back. "Is this Cyndi?"

"Yes. Are you Karen?"

The connection was good, and it sounded as if Cyndi was in another room of the hotel instead of a whole ocean and half a continent away.

"I'm glad to hear from you," Cyndi said. "You're on vacation? It was nice of you to call."

The girl was thanking *her*? She sounded like a nice kid, but she sounded scared. Karen couldn't help but compare Cyndi's upbeat voice to Louise's dead one. Maybe everything had worked out for the best, Karen hoped, but the thought didn't stop her trembling. "How are you feeling?" Karen asked.

"Oh, I'm healthy as a horse. Big as one, too. I actually lost weight the first trimester because I had morning sickness so bad. I don't know why they call it morning sickness, anyway. I had it all day long. So, I lost twelve pounds, but now I gained all of that back, and another twenty-six to boot."

"What does your doctor say?"

"He says I'm fine. But it's sure getting hard to fold the laundry. My stomach gets in the way of everything. I had to stop wearing sneakers because I couldn't tie them."

"Don't you have anyone to help you?" Karen could have bitten her tongue. Of course she didn't. "Well, why don't I tell you a little bit about myself, and my husband?"

"Sure. That would be neat."

"We both work in the garment industry. I make women's clothes."

"Oh, yeah? I used to sew in high school, but not good enough to be professional."

She probably sews better than I do, Karen thought, but let it drop. "We live in New York City. You know that, right?"

"Yeah. So did the other couple. They were from Queens. That's New York City, right?"

Karen wouldn't even attempt to explain how it was only a bridge and at the same time a world away from Manhattan. "Yes."

"Are there good schools there?"

Karen smiled. "There are some very good schools," she told the girl. "And we would be sure to send the baby to the best one we could find. We could afford private schools."

They talked for a long time. Cyndi was sweet and very open. She talked about her boyfriend, how they had been very serious and had hoped to marry some day. When she got pregnant, he'd gotten hysterical. She had three years of college to finish and he wanted to go on to law school. He'd insisted on an abortion, but she wouldn't do it. They'd broken up over it.

"I was really sad at first, you know, but in the end, I think it was a good thing. I mean I found out the kind of person he really was, you know? I wouldn't want to marry a man who couldn't love our child." Karen, for a moment, thought of Jeffrey, and wondered if he would come around to loving this baby whose own father had rejected it. Men, she decided, were not just another gender, they were another species.

Cyndi went on talking. She was the first person in her family to get into college, and she was determined to graduate. Karen thought she sounded brave. She felt lucky that the girl was pregnant and was going to bear the child instead of aborting it, although Karen wasn't sure how she could stand to do it and then give the child up.

For a moment, she wondered what the baby would come to feel: whether this unborn child would grow up with the same longing for its real mother that she, Karen, felt. But even if it did, Karen was willing to raise it.

"This must be costing you a fortune," Cyndi said at last.

"Oh, that's all right," Karen assured her. But perhaps the girl had had as much as she could take in their first conversation. "I tell you what: I'll call you from New York next week. Is that okay?" Cyndi agreed cheerfully. "In the meantime, if you have any problems, you just call Sally at Mr. Kramer's office. We'll take good care of you," Karen promised.

For the first time, Cyndi's voice choked up. "Thank you," she said. "It's nice to hear that." She paused. "I just want to be sure my baby will have a good home."

"It will," Karen promised. "I'm sure it will."

Karen sat back, sinking into the red banquette of Maxim's. After her conversation with Cyndi, Karen's trembling had finally stopped. She'd told Jeffrey all about the news, and then she'd been filled with nothing but joy. Everything had fallen into place at last, and here was the place to celebrate it. Maxim's was a classic, a relic of the Parisian Art Nouveau period. Now it was owned by Pierre Cardin, the richest designer in the world. Everything was upholstered red as a womb, from the flocked wallpaper to the patterned carpet. For some reason no one who was anyone had dinner there, but for business lunches it was de rigueur. Needless to say, when they arrived, Bill had already secured the best corner table.

Karen knew she looked good, and men's eyes definitely followed her across the room. Carl had gotten a lot of good word of mouth from the show, and models were flocking to his room for private consultations. But Karen had ten minutes after her phone call to Cyndi and she stopped by his room so he could give *her* hair some attention. Anyway, now the dim lights were kind. Plus, European men had room for women over forty. It wasn't like New York or—God forbid—L.A., where you were finished at thirty-five.

Maybe that was why European women didn't hate their bodies the way

American women did. Aside from peplums and a few other older-women-tricks-of-the-trade, French females seemed more sure of themselves the older they got. In America, most women lost their courage as they aged. Karen sometimes wondered if she would, too.

But at least right now she felt radiant and as secure and attractive as she ever had in her life. Well, why not, she asked herself? After all, her husband loved her, she was about to have a baby (even if it was by proxy), her show was the hit of the season, and—if she let him—the man sitting across the table from her was about to make her very, very rich. It hadn't been easy but it seemed it was going to be worth it.

Bill and Jeffrey shook hands warily, but not as antagonists. Karen looked at the two of them. She sometimes wondered what the mysterious world of men was like. It seemed so territorial: you were either the head of some team, a team member, or one of those poor animals not strong enough or smart enough to maintain a territory of its own. It was all about winning or losing. She knew that Jeffrey felt like a winner, but he also must feel that he was giving up some of his turf to Wolper, the man with the monogram. And Jeffrey had never been much of a team player.

"So, may I add my congratulations to the pile?" Wolper asked. "Quite a coup, Karen. You've really made your mark."

Karen made some deprecatory noise in her throat. Jeffrey beamed. The waiter came over for their order, but before Karen even looked at the menu, Wolper interrupted. "I've ordered the pâté and the special veal for you," Wolper told them. "It's the best choice in the house. Not to be missed. And I've taken the liberty to begin with this Pinot Noir." Veal! Karen *never* ate it. Just the idea of the poor calves made her sick. But the great and powerful Oz had spoken. Karen didn't know if she felt attended to or bullied. It seemed to be a familiar feeling when you were around Bill Wolper. She had to hand it to him: he always staked out his turf. She wondered how Jeffrey would take it, but he seemed amused rather than annoyed. "So, what's next?" Bill asked.

"We're taking the show to Milano," Jeffrey said. Karen turned her head to look at him. What was he talking about? Milano was finished a week ago. Were they mounting an independent show? Or was this bullshit?

Wolper simply nodded his head. "Risky, but if you did this in Paris you'll get by in Milan. And it wouldn't hurt the image. I mean, now you really *are* talking international. What's your timing like?"

Karen expected Jeffrey to begin to *phumpher,* to try and fake something. But Jeffrey began to rattle off dates and plans. "Friday we fly in. We're meeting with Bennezotti, we have an interview with Anna Piaggi, and have the show set up for the twenty-fourth. We're giving a dinner after the LaScala performance that night. *And* a big contribution to the opera."

Wolper nodded. "It should make the morning edition of *L'Espresso*." Karen blinked. Had Jeffrey actually arranged all of this? Without discussing any of it with her? She looked over at Bill. "Well, here's why I ask: I would like to get the contracts back from you by the end of the month."

Jeffrey smiled. "We're negotiating a few last issues. I'm sure Basil kept you in the picture."

Wolper smiled back. "I don't think there's anything much left to quibble over," he said. "After all, I want you to be happy." He turned and, for the first time since the conversation started, he looked at Karen. "I want *you* to be happy," he said. "So, if we have got all of the fine print straightened out, is there anything that is stopping you from accepting?" he asked directly.

She cleared her throat. Jeffrey had been right. The success in Paris *had* made them even more desirable, and for all she knew he *did* have a show planned for Milano.

Well, she'd made the Real Deal. She'd announced the buyout plan to her staff, and now, with Sally's help, it looked as if she'd get her baby, but still, she hung back. She thought of Arnold in his hospital bed. Was this a deal with the devil? She might be adopted, but she was Arnold's daughter nonetheless. The waiter came and set down three plates; the tiny slabs of pâté were frosted beautifully with a green and white dressing, all arranged with the most meticulous care. Tiny leaves of basil, small as a baby's tears, were set in an arc along one side of the plate. It was food to feast your eyes on, but she looked up and across the table to Bill.

Despite the Real Deal, despite Cyndi and the baby waiting for her, Karen realized that there was still an obstacle. "There's only one thing that's stopping me from signing," she said. "I have a last concern."

Jeffrey gave her a look. Wolper had already bifurcated the slice of pâté and had one half on his fork. He paused.

Karen continued. "Part of NormCo's reputation in the mass market has been based on your claim that you make most of your garments in the USA. But I know you do use a lot of offshore production, and I have to be certain of the condition of the workers." God, she sounded like a sociology textbook or something. She was embarrassed. He would think she wasn't business-like, that she was being "too female." She didn't want to mention the kind of rumors she had heard, but Bill must have known exactly what she was talking about. Still, if he were angry by this new factor, he didn't show it at all. He simply filled his mouth with the pâté, nodded his head, and swallowed. Then he wiped his lips on the red napkin and smiled.

"I can appreciate your concern," he said. "And I have a suggestion that might put it to bed. Because you see, Karen, this is the best of all possible worlds."

Karen wished she could believe that, but she merely nodded and kept on listening.

"Of course, we do try to employ U.S. workers whenever we can. But let's face it, we can't always get the quality at the price we want. Or at the price that that same American wants. We also like to advertise ourselves as a Made-in-the-USA kind of company. So we found the perfect solution. Our secret weapon: the Marianas."

"The who?" Jeffrey asked before Karen had a chance to. Karen imagined a group of Italian seamstresses doing NormCo's production. Who the hell were the Marianas?

"Not who. Where. The Marianas. They're a U.S. territory in the Pacific Basin. We do a lot of work there. It's legal, it's quality-controlled, and it's cheap. Plus, no import duty and every garment can be legally labeled 'Made in the USA.' "

Karen thought back to the stuff that she and Defina had looked at in Macy's. She remembered how they kept wondering how it could be so cheap. Now she knew. Well, it was within the letter of the law, apparently. But was it in the spirit of the law? Not Arnold's law, certainly. "I'd like to see those facilities," she said. "Are they NormCo plants?"

"We own one, and we contract out a lot. We also contract out in Thailand right now. I think you would be pleased with all the factories. We're not talking slave labor, Karen. Do I look like a Simon Legree?"

She smiled and shook her head. "But I would like to see them," she repeated.

"No problem. How soon can you leave?" Wolper asked smoothly. "We could all go together. A scenic tour of Asian factory production."

Karen looked at Jeffrey. "In three weeks?" she asked.

Wolper pulled out a tiny automated calendar and began beeping things into the miniscule keypad. Karen couldn't help but notice how delicate his touch was. He looked at her and smiled. "How about leaving for Bangkok on the twenty-fourth?" he asked. "We should just be ending the rainy season."

"That's when Milano is scheduled," Jeffrey said.

Karen looked over to Jeffrey, who wasn't smiling. Well, he wasn't the only one who could make plans independently. She'd finish Fashion Week in New York, then he'd do Milano, she'd do Bangkok. "That would be fine, Bill," she said.

"I think we could have the contract ready by then, don't you, Jeffrey?" Bill Wolper asked.

"I think we understand each other," Jeffrey answered. "If Basil has no further problems."

"I am sure there won't be any difficulties," Bill Wolper told them both. "So, we can plan to sign the contract before the thirtieth of the month." He picked up his glass of wine. "Shall we drink to that?" he asked.

While her aunt was choking down veal, Stephanie was in her room vomiting up her lunch. She had spent the morning going through the newspapers that Lisa had bought for her. Even though she couldn't read most of the French, she felt overwhelmed by all of the publicity that she, "The New Waif," was receiving. The black show was everywhere: the only reference to the other, the white show, was the fact that Karen showed up for the ending. And there was nothing about the other models—not even Tangela. Stephanie felt proud and frightened—she knew she'd gotten this by eating almost nothing, and now it was clear she was right not to. But how long can it go on? she wondered.

Aunt Karen was also right, Stephanie thought. I *am* good at modeling. But the pride and the fear had driven her to call room service and eat three chicken sandwiches and a whole order of delicious *pommes frites*. After she ate it all, she threw up. Then, to be certain none of the calories stuck, Stephanie got her headset and began aerobic dancing in circles, moving feverishly with joy and fear, thinking over all the possible job opportunities she would have now. "They love me, they love me," she was singing to a Soup Dragons tape, when there was a knock on the door.

"Who is it?" Stephanie asked. Quickly, embarrassed, she covered the telltale tray of dirty dishes.

"It's Tangela. Can I come in?"

Stephanie, surprised, opened the door. Tangela had completely ignored her, ever since Karen chose her to replace Maria. "Hi. Come on in."

"Thanks." Tangela strutted across the room and spread herself onto the bed. "Starting a scrapbook or something?" Tangela asked, eyeing the newspapers that were strewn around the room.

Stephanie felt embarrassed immediately. She flushed. Scrapbooks were for babies. "No. I just thought I'd collect some of them and take them back home to show my friends."

"High school? That's kid's stuff," Tangela snapped. "If you want to be recognized in this business and stay popular with everyone from your aunt to the bookers, to the agencies, to the photographers, you have to act like a woman, not a kid." Tangela squinted her long dark eyes and sized Stephanie up as if she were looking at her for the first time. "You really might be able to make it," Tangela said.

"Well, what kind of things do I have to do?"

"First of all, quit school. You've got to make your move now, while you're hot."

"Quit high school? Be a dropout?" The idea had never occurred to Stephanie.

"Of course. It's lame. You think people will remember you next year, or the year after, if you're not in the scene?"

Stephanie shrugged. "I guess not," she said. "What else?"

"Always keep yourself looking good. And keep your weight low and your energy high. Nobody would have looked at you if you hadn't slimmed down. You should be grateful to me." Stephanie noticed a glare in Tangela's eyes at the last comment. But Tangela was being nice, wasn't she?

"I am grateful. Really. And I'm careful about what makeup I use. I don't wear clothes that go against my skin color, and well, I'm trying to keep my weight . . . "

"That's the one thing that's most critical." Tangela told her. Her eyes raked the room and she saw the lunch tray. Stephanie blushed. Tangela smirked. "Uh huh. Well, you got to start smoking. All of us do."

"Forget it. My mother would *kill* me."

"Forget your mother. They're old and finished and jealous. You gotta smoke. And listen, I have something else that can help you keep your weight low, and it makes sure you *never* run out of energy."

"You mean diet pills?"

"Hell no. I gave those up a long time ago. I'm talking coke."

"Diet or Classic?" Stephanie blurted, and then nearly bit her tongue off. Kids back at Inwood *talked* about coke, but her friends didn't *use* it.

Tangela laughed wildly. "Jesus girl, what rock have you been hiding under? I'm not talking baby soda water, I'm talking cocaine."

Stephanie felt a little wave of fear run through her. She'd smoked marijuana a few times, but it had made her dizzy and hungry. Coke was real dope. "No. No way. I don't do . . . "

"Listen, you want to stay in this business and be successful at it? You're going to need something." Tangela jerked her chin at the empty lunch tray. "Hanging over the bowl is no solution. Believe me, this is *it*." Tangela put her bag in her lap and searched through it. "Ah, here it is." She pulled out a black zippered satin bag, opened it up, and took out a mirror, a tiny silver spoon, a razor blade, and a hundred-dollar bill.

Stephanie didn't know what to do. Here was Tangela, a real model and her idol, giving her advice and, for the first time, being really friendly with her. But Stephanie didn't want to do this. Still, she was too ashamed to say so. And Tangela knew about her vomiting. Tangela seemed to know *everything*. Did you get addicted if you only tried it, she wondered? Could it make you go insane? She once read about a girl who took drugs and jumped out a window. She'd thought she was a bird. Was that coke or some other drug? And what if her mother found out? What if Aunt Karen found out?

Tangela had gotten busy. She had tapped some white powder out on to the hand mirror and had now cut it into thin lines. She took the hundred-dollar bill and rolled it tightly. "All of us models use this," she said. "How else do you think we stay so thin and manage to dance down those runways? I'm telling you they're lying in those commercials when they tell you about the soda. *This* is the real thing."

She took the bill and inserted one end into a nostril. It was so gross. Stephanie was ashamed to watch, but she forced herself. Then Tangela moved the other end of the tube to the long line of powder and sucked it up her nose. God, it was disgusting! Like a vacuum cleaner. Stephanie had never hung out with the drug crowd at school. She had been with the popular, collegiate kids, not the heads. And she didn't even like drinking, plus there were too many calories in it. But when Tangela looked up at her and smiled, handing her the rolled-up bill, it was as pure a dare as Stephie had ever had and she knew that if she rejected it she would never be accepted.

Wincing, she inserted the little tube into her nose. It was wet, and that alone made her ready to throw up again. She wondered, for a terrified minute, if she could somehow fake sniffing the coke, but the line clearly disappeared when Tangela had done it. Stephanie took a deep breath, then realized she would have to expel it to have room in her lungs to snort, and kneeled down to the mirror. Quick as she could, she sucked the powder up her nose, like a good little Dustbuster.

It stung, but not enough to make her sneeze. Right away she felt her heart begin to pound, and held out the roll to Tangela. Tangela smiled, took the bill, and snorted up the other three lines.

Stephanie stood up, feeling a little dizzy. She could feel the blood singing in her ears. The end of her nose tickled and she wiped it with her hand. She sniffed.

She felt a light beading of perspiration break out on her chest and forehead and upper lip. She pinched the end of her nose again. Her heart was beating more wildly, but she didn't feel frightened. She was surprised to find that she felt good. Really good. And not scared at all. Tangela was still crouched over the table, doing something with the mirror. Stephanie walked to the window and looked out. This wasn't bad. She felt tall, thin, and important. She turned to the clippings about her lying across the bed. All of a sudden she felt as if she owned the world. She was the Waif of the Future and, in this moment, she knew she could succeed. She'd quit school. She'd make a lot of money. She could do anything. Best of all, the hunger that had gnawed at her stomach for so long seemed—at last—to have disappeared. Stephanie realized that she was free. That she would never have to eat again, that she would never have to humiliate herself by kneeling over the toilet. She felt in control.

Meanwhile, Tangela had laid out another set of lines. Stephanie was surprised. What for? She had had enough. But Tangela laughed. "Didn't I tell you?" she asked. "Didn't I give you the secret?" Stephanie nodded. Her mouth felt too dry to speak, but Tangela was making up for it. "Have some more," she said. "Have some more and afterward we'll go out and buy some things. Then tonight I'll take you to this bar. Everybody will stare, they all know us now. Ebony and Ivory." Tangela laughed, and this time the laugh sounded wilder. "We'll be like Naomi and Linda. But younger." Tangela handed the roll to Stephanie. Stephanie knelt at the table and sucked up another line from the mirror. This time she didn't mind watching as Tangela snorted the other four lines. For a moment, Stephanie wondered if you could overdose on this stuff. But then she felt her heart begin to pump again, even more strongly than before, and her blood once again seemed to sing in her ears. Tangela laughed, and Stephanie joined in, although she wasn't sure why she was laughing. She just knew it felt good. Tangela was her friend.

"Last night everyone wanted to know where you were. Every place I went, they wanted to know where *you* were."

Stephanie smiled. "That's great. I wish I could have come, but my mother and my aunt . . . "

"Fuck your aunt. Big fat bitch. Just like my mother. I didn't get coverage. I didn't get on TV. I didn't get the black dress. Whose fault was that? Bitches." Tangela bent over the table, but this time she used the tiny spoon to lift some of the powder directly under her nose. She snorted from the spoon, but that left half a white moustache on the black skin under her nose. Tangela kept on talking, but her voice was lower now. Something about her boyfriend, and Maria Lopez. Then, "Fuck them," she yelled, and Stephanie jumped. "Fuck them both," Tangela screamed. "I'm prettier than that bitch. I'm prettier than *you*."

Stephanie could see Tangela had broken out into a heavy sweat. Her eyes seemed huge, as if they were going to burst out of her head. The whites of her eyes seemed very bloodshot. Stephanie herself was dizzy. "Are you all right?"

she asked and put her hand on Tangela's shoulder. "Ssh," Stephanie cautioned. "People will hear us." Tangela twitched away and smacked Stephanie's hand.

"Get away from me. Who the fuck are you?" she spat and walked over to the bed. She picked up one of the newspaper pictures. "Fuck you," she said again. She crumpled the newspaper in her hand. "Spoiled ofay bitch!" She reached across to the rest of the papers and began to grab them, ripping and tearing them as she did.

"Hey!" Stephanie yelled. Her heart was beating even faster now. Maybe Tangela wasn't her friend. She felt a fear as total as the strength that had flowed through her only a few minutes before.

Tangela looked up at her. "Shut up!" Tangela cried. "Who the fuck do you think you are?" Then Tangela crumpled into the corner at the side of the bed.

"What the hell is going on?" Defina asked, from the doorway, where she stood with a bellman who held a pass key. Stephanie turned to her. She didn't have a clue.

26

WOMB FOR RENT

It was one of those perfect New York days, when you know the city is a better place to live than anywhere else in the world. Riverside Park sparkled, an emerald bracelet that lay along the silver sleeve of the Hudson. It was going to be a perfect day, Karen thought as she looked out of the long windows of her apartment. It was the day on which Cyndi, the mother of Karen's baby, would arrive in New York.

They had all agreed that the girl would spend her last few weeks here, and have the baby at Doctors' Hospital. Karen had been eager to fly her in from Bloomington, first class, but Sally advised her against it. "The airlines won't allow someone that close to labor to fly, and anyway she'd be uncomfortable with first class. She's just a kid, a college student. She's from a blue-collar suburb of Chicago. Don't make her feel like she's being bought. Comfort, but not luxury," Sally advised.

So today Cyndi would arrive by Greyhound and Karen and Jeffrey would meet her at the Port Authority bus terminal on Forty-first Street and Eighth Avenue. Karen didn't like to think about what the nineteen-hour bus trip had been like for Cyndi and her bladder, yet over the phone the girl had sounded not just cheerful but excited. Karen herself hadn't been inside the bus terminal in twenty years, but it would only be for a few moments and then they would whisk Cyndi up to the Hotel Wales. It was a small, family-run hotel on Madison Avenue on the Upper East Side, close to Doctors' Hospital and in an excellent neighborhood. But not in *their* neighborhood.

Sally had advised against that, too. "Not in your neighborhood, not in your home. She doesn't need to know your last name, exactly where you live, or where you work. Trust me on this, Karen. You don't want the heartbreak of lawsuits later on, or a lifetime of letters begging for money or visits. She's agreed to hand the baby over and never see it again. Believe me, it's the best thing."

Karen had felt a little chill run down her back. "But what if my child wants to find its natural mother someday?" she asked. "What if some time in the future the baby wants to know?"

"That's different. Right now we're talking about Cyndi, who's an adult who's making an adult choice. Your baby has no choice about being born or being adopted. Later on, as an adult, he can take steps to do whatever he wants."

Cyndi was carrying a boy. The other couple, the ones who had passed Cyndi on to Karen, had insisted on prenatal testing, so they already knew the baby's gender. Jeffrey didn't seem any more excited about the idea of a son than of a daughter. More than anything else, he seemed involved in ironing out the myriad of details in the NormCo acquisition final contract. In fact, since they'd come home from Paris he'd seemed more than a little distant. And maybe he was upset about her trip to Bangkok with Bill, though he didn't admit it. But Karen knew that lots of real expectant fathers felt distant from both their wives and the baby-to-be, and Jeffrey hadn't had a lot of time to get used to the whole idea. She was counting on the fact that the reality of a son in his arms would engage his emotions.

The return from Paris had not meant a rest. Karen had the New York show to contend with. Now, Karen dressed quickly in a black dress with a jumper that layered over it. It had turned out to be one of her most successful styles from the Paris show. She surveyed herself in the mirror. Too severe? Too chic? She didn't want to overwhelm Cyndi. She tore the jumper and dress off and instead wriggled into her size ten jeans and a pearl gray cotton v-neck sweater. She put on woven brown leather Botega Veneta loafers and a matching shoulder bag. That was better. Simple, easy, and young without pushing it. She didn't want Cyndi to be shocked at her age. Biologically, at least, she was old enough to be the girl's mother, the baby's grandmother. Karen shuddered. Well, she was no older than a lot of late mothers in New York right now. At the last minute, Karen pulled out a small chiffon scarf and tied her hair back. Cute. Casual. Just right.

Jeffrey walked into their bedroom. "Almost ready?" he asked. He was also in jeans, with a work shirt and a blazer in some kind of nubby cotton tweed. Very Emporio Armani. Also just right. "The car is waiting," he warned, "and I don't want the kid to have to spend any time alone in the Port Authority. God knows what might happen to her there." Karen grabbed her lipstick and they took the elevator down. Jeffrey reached for her hand. She had to put the lipstick tube into her back pocket.

"Cold hand," he said.

"Warm heart," she told him.

"Nervous?" he asked. She nodded, and checked her watch. Twenty-five minutes until the bus arrived.

"Have you been thinking of any names?" she asked.

"How about Genghis? According to you, it goes real well with Kahn."

"Very funny. Why not Attila?"

"No. That would only be good for a chicken. Attila the Hen."

"Sometimes I don't think you're taking this seriously, Jeffrey," Karen scolded.

"Listen, you pick a name. As long as it's not Max or Ben or Joshua like every other kid under five on the West Side it's all right with me."

The Port Authority bus terminal was enormous, and not as dingy as she remembered it. It was a vast expanse of ceramic tile, and at this hour there were thousands of commuters scurrying across the big open space where all escalators seemed to be disgorging their suited businessmen. The vagrants and homeless that must frequent the place were now, during rush hour, a lot less evident. "Sheep," Jeffrey said with disgust. He was a snob, and looked down on commuters.

"Don't be mean," she said.

"Well, what would you call them?"

"Men Who Run with Briefcases."

"Sounds like the companion volume to Women Who Run with the Wolves."

She giggled. "Make it a self-help book: Men Who Run with Briefcases and the Women Who Love Them." He laughed. Jeffrey had such a nice laugh.

They found the information booth and which gate would receive the Bloomington bus. It was an upstairs location, where they could stand on the tiled floor looking through big, dark glass windows onto an enormous series of parking ramps at buses that seemed constantly to be pulling in and departing. Karen checked her watch. Five more minutes, if the bus wasn't late.

It wasn't late. It was early. They watched as it pulled up and Karen felt herself struggling for breath. The thought of Louise came to her, and she closed her eyes for a moment. Please, don't let me go through that again, she prayed. The doors folded back, the driver stepped down, and right behind him was a young, dark-haired, dark-eyed girl with a belly so big that she looked ten months pregnant. The driver helped her off the bus. Even through the darkened windows, they could see the bright orange of her sweatshirt and the lime green and aqua trim on her Nike sneakers. But her face and expression were obscured by the darkness of the glass. The girl waved goodbye to some other people who disembarked, then she looked around her for a moment or two. Karen felt herself clutching Jeffrey's arm. "It must be her," she said. "You go ask."

Suddenly she felt shy. Shy to meet this teenager who was carrying Karen's son-to-be. Jeffrey looked at her. "You sure?" he asked.

"Please," was all she could say. And she watched as he walked through the aluminum doors and greeted the girl. She saw the girl nod and Jeffrey shook her hand and then the two of them walked over to the side of the bus where a tatty pile of battered luggage, mostly cardboard boxes and paper shopping bags, was being unloaded by the driver. The girl pointed to a gray-green Samsonite suitcase and a khaki dufflebag. Karen watched as Jeffrey picked up both of them and then shouldered his way through the crowd with the girl in tow. The two of them came through the aluminum door and moved right toward her. Karen felt air hungry, as if she really might fall down onto the hard, cold tile floor, right then and there. But she managed to stand.

"Karen, this is Cyndi."

"Well, hi there," Cyndi said. And somehow Karen managed to reach out and shake the warm hand she was offered.

They took her out to lunch at Tavern on the Green. Jeffrey grimaced at the choice, but Karen knew her audience and Cyndi was more than impressed; she was thrilled. She looked out through the glass of the Crystal Room to the trees of the park. Dozens of colored Venetian glass chandeliers sparkled overhead. She couldn't get over how beautiful it was.

"Boy, it's really neat," she said. "I've never seen any place like this."

"Well, I don't think you're in Kansas anymore," Jeffrey said.

"Not Kansas," Cyndi corrected, missing the allusion to the *Wizard of Oz.* "Indiana. I came from Indiana." Jeffrey nodded his head and had the good grace not to smile.

"How was the bus ride?" Karen asked.

"Neat. This really nice lady sat next to me. She was coming in to visit her granddaughter. It was her first trip to New York, too."

Karen asked about the pregnancy, about Cyndi's studies, and whether she felt badly that the MacKenzies had dropped her for another mother.

"Not really. At least not now. They were real nice, though. But I never met them, and the both of you seem, well, really neat."

The girl wasn't stupid, though she did seem to be adjectively impaired. They finished lunch and moved slowly to Central Park West, then they took a cab to Cyndi's hotel. "Maybe you want to freshen up," Karen suggested. "Or take a nap."

"Oh no, I'm just fine." The three of them took her bags up to the hotel room that looked west onto the reservoir and south all the way down Madison Avenue.

Cyndi stood, staring out the window. "It's like a grown-up Disney World," she breathed.

"Yeah, except Mickey's got a gun," Jeffrey told her.

Karen shot him a look. "Will you be comfortable here?" she asked. They had gotten her a suite—a tiny kitchenette, a small sitting room, and a big corner bedroom with four huge double-hung windows. "The neighborhood is safe. How about if we leave you here to unpack and I come back to have dinner with you later?" Karen had to get back to the showroom—buyers were flooding in from all over the country as a natural follow-up to the New York shows.

"Sure. That would be neat." Cyndi shook hands with Jeffrey, but when Karen hugged her she warmly returned the hug, though her stomach got in the way.

"I'm very glad you're here," Karen told her. "I really am." Cyndi, Madonna-like, smiled at her.

Excited, joyful as she was over the baby-to-be, Karen felt guilty about not being there for Defina during her trouble with Tangela. The blowup in Paris with Tangela and Stephanie had been heard all the way over to the Eiffel Tower. So today, the day after Cyndi's arrival, Karen had asked Defina to lunch, and as a surprise booked a table at Café des Artistes, the *haute* bohemian bistro right off Central Park. Karen was a little late, and Defina had already been seated at a window table. The dark woodwork and the murals set off Defina's skin perfectly.

"You might *feel* bad, but you *look* good," Karen told Dee as she took the chair across from her.

"The last defense of a frightened woman. You know how it is: when you can't control anything else, at least you can put on your eye makeup."

"So, what's up?"

"Jesus, Karen, I don't know. I guess I did everything wrong. She was out of control, but thank God she's willing to talk now. That man nearly killed her. I never knew a woman who couldn't be ruined by a man. I told her that she needs treatment. I told her the drugs will kill her. I fired her, and then I offered to put her into rehab. I told her if she didn't go, I didn't know how long she was going to continue to get work. Once a girl stops showing up for bookings, it doesn't take long for her to get dropped." Defina shook her head. Tears rose in her eyes and trembled on her bottom lid, silvery as the mercury in a thermometer. "What else could I do?" she asked.

Karen took her friend's hand. "You can't blame yourself, Dee. You've done everything you could. You're not in control of everything."

Dee snatched her hand away. "If I can't blame myself, whose fault is it? God's? Tangela's boyfriend? I was raised to believe I could make something of myself and that anyone who didn't had no one to blame but themselves. Am I supposed to stop believing that now? Am I supposed to give up responsibility now when it has gotten difficult?" She looked at Karen, her eyes narrowed.

Carefully, Karen tried to form the words that might help Defina. "Listen," she said. "I agree with you and I'm on your side. What you said is true: you took responsibility. So maybe now Tangela will have to learn how to do that."

Defina bit her lip and shook her head. "I should have taught her before this. I failed. Big time." She paused, fighting for self-control. "You don't know what it's like," she said. "You don't know what it's like to have a daughter. From long before she was born she was a part of me. She's *always* been a part of me. You don't know how bad it feels when there's nothing more you can do."

"You're right. I don't."

"It's too hard to raise a kid on your own," Dee said. "I probably shouldn't have tried. She only saw her dad a few times, and then, in the beginning there were those other men. They were all so useless to me and to her. All those pretty, tall, useless men," Defina sighed. "No wonder she'd found a useless one herself."

"Come on, Dee, give yourself a break. You worked to support her. You gave her a nice home. You sent her to a private school. You spent all your free time with her. You quit the men. And now you've sent her to rehab. You've done everything you can. Let's face it: this country isn't set up to help working mothers. It certainly isn't set up for single mothers. Look how much better it is in France. Beautiful state-run day care; subsidies. But here it isn't easy being a single mother, or a working mother, or a single, working mother. And that's not even *mentioning* being black."

It slid off Dee's back and she seemed to shrug Karen's words away as if she had not just dismissed them but had not even heard them. "I should have never let her model," Dee said. "You make sure you call your sister, Lisa, and tell her to keep Stephanie out of that game. You do that."

"I will Dee," Karen promised.

* * *

Karen left Defina before two o'clock. She felt sorry for her but she couldn't completely quench her own high spirits. Sales were reaching record heights in the showroom, and Cyndi seemed comfortable at the hotel. Jeffrey was busy with something or other that afternoon, which was just as well, because Karen had to call Mr. Centrillo. He knew she'd been away; she had not called him from Paris. But now, alone in her apartment, she gave him a ring. This was the last piece in her puzzle. She hoped he had some news. He answered his own phone.

"Oh. Mrs. Cohen. Back already? So how was the vacation?"

Somehow, lying to him made her feel guilty. He seemed such a nice man. "Just fine," she said.

"The lake wasn't too cold?" he asked. For a minute she didn't know what he was talking about. Then she remembered that she had told him she was going to Lake George.

"It was lovely," she told him. "So do you have any news for me?"

"Listen, Mrs. Cohen, I'm sorry. I've run into dead ends. We did contact the agency you went through. The records are sealed."

Karen felt the disappointment and anger well up in her, filling her chest so she could barely breathe.

"Wait a minute. You say you've found the agency that has my file but we can't see it?" What gave them the right to withhold her past from her?

"Well, we don't know for sure that it's your agency, but it probably is. No way to find out though. I warned you that this might happen."

It was so unfair. Why could strangers and the courts know her secret, but not her? "Is that it then?" Karen heard her voice choke up. Centrillo heard it, too.

"Listen, I have a suggestion. That is, if you're still very sure you want to pursue this. The only further lead is that I've questioned a few people there and they did find an employment record of Mrs. Talmidge's. I told them she was inheriting some money. I could work on tracing her. She's living somewhere in Florida, long retired, if she isn't dead. She might help with a lead, remember something, though it's a long shot."

Karen thought of Cyndi, her big belly and her sweet smile. Would Cyndi want to be found thirty or forty years from now by the child she was carrying today? Thirty years from now, when she had built a whole life and all of this was just a painful smudge of memory, would Cyndi want it to be exhumed? And would her son want to find her?

"Yes," Karen said. "I really do want to pursue this."

"Then I have a suggestion to make. I have a contact. A guy who's kind of unorthodox. Paige is his name. Minos Paige. Anyway, he has a few tricks up his sleeve. When it comes to helping people remember, he's good. But like I say, he's a little unorthodox and he's *very* expensive."

"What does very expensive mean?" Karen asked.

"He'd probably want a ten-thousand-dollar retainer, and more if he gets results, but he's been working in Florida off and on for some time, and he might be our best bet for finding this Mrs. Talmidge. There are still no guarantees, but it's about all I can offer at this point. Because Paige might also be able to make a breakthrough at the agency or, once he gets the info from Talmidge, he could find a wedge in the court records. Sometimes he can manage things that I—well, that we don't do."

Karen wondered whether Centrillo was talking about bribes or break-ins or something worse.

"Is he usually pretty effective?" she asked.

"Oh yes. He's effective all right."

"I'll FedEx a money order to you today," Karen told him. "I'll be gone for ten days on business, but I'll call you as soon as I get back."

"You do travel a *lot*," Mr. Centrillo told her. Karen nodded silently. And he didn't know the half of it. "I'm not sure what Minos can get together in ten days, if anything, but I'll be waiting for your call."

Karen wanted to make sure that Cyndi wouldn't be lonely during her last month. She spent all the free time she could manage with the girl but had to prepare her for the ten days that she would be gone, touring the Orient and looking at the NormCo plants. Jeffrey was immersed in Milano. She couldn't ask Defina for help: Defina had her hands full with work and Tangela. And Karen couldn't call her sister. Lisa was enraged with Karen and with Stephanie—as if it was Karen's fault that scene in Paris had taken place. Karen had ended the internship program. Lisa was furious about that, too. Damned if I do, damned if I don't. Belle, of course, was blaming everyone, including recuperating Arnold. So, in desperation, Karen brought Carl over to the hotel and introduced *him* to Cyndi. Carl was the best babysitter she could think of, especially since the baby was still in Cyndi's womb. All Carl had to do was think of little treats for Cyndi, keeping her entertained and fed while Karen was gone.

The first thing he did was cut her hair, which was a big hit. "I'd like to color it too," Carl said. "A lot of people say that coloring and perms are a bad idea during pregnancies, but that's ridiculous. They're no problem at all." Karen gave him a look. She didn't need those chemicals to be slapped on Cyndi's scalp right now. He got the message and shrugged. "Well, maybe after . . ."

None of them liked to allude to after the baby. It seemed that they were all locked in a very present tense. Still, Cyndi thought that Carl was "neat" and Carl was maternal enough to take the girl under his wing. He insisted that she spend the weekend Karen would be away at his own apartment. Karen had cleared it with Sally, who had reluctantly approved.

So, Karen was left with a free conscience as she packed for her trip to Thailand and other NormCo offshore locations. As a distraction, she asked Defina to help her pull together a comfortable, light, traveling wardrobe. In the heat and humidity of Thailand, Karen knew she would need the thinnest silks and linens.

Wolper had booked them into the Oriental Hotel in Bangkok. When Defina heard that, she grinned for the first time since Paris. "Only the best hotel on the face of the earth," she told Karen. "I was there once on a photo shoot. Well, don't worry about wrinkling this stuff. You'll have a private valet who'll press everything the minute he unpacks it for you. And anything that gets washed—even your underpants—comes back gift wrapped in a box with an orchid on top of it. It's the most romantic place in the world." Karen smiled. It did sound great, but it was strictly business. She wanted to see if Wolper really wasn't lying—if his production facilities were decent and humane. Ironic that she should be checking out the factory conditions for the lowest-level workers while she stayed at the most luxurious hotel in the world.

Meanwhile, orders kept pouring in for the black and white collection. They could hardly keep up with them. And Jeffrey was completely immersed in fights with Munchin, the final fine-tuning of the NormCo contract, and the Milano plans. He promised to have it delivered to her wherever she was when it was completed. He also promised to visit Cyndi at least twice in the week after he came back from Milano and to telephone her daily.

"Carl will do most of the work," Karen assured Jeffrey just before he left. "But you'll be back before me. Have dinner with Cyndi once or twice. It won't be so bad."

"I'm sure it will be neat," Jeffrey told her dryly.

Karen left time to stop off in Rockville Centre to visit Arnold before going to the airport. When she arrived, Belle was out and Arnold opened the door wearing his old gray bathrobe. She hugged him and was pleased to feel his flesh. He seemed sturdy, though he still didn't look great.

"I'm going back to work next week. The doctor said I could start part-time."

"Great Dad, but don't try to do too much. Relax."

"Relax? Around here? If I want to relax I have to get back to the office. I miss my work. I miss Inez." He looked at Karen. "And she misses me."

Karen only nodded.

"You know, when it comes right down to it, all that most people have are their friends and their work. And that's if they're lucky." Arnold looked at his daughter. "Are you happy in your work?" he asked. Karen nodded. "Are you going to sell the company?" Arnold asked.

"I'm going to check it out first," Karen told him, and explained about the Bangkok trip and the Marianas.

Arnold got up from the chair he had sprawled in. "I know *all* about the Marianas," he said. He rubbed his unshaven jaw. "What was it?" He looked up, as if the answer might be written on Belle's living room light fixture. "Wait a minute," Arnold said. He went into his study and Karen could hear him rooting around. He came out after a time holding a small card. "Dagsvarr," he said.

"What?" she asked.

"Lars Dagsvarr. He's written to me. He's in the Marianas. I'll have him call you."

Karen nodded. She gave her father the name of the hotel she would be staying at.

"Can you stay and eat supper?" Arnold asked. Karen shook her head. "Who could blame you?" Arnold said.

27

FASHION PLAYS

Lisa was struggling into the black control-top pantyhose she was going to wear with the black Charles Jordan pumps she'd bought in Paris. She pulled at the waistband but it continued to remain only above navel level, creating a little pucker of fat all around her midsection. Had she gained weight? It must have been all those rich French meals.

She rushed over to the mirror. Yes, she *had* gained weight. Oh God! She should have watched herself more carefully. But with all the excitement and pressure, and now with the extra tension in the house since Stephanie had been grounded, she knew she'd been eating too much.

Usually it wasn't a problem: whenever she gained a few pounds she went on the Stillman diet and doubled up her aerobic sessions until she dropped down to normal. But right now was a critical time. She looked at herself, clad only in the pantyhose, pumps, and a black lace brassiere, and imagined what Jeffrey would think if he saw her this way. Because, she thought, he *did* want to see her this way. He certainly kept showering attention on her. He'd taken her out to lunch twice in Paris, both times without Karen, and now he had called again and asked her to lunch in the city. Karen had already agreed to sell. So what else could be the reason? Lisa looked at her reflection very carefully. Although she knew she dressed to impress other women, it added a certain excitement to also try and please a man. Jeffrey, she was sure, was very critical and would not be easy. Leonard, on the other hand, hadn't noticed anything about how she looked or what she wore in years, except to ask the price.

However she looked though, and despite the couple of pounds, she knew she looked better than Karen. After all, Karen was built like a horse. Lisa had never understood Jeffrey's attraction to her sister. But then, Karen got everything, whether she deserved it or not. That was the way it had always been. Lisa was the pretty one, but she hadn't gotten the handsome, rich, indulgent husband. Lisa kept her body taut, but she didn't have a sexy man like Jeffrey in her life. She had balding, paunchy Leonard. Of course, she wasn't thinking of letting anything *happen* between herself and Jeffrey. It wasn't like she was contemplating an affair or anything, she told herself. It was just nice that she was getting this attention. Very nice.

Usually when they got together they talked about how hard he had worked to get this deal. Lisa was understanding and appreciative. He implied that Karen didn't understand all it had taken to get this offer. Lisa sympathized, and in return told Jeffrey about what a poor manager of his practice Leonard was. How it was flagging. They agreed that Karen was impractical and had never understood money. Lisa left each time promising to push Karen to sign the contract.

Lisa thought Jeffrey had sacrificed enough. She implied that *she* had given up a lot for Leonard. The dress shop had been her means of self-expression. Jeffrey was sympathetic. Then they talked about what Lisa would do and what Jeffrey would do with the NormCo money when it came through. That was always the nicest part of their lunches. Jeffrey planned to paint full-time. Lisa hoped to move to New York. Jeffrey talked about buying a loft. He told her he'd help her look for apartments. Maybe they could continue meeting and having their lunches.

Lisa looked away from her image in the mirror. She could hear Stephanie making one of her frequent forays to the bathroom. Then Lisa heard her stomp back to her room and slam the door. If it was a big drag for Stephanie to be grounded before and after her afternoon classes each day, it was just as big a problem for Lisa to be stuck with her. She had Karen to thank for the Stephanie problem. The girl was crazed about quitting school, about modeling. Well, over my dead body, Lisa thought. I don't need to be made to look old before my time by having a daughter who was out of school and working—a beautiful young daughter at that. But what the hell was she going to tell Stephanie now when she, Lisa, left the house, all dressed for her meeting with Jeffrey? Somehow neither she nor Jeffrey had mentioned their lunches to Karen. At first it had seemed natural—after all, they had met to discuss the sale of the business and what was best for Karen. But somehow, since then, the subjects had become more personal and yet they still hadn't mentioned the meetings to Karen. Lisa didn't need a pouting Stephanie to snitch to Leonard *or* Karen.

Not that she and her brother-in-law were doing anything wrong. Not at all. It just seemed as if Jeffrey had no one to talk to. Like Lisa, he was pushed away by Karen, who always had so much else going on and so many other things to do. For a moment, Lisa was filled with indignation on Jeffrey's behalf. Karen ought to take better care of him, pay more attention to him. It would serve her right if Jeffrey *did* have an affair. Men needed to feel important. They needed to feel as if they were the center of their wife's life. Lisa felt that she understood Jeffrey—she understood his loneliness. And after all, if she kept their meetings a secret from Karen, was it any worse than all the secrets that Karen had kept from her? Sisters weren't supposed to have secrets, but either Karen didn't trust her or didn't feel she was important enough to confide in. Maybe Karen preferred Defina or Carl.

Since Paris, something had changed for Lisa. The fuss that had been made over Stephanie had at first made Lisa feel important. But then there had been a bitter aftertaste. Since the drug incident, since their return from Paris, Lisa had begun to realize that the fuss wasn't over *her*. It was over her *daughter*. Stephanie was old enough for men to be interested in her—not high school boys like Jordan, but attractive men of Lisa's age. All the fuss and all the offers that had begun to come in bothered Lisa. They made her feel—well, even to herself, she didn't like to think of the word. Let's just say "uncomfortable." As if she were past the opportunity for excitement in her own life. And she wasn't even forty yet! That was why the sale of KKInc and Jeffrey's attention seemed so important right now. It was as if the clock was being turned back, and Lisa was being given a second chance.

That was not why she had grounded Stephanie, though. It wasn't out of spite. She'd done it for Stephanie's own good, and now Lisa didn't care what kind of tantrums the girl had. She could learn to pout in her room the way Tiff did. She'd be grounded until she stopped talking about dropping out of school! She could not go back to work at Karen's and she was going to spend the rest of the semester without an internship, stuck in her room.

The problem now, however, was that Lisa would have to give Stephanie some idea of where she, Lisa, was going. She kicked off the pumps and wrapped herself in her pink terry robe. She walked out of the bedroom and down the hall, stopping outside Stephanie's room. She took a deep breath before she knocked on the door.

The door was flung open and Stephanie, haggard with crying, was in her face. "What!" Stephanie asked.

"I'm going out. I have a luncheon."

"I give a shit!"

Lisa took another deep breath. Stephanie would get over this. "Just because I'm going out does not mean that you may. I expect you to wait until class time, go to your afternoon classes, and be here when I come back."

"I may be here today, but you're not going to keep me here long. Look, I'm over sixteen and I am *not* going back to that stupid high school. I hate that place, and I hate this house. And I hate this town."

Lisa couldn't tell her daughter that she hated the house and the town too. "Are you crazy?" she asked. "Of course you're going back to high school. You'll finish high school and you'll finish college too."

"You didn't. *You* didn't finish college. And I am not going back to those children. I'm calling Christian from Elite and I'm going to get work and get my *own* place."

For a moment, Lisa felt sick to her stomach, frightened. Stephanie didn't seem like a child, like her daughter. She seemed like a stranger and, despite the ridiculous head shakings and other teenage mannerisms, she seemed adult in her determination. But it was all ridiculous, Lisa told herself. Stephanie was five months from being seventeen years old. Lisa was simply going to wait out the rest of these tantrums and then watch Steph settle back into school with all her friends. Once she got used to it again, she'd come to her senses. "We'll talk about this tonight with your father," was all that Lisa said. "For now I want to make myself perfectly clear: you are to report to class, return, and stay in your room until I get back."

"Why can't you leave me alone? Why can't you let me do what I want?"

"Because I'm your mother. A mother's job is keeping her daughter from doing what she wants."

Stephanie didn't smile at the joke; instead, her eyes narrowed. "You're just jealous, so you want to ruin everything for me. Just because *your* life is boring and horrible, you want my life to be as bad. You're jealous."

Lisa went white. "Shut up," she said. "You're not too old to be spanked."

"Fuck you," Stephanie spit, and slammed the door. Lisa had already taken a step backward, so the door didn't hit her, although it was an inch from her nose. Lisa spun away and walked back to her own room. She slammed her own door. But she knew it was an empty gesture, since Stephanie had already turned up the volume of the U2 album that was on her stereo.

Tiff sat in her Language Arts class. She was supposed to be writing the outline for her essay but instead she merely stared at the empty sheet of paper in front of her. She could hear Jennifer Custiss and Becky Grossman whispering.

"Look at her butt. She's *so* fat."

"It's disgusting. Did you ever see her sister?"

"No."

"Oh, she is so awesome. She doesn't look *anything* like her."

"If she were my sister, I'd kill myself."

"Why doesn't she just go on a diet? I'm on one."

"Me, too. I can't stand it. I got *so* fat this summer."

Tiff checked Becky out from the corner of her eye. Becky weighed less than ninety pounds. Tiff was twice that.

She stared down at the blank paper in front of her. Someday she would be very thin. Someday she would be a size two. She'd be thinner than her sister, who wore a six or an eight, and when Tiff was thin, she'd wear nicer clothes than Stephanie. She had them already.

Tiff stopped listening to the two stupid idiots in Gap clothes. Tiff would look perfect. She drifted into her favorite thought: she imagined which of her blouses she would wear with each of her skirts. It took her a long time to go through all the possible combinations.

Lisa went to the closet and pulled out the Max Mara blouse and skirt she had decided to wear. Her hands were shaking. Well, Stephanie would get over it. She would have to. Imagine! Imagine, thinking about dropping out of high school, acting like some little *goyish* tramp. Had she gone crazy? This was all Karen's fault. She had put ideas in the girl's head. She had come between the two of them. Everything Karen did, Stephanie thought was perfect. Stephanie would never call Karen's life horrible. What would Stephanie think if she knew that Lisa was going to meet Karen's husband right now? Maybe her aunt wasn't as perfect as Stephanie thought.

Lisa slipped into the calf-length skirt and cap-sleeved blouse. She had bought a fabulous viscose sweater to go with it. She walked over to the closet and began to search through the chaos for the cardigan. It was missing. She stopped for a minute to think back. She had worn it once in Paris, right after she bought it, but since then she hadn't had a chance to. Had she sent it to the cleaners? She couldn't remember. Lisa was always afraid that the cleaners had not returned all of her clothes, but since she was always hiding new purchases in other places and forgetting what she had, she usually unearthed "missing" garments in the back of the hall closet weeks later. Now she looked through the guest room walk-in and then the coat closet. All the dry-cleaning was covered with polyethylene film and it was hard to see what was inside it. She tore a nail trying to unwind the wire from a group of hangers so she could get to the clothes in the center. Eventually, she just gave up. But she *couldn't* wear this without the cardigan. Could Stephanie have it? She didn't have the courage to knock on that door again, so she walked past it into Tiffany's room. Perhaps, by accident, it had been hung in here.

Unlike Stephanie, Tiff kept her room immaculate. Lisa rarely came in here. There was no reason to. She didn't have to nag Tiff about cleaning up. Since the awful *bat mitzvah*, the girl had been quieter than ever. No trouble at all. Now Lisa strode across the carpet and over to the bifold louver doors that Tiff kept neatly closed. She pulled them open and then she gasped.

There, as neatly arrayed as in the very best boutique, was grouping after grouping of coordinates. There were two Adrienne Vittidini knits. Beside them hung three Joan Vass sweaters—one white, one red, and one blue— with the knit skirts and leggings that matched. Lisa lifted her hand in wonder. There was a jacket that she herself had wanted—it was a Calvin Klein—in a beautiful raw silk. Lisa reached up and took it out of the closet. It was a size two and it still had the price tag on it: nine hundred and sixty dollars. She hung it back on the rack, and continued with the inventory. There were three Ralph Lauren dresses, a couple of Anna Suis, a Jil Sanders jacket as well as a fabulous Armani blazer, three silk Armani shirts, a tie-dye suit by Dolce and Gabbana, and some lesser stuff. It was *all* size two.

Where had it all come from? Whose was it? And what was it all doing hanging there? Tiff couldn't get one of her legs into it. She certainly had never worn it, and she couldn't have bought it. Even if she had spent all of her *bat mitzvah* money, she couldn't have bought half of this. Anyway, Leonard had put all of that money in her college account. Lisa took a step back, then grabbed the knobs of the bifold doors and pulled them firmly shut. She turned her back on the closet. Whatever Tiff had been doing, Lisa felt as if she really didn't want to know about it. She had had quite enough of both of her daughters, today, thank you. She would go see Jeffrey. They wouldn't talk about Leonard or about the girls or about Karen. Today they would only talk about what they would do in the future when all the lovely money, the money that could finance a new life, came in.

28

PULLING THE WOOL

Karen was flying to Hong Kong on one of the NormCo private jets. This time it wasn't the 707. It was a 747. Only Bill Wolper and the President of the United States would use a plane this big. Bill had explained he preferred to use them for long hauls, since they had four engines instead of three. "More expensive to run, but worth it, wouldn't you say? After all, you're one of our most valuable assets." The plane seemed to climb into the sky like a rocket. Once they had reached cruising altitude, however, it leveled out and it was a lot more comfortable than any plane Karen had traveled in before.

There were two stewards, one male and one female, as well as a chef tucked away in the galley. All three of them there to serve her. Karen sat up for a little while, reading over some of the hideously boring NormCo financials, and then decided to give up. Her ever-present *schlep* bag was filled with all kinds of stuff to read—back issues of *Women's Wear Daily*, the coverage that the Paris show was getting in half a dozen fashion magazines, and a T. Berry Brazelton book for new parents. That and a name book were the two she really wanted to look at, but she certainly didn't want to do it in front of these hovering stewards. So, even though it was only nine-thirty, she decided she would go to bed. They were eager to help, but she found herself alone at last in a double bed that was perfectly turned down and fitted with real linen sheets. Of course they had the gray WW monogram.

She got into bed and wondered what it would be like to make love in a double bed thirty-five thousand feet over the continental United States. Did

Bill often seduce women in this bed? She was going to meet him in Bangkok. Somehow, she expected that he would make a move on her then. Men, in her experience, almost needed to get that routine, knee-jerk seduction thing out of the way.

She shrugged the thought away and pulled out the Brazelton book. Back in New York, she hoped that Cyndi was being tucked in by Carl. Karen read a chapter on prenatal care, even though it wasn't her job, and felt sleep begin to overwhelm her. She was tired, but as she tucked her face into the down-filled pillow she smiled, thinking of the baby that was waiting for her, albeit *in utero*, back in New York.

Karen stepped into the white Mercedes that was parked at the curb at Bangkok's International Airport. She had been met by a Thai representative of NormCo and a beautiful, tiny woman carrying a massive bouquet. Karen had been spared all of the baggage, immigration, and customs imbroglio. Apparently, as Bill Wolper's guest, such indignities were considered beneath her. Instead she had been ushered into a pleasant room with purple silk on the walls where several government officials had done whatever needed to be done at a discreet teak desk while she sat on a gold silk divan. She still held the flowers, mostly white roses and purple orchids. There was a note affixed: "Welcome to Asia. I know you're going to love it." It was signed "Bill." Karen wondered if it would be an insult if she left the flowers there in the car? They were enormous and difficult to carry, already wilting in the sun that shone down into the limo windows.

Behind the wall of glass, inside the air conditioning, Karen got her first look at Thailand. She was woozy from her sleep and the long trip, but she had to admit that if you were going to take a twenty-hour flight, this was the only way to travel. Would she always be treated this way once she was in the bosom of the NormCo family? Or was this just the honeymoon, to be followed by business as usual? Out the windows, Karen was disappointed to see that Bangkok looked much like any other city on the way in from the airport, although all of the Thai writing was very different than anything Karen had seen before. It was decorative, prettier even than Arabic. Somewhere Karen had read that the Thai alphabet had forty-four consonants and more than half as many vowels. Well, she didn't plan to learn it any time soon. But it would make pretty patterns on fabric.

The Bangkok traffic was as desperate and mad as she had been told. Darting among the hundreds of small cars and trucks were tiny tuk-tuks, the open-air little canvas-topped taxis that buzzed around like swarms of colorfully striped insects. The noise, even through the cool glass of the Mercedes limo, was incredible.

The driver pointed out the grounds of the Royal Palace. They passed a series of canals, green and inviting, and then they were in the heart of the city, a hive of stores and crosswalks, signs and lights like any other capital. It wasn't until she pulled into the circular driveway in front of the Oriental Hotel that she felt as if she might be in another part of the world.

She was greeted by six men in pristine white jackets and the traditional skirted pants of Thailand. Everybody smiled and bowed low, their hands raised and clasped together before their faces. "*Sawadee kop*," they said, in greeting. She bowed back while her luggage was whisked out of sight. "*Sawadee kop*," she said back to them, and they all giggled. Her driver smiled. "Only boy say '*kop*,'" he explained. "Girl say '*kah*.'" Karen didn't understand, but she bowed and smiled. Then she was met by one of the managers and whisked past the registration desk and straight to the elevators. Check-in was apparently a formality she didn't have to be troubled with, just like customs and immigration. This was what power bought. Karen was taken up to a suite in the old, central portion of the building. She walked in and it took her breath away.

The living room was tiled with white marble. It had huge windows from ceiling to floor. There was a carved teak divan upholstered in purple silk— apparently the Thai national color—and a beautiful huge porcelain ginger jar beside it. There were several clusters of comfortable white cushioned chairs and a large bamboo plant growing in the corner near the staircase. The stairs brought her up to a bedroom loft that overlooked the living room and the enormous windows. Somehow, her bags had already arrived, and two valets in immaculate white jackets were almost finished unpacking her clothes. They bowed and murmured "*Sawadee kop*." A tiny bouquet of purple flowers that Karen had never seen, beautiful little bell-shaped ones with flat round leaves, sat on the bedside table. There was a note beside the flowers addressed to her. She tore open the envelope. "Pleasant dreams," it read. "I have a business dinner but I hope to see you for breakfast tomorrow. Bill." The valets bowed out of the room, while the assistant manager showed her the enormous white marble bathroom, the smaller dressing room, and the little room downstairs off the living room that contained only a table, two chairs, and some kind of a blooming tree. Its utter simplicity and its utter luxury charmed Karen. If she could pick a single room to live in, it might be this one, with its floor-to-ceiling view.

It was already dark, but the room looked out on the gardens and the pool that edged the river, a twinkling green ribbon. There were dozens of graceful boats swooping over the surface. Across the river, Karen could see some kind of temple, its gold roof shining in the reflected lights of the water. Here, for the first time, everything looked otherworldly, oriental, delicate, mysterious, and beautiful. It was the Asia she had imagined in some fairy tale, not the terrible place Arnold had often described where virtual slave laborers worked for pennies an hour.

Karen sat and watched for a long time. She was tired, but she felt happy. Soon she would be rich, and soon she and Jeffrey would have their baby. She was looking forward to settling down to a better time then. With both of these conflicts resolved, couldn't they go on to have a marriage better than it had ever been? She got out her name book and began, once again, to search through it. But happy as she was, she was restless. The gardens below looked so inviting that she felt irresistibly drawn to them. After all, this was her first evening in Asia and she had barely let her feet touch the ground. She would leave this heaven on the tenth floor and have a drink in the garden beside the pool and the river.

The lobby, which she hadn't had time to notice when she was whisked through on her way in, was now the meeting place for people dressed in evening clothes. Karen saw two beautiful Thai women, all in silks, one turquoise and one violet and both sparkling with diamonds. They were drinking with an Asian and two American men. They were breathtakingly beautiful. Karen walked passed them, feeling even larger and more clunky than usual, but once she exited through the glass doors and into the soft caress of the garden's air and darkness, she felt not just comfortable but transported. The air seemed to be exactly body temperature, as if the boundaries between where she began and where she ended became blurred. She walked along the immaculate bricked paths, palm trees and tropical vines swaying overhead, fern and orchids at her feet. A parrot shrieked from a hidden nest, and Karen, startled, laughed. She walked to the balustrade along the river, which in the gathering darkness had turned into a black satin mystery. Lights twinkled all along it and the chatter of a dozen languages from people sitting sedately at the tables overlooking the pool merged into a lulling sound, as comforting as the slap of the river water against the pilings below her feet.

Karen felt as if she had never known such peace. She had worked hard. Nothing had been easy. She existed in a man's world, a tough world of business controlled by people who didn't want to give her a share. She had struggled and she had managed, against great odds, to make a life for herself and to shape it into what she wanted. Soon all the struggle would be made worthwhile. Staring into the Bangkok darkness Karen felt the deep pleasure of success.

*   *   *

Breakfast with Bill beside the pool was charming. A Thai breakfast, at least at the gorgeous Oriental, consisted of the thinnest of omelets, rolled like a crepe over chopped vegetables and sided not with home fries, like in her local Greek joint back in New York, but with the most delicious rice. The idea of rice in the morning had no appeal—until she took her first bite. Mercedes, with her no-starch diet, would have been scandalized, but Karen smiled.

"Good, isn't it?" Bill asked.

"Beats hell out of eggs over easy and a side of pig," Karen agreed.

She couldn't remember when she had felt so pampered, so surrounded by luxury. She couldn't tell if it was the pleasant cocoon of the Oriental, of Bill's money and power, or the deference and attention of Bill himself. She wished they could spend the day staring at the river traffic, drinking and eating on the sunny veranda. It might be good to be rich.

As if he sensed her mood, he leaned across the sun-splashed table and smiled at her. "So, are we going to sleep together?" he asked pleasantly.

Karen couldn't say she was completely surprised by the question, but she was surprised by Bill's asking it aloud. And she didn't know how to answer him. Like a kid, she laughed. "I'm married," she reminded him.

"I already knew that," Bill said easily and picked up his glass of mango juice. It was one of the most exquisite colors that Karen had ever seen.

"I don't do that sort of thing," Karen said.

"But you *have* thought about it?" Bill asked. "You even thought about it for this trip, as a possibility today."

"I did not," Karen told him. She was confused. She *had* thought about Bill back when they first lunched, but that was when things weren't going well with Jeffrey, before there was the prospect of the baby. Anyway, even then it had only been a fantasy. Admitting it might make it happen, and she was fairly sure she did not want it to happen.

"I don't believe you," Bill said.

Karen laughed. "I can prove it," she told him. "Any woman who was considering an affair would have shaved her legs." She uncrossed hers and held one out, discreetly, for him to see. Her ankle just brushed his. He reached down and circled the ankle with his hand. It made her blush, but she covered her confusion with another laugh. "See?" she said. "Five o'clock shadow. I rest my case."

Bill let both the subject and her ankle drop. Smoothly, he began to talk about their schedule. Was he angry? She couldn't tell. They finished breakfast and met the entourage that was waiting.

They had a long day ahead of them. Bill was going to show her several of the factories that NormCo used, as well as two locations where they might become the major buyer of production time. Karen felt guilty, because a part of her wanted to spend the day lounging on a chaise beside the beautiful pool, but she was Arnold's daughter and she wouldn't duck out on her responsibilities. So she was whisked into another white Mercedes and they spent the morning and afternoon at the five different places. Wherever they went, Bill was referred to and treated with more than respect. It wasn't just the bowing or the deference due to a boss. It seemed to Karen that there was a natural submissiveness, an almost religious pleasure, in the rituals of respect. She mentioned it to Bill.

"You're right," he said. "I think it's a Buddhist thing. You know, reincarnation and all. If you are born to a high station it's because it's your karma. It's because you are reaping the benefits of many lives, well-lived."

"Sort of like the divine right of kings?" Karen asked.

Bill nodded. He seemed a believer. Somehow, kings always believed in the divine right of kings, but girls from Nostrand Avenue weren't so sure.

Karen *was* sure that she liked the Thai people. They were good-looking and hardworking, and seemed very gentle. The factories were clean and well lit. There were no child workers, although some of the young Thai girls looked much younger than their stated ages. Still, it was clear that these factories, at least, were not hideous sweatshops. She had an interpreter, and she got to ask a few questions, but even without the glowing testimonials of the workers, she could see that there was nothing wrong with this setup.

She was relieved, and delighted. Now she could sign the deal and she and Jeffrey and the baby (Marcus? Lucas?) would be able to live well and, she hoped, happily. Their share of the money would be close to thirty million dollars, and after taxes and fees they'd keep more than half of it. For the first time, Karen began to think about the money.

Bill took her back to the hotel at four. "How about drinks on the veranda at seven?" he asked. "And dinner? Tomorrow we fly to Korea, then the Marianas, and then we're back to the U.S. of A." Karen nodded. She was tired, and she wanted to call New York. She smiled at Bill and left him, planning to take a nap and then bathe and dress. But when she got upstairs to her room there were three messages: two from Jeffrey and one from Carl. She called Jeffrey first, at home, but there was no answer, so she tried Carl.

He answered on the first ring. "Karen?" he asked.

"How did you know?"

"Who the hell else would be calling at this time?" he asked. "Listen, the baby has been born."

"What?"

"Cyndi gave birth this afternoon at Doctors' Hospital."

"Oh my God!" Karen felt her stomach drop. "Is everything all right? Is she all right? Is the baby all right? Isn't this much too early?"

"One crisis at a time," Carl said. "The baby is three weeks early, but he weighed almost six pounds so it's right on the border of not even being premature. It has no problem breathing—that's the big worry with a preemie—but it seems its lungs are all developed. And Cyndi is fine too." He paused. "Jeffrey's back from Milan. Have you spoken to him?"

"No. He wasn't home. Maybe he's still at the hospital."

"I don't think so," Carl said. "I took Cyndi to the hospital."

"*You* did? What about Jeffrey? Where is he?"

"I don't know exactly. It took your office a little while to find him. He came in and said 'hello' but he left before I did. Anyway, you should talk to him."

"About what?" she asked. "Carl, if you are lying to me, if there's something wrong with the baby, I'll kill you."

"I promise you, there's nothing wrong with the baby. Except . . . "

"Except *what?*" she nearly screamed.

"Well, it's probably just my imagination, but something seems wrong with Cyndi. Not physically, you know. Just well . . . "

"Is she upset?" Karen asked. "Should I call her?"

"Talk to Jeffrey," Carl said. "I think Jeffrey just has to kind of calm her down. She hasn't stopped crying. I mean it's only natural. It's her first baby. This is a hard thing for her."

"Of course it is. But she is okay and the baby is okay. You promise?"

"I promise, Karen. But call Jeffrey. Now's the time to talk to him."

Karen spent the next two hours sitting beside the phone, dialing and redialing her home number. She imagined every possibility: Carl had lied and the baby was dead, or it wasn't dead yet but it was dying, or it wasn't dying but it was deformed or blind or retarded. She tried to tell herself to stop, that she was just being morbid, but she couldn't stop. It was a quarter to seven, Bangkok time, when she finally got Jeffrey. She was so upset that she forgot to ask him where he had been. "Jeffrey, what's going on?" was all she managed.

"Karen, I think I have some bad news."

She began to cry silently. She knew it! She felt her heart tighten in her chest and her stomach seemed to go bottomless. "It's the baby, isn't it? The baby is sick."

"No, the baby is fine. It's just that Cyndi may be changing her mind. I'm sorry, Karen."

Her tears stopped, dried up the way a mother's milk might. "What?" Karen nearly screamed. "What are you talking about?"

Even from seven thousand miles away Karen could hear the fatigue in Jeffrey's voice. "I think Cyndi wants to keep the baby, Karen. And if she does, there is nothing we can do."

Karen had called Bill and tried to beg off, but he had heard the distress in her voice. She tried to simply cancel without bothering to explain why. As she lay on the divan, too shocked to cry, too disappointed yet to feel the pain she knew that was hovering, waiting to swoop down on her, to demolish her, she stared sightless out of the huge windows. That was when she heard his knock. She didn't know if she could get up off the sofa, or if she could get across the room. But at the second knock she forced herself to the door and opened it to see Bill's concerned face.

"What is it?" he said. "What is it, Karen? Has somebody died?"

"No," she whispered. "It's worse than that."

She told him everything. He listened, and then he put off the next leg of the trip, canceling Korea completely, and spent that night carefully getting her drunk. He held the wine glass for her, and she drank like a baby and cried like one, too. He sat beside her on the divan, and wiped her nose and patted her back and poured more wine. He was more sympathetic than she could have imagined. "What a heartbreak," he said over and over. "What a heartbreak."

"Only for me," she admitted. "Jeffrey is probably glad, and I have to figure that this is one less child who hasn't been abandoned by its mother. This works out best for everyone except me. This is my karma." She wiped her eyes again and looked at Bill. "I could never bear to go through this again. I just can't." She cried for a while longer. "Do you think I'm making too big a deal about this? Do you think kids are that important?"

"Absolutely. What could compare?" He told her about his two sons and how important they were to him. Somehow, it comforted her. She kept drinking, and he kept talking: about how the elder boy had a weak eye muscle, a lazy eye, and how worried Bill and his wife had been; about the trouble the younger one had had in school until he was diagnosed with dyslexia, and how well he was doing now. Karen thought that Bill was more involved with his kids than most men. He seemed to be grounded by them. He had never mentioned his wife before, and if that relationship was strained or nonexistent, he seemed to comfort himself with the love of his now almost-grown boys. Together, Karen and Bill watched the lights blink off across the river, and then saw the sun rise. Karen could not count the glasses of wine she had drunk. She felt a little dizzy, but otherwise not ill. It was only the pain in her chest that still stabbed with every heartbeat.

They had been silent for a while when Bill turned her face away from the window and toward him. Gently, he bent and kissed her on the mouth. "You know, Karen, if you want to adopt a child, I could help. I know a lot of people. It doesn't have to be this hard."

"Thank you," she whispered. Even as drunk and muzzy-headed as she was, she saw how Bill made things easier for those in his care. They got private planes, the best hotel rooms, the most delicious meals, and the fastest clearance through customs. They didn't have to travel on commercial flights, and they didn't have to place ads in small-town newspapers and face endless disappointments to adopt a baby. What would it be like, Karen wondered, to *always* be taken care of by Bill Wolper?

It was the last thing she remembered thinking before she passed out.

She woke up dressed only in her bra and panties, lying under a silky blanket. Bill was gone and she remembered very little except his kindness, his arm around her shoulder, and his handkerchief. She was still holding it, crushed in her fist, and it was still wet. Now, her head hurt. She still couldn't believe the news from New York. But there was nothing she could do except believe it.

She took a long shower and called down to room service for club soda. She drank it warm because it was the only way she could get it down. She wasn't sure how much wine she'd had but she was grateful to Bill for getting her through the worst of the pain. It was already afternoon and the sun was slanting into the room, and she had to close the blinds against it. It hurt her eyes. She took a couple of aspirin and by the time the phone rang she could lift it to her head without the ghastly feeling that her brain was moving against the inside of her skull. It was Bill. He inquired about her health and asked if she felt ready to leave that evening. She couldn't think why not to, and she agreed.

She couldn't figure out how all this had happened, but she blamed Jeffrey. He had wanted the sale of the company, but not the baby, so he hadn't followed through. Why hadn't he been there when Cyndi gave birth? Why hadn't he convinced the girl, given her enough support, assurance, to give up the baby? Jeffrey was a great salesman. It had to be because he didn't want this baby and never had. Karen decided that it was a sin of either commission or omission on Jeffrey's part. And she was in a rage.

She also decided that if he gave her the opportunity, she would sleep with Bill Wolper. She knew it was partly out of gratitude, and partly out of anger with Jeffrey, but there was another part as well. She felt that Bill Wolper respected her. He was kind to her, more attentive than Jeffrey had ever been, and he respected her in a way that Jeffrey never had. Despite Wolper's success, he didn't look down on her. They were kindred spirits. She felt she needed his support, something she could count on.

When Jeffrey called an hour later, Karen held the secret of her upcoming infidelity between them. It comforted her. Jeffrey explained again how he had been busy with the follow-up from Milan and the New York show and hadn't made it to the hospital in time. But he repeated over and over how it wouldn't have made any difference if he had been there. "Karen," he assured her, "sometimes this sort of thing happens. You can't blame Cyndi, you can't blame me, and you can't blame yourself."

But he was wrong. She blamed all three of them. She felt a fury that she could never remember feeling before. If Jeffrey had been in the room with her, instead of a half a world away, Karen would have smacked his face, just as she would have smacked Cyndi's if she could. She was shocked at herself, but her rage was so enormous that for once she didn't judge it. She understood why Cyndi couldn't give up the boy, but it was exactly the same reason why she couldn't give him up either. Yet she had to. And she knew there wouldn't be another. She blamed Jeffrey, not only for not being there, for letting this happen, but also for not caring in the same way that she did. She thought of the way Bill Wolper talked about his sons. Wasn't there something wrong with a man who didn't feel that way?

Jeffrey's voice seemed more than half a world away. "Karen, this may be a bad time, but I wanted to let you know that we have approved the final contract. We've air couriered it out to you. You should have it waiting for you at the desk. I know you probably don't want to think about that right now, but at least be sure to pick up the envelope before you leave for the Marianas." Karen almost laughed into the phone. It was all Jeffrey could think about: *the deal*.

"I have a lot to consider," she told him. "It seems as if you get what you want and I lose what I want. Look, Jeffrey, you've been through the contract a hundred times but you've never mentioned to me that this deal, if it's made, will be based on me giving NormCo exclusive use of my name into perpetuity *and* signing an employment contract for twelve years. Twelve *years*, Jeffrey. That's a long time. We've only been married for nineteen."

"So? It's been a good nineteen years hasn't it? This could be another good marriage."

"But *I'm* the one who's getting married, not you. You didn't even mention that part of the deal to me." She hated to make a distinction between them in business, but there was no way he would understand unless she did. "You know I always had doubts about this deal," she said. "You told me we should go through the motions, just to see what we were worth, or to raise cash on it. I agreed. But now that the baby's fallen through it doesn't mean we accept the sale. That was never something we agreed on."

"Yeah, but we never expected the price to be fifty-fucking-million-dollars! There are certain things you can't walk away from, Karen. Not now. The staff expects the money. Our family expects the money. And Bill Wolper expects it. You *can't* walk away."

"You're wrong. I can," she said, and hung up the phone.

She felt sick with anger. All she represented to Jeffrey was a paycheck. Well, Bill Wolper might be getting Karen Kahn in a way that Jeffrey didn't anticipate. For the first time since she met him, Karen could imagine a life without Jeffrey. Lately, they'd been separated so often they nearly had lived apart. It seemed as if half a world wasn't far enough away from the man she'd been married to for her entire adult life.

29

SLAVES TO FASHION

From the air, Saipan looked like paradise. Bill had explained that Geoffrey Beene, Liz Claiborne, Levi's, and The Gap had all used the Pacific island to make their clothes. It was producing close to three hundred million dollars worth a year. As the plane landed, Karen could see palm trees waving beside the airport tarmac.

As usual, they were greeted by a delegation and ushered quickly into the waiting limos. "We're going to drive right by our factory on the way to the hotel," Bill explained. Karen was sad and tired, but she smiled at him.

Looking out the window, she saw the same shacks and down-at-heel housing that she would see in the Caribbean or any of the poorer Asian countries. But the massive factory that they drove by was modern and clean. It even had an American flag waving over the huge building. She wondered if Bill sanitized these tours for people. Well, he wouldn't have time to do it now. "Let's stop," she said.

"Don't you want to go to the hotel and clean up?" he asked. "You need to rest. I have the tour set for tomorrow morning."

. "Let's just stop now," she said. "Get it over with." Perhaps they'd spend tomorrow in bed. Bill shrugged, leaned forward, and knocked on the glass that separated them from the driver. They had already passed the entrance to the plant, but when Bill explained what he wanted, they pulled a U-turn. If he was uncomfortable with the change of plans, he didn't show it.

They pulled up to the entrance of the huge corrugated iron building. There were no windows, but it was painted a neat blue. Big as an airplane hangar, the building had a front door that seemed tiny in proportion. But as they stepped out of the car, a line of men filed out the door and lined up before them. There was a lot of bowing as the NormCo rep introduced the staff to both Bill and Karen. Introductions took so long that Karen couldn't help wondering if they were stalling while everyone inside cleaned up their room. But at last they were ushered through the portals.

The noise was shocking. Hundreds of machines were lined up, with workers at each one and runners moving up and down the aisles carrying cut fabric and finished garments. It was very hot, but despite the din and the heat, the place was well-lit and no dirtier than her own workrooms back on Seventh Avenue. A supervisor was shouting something in Chinese to an assistant, who was bowing and gesturing them toward a glassed-in office. Karen smiled but shook her head. She didn't need tea in some office. She wanted to see what was what. She began to walk down one of the aisles. There was much shouting behind her but she kept on walking and it must have been all right because Bill followed her.

On this aisle most of the operators seemed to be women, although Karen could see men's heads bowed over other machines several rows away. Several of the girls looked up curiously, but quickly dropped their eyes. One or two of them looked young, perhaps teenagers. "Is there a minimum age?" she asked. Bill couldn't hear her and she had to shout.

"I'm sure there is," he told her. He turned to his rep and asked. After a discussion with the supervisor they waited for the rep to answer.

"Minimum age eighteen," the supervisor said. "Some lie to get this job, but we must have papers. Remember that girls look very young but not be very young." Karen nodded. She wandered along, not knowing what she was looking for but simply observing. She left the huge machine room and came to a cutting room behind it, where immense tables were laid out, fabric spread upon them. Here, the workers were all men.

It was odd to think that these small, dark Asians were busy cutting stonewashed denim that would be bought in WalMarts in Nebraska. The Northern Marianas were a speck on the globe and a loophole in the import quotas. They accounted for only a small portion of the enormous offshore production of American clothes, and though the "Made in U.S.A." labels being sewn into each garment seemed to Karen to be a lie, they were legal and it looked to her as if there was nothing wrong here. She'd lost her baby, and she didn't have the strength to look for another. Now, at least, she could give her firm to Bill and concentrate on expanding her business with a clear conscience. She turned to Bill. He would be her new partner. "I'm tired," she said. "Do you think we can go to the hotel now?"

*   *   *

They had dinner together, in a restaurant that featured a wall of dripping water and a koi pool. She told Bill that she would sign the contract and she did, with a flourish, right at the dinner table. He put it in the pouch that the rep would have back to Robert-the-lawyer in New York within twenty-four hours. Exhausted with the travel and the decision, Karen went up to bed alone.

She had been sleeping for some time when the phone rang. A voice with a heavy accent was on the line. "I think you have the wrong room," she said, but the man repeated himself.

"Mrs. Kahn?" he asked. "Please, Mrs. Kahn, I must see you. My name is Lars Dagsvarr."

Oh God, she thought. What was this? Some crazy Swedish designer who was looking for a job? Some rep of a textile house who wouldn't know how to take no for an answer? Or maybe some reporter, from the trades or from the local papers who wanted an interview? How did he get her room number? She was supposed to be protected from this kind of stuff and she was in no mood for jokes. "Do I know you, Mr. Dagsvarr?"

"No, Mrs., but I must talk to you. Please Mrs."

"What is this about?" she sighed.

"People's lifes," he said, but despite the mispronunciation, the drama of his words, and the tenseness of his voice, Karen didn't hear hysteria. The voice seemed grounded. For some reason, she believed him, although there was no reason to. Then he said, "Your father, Mr. Arnold Lipsky, said for me to call."

"I'll come down to the lobby," she sighed. She trusted her instincts and her father but she certainly wasn't going to let this stranger come up to her room.

"That won't do," he said. He paused. "I am with two ladies. One is much older. May we please come up? It is of upmost importance."

Karen was tempted to smile at the "upmost," but wasn't it a logical mistake? How could this be some kind of confidence scam? She paused, and wondered if she should call Bill Wolper. "Let me speak to her," Karen said.

"Certainly, Mrs., but she doesn't have much English." There was a moment that the phone was jostled about and then an older woman's voice came on.

"Yah? Halloo?" The voice said with the unmistakable quaver of age and the lilt of the Scandinavian.

"You want to see me?" Karen asked. There was some talk at the other end of the line.

"Yah. Please. For the children. Tak," the voice said, and the man, Mr. Dagsvarr, was back on the line.

"We can see you?" he asked.

"Yes," she agreed.

They were missionaries. Karen had kept the chain on the door when they had arrived in the hallway, but Mr. Dagsvarr was indeed accompanied by a large-boned, white-haired elderly woman and a tiny young Asian girl who looked as if she were barely out of her teens. Karen had invited them in and settled them into the living room area of her suite. She offered them drinks, but they declined.

"You see, we are here on a matter of upmost urgency," Mr. Dagsvarr explained. "We have been working with the people of Saipan for three years. Mrs. Lemmon has been here even much longer," he said, deferring to the old woman, whose bright blue-eyed gaze never left Karen's face. "Your father knows of our mission. He has sometimes helped. Mrs. Lemmon started the work but we carry it on, my wife and I." Here he nodded at the Asian woman. He leaned forward, putting both of his big hands on his bony knees. All three of them wore white. Karen wondered if it had something to do with their religion. If she had known they were missionaries she would never had let them up. Arnold and *missionaries*? Arnold hated organized religion. He worshiped organized labor. Yet these people had mentioned children. She sensed something important.

"Mrs., you must not send work here. We know you are most famous and very respecting. So it is important for you to know what happens here. Here in Saipan people are slaves. Many people, Chinese and Philippine people, come here for work. Some are sold here."

Karen sat up. "What do you mean, 'slaves'?" she asked. "What do you mean, 'sold'?"

"It is so. In China, people are told there are jobs for them in America. They must pay a broker, an agent, very much money, sometimes thousands, in dollars, Mrs., to be brought here. It is not America, but the broker will not send them back to China. He delivers them to the factories. But the pay here is very bad. Pennies an hour. And people must work many, many hours. They think they will be in America but they are five thousand miles from America, and they do not make enough money even to live. They cannot pay back their families the money spent to send them here. They are shamed. They are poor. They are alone. And the agents or the factories give them holes to live in."

Mrs. Dagsvarr—for the young Asian girl was his wife—leaned forward and spoke for the first time. "Live like pigs," she said. "Live worse than pigs."

"We are trying to change this system," said Mr. Dagsvarr. "We are hoping people in America will know about this crime. Girls are sent here, young, and they must work and work with no hope to go home or to move on. It is like an island of slaves," Mr. Dagsvarr said.

"Of lost souls," the older lady, Mrs. Lemmon, said. She stood up. "Come," she said. "See." It wasn't an invitation. It was a command. And Karen stood up in answer to it. After all, this was exactly what she had been afraid of. Somehow, she'd known it all along. She could not turn her back. She was Arnold's daughter. She felt a sinking feeling in her stomach, but turned and got her jacket. Quickly, she picked up her room key, passport, and some money. Without a purse, she stuffed the small handful into her pocket.

"Let's go," she said.

The dormitories were unspeakable. There were some, like barracks, where fifty or sixty women, most of them very young, were housed with only two or three toilets, a sink at each end of the building, and no kitchen at all. The floor was bare, cracked cement. Some women had strung up tattered sheets for a bit of privacy but the place was bedlam. The heat was almost unendurable. The girls, the women, sat solemnly on beds that were little more than cots, or lay immobile on lumpy, fetid mattresses or piles of rags on the floor. Some ignored the group of four foreigners. Others ran to Mrs. Lemmon or to Mrs. Dagsvarr and chattered at them in Chinese. The smell was indescribable: a combination of dirty clothes, rancid oil, and mildew. Near the toilets the smell of sewage was overpowering. Karen thought of her suite at the Oriental, and the two air-conditioned rooms she had here, just a few miles away.

"But this isn't a NormCo dorm, is it?" she asked. Had Bill fooled her so completely?

"NormCo doesn't have housing," Mr. Dagsvarr explained. "They only contract for workers with Mr. Tang. Mr. Tang is the biggest man on the island. He owns factories, owns these barracks. He brings in thousands of workers. All think they will be in America, that they will become rich and send home money to save their families. Instead, they are paid almost nothing and are charged very much for this house and for food."

"But can't they protest? Can't they organize?"

"If they complain they will be thrown out. Then they have nothing." He looked around at the filth and the gloom. "Very little is a lot more than nothing." He paused. "Shall I show you the ones who protest? The ones who have nothing?" he asked.

In the gloom, Karen nodded. "Show me," she said.

The house was more accurately a shack. There was no plumbing, no running water at all. The floor was dirt. Fourteen women lived in the two rooms. All had been fired, either for making trouble or for producing too slowly. Some had worked eighty-hour weeks until their vision went. Mrs. Dagsvarr explained, haltingly, that several had been asked to sleep with factory supervisors. If they refused, they were fired. If they agreed and got pregnant, they were also fired. Whatever they did, the result was the same: they wound up as prostitutes, servicing the equally impoverished men who could spare a few cents. Karen wondered if Mrs. Dagsvarr herself had been rescued from that.

Mrs. Dagsvarr silently unpacked clothes and food from the trunk of their battered Toyota. The women gathered silently around the car. They were eager, but all turned their eyes away from Karen. "They are shy," Mr. Dagsvarr explained.

"They are shamed," his wife corrected.

Then, from out of the darkness, a woman began to yell. She came running toward the car and for a moment Karen thought she meant them harm. But Mrs. Lemmon listened to the girl as she shouted, breathing hard and standing before them, her legs spread as if she were ready to run again, back into the darkness she had come from. All three of the missionaries stiffened. Mr. Dagsvarr turned to Karen. "One of the girls has been taken to the hospital. She is having her baby, but there is a problem. We must go right away. The hospital won't take her in."

"I'll come too," Karen said.

The girl's name was something like Mei Ling. She sat, hunched on the floor, leaning against the cinderblock wall of the emergency room. Mrs. Lemmon knelt beside her. So did Mrs. Dagsvarr, while Mr. Dagsvarr stepped over other bodies that littered the corridor. He made his way to the desk. A fat, dark woman in a green hospital jacket sat behind the desk, blocking the mayhem before her with a sliding glass partition. Mr. Dagsvarr pushed it open. The woman, a nurse or an administrator, looked up with a bored expression.

"You must help Mrs. Ling," Mr. Dagsvarr said. "She's in labor."

"She is a citizen?" the woman asked.

"No," Mr. Dagsvarr admitted.

"She have insurance?" the woman asked.

"No. But we will pay. You *must* see her."

The woman slowly reached down into a drawer and took out a form. "You the father?" she asked.

Karen thought she saw Mr. Dagsvarr blush, but if it was with embarrassment or anger, she could not tell. "No," he said. Then, "You must hurry," he said.

"It's four hundred dollars for delivery," she said. "You have that?"

Karen reached into her pocket and pulled out five hundred-dollar bills. "Here," she said, handing the woman four. She took the last hundred and put it on the desk. "This is for you. Now, get a stretcher and bring that girl in to a doctor. Now."

Mei Ling had left a trail of blood and a baby behind her when she died two hours later. The girl was thirteen or perhaps fourteen: maybe the exact same age as Tiffany. Mr. Dagsvarr explained that children often lied about their age to be eligible for work. Mei Ling had hemorrhaged before the breech birth had even begun and didn't live to see the baby, who was, it appeared, a healthy daughter. Karen stood in the bloody hallway and wept. Mr. Dagsvarr said a prayer and then christened the little girl. Karen stepped into the room for a moment and looked down at the baby in his arms. Its hair was a halo of black feathers, and, despite the difficult birth, her skin was a beautiful soft gold color. Karen could barely take her eyes off the child. She longed to touch her, to hold the baby, but she wouldn't allow herself. Now was not a time for her to lose control. Wearily, Mrs. Lemmon went off to begin paperwork on the orphan, while the Dagsvarrs drove Karen back to the hotel. They were silent on the ride, all of them tired beyond words.

At the hotel, before turning in to the semicircular drive, Mr. Dagsvarr stopped. "I am so sorry that you had to see this," he said.

"You see it all the time," Karen said.

"Yes, but this is my work. I chose it. You didn't."

"Perhaps I needed to see it," Karen said. She turned to face the two of them. "It may be too late," she said. "It may be too late for me to stop what NormCo is doing. But I will try. And I'll make sure the word gets out back in the States. And I will send you money." She handed Mr. Dagsvarr a business card. "I won't forget and I will help," she promised.

Mrs. Dagsvarr put out her hand. It was tiny, as small as a child's. "Thank you," was all she said.

*　　*　　*

Karen didn't wait to talk to Bill. What was the point? Was he a liar, or had he been fooled, misled by his own staff? She guessed that he was a liar, but if he was only a fool, that was bad enough. And to think she had considered sleeping with him. She thought back to all the things Arnold had mentioned. Had she listened to her father closely enough? Had she not wanted to hear? Had her own selfishness gotten in the way? Or was it her ego, her ambition? Was there a difference?

She thought of the contracts, all those copies with multiple signatures that she had already signed and sent back. As she threw clothes into her suitcase, she felt sick to her stomach. The trail of blood along the dirty hospital corridor kept coming back to her mind, a sanguine scar that sickened her. How many women, how many children, were dying, or working their lives away in slavery here so that women in America could buy a bargain? Was it too late to stop the deal? Was it too late to get away from Bill Wolper and NormCo? She thought with a kind of ironic self-contempt of the special, luxurious slavery she may have just sold herself into. A slavery where she would be able to buy as many clean toilets as she could ever use, but where all of them would be tainted with blood.

Once packed, she called the concierge to find out about flights to the U.S. There would be no more private planing, she was sure of that. And while reservations were being made, she tried, once again, to call Jeffrey. Had he known about all this? Had he suspected? Would he help her break this contract? What if he wouldn't?

There was no answer at the apartment or at the Westport house, their car phone, or Jeffrey's private line at the office. If her math was right—always a risky bet—it was the afternoon of the previous day back in New York. But she couldn't locate her husband.

Karen had never felt so alone. When the concierge called back on the other line, pleased to announce he had secured the last seat on a Hawaii-bound flight, she thanked him coolly. All she could remember was the baby, and Mr. Dagsvarr's face when he said, "This is my work. I chose it. You didn't."

No. She had chosen work where she seduced women into buying clothes they often couldn't afford. And soon she would be enticing more of them, helping her clients to enslave other women a half a world away. Somehow, it didn't sound like a *Vogue* cover story.

PART FOUR

A REAL MOTHER

*Every family has a secret and the
secret is that it is not like any other family.*

-ALAN BENNETT

30

THREAD BARE

The taxi pulled up to 550 Seventh Avenue and Karen jumped out of the cab, almost running across the sidewalk into the building. With the long flight, the nightmare that the Marianas had been, and her loss of Cyndi's baby, Karen knew she was wild. Worse than that, she looked wild. She could see herself in the reflection of the stainless steel elevator doors, and it was Medusa time. She combed her fingers through her hair and, when she reached the ninth floor, strode out to the showroom. Casey, a couple of sales staffers, and some buyers looked up, but Karen had no time for PR right now. Without a word, she passed through the big space and kept moving down the hall to her own office. Janet, on the phone at the desk beside Karen's office door, opened her eyes wide in surprise and mimed that she would be one minute. Karen waved her off, threw her carry-on down at Janet's feet, and moved to Jeffrey's office. She had to tell him about this. She had to tell him her outrage and she had to stop the deal.

But Jeffrey's office was empty. Janet caught up with her. "Where have you been? I have like about a zillion messages. Mr. Wolper is going crazy trying to reach you."

"Fuck Mr. Wolper!" Karen ignored poor Janet's shocked round face, spun out of the room, and stuck her head into Defina's office. Dee was sorting through a sheaf of photos with one of the young, intense photographers who was always pitching them. When Defina looked up and saw Karen's face, she sent the guy and his portfolio packing. "The bitch is back," Defina smiled.

"It's nice to be wanted," Karen replied.

"What happened to you?"

"I tried to play with the big boys and I got my ass kicked. Defina, we can't do the NormCo thing."

"Honey, I been telling you that. But isn't it a done deal?" Defina asked.

For a moment Karen felt as if she would begin to sob, cry like a baby and never stop. She had tried hard to do what she wanted to, to create clothes and a business the way she thought it should be done. But in the end it was always the men, the corporations, the bankers, the media moguls who really controlled the business and the lives of everyone around them. She had tried to fight for her independence, but Bill, Basil, Robert-the-lawyer, and her own husband had defeated her. Still, she wouldn't go down without a fight. Karen took a deep breath and heaved an even bigger sigh. "It better not be." She gave Defina a quick rundown of the Marianas. Defina listened, sometimes shaking her head. When Karen was done, Defina stood up, crossing her arms.

"Slavery," she said.

Karen just nodded. "I never thought fashion was something people should *die* over. I mean, I design a blouse, Mrs. Cruz cuts it, they sew it up, someone buys it, and everyone goes home with a paycheck. It didn't seem so complicated or so dirty, but the bigger we get, the worse it gets. If we expand to this size, it's like I'm part of a drug ring or something. We all participate. We push fashion on society women and they keep needing new fixes. Meanwhile, working women pick up the styles. Then the blue-collar and the pink-collar workers. The lower you get on the chain the cheaper the knock-offs, and the worse the pay for the garment workers. That shit that retailed for twenty dollars in Macy's cost them a buck to make, *including* wages. People shouldn't die so secretaries in America can buy a nineteen ninety-five polyester blouse." For once, Karen let go. Her rage, her betrayal, broke through in angry sobs. Defina walked around her desk, closed the door, and then gave Karen a hug. Karen felt like melting into those big arms and that soft, warm chest. But after a moment she pulled herself together.

"So what do we do now?" Defina asked.

"You have got to help me stop the deal. Find out where the contract is, see if Robert-the-lawyer still has it. See if it's been sent back to Herb. Stop it anyway you can, if it's not too late. I have to find my husband."

Janet walked into the room. "What are *you* doing here?" she asked again. "I thought you were in Korea?"

"That trip won't be necessary," Karen said.

"But . . ."

"Janet, call Robert and see if he still has the NormCo contract." Defina snapped. "Tell him we've found an error that his office has made, and if it goes back to NormCo this way, his office will be responsible. Tell him Jeffrey is *very* upset. In fact, tell all of that to Jeffrey's secretary and have *her* call Robert," Defina instructed.

As Janet turned and left the room, Karen sunk into the only chair in Defina's office that wasn't piled high with samples, swatches, and clutter. "Where is Jeffrey?" she asked. "Defina, could you buzz his secretary and find out?"

"Well, actually, I don't have to do that. I think he's gone down to Perry's loft. He's spending a lot of time there."

"At Perry's loft?" Perry had given Karen the key before he left for rehab. She still had it on her key ring. "Isn't Perry away? What's Jeffrey doing there?" she asked.

"Beats me," Defina said blandly. "I thought *you* knew."

Maybe he was painting, Karen thought. Perfect. My life collapses, he paints. "I'll just call him."

"No phone. The place is emptied out, I think. Perry's had to sell it or rent it."

"You're kidding! God! It must have *killed* Perry. He loved that space."

Defina shrugged. "You goin' or you stayin'?" she asked.

"I'll go. I have to find out if Jeffrey knew about any of this. I'll be back in about an hour."

"Don't be so sure," Defina said. "I'll tell Janet and I'll call you a car right now."

"Thanks, but don't bother. Just get ahold of that contract before it's too late. If it's not too late already. I'll run downstairs and snag a cab."

Karen stood out on the street, almost exactly in the spot where Perry had staggered under the streetlight. She walked into the dirty vestibule of his building and the empty cage of the elevator. She pushed back the gate. These industrial-strength, high-tech old lifts scared her, but she remembered working the lever when she had brought Perry home drunk. The key to the loft fit into the keyhole beside Perry's floor. Karen inserted the key, closed the cage door, and with her hand on the lever, moved the elevator up to six.

It was very quiet. The loft had been emptied. Poor Perry. He had told her he was going into rehab and didn't know how he'd live when he came back, but she hadn't understood. The place looked stripped. Maybe Jeffrey had been packing up for Perry and already left. Defina was right. All of Perry's stuff, the old sofas, the huge canvases, the paint-spattered tables, all of it was gone except the lingering smells of linseed oil and oil paint. The loft faced north, and the huge windows washed the emptiness with cool light. Defina must have been wrong, though, about Jeffrey. No one was here in this vast emptiness. Karen turned, about to go. Then she heard the moan.

Was it Jeffrey? Had he fallen, alone in here? Was he hurt? There was an alcove, the only space not visible in the huge open area, and Karen walked—almost ran—toward it. "Jeffrey?" she cried. She turned the sharp corner into the small sleeping ell.

It was odd, but even then, the first thing she saw when she stepped into the alcove were the clothes. Jeffrey's slate blue silk Equipment shirt lying on the floor, his ostrich Bruno Magli's chucked halfway across the room instead of lined up neatly beside the bed as he did at home. A forest green linen dress (Anne Klein? Calvin Klein?) and a hot pink suede blazer was draped across the windowsill. Who would wear a combination like that? she thought, irrelevantly. What am I doing? A fashion makeover at this critical moment? I must be crazy from jet lag. Karen looked again at the shoes. Where were the woman's shoes? Then, on the other windowsill that served as a makeshift night table, she saw the crocodile Gucci pumps.

Aside from the clothes, there was also a bed, or at least a mattress and frame, all draped in white. White on white against the blank walls of the loft. All white, except for Jeffrey's warm skin, his salt-and-pepper hair, his ruddy foot, and the pale exposed leg of the woman under him.

It seemed as if the two of them had frozen, caught, as it were, in the act.

Frozen too, Karen's eyes were the only part of her that could move. She felt as if her blood had frozen, as if she had frozen to the spot in shock, embarrassment, and shame. What the fuck have *I* got to be ashamed of? she asked herself. *He's* the adulterer.

"Jeffrey?" she repeated, moronically. Who the hell else was it?

"Jesus Christ," he said, and turned to her, his face a white mask of shock. Then the color flooded back—so fast, so dense, that it was surely a blush. Well, at least he still had the decency to blush.

"Karen?" he asked, although she was as clearly there as he was.

"Karen?" the woman under him yelped. Karen knew the voice, but couldn't place it. Jeffrey's broad back shielded the woman's face. Once again Karen scanned the alcove and inventoried the clothes. And then she knew.

"Lisa," she whispered.

Karen sat with Defina at the coffee shop. Karen thanked God for her big black sunglasses: despite being dehydrated from the plane, she seemed to be producing quarts of tears that flowed ceaselessly down her face, like one of those kitsch lamps she sometimes saw in bad Italian restaurants where tear drops dripped down nylon strands. Carl had given her one once as a gag gift. Hadn't it been at her wedding shower?

Now the fountain flowed continuously down her face, and Defina removed another napkin from the chrome napkin holder and handed it to her. Hadn't Karen once been the girl who didn't cry?

"Don't rub. Blot," Defina advised. "Or else you'll get your face chapped up."

"God, Defina how could they? And how could I be so stupid? Really stupid!"

"Which question do you want me to answer first?" Karen shrugged wordlessly. "*He* could do it because he's a scum-sucking pig. It's easy for pigs to do anything. And *she* did it because she's a bored and aging woman and she just figured that out. And because she's been jealous of you since the day she was born."

"Oh, God," Karen moaned. "I think I'm going to be sick."

Defina handed her another napkin. Karen blotted up more tears. "How could I be so stupid?" she asked again.

"It isn't stupidity. It's denial. I admit they look alike. But you're not stupid. You're just very good at denial. We'll call you Cleopatra, Queen of Denial," Defina explained. Then her face softened. "Hey, don't be so hard on yourself. How could you admit that your husband was weak? That he's tried to sell you down the river. That he's dependent on you and hates it. That he blames you for everything he never did? That he envied your career and was jealous of your friendships."

"Was he?" Karen asked.

"Wake up and smell the papyrus, Cleo," Defina said. "He had to be powerful angry to sleep with your sister. A man cheats on his wife for a lot of reasons, but he cheats with his wife's best friend only when he's got something to say to his wife and he doesn't have the balls to say it. I guess he knew me and Carl would turn him down, so that just left Lisa," Defina paused. "Though didn't Carl always have a thing for Jeffrey? Maybe . . . "

"Eeuw, Dee," Karen said, almost smiling a bit at the idea.

"Sorry, girlfriend. Just trying to cheer you up."

Karen put her hand out and Dee placed another napkin in it. "People are going to think I'm crazy," Karen moaned. "Or that I'm having some kind of a breakdown."

"Hey, at this very minute there are women sobbing in coffee shops all over town. It's New York, babe. And what some stranger thinks is the least of your problems right now. I mean, you're dealing with love and death and money. It doesn't get any heavier than this."

Karen thought of the Marianas. It did get heavier than this. Somehow

Karen's experience there put everything else in perspective. She thought of Bill Wolper. How could she think he was going to save her? Or that Jeffrey would always protect her? What had been Coco's advice? All men were pimps. How had she forgotten that? But, "Oh God, Dee. What if the NormCo deal is done?"

Defina smiled for the first time that day. "Well, Cleo, when it comes to papyrus, I got some good news for you." She smiled and produced a handful of pink message slips. "Your boyfriend Bill has been calling. I took one call. He's *very* eager to talk to you. But personally, I don't think it's about a date. I think it's about this." Defina reached under the counter and pulled out a thick stack of legal documents. "Taa-daa!" she said with a flourish, and fanned the contracts out on the Formica. "I got Robert-the-lawyer so paranoid that he sent *all* the copies back. This must be the first time a Lenox Avenue black girl got the better of a white Park Avenue lawyer," Dee laughed. "What do you want to do with them?"

"Shred 'em," Karen told her.

"You sure you don't want to go up to Madame Renault's? She could burn 'em. With a little extra help, some related parties might feel burned as well."

"Forget about it. If I'm going to stick pins into people, I'll do it with my own hands and not by proxy."

"Well, if you don't do this deal, Jeffrey and Lisa are going to be punished for sure. They're counting on this money. So is your mother. Not to mention Mercedes."

Karen nodded, silent. "What about you?"

"I'll be fine. Tangela's treatment is covered by insurance, I got money in the bank, and all the clothes I can steal." She smiled, wickedly. "By the way, I had Mrs. Cruz cut me one of the wedding gown styles in size fourteen. I used the brown alpaca. You don't mind, do you?"

"Jesus! How many yards of alpaca did it take? Jeffrey will have a fit."

"Oh, I don't think so," Defina warbled. "I don't think he's gonna be in charge of inventory anymore!" Then she watched as the tears again began to roll down Karen's cheeks. "Sorry," she said as she handed Karen a napkin. "So what are you going to do?"

"I don't know," Karen said. "I honestly don't know."

31

CUT ON THE BIAS

Karen hit her apartment like a tornado. If there was anything—*anything*, god-damnit—of Lisa's there she would burn the fucking place down. She would also find any other evidence of this betrayal. And she'd be damned if she'd spend another minute in a place full of Jeffrey's things.

When she left Defina she had thought first of going to a hotel—just checking into the Royalton and waiting to see what happened. But as her anger overcame her shock she changed her mind. She told the cab to take her to the West Side and she had thrown open the door to her place with such force that the walls had shaken.

Sitting on the demilune table was an enormous vase of lilies. Karen moved toward them, mesmerized. From halfway across the room, their scent was strong, and as she got closer it was almost overpowering. The petals were the palest gold. She reached out to touch one, and the smoothness and color of the petal's flesh reminded her of the baby's skin, back at the hospital in the Marianas. Where was that baby now?

A card lay on the tabletop. It was embossed with the double W of Bill's personal stationery. Without even touching it, she went to the phone and called for a car. "I have a pick-up," she explained to the dispatcher. "Flowers to be taken to the maternity ward at Doctors' Hospital." Then she took out a card, addressed it to Cyndi, and scrawled a message. *"You've done the right thing. All your bills will be paid. Love to you and your son, from Karen."* She called the doorman and had the porter take the flowers away. Then she turned to the painting over the sofa.

She got Ernesta's favorite kitchen knife and slashed Jeffrey's canvas fifty or sixty times. She knew that she had to start being honest with herself now. No more denial. And the truth was, Jeffrey couldn't paint. Maybe he had a flair, maybe he'd had some talent once, but it was slight and long gone. Perry was the talented one.

The painting was a mass of ribbons before she was done. It felt good, but it was only a start. Karen strode into their bedroom and opened Jeffrey's closet. She pulled out the cashmeres, the melton wool blazers, the alpaca overcoat, the Armani suits, and slashed and hacked and tore away at all of them. Buttons flew across the room, pinging off the floor like bullets. She, who had always worshiped clothes, destroyed them.

She couldn't think at first what to do with his shoes. It was not enough to cut the laces, so she filled the bathtub and dropped them in: one by one, she threw in the immaculate Gucci loafers, the butter-soft Cole Haan's, the hand-made English brogues. Each of them floated for a moment on the top of the water and then slowly sank to the bottom.

The ties were easy: she merely snipped them in half with her pinking shears. She liked that effect, the pinked sawtooth ending. Maybe she could start a trend in men's wear. She opened Jeffrey's bureau and took out dozens of his folded, boxed, and starched shirts. He had always been very particular about his shirts. The pinking shears were good on them, too. On some she simply cut off a sleeve. On others she settled for collar and cuffs. In ten minutes she had enough collars and cuffs to outfit an entire hutch of Playboy bunnies. Karen looked around the room. It was piled high with the torn bodies from the massacre. She thought for a moment of setting fire to it all but she wasn't *that* crazy.

Instead, she went into the kitchen and brought out the Clorox bottle that Ernesta stored there. Karen poured the bleach liberally all over the piles of clothing. It was interesting to see the flowers and clouds that bloomed across the fabrics. Rather like a Rorschach. Maybe Jeffrey and Lisa could have a new game to play together: What does this bleach stain look like?

The phone began to ring, but she ignored it. Who would it be? Jeffrey with an apology? Or perhaps it was Lisa? What would Lisa have to say? Or—just maybe—it was another pregnant woman calling Karen to break her heart. Too late. It was already broken. No sale. The answering machine took the call. Bill Wolper's voice came on following the beep. Karen almost smiled. If he hadn't had his secretary make the call, this *was* important. "Karen, this is Bill. There seems to have been some misunderstanding that I would like to clear up. I'm confused, and I think you might be, too. I'll be at . . . " Too bad. She already knew where he was at. She turned down the volume.

Next Karen started methodically going through the top drawer of Jeffrey's bureau. The socks, carefully rolled into balls, were easy—she chucked them out the window. My God, the man must have had fifty pairs of socks! Well, not any more! Then she opened his jewelry box. There were the sapphire studs and cuff links she had given him. Exactly the color of his eyes. Her own eyes teared up for a moment, but that didn't stop her. She went to the kitchen and got the hammer out from under the sink, along with the cutting board. She returned to the bedroom and laid the board on top of the bureau, poured the beautiful sapphires onto it, and pounded them to dust. Eighteen thousand dollars worth of dust. It probably wasn't as satisfying as pounding Jeffrey's actual eyes out, but it would have to do. In fact, it was quite addictive, and so she pounded the rest of his jewelry until her hand got tired.

In fact, Karen suddenly felt more tired than she ever had in her life. She wondered if she would have the strength to move at all. At last, with a bone-weariness, she managed to make her way through the debris to the guest bedroom. There she fell down heavily onto one corner of the bed.

Her marriage, her home, her family, her work. It all seemed such a failure, so hopeless, so false, so stupid. Hadn't Defina warned her? No woman could keep track of it all. Perhaps Jeffrey had once loved her, but if he still did, his love was adulterated with rage—and she hadn't even suspected. And Lisa—well, who could tell what Lisa felt about anything? But certainly she was no best friend to Karen.

So that left her a career of making expensive clothes for women who didn't need them, with an opportunity to expand into slave labor and feed American women's addiction to "bargains." Was that what she had struggled for? All the fuss, the work, the hours, the travel, had added up to a sellout to Bill Wolper, the opportunity to put a lot of money in her pension fund, and her name on every rag that NormCo turned out.

She lay inert, too miserable to move, too tired to think of a plan. Up to now there had always been a plan, a next step, a scheme. Marry Jeffrey. Buy an apartment. Start a business, build a house, have a baby, find her mother, sell the business. Always some next step, some achievement or acquisition to focus on.

Now there was none. She'd lived half her life, maybe more, and she'd run out of plans, she'd run out of energy, and she'd run out of love. Karen closed her eyes.

When she awoke, Jeffrey was standing in front of her. She smiled sleepily. Was she dreaming? Then, painful as a brick falling on her head, she remembered everything.

She scrambled up.

Jeffrey was holding out a Chesterfield coat. It was once a navy blue cashmere with a black velvet collar, but now it had a sort of whitish-gray line of bleach flowers blooming across it and the knife slits on the back made it gap crazily.

"What have you done?" Jeffrey asked.

Karen laughed. "Isn't that *my* line?"

"You've gone crazy!" he said.

"There you go: taking *my* line again."

"Do you know how much damage you just did?"

"Jeffrey, you've got the right script but you're reading the wrong part. We are *not* going to have an argument about your wardrobe. I don't give a fuck about your wardrobe! I think I made that very obvious. We are going to talk about what you were doing in bed in Perry's loft with my sister."

"Karen, you're overreacting." Karen stood absolutely still. She could hardly believe her ears. Always, when they argued, Jeffrey had the upper hand. Jeffrey always kept himself under control while she lost it. Then he would focus the argument on her bad behavior. Did he actually think he could pull that shit now? Tell her she was being oversensitive? Ask her if she was premenstrual? Act as if *she* were crazy?

"Overreacting? OVERREACTING? My *husband* was fucking my *sister*. So far I think my reactions are perfectly normal for a woman in that situation. They've done studies of it, Jeffrey. I looked it up in the library. This is absolutely normal behavior for a woman in my position. So, I deserve to know a few things."

Jeffrey turned his head away, took a deep breath, and shifted his weight from one leg to the other. He dropped the coat to the floor and crossed his arms over his chest. "What?" he asked.

"Did you fuck up the adoption with Cyndi on purpose? Did you make her think we shouldn't get her baby?"

"No," he said. "I was nice to her. Sally thinks that once she saw the baby she would have pulled out no matter who she was with. It happens."

"Okay. I don't know if I believe you, but okay. Second question: Did you know about the NormCo blood money?"

"What are you talking about?"

"Did you know about the Marianas?"

"No. I'm still not sure what you're talking about. Bill called. There's been a big mistake. You've gotten the wrong idea. This is business, Karen, not some fuzzy liberal charity program. He wants to talk to you."

"Forget about it. Just answer the question. We're talking blood money here. We're talking indentured servitude and the worst kind of exploitation. Did you know Arnold was right?"

"If I'd known, would I have let you go there?"

Karen considered it. He was right. He probably wouldn't have let her find out if he could help it. But wasn't that a worse admission than his ignorance? She looked at the man she had married. "Last question: Why Lisa?"

Her husband shrugged. "Because she was there," he sighed.

"What? Like Everest? Who are you, Sir Edmund Hillary?"

"Karen, I'm really sorry. It just happened. It was wrong. It was *really* wrong. What do you want from me now?"

Karen paused and really thought about it. "I want you to go. Leave me alone."

"Where can I go?"

"I don't care where you go, Jeffrey. Go to hell."

He paused. "Can I call you?"

"No."

He walked to the door. "I'm really sorry, Karen," he said, and then he left her.

32

IN STITCHES

Karen sat in her chair behind the worktable in her office. Her door was closed. It was important for her now to feel she had some place, some things that belonged only to her. She felt as if, after all these years of working, this was the only space that she actually owned. She couldn't go home until Jeffrey was out of the apartment. And she couldn't leave her office and go out onto the selling floor or the workroom because she was falling apart. Plus, if she stuck her nose outside the door, she would have to tell everyone that the NormCo deal was over. Janet had stopped bothering to give her the messages that Bill Wolper continued to leave. Only he, Jeffrey, and Defina knew that the deal was kaput. Jeffrey was raging. Karen could just imagine Mercedes's reaction when *she* found out. And they wouldn't be the only ones to be pissed. Robert-the-lawyer would have a stroke, Janet wouldn't be able to make a down payment on her house, Arnold and Belle would have nothing to retire on, and God knows how Mrs. Cruz and the other women in the workroom would take it. Disappointment was difficult to deal with.

Ha! She almost laughed aloud. *Disappointment was difficult to deal with.* Now *there* was a heavy, philosophical thought, she told herself, and one she was learning to cope with all on her own. Karen actually couldn't tell if she was angry or sad or both. She thought about Jeffrey and felt murderous, until tears welled up in her eyes, at which point she was overwhelmed with self-pity. Thinking of Lisa made her crazy. She could not fathom what the fuck Lisa had been thinking. There were at least three million men on Long Island,

and if Lisa didn't want to sleep with Leonard, why didn't she try some of those other ones first, before she picked her sister's husband?

As she mulled it over, Karen came to believe that Defina had to be right. Both Jeffrey *and* Lisa were doing more than having it off in that loft bed. Both of them were sending her messages, big time, and even if she wasn't supposed to receive them like this, so soon, even if they hadn't planned for her to find out, she knew that they had still been busy telling her things. They hadn't been fucking each other—they'd been fucking *her*.

She wasn't sure if Jeffrey loved her, but he surely was angry at her. Perhaps he did feel unappreciated; he'd had to deal with the business and financial shit for years while she got the glory. And lately there'd been a lot more of the former for him and a lot more of the latter for her. If it wasn't that, if he was simply bored with her, if he found her unattractive, or felt their marriage was dying, why hadn't he just told her and left, or found another woman, a stranger?

Karen spun her chair around and stared out over Seventh Avenue—the garment district. Rush hour was just ending, but the street was still crammed with men pushing clothing racks. Trucks were blocking the street, and people were rushing around the obstructions. So much energy, so much effort, so many billions of dollars were being spent down there so that people didn't wear a simple uniform. She looked at the crowd below. Were any of them as miserable as she was? She would have to face some big disappointments and some real home truths. If Jeffrey *did* love her, then he was also in a rage so black that nothing short of this wounding would even the score. And if he *didn't* love her, if he was indifferent to her, then his act was malicious, a truly nasty, cruel gesture. Which was it? Which was worse?

Because, after considering it most of last night and this morning, Karen simply couldn't believe that Jeffrey loved Lisa. It wasn't just her ego or denial that made her so certain: she knew Jeffrey after all these years and—although a woman might never know the exact taste her husband had in mistresses—Karen knew that Lisa was not Jeffrey's style.

So, he did this because he still loves me but he's angry. Or, he did it because he doesn't love me at all. But if he doesn't love me, if he hasn't loved me for a long time, then why hadn't he left? The only answer was one that kept feeling like a kick to Karen's stomach: *the money.* He was staying with her for the money. And there was something about that for Karen, something in that, that was more shaming than anything else. It robbed her of everything—her sex appeal, her brains, her talent. It made her into something worse, for a woman, than a dupe or a wronged female. It made her into a cash cow.

A little moan escaped her. She covered her mouth and rocked herself back and forth in her executive chair. How many talented women had been fleeced by their husbands? Coco had been ripped off by her lover Iribe, Collette by her husband. No successful woman was immune. Maybe she'd just become a paycheck to Jeffrey. A payoff. She tried the thought on like an ugly garment. She played with it the way she'd tongue a painful tooth. She had loved him so much. His body had been so good to her. So what had it cost her, for each of those times that Jeffrey had sex with her? How much cash had he expected for each of those loveless fucks? Of course, she told herself bitterly, there hadn't been many of them in the last six months. There were a few times in New York, and an attempt in Westport. And there was Paris. She blushed to think of it. Had Jeffrey thought of Lisa to help him get it up? Somehow Karen didn't think so, though the idea of it made her sick. And if looking at Jeffrey's betrayal made her sick, what about her sister's?

Karen always had tried to see the best intentions in Lisa's actions. If Lisa was lazy, if she was self-indulgent, if she was dishonest to her husband and neglectful to her daughters, Karen had always tried to overlook it or give the best possible face to it. Lisa was flighty, she hadn't found herself, she had a poor self-image. But Defina was right: she, Karen, was the Queen of Denial. She hadn't wanted to see any of her sister's faults. Especially her envy and jealousy.

Why, she wondered, have I been blocked this way? She had to figure it out, because it was the reason that she was being punished now. Her life had completely fallen apart and she had to come to understand why she had been blinded to the betrayal at the center. She knew that if she couldn't make sense out of this, she could never trust her own perceptions again.

There was a tiny knock at the door. It was Janet, but this time she ignored Karen's call to go away. She put her head into the office. Her face was white. "Karen, ya sistah is heah an' ya *gotta* see huh."

"Forget about it," Karen said.

"Karen, ya gotta or ya gotta make huh go. It's makin' us sick." Karen shuddered. *What* was making them sick? Why should Karen's own grief affect Janet and the staff so deeply? They didn't know. Or did they? Oh God, she hadn't considered that. Karen's face burned with humiliation. Still, Karen wouldn't see Lisa. Not now; maybe not ever.

But then the door swung open behind Janet. The secretary fell back, as if she had been struck, while Lisa strode past her. For a moment, Karen didn't understand. Had Lisa actually hit the girl? But then she herself was hit by the odor.

Odor would hardly be the word for it, though. It traveled across the room like a wall. It was a horrible smell, worse than a stink. It was a stench so bad that Karen was ready to gag if it didn't go away. Was it Lisa who smelled like that? Karen moved to the window beside her and threw it open. There was no question of being polite. This was survival.

"What the hell is it?" Lisa asked. Her hair was wild, uncombed, and she was wearing a pair of Levi's, red high heels, and an old shirt that looked as if it might be Leonard's. Karen had never seen her sister look so awful, but the look was nothing compared to the smell.

"What the hell is it?" Lisa repeated. "How did you do this to me?"

"What are you talking about?"

"What am I talking about? WHAT AM I TALKING ABOUT? Like you can't smell this. Like the whole city of New York can't smell this! I know you and that black witch did this to me. She *never* liked me. Doctor Schneider can't figure it out. He actually gagged when I got into the stirrups. How did you do this?"

"Lisa, I didn't do anything."

"Right. My vagina smells like I've got a dead wolverine in it, and nobody did anything. I *know* it's Defina."

"Maybe you caught something from Jeffrey," Karen suggested. "Maybe it's a yeast infection or something."

"A yeast infection!" Lisa shrieked. "An ocean of Monostat wouldn't do dick about this! If this is something Jeffrey's got, his prick would've fallen off before now." Lisa began to sob, striding back and forth across the office. Karen kept the table between them and kept breathing through her mouth, staying close to the window. It was the most unbelievable stench.

"I came in by train," Lisa said, sobbing. "I stepped into the car and before we got to Jamaica it had emptied out. I was alone in an entire Long Island Railroad car, and during rush hour! When I got into Penn Station, I walked by the line of winos, the ones who live in the underpass. You know how bad *they* smell. Well, they all turned and stared at *me*. My house stinks. All my clothes are ruined. You can't go near my Mercedes without gagging. Jesus Christ, Karen, enough is enough! I never wanted Jeffrey. I just slept with him because I liked the attention. Because I wanted what you have. But you can have him. He's just a no-talent brat. Just get rid of this stink."

Karen thought for a moment. Then she turned to the intercom and buzzed it. "Janet," she asked, "has Defina come in yet?" It was only twenty to ten, and Defina was rarely in before ten-thirty. But before Janet buzzed back, Defina walked in to Karen's office.

"Hoo-eeuw! I smell a rat." Defina looked across the room at Lisa. "Is that you, girl?"

Lisa wiped her eyes and glared at Defina. "It isn't funny."

Defina looked over at Karen. "Boss, you should talk to your sister about her personal hygiene."

"Stop it!" Lisa cried. "I know you did this. You and that voodoo. I already told Karen that I'll do anything you want. Just make this smell stop."

Defina raised her eyebrows, tilted her head, and looked at Lisa. "You put dirt in your thang, don't be surprised when it smells," Defina told her. "Don't be blaming me."

Karen looked over at her friend. "Dee, did you do this?"

Dee opened her eyes wide. "Girlfriend, I ain't got the power. People ought to take responsibility for what they do. I didn't do anything."

Lisa began to wail, and sank down onto the carpet, covering her face with her hands. "Help me!" she cried. "It's not fair. You have to help me."

Dee turned on her like a big cat protecting its cubs. "Fair?" she asked. "I don't think you have any right to talk about fair. You got a big sister who's nice to you, a husband who takes care of you, and two healthy children. That's a lot more than most women get. So, when you ignore your children, cheat on your husband, and do dirt to your sister, be sure that *then* you don't talk about fair. Karen never done nothing but good by you. But her friendship wasn't enough, her gifts weren't enough, the money wasn't enough. You still had to go on being jealous and resentful. *That's* what you stink from."

"Don't you dare judge me," Lisa snapped. "My sister likes you more than she likes me. Know how that makes me feel?" Then Lisa turned to Karen. "And *you* don't have to judge me either. You've always gotten what you needed in bed at home. You don't know what it's felt like for me."

Defina walked over to Lisa and took her arm. "Get up off that carpet or we'll never get the smell out. I suggest you go home and make up a douche out of warm water, vinegar, and a few tears. Don't forget the tears. Real important. I bet that will take care of the stink," she said.

Lisa stood up, looked from one to the other with a wild expression, and then, without another word, dashed out of the office.

Karen looked across her table at Dee. "What did you do?" she asked.

"I didn't do anything. *She's* the one who done something."

"Come on, Dee. Was that something you cooked up with Madame Renault?"

Defina shrugged. "You yourself told me that mumbo jumbo doesn't work," Dee said. "You can't have it both ways, Karen."

"Dee, I *know* you did something. I know you did it out of friendship, but I can take care of myself. I'm going to have to take care of myself."

Defina walked around the desk and put her arm around Karen. "You got a lot on your plate right now," Defina said. "Carl and I both thought you could use a helping hand." Then she put her innocent face on again. "But I didn't do anything to Lisa."

"Yeah. Sure." Karen looked at her friend. "Will it go away now?" she asked.

"Uh-huh," Defina told her. "As long as she remembers the tears."

33

CASE CLOTHED

Karen sat in one of the folding chairs in the showroom, waiting while the KKInc staff assembled. The chairs were arranged in messy rows of ragged semicircles. Today's pitch had no glossy portfolios, no colored slides. It was a very different presentation than the one she had made only a few weeks ago. She tried to keep calm, but she knew that announcing loss didn't make you a popular kid. Was it ancient Greece where the tradition of killing the messenger had begun?

Karen knew that it was going to be rough. Lots of these people didn't have much between them and disaster and, since the last meeting, some of the more impractical ones may have already begun spending the NormCo money, money they now would never receive. Casey had told her that one of the workroom girls had started driving to the office in a new Cadillac, parking it out on the street, despite the insanity of the hand trucks and delivery vans, all just so the other women could see it. Karen's announcement was going to be a blow, and she didn't know how many members of the staff would stick with her.

And why should they, she asked herself. Hadn't she, as their chief, as their mother, been negligent? She could see now that despite her promises to them, once NormCo came in, heads would have rolled. Jobs would have been lost so that some other slave girl in the Marianas—one who wasn't dead yet— would be trapped in a filthy factory and in an even worse dormitory. She remembered again the poem that Arnold had on his office wall: *I have shut my little sister in from life and light/ (For a rose, for a ribbon, for a wreath across my hair).* Had she shut these women in, too? For a sheath, for a scarf, for a blazer cut just right? For a moment she felt drowned in shame.

Karen had always prided herself on the fact that, even if she wasn't saving the world, even if she was only indulging herself and her clientele, she had at least made jobs for several hundred people; that she helped them to pay their rent and buy their babies shoes. This was the first time she was ever going to take something she had promised away from them. But maybe she had taken something from them long ago. Something more important even than this money. Take, for example, Mrs. Cruz, who had given *years* to the little stitches that made up all those hundreds of dozens, thousands of dozens, of outfits that had gone into Karen's line. *I have shut my little sister in from life and light/ (For a rose, for a ribbon, for a wreath across my hair).* Just now, Karen couldn't see the point of it. Not at all.

People were talking quietly amongst themselves. Karen sat at the front and felt separated, as lonely as she ever had in her life. Jeffrey showed the good grace of not attending. Staff must have noticed but no one had said anything to her. Who, now, was she connected to in a way more visceral than habit or duty or tradition? Certainly, she wasn't connected now to Jeffrey. And her sister! Well, that was over. Her mother was useless to her, and Arnold, though a kind man, had always been distant. Now he was sick. Who was there that she was a part of, or that was a part of her? Tears of self-pity rose like a tide, but Karen bent her head for a moment and blinked them away. This was no time to feel sorry for herself. Right now she had to feel sorry for the people she was about to drop her little bomb on.

She looked to the back of the room. Defina stood, leaning against the wall, her arms crossed over her chest. Their eyes locked and Defina nodded her head. It was time to start.

"You all know that I have an announcement to make," Karen began. She was surprised to hear that her voice wavered. She cleared her throat. "When we met and went over the NormCo deal," she said, "I had every intention of moving ahead with it." There was a murmur, but she continued. "I would like to be able to say that we are going to move ahead. But we're not." The murmur grew to a buzz and Karen didn't push against it. She gave them a moment and then, raising her voice, she continued. "Quite a lot of things have been brought to my attention that make it impossible to accept the NormCo offer. This was a decision I had to make for all of us. But I felt that I did not have a choice. In the final analysis, the deal that NormCo offered me was one that I think would hurt us all in the long run. It seems clear to me now, despite their promises, that it would have meant moving jobs out of here and eventually shutting down a large portion of this operation." The murmur started up again, but Karen continued. "Of course, this means that the money that we had all expected won't be forthcoming and that, I know, is a disappointment to everyone." She bit her lip and paused, scanning her audience. Mercedes Bernard stood up abruptly, and though she was as controlled as ever, Karen could see that she was furious. Mercedes turned and walked out of the room. Many eyes followed her.

Karen looked through the audience. Only Casey was smiling. Well, he'd always felt threatened by the deal. The rest of the staff looked either angry, stunned, or confused. Karen caught the eye of Mrs. Cruz. Her brown, wide, wrinkled face showed no expression, but she nodded to Karen. It was a gesture of such generosity that Karen almost lost it, and then felt such a swell of gratitude that she could hardly stand.

"That's not all the bad news," she said. "We are also going to have to undergo a serious reorganization. We have to find a way to finance and service the debt we incurred when we started up the bridge line. Now that you're stockholders you should understand that. I can't tell you what the reorganization is going to entail, because I honestly don't know. But I promise you that as soon as we figure out how we are going to proceed, I'll share the plan with you." There was no point in telling them that without Jeffrey they had no fiscal management and that she herself didn't have a clue as to how they were going to finance themselves or anything else. She would just have to do the best she could. So would they.

"If any of you feel that you no longer want to be associated with the firm, I will understand, although I will be extremely disappointed. I don't think I have any more to tell you or any answers to your questions right now. But I will arrange for a time to meet separately with anyone who wants to. In the meantime, Defina Pompey is available to answer questions." Yeah, like people weren't afraid to talk to *her*! Karen took a deep breath. "Thank you for coming, and just let me say one more time how sorry I am if I have disappointed you." Then she couldn't help it. Her eyes filmed over with tears and she had to walk as quickly as she could out of the room, down the hall, and into her office.

Karen had barely had time to mop her eyes before the door was thrown open by Mercedes. Karen spun around from the window. Mercedes, always pale and neat, was absolutely livid. Her black hair stood out around her head as if she had either run her hands through it like a mad woman or it had been electrified. For a moment Karen had time to think that the usually stylish Mercedes looked like a cross between Morticia Addams and the Bride of Frankenstein. They were appropriate analogies, because Mercedes quickly started a horror show.

"What the fuck have you done?" she asked, her voice almost as deep as Linda Blair's dubbed one in *The Exorcist.*

"I did what I had to do, Mercedes."

"You did what *you* had to do? Well, *I* did what *I* had to do and in the last eighteen months I *made* you. I've gotten you over a dozen magazine covers this year alone. There was that five-pager in *Vanity Fair*. There was the personal profile in *Mirabella*. Not to mention all the coverage of the line. I booked you with some new angle on every goddamned TV show that mattered. I got Paris to happen. I made you a *commodity*. I cashed in every chip. And now you are telling me that I can't cash out?"

"Mercedes, there were no guarantees."

"Is that supposed to be some kind of comfort? I am fifty-eight years old. Do you know how long it took me to work my way up from the back rows to a front seat at the shows? Thirty years! I covered the industry, I knew everyone, and I sold you the benefit of that. Now what? I'm not the kind of woman who can live comfortably on a Social Security check and a partial pension from the magazines. They never paid shit! I made you, Karen, and you owe me."

Despite her exhaustion, despite her sadness, Karen felt herself getting angry. Why was it that everybody thought her success was due to them? Jeffrey had made her, Liz Ruben had made her, Bill Wolper would make her (in both senses of the word), and now it was Mercedes. Karen took a deep breath, ready to say she didn't know what when Casey stepped into the room.

"Fuck you, Mercedes," he said. "What the fuck do you know? You had the easy job. You got Karen coverage just at the time when everyone was panting for it. *I've* been here from the beginning, when she and I had to push a cart in the snow over to Bloomingdale's to show them the first line. We showed it in the freight elevator and we sold the whole thing to Marvin Traub. So fuck *you*. Karen would have got where she is with help from any flack. Don't overdramatize."

Mercedes narrowed her elegant, long eyes. "Who asked you, you little faggot?"

"I think that will be about enough, Mercedes. Unless you want to call me a nigger bitch before you get your skinny ass out of here," Defina said, joining the group and closing the door on Janet and the cluster of secretaries who stood, gaping, outside.

Mercedes looked over at Karen. She took a deep breath as if she were ready to try again. "You know that what I say is true . . . " she began.

But Karen was sick of it. She'd had enough. "Mercedes, it's time to go. Casey, would you help Mercedes pack up her desk?"

"My pleasure," Casey smiled. He escorted her out.

Karen, shaken, looked over at Defina. "She looked at me as if she wanted me to die," Karen said. "God, what an experience."

"Yeah," Defina nodded. "Experience is what you get when you don't get what you want."

Karen had worked so hard for so long, but she wasn't sure what she had worked for. Certainly not for this. The darkness outside seemed ominous, threatening. She felt that there, on the ninth floor, she was floating in space, connected to no one. If she wasn't connected anymore to Jeffrey, she was truly alone.

Karen had spent all the afternoon and evening in Jeffrey's office, going over the financials with Casey and Lenny. It had been exhausting, depressing, and confusing. Had she been guilty of too much dependency on Jeffrey? Had she made that typical woman's mistake of letting her husband do the "man's work"? But in the world of fashion there were very few businesses that didn't operate the way the two of them had. Yves Saint Laurent had Pierre Bergé; Valentino had Giancarlo Giammetti (and those two couplings had been marriages); Calvin Klein had Barry Schwartz; Christian Lacroix had Bernard Arnault. Even that master of merchandising, Ralph Lauren, had Peter Strom. And *all* of those guys were men, operating in a tough man's world. Despite that, if the designers hadn't had the help, the support, and dedication of their brilliant partner businessmen, they would have closed their doors after a season or two. The rag trade demanded too much from a designer; there wasn't time to both create *and* manage a business. Surely she had been no worse than other overworked creators. But now, figuring out where KKInc stood and coming up with a solution that Jeffrey had not been able to find, was an incredible extra burden, and one she was afraid she couldn't carry.

She knew that in 1988, one of Lacroix's best years, his sales had grown by four hundred percent but he had lost eight million dollars. The books that Lenny had laid out indicated that with the success of the bridge line KKInc might do the same thing. She felt overwhelmed, and without coming to any conclusions, she sent Casey and Lenny home. Karen was, at last, alone—alone with nowhere to go. She didn't want to go back to her apartment. She stared out the big windows of Jeffrey's office at the headlights moving down Seventh Avenue. She tried to imagine her future, alone, without Jeffrey.

Karen had never spent much time in this office. It was Jeffrey's domain. She had kept clear of the finances, the bankers, the factors, and accountants whenever she could. Now, though, she walked across the carpet and sat down in the easy chair that stood at right angles to the sofa. It was the chair Jeffrey always took during meetings. It smelled like Jeffrey in some undefinable way. Was it his soap? His shampoo? He never wore aftershave or any other perfume. The chair just smelled of Jeffrey. And, held in the arms of his chair, smelling his scent, despite her anger, Karen felt an unbearable wave of longing for her husband.

The presentation to the KKInc staff had been so hard. Running the business was so hard. How would she do it without Jeffrey's help? Was Jeffrey right? Would it be impossible to keep KKInc running unless she sold out to someone? And without Jeffrey, without KKInc, what did she have? Tears of self-pity squeezed out of the corners of her eyes. She wept silently. Once she had begun crying, it seemed as if she would never stop. Only weeks ago, she'd believed she was a woman who never cried! But clearly, she didn't have a clue who she was, or who her friends were. It felt as if she had worked so hard and achieved so little. No family, no marriage, no children, no business. The center would not hold.

There, in the darkened office all alone, Karen felt as if she could not do without Jeffrey. Not in business or at home. She'd been married late, she'd become successful late, and it seemed to her that she couldn't bear to give it up now, so soon. She'd have such a long, long time to get old alone. Was there some way their marriage could be salvaged? Perhaps Defina was right when she said that Jeffrey was only reacting to her. Wasn't his action, his terrible betrayal, just a way to cope with her absence, with her growing fame, with the baby problem? Hadn't she—Miss Goodie-Goodie—considered cheating on him?

She was hurt, and still very, very angry, but she felt that if she lost him she lost so very much: after all, she had grown up with him. All of her history was with him. And the idea of going on alone frightened her. Would she be one of those women, women of a certain age, who attended the social events of the industry with a gay man on her arm? Would she wind up, like poor Chanel had at the end, alone, loveless and childless?

Karen took a deep breath and drew that Jeffrey scent deep inside. It was hard to believe that she had considered Bill Wolper as any kind of partner. What a lying pig! He was everything she hated about men in business—their greed, their hardness, their profit-at-any-cost mentality. For a moment, the darkness of the office became the darkness in the Saipan barracks. But here there was only darkness, not the sound of rats scuttling, not the stench of sewage and filth and hopelessness. She thought of Arnold, the contemptuous way he talked of "blood money," and that reminded her of the trail of blood on the dirty hospital floor and she shuddered. What would happen to all those people, all those suffering souls? What would happen to the baby? She had already sent a check to Mr. Dagsvarr but she felt that it wasn't enough. Yet what else could she do?

Karen felt as trapped as a prisoner in a cell. She wasn't a social worker. She was a woman—a middle-aged woman—with a pleasure in, a talent for, design. But how could she go on? And how could she stop?

Perhaps she could forgive Jeffrey. It was possible. Other women had forgiven erring husbands. If he had only slept with her sister to hurt her, it was possible that there was a way to forgiveness. She wondered if it was an act of cowardice or bravery, and she also wondered if she could find that way. And even if she couldn't forgive him, they had to discuss the business, they had to make plans and begin to face the future.

She lifted the phone and slowly dialed the number Jeffrey had left her. Jeffrey answered, and at the sound of his voice Karen felt her heart begin to pound. "Jeffrey, it's Karen. We have to talk."

34

FASHION OF THE TIMES

Karen was waiting in Jeffrey's office for him. For a while she had continued to
sit in the darkness, but knowing that he was on his way up from SoHo she
forced herself to get up out of his chair. She turned the awful overhead fluo-
rescent lights on and went to the mirror behind the door to see how bad the
damage was. She needed a tissue. Hell, she needed a week's bed rest, a good
facial, an excellent therapist, a face-lift, and trustworthy legal counsel. But all
of that wasn't realistically possible before Jeffrey's arrival.

She went to the credenza behind Jeffrey's desk and she looked, for a
moment, at the picture of them taken on the night of the Oakley Awards. She
had to avert her eyes or she'd begin crying again. She reached into the first
drawer, looking for tissues. There were none. She looked in the next two
drawers. What was it? Didn't men blow their noses? In the bottom drawer she
found some paper napkins from the take-out place on Thirty-Eighth Street.
They would have to do. But when she lifted them up, she saw a locked box.
Somehow, the cheap tin case seemed very un-Jeffrey-like. What would he
keep in a ten-dollar strong box like that? She reached in and picked it up. For
a moment, despite her certainty to the contrary, she was frightened that it
might contain love letters or pictures of Lisa. She steeled herself to open it.
She'd break into it if she had to. Because she had to know. She had to know
whether Jeffrey loved her sister.

But the box wasn't locked, and it was filled not with letters but with
slides. Karen held the first one up to the light. It was a painting, one of Jef-

frey's paintings she supposed. But one that she had never seen before. It was a nude, but not like the ones in Westport. It had something of Jeffrey's style, his brush work, but this one was different. It wasn't good, but it was felt.

The woman, thank God, wasn't Lisa. Karen took a deep breath and held the second slide up. It, too, was of a nude, and again it wasn't Lisa. Karen scrabbled through the box. There were several dozen slides. When had Jeffrey had the time to do all this new work, she wondered? After looking through all the slides again, she realized that all the nudes seemed to be of the same blonde woman. Somehow, Jeffrey had managed in these paintings to gain a delicacy, a vulnerability, that she had never seen in his work before. Or maybe it was the woman. Maybe the woman in the paintings had that vulnerability. It was hard to say if the allure came from the pose, from the woman, or from the brush work. Though completely different in style, they reminded Karen of the wonderful private Degas, the ones of women bathing or stretching themselves. The woman's face rarely showed in the slides. There were several of her back, two of her in partial profile, and three where her arm was raised, obscuring all but her cheek and the tip of her nose. Karen stared at the profile. Why had Jeffrey kept *these* a secret? These were the better paintings. These were his future. What had she found?

Somehow, the secret of these glowing slides seemed more serious than Jeffrey's liaison with Lisa. Karen knew that Jeffrey had always considered himself an artist, and she had considered him an artist as well. This box of slides should not have been a secret withheld from her. Jeffrey was doing new work. It was exciting work. Maybe not great, but better than he had done since college. Why would he keep it from her?

A sick feeling began in the bottom of her stomach. She had been upset, angry, and outraged over Jeffrey's actions. But those feelings were strong, righteous ones. They gave her the energy to tear up his clothes and throw his things around. They gave her the energy to talk to her staff, to make plans, and to fight. But this Pandora's box did something much worse: it truly frightened her.

Beneath the tin box were papers. Karen took them out. There was only Jeffrey's birth certificate, a few clippings from Business Week and the Wall Street Journal with pictures or quotes of Jeffrey's. Nothing much. Certainly nothing to be upset about. She told herself she was overreacting. After all, with everything that had happened in the last three months, when had Jeffrey and she had time to talk about anything as delicate as these paintings? But she kept looking through the papers. When she found the agreement of rental with an option to buy Perry's loft she looked at it quickly. Then she stopped.

She wasn't good with legal papers, God knows, but it looked as if cautious Jeffrey had given Perry a nonrefundable hundred and fifty thousand dollars against a purchase price of eight hundred thousand! Was he crazy? Jeffrey had agreed to *buy* Perry's loft? She thought of Perry's goodbye visit. His *"mi casa, su casa"* remark. So this was how he was paying for rehab! This was why he had given her the key and said his house was her house.

Now the fear in her stomach began moving up to tighten her chest. What was Jeffrey doing? Was this just another surprise in an apparently endless list of surprises for her? She shook her head. Beneath the lease/buy agreement, there was a plan of the Westport house and a copy of the contract to build it, as well as a photo of Jeffrey and his father from some time shortly before his dad died. Karen put it aside, and paused for a minute, looking over all the clues here. It seemed as if Jeffrey had put together a cache of his accomplishments, and of the things he loved. The tin box was like a kid's runaway bag. Had he planned to run away? She turned over the papers and slides randomly. Then she saw the other photo.

It was a recent shot—she could tell by the color of Jeffrey's hair. He was standing in a street somewhere. It looked like Lower Manhattan, maybe Tribeca. And he had his arm around a woman. Thank God, it wasn't Lisa. The woman in the photo was a tall, elegant blonde, much more what Karen would have thought of as Jeffrey's style. Karen stared at the picture. In it, Jeffrey was gazing at the woman, mirroring the expression she must have had on her face. Karen recognized the look. She felt tears rise again to her eyes. How long had it been since Jeffrey had looked at *her* that way?

The woman's face was obscured by her hair and a shadow, but Karen could see part of her profile. There was very little visible, but somehow what Karen could see was tantalizingly familiar. It was, she was sure, the woman from the paintings. Karen stared and stared at the photo as if, in time, it would come to her. Then, just as she was about to get it, Jeffrey's private phone began to ring insistently. Karen kept staring at the photo. The phone kept ringing. Bill Wolper had finally gotten the message and had stopped leaving any. So who was it? Was it Jeffrey? Was he going to cancel his trip up to see her? She was afraid to answer it, to find that out. At last she got up, the photo still clutched in one hand, and with the other hand she lifted up the phone. It was Robert-the-lawyer. "Karen. I'm so glad I got you. I tried everywhere. Then I thought of this number. Look, we *have* to talk."

"It's eleven o'clock at night, Robert. And I never have to talk to you again."

"Karen, you have to listen. My life is on the line here. The firm has invested a lot of time and money. Karen, if you don't make this deal, I'm out on my ass. They're blaming me. Wolper is on the warpath. I'm going to take the fall. Throw me a bone, Karen. Give me something to go back to them with. Even if you won't do NormCo, let me get you a perfume deal. Unilever might be interested. Or I could take you public. I know it's not like the eighties, but it could still be done."

"I can't talk to you now," Karen said. "I have to talk to my husband."

"Listen, Karen, I didn't want to get involved with his private business. I'm not that kind. I didn't want to know about his affairs. Business is business; your personal life is your own. But he put me in a position here. You know what I mean. And he is family. But I want to make it clear that my loyalties are to you."

"Fuck you, Robert," she said, and hung up the phone. She sat there. Affairs? Was there more than one? What was going on?

And then Jeffrey came in.

He looked rumpled, and it was so unusual to see him anything but perfectly groomed that it surprised Karen. His almost white hair was mussed, and one of his cuffs was unbuttoned. Very un-Jeffrey-like. Somehow, it touched her and gave her confidence. If he was taking this so hard, perhaps there was a chance . . .

"What should we do?" she asked him.

"We should make the deal with NormCo, if we still can. I don't think it's too late." His voice was flat, dead.

"I wasn't talking about business," Karen said.

"All we've got is business."

It felt like a kick to her stomach. She was right, when she had figured that Jeffrey didn't love Lisa, but what had made her believe that he still loved her? She must have been crazy, desperate. Just another wife calling her soon-to-be ex-husband in the middle of the night. Affairs. Robert had definitely used the plural. Had she really thought she and her husband could reconcile? She was still playing Cleopatra, Queen of Denial. But now she was ready to know what had gone on, who the woman was, when he had done the paintings, how long since he had cared about her. All of it. She was ready—in fact, she *had* to know it all.

But Jeffrey only wanted one thing. "Karen, you have to believe me. There's no way the company can survive without NormCo. It will only be a matter of time. I've looked at all the options. This is the only one. And no matter how you feel about me, no matter what I've done, you have to do the NormCo deal. It's your future, too. Otherwise you'll be out of business in less than two years."

She didn't know that she could feel even more frightened than she had already felt. Losing Cyndi's baby, losing Jeffrey, *and* losing her company was more than she could take in or imagine. Her hands began to tremble and the tremors ran up her arms. The more she tried to tighten her muscles, the more they seemed to rebel against her. She could believe that Jeffrey was angry with her, or that he wanted to hurt her. But to imagine, to think, that he simply might not love her anymore felt like a kind of dying. Well, it must be true. Better get used to it, she told herself. The old gullible Karen, the Karen who lived in fear and lies and denial was dying. But who would replace her?

"I have other options," she said, hoping a front would work. "I could license more. Or get a perfume deal. Or go public."

"Not without me," Jeffrey said. "They'd pick your bones. Anyway, you don't have time. You don't have the cash flow. You'd wind up without the company and without your name and without any money to cushion you. Look what happened to Norris Cleveland, and to Tony de Freise and Suzanne Rowans. I know the market. I know the business. I can protect you. You can't do it alone, Karen."

"It looks as if I may have to," she said.

He sighed and shook his head. "Come on. Can't we be grown-ups about this?" he asked.

"What is it you want, Jeffrey?" she asked in a quiet voice.

"I want my life back, Karen. I gave you these years. Isn't it enough? I stopped painting. I concentrated on you. I made you. I gave you my name and then I made that name famous. You got to do what you wanted. You got to design your clothes. Now it's my turn. We sell to NormCo, I get my cut, and I get my life back. I get to paint. I get to be me. I stop being insulted by all the assholes who think that I'm just an empty suit. I take the money and run. And you get to do what you want: you can keep on designing clothes."

And then, right then, the fear hit her with all the force of a door slammed in her face. She knew, she absolutely *knew*, that Jeffrey didn't love her. "You were always going to leave me," she said. "You've been planning all this for a long time. You set the deal up so you could leave in comfort. You bought the loft in your name. But you needed more money. You *wanted* to sell me into slavery."

"That isn't true. It's the best possible deal. But things happen. People change. You made me change. How do you think I felt while you were playing creator in your workroom? You cut and draped and lived and died on every goddamn design. Meanwhile, I'm handling cash flow and dealing with the bank. And the irony is that *I'm* the one with the talent. Every stupid magazine and newspaper, every television show, focused on you. They all believed that you were the creative one. It almost made me laugh. Well, you've had your turn. Now I suggest we do the deal, we get an amicable divorce, and move on."

And then she saw just how much he hated her. How he had always competed with her. At first he had *wanted* to keep her in the back room while he ran the company, but now he blamed her even for that. She knew that he had run away from painting because he'd never be great, but he didn't have to admit that as long as she was his excuse for martyrdom. And now, when he and Mercedes had decided to use her, to make her name bigger than ever, to sell her off for profit, his ego couldn't take her fame. She saw how every achievement, every accolade she received, had diminished him in his own eyes, diminished him and enraged him.

"You're jealous," she said. She was completely surprised. He had always told her that he was the talented one and she had believed him, never questioning. But hadn't Perry and Carl and Defina tried to tell her the truth? She just had never wanted to see it. She was more comfortable, happier in the belief that her husband was greater than she was. "You're jealous," she repeated.

"Don't be ridiculous," he snarled. He looked at her. "What is there to be jealous of?" he sneered.

She didn't answer him. She held out the photo she still had crumpled in her hand. "What the fuck is this?"

Jeffrey looked at the picture and she could see the color drain out of his face. "Where did you find that?" he asked.

"Karen Kahn, girl detective," she said.

"So you know about June?"

For a moment, she thought he meant the calendar month. Had this affair, or whatever it was, started then? But it wasn't a month—it was a person he meant. And then it all made sense. It was June. June Jarrick. It was her in the picture, June he was buying the loft for. It was June all along. She'd been his fiancée back in the days when he was still an artist, then married Perry on the rebound, and left Perry after Lottie died. June, a classy wealthy woman from his own circle, a socialite who liked to marry artists. That's why she'd shown up at Tiff's *bat mitzvah*. That's why she'd been in Paris! Karen remembered the glimpse of June at the Plaza Athènèe. Those times Karen had tried to reach him, those nights at "poker games," "going over NormCo numbers . . ." Karen blushed with shame. June would bring Jeffrey back his youth, would nurture his art. That was the role she liked to play, but this time she'd get to play it with a very wealthy man, one she'd once loved and lost. Somehow, without another word from him, Karen knew everything. The pieces fit so perfectly. The last thread was tearing from the web of lies, and Madame Renault was right. It felt to Karen as if she were bleeding.

But she could see it all from Jeffrey's point of view. How he had once loved June and perhaps always regretted leaving her. How the divorce from Perry made June available. How June's money would appeal and how Jeffrey could comfort June over the loss of her child. Jeffrey was getting good at that. How many had Karen and he lost?

"How long?" she asked. "How long?"

Jeffrey looked away.

"More than a year?" Almost imperceptibly, Jeffrey nodded his head. Karen thought back to the last year. How often she'd been away for business, how often he'd worked late. She'd made it easy for him. And she'd never suspected. She thought of the Oakley Awards. And their time together in Paris. The way he'd made love to her. Was that their goodbye fuck?

She was mortified. Did Jeffrey's family know? Surely Robert-the-lawyer had. When they had come to Westport, had they looked at her with pity? Did they approve of perfect June? Blushes of humiliation washed over Karen like a light show.

"Does Perry know?"

"No. He wouldn't have sold me the loft if he knew."

"That was for June? For the two of you?"

Jeffrey only nodded.

So Lisa was only a bit of icing on the cake, Karen thought. A way to rub my nose in it, to humiliate not only me but my pathetic sister. Jeffrey might not have wanted me to find out when I did, but he'd want me to know eventually. And he knew eventually Lisa would break down and tell me.

Karen looked at her husband. And she made her decision. "Listen to me, Jeffrey. I could forgive you for cheating, and I could forgive you for lying, but not for ruining my life. You were ready to sell my talent, my name, for your future. Paint? Go ahead and paint. I never stopped you. I *wanted* you to. I could have found another business manager, Jeffrey, but I didn't want another husband. You think you're the big businessman, pulling all the right strings, but you're wrong. It was *my* talent that made the company. So, thanks for your help, but I'll hire someone else to do your job. Robert-the-lawyer has already applied. And I won't sell to NormCo, and I will continue working. And you can have the Westport house and you'll still own thirty percent of the business. But that isn't enough to control it. You'll never control it again. I'll run it, even if it doesn't make a profit. I'll run it into the ground if I have to. And you won't see a penny out of it." Her fury had built. She wasn't the kind of person who said unspeakable things, but truths had to be said. "So go see if June will marry you without the NormCo money. And see if you can afford to buy your best friend's loft out from under him without blood money from your wife. And see just how far you get with your pretty little nudes. See how you like being a minor talent."

"There's something else you should know," Jeffrey said.

Karen shook her head. She knew more than enough. There was nothing else he could say that could hurt her. But she found out she was wrong.

"June is pregnant. It changes things."

It certainly did. Karen's anger drained out of her and disappeared, like dirty water down a drain. It was replaced with numbness and shock and something that might turn into a suicidal self-pity.

Her husband was pale, his face almost as white as his hair. Karen didn't know why she looked away. Angry as she was, she still felt ashamed; ashamed, when he was the one who'd behaved so shamefully. Well, this had happened to other women. It seemed to be the fashion of the times. But, as always, she seemed to catch on late. "I'll fight you on this, Jeffrey. It will be a costly divorce. Now get out."

"You'll be sorry, Karen," was all he said.

"I already am," she told him.

35

A STITCH IN TIME

Karen lay on the loveseat in her office in the dark, staring at the moving patterns that the traffic from down below made on her ceiling. The rain that had threatened all day and evening had begun, and the lines the raindrops made on the window made the reflected light look like spiders' webs flung across the expanse of shadowy white. Fuzzily, she tried to remember what spider webs reminded her of, but it wasn't until a fire truck screamed by and the room was suffused with red that Karen again remembered Madame Renault's prediction: that Karen would tear away the web of lies but that every strand would bleed. She felt as if she were bleeding now from some internal injury too deep to show. But Madame Renault had been right about other things too. Karen had weaved her way into this corner, but she had no silk left. She was wasted. She cradled her empty belly in her arms and lay there drained.

Karen slept in her office. And despite her misery, she slept until the phone woke her at seven the next morning. Centrillo's warm voice was both comforting and confusing. She was too disoriented to say much. He just told her that he had been calling and calling her at home, couldn't reach her, and that he had news. She had to come to his office. "Now?" she asked. "I think it's worth your while," he told her.

Karen stepped out of the car onto the cracked pavement of Jay Street. She walked up the old wooden stairs to Mr. Centrillo's office. Her heart was pounding in her chest, but it wasn't from last night's scene with Jeffrey, or the exertion of climbing the stairs. Centrillo's call had been brief. She went over it again. "I think we found her," he had said in his deep baritone. "My operative has the information but he insists on giving it to you himself." Karen had held the phone, silent, her hand clutching the receiver so tightly that for a moment she thought she had choked off the connection. But then Centrillo's voice had come through again. What else had he said? She'd been too confused, too overloaded to listen. He had cleared his throat as if he were uncomfortable or embarrassed. "Uh, and Mrs. Cohen," he paused, "my operative insists on another payment in advance. In cash."

"Has he really found her?" Karen had asked.

"I believe so. But he insists on his payment. The balance. Right now. You know that's not my way but Mr. Paige is a little . . . " Centrillo had cleared his throat again. "He's a little unorthodox."

So now she stood before the wooden door with the gold painted letters. She waited for a moment, for her heart to stop pounding. It felt as if the skin on her chest was actually jumping. She put her hand up to her breastbone to try and calm herself. But she couldn't calm herself. Behind the door her mother would be revealed to her. Inside that room, perhaps, lay the secret to her identity. Her breathing wouldn't slow, nor would her heartbeat, so she took her hand off her chest and reached for the door.

The same girl with the same big hair sat in the tiny vestibule. She had her head down and was reading from a textbook that was propped on the countertop. But before the girl could even greet her, Centrillo opened the door behind the counter and nodded to her. "Mrs. Cohen," he said, "please come in."

His office was as clean as ever, though there was no sun this overcast day. In the oak chair across from Centrillo's desk a small man sat, picking at the cuticles of one hand with the long fingernails of the other. There was something rodent-like about his narrow nose and the set of his eyes, hidden under a bony ridge of brow. He was wearing a gray-white shirt that was at least two collar sizes too big, and Karen would have sworn it was a clip-on tie that hung from under his bony Adam's apple. He looked like Don Knott's evil twin. Karen glanced back over at Mr. Centrillo, his formidable bulk and his cleanliness a bulwark against this little rat-like man. Centrillo held the chair back for her and Karen was comforted to see that he had pulled it away from the other, as if the detective also felt the contamination that rolled off the little guy. "Mrs. Cohen, this is Minos Paige. I think he's been quite effective in the investigation."

She'd die if they didn't cut right to the chase. "You actually think you found my real mother?" she asked.

The man pulled a bent and crumpled manila envelope out of his jacket pocket. "I got the goods," he said. "If you got the cash."

She nodded.

"I'll show you mine, if you'll show me yours," he proposed.

Centrillo winced and interrupted. "Mr. Paige used some methods that are . . . unorthodox," he repeated.

"Since when is a bribe unusual, unorthodox, or uncommon?" Paige asked. He turned to Karen. "Look, I've done these jobs before. You get squat from the courts. With a sealed record you got two choices: find someone to talk or spread a few bucks around and maybe get a peep at a file you're not supposed to see. I did both. I got the goods, and I also got my dick on the line here. I've got informants waiting to be paid."

Centrillo leaned forward across the desk. "That kind of language isn't necessary," he said. In spite of her amusement at his paternalism, Karen was grateful to him. This sleaze-bag was a scary little guy. The question was whether she could trust his word. She reached into her *schlep* bag and pulled out the sealed FedEx envelope that she had stuffed the money into. She handed it not to Minos but to Mr. Centrillo. With the smallest of apologetic shrugs, he took it, opened the envelope, and spread the seven thousand dollars on the table. The bills were hundreds, in seven neat little packets of a thousand dollars each. He stacked them up in front of him and then looked at Minos Paige. "Let's see what you've got," he said.

Minos tore open his envelope. First he pulled out a photostat of some type. "I found Mrs. Talmidge. Old broad living in a retirement home in Saint Augustine. Got my first break. She remembered the name 'cause there had been some trouble with the adoption. I had to move into the home and pretend I wanted to date her. There's a cost to that, I can tell ya. Had to look at her whole collection of Hummel figurines, and that wasn't all she wanted to show me, neither. Got the name of the agency. Had an idea of the date. Went up to Chicago. Used the usual maintenance man cover. Jimmied a lock or two. The files had all been sent to cold storage. Found 'em, though." He pointed to the photostat. "Here's the copy of the place, the address of the home you was in." Karen looked at the photostat. The number was 2881 Fredericston, Chicago Heights. There was no zip—it was in the days before zip codes. Minos pulled out the little black and white snapshot, the one of her in front of the house. He had bent it, and Karen felt like snatching it out of his hand. But he pulled out another photo, this one a modern color glossy. "Here's the house," he said. "Same brick, same number." He handed them to Karen. She compared the two. The same numbers were arranged in the same slant, screwed into the same bricks. Now, though, they were painted white instead of the black they had been all those years ago. Whoever painted them had gotten a smear of paint on the brick just at the point where Karen's head would have reached.

Paige handed her another picture. It was a long shot of the house. "Marie and Alfredo Botteglia," he said. Karen, her hands shaking, turned the photo over and saw the name written out on the back of the photo. "He's dead," Paige told her. "She's a widow. Lives there alone. Talked to a neighbor. She remembers they once had a kid—it disappeared." He handed her another picture. It was blurry, a shot of a woman behind a shopping cart in the parking lot of a supermarket. She was short, rounded, and her hair was gray. It was hard to see her face clearly because of the shadows cast by a post she was walking by. He handed Karen another photo. It was a profile shot of the same woman loading shopping bags into her blue Pontiac. The woman's profile certainly didn't match Karen's own, but the nose *was* prominent. Karen stared at the face of her real mother.

Minos Paige handed her a photocopy of Alfredo Botteglia's obituary. He had died only two years ago. They were Catholics. *I'm* a Catholic, Karen thought with surprise. An Italian-American. But then, maybe she wasn't Alfredo's daughter. She turned to Minos Paige. "Did you speak to her?" she asked.

"I was warned not to make contact," he said. "Sometimes they pull a runner when you do that. I figure I'd leave it to you." Karen nodded. She felt breathless. She picked up the picture of Marie Botteglia again. The rest of the papers she pushed across the desk to Mr. Centrillo, who began carefully examining them. But she knew. She didn't need the nod of approval from him. She turned to Minos Paige, tearing her eyes away from her mother's face only with great difficulty.

"Thank you," was all she said.

36

NOTHING AS IT SEAMS

Karen stood outside on the sidewalk in front of 2881 Fredericston, paying the taxi driver. She had gone straight from Centrillo's office to LaGuardia and had hopped onto the two o'clock flight to Chicago. With the time difference it was only three-thirty now, but she felt as if she had lived a whole lifetime in the two hours it had taken her to get here.

"Here" was a neat, working-class neighborhood. The homes were all of the same period, clearly a postwar subdivision. The Botteglias' ranch house sat on its flat, manicured plot beside a half-bricked split level on one side and a cape-style shingled job next to it. A blue Pontiac sat parked in the driveway. She remembered it from the photo. Karen had taken the precaution of calling the telephone number that Minos Paige had provided. It had taken all of her courage to ask for Marie, and when the woman had said, "This is Marie," Karen had hung up the pay phone.

It was impossible for Karen to believe that in the last few hours she had seen her mother's face for the first time and heard her mother's voice. She looked down at the photo in her hand, the old one that Minos had folded and cracked. The crack ran through the center of her snowsuit, at the knee level. Karen looked at the little girl's face, at her face from so long ago, and looked again at the numbers beside her head. There they were, still attached to the brick wall beside the little entranceway.

She felt so odd. She knew not to count on acceptance or anything much from Marie, the woman behind the door at 2881. Karen stood there in the suburban Chicago street and felt two things. First she felt blasted by the lone-liness that she had carried for so many years: a loneliness so deep that to feel it before might have killed her. It shook her, literally, and she found herself trembling from her toes up through her legs, all along her spine to her neck. Even her head seemed to tremble with the knowledge of her own separate-ness, her terrible vulnerability. Only now could she admit it to herself. She had always, *always* felt alone and the burden of carrying that feeling was shaking her. Wasn't separation the first trauma, the original punishment? Wasn't it ironic that Belle's punishment back in Brooklyn had been to put Karen alone in the pantry? And wasn't it telling that Karen had felt no worse there than she had anywhere else?

Karen reminded herself that she had gotten this information illegally, and that Mrs. Marie Botteglia might be living in terror of this moment, a terror even greater than Karen's own. She may refuse to talk to me, she may scream at me. She may not acknowledge me at all, Karen told herself. After what Belle had done to her, Karen wondered if she could bear another rejection. The burden of rejection that an adopted child carries for life would never go away.

But then she felt herself laying the burden down or, more accurately, giv-ing it up. It seemed that merely standing there, only a few dozen yards from her real mother, had the power to melt the boundaries, the glass wall, that had always separated her from everyone else. From Belle, who had never been adequate, from Lisa, who had been the "real" daughter, from friends, who were kind but weren't adopted, from Arnold, who was distant, from Jeffrey, who had always looked down on her, and from all the people who she had been the employer to. Her separateness seemed to melt into the thin air of the suburban street and she almost laughed aloud. Her aloneness had been such a trial for so long, but somehow she had known that she could feel differently. Somehow she had known that this moment could be achieved. Now she found the courage to walk down the narrow cement path to the door of 2881. She was forty-two years old, and was doing this so much later than others, but then she had always been fashionably late.

There was an illuminated doorbell button. Over it, in a neat but faded print, she could read the name: Mr. & Mrs. Alfredo Botteglia. Karen stuck out her manicured finger and pressed the bell.

Marie Botteglia was very short. She opened the door with a jerk of her arm and looked up to Karen, who was at least eight inches taller than she. Marie looked younger and better than she had in the snapshots, her hair neatly pulled back into a low ponytail, her face pleasant, and a lot less lined than it had seemed in the pictures from the shopping plaza parking lot. The woman looked at her. "Yes?" she asked.

"My name is Karen Kahn," Karen said. She held out the bent photo to Marie. "I wondered if you could identify this picture."

Marie Botteglia frowned and then, deciding it was safe enough, reached out to take the snapshot out of Karen's hand. For a moment, Karen felt the woman's fingers touch her own and she felt an almost electrical shock. Now she had seen, heard, and touched her mother.

Marie fumbled for the reading glasses that hung around her neck. She didn't bother to push them all the way up her nose before turning the photo around and glancing at it. Then her face changed, went pale, and she glanced back at Karen and then down to the photo again.

"My baby?" she asked. And Karen nodded. Marie opened her arms. "My baby!" she said. And Karen fell into the comfort.

They both cried, of course. Then Karen had to give a brief explanation, and Marie kept shaking her head and mopping her eyes. "I can't believe you remembered," she kept saying. She also kept touching Karen, patting her knee, taking her hand, even—shyly—rubbing her back as they sat side by side on the little sofa in the dim living room. Karen couldn't help but think of Belle and how rarely she'd touched Karen at all. Marie had kissed her, and run her hand down Karen's cheek. "I can't believe you found me," she said over and over again. "I'm tickled half to death." At last she got up to make a pot of coffee and carried in a plate of *biscotti*. "Just from a can," she apologized. "I didn't know you were coming." They both giggled.

Now they had settled down to coffee in the kitchen, and Marie had brought out a family photo album. She turned to a picture that must have been taken on the same day that the other one had. In it, Karen wore the same snowsuit, but she was perched on a low wall with a dog, a dalmatian, beside her.

"Was the snowsuit blue?" Karen asked. Marie nodded. Karen pointed to the photo. "Your dog?" she asked. "I don't remember it."

"No, my sister's. Spotty. He died long ago." She turned another page of the album. She put her arm around Karen's. She was a very physical person. She kept patting and touching Karen. And Karen liked it. Karen wouldn't have minded if Marie began stroking her like a cat. She looked down at the album. There was another shot of Karen, this time being held by a tall man in a dark overcoat and fedora. "Alfredo," Marie said. "He died too."

"I know. The detective told me." Karen took Marie's hand. She didn't want to ask any of the deeper questions. Was Alfredo her father? Why had they put her up for adoption? Had Marie felt guilt or regret since then? Had she tried to find Karen? Those were too hard, and Karen felt she was already being given enough for right now. She looked again at the photo of the man holding her.

"Do you remember him?" Marie asked.

"No," Karen told her honestly. She stared at the photo. For a moment, she thought she could feel the scratchy texture of his coat against her chin. And a smell. A strong smell. "Did he smoke cigars?" she asked.

"Yes!" Marie said. Her eyes filled. "How did you know? You *do* remember."

"Just the edge of a memory," Karen said, but she was as thrilled as Marie.

There were some other photos on the page. Marie pointed out her sister, her mother, and another shot of the dalmatian being led on a leash by her brother-in-law. Then she turned the photo album page and there was the same picture that Karen carried in her *schlep* bag, the photo of her in the crib with the frog doll.

It wasn't that Karen had any doubt before, but seeing the same photo, the exact same shot that she had looked at, secretly, for so long—since she was a little girl back in Brooklyn—did something to her. She burst into tears and found that she couldn't stop crying. Marie stood up and put her arms around Karen. "There, there," she said. "Good girl. It's all right."

Belle had never allowed tears. She'd said they were childish, even when Karen was still a child. But Marie seemed perfectly comfortable with Karen's weeping.

Karen struggled to speak. "My frog," she said.

"What?" Marie asked.

"My frog," Karen wept.

Marie patted her again and left the room. Well, what could Karen expect? She must have embarrassed the woman. Still, Karen kept sobbing, sitting there at the kitchen table in this modest little house in the middle of a town she didn't remember. She tried to calm herself. Maybe she was scaring her mother. But she couldn't stop. All she could do was get up and tear a paper towel from the roll beside the kitchen sink. Then she heard a noise behind her and turned to see Marie in the doorway, tears running down her own face, wordlessly holding out the faded and cracked little green rubber frog.

Marie insisted that Karen stay for dinner. "It won't be much," Marie said—"just some pasta and maybe some breaded cauliflower and zucchini. I'm supposed to be on a diet," she confided, "but I cheat," she confessed.

Marie and Alfredo had had no other children. Marie told Karen all about her eight nieces and six nephews. Karen told Marie about her career, about her life in New York, but she didn't, couldn't, mention her marriage or Belle and Arnold. Still, it seemed as if Marie was perfectly content. She didn't seem to be the type of person who would pry. She wasn't the kind of woman who questioned or pressed. In fact, she seemed pleasantly, calmly contented. And the feeling was infectious. Karen sat in the little kitchen while Marie bustled about from the stove to the refrigerator and back. The kitchen took on the smell of good olive oil and roasted peppers. And Karen seemed to drink in the contentment, to feel it coat her and then be absorbed, as dry skin would absorb oil. It felt good, and gave her, for the moment, absolution. Jeffrey and June, the KKInc problems, Lisa and the rest of it, receded. Karen didn't worry, didn't even think about all of the problems waiting for her back in New York. She just sat in the little kitchen in the little house in Chicago Heights and felt fine.

They ate, and the meal couldn't have been more different from anything Belle had ever served Karen. Marie—my mother, Karen thought—had done more than throw together some pasta. Quickly and effortlessly she had roasted peppers, diced zucchini, and prepared a delicious cauliflower side dish. There was fresh Italian bread and good olive oil to soak it in. The dishes were only Melmac, and the glasses weren't crystal, but the food was delicious and plentiful. Karen looked around her, thinking, "This is my birth right. This feeling of plenty, of abundance, is the way I could have grown up." How could things have gone so wrong? How could it have happened that Marie gave up her daughter and Karen was cheated out of all of this?

Karen looked around at the little kitchen and across the table at Marie's round face, her unfashionable clothes, the photos of nieces and nephews and other family stuck up on the refrigerator, and in little collections on the wall. Karen stared at them all, drinking in the pictures of her family. It was funny to her that they all looked like working-class Italians. It didn't seem as if she shared any of their features. She was taller, and her hair was light brown, not black, and she was bigger boned than the women. But they were her family. She had cousins and aunts and uncles that she had never met. That she could meet now. But still, she felt as if she had missed so much.

Of course, if I had grown up here I wouldn't have gone to Pratt. I wouldn't have met Jeffrey. I probably wouldn't be a designer. Maybe I would be working in some factory. It would have been a completely different life. It might have been dull. It might have been hard. Karen knew it wouldn't have been perfect, but at that moment, hers was so bad that she longed for this one and she longed for the simplicity of Marie. God, what was so great about being Karen Kahn? What was so great about Westport, or being in WWD, or having dinner in SoHo?

"I'm just so happy to see you. To know you. To know that you're all right," Marie was saying. For a moment, Karen longed to tell her that she wasn't all right, that her whole life was falling apart around her. But that wasn't fair. She knew better than to do that. And she felt that as long as she stayed in this room, in this house, she was all right.

They ate and ate. Then Karen helped Marie clear the table, and Marie told her a little bit about Alfredo's last illness and how much she missed him, now that he was gone. "It was the cigars," she said. "Him and his cigars." She shook her head. "Stubborn," she said. "Forget about it!" Then Marie reached for the album again, wanting to show more pictures of Alfredo. They turned back to where they had left off.

Marie turned the page and there was the picture of Karen, standing beside the address numbers on the front of the house. Both of them stared at the picture for a long time. "That was the day we found out," Marie said, reaching out to Karen's hand and caressing it gently.

"The day you found out what?" Karen asked.

"The day we found out that we couldn't keep you. It was a terrible day. I couldn't stop crying. Forget about it! Alfredo thought I was scaring you and making myself sick, but I couldn't stop." Tears filled Marie's eyes again. This time Karen reached out to Marie to help console her.

It was now or never. The girl who had been given up, left alone, stuck with Belle, had to know the answer to the terrible riddle. "But why did you have to? Why didn't you keep me?" Karen asked. She tried to keep her voice gentle, free of judgment, but the little girl in the picture deserved an answer.

"The state," Marie said, wiping her eyes, "the state didn't give us no choice."

Karen looked at her blankly. Why would the state separate a mother and child? Had Marie and Alfredo been abusive? Karen couldn't believe it. Is that why she couldn't remember much? What else could be the reason? It wasn't financial. They may have been poor, but they still had the house from back then, and that was more than many people had. Marie blew her nose loudly. "It's so long ago," she said. "But it still hurts." She sighed gustily. "Well, it don't matter. You were taken care of, and it's so wonderful that you've found me and that I get to see you now."

"It's so wonderful that I get to meet my real mother," Karen said.

The older woman paused. "What do you mean?" Marie asked.

"My adoptive family was great," Karen assured her, though she was no longer sure that was remotely true. "But I always felt like there was something missing. I just felt that I needed to meet my real mother."

Marie looked at her, her eyes wide. "Karen, we had you for almost four years, from the time you were an infant. I thought for sure the state would give you to us. But then, just before the adoption was finalized, *she* came back and the state took you away. She had married and she was insisting that you go back to her. It broke our hearts, but it was only right. After all, you didn't really belong to us."

Karen stared at Marie. She couldn't take it in. "What?" was all she managed to ask.

"Karen, I love you. I always loved you. But I was only your foster mom. You were raised by your real mother."

37

CLOTHING ALLOWANCES

"Lisa, I have to see you."

When Lisa heard Jeffrey's voice at the other end of the line, she nearly dropped the phone. She didn't need this now, not after this trouble with the deal falling through, bills coming in, and Leonard ready to kill her. It had, of course, upset her that Jeffrey hadn't even tried to get in touch with her after Karen had caught them, but then came the stink and her recovery. Since then, with the terrible news that the deal was off, and with Leonard's suspicions, Lisa felt that not hearing from Jeffrey had actually been a blessing in disguise. She needed this phone call like she needed another vaginal infection.

"Come on, Jeffrey. I can't see you." It gave her a certain satisfaction to be able to say those words. She blamed Jeffrey for all this. He had gotten her excited about that stupid worthless stock. He had wined her and dined—well, lunched—her and started all this trouble. Lisa wasn't even remotely a romantic, but she did have enough ego to take pleasure in the opportunity that she'd have to reject him. It was too bad there was no one to witness it or to tell about it. For a moment, she had a flash, a stab almost, of missing Karen because Karen was the one that Lisa could tell her triumphs to. But all that, obviously, was over. To her own surprise, her eyes filled with tears.

"You have to see me," Jeffrey insisted. "And maybe you should bring Belle."

Lisa felt the breath leave her body. She stood there, clutching the phone, and could almost picture her lungs as the shrunken balloons that remain two days after a party, deflated and drained of air. She couldn't breathe. What the hell did Jeffrey want to talk to *Belle* about? She knew Jeffrey usually avoided her mother. Was this some kind of last-gasp attempt to get Karen back? Was he going to spill his guts to Belle in front of her and then beg them both to talk to Karen on his behalf? Yeah, like she would! There was no way Lisa was going to let Belle find out about her little indiscretion.

"Jeffrey, you gotta listen to me: it's over. I'm not seeing you any more and there's nothing you could do to change my mind."

"Jesus Christ! That's not why I want to see you. It's about the money. The deal. If you want a chance to cash in your stock, you and Belle have to meet with me right away."

"Where?" was all she asked, and picking up a pencil that sat beside the phone she wrote down his directions in a heavy, childish scribble.

When the doorbell rang, Lisa almost dropped the mug she was drinking from. She was exhausted. The meeting with Jeffrey and Belle and Robert-the-lawyer had taken almost two hours, and then the traffic on the VanWyck had nearly killed her. She had to be home before one o'clock, when Leonard had begun making his little "check-in" calls. So, who could be at the door? The girls were both in school, Leonard was at the office, and no one was expected. No one *ever* paid casual visits to her house. Who would just come by? Lisa ran up the stairs to the bedroom window that overlooked the front. There was a telephone beside the bed. If it was a man—a salesman or a homeless person—she wouldn't answer the door. No. She'd call the police. She cautiously moved the vertical blinds away and peeked out the front.

Lisa didn't have to call the police. They were already there, with their black-and-white and its circling blue light. What the hell was going on?

Lisa ran down the stairs and opened the front door. Two policemen—well, one policeman and a policewoman who was built like a man—stood on the front steps. Between them, her head hunched down, stood Tiff.

"What's going on?" Lisa asked her daughter, but it was the policewoman who spoke.

"Are you Mrs. Leonard Saperstein?" she asked. Lisa nodded. "Is this your daughter Tiffany?" the cop asked. Lisa nodded again. What the hell was going on?

"May we come in?" the woman cop asked. Lisa stepped to the side and the three of them walked into the house. It was only then that Lisa realized that Tiff had both hands cuffed behind her. Handcuffed like a criminal! Lisa's mouth dropped open for a moment until, by an act of will, she closed it. She followed the three stumpy figures into the living room.

400 / OLIVIA GOLDSMITH

"Can we sit down here?" the woman asked. Lisa nodded, but promised herself that was the last question *she* was going to answer. Right now she needed some answers herself.

"What's going on?" she asked.

"It seems as if Tiffany here has been doing a little shoplifting," the police-woman said.

Lisa thought of the closetful of clothes upstairs. Jesus Christ! Why did every single fucking thing in her life have to go so fucking wrong? First the *bat mitzvah*, then Stephanie, the thing with Jeffrey, the stink, the problem with KKInc, and now this! She had meant to eventually talk to Tiffany—she really had—but what with the other problems, well, she simply hadn't gotten to it. Oh, God. How much would *this* cost to fix? And what would Leonard say when he found out?

At that thought her stomach took a lurch. Since her recent medical prob-lems it seemed as if Leonard was on the verge of leaving *her*. Lisa could hardly accept that she'd been reduced to worrying about Leonard, but she was. Because, after all, what did she have if she didn't have her marriage? Without the KKInc money, she'd wind up just another divorced doctor's wife, living in some high-rise rental apartment in Great Neck and working as a personal shopper. She had to do what she'd done.

Lisa put her hand up to her forehead and brushed her hair off her face. "I don't understand," she said, and she really didn't. "Why would my daughter steal? She has plenty of money. She has everything she needs."

"Apparently not," the policewoman said. "It seems as if she needed two blazers and an eight-hundred-dollar chiffon dress."

Lisa couldn't believe this new nightmare. She couldn't believe that it was happening to her. She looked over at her daughter. The girl was standing with her fat legs slightly apart and she had her head turned as far away from Lisa as she could get it. Her face was expressionless.

"Sergeant," she said to the woman, "can't you just return the items to the store? No harm's been done."

"I'm afraid not. We're talking grand larceny. And there's a suspicion she's hit the store before. At this point, the store feels that it would like to prose-cute. And I wonder if we might take a look around."

Lisa thought of her daughter's closet, with all those tiny size twos, com-plete with their price tags, hanging up in neat rows on the rods. "I think," she said coldly, "that it's time for me to call my lawyer."

38

FOR WHOM THE BELLE TOLLS

Karen got out of the airport and went straight to the LaGuardia Airport taxi stand. She was in no mood for jokes, and didn't even notice that when she cut to the head of the line there were other people who called out to stop her. She handed the starter a hundred-dollar bill. "I'm going to Rockville Centre," she told him.

"Yes, ma'am," he nodded, and opened the yellow cab door for her.

She told the driver where she was going. He was an Israeli, one of the few left who wasn't driving a radio car. "You'll have to pay round-trip," he said, ready for a fight.

She threw another hundred at him. "Just drive," she told him.

She felt shattered. And why shouldn't she? How many times in a life could you bear to lose your mother? She had lost hers as an infant, when Belle had fostered her out. Then she had lost Marie when she was three. Now she had lost both Marie and Belle all over again. Marie, whom Karen had searched for, had been stripped away, no longer the dream haven that Karen could seek, and Belle—whom Karen had always done her best to love—was now revealed for what she was. Belle was a real mother all right, but in this case mother was only half a word.

Lies. Nothing but lies. Jeffrey, Lisa, Belle. Was there *anyone* in her family who hadn't lied to her?

It was twilight when Karen pulled up to the house. In the dusk, it looked even smaller and more ordinary than usual. Was it getting shabby? Arnold had never been interested in keeping it up, but Belle's relentless nagging had at least ensured that the paint didn't peel, or the shrubs get too long without it being taken care of. Karen strode up the cement walk and couldn't be bothered to press the stupid chimes. Instead, she pounded on the door. She felt like pounding. Pounding was a very good idea right now. But despite her noises, there wasn't any response.

There also wasn't a light visible from the street. What would she do if no one was there? She couldn't imagine cooling her heels at the Dunkin' Donut, or sitting on the stoop to wait for Belle to come home the way she had when she was a little girl in Brooklyn. Belle *had* to be there. Her mother had to be there.

And she was. It took another minute of pounding, but then Belle, wearing a lavender chenille robe, opened the door. "Karen," she said. "What are you doing here? Shh. You'll wake your father. He's sleeping in the den. Anyway, what are you doing here now?"

Karen pushed passed her. It was a good question. What *was* she doing here? Was she going to scream? Smack Belle? Pound her until she was limp on the floor? Karen didn't want blood, but then she'd never really believed Belle had any blood in her. Probably she was stuffed, like an expensive sofa. Yes, Karen would like to pound the stuffing out of Belle. For once, Karen felt good that she was taller, broader, bigger, and stronger than her mother. She'd like to grab the little woman and shake her until her teeth rattled. She stood in the center of the stupid mirrored living room, the room where lies had been told and reflected, where false lives had been lived for almost thirty years. Smashing all the mirrors might be a good place to start, Karen thought, and looked around the room wildly. Belle had followed her and crossed her arms, as she habitually did, across her chest. Sure. Typical. Belle always had protected herself, closed herself off, and refused the breast to Karen. For all Karen knew, Belle had spent her whole marriage refusing to let *Arnold* near her breasts.

"Karen, what is it?" Belle's voice sounded more than curious. Did she actually sound concerned? Frightened?

"You lied to me," Karen said. "You have lied to me for a very long time."

Belle looked at her and for once—maybe for the first time in their whole life together—Belle was silent. No justifications, no defensiveness, no nothing. Except, maybe, a gleam of fear in her eyes.

"You heard about the stock already?" Belle asked.

"Stock? What stock?" Karen asked, confused. But she wouldn't let Belle distract her. "I'm not talking about that."

"About what then?" Belle asked, but Karen could tell she knew.

"You told me I was adopted. How could you? How could you deny me?" Karen felt tears welling up into her eyes, but she wasn't going to weep now. She had drenched two pillows on the flight back from Chicago and she doubted there was any moisture left in her. She felt as if she'd been turned from flesh to something much drier and harder. Not steel, but wood perhaps. Except does wood shake the way she was shaking? She knew that her trembling wasn't from weakness; it was pure anger. She almost laughed bitterly at that thought. Anger was far too puny a word to describe this overwhelming rage.

"Not here," Belle said. "Come into the bedroom."

Like a child, Karen followed her mother down the hall. Why was it always this way? Secrets. Don't tell Lisa but . . . I'm doing this for you but don't let your father know . . . If I tell you, promise you won't tell your mother . . . Karen was sick of it all.

They walked into the bedroom. The bed was covered with various articles of clothing, bits and pieces of Belle's wardrobe that she was sorting and nursing with that obsessive care that she reserved for her garments—checking buttons, removing lint, pressing out creases. Karen ignored it all and turned to her mother. She wasn't going to let Belle control her or sap her anger. "You lied to me," she repeated. "You told me I was adopted."

"Well, you *were* adopted," Belle said. And Karen could hardly believe it. The trip down the hallway, or the comfort of being surrounded by her things, had given Belle enough time to regroup. The defensiveness had already crept back into her voice. But with her it sounded like authority, not defense. She'd already moved her hands from her elbows to her hips. Was she going to try to deny the whole thing, Karen's whole reality? This time, no cigar. Even Belle didn't have the stamina to pull that off. Belle looked away from Karen for a moment, into one of the three-way mirrors that reflected the two of them. "Arnold adopted you. I have the papers to prove it."

Karen's jaw actually dropped. In the most important conversation between them, Belle was going to pull this kind of sophistry? What length would she go to to avoid the truth and avoid admitting how wrong she'd been? "We're not talking about my *father*. You know that," Karen said.

"Well, when I said you were adopted, it wasn't a lie."

"So it was a sin of omission, not a sin of commission? That makes it okay?"

"What is she talking about?" Belle asked her closet. "Has she become some kind of Catholic?"

"Cut the shit, Belle. You know what I'm talking about. Why didn't you tell me you were my real mother? Why did you let me believe that you weren't?"

Belle snapped her head in an impatient jerk. "I *always* said you were my daughter. And I always treated you like my daughter. When did I ever say otherwise? *Never*. I *never* said otherwise. There was no difference between the way I treated you and your sister. If anything, you got *more* attention. You got everything you wanted. And from the beginning you were difficult. From the beginning you wanted your own way. And you got it. We moved out here for you, we sent you to good schools, you went to camp. When did you go hungry? When did . . . "

"Stop it!" Karen screamed. "If you keep this up I swear to God I'll kill you. We are talking about a *lie*. You robbed me all this time. I thought that you had adopted me. I thought you loved me, and I thought there was some other woman who may or may not have loved me, but gave birth to me. Now I find out that there was no other woman. There was only you. And you didn't love me or you never would have farmed me out in the first place, or denied your own child all this time."

"How dare you! How dare you judge me or raise your voice to me?"

Karen rolled her eyes. "Belle, I am asking you to stop thinking about you for just ten minutes. Just for ten minutes, Belle, I want you to try to think about *me*. I want you to try and think about what it was like to grow up in this house and blame anything that wasn't right on the adoption. I wasn't pretty like Lisa because I was adopted. We didn't get along because I was adopted. You weren't affectionate because I was adopted. And if I, sometimes, felt that I didn't love you, I had to be very careful, because I was adopted. I kept a space, a hole in me, that was reserved for my real mother's love. I had to do it to survive. And there was another space, a hole in me, because my real mother had given me up. I didn't need to waste all that space, Belle! I didn't need to be so empty. You didn't give me a bad life. You didn't beat me. You didn't starve me. A lot of kids had it a lot worse. But you gave me those spaces and you gave yourself this big burden, this wall between us. Why would you want to do that? Why would you want to lie?"

Karen paused. She shook her head. "I can't understand it," she said. "I'd never deny my child. How could you do it? Why *would* you do it?"

"Oh, don't get so high and mighty with me," Belle hissed. "You would do what you had to do. Things were different then. What do you know about it? Miss Career Woman. Miss Big Success. We sent you to school. We helped you. We denied you nothing.

"Well, it wasn't so easy for everyone else. Not like for you. I grew up in a dump. My mother was a piece worker. We moved at the end of every month when the rent came due. I wore rags to school. *Rags*. I never once—not once—had a decent pair of shoes that fit me. I was smart, good in school, but what good did that do? I was smart enough to see just how trapped I was. There were no jobs for women. Was I going to go into the factory like my mother? I managed to graduate high school and I managed to get into night school for college and I studied to be a teacher. Nobody helped me. Nobody gave me anything. I had to choose between textbooks or dinner. You think my mother was so great? She just wanted me to take a job sewing and bring home a paycheck. You think I *wanted* to be a teacher? You think I wanted to deal with other women's children all day long? But what else was there? Don't think the world back then was a Joan Crawford movie. I never met *any* woman who had a job more important than secretary. So I went to night school and I worked days in a department store. Men's haberdashery. And I met a man in each place. At night school I met Arnold, who was reliable but wasn't romantic and wasn't rich and wasn't handsome. And at the day job, I met your father. He came from a good family. He came in and spent more money on ties in fifteen minutes than I earned in a week. He asked me out to dinner. So I went. He showed me a world I'd never seen before. We ate in restaurants with linen tablecloths. He drank wine. Not just at *seders*, but every night. And he gave me a ring. I thought we were engaged. I slept with him. There was no birth control then. None that nice girls knew about. We counted on the men. Well, I shouldn't have counted on this one. And when I told him I was pregnant, he dropped me. I don't think he ever meant to marry me."

Belle laughed, but the laugh was brittle. "He took me sailing once, on Lake Michigan. He knew how to do all those rich boy things. You know, tennis and sailing. When he left me, I thought of taking a boat and drowning myself in the lake. I couldn't do it and I couldn't tell anyone."

Belle's eyes blazed. "What do you think? You think there were abortions on every street corner like there are today? You think there was counseling for girls in trouble? You think the university would let an unwed mother finish school? You think a school system would hire an unwed mother?" Belle laughed again. "You don't know what it was like, and women my age don't want to remember. Believe me, we don't want to remember. My own mother threw me out. So I moved into a boarding house. It was the lowest of the low, not for a Jewish girl, but I hid the pregnancy and worked as long as I could, and then had you and I planned to put you up for adoption. But once I saw you, once I held you, I couldn't do it. You think I'm made of stone? I kept you with me until my money ran out, but then I had to put you in foster care. What choice did I have? There was no day care back then and my mother wouldn't speak to me, and anyway she had her own kids and had to work. But I never forgave her for it. I never spoke to her or any of them again.

"So what could I do with you? And what life would I have with you? I had to give you to the state. Can you imagine? And I went back to work and I finished school and I got a job. And then, I was surrounded by women. Women and children. There was no way I was going to meet a man, not anyone decent. Not anyone who could make a living. So I looked up Arnold, and I made sure that we just accidentally bumped into each other, and we started dating again, and this time I couldn't wait until he proposed."

"So he didn't know? He didn't know about me?"

"He didn't know about *me*. He thought I was a nice girl, and I let him think that. He was willing to give me anything I wanted, and I wanted to move away, get away from Chicago, and to quit my job. I wanted a house and I wanted nice clothes and I wanted to get you back. When I told him I couldn't conceive, he didn't ask any questions. When I told him we should adopt, he agreed. And when I told him I'd seen an older baby that I just had to have, he was willing. I don't know what he knew or what he suspected. He never asked me a question, so I never had to lie. And I didn't lie to you either."

Belle looked at Karen, her lips thin, her mouth tight. "So don't play high and mighty with me, because you don't know what it was like. You don't know what *you* would have done. I did the best I could."

Karen stood there, silent. Belle moved from the center of the room to the side of the bed and sat down as if she was exhausted. Karen shook her head. As always, Belle had managed to justify herself, but it didn't mean that she was right. Maybe she *had* done the best she could do, but it wasn't good enough.

"You shouldn't have lied," Karen said. "It was still a lie, and it made our lives into a lie. Don't you see how it put a wall between you and daddy? Don't you see what it did to me? And look what it did to you! You've always been distant. I can't remember that you ever hugged me or cuddled me. Not ever."

"That was *you*. *You* weren't affectionate. I felt as if you always knew. That when I got you back from the state, that you looked at me with eyes that *knew*. You blamed me. You didn't want my hugs."

"You're talking crazy!" Karen cried. "I was four years old. I was taken from the only home I remembered. I wasn't blaming you. I was probably scared. I was traumatized." She put her hands to her head. She felt as if it might explode. For a crazy moment she imagined Belle with her trusty Dustbuster, vacuuming brains up off the carpet.

"Well, easy for you to talk. You don't have a child. If you did, I'd like to see if you'd do any better. Lisa certainly hasn't. One of hers is always puking and the other one is going to wind up in prison. You got Stephie on drugs, and Tiff was so jealous that she started stealing. Your father says the haul she was caught with was over a thousand dollars worth of clothes. That's grand larceny."

"What? What are you talking about? What has Tiff done?"

"See? Do you know what goes on in your family? No. Too busy with work. Selfish! You've always been selfish. You think you would have been a good mother! Ha! You'd be as bad as Lisa."

"Maybe Lisa hasn't done such a good job because she never saw anyone be a good mother."

Belle glared at her. "Right. Blame it all on me. I'm the bad one. Tiff is my fault. Lisa is my fault. Your father is my fault. Stephanie is my fault. Everything is my fault."

Karen knew Belle was overdramatizing to make her look ridiculous, but this time it wouldn't work. "It is all your fault," she said. "Because you lied to us all. And you never showed that you loved us."

"What? So you two never did anything of your own free will? It's my fault your sister slept with your husband? I made that happen?"

Karen felt the body blow, but for once she saw everything, each manipulation, each knife thrust, each distracting wave of the red cape, for what it was. Belle would sacrifice anyone's feelings for her own. It was the only way she knew to survive. "Yes," Karen whispered. "You did make that happen. If you hadn't always been forcing us to compete, if you hadn't always praised me to her and her to me but never praised us to our faces, then maybe she wouldn't have been so consumed by jealousy. She slept with Jeffrey to hurt me and it was because she's never felt like she could win."

"And what's Jeffrey's excuse, Dr. Freud?"

Karen stood still, absorbing the pain. She could say, "Ask my father why a man cheats on his wife," but she had the grace not to. Instead, she just shook her head. "You shouldn't have said that," she told her mother. "My marriage is none of your business. I just wanted to know if you had an apology in you." She paused. "I want you to understand that what you did has ruined a part of me that won't be fixed. I'll go on, but I won't go on with you."

She turned and started to walk out of the room. "What's that supposed to mean?" Belle asked. Karen didn't answer. She kept on walking.

"You're turning your back on your family and you've lost your husband. You could lose more. We'll see how you like being alone. It's just a good thing that you never had any children," Belle spat at her. "Because however bad a mother you think I was, I know you'd be worse."

Karen kept walking down the hallway. She passed the open door of her old bedroom and the den, where Arnold still lay sleeping, the television blaring a rerun of "In the Heat of the Night." She continued through the living room, out the front door, and to the corner. Outside, in the darkness, she realized that she had nowhere to go and no way to get there. She kept walking from streetlight to streetlight until, at last, she reached Long Beach Road and the gas station at the corner. She got into the phone booth, but couldn't find any change. So she lifted the receiver and dialed a collect call. By the time Carl answered and accepted the charges, the mouthpiece was shaking against her face and her teeth were chattering despite the warm night. He could barely understand her when she tried to talk to him.

"Just tell me where you are, Karen," he said. "I'll come and get you."

"I'm in hell, Carl," she told him.

39

WHAT'S IN A NAME

Carl had tucked Karen into his own bed, and with the help of a blue Valium and half a glass of red wine that Carl made her drink, Karen slept for nine and a half hours. She woke up and stared at the unfamiliar ceiling over her. For at least a minute she couldn't remember where she was. A lot of her recent past seemed to have disappeared as well. Karen had to back track from Paris to New York to the Marianas to SoHo to Chicago to Rockville Centre, and finally to here, Brooklyn Heights. She groaned, then, and turned over to her side, pulling the blanket up and blocking out the sunshine that shone in through the bay window and onto the ceiling. Like an accident victim, she lay as still as she could, trying to figure out where it hurt and what was irreparably damaged.

Carl tip-toed in. "Ah, Sleeping Beauty has awakened."

For some reason that made Karen think of Tony de Freise and the night of the Oakley Awards. She and Jeffrey had thought Tony was the Bad Fairy, but it was Jeffrey who was an evil spirit, not a prince. Karen moaned.

"You don't have to get up now," Carl told her. "It's still very early." Awkwardly, he took her hand. She had told him everything, and his round face drooped with sympathy—or at least it drooped as much as his round face could. "I'm so sorry, Karen," he said. "Nothing about Belle surprises me, but I'm shocked by Jeffrey's behavior." He shook his head. "You just can't trust heterosexual men," he told her. "But you'll recover. Think of Rose Kennedy and how she had to deal with Gloria Swanson. It was an inspiration."

Karen closed her eyes.

Carl cleared his throat. "Try and think of betrayals as just a part of life."

"Yeah. So are genital warts. That doesn't mean I have to like them when they happen to me. Oh, Carl, what should I do?"

"I hate to advocate catatonia to anyone, but it's always worked for me."

"I think I will try a little more sleep," Karen said. Carl tip-toed out of the room.

She couldn't bear to get up yet. Even with Carl's help she wasn't ready to face this day, or any of the others that would follow it. She lay there under the blankets and wept with self-pity. And why not, she asked herself? Who else would feel sorry for her? She wiped her eyes on the corner of Carl's fat duvet and pulled it over her head. After a little while she drifted off into a light sleep.

She was on the white duvet, but the ceiling had turned black around her. The duvet was rolling, and she realized she was on a sea. A white sea. She was in some kind of basket or boat and rolling with the waves. As far as she could see around her, there was nothing but the darkness of the sky and the shining, milky white sea. She began to weep again with loneliness, and her tears fell into the basket. She realized that if she kept crying she would sink, go down and down endlessly into the dark, cold water, but she couldn't stop crying. And then she heard someone else's weeping. It was high-pitched and came from the pool at the bottom of the little boat. She bent over and plunged her hands into the warm bath and pulled out a baby. It looked at her with slanted black eyes. It knew her, and she knew it. Karen held it close to her breast and both of them stopped weeping.

When Karen woke, she was still cradling the pillow to her side.

Karen was back at home packing when she heard the noise in the living room. Ernesta had left, so Karen stiffened with fear. But then Jeffrey called out. Funny that the fear lessened when she heard his voice. I guess that means he's not as bad as a burglar or a rapist, she thought, and turned to the doorway and walked down the hall to the living room.

He was sitting in one of the chairs at the refectory table, a pile of papers stacked neatly in front of him. The papers, the chair upholstery, and his face were about the same shade of white. "What is it?" she said, because she had nothing else to say to him. "What do you want?"

"The company," he said. He didn't move, and though he looked so pale, he sounded firm.

"Fat chance," she told him. She didn't feel safe turning her back on him, but she wheeled around and started back toward the bedroom.

"This isn't a choice you're being offered," Jeffrey told her. "It's a *fait accompli*."

She turned. "What are you talking about?" she asked.

"You won't listen to reason," he said. "So this is the only way. I met with some staff, some family. We've all agreed. With my share and theirs combined, we outvote you. We're selling to NormCo without you."

She was drained of all words for a minute, but then the ridiculousness, the nerve of it, became so obvious that she felt a surge of energy. "That's out of the question. Wolper won't buy the company without me. He wants me and he wants my name."

"He'll get your name," Jeffrey said. "It belongs to us. And if he won't pay as much for the company without you, he'll pay enough."

Karen stared at him. She couldn't believe it. "What are you talking about?"

"We own Karen Kahn," Jeffrey explained. "I've got thirty percent of the shares. With my family's shares, with the stock you gave to some of the staff, with Mercedes and . . ."

"Who is going to design the stuff?"

"Who cares? We'll get someone. Bill is talking to Norris Cleveland."

"Norris! You've got to be kidding!"

"Hey, she's interested. And she can do your kind of stuff. The customers will barely know the difference, Karen. They'll buy the label, and that'll be enough. That's all Wolper really wanted from you anyway. Wolper's dropped his price a lot, but we'll still all get enough. Better that than let you run it into the ground."

Karen blinked. All that bullshit that Wolper had fed her! About buying her talent, about respecting her work, about respecting the customer! All lies, or only true enough to count on when the going went Wolper's way. But this . . . Jeffrey. This was unbelievable. "You can't do this," she told her husband. "I'll take you to court. Robert offered to . . ."

"Robert and Sooky have already signed over their votes. So has my mother. Some of the girls from the workroom, and Lisa, and your mother have all agreed. There's absolutely nothing you can do about it."

"Lisa?" Karen asked. "My mother?"

It was too much. Karen sat down heavily. Belle! Why was Karen surprised? Belle had to have the last word, land the last arrow. But perhaps she'd done it before. Hadn't she said something about stock . . . Karen took a shuddering breath.

"Maybe you can take the company, but you can't take my talent. I'll go work somewhere else."

"Do what you want, Karen. Just don't think you'll be doing anything as

Karen Kahn. We own that name. You signed it all over as a corporate asset long before the NormCo offer. I control it now and I can do what I like with it."

She very nearly moaned out loud. Belle. Belle and Jeffrey. Working together, they'd stolen her life's work from her. Karen had a strong regret at that moment. She wished she hadn't forbidden Jeffrey to get a gun permit and a revolver for their apartment. Shooting him would be such an enormous pleasure that, at the moment, a life in prison seemed a fair trade.

"I have all the papers here," he said then, and stood up to leave. "Don't try to go back to the office. I'll have the locks changed and I'll hire new security. Janet is gone. So is Casey. And Defina. It's perfectly within my rights. You'll get your share of the money, of course. Robert will see to all of that."

And mercifully, she managed to keep standing there until after he had left. She didn't fall back against the wall and slip to the floor until she'd heard him get on the elevator.

40

A HORSE WITH NO NAME

When she looked back on it all, Karen realized that she had always had a plan B. But there, alone in the apartment after Jeffrey had gone, leaving only the legal papers that stole all her achievements from her, it took a little while for her to regroup.

Whatever Wolper had paid for KKInc, and however reduced her share would be, she would still have enough to live on. And she was sure she would have a place to live. But she wouldn't have her name, and she wouldn't have her company— her baby.

Karen lay on the white sofa, flat on her back, one arm hanging over the side, her hand on the floor. She stared through the darkness at the ceiling so high overhead. She couldn't help but see some of her designs, some of her work: Elise Elliot's wedding gown, the farm wife dress, the tunic that she had used in different fabrics for three seasons, and of course the Paris clothes. That her work would be taken away, owned by someone else, was incredible. She remembered that moment in the tent in the Place des Vosges when her name had looked so foreign to her. Well, it was only going to look more and more strange. They had her name now, and Norris Cleveland would be rooting through her designs, notes, and sketches. Karen could just imagine one of her tunics emblazoned with Norris's stupid buttons. Or Karen's new farm wife dress in poison yellow. Jeffrey would be putting out Norris's disgusting line with Karen's name on it. Would the public know the difference and would they care? Alone in the dim light, Karen blushed and she wasn't sure if it was anger, embarrassment, or both that brought the blood to her cheeks. Too bad the KKInc clothes to come wouldn't self-destruct the way Norris's perfume had.

It was so unbelievable, so unexpected, that it was surreal. Maybe that was why she wasn't in pain. Stripped of her name, her company, her family, and her husband, she didn't feel as bereft as she might have. In a way, she felt relieved. Because, like banging your head against the wall, the wonderful thing about lying to yourself is that it feels so good when you stop. The web was torn to bits at last.

Of course, she had built an entire life on lies. Well, why wouldn't she? She had always been lied to. But what amazed her was how the truth had been lurking underneath everything all along. She realized, there in the silence of the apartment, that she had always known she had a better business sense than Jeffrey: he'd fucked up with the withholding tax, made bad deals with the factors, undervalued the company when NormCo first sniffed around, and she'd ignored or overlooked it all. She'd wanted him, and she'd overlooked whatever she had to so she could stay with him. She'd been the horse that had pulled their wagon, making the money, the clothes; making the marriage. He'd known she was a horse he could ride. He counted on her strength and then resented her for it, had been a lousy painter and used her business as an excuse to run away from that reality. Then he'd been a lousy businessman, while all the time they'd pretended that she was the impractical one. She'd always known the truth, but she couldn't face it.

And she must have known about June. All those late business meetings, all those poker nights when she had been too busy working to ask questions! June showing up at the *bat mitzvah*, Jeffrey's disappearances, Perry's tip-off about the loft, the glimpse of June in Paris. There must have been a lot of other indicators but she hadn't wanted to see them. Cleo to the max.

She also realized that she knew the truth—if not in specifics, then in emotional terms—about Lisa and Belle. Neither one of them had what it takes to love anyone. This last betrayal by them was no worse than the hundreds of small cumulative ones that had come before. Karen's job had always been to give, and theirs to take. They had to be selfish because there was so little of themselves that they had to be vigilant.

How much did Belle hate herself, Karen wondered. How did Belle's panic, anger, and self-hate reflect in Karen's tiny baby button eyes? As Karen had suckled at her mother's breast, how much of Belle's remorse, anger, guilt, fear—poison—had she sucked in, too? Karen took a deep breath and sank deeper into the sofa cushions. She said a silent prayer of thanks for Marie. Without those years of love and affection from Marie, Karen would have been as bankrupt as her mother and sister.

Belle, never pretty, smart, rich enough, or clean enough, had made herself as pretty, clean, smart, and rich as she could figure out to do. But it was all lies. She'd enclosed herself in an armor of Adolfo dresses, David Hayes suits, St. John knits. They looked smooth, silky, colorful, and warm but they were armor that imprisoned and stunted all growth.

And Belle must have despised her own mother and herself for giving up her baby and lying to Arnold. No wonder there had been so little room for affection toward either of her daughters: Belle was completely occupied with her hate, living with it like a constant companion, between her and her husband, her and her daughters. Belle moved through the house in a coma, always hating, always wrong, despite the ultra-neat clothes, the cleaned bodies, the nuked meals, the unassailable rightness of everything.

And worse, Belle's self-hate had been passed on, to Lisa, to Karen, of course, and now to Stephanie and Tiff. A cascade of self-hate, taught by one generation of women to the next. I learned to be a horse, Karen thought. I was only as good as my work. That's what Jeffrey loved me for, if he loved me at all. But at least I had that. What did Belle or Lisa or her nieces have?

Karen saw her female family members as a bolt of cloth unrolled, the strands of the warp coming from the single, unrelenting skein of self-hatred. Whatever other thread was woven, whatever any generation might add to the warp, it was the skein of self-hate that gave the fabric of their lives its texture. The rest was merely the surface dye. Betrayed by men, told they weren't good enough, three generations of women had all been taught they were worthless.

If I didn't hate myself, would I have conceived? Karen wondered. And if I had, would I have passed this hate on to my child? She thought of the baby back in the Marianas: its black eyes so alert, waiting to be filled. What would *I* fill them with? she wondered.

And then she thought of Bill Wolper. He'd made a fool of her with his lies, and now with her name he'd make a fool of all the women who bought Karen Kahn clothes. They'd be overpriced, badly designed, and shoddily made. He'd romanced her. He'd made her feel like an attractive woman, but he saw her as a work horse. His had been the last betrayal.

She was a horse with no name. She turned on her stomach and buried her face in the white sofa cushion. Her makeup would leave smears—lipstick and blush and eyeliner—but she didn't care. If the slipcover looked like Veronica's Veil tomorrow, she'd have a portrait of her misery. Her punishment for being so blind and living with all her lies would be to see her name on everything from chocolates to designer napkins. Maybe even sanitary napkins. Hadn't Pierre Cardin licensed his name on plumbing? Saint Laurent had cigarettes and doormats with his initials. Karen Kahn would be sold to any woman desperate for a bit of glamour. And she couldn't do anything about it.

Or could she?

She turned over and her body stiffened. She might never be able to design anything using her own name, but her name wasn't really her after all. Her name had become a product, but *she* wasn't Karen Kahn. That had been her husband's name. She wasn't Karen Lipsky, either. Arnold wasn't her biological father. And why should she have the name of some sperm donor anyway? She knew who she was, and if the public didn't recognize her work from Norris Cleveland's, it wasn't her fault. But meanwhile, she could stop some of the abuse that was about to happen. She couldn't save her name but she could save her work.

They stood outside in the dark in the doorway of the building across from 550 Seventh Avenue. As Karen got out of the taxi, she almost grinned. All of them were in black, as if this were some rerun of an old "Mission Impossible." Janet's face was very white, but the others looked grim and cool.

Karen wasted no words. "Let's hope Casey stole the right key," she said.

Carl, Janet, Casey, Mrs. Cruz, and Defina carried the empty boxes. Carl handed two of the cartons to Karen. "Make it look like they're heavy," he told her. "If we carry stuff in and out, it's less suspicious than if we only carry stuff out."

Karen nodded. Casey looked as if he was staggering under the weight of the empty box. Clearly, he was from the Marcel Marceau School of Corporate Espionage. Janet crossed herself as they approached the security desk at 550. "What if the guard won't let us up?" she whispered.

"I'll kick his ass," Casey said. Karen grinned. She'd never seen this butch side of her marketing V.P.

The guard was dozing, his feet on the counter. "Make as much noise as you can," Casey told them. "This is *not* a covert operation."

"I can't believe those bastards won't wait till next week," Carl said loudly. The guard jerked his feet off the desk.

"Unbelievable, huh? Well, rock stars and politicians want what they want when they want it," Defina said. She waved at the guard. "Want some danish?" she asked. "Looks like you could use some coffee, too."

He rubbed at his eyes. "I wasn't sleeping," he said, defensive.

"No, neither are we. Can you believe this? Madonna got Karen Kahn out of bed to sew up a trousseau. Can you imagine the lingerie? We've got boxes of leather and rubber here. A rubber wedding gown. Can you beat that?"

"Madonna's getting married?"

"Shh, don't tell anyone," Carl warned.

"Who's she marrying?"

"Bill Clinton's brother. They're doing it on Letterman tomorrow night. Live. Like Tiny Tim's wedding." The guard whistled. "They're having a reception at the White House the day after tomorrow. We have to get all the clothes out by this morning, including Chelsea's first bustier."

"No shit?"

"No shit."

"I'll bet Hillary's ballistic," the guard said.

"To put it mildly," Defina told him as they stepped onto the elevator.

It took a little over two hours to pack every sketch, every pattern, every notebook, and all of the fashion research that Karen had collected over two decades in the business. When they had filled each carton, Karen picked up the Oakley Award plaque and dropped it on the top of the last box. Casey taped it down. Carl looked at his watch and announced it was a quarter to four. Karen looked around the empty room. She had always loved this view of Seventh Avenue, but Bill and Jeffrey had taken this room away from her. "Let's split," Casey suggested.

"Uh-huh," Defina agreed. "We got 'em. Women and gays conquer the hetero-male corporate universe."

"Damn straight," Casey agreed.

Karen nodded her head. "I want to thank you. None of you had to . . . "

"Oh, yes we did," Mrs. Cruz smiled.

"What will Norris copy now?" Casey giggled.

"There's one more thing I have to do," Karen told them. "Janet, I need your help." Her secretary nodded. "I need to dictate a letter."

"Yah need ta dictate a lettuh *now?*" Janet asked.

"Yeah." The others started dragging the boxes to the elevator while Karen sat beside Janet at the word processor. They worked together for a few minutes as Defina supervised the others while they got the boxes into a taxi and took off with them to Carl's place for safekeeping.

Defina returned alone to Karen's stripped office. "Aren't you ready yet?" she asked. "I got a security guard down there who's asking for a private visit to the Oval Office."

"We're done now," Karen said, and handed the letter Janet had just finished over to Defina. Karen read it over Defina's shoulder.

Dear Bill,

I wanted to thank you for the trip to Bangkok and the Marianas. It has given me a lot more than either one of us ever bargained for.

I also want to say that you did an excellent job of duping me, just as you have fooled other women in your private life and all the women customers of NormCo. You're very good at selling dreams and playing to a woman's weakness. I know it makes us look foolish, and that you have no respect for any of us. You exploit the lowest of us, from the slave girls in your factories, to your customers who don't know what they're buying, to me, a woman whose work you will steal.

You've won, as men like you always do.

I'd just like to point out that even men like you have to live with women, and when you have made all of us into fools you may find yourself very lonely.

Very truly yours,

The Ex–Karen Kahn

Defina opened her eyes wide, nodded her head, and smiled.

"It's okay?" Karen asked.

"All except for the P.S. You forgot to call him a dickweed. Are you leaving a note to Jeffrey?"

Karen smiled grimly, reached into her *schlep* bag and pulled out the can. Then, starting at the left-hand side, she spray painted her goodbye across the office walls and windows. "ALL MEN ARE PIMPS" she wrote in letters six feet high.

If it wasn't completely true, it was true enough.

41

A FRIEND INDEED

Arnold was closing his practice, but Karen reached him at his office and he told her to come right out.

She hadn't been to the two-story brick building in Hauppauge since they had first incorporated KKInc. It was as messy and cluttered as usual. Inez buzzed her in and smiled, perhaps shyly. Karen said hello, and then Arnold called out to her.

He was sitting at the big scarred gray metal desk that she remembered. Arnold was a no-frills guy. She sat down in the chair in front of the desk. "I'll just be a minute," he said. "I'm separating the cases that might be active from the rest." Karen nodded and looked up at the wall, where the same poem she remembered still hung in its tarnished frame: *I have shut my little sister in from life and light/ (For a rose, for a ribbon, for a wreath across my hair)*. It reminded her of the nightmare of the Marianas. Karen looked away.

Arnold dumped a few file folders into a box and threw another into a garbage bag. "So," he said, "you gave away your majority. Belle told me this morning that she signed the stock over to Jeffrey. It was unconscionable."

Karen nodded.

"I've always tried to see your mother's point of view. I've always known that she operated out of fear, not hate. At least, that's what I always thought." He shook his head. "I've made a lot of mistakes, Karen. Any mistakes I made that hurt you I regret most deeply."

Karen felt her throat close, but she wasn't going to cry anymore. Did her father know she was Belle's real daughter? Should she tell him? Did it really matter in the end? Best to stick to business. "I just wanted to ask you one thing," she told Arnold. "You incorporated us. Is there anything I can do to hold on to the company?"

Arnold shook his head. "I didn't know you transferred the stock. I would have advised you against that, but it was a generous gesture. Maybe it was even the right thing to do. You're a good girl, Karen. I got a fax from Lars Dagsvarr. He thinks you walk on water." He put his hand on her shoulder. "I'm proud of you," he said.

"Are you really? It feels as if I've really screwed up."

"You've been brave and hardworking. And you were working in a bad man's game. There's nothing tougher than the garment industry, Karen. You know that. We're talking fifty billion dollars a year, bigger than the auto industry. It's controlled by men and it feeds into a sickness in women. I used to watch Detroit pull that planned obsolescence on men in the fifties and six- ties. I had nothing but contempt for guys who got sucked into the 'new model,' and I thought that women would never be so stupid. But they are," he sighed. "You did good. You tried hard. You have nothing to be ashamed of."

He sat down slowly, holding the arms of his swivel chair. "So, what are you going to do?" he asked.

"I have an idea," Karen told him. "Another business venture. But there's something more important. I've been thinking about a baby—adopting a baby." She paused. She wasn't used to talking to Arnold like this. She took a deep breath. "Do you think it's a good idea?" she asked. "Belle said that I . . . "

"Let me tell you this, Karen: I'll never regret marrying your mother because through her I got you. And I think you'd be a wonderful mother. Does that answer your question?"

Karen nodded her head.

"I'm leaving Belle, Karen."

Karen nodded her head again. "Will you handle my divorce?" she asked.

It was Arnold's turn to nod silently.

Once again, Karen thought of Madame Renault and her prediction. Now, after her talk with Arnold, Karen knew exactly what she was going to do. She was going to find the baby in the Marianas who was meant to be hers. And she was going to call Bobby Pillar, because he was a no-bullshit kind of guy, and they needed each other right now. He needed her class and she needed his clout to cope with Bill Wolper and restructure her life. After sitting there for a time, she dialed Bobby's West Coast number and, amazingly, he was not only in but he took her call. It took her only a few minutes to explain the situation. Bobby seemed to know a lot of it already. And when she was finished talking, he laughed.

"The *momzers!*" he exclaimed. "They think they can fuck with you like that? Listen, *mammela*, I have several ideas, but the neatest one is for you to come on my channel with a new line of stuff. Good stuff, but moderately priced."

"But I can't use my name," she reminded him.

"Who needs it? You got something better than your name: you got *you*. And you'll be unbelievable on TV. No, that's wrong. You'll be *believable*. We do a whole fashion show, show 'em all kinds of stuff—stuff you like and stuff you don't. And you talk about what you like and why, and *then* you sell your designs. Not to the rich bitches you've been catering to, but to real women, regular working women who will recognize not just your name but your good design. Why don't you stop with the fancy-shmancy for the ladies who lunch and dress America?"

Karen smiled. She liked the idea. "Designs that will look good on women who weigh more than a hundred pounds?"

"Yeah! You might even put a few of those anorexic models out of business. Can't you see them now, holding cardboard begging signs on Seventh Avenue that say WILL WORK FOR VERSACE."

"But my name. I've lost my name."

"Hell, we can call you Madame X! We'll tell the world how your husband done you wrong. Stole your company. *Stole* your name. Anyway, you got your name—you just can't use it on the same product. The Gallo case set the precedent. You know, the brother of the wine guys who wanted to sell cheese or something. They can't keep you out of all businesses. Plus, I've got a file on Wolper I've been dying to use since he fucked me on that cable TV deal. Hey, we'll get backlash power! Look what it did for Loni Anderson. Look what it did for Ivana," he paused. "And think what it will do to Jeffrey and NormCo! Nice acquisition, Bill. You think you're buyin' class, but all you're getting is backlash and bullshit." He paused and laughed. "Don't you love it?"

She did.

Her next call was to Sally at Harvey Kramer's office. Sally was supportive, but cautious. "It *could* be done," she said. "But not without pulling a few strings. Technically, you *are* married and you *have* been approved as adoptive parents. But with this breakup, I'm not positive about where the court will stand. On immigration I can help you."

"Two senators' wives are good clients. Call them," Karen told Sally. She wasn't above pulling strings for this. "And I've dressed Ambassador Scranton since she first ran for councilwoman. She's in China. Pull out all the stops."

Karen had made a few more calls, one of them to Carl, who had changed her reservations and arrived to help her finish packing. He had even taken the car with her to the airport. "Do you think I'm crazy, Carl?" she asked.

"Not at all. I think you know what you want and you're going to get it. This didn't happen overnight Karen. It's not just a whim."

"Carl, there's something else I want you to do for me," she paused, trying to put it delicately. "Look. I'll be getting some money because of the sale. And I want something good to come out of it. So I want you to open up a shop in Manhattan. Since Paris, all the models love you. You're hot. Do it, Carl."

He shook his head. "I can't take the money from Jeffrey's deal. It makes me sick."

"It would make *me* happy. Please?"

Carl considered. "A business loan. Strictly business." She nodded. "Thank you, Karen." She took his hand, gratefully, and held it all the way to JFK International.

With the help of Carl's Valium she slept most of the way to Hong Kong, where she had an hour to wait before catching the flight to the Marianas. She used the time to call ahead, check in with Sally, and continue the arrangements that she and Carl had started back in Brooklyn. Then she got on the plane for the six-hour leg of the flight, but she didn't sleep. She was too excited. In the six hours she probably changed her mind more than a dozen times: this was a great idea, an inspired idea; no, it was total foolishness. It was sentimental, stupid, and not thought-out. She'd always regret it; she'd never regret it. Each time she felt as if she might jump out of her skin. Each time she felt that it was impossible—that going forward was impossible—she remembered that turning back was impossible, too. Always, each time she came to a dead end, she would remember the eyes of the baby, the baby that was meant for her.

She and Bobby Pillar had agreed not to make their deal public until after she collected the Wolper money. But then they would go public in a big way. It meant that she would have to give up her snobbery: she wouldn't be dressing the wealthy anymore. But when she thought of some of the sad and desperate women who bought her couture line, she couldn't feel too bad about it. She would regret giving up the luxury of buying any fabric she wanted, and she felt regrets that she would never design for the French and Italian mills. Hey, but what the hell, Yves Saint Laurent always got Gustav Zumsteg's best cuts anyway. Karen thought of all the women she saw on the street, on airplanes, and in the malls. It would be an exciting challenge to come up with good designs in fabrics with integrity at a price that mass market could afford. A whole new world. The hell with Paris, France. Let's sell Paris, Texas!

Would the mass market understand her clothes? she wondered. Would they reject things that didn't have extra flowers or flounces tacked on? Karen was gambling on the fact that they wouldn't, and Bobby was willing to put his money where her mouth was. Plus, it would be such a joy to show bad designs like Norris Cleveland's and tear them apart on screen. She might not make new friends in the fashion industry, but she just might become a heroine—a kind of Everywoman's Elsa Klensch.

And she would adopt this child and raise it. She prayed she would do a better job than Belle had done. It wasn't easy to be a single mother and raise a child alone, but what was easy? She had been raised by Belle and Arnold, and so had Lisa, and look what a fiasco that had been! Karen thought of Marie Botteglia: Marie had loved her; Marie had cuddled her and touched her and looked at her and kissed her. Thank God for that! It must have been what made the difference between herself and her sister. As a child, she had basked in Marie's love and approval. In a way, I've been lucky, Karen thought. I didn't get enough and I didn't get it for as long as I should have, but at least I got it sometime. At least I got something. The thought of Marie, back in Chicago Heights, even now made Karen smile. In just a few hours, I'm going to make you a spiritual grandma, she thought.

And what about Lisa and Belle? Could she forgive them? *Should* she forgive them? Karen wasn't sure. Was blood so important that it tied knots that should never be untied? What had Madame Renault predicted? That she would tear away the web, but that the strands would bleed? Now she smiled. Hadn't the fortune-teller also told her that she had a dark child waiting? Madame Renault had been right about everything.

Karen thought of the feathery black hair of the baby, of the black, black eyes that had stared up at her. She didn't care how young the infant was. The baby had *seen* her. The baby had chosen her, and in the years to come when Lily—that would be her name—when Lily asked how she had been adopted, Karen would tell her all of the truth. Karen would tell her about her poor mother and about the way the world was made. She would tell her how women and children sewed cheap clothes in the dark, in filth, so that other women half a world away could spend money on but never satisfy their vanity. And how men controlled it all: the women who slaved and the women who were manipulated by photos in magazines and store windows and catalogues. She would tell Lily how and why her mother had died, and how Lily had picked Karen out.

The time might come when Lily felt angry, different and separate. The time might come when Lily would regret being taken from her culture. But Karen had to believe that she wasn't making a mistake. She would let Lily go to do whatever she needed to do, and she would help her in any way she could. And, meanwhile, Karen would stop feeding the status machine, the inexhaustible appetite women had for fashion. She'd build good clothes that lasted and they'd be made by women who were paid a decent wage and bought by women who worked hard for their money. No more glamour, no more exclusivity. She'd work for a new clientele. Karen hoped she wouldn't disappoint any of them. Or Lily. In the meantime, all she wanted to do was be granted the privilege of loving her.

Mr. Dagsvarr met Karen as soon as she had moved through customs. "Are you surprised to see me?" she asked. He shook his head and smiled.

"Not at all," he said. "Not at all."

"Can we go right to the hospital?" she asked.

Mr. Dagsvarr shook his head. "I'm afraid that the baby has been moved. She isn't at the hospital anymore." Karen opened her eyes wide.

"Why not? Is she all right?" Unlikely as it was, had some family member shown up to claim her? Fear clutched tightly at Karen's chest. She couldn't breathe. Was she destined to lose yet another baby?

"They have removed the infant. She wasn't ill, so she had to be released from the hospital. She was supposed to be transferred to the United Marianas Orphanage."

"So? Is she there? Is she all right?"

"Well, she never arrived there. There was some up-mix in the paperwork. She is being located right now." They had already walked out of the airport. The heat and humidity hit Karen like a wall and, heavy as bricks, it seemed to gather and weigh her down. She felt as if she were walking under water.

"How could that happen? How could they lose a baby?"

"Babies are something we have a lot of here," Mr. Dagsvarr said with a sigh. "I wish I could tell you that they are reared carefully." He sounded tired.

"Let's go to the attorney general's office," she said. "I've already spoken to them."

"Perhaps we could just start with *your* attorney," he said. "Have you got his address?"

Karen pulled out her Fil-o-fax and gave him the card. She couldn't believe it! Lily was lost! She bit her lip. She had come almost ten thousand miles, halfway around the world, and these idiots couldn't even keep track of one infant. Well, if she had to comb the entire island, she would find her baby.

They drove by some of the factory buildings, and some of the slums where Karen knew there were other girls suffering, as Lily's mother had suffered. She hoped that the NormCo check would be a big one, because half of it would come back here, to the women who had been robbed. She'd talk about them on television, too. It wouldn't do enough, but it would do something.

When they hit the main business street, Mr. Dagsvarr turned his rattling old car at an intersection and managed to wedge it between a new Toyota and a truck made of so many tied-together rusty parts that it was impossible to tell what make it was. He helped Karen out of her seat and the two of them made their way up to Mr. Ching's office.

They didn't have to wait long. Mr. Ching, a pleasant-looking man with graying hair, ushered them into his office. "I have some good news," he said. "The baby has been located." Karen looked from him to Mr. Dagsvarr. Was it true? Could she relax? Or were they afraid that she would make a fuss and had they found another baby, any baby, instead of Lily?

"May I see your papers?" Mr. Ching asked.

Karen took out her passport, the home study that had been done in another lifetime, the application that she had made to the State of New York, and all of the information that Sally from Mr. Kramer's office had provided. "I will have to contact Immigration, of course," Mr. Ching said.

"Why?" Karen asked. "The child is an American. She was born here. Isn't this a part of the good old U.S.A.?"

"Well, she was born of a Chinese mother. We do not know the nationality of her father. I think it would be best to cover every eventuality."

"Do whatever you think is necessary," Karen told him. "I just better be able to take home my baby. Now, I'm going to her. Where is she?"

Karen strode down the hallway of the Marianas Methodist Hospital. They had sent Lily to this hospital because she was running a slight fever. At least that was what Karen had been told. It was the only way the child had been found. Otherwise, she might still be in the place she'd been sent off to, on the other side of the island. Now she and Mr. Dagsvarr walked up the stairs to the maternity floor. Kindly, he was carrying her bag for her, since it couldn't be left in his car with doors that didn't lock and windows that didn't quite close. Karen was grateful for his help. But not so grateful that she would slow down and let him keep up with her. By the time they reached the nursery at the end of the hallway, she was flat-out running.

A nurse in an old-fashioned starched cap stopped her at the desk beside the nursery window. "Can I help you?" she asked.

"I'm here for my baby," Karen said.

The nurse looked at her for a moment as if she were mad. Karen reached into her *schlep* bag and pulled out the temporary custody papers that Mr. Ching had given her. "I want to see my baby," Karen said. She handed the papers over as Mr. Dagsvarr arrived. The nurse looked at him and her face softened.

"Oh, hello Reverend," she said. The two of them began to talk, but Karen turned her back on them and turned to the glass window. Inside, there were a dozen bassinets; all were full. But Karen's eyes swept over them and, despite the two Asian babies, she knew that Lily wasn't there.

"Where is *my* baby?" she asked.

And then she saw her. The baby was in an isolette, but the plastic of the cover was clear, and even from this distance, some twenty feet, Karen recognized the child.

"There she is. There's my baby," Karen told them.

42

FASHIONABLY LATE

It had taken Karen hours to clear Immigration, and that was *with* the invaluable help of Sally, a state representative (the husband of a good client), intervention from a U.S. senator's office, and, finally, a visit from Harvey Kramer himself—at a cost of who knew how many billable hours. Karen wearily wondered what kind of security risk to America a four-week-old Chinese-American female infant posed, and what the whole horrible process was like for people who didn't have her privileges, her money and connections, those who couldn't take catnaps in the VIP rooms at the airport. Thank God Lily slept most of the time, wrapped in a blanket that Mrs. Dagsvarr had embroidered when she learned Karen was coming back for the baby, and had shyly given to Karen. It already was soiled, but it did have Lily's name sewn neatly at the corner.

Wearily, Karen had called for a company car to pick her up. What the hell! It might be the last privilege KKInc ever gave her. She couldn't face a taxi for the last forty minutes of this round-the-world tour. The ride from JFK into Manhattan was a blur of fatigue, and Lily and Karen both dozed fitfully in the back seat.

Karen woke up on the Grand Central Parkway. For a moment she didn't know where she was and clutched at the baby. Thank God! She hadn't lost or dropped her. But what a responsibility the little sleeping bundle represented. Could she be a good mother? Could any woman in the nineties? Defina had tried so hard. Maybe her working had made things difficult for Tangela. But had Defina had a choice? Of course, Lisa *hadn't* worked, and look at how her girls were turning out. Karen suddenly felt old and tired. Would she have the energy, the stamina, to be a good mother? She crossed her fingers and hoped that love and money would be enough. Then she fell asleep again.

When they pulled up to the green canopy of her West End Avenue apartment, she was jerked awake. "Well, Lil, for better or for worse, you're home." She looked down at the little face. Lily's eyes were closed and the baby's black lashes, tiny and indescribably sweet, pushed against the fat of her cheek. Her fist was curled tightly against her chin, and Karen had to smile down at the child. Maybe this choice was irrational. Maybe she should not be doing it. Maybe at some time in the future she would have regrets, and maybe Lily would regret it as well. But even so, Karen would not choose to do this any other way. If it was self-indulgent, if it was the act of a desperate woman, she still felt good about it. In fact, she had never felt so good. Holding Lily to her breast, she felt more real, more complete, and more joyful than she ever had before in her life. Some things are beyond analysis, she thought. Probably all the things that create joy.

Karen got out of the car. The driver helped her with her scant luggage and the bag full of improvised baby paraphernalia. George, the doorman, late and slow as usual, only got to her side after she had managed to get the luggage and the baby into the foyer. The more things change the more they remain the same she thought, but she smiled.

She fit the key into the lock, and as she opened the door she wondered if Ernesta would still be there. It was already almost one o'clock in the afternoon, and Ernesta only worked half days. Karen kicked the bag into the hall and walked into the living room.

"Surprise!" whispered twenty voices. Karen jumped, but Lily slept on. Defina, Casey, Carl, Janet, Mrs. Cruz, Ernesta, Perry, Arnold, Inez, and another dozen people stood in a loose semicircle clutching pink helium-filled balloons. Karen was shocked to see Elise Elliot, carrying a big robin's-egg-blue Tiffany box. Alongside her stood Annie Paradise, her hand on Ernesta's arm. Even Brenda Cushman was there, and Karen couldn't help but notice Brenda was wearing the dress Karen had designed for her.

"Oh, my God," Karen whispered back. "What are you all doing here?"

"You have to have a baby shower," Janet said.

"Tangela was here. She's doing okay, but had to get back to rehab. She sends her love. The rest of us have been waiting for hours," Defina said.

Karen smiled. She'd been a late bloomer her whole life. She'd been adopted late, she reached puberty late, she'd been late to marry, to search for her roots, and to realize the betrayal of others. Now, she was late at starting this motherhood gig. "Defina, do you think I'm too old to be a good mom?"

"Honey, you're not old, you're just fashionably late."

Karen looked around her and saw all her loyal friends from KKInc. That wasn't all. Against the window, the tall, dark figure of Madame Renault leaned gracefully. What was *she* doing here, Karen wondered. Not that she wasn't welcome. Karen watched as Madame Renault walked forward, toward Karen and the baby. Karen blinked. Well, wouldn't she come here now? Hadn't Madame Renault known all about Lily? Hadn't she known about a dark child who had to take a long journey to get here?

"I'm completely shocked," was all Karen could say.

"Haven't ya ever had a baby shower before?" Carl asked. He approached her and looked down at the wrapped bundle. "Let us see," he whispered. "Introduce me to my niece."

"*My* goddaughter," Defina said.

"My granddaughter," Arnold added.

"My granddaughter, too," someone echoed. Karen felt her stomach flip and looked up from Lily's perfect tulip face. But it wasn't into Belle's eyes that she had to stare. Instead, there were the warm brown eyes of Marie Botteglia. How had they found *her*? Who had invited her? Karen didn't know, but she was thrilled to see her. The tiny dark woman smiled up at Karen, just on eye level with Lily. "Ohhh, she's beautiful," Marie whispered.

"Let us all see," one of the kids from her design staff cried. Still shocked but also transported, Karen floated over to the sofa and spread out the blanket, putting Lily down and wedging her between two pillows.

"That's the last time *that* sofa is gonna be white," Defina said. Everyone laughed and crowded around, looking at the sleeping beauty.

"What's her name?" Perry asked. He hung back a little bit from the crowd and Karen wondered what it cost him to be there. Was he thinking of Lottie? Was he still drinking? She would never again blame him if he did. She already knew that it would kill her if anything happened to this baby.

"Have you picked a name?" Defina asked. "If you don't like 'Defina,' Latosha is nice."

"Latosha?" Carl asked. "It sounds like a French Macintosh apple. How about something more practical? Lanoleum might work."

"I don't think so, Carl," Karen said.

"Nothing wrong with Latosha," Defina huffed.

"Her name is Lily," Madame Renault told them all.

Karen blinked. She looked into the woman's dark face. She felt the hair on the back of her neck rise. Did the woman know *everything*? Then Madame Renault smiled. "It's on her blanket," she pointed out.

Perry walked over to the baby, reached down, and covered Lily's little foot with his hand.

"Welcome, Lily," he said, and tears filled Karen's eyes. Mrs. Cruz must have seen that and came up to hug her.

"She have no clothes, your baby. So we fixed that," Mrs. Cruz said. And then they started bringing out the packages. Hand-smocked little cotton batiste dresses. A tiny pink taffeta party dress. A dotted Swiss nightgown with hand tatting. Little knitted booties out of the softest boucle wool. An entire hand-stitched, perfect layette! When did they have the time? How could they have known? Karen couldn't help it then. She did begin to cry.

But that wasn't all. From the kitchen Ernesta wheeled in a blue perambulator, the Rolls Royce of baby carriages, sent air express from England by Bobby Pillar. The note said, "Dear Partner. *Mazel tov*. If you design a line of baby clothes, I'll pay for her college education (all Ivy League)." Karen cried harder.

"There's something else Bobby is giving us," Karen told them. "I have jobs for all of you if you want them." She turned to Defina. "And for Tangela, too." People cheered. Karen cried harder.

"Now look what you made her do," Carl mock-pouted. Perry handed Karen a clean but paint-spotted handkerchief.

"It's so nice of you all," Karen said. "It's just so nice."

Janet took the baby. "Will she speak Chinese or English?" she asked, innocently.

Karen smiled. Janet was a nice girl but a space kitten. "She'll probably speak with a Brooklyn accent," Karen told her.

And somehow it didn't seem to matter, at least right then, that Belle wasn't there. That Lisa and Jeffrey weren't there. That anyone who had legally been defined as family wasn't there, except Arnold. And to Arnold, she had no ties of blood! Karen looked around the room at the people she had been kind to, the people she had connected with, who in turn had been kind to her. This is enough, she said to herself. I'm lucky. Lily will be lucky, too. This is *more* than enough.

"Best stroller?" Defina asked.

Karen opened her mouth and was about to speak when she realized she didn't know the answer. And she didn't know the best diaper service, or the best play school, or the best pediatrician. For a moment her confidence deserted her. Maybe she wouldn't be able to do this well. Defina saw her hesitate.

"Best new mother?" Defina asked softly. Before Karen could say anything, Defina answered the question herself. "Karen Kahn," she said, and squeezed Karen's hand.

The buzzer rang, and Ernesta went to get the door. She came back followed by Mr. Centrillo, who was lugging a huge box. "Mrs. Kahn," he said. "Sorry I'm late, but something came up. You know how it can be." He shrugged apologetically. "Anyway, I heard the good news and I wanted to bring this along to the little lady. If she's anything like her mother, she'll do okay."

"Mr. Centrillo . . ." Karen was embarrassed. She'd been careful not to use her real name, and to pay in cash. How had he known?

"We have television in Brooklyn, Mrs. Kahn," he said smiling. "We even sometimes get *Women's Wear* over there."

After Karen blushed and apologized, she opened the boxes of diapers he had brought. She exclaimed over the bassinet, the crib, and the baby quilt. Then there was only one more box, which Carl brought out to her with a flourish. It was wrapped in plain brown paper, and Karen expected some basic for the layette. That was why she was so surprised by the gleam of satin under the tissue paper. She pulled out a quilted bed jacket, a beautiful white one with hand-carved buttons and the most perfect French lace trim at the neck and sleeves. It was a dream out of some Harlow movie, and Karen stopped sniffing and began to sob in earnest. "My bed jacket," she said. "You got me a bed jacket." Lily, now over on the sofa, woke up and began to cry too. Ernesta, with the authority of years of practice, scooped the little baby into her big arms.

"I'm her *other* grandma," she told Marie, and began to pat Lily gently. She looked over at Karen. "You got a bottle for her?" she asked.

Mutely, Karen nodded. "In the bag," she managed to say, and pointed at one of the carry-ons.

"Put on the bed jacket," Carl demanded. "America wants to know what you're going to wear under it."

She laughed and then slipped into it. She sat herself down on the sofa and cradled Lily while Lily sucked down almost half a bottle of formula. Everybody else ate too, and Perry held a bagel for Karen that she managed to take bites of while the baby nursed. "How was Minnesota?" she asked him quietly.

"Cold and dry," he said, "just like I was. Still am dry," he added and lifted a glass of bottled water to his lips to toast her.

When Lily was finished, Karen put her up to her shoulder and began to pat out the air. She forgot a rag. In a second, before Karen had had a chance to think about it, Lily spit up all over Karen's satin-clad shoulder.

"Oh, no!" Karen cried. Perry laughed. Mrs. Cruz shrugged. Ernesta mopped up Karen's shoulder with a dishcloth. And Defina stood back and smiled.

"That's what clothes are for," she said.